Labyrinth War

Tim Goff

Published by Tim Goff, 2024.

This is a work of fiction. Similarities to real people, places, or events are entirely coincidental.

LABYRINTH WAR

First edition. November 12, 2024.

ISBN: 979-8227213402

Written by Tim Goff.

Also by Tim Goff

Empire

Empire: Country

Empire: Country

Empire: Capital

Empire: Capital

Empire: Estate

Empire: Estate

Empire: Metropolis

Empire: Metropolis

Empire: Spiral

Empire: Judgment

Empire: The Complete Collection

Standalone

Labyrinth War

Table of Contents

Eastern Solaria

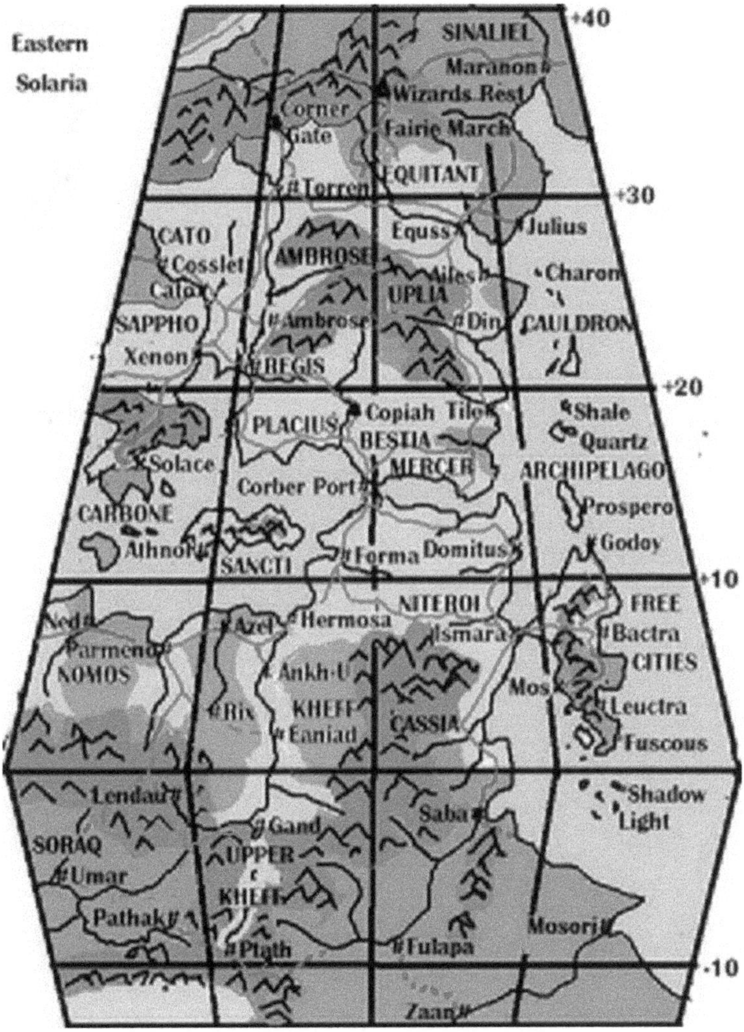

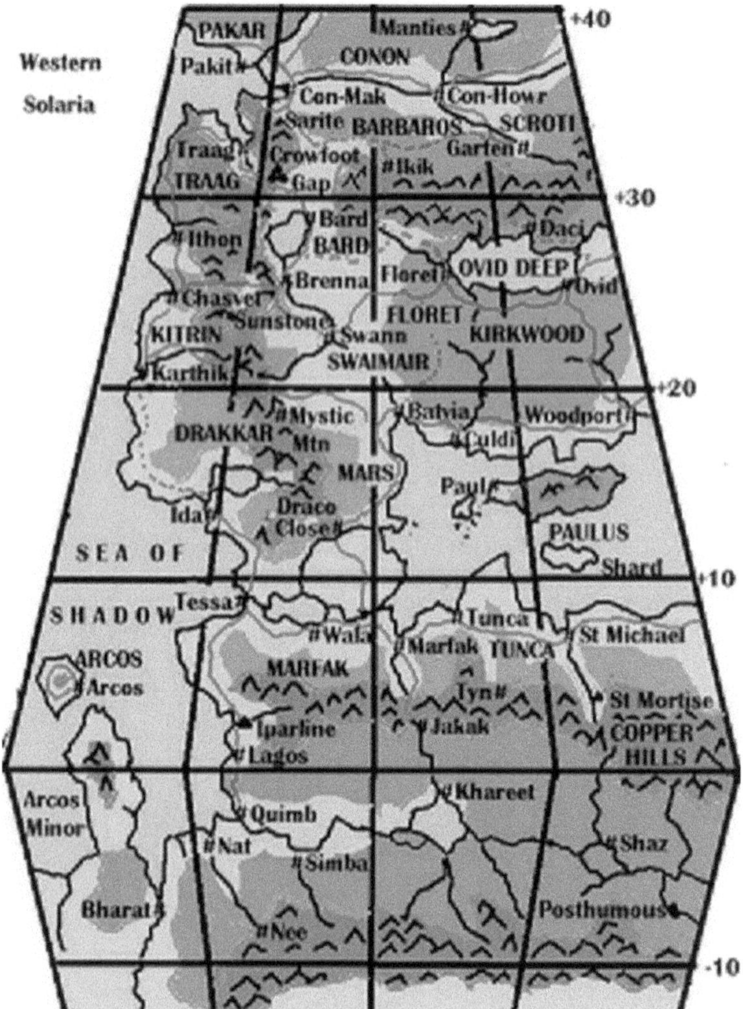
Western
Solaria
PAKAR
Manties
+40
Pakit
CONON
Con-Mak
Con-Howr
Sarite
BARBAROS
SCROTI
Traag
Crowfoot
Gap
Ikik
Garten
TRAAG
+30
Bard
Daci
Ithon
BARD
Brenna
Floret
OVID DEEP
Ovid
Chasver
Sunstone
FLORET
KITRIN
Swann
KIRKWOOD
SWAIMAIR
Karthik
+20
Mystic
Mtn
Batvia
Woodport
DRAKKAR
Culdi
MARS
Paul
Draco
Close
Ida
PAULUS
SEA OF
Shard
+10
Tessa
SHADOW
Wala
Tunca
St Michael
ARCOS
Marfak
TUNCA
Arcos
MARFAK
Tyn
St Mortise
Iparline
Jakak
COPPER
HILLS
Lagos
Khareel
Arcos
Minor
Quimb
Nat
Simba
Shaz
Bharat
Posthumous
Nee
-10

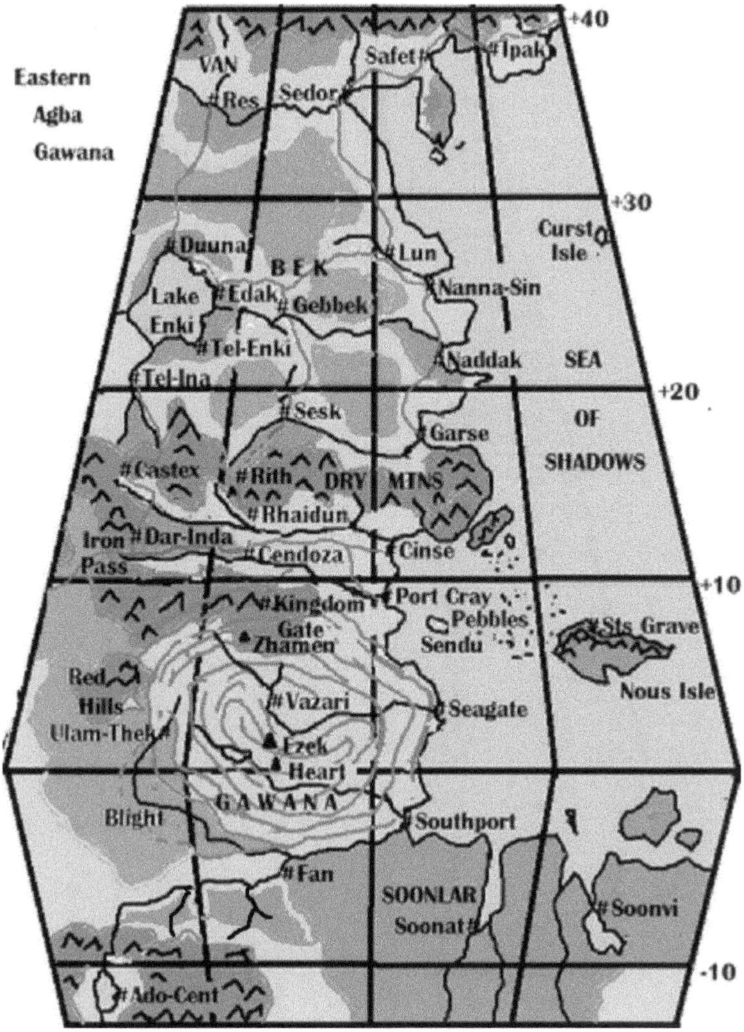
Eastern
Agba
Gawana
+40
+30
+20
+10
-10
VAN
#Res
Sedor
Safet#
#Ipak
#Duuna
BEK
#Lun
Curst
Isle
Nanna-Sin
Lake
Enki
#Edak
#Gebbek
#Tel-Enki
#Tel-Ina
Naddak
SEA
OF
SHADOWS
#Sesk
#Garse
#Castex
#Rith
DRY
MTNS
#Rhaidun
Iron
Pass
#Dar-Inda
#Cendoza
#Cinse
#Kingdom
Port Cray
Gate
Zhamen
Pebbles
Sendu
#Sts Grave
Nous Isle
Red
Hills
Ulam-Thek#
#Vazari
#Seagate
Ezek
Heart
GAWANA
Blight
#Southport
#Fan
SOONLAR
Soonat#
#Soonvi
#Ado-Cent

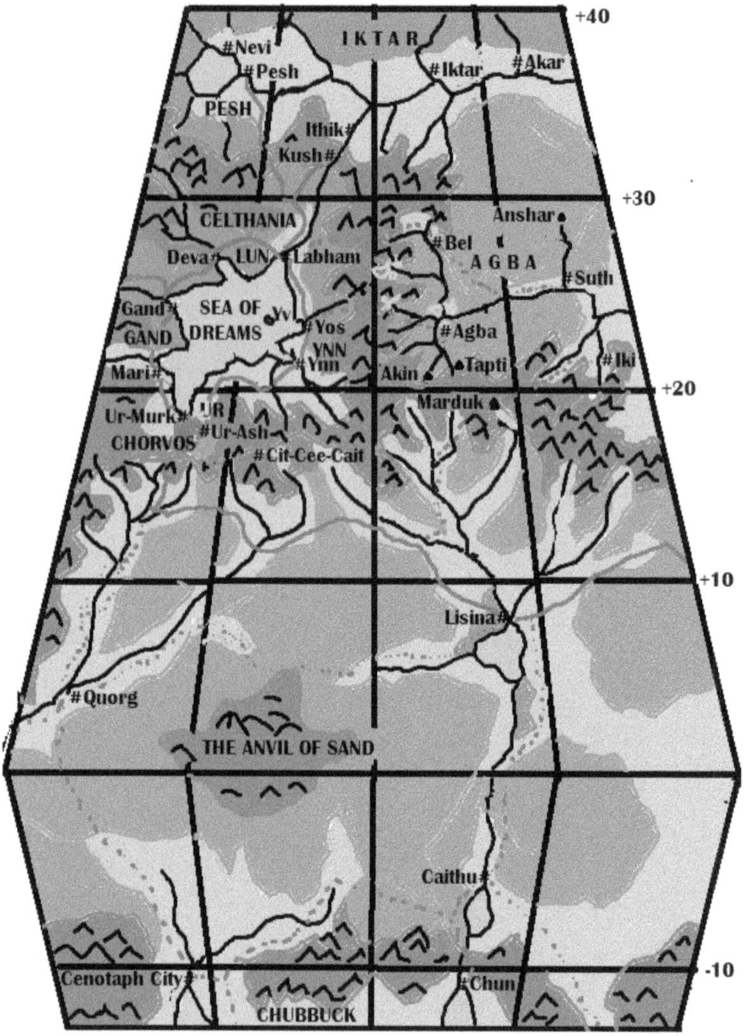
+40
IKTAR
#Nevi
#Pesh
#Iktar
#Akar
PESH
Ithik#
Kush#
+30
CELTHANIA
Anshar
#Bel
Deva#
LUN
#Labham
AGBA
#Suth
Gand#
SEA OF DREAMS
Yv
#Yos
GAND
YNN
#Agba
#Ynn
Tapti
#Iki
Mari#
Akin
+20
Marduk
Ur-Murk#
UR
#Ur-Ash
CHORVOS
#Cit-Cee-Cait
+10
Lisina#
#Quorg
THE ANVIL OF SAND
Caithu#
-10
Cenotaph City#
#Chun
CHUBBUCK

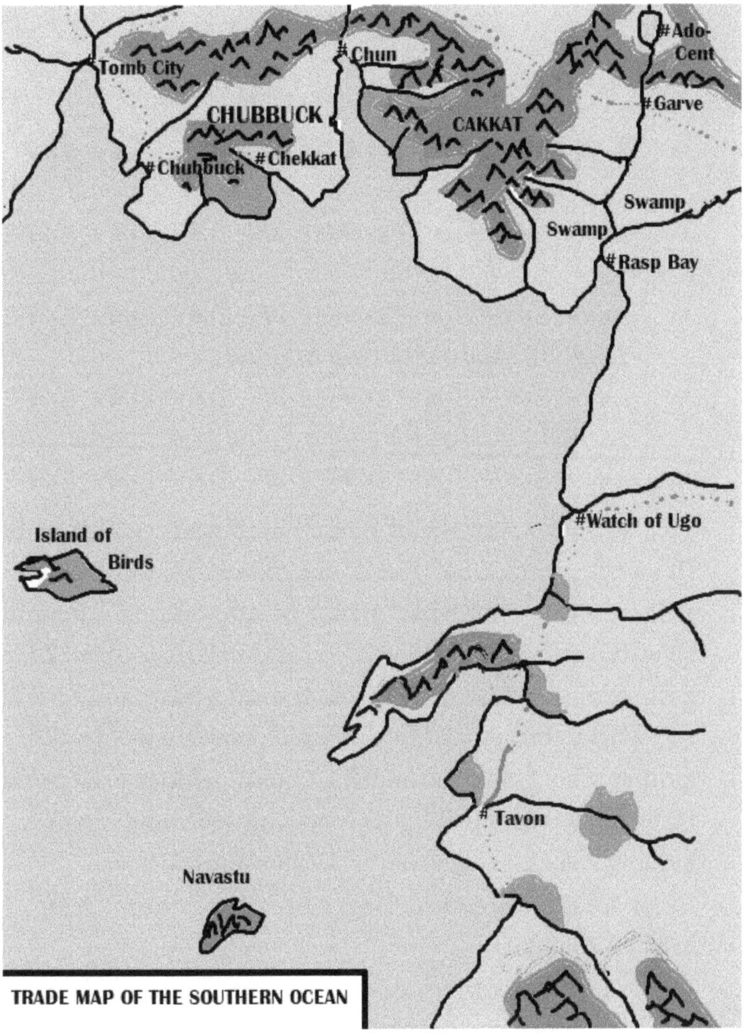

TRADE MAP OF THE SOUTHERN OCEAN

LABYRINTH WAR I – Singer

'I began this record as Titus Maximus, a Lord of the Solarian Empire.

I conclude it as Titus Maximus, a Lord of Gawana.'

– From 'The Journal of Titus Maximus.'

The man who thought of himself as 'Singer' closed the book. "It's a fake. It must be." But doubt colored his words. He stared at the tome on the table, drew a breath, hooked a long finger beneath the book's leather cover, and flicked it open. Lines of neat script stared back at him, each word a truth, and each a lie.

Worse, those words unlocked unwanted memories. A mother who drank too much. A stern, seldom present father. Halls filled with hustling servants and scheming relatives. Red blood on an exquisite green and yellow mosaic floor.

A tolling bell jerked Singer from his reverie. Damn. He'd been up all night.

I missed my engagement at the Pelican. Steric will be furious.

Two steps brought Singer to the apartment window. His gaze settled on a collection of spires and domes lined in dawn's red light. He needed answers. And he knew where to get them.

Once, the Empire's best scholars, philosophers, and musicians attended the University of Solace. Scholars probed the mysteries of electricity and alchemy. Healers discovered ways to cure and prevent diseases. And the musicians mingled melodies from around the world to create songs never before heard. That was before the Purge, when zealots rampaged through the halls, burning sorcerers and bullying scholars. Now, the University was a shell of itself. But Singer loved it all the same.

He descended three flights of stairs and stepped onto the street.

"Singer!" The hail originated from a fat man with a black mustache behind a pushcart piled with steaming loaves.

"What's the special today, Rollo?"

Rollo smiled. "Sticky bun and sweet tea."

"Sounds delicious." He dug a copper bit from his painfully thin pouch and handed it to the vendor. He needed a paying gig.

"I am pleased." Rollo handed Singer a hot bun and a paper cup of tan liquid. "A man asked for you last night."

"Oh?" It was probably a client.

"He wore green livery with a gold chain across the front." Rollo shook his head. "Very arrogant. He took three buns without paying."

Green livery with a gold chain. Red blood on a green and yellow floor. His past was catching up to him. "Thank you." He took a large bite from the loaf.

"You know this man?"

He nodded around a mouthful of bread. It should have been delicious, but he couldn't taste it. He washed it down with equally bland tea. Then he strode across the Sophocles Bridge and onto the University's campus.

A large sphere beneath a gazebo caught Singer's eye: the globe of Vertis the Geographer, the best public map of the known world. That infernal book mentioned multiple distant locations. Here, he could match its lies against reality. He strode past the placard that denoted the Great Geographer's accomplishments.

The wagon-sized globe rotated with clockwork precision atop its axis. Dawn's chill light illuminated the hemisphere nearest Singer. He walked around the sphere's base. There: Solace, the city where he now stood, perched on the Carbone Peninsula in the Mare Imperium. Singer's gaze traveled west, past the Imperial Sea, to the bloodstained lands of Kitrin and Drakkar to the Mare Umbra, the Sea of Shadows. A long isle that almost split that watery expanse in twain caught his attention: Nous Isle, with a dot marked 'Saints Grave' on its northern shore.

A chill lump formed in Singer's gut. "This proves nothing." He directed his attention to the Shadow Sea's far coast. More names from the manuscript leaped out at him: Port Cray, Cendoza, Rhaiduni...and Gawana. Those places did exist! He blinked. Then he whirled and stumbled from the gazebo.

Singer paused briefly outside a colonnaded building with a façade cracked by fire – the Arcanum of the Celestial Circle, Solaria's preeminent order of sorcerers. They could have answered at least some of his queries. But they were gone - fled or burned along with a hundred other wizards by the mad witch hunter Appius Ambrose. Now, their hall stood empty and shunned, and the arcane arts once openly taught at the university were banned, their remaining practitioners studying in secret. He considered ferreting out one of these hidden wizards but decided against that course. He had enough trouble without adding banned magic to the list. He shook his head and pressed on into the campus.

Nothing moved in the Grand Athenium. He strode to the polished counter that separated the library's public area from the stacks and peered into the dim recesses. He didn't see a clerk, let alone the old woman.

"I knew you'd be back." The aged voice came from behind Singer. The old woman lounged in a chair beside the entryway, gray hair sprouting from a shapeless black academic gown. "I brought something for you."

"More lies?" He fought to keep his voice from rising. "My father did not write that book."

The aged woman appeared unperturbed by Singer's accusation. "My, you're a quick one. And you're right. Titus Maximus did not write that book." A palm-sized notebook appeared in her hand. "He wrote this one."

The booklet was yellow with age. Cuts and stains marred the pamphlet's cover. "More lies."

The old woman shook her head. "Not lies, Octavos."

The man started. That name belonged in the dead past.

"Elaborations," continued the woman. "Titus omitted items from his record you needed to know. So, I expanded his account."

"The past is dead."

"The past lives, Octavos. As does Titus Maximus."

Singer reeled. He clenched the wall for support. "You've spoken with him?" He couldn't keep the eagerness from his voice.

The woman tapped the packet. "Titus and I exchanged a few communications," she said. She hesitated. "He asked about your well-being."

"How is he? What did you tell him?" Singer loomed over the woman as he spoke.

"I said we communicated," said Doctor Isabella Menendez. "I have not seen Titus Maximus since departing Gawana."

Octavos glared at her. By all rights, the woman before him should be dead, burned along with the rest of Solace's Sages by the mad witch hunter Appius Ambrose. But here she was. For a moment, he wondered how many other sorcerers here had escaped the purge – ten? Twenty? A hundred? He pushed the thought aside.

Isabella did not meet his gaze. Instead, she thrust the booklet and a thick packet at him, "Here."

Octavos took the material. His gaze flicked over the papers. Maps. A list of phrases. Drawings. "What is this stuff?"

"Knowledge," said the old woman, "You'll need this knowledge. You can peruse it aboard the ship."

"Ship? What are you talking about? My place is here, not the far side of the world."

Doctor Menendez put a finger to her lip and pointed to the door. "They're here."

Singer's blood chilled. He peered through the entry. Nothing. He faced the old woman's seat. Empty. Wretched trickster. He stumped from the Athenium in a huff, ignoring his surroundings.

Octavos opened his chamber's door and stopped short. A figure both familiar and unwelcome sat in his chair.

"Greetings, cousin." Manias Maximus smiled. "I apologize for the inconvenience, but you are a devilishly difficult person to find. Why, one might almost think you are trying to hide from your kin."

Octavos exhaled. "What do you want?" He remembered Manias as an obnoxious young prick. He wanted to step across the room and wipe the smirk from his cousin's face with his fist. The large men standing to either side of Manias dissuaded him from that action.

Manias rose to his feet. He stood a good half-head shorter than Octavos. "It's not what I want, it's what the family wants."

He means Varro. Again, Singer saw the body lying in a pool of blood on a tile floor. "I have nothing to contribute to the family," Octavos chose his words with care.

"I am inclined to agree." Manias made a sweeping motion with his right hand, taking in the entire room. "It appears you don't even have a pot to piss in. I have heard tales of you playing in taverns for copper bits. I waited half the night in one establishment whose proprietor insisted you'd be gracing the premises." He gestured at the bruisers. "When you didn't appear, I had the lads toss the fellow off the wharf for lying."

Singer's face flushed. No doubt Manias regarded his action as both restrained and appropriate.

"And here I thought academics enjoyed at least some perks with their profession. But piss-poor or not, Lord Patriarch Varro Maximus demands your presence in Hermosa."

Octavos ignored the insult. "Why am I going to Hermosa?"

Manias' eyebrow lifted. "Two reasons. First, we save the Empire. Then you serve the family."

LABYRINTH WAR II – Curtis

"I spent much of the past year sailing from one end of the imperial sea to the other, encouraging the aristocracy to support Thomas for Emperor." Father launched into a spiel about how superior Cousin Varro's boy was to the other heirs. "Plus, Thomas boasts enough DuSwaimair blood in his veins to make him one of the family. Most of those notables agreed with me." His face hardened. "Then you had to go and rip open old wounds."

- From 'The Journal of Titus Maximus.'

"I haven't seen you in forever!" Emperor Charles DuSwaimair extended his hand as Sir Curtis DuFloret entered the emperor's private suite. "You haven't changed a bit since the old days."

I can't say the same for you. Curtis inhaled air that smelled of sharp herbs and sour medicines. The emperor was a scarecrow of a figure, with yellowish skin stretched across his face and stick-thin arms protruding from the blue and white tunic covering his frame. He looked like a plague victim.

"Thank you, Supremacy." Curtis made what he hoped was a passable bow.

"No, no, no! Lay off the bowing and scraping and 'supremacy' crap. I get a bellyful of that every day. We're alone. Curtis, it's me, Charles, your old comrade in arms."

Curtis straightened and smiled. "I never did take well to the whole court etiquette thing. I haven't had much opportunity to practice these past few years." *Because I was in Agba, the ass end of creation, helping my brothers turn decadent heathens into imperial subjects with no support whatsoever.*

"There's the Curtis I remember," said the emperor, stepping forward and wrapping his arms around the knight in a mockery of a hug. His thin arms lacked any strength. Curtis returned the motion but retrained himself for fear of injuring the Emperor.

The two men separated. The emperor motioned to a trio of armchairs upholstered in red velvet next to a small round table. "Have a seat. How's Beatrice doing?"

"My wife is renewing acquaintances among the ladies of the court." His marriage to Beatrice was purely political, especially after the second miscarriage.

"Hah! She's still the social climber." The Emperor made a dismissive wave. "No, don't answer that." He leaned toward Curtis with a mischievous smile on his face. "I wish to hear about you."

Here is the Charles I remember! He began reciting an anecdote about an amorous merchant's daughter who'd spent time at his brother's estate.

"...So, she's standing there stark-naked staring at the both of them, saying, 'but I thought he was Liam,'" finished Curtis.

Charles laughed and slapped his knee, a rich, deep sound roiling from his chest, at odds with his skinny frame. Tears ran down his face. "Ah, what a sight that must have been! I tell you, Curt, I live for moments such as this."

A knock sounded at the door, followed by the silent entry of an immaculate servant clad in silver and blue. "I apologize for interrupting, Supremacy, but the Admirals of the Fleet await without." The butler's chiseled face conveyed no expression whatsoever.

"Drat. I need to change." The emperor looked at Curtis. "Your garb will suffice."

"What is this?"

"A traditional ceremony prior to dispatching the fleet." The emperor rose and walked to a desk across the room. "Nikolas, show Curtis the document."

A middle-aged man with short curly hair emerged from a doorway Curtis hadn't noticed. He raised an eyebrow. "Supremacy, that might not be wise."

"Just do it, Nikolas. Remember our agreement." With that, Emperor Charles passed through another door.

Agreement?

"As you command." Nikolas bowed and retreated into the other room before emerging with a sheet of parchment. "This is a confidential document. Its contents are known only to His Supremacy and myself."

Secrets. "I understand." Curtis took the proffered manuscript festooned with seals and scribed in legalese. Still, the gist was clear, even to a backwoods knight like himself.

Nikolas vanished back into his lair.

"There must be something in here the right size!" Charles' voice sounded through the door.

"Perhaps this," said the servant's deep voice.

"God, that's hideous. That shade of purple should be outlawed as a threat to people's vision."

"Hmm...This assemblage may be appropriate." Richard's voice was as impassive as ever.

"It's more subdued, anyhow," said the emperor. "Do you think it will fit?"

"It should. Let me...there," a note of satisfaction entered into Richard's voice.

"It's heavy."

"Supremacy, you can bear the weight. And the Admirals are waiting outside."

"Oh, very well." The emperor strode into the main room, wearing a naval uniform dominated by a blue coat larger than some tents Curtis had seen, secured by a double row of gold buttons, head covered by a tricorn hat. "How do I look?"

Like a child playing dress up. "Very...nautical. It compliments you." That much at least was true, the uniform called more attention to itself than the man wearing it.

The emperor whirled upon Richard. "I told you it was hideous."

Richard's hands fluttered. "Supremacy, the Admirals"-

Charles stamped his foot. "Oh, all right. Bring them in. Is the wine ready?"

"Of course." The butler's voice carried a note of distaste. He swiveled on his feet and headed for the door.

Charles turned to Curtis. "You read it? What did you think?"

"It's...clever. But doesn't the Privy Council have agents among the fleets?"

"They do – but they pay far more attention to the legions - which is why I had to dispatch Auxiliary troops to Agba – they pay less heed to peripheral forces."

The emperor took the parchment, folded it, and dribbled wax across the seam which he pressed with his signet ring. He tucked it inside the jacket.

The door opened. Three men in uniforms almost as gaudy as the emperors entered the room.

Richard put himself between the emperor and the new arrivals. "Supremacy, I present the Admirals of the imperial fleets – Admiral Horace DuMars of the First Fleet, Admiral Peter Merrywood of the Second, and Admiral Gerald Whiteraven of the Third." Each officer bowed in turn as they were named.

"Today the empire requires your service," said Charles. "Rise and hear my words: the pirates of the Free Cities are hounding our coasts, raiding villages, and capturing merchant vessels from Prospero Isle, which rightfully belongs to Solaria. It would greatly please me to see this situation corrected." He handed Admiral DuMars the missive. "Your sealed orders."

"Supremacy, we are honored," said Admiral DuMars.

"And now for the farewell cup," said the emperor. He clapped his hands. Richard carried a silver platter with a dark blue bottle and five tiny crystalline flutes into the chamber.

"Sidon wine, from my private stock," said the Emperor.

Richard uncorked the bottle and the aroma of wildflowers filled the room. With efficient motion, he poured a small measure of deep blue liquid into each cup.

Admiral DuMars sniffed his carafe. "I haven't had this stuff in years."

"It's quite rare," said Admiral Whiteraven. "Sidon berries grow in a single valley on Sancti Isle." He swirled the liquid with a nut-brown finger. "In ages past, pagan priests would eat the berries to garner visions from the gods."

The emperor tapped his glass. A chiming sound rang through the room. "Gentlemen. A toast to victory!" He drained the contents of his glass in a single swallow.

"Victory," repeated the Admirals and emptied their flutes.

Curtis followed suit. The liquor was sweet and tart at the same time. His head seemed to expand, and stars filled his vision. Then the cup was empty and there was a pleasant warmth in his belly. He turned to see Admiral Merrywood staring at him with a puzzled expression. "I know you, I think," said the Admiral.

"I am Sir Curtis DuFloret," said the knight. "You commanded the squadron that took Nadak during the war, right?"

Merrywood nodded. "Bloody work, charging ashore in the dead of night and seizing the wall. That escapade is how I made Admiral." He snatched a pastry from a tray. "But Horace there was in overall command." He gestured at Admiral DuMars, who regaled the emperor with a fearsome tale of ship-to-ship combat.

At length, the admirals departed.

"Thank you, Richard," said the emperor. "Sir DuFloret will be remaining with me for lunch."

"Certainly." Richard opened the door and exchanged words with somebody on the other side before pulling a metal-wheeled cart into the room, laden with covered dishes. "Cardinal Cyril waits without."

The emperor made a face. "Send Nikolas out here. Then help me change."

"Very well." Richard bowed deeply, turned, and rapped once on the door to Nikolas's room.

Nikolas stalked into the room and lifted the silver platter from the centermost dish, exposing a savory expanse of diced meats and vegetables swimming in brown sauce. Curtis's mouth watered at the aroma.

Nikolas noticed the knight's stare. "Smells appealing, doesn't it?"

"It does."

"It is a delicious repast, fit for an emperor." Nikolas scanned the contents of the pot. "Alas, it is a trifle over-seasoned for the Emperor's health."

Curtis sat erect. Poison?

Nikolas read the knight's expression. "No need to get excited." He reached into his jacket and extracted a tiny vial filled with a clear fluid. "Here. Drink this. It will keep your stomach settled."

Curtis looked at the vial and then at the platter. "I – what?"

"You'd have a bellyache that would last through the night."

Curtis stared at Nikolas. "Who are you?"

"A loyal servant of the Empire." Nikolas stirred a tiny packet of brown powder into the stew.

"What is that?"

"A special spice."

"I don't understand. Why?"

Nikolas eyed the door. "Choose swiftly."

Curtis grabbed the vial and downed its contents in a single gulp. It had no flavor at all.

"There. That's more comfortable." Emperor Charles reappeared, clad in his original blue and silver. He eyed the cart. "Did they add something extra to the stew?"

"They did." Nikolas bowed and presented the emperor with a second vial. It would have left you incapacitated for tomorrow's meeting."

"Well, I shall just have to disappoint them." The emperor drained his vial.

"I'd best get out of sight." Nikolas exited the room without waiting for a response.

Curtis couldn't restrain himself. "They tried to poison you!"

Curtis smiled. "It happens. They don't want me dead, just out of the way. Now, compose yourself."

Curtis took a deep breath as Richard placed the cart's contents on the table.

The emperor surveyed the repast. "Very well, Richard, I suppose we'd best admit the good Cardinal."

Cardinal Cyril's great beak of a nose and small head reminded Curtis of the vultures that flew over Agba's wastelands, ever alert for carrion. His beady eyes flicked over Curtis. "Who is this?"

"Cardinal Cyril, I present my old friend Curtis DuFloret, who recently returned from Agba."

"Hah. Just as well he's back. Agba is naught but a drain on the Empire." With those words, Cyril dug into the meal, shoving spoons full of the stew into his mouth. "A most excellent repast."

"One of the perks of being Emperor," said Charles.

Curtis had to admit the Emperor was correct – the stew was delicious.

Cardinal Cyril finished his bowl and a small glass of wine. "Now to business."

Curtis glared at the cleric. "Can't I finish this superb repast first?"

"The Empire's business cannot wait."

Curtis placed his spoon on the table. "What now, Cyril?"

"The Church finds your 'Decree of Toleration' unacceptable. Supremacy, we cannot have all these sorcerers, dissidents, heretics, and other free thinkers roaming about the empire causing trouble. They detract from the Empire's greatness. I insist you retract it immediately less it creates complications."

The Emperor cocked his head. "Strange. Your second, Archbishop Green, supported the Edict. He called those people the best and brightest minds of the Empire – a position I agree with."

"I represent the Church, not that milksop!" Cyril's face colored. "Cassius Maximus has expressed his family's displeasure with this edict."

"Cassius Maximus does not head the Privy Council. Lord Stewart DuPaul heads the Privy Council. He supports the Edict."

Cyril's face colored still further. "Don't be ridiculous. DuPaul will not," Cyril leaned forward and violently coughed,

"Defy the Church." A great wracking cough shook the priest's body.

The Emperor watched the clerics convulsions. "I say, Cyril, are you all right?"

"I am fine." Cyril made a weak hand motion. "Something went down the wrong pipe, is all." He finished the statement with another cough.

"I must disagree." Charles faced his butler, who'd stood silently against the wall the entire time. "Richard, fetch a priest of Asclepius. Tell him Cardinal Cyril is ill and requires immediate attention."

"At once, Supremacy." Richard opened the door.

"Nonsense. This. Will. Pass." With those words, the priest toppled sideways to the floor right as a pair of priests with the serpent and stick symbol of Saint Asclepius entered the room, accompanied by a hulking bodyguard with a scarred face.

They scooped the still protesting priest onto a stretcher and carried him from the room while Curtis sat there open-mouthed. "What just happened?" Curtis asked once the door closed.

"One of the worst Privy Councilors is taking a forced retirement. His replacement, Archbishop Green, has a much more reasonable nature. He will support the Edict of Toleration and other proclamations."

"But Cassius Maximus"-

"Cassius Maximus will be distracted by family matters and be unable to attend tomorrow's meeting. Without his presence, Lord DuPaul will consent to the decree."

Curtis stood stock still for a moment. "I prefer battlefields to this sort of intrigue."

"It is necessary." The Emperor moved to a large window.

Curtis joined him. Together, they gazed at the city below: noblemen's townhouses, shops, stables, barracks, churches, and government offices.

After a time, Charles spoke. "Ah, there she is, Ingrid, the light of my life." He motioned at a muscular lady with flowing blond tresses holding court over a group of noblewomen seated in a semi-circle on a terrace below the window and to the left. "Ingrid DuSwaimair, my very own ice princess from far off Gotland." His voice turned wistful. "I would have liked to have seen her homeland."

Curtis picked out Beatrice among Ingrid's courtiers. "She certainly has a commanding presence."

"Yes, Ingrid is formidable. She's tougher than many of my palace guards. That toughness is why I married her – the scholars said the DuSwaimair line was breeding too close. She almost killed me on our wedding night." A band of youths led by a tall blond boy burst onto the terrace and launched into an impromptu battle with toy swords and spears. "And there's my son Thurmond. Quite the rascal, isn't he?"

Curtis eyed the mock combat. "He's good. He'll make a fine knight."

"Flattery?" The Emperor raised an eyebrow.

"No, I'm serious. Thurmond has excellent form and knows how to press the advantage. See?" He motioned right as Thurmond disarmed his opponent.

"Heh." Charles shook his head. "I envy your robustness. The view through this window is what I see of my realm. I seldom leave the Capital. Hell, I seldom leave these chambers, let alone the palace. The weekly audiences invariably leave me bedridden."

"That sounds horrible."

Below, the children vanished back into the palace's innards. Ingrid spoke quietly with Beatrice.

"I have become accustomed to my limitations. They do not keep me from my duties." The Emperor faced Curtis. "Now, tell me about the true conditions in Agaba."

This is what I am here for. This is why I traveled four thousand miles. "Agba fares poorly. We are deluged with refugees from turmoil in Celthania, a western cousin-state of Agba." *He'll think I'm mad if I tell him what prompted their flight.* Many are decent folk but others demon-worshipping filth who infiltrate towns and institute reigns of terror. Good men are murdered in their sleep, riverboats vanish, and there is scarcely a legionnaire in sight. Put bluntly, we need troops or Agba will be lost."

"Troops," repeated the Emperor. "Thomas Maximus is leading a hundred thousand legionaries and another twenty thousand Church Liberators south to repel the Nations of the Plains, who are amassing the largest horde in four centuries."

"I'd heard about that." Every bard, tavern keeper, and petty official he'd encountered on the trip here gossiped about the Horde and the massive Southern Expeditionary Force summoned to repel them. The gossipers spoke of reserve legions called to active duty, jails emptied, and press gangs pulling farmers from the fields to fill the ranks. He'd hoped the rumors were exaggerated. *He won't do it. He can't spare the troops, not with an invading nomad horde. Agba could fall.* "There are no soldiers to spare, then?" He tried to keep the despair from his voice.

"True, most imperial troops are committed to the Southern Expeditionary Force," said the Emperor, "but not all of them. Two Auxiliary Brigades are mustering in Conon. When their ranks are filled, they'll pedal to Agba along the northern route."

Relief flooded Curtis. Two brigades – five thousand men - equaled half a legion. "Thank you. They'll be a godsend." *We could take the war to the cultists instead of cowering in our strongholds.*

"You are welcome. Now, tell me about the upheaval that spawned the havoc in Agba. Tell me about the Gotemik."

Curtis started. "You know?"

"I do." The Emperor motioned at a cubby crammed with papers. "I receive hundreds of missives each day from across the world, each containing a plea, a threat, an offer, or some obscure tidbit. Most are deadly dull. Nikolas sifts through the pile each morning and presents me with the more interesting specimens. The ones from Agba often mention these Gotemik."

"Oh." Curtis thought for a moment. "I have not seen the Gotemik myself. The more trustworthy refugees say they resemble giant crabs. Supposedly, they appeared from parts unknown a decade ago, conquered Celthania, and pushed into the southern plains. Some rumors say they attempted to invade Gawana but were repelled.

"They have functional mechanisms from the Dawn Times, most notably flying disks and weapons that can burn through a stone wall. They use captive warriors fitted with magic collars that compel obedience."

"I see." The Emperor stared into space.

He's going to change his mind. Nobody sane wants to confront a foe equipped with the weapons of the Dawn Races.

"You are a loyal friend and a doughty warrior," said the Emperor after a long silence. "Furthermore, you possess esoteric knowledge. Those qualities make you suited for a special task."

"Name it."

"I wish you to join the Southern Expeditionary Force as my private agent."

LABYRINTH WAR III – Carina

'The witch hunter Appius Ambrose went south to Ismara, where he instituted a reign of terror that angered the entire populace. He fled the city when the Edict of Toleration was proclaimed.'

- From 'History of the Great Purge.'

Carina sat cross-legged on the flat boulder, trying to reach her magic. Eyes closed, hands on knees, she took a measured breath and recited the first focusing ritual. In her mind's eye, she stood at the base of a towering mountain of broken red rock.

She released the wind from her lungs. The image held. She began the second cantrip. She approached the mountain, grabbed hold of a projecting outcrop, and began to climb, pulling herself up the cliff to a wide ledge leading to a plain door of white stone.

As she approached the door, a cowled figure materialized and blocked her path. "Your greed will not let you pass," the being hissed.

"Then you may have my greed," said Carina. A black and green mist seeped from her body and formed itself into a serpentine shape which undulated towards the hooded being. When it touched, serpent and spirit vanished, and a key of plain black iron tumbled to the ground. Carina lifted the key and inserted it in the door's lock, revealing a small space dominated by a large glowing diamond. Her long fingers closed about the gem, which erupted in golden light. Carina blinked.

Carina opened her eyes to find the diamond, door, and mountain were all gone. "Drat," she said under her breath. She'd hoped to break the block this time. Instead, she'd merely chipped the barrier. She sighed. It was more than she'd had before.

Carina rose to her feet and considered the sun's position. The others would be waiting for her. She began picking a path along the stony hillside, keeping an eye out for snakes and scorpions. She detested the creatures. A scorpion sting had killed Anatolia. Given the chance, she'd roast every last one of the vermin. Her vision started turning red. She smelled smoke and heard distant screams.

Carina blinked. The smell and sound were both real. A chill sensation flooded her body. She lifted her skirt and darted around a final outcrop, giving her a view of the Estate, two miles in the distance. A column of smoke rose from its center. The Witch Hunters had found this place.

"Dear God, no," Carina muttered under her breath. Then she was running. *Maybe they won't kill everyone. Perhaps somebody got away.* Both thoughts were futile. The Witch Hunters held a scorched earth philosophy, burning not just magic users, but their families and associates.

The screams stopped as Carina reached the fieldstone wall encircling the complex. Lazy plumes of black smoke hovered above a wide circle of ash in the courtyard between the main house and the shed. Two men in grey armor emblazoned with the sword-and-sun symbol of the Mithraic order walked about the scorched area. One kicked a stone into the herb garden. The other muttered snatches of scripture under his breath.

The stone kicker paused and looked in Carina's direction. Heart pounding, she dropped flat to the ground. *Did he see me? I can't stay here.*

Voices came from the wall's other side. "I thought I saw something." The voice was cultured. Aristocratic. It was also familiar.

Ambrose. Carina stiffened.

Unbidden, an image appeared in her mind.

A row of tall wooden posts outside a stone wall, each holding the bound form of a woman or man – most of the petty wizards and charm sellers of Ismara. A slender golden-haired man in aristocratic garb swaggered before the posts, addressing a crowd of Ismara's citizens: Lord Templar Appius Ambrose, noble scion, and a power within the Church. "For too long," said the speaker, "Ismara has been a byword for decadence and debauchery, a den of whores and addicts and pagans sapping the Empire's strength." He raised his arm. "I intend to remedy this situation by purifying these sorcerous vermin." His hand dropped. Torches flew, igniting the oiled wood piled around the stakes. The screaming began.

Carina blinked. The past dissolved into the present.

"This place is unholy," said a second voice. "I say we finish the last one and leave."

The words hit Carina like hammer blows. Superstition claimed bedded witches lost their power – a loophole eagerly exploited by sadists like Ambrose.

"Tomorrow," said Ambrose. "I grow weary."

Weary from raping Cassie. Her curvaceous body made men howl. Ambrose would save her till the end.

Carina shifted, dislodging a pebble. It sounded as loud as a thunderclap upon striking the ground.

"I tell you, there's somebody out there."

"Then look. I'm going inside."

"I shall."

The sound of footsteps crunching on gravel approached Carina's position. *I can't stay! I must flee! Hide!* She drew a breath. *Calm. Reach for the magic.* She focused her mind, reached for a dollop of golden power, and uttered a spell.

"Huh – must have been a rabbit or stinger."

Carina could feel the man's hot breath on her left ear. She didn't dare breathe. Moving was out of the question.

A gauntleted hand dropped right in front of Carina's nose. Metal-wrapped fingers seized a stone and lifted it out of sight. A moment later a dull 'thud' sounded in the field. "The deeds I do in God's Name." Distaste filled the Witch Hunter's voice. Perhaps a spark of decency lingered beneath the mask of piety he wore. "True God above grant me strength."

Footsteps sounded as the witch hunter retreated towards the house.

Carina raised her head. Nothing moved in the courtyard. Exhaled. The bastards were all inside the house.

The sorceress's gaze fell on a shed past the dwelling. Her lips curled into a smile. If Ambrose wanted fire, then she'd give him one.

Carina skirted a group of picketed horses and reached the shed. A minuscule amount of magic ensured the hinge's silence as she pulled the door open, and a flick of her wrist sufficed to conjure a glowing yellow ball. Racks of tack and tools lined the left wall. She moved the light, illuminating a row of amphorae: The Estate's supply of cooking oil.

Outside, footsteps cracked on gravel.

Carina froze. Her heart thudded like a drum in her ears. The last Witch Hunter hadn't entered the house. Instead, he'd walked around it.

"Whose here?" The sound of metal on leather accompanied the words.

Damn. Carina grabbed an ax from the rack. Then, not stopping, she twisted into the entryway. She caught a glimpse of the Witch Hunter's plain face right before the ax split his skull.

Carina shuddered. It'd been a dozen years since she'd killed another person, back in the Traag War.

"There's something out there." A shadowed figure appeared in the entryway of the house.

Carina forced herself to move. She broke the cap off the nearest amphorae. The lid clattered upon striking the floor.

"Somebody's in the shed!"

"It must be Thomas."

Booted feet crunched across the yard.

Carina grabbed a jug and tilted the big jar. A portion sloshed into the smaller container but most struck the floor.

"Thomas is dead!"

Raised voices followed the exclamation. "Get her! We missed one!"

"I got you, witch."

Carina turned. A brown-haired man stood in the shed entry; blade raised. She threw the jug at him.

The Witch Hunter dodged the missile. The jar struck the stones behind him and shattered. "Women can't throw worth shit."

Carina muttered a spell that should have knocked her assailant off his feet.

The Witch Hunter stood there, unmoved. "God protects me against your vile magic, witch." He took a step towards her.

Carina's grabbed the ax haft and heaved. The tool seemed to weigh ten times what it had moments earlier. She swung at her foe's midsection.

The fanatic stepped back and let the ax-head strike the doorframe. "Pathetic little murderer, aren't you? Weapon-play is man's work."

"You're the murderer!" Carina screamed. "And a filthy rapist!"

The Witch Hunter advanced a step. His face tightened. "I am God's hand. I do His will."

Carina took a step back. She didn't have the strength to swing the ax again. There was nowhere to run. She was going to die.

The Witch Hunter raised his blade.

Carina threw herself sideways. She heard the sword 'whisk' above her head.

"You have fire." A smile creased the Witch Hunter's face. "I like that."

Carina's hand contacted something liquid. Oil. The broken amphorae lay on its side, amidst a pool of flammable liquid spreading across half the floor. "Then have some." Carina focused her will. The oil ignited.

The Witch Hunter's pant leg ignited. He shrieked and dashed from the shed.

Carina curled her lips into a savage grin. But flames licked at her clothes, so she dashed out the door – and almost lost her head to the blade of another Witch Hunter.

"What's going on?" Ambrose, from the entrance.

"We missed one, Excellency." The Witch Hunter before Carina shifted position as he spoke. "She killed Thomas and set Mark's clothes afire."

Carina started to run.

"Well, Dominic, kill her!"

Dominic positioned himself before Carina. Mark rolled on the ground behind him and howled.

Carina tripped and fell.

Dominic crumpled to his knees. Blood burbled from his mouth. Then the Witch Hunter fell face-first to the ground, a long dark shaft protruding from his back.

Carina blinked. She recognized that shaft. Xenia! She must have been out hunting.

Mark clambered to his feet. "Excellency! There's more than one! They just killed Dominic!"

"What? How!" Ambrose's dark silhouette filled the doorway. "I shall settle this myself."

Fear fueled Carina's limbs as she dashed past the flaming hut and into the darkness. "One ran that way." Mark's voice.

"Good God, that's a Monster Hunter's spear." Ambrose's voice trembled.

Carina's leg slammed into a hard stone – the paddock. Hot pain flared along her shin. She gritted her teeth and clambered over the barrier.

"I hear something," said Mark.

"It came from the fence." Ambrose.

Carina craned her neck. She couldn't see the Witch Hunters. Where was Xenia? Had she turned herself invisible? Invisibility was the upper limit of the Saban girl's magic.

Leather slapped against the stone left of Carina's position. At the same moment, she caught a glimpse of a dark outline against the glow cast by the burning shed. The Witch Hunters were flanking her.

Carina rose to a crouch and ran alongside the fence.

"I see her!"

Carina ducked, grabbed a stone, rose, and hurled it at the voice. She heard the missile 'ping' against metal.

"The damn bitch threw something at me!"

"Go on," ordered Ambrose. "She's a woman, armed with a bloody wood ax. You're a trained Mithraic knight."

A long, thin object flew through the murk and struck Ambrose in the shoulder.

"Dat be a Night Adder," said a deep Saban voice from the shadows. "It bites, you die."

"Get it off," shrieked Ambrose. "Aeeii!"

Carina leaped over the fence and charged. The ax caught Mark square in his chest, knocking him to the ground.

Ambrose seized the snake and threw it into the night. "Now, we'll finish" – he caught sight of Carina. His gaze flicked to Mark, squirming on the ground, and clenching his chest.

"Not so brave, now, are you?" The Saban voice came from behind Ambrose.

Ambrose halted his advance. "Leave!" He fled for the picketed horses.

Mark rolled to his feet and hobbled after Ambrose, clenching his gut.

Hoofbeats sounded in the dark.

Xenia's tall, thin frame materialized in the gloom; face framed by the dreadlocks that dangled almost to her waist. She carried a shortsword in one hand and a snake in the other.

Carina took a breath. "Where were you?"

"Hunting."

Together, the two women entered the cottage. They found Cassie sprawled on the floor with her throat cut.

The next morning, they dumped the Witch Hunter's corpses in a deep pit, salvaged what they could from the wreckage, and began walking west, towards the Tefnu River.

LABYRINTH WAR IV – Bao

'Secrets and sorcery fill the air in Kheff.'
– Old proverb

Bao fumed as the litter carried her through Hermosa's crowded streets. She'd spent three years studying at the Grand Librium, and now she was being packed off like some prize cow. Naturally, she'd not been consulted about her impending nuptials. Her prior engagement to Amentep had been ignored – what would he think? But the crowning insult, the greatest humiliation, was her prospective husband – a Slaver!

The litter halted. Its bearers gently lowered its poles until they kissed the paving stones.

Bao took a breath and forced her features into a blank mask. Composure was crucial to the aristocracy, who had to appear calm and rational in all circumstances. Right now, true composure was beyond her. The mask would have to suffice. She thrust aside the curtains.

Ebony-skinned Maaike, Bao's Saban bodyguard knelt and extended her mistress a hand. A pair of dark eyes framed by black dreadlocks peeped from within Saban's hood, gateways into some hidden place. Maaike pulled Bao erect without effort; but she'd been a Monster Hunter, stalking and slaying the thunder lizards and swamp dragons of the southern jungles prior to becoming a bodyguard.

Bao acknowledged Maaike's service with a single nod before letting her gaze slide over the massive edifice before her: The Cabinet Obscure, a depository of odd relics attached to the Grand Librium.

Inside, Bao strode past quasi-magical trinkets: fertility idols with huge penises, feathered tokens intended to ward off dream demons, divination cards, crystals, and fractured clay tablets written in obscure tongues. A worn and vaguely disreputable air clung to the contents of the structure. Were it human, the Cabinet would be the shady uncle fond of filthy jokes and pointless stories – much like its Master.

Bao found that Master, Uday the Fat, in his workshop. Uday boasted a bald spherical head atop a short round body draped in thin blue silks. Talismans hung from a wide belt about his midsection. His workshop boasted tall shelves filled with jars of glass and clay or metal, and flasks of colored liquid bubbled and hissed above the burners on the long table that dominated the center of the chamber.

The mage held a vial filled with brilliant blue liquid to the light as she entered, assessing its contents. "Ah, Lady Bao." Uday's gaze remained focused on the miniature bottle as he spoke. "I understand congratulations are in order."

That confirmed it. Bao's already taunt nerves snapped. "It was you, wasn't it?" She jabbed a finger at the wizard. "You arranged my betrothal to the Slaver Prince."

Uday lowered the vial. "I merely made a suggestion to the Maximus Patriarch."

"But why? I was engaged"-

- "To a man you'd not seen in three years." Uday wagged his finger. "A childish infatuation. Besides, he's little more than a commoner. Octavos Maximus will be a Prince of the Empire when his cousin ascends to the Luminous Throne."

Bao stamped her feet. "I don't want to marry a Slaver! I'll be an outcast, beset by false friends and status seekers."

Uday's face hardened. "Show respect, young lady. The Maximus are more than mere slavers."

"But" –

"Enough, Bao. You are overcome with female passions." Uday tapped his workbench. "You must restore your center." The mage's broad face changed. "I have just the task. There are three boxes of relics in Chamber Four that require sorting."

Bao's heart sank. Her fury evaporated, replaced with resignation. "Yes, Master Uday."

Bao held the palm-sized metal box to the light, squinting at the gears and strikers inside it. A figurine of a veiled dancing girl stood on a disk atop the container. A flat bar protruded from the side. She fingered the projection and felt it move. Encouraged, she twisted the key a full turn and removed her fingers. High-pitched chimes and bells came from within the device. The disk with the dancing girl rotated.

Bao placed the device on the table. It was a music box, a trinket crafted by an infernally clever artisan in Equitant and sent here as a gift or toy to a petty potentate, who wrongly regarded it as magic, not mechanics.

The Slavers preferred their subjects ignorant, and superstitious. Elsewhere in the Empire, priestly orders, guild instructors, and government scholars taught promising youths how to read, write, and do sums. The Slavers forbade such endeavors in Kheff. The Grand Scriptorium outside Ennead had been burned to the ground by Maximus agents disguised as desert marauders. The Advanced Engineering Academy in Gand had shut its doors amidst scandals and crippling fines. Apart from the Great Librium here in Hermosa and the Sorcerers

Pyramid in Ankh-U, there were no schools in the lands watered by the Tefnu.

However, Ptath was far to the south, at the Empire's literal edge. A third of the city's populace claimed descent from imperial troops, giving it a different character than Kheff's other population centers. Maybe, just maybe, the Slavers would overlook a school there. At least, she and Amentep hoped such might be the case.

Except now, she was being married off - sold - to a Slaver who'd no doubt frown on such an endeavor.

The music box stopped. Bao sighed, pushed it to the side of the table, reached into the crate of relics, and extracted a rack of tiny glass vials filled with colored powders and liquids. She squinted at the labels affixed to the bottle's sides: mercury, sulfur...what was this?

Bao's gaze flicked to the fat green gem on the ring adorning her index finger. That ring had been a gift from her grandmother. 'Spiders and Toads are both mortal,' she'd said upon slipping the circlet onto Bao's finger.

A smile creased her face. Perhaps her marriage need not be permanent. She slipped the bottle into her pocket.

Bao peered into the crate. Empty. No, wait – was that a reflection? Perhaps something shattered? She didn't remember any broken glassware. Bao reached into the box. Her fingers clasped onto something solid, transparent, and flat. She pulled her discovery to the light – a flat piece of glass inset with tiny wires and gems, etched with tiny letters along one edge.

Bao read the symbols. Gasped. After all this time...

LABYRINTH WAR V – Singer

'Nimuk lifted his eyes. "Name your ancestors." His tone was formal and distant.

I recited my lineage on both sides of my family.

Nimuk checked his papers. "What seven praenomina's are appropriate for Maximus males?"

I smiled at the clumsy attempt to entrap me. "There are six, not seven: Cassius, Manias, Octavos, Quintus, Titus, and Varro; the praenomina of past emperors."

"Yet you claim Victor Maximus as an ancestor."

"On occasion, another praenomen will be awarded for political reasons. Victor's mother was of the DuSarite family, a clan with imperial aspirations."

"Thomas Maximus being another of these exceptions," said Nimuk.

"Yes." How did Nimuk know of Thomas? "Thomas is a cousin of the imperial family."

Nimuk frowned at his papers. "Ranking Solarian aristocrats have three names: praenomen, nomen, and cognomen. You provided praenomen and nomen; what is your cognomen?"

I smiled. Nimuk Brote displayed impressive knowledge. "Lesser aristocratic families have praenomen, nomen, and cognomen. When one's ancestors are emperors, no other name matters."

– From 'The Journal of Titus Maximus.'

Singer's head pounded. *Too much wine.* He'd been drinking far too much since Manias had loaded him onto that leaky tub back in Solace. *Insufferable little prick. Being with him would try a Saint's patience. No wonder his wife is sauced out of her mind.* He put both feet on the floor and bent forward. Fireworks exploded in his skull. Elbows on knees, Singer grasped his head. *At least we're on solid ground.*

The throbbing in his skull eased a fraction. The colored tile floor receded in and out of focus. No, not tile. A mosaic. He remembered Manias saying something about their accommodation's once being an old palace, built by a merchant adventurer from Carbone. Singer's eyes tracked the colored stones. Most of them were faded. Others were missing. But the pattern reminded him of something...

He walked along a pastel hall, anticipating the sweet and spicy fruit medley at Cousin Varro's. He'd spent the evening resolving the chords of his latest composition. His cousin's door loomed. He knocked. No answer. Instead, the door pushed open, exposing a neat chamber with a mosaic floor and the back of an overstuffed couch. A table laden with cups, plates, and bowls dominated the room's far end.

"Hello?" He took a cautious step into the room. Perhaps they'd stepped out for a moment. The apartment fronted a courtyard dominated by a large pool; Varro was fond of sitting out there, drink in hand. Yes, that was it. He took another step, moving past the couch. Something caught his foot, making him trip. He turned to see two bodies lying face down on the floor, blood seeping from beneath them.

And he fled.

He lifted his head. His gaze focused on a pile of documents atop a nearby desk – his father's original journal and Doctor Menendez's expanded version. In a sense, he couldn't blame her for the forgery. Titus had been terse to the point of frustration throughout the manuscript. He'd written two sentences about the passage through Drakkar: 'This place is cursed,' and 'Louis DuPaul is still an idiot.' His account of the voyage west took two pages, with one describing Cousin Quintus's death. He'd never once mentioned the Maximus Seal. In the maze, Titus used pictograms more than words – but his text matched those in Menendez's edition.

The sound of marching chants and clashing metal drifted in through the open window. The Solarian legions were encamped on the next island over. He rose to his feet, strode to the window, and peered at the long barges filling the channel outside his window. Nut brown laborers in white loincloths tossed barrels and crates onto craft tied to the piers, while soldiers loaded themselves onto others. *We leave today.*

A knock sounded at the door.

An old servant he didn't recognize stood there. "I am Master Pindar. Lord Varro Maximus requests your presence within the hour."

Singer nodded. "I need to bathe and eat first."

"A bath is in order." He clapped his hands, and half a dozen men and women entered, bearing a small tub and a platter of honeyed neat and sliced fruit, along with a pitcher Singer hoped contained wine but was willing to bet held juice.

Singer stripped and settled into the tub without embarrassment while a stern-faced woman inspected his wardrobe, pulling and rejecting garment after garment. At length, she settled on his old Maximus House tunic. Her expression said, 'This will have to do.'

Another woman began combing and molding Singer's hair. He stepped from the tub and reached for his tunic.

Pindar halted Singer with an outthrust hand. "Prince, you are clean but must be made palatable." He clapped his hands again and more women entered, carrying sponges and stoppered jars.

He eyed the containers. "I don't understand."

"You are in Kheff." Pindar motioned at the servants, who unplugged the bottles. "You must look the part. Your skin is much too pale."

"But I'm a Maximus!" He shook his arms in frustration.

"Yes, you are." Pindar motioned again, and a muscular woman forced Singer to sit on a marble bench. "But conformity is important. Your family has ruled Kheff for so long because they are perceived as Kheffian."

"Oh." The woman rubbed oil into his frame. His skin darkened where their hands passed. They made him lay on the slab and massaged the fluid into every part of his body. Then they rubbed a salve into his hair darkening it as well. When Singer gazed into the mirror afterward, a Kheffian gazed back, albeit one with a long nose.

Pindar nodded. "Your appearance is adequate."

Singer slipped into his tunic. Servants strapped his sandals into place. He sighed and squared his shoulders. It was time to face the author of his past nightmare.

The old servant led him along a cool corridor and across a courtyard filled with gossiping women, before passing through another set of double doors. Here, he motioned Singer to wait while porters in the Maximus colors swung the portals open.

The elderly servant stepped within and bowed to a figure perched on a throne-like chair, surrounded by servants and aristocrats. "Patriarch Varro Maximus, I present your esteemed cousin Lord Octavos Maximus."

Octavos took a breath and entered the room. Varro looked just as he remembered; a narrow face with the protruding Maximus proboscis and a blocky body wrapped in a formal purple toga. He was speaking to a much younger square-faced man next to him: Cousin Thomas, prospective heir to the Luminous Throne, should the Maximus be able to garner sufficient support.

Varro deigned to notice his entrance. "Cousin Octavos, I am pleased at your prompt arrival. I have not seen you in ages!"

Octavos inclined his head. "I live to serve, Patriarch." He wanted to say, 'You left me no choice.' Such bluntness was both politically infeasible and personally dangerous.

"Cousin Manias tells me you lived in poverty." Varro's voice held a slightly mocking tone.

"My income vanished during the Coin Crash in Equitant last year." He kept his voice even. Then and now, he suspected the Maximus Family had a hand in that fiscal calamity. "But my needs are modest."

"Nonsense," Varro snapped. "You are a Maximus. We are not modest." His gaze pierced Singer. "You should have returned to Forma."

When Hell freezes over. "Solace seemed healthier," he said, regretting the words as he spoke. His heart pounded.

A shocked silence descended over the court. Even veiled references to the wave of deaths that had propelled Varro to the Patriarch's chair were bad form. "I see," said Varro in a tone radiating menace. "So how did you pass the time in Solace? Still plucking lute strings and singing old ballads?"

"I studied history, mathematics, and physics, sciences needed for success in today's world."

"Quite the scholar," said Varro. "Just like your namesake."

"Octavos did rule longer than any two other Maximus combined."

"He sat on the throne for longer than any other Maximus." A sneer entered into Varro's voice. "Apart from that, he did nothing: he conquered no new lands, founded no new cities, and added nothing to the Empire's glory."

"He commissioned the Cornucopian Bridge in Corber Port, an acknowledged wonder of the world, and granted Solace's University its charter." The court was so silent Singer could have heard a pin drop on the chamber's far side.

"Those are the acts of an administrator, not an emperor," said Varro.

"Emperor Octavos made treaties with Kitrin and the elves."

"He ceded imperial territory," said Varro. "Solaria would have bested both those realms, given time, but your namesake's treaties ended that avenue." Varro shook his head.

"Octavos's education has its place." Thomas addressed his father. "Good warriors often make poor administrators, and vice versa."

"True," said Varro. "Octavos' father was a perfect example of that dictum." His tone became more informal. "Octavos, I respected your father. He was a first-rate soldier, a demon on the battlefield. The way he trounced a superior force at Iron Water was sheer brilliance. At the war's end, he should have been promoted to General and given command of a frontier garrison. Instead, my predecessor made a warrior into a clerk with predictably disastrous results. I shall not repeat that mistake with you."

Varro clapped his hands. A young woman entered. Hard dark eyes pierced Octavos above the pink and blue veil that concealed her face. Gold earrings and locks of auburn hair peeped out from beneath the girl's head covering. A necklace of flat gold plates set with gems hung over the front of her creamy white dress, trimmed in gold and blue. "Lord Octavos Maximus," said Varro, "I present Lady Bao Vada Falun Des Ptath, daughter of Abbas Vadim Des-Path, Governor of Upper Kheff. You should find her most compatible. She is intelligent and attended the Librium here in Hermosa."

My bride-to-be. Octavos smiled. "Pleased to meet you, my lady."

The girl didn't smile. Her expression stiffened.

Varro scowled. "Bao is a little shy," he said in a low voice.

Bao doesn't look shy, thought Octavos. *She looks furious.*

Bao nodded, the barest acknowledgment of Octavos's existence. "Hello." Her voice could have chipped stone.

I foresee a long and unhappy marriage ahead of me, thought Octavos.

LABYRINTH WAR VI – Carina

'The 'Edict of Toleration' undoubtedly saved the lives of many wizards. It did not, however, restore the old sorcerous institutions. Ever distrustful, many arcane practitioners elected to remain hidden, masking themselves in mundane trades...'

- From the 'History of the Great Purge.'

"I know herbs." Carina eyed the assortment of containers spread on the table between her and Demetrius, one of several hedge doctors with the army. Rumor insisted the skinny, pinch-faced man desperately needed an assistant. That Carina found him here, engaged in mundane herbal preparation normally performed by apprentices, led credence to the stories.

Demetrius looked disdainfully at Carina. "Prove it."

He motioned at the array of containers spread across the counter.

A smile creased Carina's face. "All-Heal." She pointed to a bowl filled with purple flakes. "Good for bruises, cuts, sexual pox, and sore throats." Next, she indicated a jar filled with dark oil. "Castor Oil. I bet you sell a lot of that to the camp followers. This next one is Quassia, a treatment for malaria. Chamomile, for burns and female issues. Then Angelica Root, for coughs, digestion, and childbirth." Carina gave a sweet smile. "I wager you keep the Goji berries under the counter."

"Goji berries are under Church ban." The herbalist betrayed not a trace of tension. Goji berries imported from the far-off Yellow Kingdoms were used as abortifacients. "But you do appear to know a fair bit of herb lore. Let me guess: Ismara?"

"No, Corber Port." Carina overemphasized the name.

A thin smile played across the herbalist's lips. "There are many herbalists in Corber Port."

"Too many." Carina fought to keep her voice casual. If Demetrius reported his suspicions...Ambrose was with this army. "That's why I'm here."

"You are familiar with distillation and preparation procedures?"

Carina smirked. "Of course."

"There are three patients in the tent behind me," said the herbalist. "I am most interested in your diagnoses and treatments."

Carina entered the tent, where she found a muscular blond man, whose carriage screamed 'aristocrat' parked next to an attractive brunette camp follower. Another woman read a scroll by candlelight, probably an officer's temporary wife.

The aristocrat came first.

Carina bowed. "My Lord, I am here to diagnose your ailment."

"I have been waiting long enough." Aristocratic disdain filled the man's voice. "Yon bean grinder wouldn't budge his ass."

"Apologies, my lord." Carina eyed the shirtless man, noting the scars creasing his body.

The knight grimaced. "Just rid me of these cramps."

"Cramps?"

"Yeah." The man rubbed his belly. "My gut is tied in a knot."

Carina pursed her lips as she ran through a mental list of possibilities. "Any other symptoms?" She pressed the knight with questions about aches and ailments. Finally, she nodded. "Bad food."

"I thought that beef tasted off."

Carina stepped outside the tent and snatched a jar from the counter. "Aloe Vera." She measured three doses. "This should help, though I also recommend rest."

The knight stumbled from the tent. Carina turned her attention to the other patients. The Reader's head almost touched that of a Kheffian in the cream-colored tunic of a petty official.

The blond glanced at the Reader, who responded with a quick 'go ahead' motion. She faced the fug. "Guess I'm next," she said in a bubbly voice. "I'm Chrissy. I did five men last night. Now, I have a rash."

"Are you taking precautions," asked Carina. "Keeping yourself clean?"

The blond woman nodded. "Course. Don't need no little one, and they'll boot me out if I got pox."

"Let me see."

Chrissy dropped her shift with no shame whatsoever and presented a cute butt marred by a red rash for inspection.

Carina probed the mark and asked a few questions. "You should be all right." She fetched doses of All-Heal and Tamanu oil. "No screwing for a couple of days."

"Sure," said the brunette. "Could use a break anyhow. Maybe I can write letters for the troops." That comment prompted a raised eyebrow from Carina and a slight scowl from the reader. Camp followers weren't normally literate, especially here in the southern reaches of the empire. Maybe Chrissy was a disgraced student?

Chrissy left. Carina emerged from the tent to find Demetrius grinding herbs with a mortar and pedestal. "Where's the Sin Book?"

Demetrius cocked an eyebrow. "My, you are experienced." He reached under the counter and extracted a large thin book secured by a tiny lock. "Chrissy?"

Carina nodded as the herbalist undid the book's clasp and scanned the notations. "Miss Chrissy has been busy. Very busy."

"Popular," said Demetrius as Carina scribbled. "You'd best get back inside."

The Reader waited within the tent and placed the tome on a folding table. "I am Lady Jazmine Bottle, Mistress of the Camp." Jazmine leaned closer to Carina. "Managing the Tail is something of a family tradition."

Carina blinked. The Bottle Clans lifestyle revolved around outrageous parties and drunken orgies. "My Lady."

Lady Bottle cocked her head. "Yes. You are an escapee sorceress from Ismara."

Carina's heart pounded. "My Lady, I"-

"No, don't say a thing." Lady Bottle pursed her lips. "You need not fear I'll hand you over to that animal Ambrose. This army needs all the healers it can get, a point lost on pious assholes. That is why I informed Demetrius he was hiring an assistant."

"Uh, thank you, Mam."

Lady Bottle plopped her curvaceous rump on a cot and smiled. The fine dress slipped from her shoulders, exposing olive-toned flesh. "It's time for my beauty treatment – the essence of coconut and Maharajan oil."

Carina blinked. The former component came from the Black States. The latter was imported from Chou. Both were sinfully expensive. "You know the procedure?"

"I have done it." Twice. Carina rummaged through the supplies and found a tall bottle filled with the Chou oil. But she didn't see the essence of coconut. "One moment." She stepped outside the tent and found Demetrius wrapping the hands of a chunky man in an artisan's smock.

"Return tomorrow," instructed Demetrius.

Carina surveyed the containers spread across the counter.

"Ah," said Demetrius. "Lady Bottles beauty treatment?"

"Yes." Carina frowned. "I need the essence of coconut."

"Here." Demetrius reached beneath the table and produced a stoppered jar.

"Thank you." Carina smiled and ducked into the tent, where she found the now nude aristocrat speaking in a hushed tone with a blushing young man in the gold tunic of an imperial messenger.

"I'll have a reply for you tonight." Lady Bottle waved the courier away and reclined on a padded cot.

Carina rubbed oil on her hands and knelt by the woman. "You seem busy."

"Always." Lady Bottle sighed as Carina rubbed the oil onto her body. "That feels simply divine."

Lotion applied; Lady Bottle plucked a scroll from the table. She scanned its contents and eyed Carina. "This may interest you."

"Oh?" Carina washed her hands.

"It's from my brother Caspar, adjunct to Admiral DuMars."

"I thought the fleet was blockading Prospero Isle."

Jazmine smiled. "The fleet didn't blockade Prospero Isle – they captured it.

Admiral DuMars made a big show outside the harbor while the Marines landed on the other side in longboats. The pirates never knew what hit them. Then they went to Ismara to celebrate."

"That must have been an impressive celebration."

"Oh, it was," said Jazmine. "Three fleets filled with horny sailors stormed into Ismara's fleshpots. Caspar had quite the time." She frowned at the paper. "The scoundrel claims he bedded a rachasa! Imagine that!"

"That's impressive," said Carina. Not to mention perverse and suicidal. She remembered the rachasa cat-folk from the Traag War: short furry creatures with thrice the strength of a man and fingers boasting retractable claws capable of punching through armor.

"Hmm...we may encounter rachasa," said Jazmine. "I wonder..."

The tent flap parted. A woman in a stained smock stepped inside and bent her head next to the aristocrat's ear. "Very well," Lady Bottle told the woman. "I shall see to it." She faced Carina. "Walk with me."

The women exited the tent. To their left was the low earthen wall of the legion encampment. The legionaries routinely constructed such a fortification after a day's march but these walls had been erected centuries earlier. Long lines of soldiers moved barrels and bundles hand to hand from squat buildings to the barges pulled alongside the riverbank. This encampment was one of several supply depots along the Tefnu River. A mishmash of colorful tents to their right marked the knight's camp. And in between lay the mad mix of tents which comprised the brothels, shops, and taverns of the tail.

A group of veiled women watched the anarchy from the aft deck of a barge painted in bright colors. Rumor said one of those women was the future bride of Octavos Maximus. Rumor also insisted the future bride guarded her virginity with a miser's zealousness. *That is going to be a fun marriage.*

A long narrow dispatch boat shot past the barges, heading upstream. Kheff was too backward for signal towers.

They skirted a field where soldiers played an impromptu football game to raucous cheers and jeers. The sport was insanely popular among the Empire's commoners, who celebrated their team's victories and rioted when they lost.

The aristocrat's course took them next to a rude table where two legionaries and a drunken squire tossed dice amidst jeering spectators, and then past a cluster of men gathered around an 'L' shaped table of planks on barrels where more troops drank themselves insensate.

"There are a hundred thousand legionnaires and another twenty thousand Church soldiers in this army," said Lady Bottle. "There are also two thousand knights, plus cohorts of scouts, sorcerers, and special units, each with its own officers. Then there is my domain" - Lady Bottle paused and spun in place – "The Tail - ten thousand colorful and contemptible individuals whose services are as necessary as any sword swinger. Here, my word is law. But I cannot be everywhere at once."

Their guide halted and gestured at a large man speaking to a knot of civilian guards and a mangy crew in the green tunics of imperial scouts. "That's him, my lady. The big one."

Carina studied the fellow. Past fifty, with short cropped gray hair and a bulging belly. Stretched and faded military tattoos lined his arms where they protruded from the battered leather shirt that covered his torso.

Lady Bottle cleared her throat. "I would speak with you."

The man broke off his conversation with a long-limbed legionnaire so covered with hair he resembled a monkey. "Yes?"

"You are Cam, senior agent for Tiberius of Arcos?"

"I am. What of it?"

"I am Lady Jazmine Bottle, Mistress of the Tail. I have a proposition for you."

"We'll talk more later," Cam told the apish soldier. Then he faced Jazmine. "What sort of proposition?"

"I am informed you are a decorated veteran of the Traag War." Jazmine approached Cam and pointed at the tattoo on his right bicep. "Impressive. Primus Pilus – First Spear - of the Sixth Gemini. The Islanders."

"That's right."

Carina wasn't so sure. The 'VI' looked more like a 'VII' to her, and the 'twin' or reserve notation seemed tacked onto the rest of the tattoo. The Seventh Marfaki had a much more interesting reputation than the Islanders.

"What happened," asked Jazmine. "As First Spear, you were entitled to lands and wealth upon discharge."

Cam's face colored. His features contorted. Then he took a breath. "Wine, women, and slow horses happened. I left the Empire for a time and fell in with Tiberius. Now, what do you want? An Enforcer?"

"A Commander." Lady Bottle made a sweeping motion. "I wish these people trained at arms, should the Tail come under assault."

"You want me to turn this pack of whores, peddlers, servants, and riffraff into a militia."

"Yes." Lady Bottle nodded. "And I want you to police the camp."

The football game ended. Several of the spectators headed in their direction.

A gap-toothed smile appeared on Cam's face. "I can do that."

"Go away, pale boy." The familiar voice came from Carina's side.

"Oh shit." Carina climbed a hillock. "Xenia."

"Interesting." Lady Bottle spoke from beside Carina. "A Saban Monster Hunter. You know her?"

"We traveled together." Carina kept her gaze on Xenia. A barrel-chested soldier latched onto the Saban girl's elbow.

"Go away." Xenia dipped her spear point. "I ain't no light skirt."

"True," said the soldier mauling her. "You're not wearing a skirt. Or much else either. Just that vest and those little pants."

"You tell her, Gordy!" The second trooper shouted to a squat fellow whose body resembled broken yellow bricks piled atop each other.

"Shut your trap, Paul," said Gordy.

Xenia jerked away from Gordy and waved her spear. "I gonna hurt you!"

"Put that toy away before you get hurt," said Paul.

Xenia's unwanted suitor lunged for the spear.

Xenia sidestepped and twisted, her foot hooking the soldier's ankle.

Gordy landed hard on his rump.

The butt of Xenia's spear hovered an inch above his nose.

Lady Bottle pursed her lips. "Your friend is good with that spear."

"She can take care of herself." Carina glanced around. Was Ambrose or one of his agents snooping nearby? Raised voices drew her attention back to Xenia.

"God cursed Saban bitch," said the third trooper, whose neck was hung with a pantheon of saint's symbols.

"Time to put you in your place." Paul rushed Xenia.

Xenia's spear spun, its shaft slamming into the back of Paul's neck, knocking him face-first to the ground.

Gordy came off the ground and slammed into Xenia's midsection, knocking her backward.

The haft of Xenia's spear cracked against Gordy's neck.

"Ow!" Gordy forced Xenia to the ground. "You'll pay for that!"

Paul rose to his feet. "Told you to put that toy away. Now I'm gonna"-

A massive fist slammed into the side of Paul's head, knocking him off his feet. "Now," said Cam, "you are going to find something else to do."

Gordy craned his head. "Who the hell are you? This ain't none of your business."

"He works for me." Lady Bottle's voice carried across the clearing. "And I run the Tail."

"Move!" Cam's face colored.

Gordy and his friends departed.

Cam turned to Xenia. "Nice footwork. You want a job?"

LABYRINTH WAR VII – Singer

"Know this, the Maximus name carries immense weight in the Solarian Empire. My ancestors include emperors, statesmen, generals, and men of wealth.

"Servetus Rufus was a merchant in Corber Port with a tortuous kinship to my family. He used this alleged relationship to profit in his enterprises, falsely naming himself a Maximus agent and confidant. When some of his schemes went awry, he would take refuge behind the family name, and none dared touch him.

"Eventually, my grandfather decided he'd had enough of this merchant muddying our name and took subtle action. Servetus began to suffer one misfortune after another: his dockside warehouse burned to the ground, moneychangers denied his loans, and a major shipment vanished. His wealth evaporated. Somehow, the sums demanded by his creditors matched the value of his worldly possessions. Servetus barely had two silver pieces to rub together afterward."

"Masterful." Varian sipped from his cup.

"Ah, but there's more," I said. "Despite being ruined, Servetus still possessed many contacts, a shrewd business instinct, and the ruthless acumen to employ both. Ten years after losing his first mercantile empire, he'd built a second. But now, he had a different reputation: as one who'd defied the Maximus clan and prospered."

"Some people never learn," said Varian.

"True. Servetus fell victim to footpads who pressed their attack despite losing four of their number to his bodyguards."

- From 'The Journal of Titus Maximus.'

"Damn, that cliff is a monster." Singer stared at seven waterfalls that dropped from the clifftop and split the city. He spotted two bridges across the river, one at the base, the other near the summit.

Prince Thomas Maximus pointed at a diagonal line climbing the cliff on the waterfall's right side. "That must be the Portage." Shops and dwellings lined the portage route.

Octavos scanned the area left of the waterfalls. "I don't see the Elevator."

"There." Thomas pointed at a tongue of water sliding into the Tefnu. "That must be the access channel."

Octavos sighted along the channel. His gaze settled on a patch of cliff that seemed too straight and regular. "So that would be the Elevator. Doesn't look like much."

"Octavos, we're miles away yet."

"True." Octavos felt his cheeks flush. *What an idiot.* He turned from the distant city and focused on the riverbank two hundred yards in the distance. The barge passed a bland row of single-story mud-brick farmhouses, each surrounded by an identical patch of brown dirt. From this distance, the farmers working those fields appeared identical: skinny dark brown men wearing dirty white skirts. No doubt they shared the same thoughts. Kheff placed a great emphasis on tradition and continuity. 'Not an original thought in the whole damn country,' one of his professors at Solace had said of Kheff.

"So, how went the big date last night?" asked Thomas.

"Terrible. That horrible chaperone hovered over us the entire time. When I offered to strum a tune, the hag started talking about the 'loose morals of minstrels.'"

"God, I can just imagine," said Thomas. "Did Bao at least talk this time?"

"She quoted entire passages of Pliny and Thucydides," Octavos grinned. "This time we held hands. I thought the chaperone was going to faint. The best part of the night."

"I wager it was." Thomas laughed.

"What news from your wife?"

"Celia assembled a vast mob of waiting women from the other left-behind wives. They've been visiting the theaters each day." Thomas winced. "They took in Decker's 'Ladies of the Camp' last week."

Octavos smirked. "That must have been an eye-opener for her." To say 'Ladies of the Camp' was lewd was a serious understatement.

"Oh, it was. Celia's promised 'consequences' should I visit the Tail."

The floor jolted beneath Octavos' feet. "We've stopped."

An almost solid wall of wood choked the river from bank to bank. "Gand's docks must be out of space," said Thomas. "Poor planning."

Octavos spotted a regal figure making imperious motions on a craft ahead of theirs.

"Is that your dad?" Octavos pointed at a regal figure making imperious motions at a flock of underlings with bobbing heads.

"Yep," said Thomas. "He just can't resist imparting his own brand of confusion."

"We'll be the rest of the day getting through that mess," said Octavos.

"Maybe, maybe not." A gleam appeared in Thomas's eye. "How about riding in the Water Elevator instead of just seeing it from afar?"

"Varro will be pissed," said Octavos.

"I am exercising initiative." Thomas grinned. "I'll find Captain Zamir."

Octavos watched Thomas disappear. Thomas was the only person in the army who could disobey Varro's orders without penalty. Varro's path to the throne lay through Thomas.

Octavos was still mulling the point over when a flurry of signal flags sprouted from the barge, and they altered course towards a line of barges heading for the Elevator channel.

Thomas reappeared with an ear-to-ear grin splitting his face. "Zamir didn't say a thing – just started issuing orders."

Of course – only fools objected to orders given by the future emperor.

They inched into the channel, closely followed by a massive supply ship.

Pandemonium erupted among the Maximus Patriarch's syncopates. Varro ignored his agitated underlings, instead rotating in place to view Thomas's barge, impassive as a statue.

Thomas saluted and deliberately turned to face the ancient stones of the Elevator wall.

Varro countered with his own salute, followed by a chopping motion directed at his minions, who instantly found other tasks.

The rock wall grew ever taller. Large pools dominated the landscape to either side of the channel, runoff ponds for the Elevator. And then they were before a huge gate of thick oak planks bounded with iron. Near naked laborers with huge thighs and biceps strained at a horizontal spoked wheel, and the portal jerked into the air, exposing a damp tunnel.

Captain Zamir's blocky form strode the deck, screaming curses and orders to his crew as the barge slid inside the tunnel.

"Cool in here," said Thomas.

"And dark," added Octavos. He hadn't felt this cool outdoors since Solace.

The barge burst into the light, at the bottom of a deep crater.

Captain Zamir steered his vessel alongside two other craft already present. Four more barges emerged from the tunnel and were made fast to the others.

Thomas pointed to a deep vertical gouge in the walls. "Those must be the spouts."

No sooner had the words left his mouth than a gong sounded, and water poured through these channels. Thomas heard a distant 'boom' as the tunnel door closed.

Octavos studied the rising water, comparing it against marks on the cliff. "This is going to take hours."

"At least it gets me away from Varro," said Thomas. Octavos had noticed that about his cousin: He never called Varro 'father.' "That's been getting increasingly difficult these past few years. He used to check on me every few months. Now, though, he is always close at hand. Titus this and Titus that." He sighed. "God, I hate that name. It's cursed, you know."

Octavos nodded. Nine Titus Maximus's had sat upon the Luminous Throne. None reigned for more than a decade before meeting a violent end.

Titus was Thomas's official Maximus name, one that he'd rejected in favor of Thomas. He faced Octavos. "You had it lucky."

Octavos shook his head. "My father went missing when I was little. Mother died in Equitant. I miss them both."

"Well, he was a Titus. They always get themselves killed." Thomas's voice radiated false sympathy. "But cheer up: soon you'll be married, and soon after that you'll be governor of Upper Kheff."

"While you contend with Chancellor Varro Maximus."

"Killjoy."

"Maybe he'll eat himself to death. Remember how his brother perished from too much food?"

Thomas laughed. "I can hope."

The ascent continued in silence.

Manias awaited the barge at the crater's summit. Like Octavos and Thomas, he was decked out in royal Kheffian garb but Varro appeared more animalistic than regal. "Father wants to see both of you now," he said without preamble. "I have a litter waiting."

Thomas and Octavos looked at each other. "Had to end sometime," said Thomas.

They climbed into the litter, a giant thing bigger than a wagon, with a score of stout bearers standing ready. Manias shouted directions. The porters heaved and began walking at a measured pace, singing a tonal chant.

Octavos caught glimpses of the upper city through the litter's curtains. First, their course took them alongside blocky warehouses and then they cut across a wide market plaza. Flashes of leather and white ivory caught Octavos' eye. "These people deal with the Black States."

"And with the nomads and others," said Thomas.

"Pack of sneaky bastards," said Manias. "Not like Lower Kheff, where the darkies do as they're told.

The litter ducked into a street between two tall buildings and stopped. Manias poked his head through the curtain for a moment. "Crap. Goddamn ship blocking the way."

Octavos stuck his head through the curtain. A row of bulky porters strained at poles projecting from the side of a barge on a giant wheeled cradle, moving it step by plodding step along the street. Like the litter bearers, the boat movers chanted under their breath. That song, Octavos was certain, predated the

Empire. It might even date back to when Kheff was a mere puppet state for the inhuman Old Races.

"There must be at least a hundred porters on this side alone," said Octavos.

"Closer to two hundred," sighed Manias. "And by ancient writ, they have the right-of-way."

"They work fast," noted Thomas. "The Portage is two miles long and they almost beat the Elevator."

"They did beat the Elevator," said Manias. "This is the tenth or twelfth ship."

The barge passed. The litter resumed its journey. When Octavos peered through the curtain, he saw another ship pulled up the street.

The litter passed into a respectable neighborhood, where wrought iron gates opened into courtyards fronting manors sporting carved columns and animal-headed sculptures. At the fourth of these estates, the litter turned and entered a yard studded with lemon and pomegranate trees before halting before a pair of double doors.

"Remember, we are aristocrats, not brawling children," said Manias.

The trio approached the mansion with their backs straight and heads held high. The watchman saluted and swung open the portal. "Straight through the hall and up the stairs to the left," said Manias.

A short corridor opened onto a wide hall with scattered tables where robed men and women hunched over papers stacked next to bowls of fruit, bread, and cold meats. Servants bowed before them, their heads touching the floor. Manias took measured steps to the chamber's far side.

Octavos belly rumbled. He hadn't eaten since morning.

The stairs proved empty, though a pair of legionaries lounged in the upstairs corridor. "He's waiting for you," one said as they approached a green portal carved with vines and trees.

Inside, Varro waited for them across a table perched on a low dais. Behind him, a tall map depicted Lower and Upper Kheff. The contrast was stark: Lower Kheff was dominated by the wide Tefnu valley, while Upper Kheff was a triangular plateau. Other imperial provinces framed Lower Kheff. Upper Kheff was a jutting finger with Soraq to the west, the Black States to the east, and the endless plains to the south.

"Titus, what were you thinking?" Varro began without preamble once the door shut. "You were supposed to ascend the Portage with me so you could be seen."

"It's Thomas, not Titus." Defiance rang in Thomas's voice.

"That's enough of that nonsense." Varro made a furious chopping motion. "Thomas suited you when it suited the family. Your name is Titus, and you will use it!"

"No."

Varro colored. "If I didn't need you – I have no time for this. Do you wish for a measure of independence? Very well, you shall have it. As of tomorrow, I am returning to the Capital."

"What happened?"

"That meddling idiot on the throne happened. First, he snuck troops into Agba. Next, he had the fleet conquer Prospero Isle outright instead of establishing a blockade. Now, he's taken advantage of Cardinal Cyril's ill health and cousin Cassius's stupidity to weaken our alliance with the Church with this ridiculous 'Edict of Toleration.' Worse, he managed this without alerting my spies – and my spies are everywhere."

"You fear we are compromised," said Thomas.

"I fear more than that," said Varro. "Left unchecked, that imperial idiot might cripple my plans. Hence, I must return to the Capital and explain to him why one never crosses the Maximus Family. So, you get to defeat the nomad horde without me looking over your shoulder."

"But I will be there," said Manias.

Varro nodded. "Yes, Manias will be accompanying you as my representative. General Tullos will oversee the army."

"Thank you," said Thomas.

"Don't go thanking me just yet." Varro waved at the papers covering the desk. "We have much to discuss tonight and more to hammer out tomorrow. Disturbing reports have reached my ears." He tapped one of the papers. "The Ptath garrison almost fell to a nomad probe yesterday. Nobody knows how they slipped past the forts. Worse, scouts returned with word of three more tribes joining the horde."

"It sounds dangerous."

"It is dangerous, so personal preparations are in order." Varro pulled a rope hanging from the ceiling. A bell tolled. A door to the left opened, and a burly Westerner entered the chamber. "Octavos, this is Sir Curtis DuFloret, your instructor in the martial arts."

LABYRINTH WAR VIII – Curtis

'The questions began.

"You abducted Bethany Euripides, scion of the imperial family, from the Parthenon manor."

"No," I said.

Cora's expression twisted.

"What?" Simon's face colored.

"No. I attempted to rescue Bethany Euripides before the Parthenon family could murder her."

Simon appeared baffled. "Titus, Eugene Parthenon was not about to kill the emperor's cousin. You had to know that. The emperor would have retaliated."

"The old emperor did not retaliate when the Parthenon Family murdered Bethany's parents."

Simon shifted in his seat. "Charles DuSwaimair was in a different political situation. Besides, the Parthenon's had plenty of allies during that fiasco."

"Bethany Euripides was alone and presumed dead since childhood. Her claim, her very identity was uncertain. The Parthenon Family could easily have killed her without consequence. That is what I believed." A tingling sensation ran across my scalp as I spoke.

"You're lying." Simon's words were a flat declaration.

"He's not," said Cora.

Simon turned his head. "What? Are you sure?"

Cora returned his look. "I am Godborn, able to sift lies from truth. Despicable though he is, this man believes he rescued rather than kidnapped Bethany Euripides."

Simon shook his head. "Well, Bethany didn't think so."

"She is not here," said Cora.

Simon glared at me. "You knew nothing of my negotiations with Eugene Parthenon?"

"Not until I saw you speaking with him outside the city gate. Until then, I believed you were in Saba to hunt thunder lizards."

"Gaius is right." Simon shook his head. "You are ignorant of politics."

"My purpose in Saba was purchasing slaves, not intrigue."

Cora's face twisted in disgust at my mention of slaves.

Simon rubbed his head. "What of my brother?" His voice was low and dangerous.

My palms grew slick. "Self-defense. Carl attacked without warning when I emerged from the carriage." My words were true, but there was no way Simon could accept them.

Simon's face turned red.

"He speaks true," said Cora.

"No!" Simon lunged across the table.'

- From 'The Journal of Titus Maximus.'

Curtis swung. His wooden practice sword slammed into Octavos' stick.

Octavos twisted away from the blow and smoothly dropped to his knees. His stick slammed into Curtis's right ankle. "Ha! Got you!" Octavos shouted.

"Ouch!" The boy's blow stung. Curtis dropped the tip of his sword against the back of Octavos's neck. "But you're still dead."

A part of him wished for a steel blade instead of a stick. *One less Maximus to infest the world.* He dismissed the thought. Octavos was an innocent soul, unlike the rest of his clan.

Octavos laughed and rolled to his feet. "That makes, what, fifty times you've killed me?"

Curtis winced. "You're getting better. I'd say you're a match for a legion recruit." Curtis waved across the field where legionaries battered at each other with wooden swords or practiced marching with interlocked shields.

"So, I might survive a real bout."

"You might." Curtis grinned. "If you keep up with your practice and exercises. Speaking of which, why don't you take a nice jog around the field?"

A mock groan escaped Octavos's lips. "But it's almost lunch!"

"I'll save you a plate." Curtis motioned at the field. "Now go!" He watched the boy begin a deliberate jog. *I should have made him run with a log strapped to his back.* Curtis sighed and started for his tent, intending to shrug out of his armor in private.

I need a squire, Curtis thought not for the first time. But this army was short on squires. And other retainers required by proper knights. *It didn't used to be like this.* Curtis remembered listening to Uncle Rood's tales about the old days. 'Being a Knight meant something back then. I had three squires, four grooms, a blacksmith, and five servants. Your Uncle Ghent had more.'

The final battles of the Traag War ended those glory days. The histories said ten thousand Knights charged the enemy at Crowfoot Gap. But the histories lied. Ten thousand armored men on horseback made that charge. But only half of them were proper knights. The rest were jumped-up squires and sellswords.

Some – maybe a hundred, maybe more – weren't even men, but women. And of those ten thousand, just two thousand lived.

Cheering voices drew the knight's attention to a rowdy crowd watching a football game in a muddy field. Sir Fury was taking bets on the sidelines. Curtis shook his head and detoured around the mob to an improvised archery range.

"Draw!" The voice came from Cam, the former legionnaire who bossed the tail camp. Curtis watched him stride along a line of archery students, correcting stances. "Feet there," Cam shouted at one pupil. "No, hold the bow like this." He took the bow from a skinny woman and demonstrated the correct grip. "And again! Draw and release!" A ragged flight of arrows shot from the line of would-be archers. Perhaps a third hit the archery butts.

"Damn pussies." Sir Richard Fury appeared, waving a wine bottle. "Women belong in the bedroom or the kitchen, not on a battlefield." He punctuated the statement with a pinch to the ample rump of a brunette struggling to draw a bow.

Fighting, fornicating, gambling, and getting drunk - that was Sir Fury for you. He'd spent most of the last decade as a hanger-on at Sir Hugh Allergan's steading in Agba until some drunken impulse made him decide to accompany Curtis back to the Empire.

Curtis spotted a bucket beside Sir Fury's boot. "did you find us any provender?" He'd begun the river voyage with seven barrels of beef, bread, and vegetables, along with a pile of hay. Three of those barrels and half of the hay were stolen in the first week. He'd pooled his remaining provisions with two other knights out of prudence.

"Provender." Fury cocked his head and spat. "Fancy word for moldy bread and green meat." He held up the bucket. "No, I have figs and fish taken from a local girl too plain to poke."

Curtis sighed. "Did you pay for them?"

"I showed her my dick. That was payment enough."

The last thing they needed was trouble with the locals. "Richard"-

"I tossed in a brass ring and two coppers." Siry Fury scowled and kicked a stone. "Happy now, Sir Shit-Don't-Stink'?"

Curtis started for their tent. "Maybe the army quartermasters will part with a sack or two of grain."

Sir Fury shook his head. "The Tribunes put the fear of God into those rascals when their tallies came up wrong. Now they guard that grain better than their virgin daughters."

"Maybe the officers didn't get their cut." Selling army goods was a quartermaster corps tradition.

"No, this is different," said Sir Fury. "Things have gone missing that shouldn't, it seems. Maybe you can get that pansy-ass kid to cough up something."

"Octavos depends on his cousin's generosity," said Curtis. "Though he might send a few bottles of wine our way."

"That would be something."

Curtis's small, plain tent hove into view, scrunched against three others. A gray-robed figure stirred a pot between the tents. *Then there's my retinue: Julie the Whore-turned-Cook and her sister Sadie.* Curtis shared the sister's services with his partners.

"Ho, Julie, what's for lunch?" *Please don't let it be fish.*

"Fish stew," said the crone without lifting her head from the cauldron.

"You got mail." A second crone came out of the tent, clenching a pair of scroll tubes. She handed one sealed with the DuFloret insignia to Curtis. "You got one too, Sir Fucks-A-Lot." She held out the second cylinder marked with the crossed blades of the DuMars clan.

"Give it here." Fury angrily wrenched the tube from Sadie. "I wonder what those pricks want?"

Curtis popped the seal on his tube, It was a long letter from his wife Beatrice who'd ingratiated herself among Lady Maximus's companions. She described watching 'Ladies of the Camp' in one of Corber Port's seedier theaters ('You better not take a Campaign Wife,' she'd written) followed by a shopping spree in the city's Grand Market. *I hope the Maximus are footing the bills.*

That thought reminded him of his obligation to the Emperor. *I should scribe another missive to 'Cousin Rock.* He sighed. *I'll be talking about 'barren fields' again, though.* He reported via simple codewords inserted into otherwise innocuous letters to 'Cousin Rock.' 'Barren fields' meant 'nothing new to report.'

Something sailed past Curtis's head and bounced off the tent.

"Fucking busybodies!" Sir Fury held his letter in a grip so tight he'd torn the paper.

Curtis glanced over and saw the scroll tube beside his boot. "What now?"

"It's about my bastards. The eldest is a hulking dimwit, the second is a sneak thief, and the third is a homily girl who mixes potions and poultices. They're worthless! Yet my asshole brother went to Lord DuMars, saying I must do the honorable thing and legitimize them. Hah!" He crumpled the paper. "I started with naught but a horse and a sword. Everything else I have comes from the battlefield, dueling ring, or gaming pit. Why should they be any different?"

Curtis sighed. "You had the advantage of your Name."

Sir Fury exhaled. "Yes, my Name did open a few doors. But I had to earn the rest."

"So, have them earn the Fury Name."

"Huh." Sir Fury stroked his chin. "Well, the dimwit is handy with Grandad's old broadsword. He might make a passable knight despite being dumber than a rock. The Sneak can swing a sword, but he's better at skullduggery."

"Maybe he'd make a good scout?"

"Maybe." Fury shrugged. But that leaves the girl. She's a potion mixer for God's sake!" He paused. "She did give me a salve that worked wonders on my joints." He strode off muttering to himself.

"Sir Curtis?"

Curtis turned to see a youth in Maximus's livery. "I'm Curtis." Had Octavos gotten in trouble?

"Thomas Maximus requests your immediate presence."

"Immediate," said Curtis. "As in right now, not after lunch."

The youth nodded.

Curtis sighed. "Well, lead on then." He wondered if there'd be food.

Thomas was at a table when Curtis reached him. Bowls of fruit and platters of bread covered half its surface. However, Curtis lost his appetite upon glimpsing Thomas's companion, the Witch Hunter Appius Ambrose, known throughout the ranks as 'Asshole Ambrose.'

"I tell you," Ambrose told Thomas, "I smell witchcraft."

"Your man perished from a knife through his throat," said Thomas. "No great surprise, considering his behavior." The prince tapped a stack of papers. "I have a dozen complaints against him right here."

Curtis was willing to bet Thomas had even more complaints about Ambrose.

"I tell you; Sir Russo was on to a nest of witches." Ambrose made a pushing motion. "He found them out and they killed him."

"Cousin, what gives?" Octavos approached the table. With him was a big, bearded man whom Curtis recognized as Sir Dominic Falk. "Why am I missing lunch?"

Thomas gazed at the assembled group. "Good. You are all here." He focused on Dominic. "Sir Falk, I understand your father has a steading near here."

Sir Dominic bowed. "Step Keep, where the Snake drops into Soraq."

"You were planning on paying him a visit?"

"I was," said Sir Dominic. "Has something arisen?"

"Something has," said Thomas. "Sir Russo, vassal to Lord Ambrose, was found murdered this morning."

"Sir, I assure you, my father had naught to do with this," said Sir Dominic.

"I make no such accusation," said Thomas. "Yet the scouts tell me Russo's murderers fled along the Snake, and I have received many disturbing reports out of Soraq."

"That's where the witches must be hiding," said Ambrose. Everybody ignored him.

"You desire intelligence, not rumor," said Octavos.

"Yes. My magicians report a presence that impacts both the mystic and the material realms in Soraq."

"Witches," said Ambrose. "They must be destroyed."

"That is one possibility," said Thomas. "But until an investigation is made, I will not know. Hence, I am sending the lot of you to Sir Rodger Falk's steading."

Sir Dominic stroked his beard. "That's a day and a half each way."

"We'll be taking on provisions here until late tomorrow," said Thomas. "Kane village is a few miles south of here, but the river makes a great dogleg from this depot. We should reach Kane at the same time."

Sir Dominic nodded. "That could work. But we must depart now."

"Of course." Thomas motioned behind the knight. "Your mounts are behind that tent."

Curtis started for the tent in question, paused, then spun and grabbed a loaf of bread and a pair of pomegranates from the platter.

Thomas smiled. "Help yourself."

Curtis did so as did Sir Dominic and Ambrose. Naught was left of the repast but a solitary biscuit and a wedge of cheese when they mounted their horses and left the camp.

The party's course took them west on a rutted road parallel to the Snake.

"We're at the edge of the Empire," Octavos remarked.

"Almost," said Sir Falk. "The Upper Tefnu flows west and north. South and East, aye, that's the Black States. But north"- he waved a hand at the dusty brown hills to their right, "that's the Empire. Or at least the tribesmen dwelling in those hills pay taxes to the Empire, and their sons join the legions."

"Falk is an Avar name," said Octavos. "What brought your father here?"

"Hammerford," said Sir Falk, naming the bloodiest single battle of the Traag War. "Father rode with Prince Morgan. Afterward, when Morgan was handing out awards, Father asked him for lands in a place where it never snowed." He smiled. "Morgan kept his word. Didn't see snow until I rode north. Thought Pa was pulling my leg."

"Any other Avar hereabouts?"

"Yeah," said Sir Dominic. "Six or eight have places along the old Copper Road. I used to ride over to Bruin Steading all the time. I damn near married Richard Bruin's daughter Stacy."

"The Copper Road," Octavos mussed. "Is that the old caravan route to Nomos?"

"It used to be," said Sir Dominic. "Now it's the main route through tribal country."

They spent the evening in a roadhouse manned by a plump Kheffian who sweated too much. "Our host is too nervous, to be honest," said Ambrose. "This place is watched."

None of the others disagreed. They departed at dawn.

A band of ragged, brown-skinned figures plodded towards the imperial party along the rutted track, towing a pair of rickety carts piled high with jars and bundles. Caged chickens squawked from atop the second cart. Upon seeing the imperials, the procession stepped to the side, eyes downcast.

"Poor bastards don't look like they've had a decent meal in weeks," said Curtis.

"They're from Soraq," said Sir Dominic. He stopped next to one of the older men and said a few words in a language Curtis didn't recognize.

The elder mumbled a response.

Sir Dominic made a cutting motion and spoke a second time.

Another member of the band, a child of twelve or fourteen, approached the knight and commenced an impassioned monologue, complete with expansive hand gestures. This speech prompted black looks from the older people. A baby began wailing.

Sir Dominic scowled and asked more questions. He received short, fearful responses. At length, he turned to Curtis. "These people are refugees, fleeing the town of Pathak." He shook his head. "I thought my grasp of the tongue fair enough, but maybe not. They say the Demon Citadel claimed Pathak."

"See, I told you black sorcery laid at the heart of these troubles," said Ambrose.

Curtis ignored the Witch Hunter. "A warlord conquered the village?"

"That's what I thought," said Sir Dominic. "But these people insist there was no army – just walls that sprouted overnight from the ground."

"Gawana," said Octavos under his breath.

Curtis glanced at the youth. Octavos's skin had turned pale. His body trembled. "What are you going on about?"

"Walls sprouting from the ground," said Octavos. "I have read similar tales about Gawana, the great labyrinth."

Sir Dominic snorted. "Gawana is thousands of miles from here."

Curtis held his silence. Octavos had reached that conclusion far too quickly for his taste. The boy knew something. *Maybe I do have something interesting to tell Cousin Rock.* He considered what codewords might be appropriate.

They resumed riding.

At midday, they approached a squat fortress next to a small lake. "Pa's steading," said Sir Dominic.

"Somethings wrong," said Curtis. He'd seen plenty of abandoned buildings. Regardless of the country, they all had the same look.

"You're right." Sir Dominic spurred his steed into a gallop.

"Wait, damn you," Curtis shouted.

But Sir Dominic did not slow his steed, instead galloping towards the fortress. Then the arrows began to fall. One caught the Knight in the throat, hurling him backward off his steed.

"Witches," said Ambrose.

"Enemies of some sort," said Curtis.

"Now what do we do?" Octavos asked.

Curtis looked at him. "Now we go back. Thomas will send a company to reclaim the property."

"We're just going to leave him?" Octavos's eyes were wide. His hand trembled.

An innocent no longer. "Yes," said Curtis. "There's nothing we can do."

"Except pray," said Ambrose.

LABYRINTH WAR IX - Chimp

'Unlike many other Church Leaders, Bishop Sybil of the Fabian Order was sympathetic to sorcerers. She employed her authority to persuade many of Corber Port's magicians to take vows as lay brothers and sisters, bringing them under Church protection, thus negating the charge of wizards stealing divine power. Those who did not take such vows she charged as common cheats and frauds, devoid of magical ability. She steered others into positions with powerful patrons, especially the military.'

- From 'The History of the Great Purge.'

Lines of fire shot through Chimp's arm as he wrapped his fingers around a protruding stone. His long toes dug into a crack in the wall. Above him, yellow lantern light spilled from an open window – his target.

Sticks's mangy paw latched into the same crack as Chimp's foot. It was time to move.

Voices wafted through the opening. Chimp froze. God damnit, it was night. These people were supposed to be asleep. Instead, they were wide awake and jabbering in some heathen lingo. He cocked his head. They sounded agitated. Did they know about the army? Had he been discovered? He did his best to melt into the wall. The thick dark hair that covered his body helped make him invisible.

That half-elf loon Bramble was nowhere to be seen. Had he wandered off? Stick's labored breath sounded like a muffled trumpet. Dogface's sword 'clinked' into the rock. To top it off, a vile odor reached Chimp's nostrils. Skunk. A walking cesspit of smells. Idiots. Bloody wonder they hadn't woken half the castle.

Wood slammed into stone. The speakers had closed the shutter.

Chimp sighed. Now he'd have to pick a different window. Shades enchanted spectacles threatened to slip from his nose as he studied the overhead stonework. The petty wizard couldn't see color, but to him darkness was daylight. His lenses transformed the pitch-black night into dark twilight, making it possible to discern features. Shade had other tricks that would be handy here – spells that twisted shadows and made men invisible, but the skinny shit couldn't climb worth a damn, so he was down with Razor and Snuffles the shifter girl trying to take the gate.

There. Chimp selected a new handhold, found a nub to plant his foot, and heaved himself towards a dark gap. Two more pulls and he'd be there. He reached and straightened his leg – and the rock beneath his toe snapped, leaving him held aloft by three fingertips and two toes as the broken shards cascaded towards the wall's base.

Chimp's heart pounded. His fingers slipped. He took a breath. He'd been in worse spots in his thieving days. Scaling Raven Tower had been bitch – no handholds to speak of, no magic glasses, and ward spells set into the tower. This backcountry keep was downright easy by comparison. His free hand curved over a nice, deep projection, three finger joints deep. He exhaled, steeled himself, ignored the fire in his muscles, and resumed the climb.

Chimp reached the window, peered through, and picked out a narrow hall that transformed into a descending stairwell. He was willing to bet Lord Fire had half his troops bunked in the underlying level.

Chimp got one leg inside the room when a skinny kid in blue came into view. The kid opened his mouth.

Shit. I can't have him raising the alarm.

Chimp got his other leg inside the room and drew his sword. He hated having to do this –

Then a wild-haired figure dashed past Chimp and touched his fingertip to the kid's forehead. The youth crashed to the floor.

Bramble turned to face Chimp. "You weren't going to kill him, were you?"

Chimp stared at the half-elf. Damn the insubordinate bastard spell slinger. "We got a mission.

Agitated voices rose from the stairwell. Were they onto Razor's bunch?

A door popped open and light spilled out. A big, gray-skinned man in a fancy leopard robe entered the hall.

Shit. That man had to be Lord Fire. If he rallied his troops...Chimp grabbed Bramble and pointed at the stairwell. The petty wizard had a couple of spells that might buy them a minute or two.

Bramble glanced at Lord Fire and then at the stairs. Then he grinned and jabbed a finger into his arm, the sign for the Stinger Spell. The Stinger was like getting hit with a swarm of bees – the jabs hurt enough to make six or eight men stumble and drop stuff but didn't inflict true damage.

Chimp watched Bramble glide towards the stairs. Then he ran straight at Lord Fire, who'd turned to face somebody else inside the room he'd just exited, intent on driving his sword through the man's back.

Lord Fire twisted right before Chimp's blade struck. Worse, the rebel leader grabbed Chimp's wrist.

Desperate, Chimp wrapped his free hand around the rebel's neck.

Lord Fire slammed his back – and Chimp - into the wall so hard the timbers cracked. Shade's magic glasses fell to the floor.

Agony exploded in Chimp's chest. The breath left his body in a 'whoosh.' His grip on the big guy's neck faltered.

A huge racket featuring curses, shrieks of pain, and animal howls blasted from the stairwell.

Then Sticks's sword left a red slash across the big guy's chest.

A helmeted head popped into view in the stairwell.

Lord Fire shouted. His oversized fist collided with Stick's cantaloupe-sized skull, knocking him halfway down the corridor.

Helmet Head reached the summit of the stairs.

Dogface tackled Lord Fire.

Helmet Head shouted and planted his blade in Dogface's backside.

Dogface screamed, spun, and slammed into Helmet Head, knocking both into the stairwell.

Sticks picked himself off the hallway floor just as a pair of teenage boys with clubs burst through a door. The skinny soldier sheathed his sword in the first kid's gut. The second youth walloped Stick's head.

Chimp managed to take a breath despite being squeezed against the wall.

Skunk slithered through the window as Helmet Head, or his first cousin reappeared in the stairwell.

Chimp grunted, braced his legs against the wall, and pushed Lord Fire.

Wounded and off balance, Lord Fire tottered two steps and went head-first through the window.

Skunk's sword cut Helmet Head's throat.

Sticks and the second kid rolled on the floor.

Another door opened in the hall. A white-haired geezer entered the fray, backed up by a huge woman with a frying pan. They drove Sticks back from the second kid.

Chimp grabbed his sword.

Blaze, the last squad member, stuck his head in the window. "A great big guy fell right past me."

Chimp took a pain-filled breath. "That was Lord Fire."

Blaze hauled himself inside as Skunk's sword clanged off the gal's frying pan. "Mission accomplished."

Screams of pain came from the stairs, followed by a dog-like creature with bloody fangs and crimson claws – Snuffles.

The shifter leaped past Chimp and knocked the geezer into the wall where he slid to the floor.

The frying pan fell from the stout woman's hand as her face contorted in terror.

The shifter raised a claw.

"Please." The woman sank to her knees.

Chimp glanced around. He didn't see any other opposition. It was time to end this. "Scout Recruit Sammy! Cease!" 'Sammy' was the shifter's real name. Chimp put every bit of authority he could muster into the word. Shifters, never the most stable of people, sometimes went berserk, and Snuffles was new to the army. If that happened...

But the shifter's claw stopped its descent. Her form blurred, rearranging itself. Then Chimp was staring at a nearly naked woman, shorter than himself, covered in thick hair. She faced Chimp. "Killing done?"

Chimp took a breath. "Yeah, the killing is done for today."

"Good." Snuffles sniffed the oldster's hair. "Spicy. I like." She eyed the frying pan. "Got food? I hungry."

The plump cook gave a slight nod.

That was Snuffles for you – a murderous monster one moment and complimenting folks the next.

"I could stand some grub myself." Bramble came up the stairs. "Where's Dogface?"

"He got his head bashed in."

"He ain't the only one." Sticks rolled to a sitting position. Blood leaked from his scalp.

"Bramble, get Sticks patched up."

"I want to eat." Snuffles stared at the frying pan, apparently willing food to appear.

"Get cleaned up first."

"There's a tub in this room." Blaze pointed at a doorway.

"Bath?" Snuffles glanced at the blood and other substances matting her fur and sighed. "Yes. Need bath." She latched onto Blaze's wrist. "You need a bath too."

"Uh." Blaze shot Chimp a nervous look.

"Go with her," said Chimp as Snuffles pulled Blaze into the room. He turned his attention to Bramble, who massaged Sticks's skull with his fingertips. Bruises and scars vanished in his digit's wake. Bramble's healing knack made it worth putting up with the rest of his crap.

"That feels better." Sticks leaned against the wall with a blissful expression on his face.

"The Tribune wants a report." The hollow voice came from a tall skinny fellow with pasty skin wrapped in gray rags. Shade. "Where's Sammy?"

"With Blaze, taking a bath."

Shade raised an eyebrow. "Well, she was dirty. That reminds me." He extracted a bundle of leather and cloth from his robe and tossed it at Chimp. "Her uniform. Tribune Bates is a stickler about such matters. Ah." He knelt and retrieved the spectacles. "Intact. Good."

Chimp and Sticks exchanged glances as orange dirt dropped on Dogface's body.

Sticks's limbs twitched as he dropped another pile of soil atop the body. "He was an asshole. Owed me ten denarii. Wouldn't pay."

Chimp's shovel bit into the ground. He stared across the shallow grave at Sticks. "He was one of us." By 'us,' Chimp didn't mean the imperial army – the V Nomos, or 'Sand Runners' in their case. He referred to the 'Sweepers,' the ragtag band of rogues they'd run with back in Corber Port until things went sideways, and joining the army seemed the best way out. "Old crew."

"He was an asshole back then." Sticks plopped more orange soil on Dogface's corpse.

Chimp couldn't dispute Sticks's words. Dogface had been a bully back in the old days – all of four years ago. "Still." He emptied his spade, covering the body.

A whiff of bad air announced Skunk and Shade's arrival at the burial site. "Tribune Bates wants to see you, Chimp," said Shade.

Chimp planted his shovel. "That so? Wonder what he wants now? We made our report."

Skunk shrugged. "Maybe he wants us to check out that mess in Soraq. Us being scouts and all."

Sticks threw more dirt in the grave. "Think there's anything to this Demon Citadel hoodoo?"

Chimp shrugged. "I don't know." He didn't care to find out, either. He handed his shovel to Skunk. "Finish up here."

Skunk stared at the shovel like it was a poisonous snake. He considered 'work' to be a dirty word.

Chimp faced Shade. "How's Blaze doing?" The redheaded giant was New Crew, not old, but still part of the squad.

"Bramble says Blaze's injuries are superficial."

Well, that was something.

Fifty legionnaires were busy in front of the fort, affixing manacles to Lord Fire's former subjects. Rumor said the prisoners were being shipped north, to spend their remaining days as farm slaves in Lower Kheff and Niteroi. The luckier ones might get spots as house servants or artisans.

Other legionnaires tinkered with the bicycles that had brought the cohort here. Bicycles. Chimp had pedaled the contraptions from Hermosa to Marfak and back since joining the legions - twice. A hundred miles a day, easy. Versus maybe half that on the barges – on a good day. If he'd had his way, the army would have biked the whole way to Ptath. But Kheff's roads weren't worth spit and the Maximus wouldn't allow it. They didn't want the locals to see bicycles.

Bramble came by and traded a few quiet words with Razor. Those two shared a history that went back to a frozen tunnel in the northern part of the empire during the war. That tunnel opened into a hidden city filled with elves and goblins who hated Traag with a purple passion. The imperials figured they'd found allies. They were wrong – that bunch was into serious black magic. Bramble and Razor were damn near the only ones to make it out. The army rewarded them with a flogging and five more years tacked to their hitch.

Chimp found the Tribune parked behind a field desk in the gatehouse, stuffing papers in scroll tubes. He halted at the desk and saluted – Bates was a stickler for such things. "Decurion Chip Cobble reporting as ordered, sir." It felt weird using his real name.

Bates stuffed another sheet into an already packed canister. "Your squad ready for travel?"

"Yes sir." Chimp hoped Bates didn't send him into Soraq.

The Tribune motioned at the tubes. "Good. Take these back to the main army."

Chimp did a double take. "You're not sending us into Soraq?"

"No need." The Tribune tapped the tubes. "A couple of the prisoners were talkative about conditions there. The Generals want that intel straight away."

"Courier duty."

"Yeah, courier duty." Bates nodded. "You get to leave this glorious shithole for an even bigger shithole. Get your squad together."

LABYRINTH WAR X – Bao

'Octavos produced a black flute as long as his arm. He climbed atop a low table against the far wall and bowed. "I will now perform 'Winds of Summer' by the great minstrel Marabous." He put the flute to his lips.

I expected childish whistles. Instead, Octavos coaxed a smooth, pleasant melody out of the instrument.

"He possesses true talent."

"He's been practicing," said Ann.

Octavos finished 'Winds of Summer' and started 'Raven's Flight.' Ann snuggled alongside me on the couch.

Octavos finished 'Raven's Flight' and began a dance tune whose name escaped me.

I rose to my feet. "Shall we?" I asked Ann, extending my hand to her.

A twinkle appeared in her eyes. "I'd hate to disappoint the musician," she said as I lifted her from the couch.

We embraced.

The music was smoother than our dance steps. But it didn't matter.'

- From 'The Journal of Titus Maximus.'

"I think he's cute," said Fatima to Princess Bao as they came on deck.

Bao glared at her maid. The silly girl was concerned only with superficial things.

"He's weak," said Maaike. Bao's bodyguard awaited the pair on deck. "An advisor, not a leader. Most definitely not a warrior."

Bao disagreed with that assessment. Octavos displayed subtlety and intelligence.

"He will be your husband," said Wafa from within the companionway. Why must there be so many stairs on these wretched barges?" The older woman's breath came in heavy gasps as she reached the deck.

"He's a Maximus," said Bao. "A Slaver."

Wafa clumped over to the rail and grabbed it with both hands. "That makes no difference. He is still your betrothed." She eyed the military encampment on the Tefnu's bank, neat rows of tents hard against a walled compound dominated by large stone warehouses and a trio of grain silos. "What transpires here?"

Bao glanced at the depot. Muscular legionaries made human chains that passed heavy sacks and tall clay jars from the station to ships tied to the piers. "I don't – oh." She caught sight of a cluster of imperial soldiers and Kheffian officials on the dock. Tall General Tullos, resplendent in his plumed helm and gold breastplate, confronted a short, stout, dark-skinned Kheffian in a green silk robe bisected with a red sash.

"General Tullos is displeased with Depot Master Bashir." Maaike waved her spear at the pair.

"I hope the General doesn't crucify him." Fatima furiously waved a hand fan before her face as she spoke. "I had nightmares last time."

Bao repressed a shudder. Tullos was the epitome of Solaria – arrogant, brutal, efficient, and intolerant of flaws in others. She didn't doubt the General would nail the depot's entire staff to crosses if he concluded they were guilty of pilferage – which they no doubt were. Corruption figured into all transactions in Kheff.

"Your inventory claimed nine silos of grain, twelve thousand amphorae of marinated meat, and another twenty thousand bushels of figs." General Tullos's voice carried clearly across the open water. "Yet, I find two towers empty, half the listed amount of meat, and a mere nineteen hundred baskets of figs."

"I told you, the caravan"-

Tullos made a cutting motion. A massive centurion clouted Bashir's head.

"I disbelieve you," said Tullos. "Can't you curs grasp the simple fact that without the imperial army, the nomads will slaughter the entire country?"

Bashir stared at the planks. "I do, but"-

A red-cloaked Tribune dashed onto the dock and saluted. "Sir, a caravan approaches. A large one."

Tullos glared at the officer. "How large?"

"Two hundred wagons, perhaps more."

The General returned his attention to Bashir. "What do you know of this?"

"Excellency, it is the supply train from Kamu." Bashir's face was shiny with sweat.

"For your sake, it'd better be." The entire procession marched along the dock to the station's corner, where the Tribune pointed at a line of carts cresting the valley wall.

"Centurion!"

"Sir." The soldier saluted.

"Get the caravan's cargo inventoried immediately. Then, form another chain and load the goods directly onto the transports."

"Yes sir." The centurion took two steps towards the slope.

"One other thing."

The Centurion paused.

"Depot Master Bashir appears to require a bath. See to it."

"With pleasure, sir." The muscular soldier yanked Bashir clean off his feet and hurled him into the river.

"I suppose a bath is better than being nailed to a post," said a voice from behind Bao.

Bao and her maids whirled in unison. The Slaver Scion stood on the small deck, clad in pastel silks, clenching his lyre case in one hand. She wanted to demand how he'd gotten aboard her barge. But a display of temper would be inappropriate. As would any other emotion. "My Lord, you dressed...informally...this time."

The Slaver smiled. "Toga's are beastly hot and uncomfortable. I never got used to the things."

"Much that is necessary in life is uncomfortable." Like having to marry a Slaver.

"True." Octavos ran his hand over the circular case. "But many discomforts can be avoided. And life has pleasures as well as sorrows. During our previous engagements, I played traditional court songs. Acceptable, but dry as dust. Tonight will be different." He motioned at the hatchway. "Shall we?"

The Slaver's music matched his boasts. His fingers thrummed across the lyre's strings, evoking wondrous sounds. Subtle and bold melodies transported Bao from chill northern forests to stormy seas to pastoral landscapes. Octavos sang of daring lovers parted by circumstances, followed by a saga of youths venturing into the world seeking fame and fortune. He sang about ordinary people finding joy despite adversity, halting only when the watch blew the midnight trumpets.

When the Slaver departed, Bao turned to her maids. "What do you think?

Wafa stretched. "My father warned me to beware of minstrels for their music could lead even the most poised women into temptation. Tonight, I see what he meant." She rose and shuffled towards her tiny sleeping compartment. "Fortunately, he is also your betrothed."

"This Maximus uses music the way soldiers use swords," said Maaike. "He thinks, something most men never do. That makes him dangerous."

Bao turned to her third maid. "And you, Fatima? You are a skilled musician."

Fatima stared across the room. "I can sing, play, and dance. But that one, well, he possesses a musician's soul. He's wasted as an aristocrat."

Bao nodded in agreement.

LABYRINTH WAR XI - Singer

'Grandfather reached beneath his desk and produced a sheaf of papers that he made a show of examining. Inspection complete, he stared me in the eye with such force I lowered my head.

"Titus, what were your instructions in Saba?"

"To purchase slaves suited for quarry and fieldwork." I kept my head low.

"Did your brief include kidnapping, arson, and homicide?"

"No sir."

Grandfather's hand tapped the papers. "So, tell me, why am I reading of the botched abduction of a lost imperial heir, riots, and aristocrats dying in the streets?" He tapped his fist on the desk for emphasis.

"Well?" Grandfather demanded.

I swallowed. "I sought to act in the best interest of the family."

"Bethany Euripides had been missing and presumed dead for a dozen years without affecting the family interests in the slightest!"

"I believed she should be under our control," I said. "I saw an opportunity for the family to profit."

"She slipped your grasp!"

"She used magic." The words escaped my mouth before I could contain them.

"She used something you neglected when you embarked on this scheme – her wits!"

- From 'The Journal of Titus Maximus.'

Octavos joined Thomas on the barge's prow.

"There it is," Thomas waved at the blocky shape rising in the distance. "Ptath, font of the Tefnu River...and ass-end of the Solarian Empire."

"Hey, that's my future home you're talking about." Octavos craned his neck, taking in the scenery. The Tefnu flowed arrow straight from a gap in Ptath's battlements, a gap aligned with a tall triangular shape behind the city wall. Orchards and fields thick with crops lined the river to either side. Octavos thought he could leap from the barge to the riverbank. And even if he fell short, the Tefnu was only waist-deep here anyway.

"Your presence will improve the place." Thomas laughed.

The barge approached a channel jutting westward towards a large, fortified compound. "The legion docks," said Thomas.

"Think there's room for all the barges?" Octavos asked.

"No," said Thomas. "I discussed this with Captain Zamir earlier. "Not by half. We'll have to commandeer berths in the Outer Market – that's it on the left – and the Aeolia Fountain as well."

"Barges in the Grand Fountain?" Octavos raised an eyebrow. "That'll piss off half the city."

"Better pissed off than dead," said Thomas. "We'll also need to erect Marcher Camps to house the troops. The locals built more barracks but it's still not enough to house our numbers."

Behind them, Pindar cleared his throat. "My lords, we have sufficient time to make you presentable before the barge docks." He bowed and waved at the stairs.

"If we must," said Thomas.

"Appearances matter," said Pindar. "Speaking of which, might I suggest toga's instead of Kheffian attire?"

"I'll be roasted alive," said Thomas. Octavos nodded in agreement.

"Proper attire will remind these provincials just whom they answer to." Pindar made vertical motions with his finger. "Remember: Impressions matter."

"And first impressions matter most of all," finished Thomas. "Lead on, then." He waved at Octavos.

They retreated below decks, where Manias was already being fussed over by half a dozen attendants, striving in vain to make him look regal instead of rodent-like.

"Do Octavos up special," said Thomas. "He has some courting to do and must look his best."

An hour later, Thomas, Octavos, and Manias stood on the barges foredeck as it squeezed through a dark, narrow tunnel. Then the craft burst into the brilliant sunshine illuminating the Grand Fountain of Aeolia, the source of the Upper Tefnu. The 'Fountain' was a large square the size of a lake, its points aligned with the sides of a larger square, creating four triangular markets or plazas, now packed with nobles and curiosity seekers clad in light flowing robes of pale blue, soft pink, or translucent yellow. Few wore the traditional white kilt and vest prevalent throughout Lower Kheff.

But it was the Great Pyramid of Zep that attracted Octavos's attention. This ancient pile of cracked and pitted stone rose from the Fountains center, climbing over two hundred yards into the sky. Common superstition claimed ancient gods built the Pyramid. Others insisted it was a lingering vestige of the alien Old Ones. *I'll have the rest of my life to determine which tale is the truth,* Octavos thought as the barge docked.

"By the numbers," said Pindar.

Imperial troops, resplendent in crimson capes and armored leggings, wheeled and marched off the barge.

"Our turn now," Thomas smiled and waved. Then the three cousins joined the others.

"This wretched thing is hot." Manias tugged at his toga. "And heavy."

"Don't embarrass me," said Thomas.

"Greetings, brave defenders," said a white-haired aristocrat on a low dais. Vestments of black and white were draped over his pastel pink and blue robes. "I, Governor Abbas Vadim Des-Ptath, welcome you to our fair city and pray for your speedy victory over the Southern Horde. Come, enjoy Ptath's renowned hospitality."

The three Maximus dipped their heads. "We are pleased to accept your offer." Thomas faced the crowd. "I am Prince Thomas Maximus, commander of The Southern Expeditionary Force. We come here to repel the barbarians threatening the Solarian Empire. Victory!" He raised his fist.

The onlookers cheered. "Victory!"

The governor waved at a flat cart equipped with luxurious purple benches. Brown-skinned men in sandals and kilts stood before the wagon. "My personal conveyance."

"You are most thoughtful," said Thomas.

Manias barely made it onto the conveyance before collapsing. A loud sigh escaped Octavos's lips when he sat. "At least I don't have to walk across the city wearing this thing."

"Smile and wave," said Thomas. "Smile and wave." They did plenty of both as the imperial procession inched along a broad avenue to a huge villa with a red tiled roof. The crowds waved back, though not with great enthusiasm.

Here, the imperial column filed through a gate of brass and wood to an inner courtyard arrayed with linen-covered tables, set with silver plates, rose-colored crystalline goblets, and gleaming eating implements. The Maximus, as befitted their exalted status, were seated alongside Governor Des-Ptath and his family on a long platform at the courtyard's far end.

Musicians played a succession of upbeat imperial tunes.

The Governor himself escorted Lady Bao to an empty chair next to Octavos. Dreadlocks secured with rings of gold and ivory framed her face, while a floor-length dress of pink and blue concealed her body. *At least she's not wearing a veil this time,* Octavos thought.

A wide smile appeared on Governor Abbas's face. "My daughter looks forward to renewing the bond between our respective families."

The girl glared at her father.

The Governor's smile remained fixed as he pulled back the empty chair. "Alas, other business awaits."

Bao gave Octavos a disdainful glance and sat, eyes focused on her empty plate.

Rows of kilt-clad servers appeared, each bearing large platters or jars. One placed a savory-smelling bowl of meat and vegetables on their table. Octavos speared a portion with a convenient fork and put it on Bao's plate.

Bao ignored the gesture.

Another server materialized and poured rose-colored liquid into the goblets. Octavos took a sip. *Spicy – but good.*

Servers sat more dishes on the table: a large bowl of creamy white soup, a platter of hot bread laced with spices, and fruit.

The musicians switched to a local ballad, featuring a long wailing monologue.

Octavos snagged two of the buns and placed one on Bao's plate.

"Don't." Bao's voice was soft, almost a sob. "Just don't."

What's wrong with this girl? "My lady"-

Bao's head rotated in Octavos's direction. "Don't speak to me." Then her head dropped.

"But you need to eat," Octavos spoke in his most soothing voice.

Bao said nothing. Still, she lifted a fork and took a tiny bite. *Well, that's something.*

"I tell you it is getting worse!" The raised voice came from a plump man in a red vest and white shirt three chairs away. Like the governor, vestments of black and white were draped around his neck, marking him an important member of the Des-Ptath clan.

"Odalis, it won't spread past Soraq," said the man next to the speaker. He wore the crimson dress shirt of a Solarian officer.

"Just like it wasn't supposed to claim Pathak," said Odalis. "Well, it did, and now it's a day's walk from Dessau."

Singer stiffened; his food forgotten. *They're talking about Gawana. Or something like Gawana.* He remembered his father's claim that Gawana would someday swallow the world.

"Dessau is a small town," said the officer.

"Dessau is twenty miles from here," said Odalis.

"Dessau sits atop of a thousand-foot cliff! The walls can't scale it."

"But they can claim the trade road below it," said Odalis. "Ptath depends on that highway for lumber and herbs. Plus, Dessau is swollen with refugees from Tarrit and Olin."

"My concern is the nomads assaulting us to the south." The officer focused his attention on the food before him.

Odalis started to speak again but stopped. Octavos wondered if he should introduce himself. *Odalis knows things. But what do I say? No, I need to think.* He returned his attention to the plate. The once savory meat and vegetable dish had gone cold. Unappetizing. The soup tasted flat. The spiced bread...was just bread. And Bao was gone.

Where did she get off too? Octavos glanced around the courtyard. There. He spotted Bao and a fit young man wearing black and white vestments entering a doorway.

Singer's stomach clenched. *Now the damn food doesn't agree with me. I'd best find the jakes.* He rose to his feet.

The mansion's interior proved a bewildering maze of corridors and stairwells populated with rushing servers, statuesque guards, and petty officials. Finding the jakes took a while. Then, when finished, he took a wrong turn on the way back to the courtyard. Naturally, the once-filled halls were now empty as a tomb.

Great. I could have sworn there was an intersection here, Singer thought as he contemplated a blank wall. Well, the wall wasn't blank. Lanterns placed in niches illuminated mosaics of long-ago court scenes to either side. But those images were so repetitious that they might as well have been a blank wall. *Screw it.* He took the lefthand corridor. *It has to go somewhere.*

The hall rounded a corner and halted. Singer reached a group of three unimportant seeming doors: one left, one right, and one straight ahead. *Maybe I have found the servant's quarters.* This explained why this portion of the palace was so empty – the servants were all busy with the big feast. Raised voices sounded through the rightward door. He started to retrace his steps. *The last thing I need is more drama.* But then one of the voices caught his attention. *That's Bao!*

"You think I chose this!" Bao's muffled voice penetrated the door. "I don't want him."

"He's attractive. Intelligent." This voice was male, deeper, laced with arrogance and contempt. "As is your other swain."

Does Bao have a boyfriend? He blinked. This explained much. Of course, a noblewoman such as Bao would have suitors, perhaps even lovers. But none of that would have mattered to

Varro and Abbas. *With my luck, Bao's boyfriend will murder me while I'm asleep.*

"Amentep is the one I desire," said Bao.

"Forget Amentep, unless you desire to be executed for adultery," said the male voice. "The Nebos Family is queer, clinging to secrets best forgotten."

"Amentep's uncle ranks high in the court," said Bao.

"The Nebo's power is as much a chimera as their secret lore," said the male voice. "Besides, Amentep has found another bride."

"Liar!" Bao screamed the word. "I will not – cannot believe that!" The word ended in a sob.

"Clean yourself up and return to the feast," said the male voice. "I must consult with the other officers."

He heard the thud of a distant door closing. Bao continued to sob.

Ok, I need to leave. The door popped open. Octavos found himself staring at Bao.

Bao stood stock still. Then she jabbed a finger at him. "You? Are you spying on me?"

"No, my lady, I entered to use the toilet"-

"Back the way you came, then left, left, and right."

"I found it but became lost, and then"-

Bao let her arm drop. "Octavos Maximus, you really are an innocent." A sigh escaped her lips. "Come with me." She began trotting along the corridor without waiting for a response.

Gut churning, Singer followed Bao through a tangle of shadowy passageways to an unadorned door.

"This belongs to my maid Fatima," said Bao. "She is occupied at the feast, so we will not be disturbed."

The chamber beyond the door met Octavos's mental impression of a servant's room: small, cramped, dominated by a narrow bed lit by a shaft of light from a window opening onto a garden. Next to it was a large mirror suspended over a dresser whose surface was covered with tiny pots and bottles.

"Fatima is an expert with cosmetics," said Bao as she checked herself in the mirror. Her hands passed over the containers, opening one after another. "Ah. This one." Bao dabbed a brush into a clay pot and brushed a dark substance onto her tear-stained cheek.

"Can I be of assistance?" Octavos asked.

"Do you know anything about cosmetics?" Bao squinted at a vial.

"Well, I was in the theater a few times at Solace."

"True God above, that's right, you're a musician." Bao replaced the vial and lifted another bottle. "But I wager what makeup you wore was applied by others."

Octavos sighed and sat on the bed. "You'd win that wager."

Bao applied gloss to her lips. "That should suffice."

He began to stand.

"Sit." Bao's tone made the word an order. She remained focused on her image in the mirror. "What do you know of your family's involvement in Upper Kheff?"

Octavos shrugged. "Not much. My great-aunt Cassandra was married to one of the past governors. Uncle Cassius was governor for a while."

"Hah!" Bao faced him. "We called your great-aunt 'The Spider' because she kept a web of spies stretching across the province and did not hesitate to use their information to advance her goals. I suspect at least three of my relatives died because of her machinations."

Singer's cheeks turned hot. "My lady, I didn't know!"

"That is obvious. Your 'Uncle Cassius' was a fat slob with a penchant for young girls, at least two of whom died because of his attentions. We called him 'The Slug.' He spent twenty-two years in Upper Kheff, but his term as governor lasted just twenty-three months before his heart failed." Bao gave Octavos a level look. "What does this tell you?"

He thought for a moment. "My family rules Lower Kheff openly." *But the old traditions bind Lower Kheff, and my family goes to great lengths to adhere to them. In Upper Kheff is a military fief.* He remembered the patriarch wearing the garb of Kheff's old pharaohs. "But in Upper Kheff, the Maximus is the power behind the throne."

"Wrong." Bao's dark eyes glinted. "In Upper Kheff, you Maximus are one faction among several. My father is governor - but he must contend with the imperial army and your family. Uncle Odalis or my brother Adar will become governor upon his passing. But barring a direct imperial appointment, you will not be Governor. And even then, your reign would be short."

Uncle Cassius died after twenty-three months as governor. Poison? "But"-

Bao jabbed a finger at Octavos. "Your family's chief concern in Upper Kheff is maintaining the slave trade with the Black States."

"My lady, I despise slavery."

"As does my family. Yet ensuring the continuity of the slave trade will be your chief duty. My brother Adar is especially furious with me for marrying a Slaver."

"He's the one you were talking"-

"Yes!" Bao made a cutting motion. "Do not speak of him."

"I'm tempted to change my name and leave the Empire." Octavos managed to have a weak smile. "Given your circumstances, perhaps you should join me."

"Ridiculous." Bao swept past Octavos and out of the room.

LABYRINTH WAR XII – Curtis

'We climbed a slight slope, passed through a narrow opening, and found ourselves confronted with a wretched sprawl of huts and hovels encircled by hills and the brown plants of the hedge. Filthy men and women stared at us with dead eyes. A mob of almost naked children barreled out of a hut and converged upon Kellicks wagon.

"Away, beggar's," a voice shouted in Solarian. A thick, hairy arm batted one child to the ground. "Titus Maximus – is that you?"

The children vanished as quickly as they'd appeared.

"Julius Servetus Longinus," I said, taking in the unshaved features and the filthy tunic of a man I hadn't seen since quitting the legions. "What brings you here?"

"I might ask the same of you," said Julius. "Fact is, I'm supposed to ask that question, on the orders of General Kevin DuMars."

"I'm here on family business," I said.

"Yer granddaddy is scheming again, is he?" asked Julius. "Nah, don't answer." He waved his hand and almost fell to the ground.

I descended from the cart and followed Julius into a nearby hovel, larger and more solidly built than its neighbors. Trash and empty bottles littered the floor.

Julius took a seat at a large table.

"Yer going inside, then," he said, leaning back and motioning towards the far wall.

"Tomorrow or the next day, if I can manage it," I said.'

- From 'The Journal of Titus Maximus.'

Curtis filed into the command tent with several other knights. Thomas Maximus and dapper General Flynn of the Sand Runners hovered over a large table covered with maps. Squat, blocky General Masters, commander of the II Equitant stood with them, jabbing his finger at this or that fortification. General Tullos, the aged administrator who commanded the I Imperial, methodically perused a pile of reports. Near-useless Manias lounged in a chair to the side, hand wrapped around a bottle.

Octavos was nowhere to be seen. No great surprise as he was a civilian, not a soldier.

Thomas nodded at the assembled officers. "General Flynn, you will dispatch patrols along the ridge road while the Second begins reinforcing the forts. Tullos will deal with the local officials."

"Our knowledge of the enemy's dispositions is deficient." The speaker was a bland fellow Curtis didn't recognize.

"The gasbags will help," said General Masters.

"Ready them." Thomas surveyed the room. "In the meantime, I shall inspect the closer forts." His gaze settled on Curtis. "I would appreciate your company."

Curtis bowed. "Of course, my lord. When do we depart?"

"As soon as my horse is brought around," said Thomas. "Fort Siccas is half an hour's ride away, and Fort Saxum is an hour westward. Tribune Basil tells me those two forts offer the best view of the enemy."

An aide entered the tent and approached Thomas. "Sir, your mount is ready."

Thomas rose to his feet. "Let's go."

"Sir, I must protest," said General Tullos. "We have not covered a tenth of the matters here."

"I suggest you deal with those issues. Evaluating the enemy takes priority."

General Tullos stared at Thomas. Technically, he outranked the prince. But his clan was politically insignificant. Moreover, the General had spent the past decade in administrative duties. And Thomas was correct. "A firsthand assessment of the enemy appears appropriate."

Officers around the tent nodded in support or frowned at the apparent insubordination. Thomas paid them no heed.

Minutes later, Thomas, Curtis, and a handful of knights rode south along a stone paved road through parched fields, heading towards a line of low dead brown hills.

"Ware!" A voice behind them shouted. Curtis edged his horse off the road as a long column of bicycle-mounted legionaries shot past the knights.

"Arrogant curs," said Manius Maximus, "passing their betters without so much as a by-your-leave." That the legionaries who completed their twenty-year stint would be granted lands and full citizenship further irked the aristocrat.

Thomas cast Manius a look. "I am pleased."

"But why?" Manius started to say more but thought better of it.

"Because their presence means the army's organization is not as dire a mess as General Tullos claims."

The road scaled a low ridge and then dipped into a dell with a cottage set between a large pond and a stand of leafless trees. The cottage door was stamped with the crossed swords of the militant DuMars clan.

"Built by an exile, no doubt," said Manius as they passed the dwelling.

Curtis nodded in acknowledgment. The DuMars had a long history of exiling disgraced family members to places like this.

A crossroads awaited the prince's party atop the next hill, next to the square dirt walls of a legion fort. Soldiers with the hammer-and-sword badge of the 2nd Equitant swarmed over the structure.

"Ho, what report," called Thomas.

"Still solid, sir," said a barrel-chested Centurion. "My lads are patching the east wall now. It crumbled some years ago and the local incompetents didn't properly repair it. But we'll have it fixed by sundown."

Thomas saluted. "Good work."

The Centurion returned the salute. "Thank you, sir. If you'll excuse me, I have a fort to rebuild."

"Fort Siccas is straight south," said Thomas.

The highway devolved into a narrow track with many missing paving stones.

"These wretched mounds didn't seem near this height from a distance," Sir Sate groused as the party climbed the slope.

Then the slope leveled, and the knights rode alongside a withered vegetable patch outside the cracked stone walls of Fort Siccas. A squad of legionaries hammered nails into the closed iron-shod oaken gate, but a postern door stood open, watched by a trio of sentries.

A guard ran inside upon spotting the prince's party. He returned a moment later with a massive unshaven thug bearing a Centurions hash mark on his sleeve. "Ho!" The lout cried. "I am Centurion Julius Servetus Longinus, current commander of this fortress, as Tribune Delano took an arrow to the gut last week. Who the hell are you?" He finished this speech with a massive belch. Curtis fancied he could smell rotgut on Longinus's breath despite the thirty paces separating them.

"I present Prince Thomas Maximus of the Southern Expeditionary Force," said Curtis, "come to inspect the border forts in person."

Julius considered this for a moment, unfazed by Thomas's presence. "The reinforcements?"

"Yes, the reinforcements," snapped Sir Fury. "We reached Ptath yesterday. Surely you must have heard."

"Been busy fighting." Julius let loose with another massive belch. "We fought all fucking night. I was trying to catch some shut-eye."

"Far be it for me to interrupt your repose," said Thomas, "but I am here to ascertain the enemy's disposition."

Julius squinted, attempting to comprehend Thomas's words. "Oh, you'll want to climb the prick." He waved a hand inside the compound. "Come on in then."

Legion forts were typically perfect squares with a gate at the center of each wall. Fort Siccas boasted seven corners with no two walls the same length. Narrow barracks, workshops, and sheds clung leach-like to the inner perimeter of this barrier. A three-story abomination with wings and protruding balconies crouched at the center of the fort like some lurking beast waiting to pounce. And everywhere squads of legionaries lifted, hammered, and pushed.

Julis paused in the courtyard. "We got visiting gentry! Best behavior, everybody!" His words had little effect on the soldiers.

"Arrogant curs," growled Manius.

"They are doing their jobs," said Prince Thomas as he dismounted.

"You three!" Julius motioned at a squad sharpening their swords. "Get these horses stabled and fed."

"Sir." One of the men threw a lazy salute.

"That's the prick." Julius pointed at a thick pole sprouting from the central structure's middle like a monstrous horn. He cupped his mouth. "Yo! Rodger, Jabari – two coming up!"

"Lord Thomas needs to have that imbecile flogged," said Manius under his breath.

Curtis shrugged, remembering the desperate days on the Agban frontier. At times, he hadn't looked any different than Julius. "He was here. We weren't."

Julius guided Thomas and Curtis through a dim room that reeked like a distillery and then up a winding flight of stairs. Graffiti adorned the walls: officers in impossible sex acts, naked women executed with fanatic skill, lists, slogans, and curses. 'I am going to die here,' read one lament. 'Shithead Stephen DuMars,' read another. The stairs opened on a flat roof next to the post they'd spied from below: a monster of a shaft thicker than Curtis's armored torso, reaching at least a hundred feet into the air. Thick, flat spikes had been driven into this massive bole, creating a dangerous spiral staircase. Julius pointed to a curving pipe screwed into the post. "Best keep a hand on that." He turned away.

"Aren't you coming with us," Curtis asked.

"Nah." Julius made an indeterminate motion. "Not enough room. 'Sides, the heights get to my head. Rodger will set you straight."

Curtis turned to the post. Thomas stood there with a grin on his face. "Lead on, Sir Knight." He bowed a fraction and waved at the post behind him.

Keeping a firm grip on the rail, Curtis climbed the stair of spikes. The flat bolts projected less than two feet from the trunk. His boots rang with each step. Twenty steps up, his boot slipped, and only a white-knuckled grip on the rail kept him from falling. The post seemed to sway as he ascended. Then he passed through a square hatch onto a round platform just long enough for a man to lay down. A stout wooden rail encircled the deck. Two men stood there, one brown, the other white.

"Welcome to the knob, Sir Knights," said the brown man. The white said nothing, his eye pressed against a spyglass pointing south.

"Charming place," said Thomas. "Have you another spyglass?"

The black opened a locker. "Two spyglasses, three flares, and a trumpet, sir." He handed one telescope to Thomas and another to Curtis. "They fix to the rail."

Curtis locked his spyglass in place and turned his gaze south. The ground fell away in steep ridges and sub-peaks, making the lower slopes invisible. But past them stretched an immense flat expanse, marred only by a blue lump in the distance.

"That's Arcus Australis, the Southern Redoubt you're looking at," said the white without turning away from his spyglass. "In better times, we kept a company of scouts posted there with fast horses. Twenty days past it is Rostra."

"The lost city." Thomas glanced at the watchman.

"Yep." The white man pulled away from his spyglass. "One of the old emperors sent a full legion of men to die in the southern wastes. Instead, they survived and founded a city. It might have been better if they hadn't. Rostra is a stinking cesspit – slavers, bandits, murderers, deserters, you name it, they're there."

"You sound as though you've been there," said Curtis.

"Twice. But Rostra isn't why you're here." He pointed to the left, at the near part of the plain. "That's why you're here."

Curtis put his eye to the spyglass and aimed it in the indicated direction. A vast encampment swam into view. Tens of thousands of tents. Thousands of wagons. Entire herds of horses and droaths and reptilian riding beasts. "God above, but there's a lot of them." The visible portion of the horde outnumbered the expeditionary force two to one. "Looks like humans and goblins," he commented. "No cat-men?"

Rodger shuddered. "Oh, there are thousands of Cats out there, or there were. The scouts say a big mob decided to try their luck in the Black States."

"Well, that's something."

"I require a better vantage," said Thomas. "The bulk of their camp is hidden from view."

"Sir, we might have obliged you yesterday," said the black man. "Dragon Rock offered a grand view. But the nomads hold it now. We lost three men there this morning."

"You might get a better view from Fort Saxum," said the white. "The cliffs are steeper there and stick out into the plain."

"Fort Saxum it is then," said Thomas. He handed the telescope to the black and began descending the staircase.

Curtis found the descent even more nerve-wracking than the ascent.

Manius waited for them in the courtyard with a scowl on his face. "This place disgusts me."

"Imagine being stuck here for twenty years," said Curtis as he climbed into the saddle.

Another knight helped Thomas mount.

"I'd sooner spend twenty years posted in hell." Manius scowled and swung into his saddle.

A few minutes later they were descending the hill towards the crossroads. Bicycles littered the nearby fields like metal plants. The site swarmed with activity as shovel-wielding soldiers erected a new earthen berm next to the fort. The Centurion they'd spoken to earlier stood atop this wall, cursing a blue streak at the digging men.

They didn't stop, instead turning onto the western road. Here the terrain became more rugged: one section of the road had been gouged from an almost vertical cliff, and past it, a long stone span crossed a deep gorge with a trickle of water at its bottom. "This might make for a suitable defensive location," said Curtis.

"It has," said Thomas, pointing to a hillock covered with grave markers. "More than once."

Another long column of pedaling legionaries raced past the knights. "General Masters didn't waste any time."

"Reinforcements for Fort Saxum and Fort Cox," said Thomas. "Some will continue to Dessau."

The road forked west and south a mile past the bridge. A crisp squad of soldiers directed the knights along the southern way. "Fort Saxum is around the bend and atop the hill, sir," said the baby-faced corporal leading the squad.

Fort Saxum proved altogether different than Fort Siccas. Here, an utterly typical square fort crouched behind a wall of rubble that extended between two cliffs. Hundreds of troops marked with Church insignia piled more stones on this barrier.

The haughty officer who greeted the knights named himself Captain Adar Vadim Des Ptath, making him a member of the governor's family. *Stuck up bastard,* Curtis thought. He wondered if Adar's formal manner hid a grudge.

But to his credit, Adar listened carefully to Thomas's request and guided the knights to a low stone tower perched atop a jutting mastiff. Curtis's stomach churned when he peered over the edge. This was no slope, but a vertical cliff that dropped a thousand feet to the grassy plain.

"Better," said Thomas as he scanned the nomad's encampment. "But that hillock to the southeast conceals part of their camp."

"Those slopes are a fierce battleground," said Captain Adar. "I lost two squads to an ambush this morning."

"Will the enemy be able to scale those cliffs to the summit," asked Curtis.

Adar shook his head. "They can ascend partway, but then the cliffs become unclimbable."

Curtis inspected the rock face. "Rachasa can climb that."

Adar hesitated. "A few have. But my men are vigorous about patrolling the edge. West of here, though, a band of rachasa destroyed the signal tower."

"An interesting target." Thomas thought for a moment. "Is there a western vantage?"

Adar shook his head. "Not a good one."

"Show me the best location." Thomas began descending the tower.

LABYRINTH WAR XIII – Carina

'The Master's brought our ancestors here to serve in the fields and mines. Those who proved their worth were taught a tiny fraction of the Master's secrets. And those who excelled were imbued with magic.'

- From the 'Kwintath Chronicles.'

Hawkers and soldiers swarmed around Carina and Xenia as they walked along the Aeolia's shore.

"You gonna try that ritual again?" asked Xenia.

"I need the magic." *Especially if I'm going to be in the middle of a fight.*

"You don't need Asshole Ambrose catching you," said Xenia. "He has been snooping."

"I'll be careful." Carina embraced the Saban woman. Then she walked south into Ptath's center. This was a placid working-class district, not prosperous enough for Ptath's elite, nor seedy enough for its criminal element. Just row upon row of tenements perched over shops and working-class taverns, interspersed with the occasional other structures – mostly drab warehouses. A few were freestanding cottages. Carina's destination was neither.

Square and squat, the crumbling stone building rose from an overgrown courtyard near Ptath's southern wall. Too big to be a tomb and too small for a nobleman's townhouse, Carina judged it a pagan temple fallen to ruin and wrack. This impression was heightened by the bizarre broken statues littering the courtyard and the merest trace of old magic clinging to the ruin. An ancient doorway bound with a rusted iron lock barred entry into the temple.

Carina decided the edifice suited her purposes.

A rudimentary levitation spell put her on the temple roof. More broken masonry and shattered statues awaited on the roof.

A stone shifted beneath Carina's feet. She flailed for balance and grabbed a headless gargoyle for balance as a distant 'crack' reached her ears. Still holding the statue, she turned to see a hole in the rooftop. Heart pounding, she spotted jagged shapes on the floor.

"That would have hurt." She wondered if anything of interest remained inside. "Not likely." In the meantime, though, she needed a stable place for the ritual. Her gaze settled on a relatively debris-free corner shielded by a parapet.

No stones shifted under Carina's cautious probing, so she chalked a mystic circle and sat in its center.

Then she closed her eyes and focused, working through one meditative cantrip after another. There was power in this place. Strange. Alien. Mechanistic. A vision formed in her mind's eye.

Red and gold gears clicked and spun before Carina, a barrier of moving parts. Cream-colored lights snaked along metal columns. And deep within this mechanism, a glowing ruby. The gem was just within reach, just past a big gear and a column sparkling with electricity. Carina extended her arm. No. She withdrew the limb just as an ax-shaped pendulum cut across the gap.

No, Operant. That path is closed.

Like the power pervading this place, the mental voice was cool, detached, and alien. Mechanical.

Operant. The Old Ones designation for their sorcerer-slaves. The Dawn Races were gone, but their relics remained. Did this vision stem from such a device? Ptath was ancient enough.

Carina studied the assemblage. The pendulum blocked the obvious approach, but what of this smaller gap between two gears and a vertical spring? Again, she extended her arm. And stopped right before a hammer dropped from above, blocking the approach.

No, Operant. That path is closed.

Carina grimaced in frustration. The glowing ruby – another portion of her suppressed power – was right there! Why couldn't she reach in and grab it? *Because it's a test. That's why. Which means there's something I'm missing.* She resumed studying the mechanism. There were so many moving parts! So complicated! It reminded Carina of her truncated mystical training; of the problems the instructors had foisted upon her - complex tests that required precise solutions. Each solution provided a clue to the next part of the problem. And with each solution came a bit of mastery.

Carina permitted herself a small grin. Her nimble fingers tapped the machine's components in a precise pattern. A gear rubbed across her wrist, drawing blood. The mage's body shivered when energy sparked against her hand. But Carina persisted.

Portions of the machine withdrew. Other sections altered shape. A mechanical claw plucked the ruby from its cusp and deposited it in Carina's outreached hand.

Excellent, Operant, said the alien voice as Carina's vision turned red and the machine dissolved into gold and green sparks.

"Amentep, my love, I didn't see you!" The female voice penetrated Carina's trance. She opened her eyes.

"It's been a long while," said a male voice. "My circumstances have changed."

The voices came from the courtyard. *Just my luck,* she thought. *Of course, this would be the local trysting place. Isolated, yet close at hand, and somewhat romantic. Now how to depart without disturbing the love birds?*

"But I have the glass key, Amentep! It was just sitting there in a musty old storeroom. Are you not glad?"

Who makes a key from glass? It sounds like a relic of the Old Races. Carina peered through a crack in the base of the statue. A woman in the colorful attire of the local nobility faced a man in a long tan cloak.

"Bao, you shouldn't be here," said the man. "Neither should I."

"But you loved me. We had such plans!" The girl balled her fists.

"We were a pair of young fools," said the man. "Bao, I am married now. You are betrothed to the Maximus prince. We cannot be seen together."

Maximus prince? Disparate pieces clicked together in Carina's mind. *That is the future bride of Octavos Maximus down there!*

"Then we shall see each other in private! If I cannot have you as husband, then I shall have you as a lover!"

The man shook his head. "No, I cannot betray my wife in that manner. And I cannot associate with the Slaver without losing status."

"But I'm not"- Carina could envision the tears welling up in Bao's eyes.

"You will be," said Amentep. "But I will accept the key in remembrance of our past relationship."

"You want the key!" Bao screamed. "Then find it!" She made a throwing motion. A glittering object flew over the roof. Carina caught the object before it hit the stones.

"You should not have done that," said Amentep to Bao's retreating backside.

Carina inspected her catch. She held a transparent flat square the size of her palm, its interior studded with tiny green and red gems.

A noise from the courtyard caught her attention. Amentep was picking a path through the detritus along the temple's side. Words floated to Carina's ears. "It might still be intact."

He means to scale the building. I'd best depart.

LABYRINTH WAR XIV – Curtis

'Another short passage brought us to a miles-wide open area, dominated by a mad quilt of gardens, alleys, hovels, tents, and dilapidated houses of ancient aspect. A line of tall aquamarine towers to the north caught my eye, but Duun Var escorted us west across an irregular market space to a tall building with crumbling walls and nomads dicing on its front steps.

Inside we waited under the watchful eyes of his men in a once elegant foyer while brown women in simple shifts brought us trays with pitchers of wine, sliced punto fruit, and strips of spiced meat.

At length, a voice called from above and Duun Var guided us to a tent perched upon the roof. Three nomads sat at a long table: an oldster in a maroon silk robe, a glaring youth in leather armor, and a barrel-chested fellow wearing a tan vest over a yellow robe.

The yellow-clad nomad stood and thumped his chest. "I Haman Zeer. I First Chief."

Haman indicated the armored youth. "War Chief Kotef Zumar."

The War Chief stared at me with the flat, dead eyes of a killer.

Haman Zeer waved at the old nomad. "Elder Chotuck." The elder contemplated the inside of his eyelids.

Haman Zeer pointed at me. "Who are you?"

Following what seemed to be the local custom, I pointed at my chest and said, "Maximus."

Haman Zeer's face went slack. He turned to the old nomads. A great burst of incomprehensible chatter followed.

"It appears the Maximus name is known here," said the Doctor.

"The Maximus name is known everywhere."

- From 'The Journal of Titus Maximus.'

Curtis ducked his head and entered his temporary home, one of a hundred-odd hovels erected by enterprising locals for knights and officers. It boasted two rooms, a packed dirt floor, and a low ceiling. Plus, it stank of sweat and piss. But it beat sleeping in a tent.

Inside, Julie cackled over her iron kettle.

"What's for dinner?"

Past her, lanky blond Sir Adam Marbrand diced with Sir Fury and the ape-like Centurion Chimp for a bottle of Carbone Red. Rumor insisted it was one of five such bottles left in the camp.

Julie dropped something unidentifiable into the pot. "Guess."

Curtis winced. "Steak and eggs?"

Julie laughed. "You been sucking dreamweed? No, it ain't steak. It's fish, though I did dress it up a bit."

"Better than snake stew, I suppose." Julie had cooked that a couple of times as well.

"Ten! Beat that!" Sir Marbrand raised both arms. "The wine will be mine!"

"Yer rhyming sucks." Chimp rolled a three. "But my luck sucks worse."

The bones passed to Sir Fury. "I want that bottle." His toss resulted in a pair of fives. Sir Sate glared at Sir Marbrand. "Hah! Matched you."

Sir Marbrand grabbed the dice and threw them so forcefully that one ricocheted off the ceiling. "Nine!" He turned to the Centurion. "You want another roll?"

"Nah." Chimp climbed to his feet. "I'd best quit while I'm behind." He took a step towards the door.

"My turn," said Sir Fury. "I can beat a nine." One of the cubes bounced off Curtis's boot and into Julie's stewpot.

"Hah!" The hag waved her ladle. "Your game is over until after dinner."

"Damn klutz," said Sir Marbrand.

Sir Fury twisted his body. "It's gone!"

"What's gone," asked Sir Marbrand.

"The wine!" Sir Fury's fist pounded the floor. "That wretched peasant filched the bottle! Now what am I to do? I can't get drunk, the dice are gone, and dinner is an hour off yet!" He deflated. "Oh, piss it. I suppose I could pen a response to Lord DuMars."

"Are you going to tell him to 'Fuck off?'" asked Sir Marbrand.

Sir Fury's response surprised them both. "Lord DuMars made me an offer – I get the bastards all properly legal and he'll deed me that tract in Agba, the one just upriver from Curtis's place."

"Huh."

Fury's statement made Curtis think about his last missive from 'Cousin Rock' – 'Investigate Soraq Fortress.' He'd sent acknowledgment but had no idea how to carry out that order.

"Here you are." Manias Maximus's voice came from behind Curtis. "God above, what a stinking hovel. I have seen cleaner goat pens."

"It was the best we could find." Curtis faced the Maximus scion. "What's going on?"

"Command meeting. Now." Manias's tone allowed no dissent. "Though why Thomas wants you present..."

"You're interrupting my dinner," Curtis complained as he emerged from the hut. The sun sank towards the horizon, casting an eerie orange-red light across the city.

"There will be food at the meeting." Manias's bruisers emerged from the shadows and flanked the pair as they walked across the city.

"The camps that way." Curtis pointed in a diagonal direction to their course.

"This meeting isn't at the camp." They passed through a postern gate.

An uncomfortable horseman waited beyond the portal. Thomas. Half a dozen horses cropped the sparse grass.

One of the horses raised its neck at Curtis's approach. "That's my horse!"

"I had the boys bring him here," said Manias. A bruiser helped him into an empty saddle. "Get mounted. We have some distance to ride."

A moment later they were traveling south.

"Here." Manias raised his hand. They were at a cottage between a small pond and a clump of leafless trees. He dropped from his horse and began walking towards the dwelling.

"Stop right there, Empire man," said a voice in the trees.

"I'm expected." Manias's voice and body both quivered.

Nomads! Curtis grabbed for his sword.

A large hand wrapped itself about his wrist. "Do not try," said a voice close to Curtis's ear.

Curtis turned his head and found himself face to hair with a veritable giant of a man, clad in rough brown fabric covered with leather. "Talk today," said the giant. "Maybe fight tomorrow."

The cottage door popped open. "Get in here," said Pindar.

"Keep watch," Manias told his bruisers. Then he entered the cabin, trailed by Curtis.

A large plank table with a lantern at either end dominated the domicile's main room. Three nomads sat on the near side. Thomas sat across from them. Two bottles sat between them.

Thomas has balls. Then he caught sight of Octavos and a pair of bodyguards standing against the wall.

"Glad you could join the party." Thomas gestured at the people across the table.

"Ganbaatar, a chieftain of the Chonju tribe." Ganbaatar sported grey hair and a wrinkled face. A long, checkered cloak encompassed his frame. *Chosen because he's expendable,* Curtis thought.

"Kylan, a chieftain of the Ubaki tribe." Kylan was short and wide with a wild expression on his sallow face. Dangerous. And tough. He wore a silver sash across a black tunic and drank from an earthen cup.

"Oyunchin of the Baandar Tribe." This one was female, old, and calm. Long necklaces of beads, coins, and unidentifiable objects spilled over her cream tunic.

"Together, they represent the largest human tribes confronting us."

"What of the goblins and rachasa?" Curtis spoke before he could think.

"We feared their presence disruptive," said Ganbaatar. "We know Empire detests goblins. Why make talk harder?"

"They maybe listen, maybe not." Oyunchin fingered her talismans.

Kylan said nothing and grinned, rocking back and forth on his chair.

Curtis, Manias, and Octavos took seats on either side of Thomas.

"Gentlemen," Thomas addressed the nomads. "Let's get straight to the point: What do you want? Why are you here?"

"Good. You speak your mind," said Ganbaatar. "We want Kheff."

"Kheff is an Imperial province," said Thomas. "You can't have it. The Empire has bested previous hordes."

"No," said Ganbaatar. "Empire beat one, two, tribes, not Gathering." He tapped his chest. "When I young fighter, I climb wall, fight Empire."

"And you were soundly defeated," said Thomas. "Now you face a bigger army."

"We got enough fighters to take Ptath," said Ganbaatar. "Damn big fight, many die. Maybe make an offer instead."

"What sort of offer?" Thomas asked.

"You take your army, take people, leave forts, leave Ptath." Ganbaatar glanced at Oyunchin. "Three days."

"Evacuating a city Ptath's size would take weeks," said Thomas. "And I doubt you'd stop there."

"Stupid root feet," said Ganbaatar.

"It's called civilization," said Manias. "People living in one place and building things."

Kylan seized his rocking. He locked his gaze onto Manias's face.

"You keep the rest of Kheff," said Oyunchin. Again, a look passed between her and Ganbaatar. "We maybe let Ptath people leave. Maybe we take Soraq."

"Why Ptath?" Thomas asked. "The city couldn't support your tribes even if we did evacuate."

"Soraq plenty big," said Ganbaatar.

"You're afraid," said Octavos.

Ganbaatar eyed Octavos. "You too be afraid of flying demons."

Impossible. But it makes sense. Curtis leaned across the table. "Flying demons – or flying shields bigger than a chieftain's tent?"

"You know?" Ganbaatar and Oyunchin exchanged rapid words in the nomad dialect. Then he faced Curtis. "Flying shields come Empire?"

"No," said Curtis. "Agba."

"Agba." Ganbaatar exchanged more rapid-fire words with Oyunchin. Then, "Yes, Empire rule Agba now."

Thomas glanced at Manias. "Silence."

"But this is nonsense! Superstition! A means to gull us!"

"Manias shut up!" Thomas's voice radiated menace.

Manias paled and quieted.

A thought occurred to Curtis. He looked at Ganbaatar. "Agba...or Celthania?"

"Ah." Ganbaatar's head bobbed. "Celthania be west Agba. Far away. Yes, flying shields kill Celthania. Big magic. Ground shake. Tribes see smoke, see fire, go try to take."

"Celthania scum," said Kylan, the first words he'd spoken. "Demon talkers. Liars."

"Yes, yes," said Ganbaatar. "Celthania scum. But they fight. Got big magic. Some flying shields fall and get smashed on the ground. We see a chance, go take Celthania. We go to two cities, kill demons, and take prizes. Then flying shields come back and kill fighters. No way to fight, so flee. Flying shields come, go, attack more tribes."

"So, you came here." Thomas placed his hands on the table. "But why Ptath?"

"We were desperate," said Oyunchin. "Flying shields come again and again, and more die each time. Seer's cast bones and read entrails, look flames. See a city with a stone peak, see hope."

"Ptath," said Thomas.

"Yes, Ptath," said Ganbaatar. "Ptath horde's future."

"Well, I'm not ceding Ptath to you," said Thomas.

"Then we fight," said Kylan. He barked a couple of words. All three nomads rose and left the cottage.

"You should have them killed," said Manias.

"That's dishonorable," said Curtis.

"Stinking Westerners and their stupid code of honor," Manias snarled. "The world doesn't work that way."

"Killing them wouldn't accomplish anything," said Thomas. "Permitting their departure does."

"Like what?"

"Like finding out which way they go," said Thomas.

"Huh?"

"Those weren't the top chiefs," said Octavos. "They were trusted people the real chiefs could afford to lose."

"How do you know that?" Manias demanded.

"I'm a minstrel. Reading people is what I do."

"You are a Maximus, not a common minstrel," said Manias.

"Enough, cousin," said Thomas. "I believe we are done here."

Manias, Curtis, and Octavos started for the door. "Sir Curtis, wait a moment," said Thomas.

Curtis paused. "What's this about?"

"Private business," said Thomas.

Manias started to say something and changed his mind. He and Octavos departed, leaving Thomas and Curtis alone in the cottage.

Thomas waited until his cousins had mounted their horses and departed. Then he reached for the bottle and poured two cups.

"Carbone Red," he said, "One of seven bottles left in the camp."

"Seven?" Curtis asked. "I thought there were five."

"The camp gossips don't know about the two bottles I keep under my bed."

A humorless smile appeared on Thomas's lips. "I have spies everywhere – just like the emperor." He handed Curtis a cup.

He found me out. "You know," said Curtis.

"That you are Emperor Charles DuSwaimair's personal agent? Of course. If the need arose, you were to be our private messenger. That status was why you became my Cousin's instructor at arms – it kept you close."

LABYRINTH WAR XV – Singer

"You should be able to see the walls past this next bend," said Kellick as we jounced along the road.

Sure enough, a long, tan line appeared in the south. Kellick waved at the distant image. "There. That's the demon-spawned thing eating the country." He spat. "It done ate my family's farm."

Father Joseph asked. "You witnessed this?"

Kellick shook his head. "My granddad told me about it. He was out in a field near the wall when the ground shook. The next morning sinkholes covered half the fields, and knee-high berms of raised dirt crisscrossed the rest, the last a stones' throw from the house. Next year, vines started sprouting from the berms. A hard shell formed over the dirt, turning the berms into walls. A few years later the walls were taller than Gramps."

"Incredible," said Father Joseph. "Didn't he try to dig up the berms or burn the vines?"

Kellick spat. "Of course, he did. It didn't do any good – those berms were rock-hard. And the vines wouldn't catch fire. Nah, what stopped the walls were the monks." He spat again. "Gramps saw that too."

"Do tell," said the Doctor.

"The monks had a camp next valley over from Gramps farm. He'd watch them sometimes. First, they'd drive long stakes way deep. Then they'd pull them out and drop in a white seed, blue stone, and a bit of blood in each hole. The hedge sprouted the next year. The wall stopped growing, but it had already eaten the farm."

"It sounds like a steep price," I said.

"Yes, it was. Damn hedge is poison. Touch it and you'll get sicker than a dog. But better the hedge than the walls."

- From 'The Journal of Titus Maximus.'

Octavos flipped open his father's journal and slammed it shut without reading anything. He stalked to the window and stared at the immaculate garden surrounding the Maximus Manor. But images of Gawana's vine-draped walls overlaid the pomegranate trees and alabaster benches. A fluttering bird transformed into a flying shield.

Octavos blinked. The garden reasserted itself. He spun from the window and strode to the kitchen nook, where he fetched a bottle of the thick spiced wine favored by the local aristocracy. He poured a quarter glass, took a single sip, and walked to the desk.

Impossible. Gawana is past Soraq and across the Shadow Sea. And yet... Octavos paged through the journal. Yes, the carter's account of Gawana's expansion read like the tales he'd heard from Soraq. More pages. 'Gawana grew from a seed the size of a chest.' Octavos's gaze flicked to the trunk in the apartment's far corner. A group of men could load something chest-sized onto a ship, cross the Shadow Sea, carry it into Soraq's depths, and plant it. How long for the seed to sprout? A year? Five?

And it wasn't just Gawana. The journal mentioned flying shields as well. But unlike those assailing the nomads, men piloted those machines. And then there was his father's bizarre declaration in that letter added to the tome, speaking of cosmic powers and human feebleness.

Thomas needs to know. Octavos closed the journal and cradled it under his arm. Then he left the apartment and stalked through empty halls with marble floors and walls decorated with pastoral mosaics. As usual, there were no servants. Clean clothes and cooked food appeared as though by magic.

A few listless junior officers stared at maps in the War Room. "You just missed him," said one skinny scarecrow of a clerk. He directed Octavos to a private conference room across the manor.

Sentinels stood in the hall outside the specified chamber.

Octavos stared into their impassive features. "I must speak with Prince Thomas."

Their expressions didn't change. Would they turn him away?

"The prince meets with his wizards," said the largest of the lot, a clean-shaven fellow with a scarred cheek.

Octavos felt his heart skip a beat. He'd encountered Thomas's mages perhaps a dozen times since joining the expedition. "It's important."

"Wait here." The scarred guard opened the door and vanished inside.

Wizards. Scores of mages accompanied the army, many seeing military life preferable to taking holy vows. Thirty cloistered Godborn healers staffed the mercy tents, and a dozen furtive wizards provided potions and talismans to select soldiers. Rumor insisted a few sorcerers lurked amongst the riffraff in the Tail.

Those were not magicians his cousin consulted. No, Thomas met with the Kheffian sorcerers. Twelve of Kheff's sorcerous clans swore service to the Maximus Family at the Empire's founding. Their spells secured victories on the battlefield and at the imperial court. In return, those clans were exalted – and protected. These wizards owed their very survival to their Maximus patrons.

The door opened. The soldier emerged. "You may enter."

The chamber was simple and stark: hard cane chairs flanked a dark, polished table with a pile of manuscripts at one end. A detailed map of the province dominated one wall.

Thomas greeted his cousin with a curt glance. "Sit."

The Kheffian mages numbered three. Each spared him a hasty glance before looking at Thomas. Quadir, thin and acetic stood closest to Octavos, hands clasped inside a soft black robe covered with silver runes. "Cousin Octavos, I present my sorcerous advisors. Quadir, an expert in fire magic, illusions, and ritual work."

The tallest of the three sorcerers bowed deeply. "I am honored, Prince Octavos."

"Uday, an expert in alchemy, amulet making, and the healing arts."

The plumpest of the three bowed. "Greetings, honored prince."

"And Halima, considered a prodigy by her peers."

The attractive female sorceress inclined her head. "It pleases me to see you, honored prince.

"Gentlemen and Lady," said Thomas with a nod at Halima, "what follows remains secret. Am I clear?"

The mages nodded in unison.

"Good." Thomas cleared his throat. "Yesterday I treated with envoys sent by the horde. They made an offer I cannot accept, and when pressed, explained the reason for that offer." Thomas continued with an account of the conversation. "So, tell me, what does Ptath offer that would cause twenty tribes to march halfway around the world?"

Quadir shifted his feet. "Great Prince, Ptath is ancient."

Thomas made a cutting motion. "Of course, Ptath is ancient. Older than the Empire, maybe as old as Kheff."

Uday stroked his chin. "No, Great Prince, Ptath is older than Kheff. The Dawn Races erected the Pyramid of Zep and founded Ptath to service it."

"Do you know the pyramid's purpose?"

Uday shook his head. "No, Great Prince. Many thousands of years have passed since the Dawn Races ruled these lands. Much has been lost since those days, including the pyramid's true function."

"You must have some inkling," said Thomas.

"Great Prince," Halima spoke in a soft yet breezy voice. "Ptath's pyramid has been prominent in my divinations for years. It appears when I gaze into scrying mirrors or through fire."

"Great Prince, the Pyramid of Zep has long been indicated in my rituals," said Quadir. He motioned at his plump companion. "Uday spent a year here searching for answers and found nothing."

Uday's head bobbed. "Great Prince, Quadir speaks true. My investigation was both thorough and fruitless."

"If your research were thorough," said Thomas, "it would have yielded answers."

"The shame is mine, Great Prince," said Uday.

"Shame doesn't interest me," said Thomas. "Results do. So, like the nomad shaman's, you know Ptath is important, but do not understand why."

Quadir bowed. "This is so, Great Prince."

Thomas took two paces to the left, whirled, and then two more to the right. Then he stopped and faced the mages. "The nomads spoke of giant flying shields and creatures of alien aspect possessed of superior weaponry."

Quadir blinked. "Great Prince, can the accounts of such primitives be given credence?"

"I have similar reports from imperial agents in Agba. They mention a name. Gotemik. Are you familiar with that term?"

The three wizards exchanged glances.

Uday bowed deeply. "Great Prince, the Gotemik are occasionally mentioned in the ancient records. They were a Dawn Race. They went elsewhere after a dispute with the others." He paused. "The records say they held most other races in disdain."

"The return of the Gotemik would be most alarming," said Halima.

"It is alarming," said Thomas. "Now to determine what makes Ptath so important. Uday, were there any avenues you did not pursue during your earlier investigation?"

Uday frowned. "Great Prince, there were options I deemed impractical at the time. But with sufficient resources...I cannot say for certain."

Now it was Thomas's turn to frown. "What resources would you require?"

Uday considered the question. "Authority over civic officials. Manpower."

Thomas nodded. "Ptath is under martial law. I can issue a decree granting you substantial authority. In addition, the II Equitant is part of this army – the best military engineers in the Empire. They can supply labor and perhaps their technical knowledge will be of use. I can dedicate a full cohort to this project without impacting other operations."

The magicians exchanged glances. Quadir spoke. "Great Prince, the legion engineers possess marvelous skills. But their knowledge is insignificant compared to the Dawn Races." The wizard's voice carried a hint of disdain.

"They are the best available," said Thomas.

"The engineers may prove useful," said Uday.

"Good," said Thomas. "You will have the necessary authorizations within the hour. I expect your investigation to begin immediately."

"Great Prince, I must review my notes." Uday grabbed the manuscripts.

"We live to please," said Quadir, a note of excitement in his voice.

Thomas took note of the wizard's tone. "Permit me to be clear. The resources I am granting you pertain to this specific project. Having the engineers dismantle part of the pyramid or digging up a street is acceptable. Mass confiscation of goods or arrest of Ptath's residents without excellent cause is grounds for arrest."

The magician's heads bobbed. "Your words are clear to us, Great Prince," said Quadir.

"Good," said Thomas. "Begin your preparations."

The magicians filed from the room, leaving Octavos alone with Thomas. A long breath escaped Thomas's mouth. "Our family depends on Kheff's magicians," he plopped in a chair, "but dealing with them makes me uncomfortable." Thomas looked at Octavos. "But what brings you here?"

Octavos placed the journal on the table. "This was compiled from my father's notes. It describes an expedition he made into Gawana."

"Gawana is thousands of miles from here," said Thomas. "I am faced with a nomad invasion right now."

Octavos tapped the book. "The accounts match the reports we received from Soraq's refugees. Walls sprouted from the ground overnight, decimating farms and villages. I wish to go to Dessau to investigate."

Thomas leaned back in his chair. "The disturbances in Soraq may have other causes – rogue magicians or some device of the

Dawn Races emerging from dormancy. But...mitigating Soraq's strife would make my job much easier." Thomas stretched his arms and yawned. "God above, I have not slept in two days now."

Octavos waited.

Thomas considered him. "When did you wish to depart?"

"Right away," said Octavos.

A thin smile appeared on Thomas's lips. "You just want to escape your hellcat wife-to-be."

Octavos smiled in return. "Am I that obvious?"

"Yes." Thomas sat erect in the chair. "A major relief column departs for Dessau this afternoon. The town is well fortified, so you're as safe there as anywhere."

"Thank you," said Octavos.

Thomas waved a hand. "Don't. Damn, I am so tired."

"Get some sleep."

Thomas sighed. "Maybe tonight."

A sharp rap sounded at the door, followed by the entry of a harried scribe.

"Report," said Thomas as Octavos slipped from the room.

"Pardon sir." The request came from a blond soldier with a huge bundle thrown over his shoulder.

Octavos stepped to the side and tried to spot an officer in the madhouse activity before him.

Being granted permission to join the relief column to Dessau was one thing. Finding a place in that company was another. Each legionnaire and each wagon had a designated place and a designated cargo to go with it. Octavos's queries were meant with, 'Not my department. Find the Tribune.' Except the Tribune was nowhere to be seen. *How could there be mounts and wagons to spare yesterday and none now?*

"You look lost," said a big man wearing a leather breastplate over a tan tunic. Brown eyes beneath a helmet of grey hair surveyed the young aristocrat.

Octavos managed a wry grin. "I am looking for passage to Dessau. Everybody says, 'speak to the Tribune,' but I can't find him."

"Officers are good at hiding. I should know." He extended a beefy arm towards Octavos, the skin marred with spreading blue-green blobs.

"Those are legion tattoos."

The big man nodded. "I did my twenty. Now I do other things." He claimed a seat alongside Octavos. "Now, why did you want to join this bunch?"

"I have business in Dessau." The big man puzzled Octavos. *I should know him.*

"What a coincidence," said the big man. "So do I. Got three wagons out back, be following in the wake of this bunch."

"Cam!" The speaker was a compact man in an officer's cloak. "I hear you're leaving us."

"I got business in Soraq, Michael," said Cam. "I told you that at the outset."

"Sir, are you the Tribune in charge of this column?"

The officer's eyes flicked over to Octavos. "I am." His eyes widened. "You're the Prince's Cousin. What brings you here?"

"I seek passage to Dessau," said Octavos. "A special project."

"Horses are in short supply," said the Tribune. "No room left in the wagons, either. I suggest asking if Cam has a spot."

Cam nodded. "Matter of fact I do, Michael."

"Good, it's settled then," said Michael. "Prince Octavos, you ride with Cam. Don't worry, he's a good fellow." The tribune spun and vanished back into the mob.

Octavos followed Cam through the postern gate to a trio of wagons laden with large boxes. "Get your asses ready," shouted Cam at a knot of men lounging beside the middle wagon. "And no, Louis, you're not taking the floozy."

A squeal of indignation emerged from the third cart, followed by a tanned girl running off in a flurry of pastel robes.

Cam slapped a beefy palm on the driver's bench of the lead wagon. "Get aboard. I have to check with some people."

Octavos climbed onto the seat. Am I really doing this? He glanced around for Cam and finally spotted him speaking with a trio of soldiers in green scout tunics. The conversation ended with Cam tossing a small pouch at one of the scouts.

Trumpets sounded with an ear-splitting screech. The fort's main gates swung open, and five parallel lines of bicycles emerged onto the road.

Cam stumped over, unconcerned with the bustle, and heaved himself into the wagon.

The flow of bicycles transformed into military wagons. "It'll be our turn next," said Cam.

The last wagon rumbled through the gate. Cam flicked the reigns. A jolt ran through Octavos as the cart moved. The hills grew near.

Something bothered Octavos. *Cam does seem familiar. But I don't remember seeing him anywhere! He didn't bat an eyelid when the Tribune called me 'prince.' He already knew who I was.* "So, what's your business in Dessau?"

Cam shrugged. "Just passing through. I got an investment to check on in Soraq. Then on to the coast." He looked at Octavos. "What about you?"

"Just Dessau. What sort of investment?"

"Construction. My boss has big plans for Soraq."

"He sounds ambitious."

Cam looked at him. "Yeah, he's ambitious all right."

Cam adjusted his grip on the reigns. Octavos caught a glimpse of the blurry legion tattoos. "You were Pilus Primus?" The First Spears were the biggest badass in the legions.

"Yeah, in the Sixth," said Cam.

Octavos squinted. That 'VI' looked more like 'VII.' The VII Marfaki, not the Islanders. If so, that made 'Cam' – "Leander Casein."

"Took you long enough."

LABYRINTH WAR XVI – Git Vik

'The Nitivi keep crucial knowledge from the People.'
- Coordinator Brik-Jute immediately prior to losing his office.

"Brik-Jute nears completion." The liquid voice originated from a black bulbous head protruding from a shell large enough to hold a dozen People. The speaker was Intiviki, one of the alien Nitivi, who'd advised the People since...nobody was certain. That knowledge was lost with the Prior World. Brik-Jute voiced the opinion that the Nitivi deceived the People about the depth and nature of their alliance. Git-Vik was certain that opinion contributed to Brik-Jute being made into a Shull. He thought it strange that the Nitivi knew more about the creation of Shulls than the People. Unlike Brik-Jute, he did not vocalize his suspicions.

"Acknowledged." Git-Vik tapped three of his manipulator appendages together as a sign of respect. One did not offend the Nitivi. Their knowledge and peculiar abilities made them dangerous. "I will proceed to the Transformation Pit at once."

"Intiviki will accompany Git-Vik." The Nitivi squeezed its squid-like bulk from the shell, the metal bands, and plates affixed to his soft parts rattling and clanking.

Git-Vik's six crab-like legs propelled him into the shattered streets of Tet-Gheg-Vu.

Once, Tet-Gheg-Vu must have been impressive – soaring crystalline towers linked by graceful bridges rising from the summit of a plateau. Now, most of those towers were jagged stumps. Mounds of debris blocked half of the streets.

Git-Vik's course took him past the cause of that catastrophe – a place where a large section of the plateau had broken away and slid into the depths. Brik-Jute claimed the damage was consistent with a kinetic strike – a giant rock dropped onto the city from space. He had no explanation as to who was responsible for that assault. Had it been aimed better, that projectile might have ended Tet-Gheg-Vu completely. As it was, the city was an occupied ruin.

The meddlesome kwintath occupied most of Tet-Gheg-Vu. Still, the insectoid-like race preserved considerable technological expertise even in this ruinous era. That lingering technology, combined with nitivi knowledge, made it possible to transform aging People into Shulls.

People who survived long enough underwent a metamorphosis from male to female, a process that made their carapaces swell to immense size, filled with egg sacks. Swarms of males inseminated these sacks. The hatchlings then devoured their mother from the inside out before being captured and trained. The transformation to Shull altered this process – granting an extended lifespan and a new form of mobility for those who survived the transition. Git-Vik's course took him past pits filled with the rotting corpses of those who failed to make the transition. There had been too many failures. Git-Vik hoped that Brik-Jute would not be another casualty.

Inarticulate screeches emerged from a pit ahead of Git-Vik and his unwanted companion. Bipedal thralls with control collars around their necks heaved vegetable matter and corpses of various species into the hole under the supervision of silver-robed kwintath. One of these aliens faced the pair as they approached the pit.

Intiviki moved closer to the kwintath. "What is the status of this Shull's transformation?"

"We find the transformation process problematic and prone to failure."

"Shulls are necessary." That statement came from Intiviki.

"We believe mechanizing the gliders would be an easier option."

"Mechanical fliers are inferior to Shulls."

"That assessment is dubious."

Git-Vik quivered as Intiviki loomed over the kwintath. The nitivi did not like being contradicted. Nor did they care for the kwintath.

Git-Vik thought the kwintath made a valid point. Purely mechanical fliers would be much easier to construct. He did not voice that opinion.

A loud screech from the pit and a cloud of toxic gasses interrupted the confrontation.

The kwintath faced the hole. "Brik-Jute is experiencing difficulties completing the transformation."

"Elaborate." Git-Vik moved towards a viewing platform that protruded over the pit as he spoke. Thralls toting dead and dying creatures stepped aside.

Brik-Jute-Shul's swollen carapace filled the circular depression. The former Gotemik's inarticulate screeches filled the air, accompanied by the whistles of escaping toxic gasses. A net of woven plant fiber covered the cradle, to prevent the Shul from taking flight.

"Brik-Jute's organs interact poorly with certain of the mechanical augmentations." The kwintath moved to join Git-Vik.

"Those mechanisms are inferior." Intiviki did not approach the hole.

Brik-Jute's bloated body almost filled the pit, resembling a partly inflated ball studded with chitinous plates. An orifice large enough to swallow a thrall dominated this grotesque balloon's edge. Git-Vik watched a dead beast plummet into that mouth.

Git-Vik remembered being larger than Brik-Jute. The old Gotemik mentored Git-Vik, making him his assistant. Back then, Brik-Jute had been a Coordinator, orchestrating thousands of People, and thralls. That was before the fall that saw both posted to this remote outpost. Even that exile had been deemed insufficient punishment for Brik-Jute. No, for his offenses, and the People's greater need, Brik-Jute was being made 'Shull.' And Shul's were immense – their disk-shaped carapaces were a dozen times the diameter of their land-bound cousins.

"No more." Brik-Jute's screeches attained coherency. "No more food." The Shul's maw closed. "I hurt!"

Git-Vik's six legs clicked against the platform as it shifted position. "Hold," it informed the thralls, who were about to hurl an aged biped into the Shul's maw.

"We believe these units can properly repair the Shull." The kwintath motioned at a pair of thralls carrying tools and bulky equipment – a power modulator and a filtration unit.

"Hold." The thralls stopped at Intiviki's command. "The damage to Brik-Jute is too severe. I recommend termination."

"No." Git-Vik surprised himself with the defiant statement. "I possess the requisite skills to repair Brik-Jute."

"The procedure is likely to fail," said Intiviki.

"The mechanisms will suffice," said the kwintath.

Enough. "Brik-Jute! I am here."

"Git-Vik?" The Shul's voice terminated in a pain-filled screech. "I hurt!"

"I can assist you." He secured the power modulator and filtration units to his carapace. "Will you permit me entry?"

"Yes." The word was a vast sigh, accompanied by outgassing from the Shul's thruster modules. A curved segment of Brik-Jute's shell popped open, exposing the Shul's internal organs.

Git-Vik didn't hesitate—no time for a gradual descent in a cage. The Gotemik leaped from the platform. Pain shot through Git-Vik's legs upon impact with Brik-Jute's carapace, including the grinding sensation of a fractured joint. The Gotemik ignored the pain and scuttled through the hatch, edging past the drooping flesh.

This maneuver put Git-Vik in Brik-Jute's cabin; a space big enough for three Gotemik plus a dozen tightly packed thralls – though the latter would be unable to stand erect in the cramped space. Bioluminescent lights attached to Git-Vik's shell revealed various organs that intruded into this space. Chief among these organic components was a tight bundle of ropy nerve cables that emerged from the floor and entered the ceiling. The conglomeration sparked and hissed at irregular intervals. Unless repaired that malfunction would eventually kill Brik-Jute.

Git-Vik detached the power regulator and approached the nerve bundle. Care was called for; enough raw power pulsed through those cables to fry the Gotemik to a crisp.

Git-Vik edged the regulator closer to the mass. It was a grotesque abomination, thrice the proper size, cobbled together from a dozen other pieces of equipment. Moreover, it lacked efficiency. Worse, it was a salvaged kwintath mechanism. But it was what he had to work with and was Brik-Jute's sole hope of survival.

Git-Vik applied insulating gel to its manipulative cilia and carefully severed a cable. Sparks flew from the severed end before he jammed it into the regulator. He repeated the process sixteen times. The pops and sparks faded, replaced by a dull glow from the regulator. The Bug had assembled the device correctly.

"I can think." Brik-Jute's voice sounded all around Git-Vik. "But my innards are clogged."

"I shall repair them." Git-Vik scuttled across the chamber and popped loose a panel that provided access to the Shull's guts. Then he slithered into Brik-Jute's belly.

Giant sacks held half-digested meat and the fuel that would enable the completed Shul to fly. Solids and fluids leaked from some of these sacks; Git-Vik's path traversed the bones of beasts and thralls, including other People, no doubt at Intiviki's command. *We are being culled.*

Git-Vik located a clogged digestive bag attached to a fuel cell. The sack was bloated with bones and undigested corpses, swollen to five times the proper size. Git-Vik lifted a sharp-tipped mandible and made an incision. The sack's contents plummeted to the floor.

"Ah, that feels better," said Brik-Jute.

Git-Vik didn't respond, being busy installing the filtration unit. He sealed it in place. "There. You should be able to resume feeding without discomfort."

"That is good." Brik-Jute's innards trembled, making Git-Vik fight for balance. "I hunger."

Git-Vik started for the exit. Rope-like cables, used by the Shul for internal repairs, emerged from the walls, blocking his path. "Have you another concern?"

"I do." Brik-Jute fell silent for a moment. "This thing we do. Is it right?"

"Yes," said Git-Vik.

The cables didn't move. It dawned on Git-Vik that Brik-Jute could kill him here and escape all penalties. "I do, however, have concerns." Git-Vik could never admit something so treasonous to any other being. Otherwise, he might become a Shull.

The cables parted. Git-Vik scuttled through, his thoughts focused on the task for which Brik-Jute and the other two Shul were being prepared: eradicating the vermin who'd dared assault a superior race.

LABYRINTH WAR_XVII – Singer

'Samual turned and then he was on the ground with an arrow in his throat. It could have been me.'

- Statement of Legionnaire Tiberius after his squad was ambushed on the road to Dessau.

The brush parted. A battered legionnaire stepped into the road near Casein's wagon. "Don't stop," said the soldier. "There are infiltrators in the brush." He motioned to the steep tree and shrub-covered slope rising south of the road. "We took out one bunch, but more are still out there."

Octavos's foot bounced. His tunic chafed. He glanced at the deep chasm paralleling the road a dozen yards to the north. *Hill on one side, gorge on the other, and enemy all around.* He gripped the sword hilt with sweat-slick palms. *I might have to use this thing for real.*

Casein nodded. "Thanks for the heads up."

The soldier nodded and vanished back into the bramble.

"Listen up, losers," Casein shouted. "The enemy is here. Eyes open and weapons at the ready." He glanced at Octavos. "That goes for you too."

"That includes the specials, boss?" The voice came from the rear wagon.

Casein muttered under his breath. "No."

"Specials?"

"Don't ask, kid."

They resumed travel, climbing a hill shaded by the setting sun. Caseins eyes flicked back and forth. Octavos saw goblins and nomads in every shadow. The view from the summit revealed a long empty straightaway, and a distant bridge crossing the gorge to a walled city. "Dessau," said Casein.

They descended the slope. "There." Casein pointed to a gap in the brush.

"What?" Octavos didn't see anything.

"On the ground next to those flowers."

Octavos looked a second time and spotted an outthrust arm and face covered in blood. The yellowish corpse wore rough leather armor. Octavos's stomach clenched.

The grass ahead parted. A sallow-skinned man in leather stumbled onto the road, clenching his gut. He took three steps and fell face-first into the dirt. An arrow protruded from his back.

Casein wrapped a meaty fist around the hilt of the crossbow in the seat next to him.

The wagon rumbled past the second corpse. Octavos's gut refused to unclench itself.

The highway rounded a corner and entered a squat block of a building straddling the road, next to the earthen square of a legion fort with a tall fieldstone wall. Past it, a switch-backed dirt track ascended the hill. A long drawbridge connected the fortress with a similar structure attached to the city wall.

Dessau's not much of a city. More of a town, or a large village. It wasn't big enough for more than a few thousand people. "Where's the camps?"

Casein motioned at the fortress. "Past there, down the slope a bit."

A framework projecting from Dessau's wall caught Octavo's attention.

Casein noted Octavos's interest in the mechanism. "That's the chain lift. Five hundred feet to the bottom of the gorge. Hell of a lot quicker than the road."

"Are you taking it?"

"If I must." Casein's face remained impassive. "I'm taking a little road going north and west."

"To Pathak," said Octavos. "Am I going with you?"

"I dunno," said Casein. "Are you?"

Octavos found himself at a loss for words.

Inside the blockhouse, Casein handed coins to a harried officer and then directed the wagon towards the bridge. Another soldier opened a portcullis opening onto the span. "We were just about to raise the bridge for the night."

"That bad?"

The soldier nodded.

As the wagon trundled onto the bridge, Octavos realized this was two separate drawbridges set to either side of the chasm that almost met each other, leaving a gap wide enough for a thin man to fall through to the chasm floor.

Casein didn't seem to notice. The horses stepped over the void and the wagon followed with a disquieting bounce that did nothing for Octavos's stomach. Then they were through the portcullis on the far side amidst a cacophony of pushing people and raised voices.

"Move, damn you!" Casein raised the buggy whip. Locals in pale robes and tanned people in rags retreated enough to allow the wagon passage.

The street past the blockhouse was not an improvement. Mobs of people in rags and robes thronged a dirt street lined with mudbrick huts, arguing, bartering, or loafing. *What was I thinking of coming here?* He'd just assumed his name would be enough to infringe upon the hospitality of the local aristocracy.

He'd known Dessau was crowded, but knowing and experiencing were different things.

Casein drove the wagon a short distance along the street and veered through a wide portal set in a stone building that protruded from the city wall.

"The Chain Lift," said Casein. Stout wooden doors dominated the wall directly before them. Given their location, they had to open onto the lift.

Casein nodded. "Last room left in town."

A plump-robed man emerged from a dark opening and began a rapid-fire conversation with Casein that ended with the transfer of a thick pouch. The man smiled and waved at a tight spiral stair to the side.

The second and third wagons pulled into the cramped space. The men driving them dismounted and began unhitching the horses.

"Let's see what accommodations my coin bought." Casein jumped from the cart and started for a dark stairwell. "Not much, I reckon."

Their quarters were a long, narrow room bisected with thick timbers. Walking from one end to the other meant ducking under or stepping over these supports. There was no other furniture. Octavos saw three other occupants, men clad in brown and black rags, sitting with their backs against the wall.

"It'll do," said Casein.

Octavos found a stout door next to one of the beams. "This must open onto the gantry."

Casein glanced at the portal. "Probably. Not sure I care for that."

Two of Casein's men tromped into the room. "Louis and Goji are watching the horses, boss." The speaker boasted a thick leather-covered torso and a wide face framed by long dirty blond hair.

"Good job Luther." Casein gave the room a final glance. "Let's see about some grub."

"I'd like to check in with the Mayor's Office," said Octavos.

Casein gave Octavos a blank look. "Tomorrow."

They descended the stairs and ventured onto the street, still a madhouse despite the hour. Dessau boasted three inns. Two were packed full of soldiers and a ring of locals five deep surrounded the third. Casein finally gave a street vendor good silver for half a dozen skewers of meat and vegetables and a pitcher of weak wine.

"He screwed you over." Octavos eyed his skewer and attempted to determine if he was looking at turnips or onions. The meat had a strange texture to it.

"Seller's market." Casein took a bite. "Snake."

"Never had snake before," said Octavos.

"Pretend it's chicken." Casein took another bite.

Octavos took a bite. Spices exploded in his mouth. Sauce dripped from his mouth. "Not bad."

"Back to our room," said Casein.

Once there, though, Octavos found the chamber stuffy and oppressive. "I'm for the roof," he told Casein.

"I'll join you." Casein finished the last of his skewer. "Should be a good view."

An impulse made Octavos grab his lyre case before ascending the stairs.

The tips of Casein's lips curled. "You are pretty good with that thing."

Octavos whirled. "This 'thing' is a model nine lyre made by the master Rufus Brassicas, one of the best living fabricators of musical instruments in the Empire. Imperial court musicians play his instruments." *It also cost me far too much money. But I was prosperous in those days.*

"Sounds impressive."

The roof proved as crowded as the rest of Dessau. Tan men in rags offered strange wailing prayers to pagan deities, prompting catcalls and insults from the Kheffians. Octavos spotted a large family huddled at the far end of the roof. Bands of legionaries stomped across the surface, brutally knocking Kheffian and Soraq refugees alike to the side.

Casein crossed the parapet to the gorge side. "Too many torches," he said. "It'll ruin the sentry's night vision."

Octavos scanned the descending slope past the blockhouse, noting a large constellation of small fires. "That must be the refugee camp."

"One of them." Casein strode to the roof's opposite side.

Octavos joined him. This perch provided a commanding view of Dessau: a tight tangle of skinny lanes between almost identical flat-roofed mudbrick huts. Even now, people packed the streets.

"There." Casein pointed at a twice normal-sized hut across the town, surrounded by a brick wall. "That's the mayor's house."

Octavos studied the distant domicile. A solitary light gleamed in a second-story window. "Looks closed for the night."

"I'll see about getting you there in the morning." Casein sounded ambivalent.

A scream of panic prompted both men to turn to the roof behind them. A Kheffian had leaped atop one of the praying men, thrashing him with a club. Another leering Kheffian dangled a young child over the parapet while a haggard woman screamed and pleaded.

Casein grabbed the club wielder and yanked him off his victim, who lay moaning upon the boards. Then he turned his attention to the infant dangler.

An outraged cacophony emerged from the beater's companions. Seeing Casein approach, the child dangler whirled, handed his victim to the mother, and fled.

These people have given up hope. But maybe I can change that. A sense of determination filled Octavos. *I may not be a warrior of legend, but I can make a difference.* He placed the lyre case on the ground and opened it with deliberate movements. Next, he removed the instrument, casting a critical eye over its strings. *It will do.* Then he leaned against the railing and began to play. He started with a tuning piece, not a true song - just something to assess the chords.

Heads turned in their direction at the sound. People stopped speaking.

Anaximander's 'Flower Mountain' was his first piece. Octavos became lost in the melody after the first few chords. 'Rain at Dawn,' an old folk tune, was his next selection. This one gave him some trouble. After that, 'Farmer Polk's Journey,' a comical romp with a dozen different versions. A dozen voices joined him in the choruses.

Then Casein was at his side with a broad smile plastered on his face. "Damn, kid, you are good with that instrument." He handed Octavos a cup. "I figure you're getting parched.

"Thank you." Octavos took the cup and drank a long swig of weak wine. Then he looked around the roof. Nobody argued. No fighting. A glance over the rail revealed more of the same: large silent crowds, staring at the rooftop, all staring at him.

Casein's minion Luther appeared, carrying a drum. "I'm not the best," he said, placing it on the planks, "but I can bang out a few tunes."

Octavos thought a moment. Luther was an Avar. "Do you know 'Donegal's Ride?" That one had a simple enough drum section.

Luther grinned, exposing a pair of missing teeth. "I do."

"Then let's have at it." Octavos's fingers began to fly over the lyre. Luther joined in at the appropriate point and managed a credible job. Most of the audience didn't know the words, but the ones who did sang the chorus.

From there it was 'Belasco's wedding,' which many of his listeners did know. Luther botched the drum work on that one, but nobody cared. Then a legion marching tune had the soldiers stomping their feet.

Octavos finished with 'Firefly Melody,' which left him exhausted.

Casein steadied the youth. "Not bad." He guided Octavos towards the stairs, the youth still clenching his lyre with bloodied fingers. "Now it's time for some shut-eye."

LABYRINTH WAR XVIII – Carina

'Outside, I stepped into a scene of chaos. Scores of people ran in different directions or huddled in small groups.

A stout bald man in a baker's apron shouted, "They're outside the gates!"

"Which army?" I asked. Rumor insisted an imperial legion was in the province.

My words met empty air. The baker was gone.

Three thin men in brown leather stumbled by, sharing a bottle. One paused long enough to vomit.

Bruno the Butcher lumbered past, swinging a meat cleaver, vowing to chop off the head of Traag's general.

A woman in a purple checked dress crouched over a small child against a crumbling brick wall.

I skirted a small mob gathered around a balding man in a tattered black robe standing atop a broken crate, proclaiming that the End of the World was nigh.

Past the street preacher, a busker played his lyre and mangled a patriotic song to an audience of children and drunkards.

An old woman in a brown dress pressed an apple against my chest and demanded a silver dinar. I declined her offer.'

-From the wizard Lysanders account of the Siege of Brenna during the Traag War.

"I don't like it," said Xenia. The Saban girl paced back and forth along the summit of the wall, fingers constantly moving along the haft of her leaf-bladed spear. She'd had just one upon their arrival. Now she boasted three. "Something is going on east of here. Way too many Black State boys in dem hills."

"They're probably just keeping an eye on Ptath." Carina cast a glance at the low scrub-covered hills east of the city. Nothing moved. That meant nothing. "After all, this is the biggest nomad invasion in four hundred years."

"Maybe." Xenia stepped aside as a line of soldiers passed. "But dares other folk out dare too. Cats – and I ain't talking leopards and tigers."

"Scouts for the nomads," said Carina.

"I told Centurion Briscoe and Tribune Strong, but day just look at me."

Carina sighed. Misogyny was a given for the officers. Women couldn't know anything about martial arts, period.

"Don't worry," said a youthful voice. "Me and the lads will stop them." The speaker was the fifteen-year-old apprentice to Brassicas the Butcher. He sported a dented helm, leather breastplate, and an ancient sword clenched in his right hand. An equally ancient crossbow was strapped across his back. His half dozen 'lads' ranged from ten to fifteen years old and bore even less impressive weaponry.

"Tyler, get your ass out of here," said Xenia.

"Hey, I've been practicing." Tyler's face contorted. "Cam said I had potential." His tongue tripped over the word. "Dat means I'm tough."

"No, that means you are an idiot." Xenia whirled her spear and tapped the boy's wrist. His sword clattered to the stones. "Now git."

"You shouldn't have done that." Tyler knelt, grabbed the sword by the blade, and darted off along the wall.

"I do miss Cam," said Xenia. Over the past month, the former soldier had turned a collection of servants, apprentices, grooms, boatmen, and even whores into something that might almost be mistaken for a militia. Tyler was one of Cam's more promising students.

"He's gone," said Carina. "Get over him."

Raised voices came from the Pyramid of Zep where hundreds of legionaries dug into the ancient monolith like termites devouring a savory plank. A block the size of a wagon escaped their grasp and tumbled down the structure's steep slope and into the font.

"Why day doing dat?"

"Because somebody told them to." Carina pointed at the pair of figures in wizard's robes among the soldiers, one thin, and the other plump.

"Best let sleeping spirits lie." Xenia shook her head. The rings in her dreadlocks knocked against each other. "Day wake up, dare be hell ta' pay."

"Here you are," said a familiar voice. Demetrius came into view.

"What now?" Annoyance filled Carina's voice. "The shops ready."

"Not my chores," said Demetrius. "Lady Bottles." The gaunt herbalist handed Carina a slip of paper.

Carina inspected the document. "I thought that was just a rumor."

"Lady Bottle says otherwise." The herbalist placed his hands on the rail and stared at the distant hills. "And in my experience, she is usually correct about these things."

Another massive block of stone bounced from the summit of the pyramid.

Carina looked at the paper. "I'd best get moving."

Carina stalked through Ptath's near-deserted market, left elbow draped through the handle of a large straw basket. Just four of the stalls remained open. Of these, two were doing a raucous business selling intoxicants. The third was a pawnshop whose owner possessed more greed than sense. Carina's destination was the fourth, a lonely stall near the Grand Font with just a solitary customer.

The most recent barges had brought All-Heal, Aloe Vera, Angelica Root, and other medicines destined for the healer's tents. But Lady Bottle's note said Talib the Fat had somehow claimed a percentage of these herbs. Talib dealt in cosmetics and cure-alls, with sidelines in combs, brushes, and junk jewelry. Those wares made the vendor popular with whores and working women alike. But his real profits came from the trade in semi-licit stimulants such as Blood Weed and hallucinogenic Blue Dust.

Talib's client left clenching a parcel as Carina approached the stall. A wide, false smile appeared on the merchant's broad face. "Ah, Demetrius's assistant, no doubt here for my latest stock." The false smile dissolved into an equally false expression of despair. "Alas, you are late."

"Not bloody likely." Carina wasn't in the mood for bargaining. She recited a list of herbs, watching Talib smile or wince at each name.

"Lady Carina, your bland list takes the joy from my day." Talib rubbed his hands together.

"Your sole joy is counting coins," said Carina.

"You malign me." Talib's expression turned to indignation. "Perhaps the dour attitude afflicting the rest of the market has affected you?"

"In case it escaped your notice, Ptath is facing the biggest nomad invasion in four hundred years."

"I am not concerned." Talib rubbed his hands. "The sand dwellers have attacked Ptath many times. The legions thrashed them on each occasion."

"A commendable attitude," said a new voice.

Carina stiffened. She knew that voice.

Talib's false smile reasserted itself as he faced the new customer. "Ah, Lord Ambrose. How might I assist you?"

"My throat burns and my stomach churns," said the Witch Hunter. "I am informed you offer a cordial for these ailments."

"Of course, of course, great lord!" Talib's head bobbed. "Preparing the potion requires a few moments." The merchant spun with surprising agility, pudgy fingers darting beneath the counter, extracting pots and jars.

Carina dared a quick glimpse at the Witch Hunter. Ambrose's face was pale and gaunt. His legs wobbled. *The bastard deserves to suffer more.*

Then the Witch Hunter looked at her. His brow furled. "You appear familiar."

He can't know who I am. It was dark. He couldn't see me. Carina dipped her neck. "I work in the healing tents, lordship."

"Strange. I don't recognize you."

"My master is Demetrius," said Carina. "His tent is with the tail."

Ambrose nodded. "Ah, that explains it. Are you whore as well?"

"No, my lord." Carina kept her head lowered. *Fool! I should have answered 'yes.' Whoever heard of a woman with the tail camp who was not a whore?* "I left that life behind me."

"Commendable," said the Witch Hunter. "Your renunciation of sinful ways proves that even fallen women can seek redemption."

Shouts came from the pyramid.

"Now what?" Ambrose stepped past Carina to get a better view of the pile.

Carina raised her face. A knot of soldiers clustered about a great gouge they'd made in the stonework, staring at something that reflected the light with a rainbow of colors. The Kheffian wizards clambered over the stones to investigate.

"Fools." The Witch Hunter's fingers clenched and unclenched. "Fools stealing God's power to pry into secrets best left buried."

Carina almost agreed with the fanatic. Tampering with ancient magic was seldom wise.

"Ah, lordship," came Talib's voice from within the stall. "I have your medication."

"Good." Ambrose lurched over to the counter and dropped a coin. Talib handed him a tall cup. Ambrose's face contorted as he gulped the liquid. "Gah! Must these cordials always taste like shit?"

Carina smiled. Properly prepared, the potion should have been tasteless. *Talib spiked it.*

More shouts came from the pyramid as another block of stone slid into the font. Near the summit, the mages fiercely argued with each other.

"What are the fools doing now?" Ambrose resumed his former viewing position.

If Asshole Ambrose is watching the pyramid, then he might not notice me leave. Carina scuttled to the counter. "I am here for Lady Bottle's special order."

"Ah." Talib placed three small packets on the counter. "That woman – how did she know?" He shook his head. "The city's melancholy affects me. You shall be my last customer for today." His hand reached for the visor handle above his head.

Carina nodded and swept the bundle into her basket. Then she began walking towards Ptath's southern quarter. The address in Lady Bottle's directions was close to the ruined shrine. Carina's fingers fumbled at the glass rectangle in her pocket. *Perhaps I can visit that place and find out what this does.*

"That's it! I'm out!" The words came from the proprietor of the nearest drink stall.

Flaming idiot, Carina thought as mutters arose among the customers.

"I don't believe you," shouted a beefy soldier.

"Greedy bastard! You can't turn us away now!"

Carina increased her pace.

"He's holding back!"

"Get him!"

Two soldiers grabbed the bartender. Others jumped over the counter.

"Enough!" Ambrose's voice cut across the din. "Cease this conduct at once or be flogged!"

A few members of the incipient riot turned in the Witch Hunter's direction.

"Stuff it, Asshole," shouted an anonymous voice from within the mob.

"Spoilsport!"

"He can do it," said another voice in the crowd.

The mob quieted; its members began to disperse.

"Damn it, he was telling the truth." The voice came from the interior of the stall. "Not a drop left."

Raised voices ahead attracted Carina's attention. A squad of soldiers emerged from a side street, accompanied by a third Kheffian magician: Halima the Witch. Halima pointed at a modest standalone house. "Bring everything and everybody to me."

Great. Carina ducked into an alleyway. That house was her destination. She moved to the alley's far end and craned her neck. A pair of figures darted across the street to the south. Amentep was one of them.

"Some escaped out the back!"

"Find them," ordered the mage.

Carina heard the sound of tramping boots as soldiers neared her position. *Shit. I must leave.* She ducked into the alleyways, searching for a refuge. Dust Dens and the local taprooms were out. She considered the ruined shrine but decided against it. Too close to the house being searched. And likely to be searched in turn. There. Carina spotted a small church with an open door. She slipped inside.

Four or five figures in drab robes huddled in robes near the entryway. Past them, a double row of people prostrated themselves before a candlelit altar. Carina sidestepped the huddle and found herself next to the back bench, occupied by a white-bearded oldster and a solitary woman sitting with a bowed head. Lady Bottle.

Carina slid next to the camp mistress. "There you are, dear," said Lady Bottle. "Talib came through?"

Carina nodded. "But"-

Lady Bottle put a finger to her lip. "I know."

"What happened? Why were you there?"

"Keep your voice down, dear." The aristocrat rummaged through the handbag on her lap. "Business. The Nebo clan mines crystal." She extracted a faceted blue and white stone from the pouch.

Nebo. So that was Amentep's family name.

"Junk jewelry." Carina eyed the stone. She'd seen similar specimens adorning the local whores. Chrissy had acquired a pendant made of the stuff.

Lady Bottle nodded. "They were willing to trade in exchange for certain services. If I hadn't been running late..." She shook her head. "Whatever did they do to attract such attention?"

Carina thought she knew but didn't speak. Her suspicions involved an abandoned pagan shrine and a glass square in her pocket.

"At least you obtained the herbs," said the aristocrat. "My original deal is no longer practical, but another option presents itself."

A black-robed priest with a bushy beard navigated the huddle. "Lady Bottle?"

"Father James." Lady Bottle dipped her head. "I have the medicinal supplies you requested. Shall we negotiate in private?"

The priest smiled. "This way, my lady."

Lady Bottle rose to her feet and took the basket from Carina. "You'd best run back to Demetrius."

But how did she know I'd come here, Carina wondered as she exited the church.

The lowering sun cast long shadows across the deserted street. Carina strained her natural and supernatural senses. *Damn.* The street west of here buzzed with activity. And Demetrius's improvised shop was near the western wall. Rather than tangle with the soldiers, Carina decided to head to the market. Ptath's major avenues converged there anyhow.

Ambrose should have left by now.

The drink stalls, pawnshop, and Talib the Fats booth were all shuttered. But the market wasn't empty. A large crowd milled along the edge of the Font, watching the pyramid and muttering. The legionnaires toppled another stone into the water. Carina barely noticed. She was focused on the two figures beside a huge glittering patch on the pyramid.

They made elaborate arm movements. Snatches of words reached Carina's ears: "Dangerous...foolhardy...unknown...necessary."

The troops formed a line where the pyramid's stones struck the water and stood there, gazing at the arguing magicians.

The thin figure pointed at the glistening patch. The thick figure knelt and extended a hand, touching the material.

Carina's skin prickled. There was no way the Kheffian magicians could know what they were doing.

The stout magician began an incantation. Carina cocked her head. That spell was old. Downright ancient, from tomes few bothered to consult anymore.

The glistening substance began to glow. The stout magician kept chanting, though his voice wavered. A burst of blue-tinged light erupted skyward from the alien material. The stout magician cried out and fell backward.

An electric jolt ran through Carina's body. Symbols she could not comprehend appeared in the sorceress's mind, making her head throb. Her knees threatened to buckle. She reached for a nearby wall to steady herself.

Then it was over. Carina blinked. The thin magician helped the stout mage to his feet. The soldiers still stood at the base of the pyramid. Some clenched their ears while others covered their eyes. Half the market crowd had collapsed.

A familiar and hated figure stepped from the shadows of Talib's shop and faced the pyramid. "You fools!" Ambrose raised his fist. "You have awakened demons, bringing ruin upon us all!"

Others in the crowd echoed Ambrose's call. The soldiers on the pyramid cast uncertain looks first at Ambrose and then at the Kheffian mages, who huddled in private conversation.

Downed men and women began climbing to their feet, moaning, and clenching their heads. Others in the crowd shouted epitaphs at the mages.

This could get ugly. Carina glanced to her left. Empty. *That street goes to Demetrius's shop.*

The Kheffian wizards ended their conversation. The thin one stood atop a projecting stone. "Return to your units," he ordered in a booming voice.

"Why should we heed the orders of a demon caller," Ambrose shouted back at the mage.

"We hold direct authority from Prince Thomas Maximus," said the thin mage. "Now, return to your units!"

"Liar," Ambrose shouted. "With the Prince gone, I hold the authority in this city. I hereby place you under arrest."

Crap. Ambrose has lost his mind. The prince might be absent, but there was no way he'd put Ambrose in charge of the city. Right? Carina edged towards her chosen street.

Horns sounded from the eastern wall.

Carina froze. *That's the alarm! We're under attack!* Moreover, the eastern wall was Xenia's station. Carina threw caution to the wind and began sprinting across the plaza.

"Move," bellowed a petty officer's voice on the pyramid. "Get your kits. Grab the specials."

Carina reached the eastern wall and climbed the stairs three at a time. She glanced over the parapet. Long shadows cast by the city walls covered fields of stunted crops and withered grass. But beyond them, loping tan and orange-furred figures lopped towards the walls. Rachasa. Lots of rachasa.

Xenia appeared alongside Carina. "We in for Hell's own fight."

LABYRINTH WAR IXX – Curtis

"I lived in a hell of war and battle for years, fighting men and vilekin and conjured things. I didn't even draw my blade in my first battle, but my childhood friend Richard took an arrow in the eye. I rode over three men in the next contest before being knocked from my horse. Even so, I was more fortunate than Cousin Thomas who took a spear through the gut and spent a day dying. We had to hew our way out of the next ambush. I escaped, but my brother Jon did not. We sought refuge in some stinking village, but they tried to murder us in our sleep, so we...did things, then and afterward." Dark shadows haunted the knight's eyes as he spoke those last words.

Sir Benedict pulled a leather thong around his neck, exposing a mangled metal disk. He rolled it between his fingers while staring into space with a haunted expression. The amulet featured a standing figure with a raised sword and the sun behind him. It was deeply gouged in the middle.

After a time, the knight spoke. "God works in mysterious ways. After years of fighting, I cared about little and less – family, honor, death, life, God – nothing mattered. Then a priest gave me this." He gave the medallion's thong a little shake. "I thought nothing more of it. Then came Crowfoot Gap, where the empire's full might clashed with Traag. My company's charge broke the ranks, but the enemy foot surrounded us. Those I might have bested, but squads of Invincible's were mixed into their ranks – and those sorcerous warriors are hard to kill. One stabbed me through a chink in my plate. Only this," he held up the amulet "deflected his sword from my heart. I fell from the saddle as the sky overhead exploded in flame."

"Equitant's blasting powder." Jot nodded.

Sir Benedict ignored the comment. "I lay on the field tormented and astounded by visions of heaven and hell." He put the small icon back on his shirt. "I found my soul again that day." He put the talisman back in his shirt.

Silence reigned for a moment. Then Sir Benedict drained his cup and sat it on the platter. "God above," he said, "but I am weary."

- Sir Benedict DuPaul's account of the Battle of Crowfoot Gap during the Traag War

Julie wrapped her bony limbs around Curtis's armored form. "Take care," she said. "Remember, I'm gonna be your new Steward."

Curtis smiled. "I told you. I don't have a Steward."

"See, you need one." Julie released her grip. "Come back in one piece, now." She looked at Sir Sate's dour form. "That goes for you too."

Sir Sate snorted and climbed onto his steed.

"Take care of yourself, Julie," said Curtis.

Julie made a dismissive wave. "Oh, I'll be all right. It's you stupid menfolk that get yourselves kilt."

Curtis mounted his horse and eyed the long column of horses and bicycles snaking towards the hill forts. *This is it.* Word from on high had the nomads making a major push at Fort Saxum. The army could be flanked. Hence, Thomas's move, emptying Ptath of everything but three cohorts.

A trio of youths waited next to a cluster of flags planted atop a low mound outside the Crossroads Fort. "That way, Sir Knights," said a round-faced lad when Curtis reached the hillock. He pointed at a trail of armored figures working their way to a large field behind the fort. "General Maximus awaits."

"We will probably be there all damn day," said Sir Fury. "I hope there's wine."

"I hope there's food," said Curtis. The provisions in his saddle bags would be exhausted after two or three days. And he was heartily sick of fish.

Sir Fury's concern proved unfounded. Before they could even dismount, Thomas Maximus, clad in magnificent armor of gem-studded silver, appeared on a low platform. "Infiltrators attacked Fort Saxum, Fort Cox, and Dessau enmass last night. s. Fort Saxum held. Fort Cox and Dessau did not. I find this intolerable. We march now to relieve Fort Saxum and reclaim Dessau."

"What intelligence have we of the enemy?" Curtis couldn't see the questioner.

Thomas raised his hand. "We have reports of humans, hobgoblins, and rachasa. No cavalry as yet."

Sir Fury nudged Curtis. "Such rabble and vermin are no match for mounted warriors."

"Rachasa are formidable foes," said Curtis. Uncle Rood had spoken often of the catmen, ascribing them with speed and strength just shy of supernatural.

"I bested cats during the war," said Sir Fury. "I'll best this bunch as well."

Curtis had doubts. He'd not fought rachasa, but other DuFlorets had faced the creatures. 'A cat did for your Uncle Ghent,' Rood had told Curtis. 'Its claws speared him through the chest, armor, and all. Hurled him from the saddle. Gutted the horse, too.' Uncle Rood's account left a lasting impression on Curtis. But Sir State didn't believe such tales.

"No," said Sir Fury, "I'm more concerned about the hob's war lizards."

"So am I," Curtis remembered his clash with a hobgoblin riding a war lizard at Crowfoot Gap. He'd gutted the hob with his lance, but not before the war lizard gutted his steed. *But Dessau fell hours ago. Could the hobs have gotten mounts through the gap by now?*

"We came here to defend the Empire," said Thomas. "Now's our chance. Victory!" He raised both arms in the air.

"Victory!" The Knights repeated, a ragged chorus at first, but one that grew in strength. Curtis shouted along with the rest, fist-pumping the air.

"Ride!" Thomas shouted. "Ride for the Empire!" Again, the Prince's hands shot skyward, this time clenching his sword.

"For the Empire!" The knights shouted. Some imitated the prince, waving swords overhead.

Thomas strode from the stage and stepped onto a waiting horse held by a youth. He left the field, trailed by the knights. Behind the knights came rank upon rank of bicycle-mounted legionnaires.

Curtis expected the enemy to await the army at the bridge. *It's a fine chokepoint. That's what I'd do.* But the bridge proved deserted save for a few crows, pecking at a bloodied mass. Bits of legion-issue armor clung to the corpse.

"Infiltrators." Sir Fury scanned the wooded slopes to the south.

Curtis did the same, but the thick vegetation offered no clues.

Past the bridge, the road traversed a wide uneven shelf between a steep slope and a gully that grew deeper with each mile.

Legionnaire and nomad bodies littered the Saxum Road intersection. Two of the dead had orange skin, four-fingered hands, and pig-like snouts in place of noses. Hobgoblins.

"Hell of a fight," said Sir Fury.

"A small part of a greater conflict." Curtis surveyed the wooded slope and saw nothing. "Those hills must be crawling with infiltrators and imperial scouts."

A messenger rode along the column. "Prince says for the knights to keep going. A cohort is being dispatched to Saxum."

The highway topped a low ridge and rounded a corner. Ahead, a pair of horsemen galloped in the column's direction.

"Nomads," shouted one knight from ahead of Curtis.

"No, you fool, they're imperial scouts," said another. "Don't you recognize their uniforms?"

The horsemen reached the column. Their horses were lathered. Blood dripped from one of the arms of the rider.

"What news," called Sir Sate.

One of the scouts faced the knight with wide eyes. "Hobgoblins on war lizards. Half a mile ahead. We must alert the prince."

"Shit," said Sir Fury.

Curtis's stomach churned. His mouth was drier than a desert.

Dots appeared in the distance and rapidly resolved into grayish-green lizards, each taller than a horse. War lizards. Savage beasts with fang-filled maws and limbs that terminated in needle-sharp talons longer than daggers. Hob's with long spears rode the creature's neck in a parody of knighthood.

Curtis dropped his visor, limiting his vision to what could be seen through the eyeholes. The knights fanned out to either side of the road, making a wall of armored flesh across the ledge's width. Curtis found himself mere yards from the chasm.

Trumpets sounded. Curtis lowered his lance, raised his shield, and charged. *This is what I trained for.* All emotion fled.

Curtis picked an onrushing reptile ridden by a hob clad in mismatched bits of armor. Other sights and sounds faded.

Curtis's world shrank to him, his steed, foe, and the ground between them.

The hob boasted a rectangular shield smeared with random colors and a lance thinner than Curtis's. *That spear could break. The shield looks light. My lance should go right through it.*

The hob spotted Curtis. Its dark eyes bored into his. The hob tugged at the war lizard's reigns. An ear-splitting screech escaped the reptile's maw.

The lizard is the greater danger. Curtis lowered his lance tip, hoping to strike the creature's less armored underside.

Curtis's horse neared a low patch of scrub. He tugged the reigns, adjusting his course. The lance tip bobbed. *Focus.*

The hob was mere yards away, pulling back on the war lizard's harness, spear held high.

He means to throw! Curtis tilted his shield.

Contact! The hobs spear skittered off of Curtis's shield. Curtis's lance was ripped from his grasp as the war lizard's grey-green claw shot by, screaming in fury and agony. Then the beast was behind him.

Another reptile rider loomed. Curtis pulled the broadsword from the sheath on his back and swung. The war lizard ducked. The hob riding it didn't and tumbled to the ground with orange blood spurting from his neck. And then an empty road loomed before him.

Curtis pulled on the reigns, slowing his steed's charge. Sensation returned in a rush. His arm hurt like unholy hell. Had he broken it? Other knights slowed to either side of him. Agonized screams and cries of victory filled the air.

Curtis turned and raised his visor. Armored bodies and writhing beasts littered the field behind him.

Sir Fury's familiar armor appeared. "We beat the bastards!"

"Oh shit!" Another knight pointed at the massed legions behind the troops.

Curtis squinted. A weird cloud had appeared above the troops. *No, not a cloud. Arrows. There must be thousands of archers in those woods.*

Shouts rose from the imperial ranks. Soldiers dismounted their bicycles and lifted their shields in a single motion.

A gauntleted hand smacked into Curtis's side. Sir Fury pointed west.

Curtis turned. A mob of nomad horsemen crested the hill, gaining speed, weapons lowered. *The hobs were there to break our ranks.*

Sir Talltree stood in his stirrups. "Form up! There's more killing to be done!"

Curtis understood. The well-disciplined legions could fend off both lines of attack – if they had time to form ranks. The knight's task was to buy the legions that time.

Curtis turned his horse. A knight he didn't know thrust a bloody lance into his palm. He sheathed the broadsword. For the second time that day, he faced the enemy. But this time his energy had fled. His arm throbbed.

A mob of mounted nomads wearing big checkered vests and pantaloons rushed towards the knights, waving swords and spears. Others produced small bows.

Curtis resumed his place in the ranks and tried not to think about the empty spots. He dropped his visor as Sir Talltree called the charge. *I may not survive this.*

He couldn't focus. The lance tip bobbed. The nomads kept shifting positions making selecting one difficult. And there wasn't time to reach a full gallop. Dark shafts with bright feathers filled his vision. One creased his helm.

My arm can't stand another collision. I must try something different. Curtis shifted his grip on the lance.

The approaching riders bobbed around a protruding patch of brush, exposing their flanks. *Works for me.* Curtis picked a rider and hurled the lance. And then the ground dropped away beneath his horse's hooves.

Shit! The bushes had hidden a transverse gully feeding into the gorge. Now his horse galloped full tilt down a steep slope. Divots of dirt tore loose as the beast tilted and turned towards the main gorge, trying to slow its descent. Then it was running at an angle along a steep talus slope, inside the chasm.

And then knight and rider were at the canyon's bottom, a few hundred yards and a world away from the battle above them.

Curtis raised his visor and gasped for breath. Then he removed the helm altogether and shook his head. *I can't believe that just happened. I should have died.*

He gazed at the steep walls rising to either side. *Returning that way is out, even if it didn't put me in a battle. Can I go east?* He rotated his head. A pretty little waterfall shot over a sheer cliff in that direction. *That leaves West.*

LABYRINTH WAR XX – Chimp

"Legions are often compared to mobile cities, complete with artisans, cooks, carter, healers, and members of many other professions. But at the end of the day, we are warriors."

- Induction speech of General Fabius to recruits.

Centurion Chimp eyed the branch. Maybe ten inches between it and the top of the big mossy rock he laid upon – at the tall end. Ahead of him, Sticks made a come-hither motion with three fingers. Those fingers and the soles of his boots were about all Chimp could see of the skinny legionnaire.

Sticks repeated the motion, more urgently this time. Ok, ok. Chimp slid forward on his belly. He prayed he'd fit under the twig without betraying his presence. Inhale. Exhale. He slithered along the moss. The branch didn't quiver. His face reached a tuft of weeds that climbed the boulder's far side. There. A gap just large enough for a peek. His heart threatened to quit beating.

The whole damn nomad army was on the march - or rather, on the climb. They'd felled trees to make ladders and pounded them right into the slope. And now, thousands of grease-ball warriors swarmed up those timbers like rats on ropes.

Sticks gave Chimp a nudge. His face asked a silent question: 'Now what?'

Chimp jerked his thumb back the way he'd come. The nomads weren't supposed to be here. They were supposed to be ten miles to the west. They had to alert the army.

Fifteen minutes later, Chimp and his squad huddled in a stone bowl just shy of a rocky summit, nomad warriors filing around their perch to either side. Well, most of them - Snuffles were nowhere to be seen. Likely, the daft shifter was out chasing squirrels or sniffing flowers.

They were trapped. They needed to fire the Marker; the special crossbow bolt that'd let the army know a world of pain was coming through these hills. But they couldn't do it without getting killed. Not good enough. There had to be a way to alert the army and survive.

Chimp prayed that none of the grease balls were looking their way and raised his head. Maybe the weeds he'd stuck to his helmet would help hide him.

His head cleared the brush. Fifteen feet below, humans and hobs in leather armor strode along narrow paths through the brush. They weren't silent about it, either. He twisted his neck. More grease balls. More hobs, too. But no cats. Well, that was a small mercy. But it still left him, and his squad surrounded by a dozen legions worth of grease balls.

A bush moved behind the hobs. A pebble fell from a tiny ledge and bounced into the weeds. The hobs didn't notice. He felt an invisible presence settle onto the ledge beside him – and then that pointy-eared bastard Bramble popped into view with a shit-eating grin. Naturally, the crazy half-elf thought this was a lark.

Chimp's gaze settled on a funky tree with a protruding branch fifty yards downslope from their position. Then he eyed the knurly fir at the back of the bowl. Lunacy. But it just might work. He ducked back down into the pit and elbowed Blaze.

Blaze opened his mouth. Idiot. Stick clamped a filthy hand over Blaze's lips, letting him see the edge of the knife he carried. Blaze nodded. Then, Chimp used hand signs to explain his plan.

Sticks looked sick. Skunk gritted his teeth. And Blaze got a crazy gleam in his eyes.

Chimp motioned. Skunk slid an arrow with a grappling hook into his bow and a long, slender rope attached to the shaft. Then he stood, turned, pulled, and released. Loops of rope vanished in a hurry.

Chimp held his breath along with everybody else. Could the grease balls be so damn blind they'd miss the arrow flying overhead? What if Skunk missed?

But no, Bramble made a little twisty motion. A bunch of twigs wrapped themselves around the hook.

Enough rope remained for Chimp and Blaze to cinch it around the fir and twist it tight.

Skunk pulled a metal hook from his kit and gave it a dab of grease. Then he stood, set the curved metal on the line, and kicked off.

Again, Chimp and the others stopped breathing. No shouts from the grease-balls. Maybe they were that blind.

Skunk went next, followed by Bramble. That left just Chimp and Blaze, who fiddled with a fat crossbow bolt – the Marker.

Chimp slid his bracket over the rope.

Blaze raised his thumb. Chimp figured the goofy redhead had maybe three seconds between the moment he pulled the trigger to when the Marker went off. The nomads would need a few more seconds to find the launch point. Call it six or eight seconds in total. Was that enough time to escape?

Enough. Chimp kicked away from his perch. Brush flashed past underneath. His arms burned. A spindly fir loomed ahead and then shot past his left shoulder. His right foot almost collided with a hobs head. Somehow, the creature didn't see him. Then the hook slammed full tilt into the branch, and he lost his grip.

Chimp tumbled ass over appetite through a brushy tunnel before rolling to a stop next to three dead grease balls. Freaking wonderful.

Then a brilliant orange flash and a blast of thunder erupted overhead. Chimp got out of the way about two seconds before Blaze bounced into the patch.

The grease balls weren't silent anymore. Guttural words flowed from all around the squad. Harsh voices issued orders. Then the whole mob took off, whooping and hollering.

Another bright flash and a burst of thunder came from overhead. One of the other teams had launched their Marker. Hopefully, the army had time to do something with the warning.

Distant trumpets sounded the call to raise shields.

Blaze picked himself up and almost got run over by a scrawny hobgoblin with bulging eyes. Stick stepped out from behind a tree and ran a wicked blade across the hob's throat. The creature gagged, took three steps, and collapsed at Chimp's feet.

Skunk popped from behind a log. "We can't stay here."

Chimp flipped over one of the grease balls. "You're right." He pulled off the corpse's filthy coat. "Slip this over your armor."

Blaze helped himself to another cloak. "Can't beat them, might as well join them."

Bramble stepped out in front of a trio of running greaseballs and made a slow clapping motion. Two big tree branches swung in from either side and poleaxed them. That gave them two more coats and a vest.

Chimp draped the cloth over his kit and faced downslope. His heart pounded. He stepped onto the trail. This plan was stupid. The grease balls would see right through this pathetic ruse. But there was nothing for it. Chimp's gut tensed as he stepped onto a path. "Let's move." Then Blaze was past him, and they were running.

Chimp caught glimpses of ragged nomad cloaks and armor through gaps in the brush as he ran. The grease balls never looked his way. Their attention was focused on the trail and the sounds of clashing weapons, screams, and whoops from the road. The whole mob flowed downslope like sewage through a gutter.

Then the forest turned into an anarchy of battling bodies. Grease balls clustered around knots of imperials in scale armor. Bodies and bikes littered the ground.

Chimp stopped short.

Sticks nudged Chimp in the ribs. "Now what?"

"Now we get behind the shield line."

"I don't see one." Sticks rotated his head. "Just squads."

A two-legged lizard with a greenish hide pounced atop a band of legionaries. The creature grabbed a screaming soldier in its fang-filled jaws and hurled the fellow through the air. The armored hobgoblin atop the lizard backstabbed another imperial through the throat with a long spear. Chimps blood chilled. Somehow, the nomads had gotten war lizards past the forts. This wasn't good.

Sticks turned and started to run.

Chimp stopped the skinny soldier with a hand on the shoulder.

Sticks tried to twist away. "We can't fight those things!"

"We will. Drop the grease ball gear." Nomad rags hit the ground.

Centurion Chimp grabbed a fallen legion shield and took a breath. "Form up on me!"

Skunk, Sticks, and Blaze picked up shields and stepped beside him like they'd done in the drills. Bramble grabbed a shield, gave it a sideways look, and slid alongside Blaze.

"Form up on me!" Chimp combined the cry with a gesture at a dissolute band of legionaries threatened by a pair of mounted nomads.

Heads swiveled in his direction. Bodies and metal plates came together. A legionnaire put a spear through the first horseman's gut. Another stepped forward, ducked, and slashed the throat of the second's steed.

The war lizard let out a bellow and stomped towards them. Three imperial crossbowmen in another squad unleashed bolts at the beast. One, by skill or luck, penetrated the creature's eye. It fell in a heap.

A greaseball came flying out of the woods with half his throat missing, followed by Snuffles. Before Chimp could say anything, the shifter girl let out an ungodly screech and leaped at three more nomads. Well, she wasn't one for line fighting anyhow.

"Form up on me!" That got the attention of twenty or thirty troopers, who joined the line with Chimp's crew. More legionnaires joined in.

Chimp rotated his head, matching troop numbers against distance. They didn't have enough to form a proper line. "Make a square!" Soldiers slid into place and locked shields. Chimp found himself beside a dandy in gleaming silver armor festooned with intricate designs.

"Thanks for the assist," said the dandy.

"Damn sluggards should have formed up quicker," said Chimp.

Then about ten thousand grease balls came swarming out of the woods and there wasn't time for anything but blood and death. Chimp swung his sword until his arm ached. A goblin slashed his leg. A big smelly brute bashed Skunk's shield so hard it bent the metal. Blaze was bloody to the elbows.

The dandy took a cut across his face.

But somehow, impossibly, the square held together.

Three armored soldiers on bicycles flashed across Chimp's field of vision and plowed headlong into the nomads. Dozens – no hundreds - more cyclists came after these, careening into befuddled grease balls and wreaking havoc. A proper line took shape.

An officer flanked by aides and bodyguards detached himself from the new arrivals. "Highness! You're safe!"

"A bit banged up but still here, General." The dandy's lips curled in a smile.

Chimp stared at the pair in confusion. General Flynn he recognized from drills and occasional briefings. But the dandy? Highness? "Prince Maximus?"

Both officers stared at him. Centurion Chimp got weak in the knees. "Yes." General Flynn turned to the prince. "What happened to your bodyguard?"

"Killed in the first attack," said Thomas. "I'd be dead but for" – he looked at Chimp.

"Centurion Chip Cobble of the Sand Runners, sir!" Chimp saluted automatically. "We were in the woods."

"You fired the Marker," said Flynn.

"Sir, yes sir. Then we took nomad clothes and ran downslope."

"That took balls," said Flynn.

"Then he organized the square that prevented a total collapse." The prince eyed Chimp. "Centurion, you will be joining my personal detail."

"Sir, I'm just a scout"-

"You demonstrated bravery and ingenuity. I appreciate such men." The prince faced General Flynn. "With your permission?"

"Of course, sir. Centurion Chip is one of my most promising officers."

Then Snuffles popped out from beneath a pile of dead greaseballs, face and arms stained crimson, wearing nothing but a kilt.

The prince took a step back. Flynn reached for his sword.

Chimp raised his hand. "That's Sammy. She's one of mine."

Snuffles crouched, her head moving in about eight different directions.

"Centurion Chip," said Flynn.

"Scout Sammy!" Chimp put all the authority he could muster into his voice. "Attention!"

Snuffles stood erect. "Sir!"

"At ease."

Snuffles relaxed.

The Prince faced the General. "What of the woods assault? Is it general or localized?"

"General. They attacked along a mile of road."

A hue and cry came from the trees, accompanied by another wave of fresh grease balls. The nomads slammed into the newly formed line of imperials.

Prince Maximus exchanged a glance with the General. "Looks like bloody work awaits us."

Chimp cocked his head. "Sir, somethings wrong."

The Prince and General both glared at Chimp. "What," asked the prince.

"Those aren't war cries. They're afraid."

Flynn surveyed the fresh wave of grease balls. "He's right. I see a lot of kids and oldsters."

A high-pitched hum filled the air. Then a flying disk crested the ridge.

He stared at the aerial device. "Is that a gasbag?" The nomads weren't supposed to possess such gear.

"No," said the prince. "It's something else."

Two more airborne disks came into view. "They look like flying shields," said Chimp. "I put them at twenty yards across, give or take."

The alien machines drifted over the battlefield. Then they sped away south and east – towards Ptath.

The new pack of grease balls gathered their wits and charged the legionaries.

The imperials responded with point-blank crossbow bolts and a hedge of swords and spears. A one-sided slaughter ensued.

The nomads fell back. A squat, swarthy fellow gestured and bellowed commands.

"Kylan." An intense expression played across the prince's face.

"You know him?"

"We spoke once."

"Here they come." Flynn pointed across the road where Kylan spearheaded a huge pack of nomads.

Kylan's mob made contact in a flurry of blood and screams.

Imperial soldiers fell. The line thinned. And then Kylan was inside the imperial lines, with hundreds of men at his back.

"Plug that gap," shouted Chimp and Flynn simultaneously.

The square surged into the opening and plugged it.

Kylan's mob charged into the square, only to be repulsed. Imperials pecked at his flanks.

Kylan's eyes settled on the prince. He shouted an oath in the nomad's tongue and charged the broken square with about forty of his friends. Such was their savagery that they managed to pierce the shield wall. Then Chimp stepped forward and planted steel in the grease ball's gut.

The remaining nomads didn't last long.

Chimp took a long swig from his wineskin and surveyed a landscape of blood and corpses. Dead horses and war lizards made miniature hills. "We beat them."

"Ho, the camp!" The cry came from an approaching cyclist. "I bear a message for Prince Maximus."

The prince stepped forward to greet the rider. "What tidings?"

The messenger, a skinny kid of maybe sixteen, took a breath. "Ptath is under attack. Monster Hunters and rachasa have breached the walls."

LABYRINTH WAR XXI - Carina

'Today, it is common to say the Old Races dwelled in this place or that place. Those who make such claims forget the Dawn Races reigned for thousands of years and their civilizations spanned the world. They left their mark everywhere.'

civilizations

- - Doctor Isabella Menendez, 'Commentary on the Kwintath Chronicles.'

Carina stood wide-eyed atop Ptath's eastern wall with her hands locked onto the stone rail. At least a hundred rachasa catmen loped across a fallow field towards the city. Behind the catmen came scores of ebony-skinned Monster Hunters waving leaf-bladed spears and a thousand or more nomads carrying short bows and curved swords.

Carina let her gaze drop. Ptath's crumbling stone walls rose five yards above a grassy field, with the railing on top adding another yard. The sorceress knew from experience that rachasa could leap twenty feet into the air. *We're screwed.*

"Ah knew dem Faas boys were up to no good."

The nearest rachasa was seconds away from the wall.

"Form up!" Centurion Briscoe ran along the parapet, shoving legionnaires and ill-trained militia into place.

Carina found herself sandwiched between Tyler the Butcher Boy and the legionnaire everybody called Preacher because he spoke in scriptural quotes.

Xenia pressed a spear into Carina's palm. *It is better than no weapon.*

"Ready!"

Tyler fumbled a bolt into his ancient crossbow with trembling hands.

Carina braced the butt of the spear against the stones. Let the spear do the work.

"The Devil shall claim his own!" Preacher slid a long flat quarrel into his crossbow and yanked a metal pin from its midsection.

"Aim!"

Tyler placed his bolt-thrower on the rail. The tip wobbled.

Preacher squinted along the sites of his weapon.

"Release!"

A thicket of bolts and arrows shot toward the oncoming catmen.

Preacher's missile went wide, struck a stone, and exploded, raining shrapnel into a leaping catman's backside.

Astonishingly, Tyler's bolt struck a big brown-furred rachasa, punching clear through its shoulder. The catman spun and fell to the ground.

And then the catmen leaped.

"Swords!"

A catman landed on the wall in front of Tyler, talons extended. Gold rings gleamed in the beast's ears, and necklaces laced with gems and bits of metal dangled from its neck. Severed human hands hung from the belt holding its cowhide breeches.

Xenia's spear flashed, severing the necklaces, and scoring a red line across the catman's throat. It toppled from the wall while gems and bits of metal bounced along the parapet.

A bloody catman disemboweled a screaming Preacher, its talons punching right through the soldier's ring shirt and leather.

Carina struggled to bring her spear to bear.

Tyler unsheathed his ancient sword.

The catman tore the weapon from Carina's grasp with a casual swipe. It clattered to the ground.

Carina raised both hands and unleashed a telekinetic blast at the rachasa, knocking the catman off balance even as those terrible claws swung in for a death blow.

The beast's claws struck Carina at an angle, propelling her from the wall.

Tyler nicked the catman's arm with an overhand swing, missed his step, and plummeted from the walkway.

Carina rolled as she struck the flagstones. Hot pain burned in her side and arm. She rose to her feet as the rachasa dropped into the courtyard. Everything hurt.

The catman took a step in Carina's direction. Its muzzle parted, exposing needle-sharp teeth. Talismans of bone and metal hung from the catman's neck.

Carina inhaled. Her chest hurt. *Fire,* she thought. *Fire and magic are two of the few things rachasa fear. I have both.* She focused her mind. *Fire is matter given motion. Fire is part of us.*

The rachasa advanced, claw raised for a killing swipe. Then sparks played along its fur. The catman halted. And then it was a living torch.

Carina wavered on her feet, exhaustion warring with exultation. *I did it!* It had been a dozen years since she'd last cast that spell in battle.

Horns brought Carina back to reality. Rachasa rampaged along the parapet, supported by monster hunters and nomads. A tight knot of legionnaires and militia retreated to the Gatehouse, Xenia among them. *'They're giving up the wall.*

Tyler rose to a sitting position and rubbed his head, his helm in the fall. His fingers fumbled for the sword.

A pair of monster hunters descended the stairs. A furry shape darted across the courtyard.

"We must flee!"

Tyler nodded and lurched to his feet.

Carina scanned the market and spotted more rachasa and monster hunters. The legionnaires dismantling the pyramid now stood in a line along the Grand Font, leveling crossbows. *Too far. Too exposed. And I bet they're loading Specials. There.* She began running at an angle across the plaza, avoiding the font. Behind her came bestial roars and the sounds of explosions.

Carina reached the nearest building and turned. Tyler trailed her by a few yards, sword in one hand, crossbow in the other. Fierce cries and the sound of clashing metal came from the blockhouse. Nomads poured over the walls and into the plaza. The legionnaires unleashed a second round of explosive bolts, though catmen and monster hunters swarmed around their ranks.

"Look!" Tyler pointed at a phalanx of imperial soldiers entering the plaza. "Reinforcements!"

But from where? Did they pull the guard from the north wall?

Carina spotted the two Kheffian magicians behind the troopers. The thin one walked in a tight circle while his hands made complex motions. The plump magician held a length of rope to his nose, inspecting it inch by inch.

Groups of marauders confronted the imperial reinforcements. Monster hunters threw spears. Nomad archers shot arrows.

None of the missiles had any effect, though several appeared to strike the legionnaires. Moreover, the soldiers did nothing apart from marching with raised shields.

A rachasa loped close to the phalanx, halted, and swiveled its head.

A tall monster hunter with grey fringed dreadlocks turned from the imperial reinforcements, hefted his spear, and threw. The spear passed over the heads of the engineers by the font and into the thin magician's chest. A warbling screech escaped the wizard's chest as he toppled into the water.

In the square, the imperial reinforcements flickered and vanished.

"What happened," Tyler asked.

"Illusion." Carina kept her gaze focused on the plump magician, who'd finished his inspection of the cord and began twirling it over his head. He barked a mystic word. The rope burst into flames and left his hand, still spinning as it entered the market.

"Not bad, Kheffian." Carina recognized the spell from her army days.

One end of the fiery rope struck a nomad, setting him ablaze. He screamed and collapsed to his knees. A catman leaped sideways to avoid the burning cord, knocking a monster hunter off his feet. A second rachasa howled as the fur on its arm ignited and ran for the Font.

The rotating rope altered course, igniting a trio of nomads who didn't flee fast enough. The flames became sparks as the cord turned to ash.

The plump magician wavered on his feet.

More shouts came from the wall. Dozens more nomads and monster hunters dropped to the ground.

"Look out," Tyler cried.

Carina felt something pass close to her skin followed by a screech of pain. She turned just in time to see a monster hunter fall to his knees with a feathered shaft protruding from his chest.

Tyler reloaded his crossbow. He had three bolts left.

The invaders are loose in the city. I am in no shape to fight. But I know a safe place. Carina motioned to Tyler and began to run, seeing rachasa and monster hunters in every shadow. Rachasa had excellent night vision.

Carina paused at an intersection. *It's this way –I think.* She turned left and found herself at the broken stone wall that enclosed the ruined shrine. A moment later the fugitives climbed over a rubble heap and entered the dilapidated courtyard.

"What is this place," asked Tyler as Carina stalked the perimeter of the building.

"Someplace safe." Carina didn't turn from her inspection of the walls of the shrine. *There must be a ground-level entry.* But iron chains bound the doors and she could find no other ingress. *Then it's the roof.* She began climbing a broken statue set into the stonework.

"You're a witch, aren't you?" Tyler sounded thoughtful. "You used magic on that cat devil. That's why it caught fire."

"Quiet." Carina found hand and footholds which permitted her to scamper to the roof.

"Don't leave me."

"Then follow. Quietly." Carina crossed the roof while Tyler scaled the wall, his sword banging against the stones.

There. The same hole she'd found before, near the edge. Whatever it opened onto was lost in blackness. *I wonder if there are handholds.* She didn't have any rope. *I could make a light spell. That's easy enough.*

Tyler reached the hole. "It's dark. Are you going in there?"

Carina nodded. "We should be safe."

More trumpets sounded from the south, accompanied by rachasa screeches and nomad war cries. *Shit. More attackers. Where did this bunch come from? Have the forts fallen?*

"What are those?" Tyler stared into the sky above Carina's shoulder.

Carina turned. A trio of airborne, red-tinted disks approached the city from the west, moving in a triangular formation. "I don't know." Judging the contraption's sizes was difficult – maybe the size of a river barge. A ring of violet half-spheres was imbedded in the things undersides.

"Maybe they're gasbags," said Tyler.

"I doubt it." *These things came in response to whatever those Kheffian idiots did on the pyramid.*

The violet hemispheres began to pulse. Carina's skin prickled. *Immense power is being generated.* "Into the hole now!"

"I can't see!"

Carina exerted her will. Energy pulsed through Carina's body to the tip of her right index finger, forming a globe of yellow light. She flicked her hand, and the sphere left her finger and descended into the chamber, giving shadowy illumination to cracked stones and broken statues.

"You are a witch!"

"Go!"

Tyler dropped into the hole. His probing foot found a toehold. Then another. Hold by hold, he descended into the dark interior.

Carina cast a last glance at the nearest disk. The violent hemispheres were too bright to look at. Then they pulsed. And an invisible giant foot flattened a nearby tenement. The shrine shook. *God above, what did those fools summon?* Cold sweat broke out across Carina's body. She dropped into the hole.

"What was that?" Tyler asked as Carina reached the floor. "The whole place shook. Stuff fell off the walls."

"Trouble." Carina scanned the chamber. The interior didn't look like much. More broken statues. Defaced friezes depicted bug-like things bigger than a large dog. A crude image of the church's sun symbol dominated one wall.

Carina walked around the perimeter of the chamber, accompanied by the glowing sphere, inspecting the chamber with darting eyes. Here. Debris had been swept away from this corner. Blocks of stone had been shoved to the side, revealing a round hatch in the floor.

The shrine shook. "What is that?" asked Tyler.

"The flying things are attacking the city," said Carina as she inspected the hatch.

"Why?"

"I don't know." Carina found a stud that slid a finger's length. The hatch slid to the side, exposing a long ladder dropping into a shaft of cream-colored metal.

Tyler peered into the tube with wide eyes. "Where does that go?"

"Let's find out." Carina slid into the shaft.

Carina's world shrank to the shaft's pale confines and the aches in her limbs. There were no landings, portals, or intersections. Despite having no source, the wan illumination remained constant. Cantrips of mind and heartbeat kept Carina calm.

Above her, a white-faced Tyler took each rung in turn. The crossbow hanging from his belt clicked against the side of the shaft each time his leg flexed.

Then the shaft's sides flared, and the ladder dropped into a hemispherical chamber.

"Hold a moment," Carina spoke in a low tone while she surveyed this new space.

"My arms hurt," Tyler complained. "I don't like this place."

"Would you rather be out there?" Carina's probing gaze found curved and rectangular lumps protruding from the round wall and floor of the chamber, all made of the same material as the shaft. She also spotted a much more prosaic wooden barrel and a carpenter's vest draped over a sawhorse. Three waist-high circular portals exited the chamber to the east, south, and west. Nothing moved. Carina heard no sounds.

Carina walked among the protruding shapes while Tyler slumped against the ladder. *What's this?* Her fingers brushed against a patch of lime green material. The rest was mostly beige. Tiny sparks danced along her fingertips and soft musical notes filled the air.

"What did you do?" Tyler's voice was shrill.

"Nothing," said Carina.

"You most certainly did something," said a new voice. A man in the purple robe of a civic official rose to his feet near the southern portal. Amentep. He clenched a mason's hammer in one hand. "It never did that before. Are you a magician?"

"Honey, what was that? Did you fix it?" A brown woman's face framed by long black hair appeared near the western entrance. She spotted Carina and Tyler. "Who are they?"

Tyler's head turned. His left hand fumbled at the crossbow, though his left remained attached to the ladder.

"Intruders," said Amentep.

"Demon worshippers," said Tyler under his breath. "This is a demon's place." His head spun to face Carina. "You're in league with them! Did you mean to sacrifice me?" His right hand continued to fumble with the crossbow.

"Tyler shut up." Carina used her most authoritative voice. "They're not demon worshippers."

"Don't hurt us!" The woman's voice was a squeak. Her eyes darted back and forth.

"Then who are they? Why are they down here?" Tyler's voice rose in pitch.

Carina motioned. "This is Amentep, a city engineer. Aqueducts, sewers, things like that. He found this place long ago. Now he's hiding here."

Tyler considered Carina's words. "But what is this place? Nobody builds things like this."

"Says a boy who has seen little of the world," said Carina.

"I am a soldier," said Tyler.

A faint wail sounded behind the woman. "Yusuf is upset."

"Go see to him," said Amentep without removing his gaze from Carina.

The woman's head dropped from view.

The room shook, knocking Carina and Amentep off balance. Tyler fell despite his grip on the ladder. Yusuf wailed from the western portal.

Amentep's eyes darted. "What is that?"

"The city is under attack," said Carina.

"Did the nomads obtain blasting powder?" Amentep glanced at the ceiling. "Mere swords and arrows would not make this place tremble."

"You don't know?" Tyler picked himself off the floor.

"Tyler, they were here before us. They don't know about the flying shields."

"Flying shields?" Amentep stroked his chin. "The Old Ones had devices like that. Have they returned?"

"Somebody is using flying shields to attack the city."

"Ptath cannot stand against the weapons of the Old Races. However," Amentep stroked his chin. "The Grand Pyramid of Zep is also one of their creations. The legends say it is imbued with potent defenses. But those will require sorcery to activate." Amentep's dark eyes focused on Carina. "You must possess power."

"I know magic," Carina admitted. "I trained at Mystic Mountain during the war."

Amentep blinked. "Please follow me." He dropped to the floor and scuttled into the tube.

Carina went after Amentep.

"Don't leave me." Fear laced Tyler's voice.

"Then come with me." Carina reached the opening.

"I-I can't." Tyler glanced around the chamber.

"Maybe you can help Amentep's wife." Carina dropped to her hands and knees. Amentep had made considerable progress along the shaft.

A clattering sound came from the ladder as Carina entered the tube. Carina's knees hurt. Her arms were ready to buckle. And still, the cream-colored shaft went on and on, descending at a slight angle. Then her head popped into another hemispherical chamber filled with more curved and boxy shapes.

Amentep stood near a cabinet studded with dull gems in a rainbow of colors. "This controls the mechanism...I think." His finger touched a yellow gem. "This one flared a while ago but faded." His face fell.

Carina's eyes were drawn to a vertical slot near the cabinet's edge. She extracted the glass square from her tunic.

"The Glass Key," said Amentep. "I thought it shattered when Bao – wait, you saw us, didn't you? That's how you knew my name."

"Yes." Carina took a breath and shoved the key into the slot.

Several of the colored gems flared with light. A section of the wall slid away, exposing an indented ovoid. It looked like the reverse side of a mask.

"The interface," Amentep breathed. "It's been centuries – I thought it a myth. The device can be controlled from here." He faced Carina. "By a mage."

"How?"

"Press your face against it. The machine will contact you." Amentep shrugged. "Or so say the family legends. We tended this machine since before the Empire."

The chamber trembled. This time, the ceiling rippled.

The ovoid had a sinister cast to it. Carina's stomach went queasy at the thought of pressing her face into that thing. *Do or die.* Carina's forehead contacted the ovoid's surface. Sight vanished. It felt cool. Then myriad pinpricks filled her skull. And the world opened.

SYSTEM ACTIVATED.

POWER LEVEL: 17%

EMITTER 73% COVERED

TRANSMITTER 11% FUNCTIONAL

SATELLITE CONNECTION ESTABLISHED

STATE REQUEST.

A mélange of images accompanied the voice in Carina's head. Creatures that resembled giant centipedes. Tanned men and women in grey one-piece uniforms. Machines. Equations. Alien cities rising from the plains.

Carina's head throbbed. She struggled to formulate her thoughts. "The city is under attack." She formed a mental image of one of the flying disks.

CONFIRMED. THREE GOTEMIK SHULLS ASSAULTING SURFACE INSTALLATION.

More images appeared in Carina's mind: six-legged crab-like creatures with cilia-topped towers rising from their backs. *Those bastards are ugly.*

ACTIVATE DEFENSES?

An image accompanied the words: three flying disks seen from overhead crisscrossing a flaming metropolis dominated by a pyramid rising from a square pool. *Is that Ptath?* "This is what's happening outside right now?"

YOU ARE VIEWING AN OVERHEAD SATELLITE IMAGE. ACTIVATE DEFENSES?

Carina would have blinked if she'd been able. The machine was asking her for permission to defend itself. *But it is a machine. It can only obey instructions.* "Yes." Carina's head throbbed. *It's like a bad hangover without first getting drunk.* "Activate defenses."

DEFENSES ACTIVATED.

In Carina's mind, the tip of the pyramid pulsed. One of the flying disks exploded. A second wobbled and began to plummet towards the ground. A dark mist leaked from the third craft.

TWO GOTEMIK VESSELS NEUTRALIZED. NEUROTOXIN DETECTED. ORGANIC FATALITY RATE FOR SURFACE INSTALLATION ESTIMATED AT 73%. ACTIVATE COUNTERMEASURES?

"Yes." The pain in Carina's skull intensified.

A faint pink radiance erupted from the pyramid's summit. Sparkles erupted where the radiance contacted the dark mist.

NEUROTOXIN NEUTRALIZED.

Carina's mind went blank.

LABYRINTH WAR XXII – Bao

'Power has no friends, only allies of convenience.'
- Popular truism

Bao's father turned from the elegant dish and stared at Bao. "Where is your betrothed?" His inflection was perfectly flat, devoid of emotion. It implied a casual question.

General Tullos, seated next to Bao's father, took no heed of the question, instead frowning at the wine cup before him. The DuPaul brothers next to Bao remained engrossed in their private discussion.

One might think that Tullos and his minions would be off managing the battle – but they saw no need to trouble themselves with such trivial tasks. Politicking was much more important. Their attitude was shared by the other twenty-odd aristocrats in the dining hall.

Bao's gut clenched. The cup in her hand trembled. "He – I" – the glass slipped from her fingers, spilling its contents across the table.

Uncle Odalis and Lord Yusef took note of Bao's discomfort.

So did her father. Abbas Vadim Des-Ptath's eyes flicked to the stain, then back to Bao. "Poise, daughter. How often have I told you poise is the essence of the aristocracy? Act like you are in charge, and people will offer deference."

A female Saban servant mopped up the mess while a second refilled the goblet.

Bao's cheeks grew hot. She took a breath. Swallowed. "Father, I received word that Octavos Maximus traveled to Dessau yesterday with a relief column."

Fatima claimed to have overheard that tidbit from one of her boyfriends in the barracks.

Abbas's eyes narrowed. "Why ever would he do that? Dessau is an overgrown village stuffed full of refugees."

Bao lowered her eyes. "I-I don't know." Her stomach churned. She didn't dare touch the drink.

"The young Maximus displayed interest in the Demon Citadel." Uncle Odalis finished the statement with a bite of beef washed down with a swallow of wine.

Abbas's head rotated to face his younger brother. "Strange."

"Indeed." Odalis's head bobbed. "I have also received a report that imperial soldiers arrested Jamal and Zora Nebo and have begun demolishing the Pyramid of Zep." He took another bite. "Most strange."

"Prince Maximus ordered General Masters to provide a full cohort for that task," said General Tullos, showing that he retained at least some interest in his job. "He was most displeased."

A nest of twisting vipers settled in Bao's gut. She barely heard her father's response.

A guardsman entered the dining hall, bowed, and approached the Governor. Isolated words reached Bao's ears: 'Attack.' 'Rachasa.' 'Faas.' 'Wall.' Abbas's face paled a fraction. His features stiffened. "You know what to do," he told the soldier.

The guardsman saluted and exited the chamber.

Governor Abbas stood and regarded the assembled aristocrats. "I am informed Ptath's walls are under assault. The Palace is well fortified, but the garrison is with Prince Maximus to the north. We may have to retire to the vaults."

The vaults were dreary tunnels and rooms beneath the palace proper that always seemed dark regardless of how many lanterns one lit. Rumor insisted restless spirits roamed those spaces. Just the thought of entering them made Bao's stomach clench. She rose to her feet.

"Daughter, where are you going?"

Bao shot her father a pained grin. "Woman's matters."

Her father nodded, instantly losing interest. "Be swift."

"I don't feel so well myself," said Odalis.

"I will." Bao strode from the room. Outside she clenched her belly and wobbled to the jakes. She reached the hole just in time. Bao's belly heaved, and a great brown mass gushed from her throat, leaving behind a sour aftertaste. She winced and steadied herself against the wall. Her stomach wasn't near as tumultuous. Bao frowned – perhaps the food had been undercooked? She shook her head. No. She'd barely eaten. Instead, she'd drank a little – "the wine. There was something in the wine."

Screams erupted from the dining chamber when Bao opened the door. She ducked across the hall – and gazed into a scene from Hell. Upended chairs and dead aristocrats in gaudy clothes with red lines across their necks littered the floor. Her father was slumped over the table with two knives protruding from his back. Odalis stared at the ceiling with sightless eyes. As she watched, a Saban servant plunged a long kitchen knife into General Tullos's gut.

Bao's hands went to her mouth. She tried to suppress the scream that fought its way from her gut. *This can't be happening. It must be a fever dream or a bad jest.*

A Saban woman carrying a spear entered the hall's far end and approached a muscular servant. "Dis all of dem," asked Maaike.

"One of the DuPauls kilt Irma and ran off," said the servant. "We can't find Jamar, Yusef, or Bao."

"Hmm." Maaike turned to survey the room – and locked gazes with Bao. "Time to die, princess."

General Tullos chose that moment to produce a dagger and ram it through the throat of his assailant. All eyes turned in his direction – except Bao's. She stumbled along the corridor. Behind her, Maaike's spear clattered into the wall.

I need to find help. Or, failing that, a place to hide. But where?

Deep Saban voices came from an intersection.

Bao ducked into a servant's corridor that passed by her suite. Maybe she could hide there.

She rounded a corner. Halted. Maaike led the search for her. She'd check Bao's quarters first. So, her apartment was out. But where? There had to be someplace. Bao pondered. The Low Hall. A long chamber where the elite servants dined and amused themselves. Fatima had gushed about a gala being staged there all week.

Bao retreated three steps and took another corridor. There. This should be it. She could find help here. Sanctuary. She pushed the door open. A scream threatened to climb from her throat. The Saban murderers had visited the Low Hall, bringing gifts of death. Assad, her father's body servant, was sprawled on an oversized throne-like chair, pinned through the gut by a long knife. Jackman, a DuPaul bodyguard, lay atop a tangle of broken furniture, bracketed by a pair of dead Sabans. Fatima stared sightlessly at the ceiling; her pretty neck marred by a red crescent. Wafa was slumped over the table, her cassock framed with crimson liquid.

Footsteps sounded in the hall outside the chamber. "We'll check here first," said Maaike's voice in a Saban dialect.

More footsteps sounded, rushed this time. A clamor reached Bao's ears through the left wall: battle cries, the clash of weapons, and screams of pain. Somebody was fighting back.

Bao heard urgent words through the door. She searched for a hiding place.

"I'll check here, then join you," said Maaike. The door opened.

Bao grabbed a kitchen knife from the table.

"Put dat down." Maaike entered the room. She didn't have her spear with her. "You know nothing about weapons."

Bao tightened her grip on the hilt. "Why? We're friends."

"You fell for da Slaver, that's why." Maaike moved closer to Bao.

"Octavos? He's a musician." Bao took a step back. "He hates his family."

"Dat's what he wanted you to think." Maaike rushed forward and grabbed Bao's wrist. The knife went flying. Bao felt cold steel at her throat. "He made you soft in da head. I'll make this quick."

Bao shifted her feet, but Maaike's limbs were made of iron. She moved her hand. Her fingers caught against the dress she wore. No. Not her fingers. The rings on her fingers. Including the special circlet given to Bao by her grandmother. A desperate notion entered Bao's brain. She twisted her digits. The ring writhed. Then she jabbed it into Maaike's side.

"What you do?" Maaike took a step away from Bao. "I don't feel right." The Saban girl trembled. A long knife fell from her fingers and clattered to the flagstones. Then she collapsed and went into convulsions. Dark fluid came from her mouth.

Bao stood over the corpse of her friend and would-be assassin, heart pounding, body shaking. Then she picked a path through the Low Hall to the door at its far end. It opened into a deserted kitchen. She found a mostly empty cabinet, climbed inside, and waited for the madness to end.

LABYRINTH WAR XXIII – Git-Vik

'The nomadic vermin contribute nothing and need to be eradicated. The more technologically sophisticated vermin may prove useful.'

- Gotemik Coordinator Zut-Zab

Git-Vik studied the encampment beneath Brik-Jute-Shull. Bipedal forms streamed towards the nearby forested slopes. Their flight was futile. "Release!"

Brik-Jute-Shull moaned, the noise pressing against Git-Vik from all sides. Wailing words formed in the clamor. "Is this right?"

A chill ran through Git-Vik's appendages at the Shull's question. Such queries were abnormal. Dangerous. "Yes! It must be done!" He wrapped three manipulators around a lever and gave a fierce tug. It stubbornly refused to budge, locked in place by Brik-Jute-Shull's stubbornness.

Jib-Kit's voice came over the communicator, demanding to know why Brik-Jute-Shull had not released its allotment of toxins.

Below, vermin dropped in their tracks beneath the other two Shul's. A fair percentage of those targeted by Git-Vik had reached the forest, which offered a modicum of protection against the poison.

Git-Vik ignored the communication. Jib-Kit was ignorant of Brik-Jute-Shull's true limitations. Instead, the Gotemik pilot addressed the flying craft. "Friend Brik-Jute-Shull – we will speak of your concern later."

"Promise," asked Brik-Jute-Shull's massive wailing voice.

"Yes, promise." Git-Vik had no idea how to fulfill that vow without getting them both terminated. "Release. We have no choice." True. Jib-Kit would issue a devastating report upon their return.

"Ok." Brik-Jute-Shull's bulk flexed. Orifices opened in the Shul's underbelly, releasing a near-invisible cloud of lethal particles. Minutes later, the pestilential bipeds fell writhing to the ground.

"Continue towards the Installation," said Jib-Kit over the communicator.

Git-Vik and Tab-Cade, the pilot of the third Shull, offered acknowledgments.

The Shull left the dying bipeds behind and drifted over the ridge. More vermin came into view.

Git-Vik inspected the new concentration of vermin. A battle! "Interesting. The vermin contest with each other."

"The vermin always attack each other." Jib-Kit's voice carried a warning note. "Proceed to the Installation."

The Shulls left behind the battling biped filth. Moments later, the installation came into view.

Jib-Kit and Tab-Cade's shulls sent energy beams against prominent structures.

"My Shull reports increased energy signatures," said Tab-Cade.

"Confirmed," said Git-Vik. "Perhaps the vermin are meddling with the Installation."

"Ridiculous." Jib-Kit sounded irked over the communicator. "The equipment is beyond their comprehension." An energy beam from his shull turned a building into rubble.

"The transmitter is partly exposed," said Tad-Cade. "I detect organized teams of bipeds removing the sheathing."

"Strange," said Git-Vik. "Perhaps the vermin grasp the installation's importance, even if its purpose eludes them."

"Irrelevant," said Jib-Kit. "Assume positions. Prepare to release the toxin."

Tad-Cade's Shull flew past the transmitter and banked. Its orifices opened. "I detect a massive energy surge!" Then the Shul exploded.

Simultaneously, Jib-Kit's Shul sprouted a massive plume of black smoke and violently wobbled.

Brik-Jute-Shull howled in agony. "It burns! It burns!"

"Turn!" Git-Vik wrenched at the Shul's controls with all its manipulator appendages. Somehow, impossibly, the vermin had activated the installation's defenses. Brik-Jute-Shull had been spared solely because stone blocks still covered the portion of the transmitter facing it.

Brik-Jute-Shull turned. Its carapace vibrated around Git-Vik. An organ burst apart, spewing an acidic compound. Smoke poured from the power regulator. The Shul was going to crash unless Git-Vik acted now. The Gotemik pulled itself from the flight couch and approached the regulator. The damage appeared concentrated along one side – but the device was improvised, with many redundant components.

Git-Vik tore away the regulator's panel. There. That component would suffice for the damaged section. Pain flared through the Gotemik's manipulators as he grasped the sparking, burning mess. He tore away the damaged section and grabbed the replacement component. Burning flesh dominated Git-Vik's senses as it shoved the new part in place. Then, miraculously, the smoke and sparks subsided. Brik-Jute-Shul stopped wailing.

The Gotemik pilot returned to its couch just as Jib-Kit's Shull slammed into the ground and bounced, leaving a trail of wreckage. There would be no survivors.

"We must return to Tet-Gheg-Vu," said Git-Vik. "Are you capable of the journey?"

"I hurt." A hissing whine accompanied the Shull's voice.

The Shul passed over the battlefield, now covered in dead vermin.

Brik-Jute-Shull acted sluggish. The half-functioning regulator didn't permit the Shul enough energy for sustained flight. Git-Vik consulted its instruments and maps and chose a flight path to the west of its previous course.

Yes, the mountains were lower here. Git-Vik steered the Shull towards a vegetation-lined gap.

An instrument chimed for attention on the control panel. Git-Vik diverted a portion of his attention to consider the device. A communication? Impossible. The other two Shul were destroyed. Tet-Gheg-Vu was out of range. A malfunction? Possible. Git-Vik adjusted the instruments.

No, not a malfunction. A signal, not on the usual frequencies. No Gotemik used those bands. Did the bugs have a Hive here? Something about the transmission seemed familiar. Realization dawned upon Git-Vik.

Not a Bug Hive. Instead, a rogue Bug Construct. A juvenile, in communication with its parent across the sea. An opportunity.

LABYRINTH WAR XXIV – Singer

'Casein woke the entire vessel with a nightmare this morning. "I couldn't help myself, Titus," he said as he blubbered into his morning beer. "I closed my eyes and then I was on Snake Ridge again with the catmen striking from the shadows."

I patted his arm. My friend spent two months recovering from that savage encounter. He couldn't even stand, let alone walk for the first week.

This afternoon, we passed a scene from my personal nightmare: Iron-Water Fortress, my legion's base for much of the war. Here, I saw an opportunity and led the legion to victory. Instead of the accolade and promotion I deserved, that worthless do-nothing prick Grand Marshal Arthur DuMars berated me in public and vowed I'd never make General as long as he held office.'

- From 'The Journal of Titus Maximus.'

In his dream, Octavos conducted a symphony in the Grand Auditorium at Solace. Lyres, flutes, and drums combined to make an epic opera. But the horn section became discordant. The chorus lost coherency, trading volume for voice. And then some infernal oaf was tugging at his arm.

"Wake up." A stinging pain flared across Octavos's face. "Damnit wake up."

Octavos opened his eyes. Casein stood over him. But the discordant horns and shouting continued. "What happened?"

"Night attack." Casein's voice was grim. "A big one. The southern blockhouse might not hold." He cradled a crossbow in one beefy arm.

"But surely, they can't cross the gorge. Octavos sat up, heart pounding. "Not with the bridge raised."

Casein made a cutting motion. "Listen."

Octavos did so. A vast screaming roar reached his ears, a sound no human throat could duplicate.

"Rachasa," said Casein. "A bunch of them from the sound of things."

Octavos eyes widened. The catmen were almost supernaturally tough, far stronger, and quicker than humans. They were also savages with reputations for eating their fallen foes. "But they still can't cross the gorge."

"They can." Casein's voice was flat. "They only need half the bridge. With a running start, they can leap the rest."

"But that's still thirty yards!"

"I have seen them jump chasms," said Casein. "If enough rachasa get across, Dessau is doomed."

"The wall guard"-

"Kid, I was a Pilus Primus during the war. First Spear, biggest, baddest bastard in the legion, boss of the first cohort – a thousand of the toughest, meanest legionaries you'd ever have the misfortune to meet. My cohort and I tangled with two hundred of those furry devils at a place called Snake Ridge. We were ready – armed and armored. Do you know what happened?"

"You lost." Octavos's eyes widened even more.

"That's right," said Casein. "Those two hundred catmen tore my cohort to shreds. Nine hundred men dead in minutes. We killed half of them."

"But you survived."

"Only because Marfaki horsemen attacked them from behind." Casein pointed at the wall facing the gorge. "There's one cohort across the gorge and another here. Two hundred catmen will tear them to shreds."

Luther came into the room. "We got the horses loaded onto the lift, boss."

"Good, send Daki and Goji with them."

Octavos faced Casein. "What are you doing? You can't just run away!"

"If those catmen get across, I can't make a difference here." Casein started for the stairs. "Stay or grab your kit and go. The choice is yours."

Something slammed into the door opening onto the gantry. Shouts and cries came from above. *True god above, they're here.*

Octavos rolled to his feet, grabbing the lyre case with one hand and his pack with the other.

The door blew inward. A dark-furred humanoid with a cat's muzzle ducked into the room.

"Down, kid!"

Octavos didn't think, he dropped. Something 'whooshed' past his right ear. The catman emitted a choked roar and toppled to its knees.

"Come on!"

Octavos ducked into the stairwell.

They found Luther prying open a crate. "Figured it was time to break out the specials, boss."

"Good thinking." Casein recocked his crossbow. "Give me a rack."

Luther extracted a wooden frame from the crate holding six fat crossbow bolts.

Casein pulled a bolt from the rack and showed it to Octavos. "See that pin?" He jabbed a gleaming bit of metal in the shaft's midsection. "Pull that and it's armed. It hits, it explodes." He pulled the pin and loaded the bolt.

"Aeeii!" An armored legionnaire fell past the open doorway.

"Shit." Casein glanced through the open door, then back at Luther. "They reach the bottom yet?"

"Yeah." Luther loaded a special into his crossbow. "Lift is on the way back."

Fascinated and horrified at the same time, Octavos stared through the portal.

The blockhouse on the gorge's far side burned. Shadowy figures raced along the half-lowered drawbridge, reached the end, and leaped. Some fell short and screamed all the way to the bottom. Others reached the far side.

Octavos's gaze settled on two sprinters running at an angle to the others. "They're trying for the gantry!"

The leapers landed even as the words left Octavos's mouth.

The catmen were halfway to the opening in the time it took for Casein to raise his crossbow.

Casein's bolt took the rachasa square in the chest. The metallic plunger sparked against the blasting powder within the quarrel, blowing the catman to bloody bits.

"Got him, boss!"

Octavos's ears rang. Bright flashes played against his eyelids.

The second rachasa thought better of entry here and climbed the heavy beams.

Octavos blinked. His vision returned. The ringing in his ears subsided.

A twelve-by-twelve-railed platform was suspended outside the door.

Casein and Luther strained against the nearest wagon. "Come on kid, give us a hand!"

Octavos hesitated. More catmen ran across the half-bridge. The wagon moved. *Hell with it.* Octavos took a spot next to Luther and pushed. The cart moved onto the platform.

Another leaping catman reached the framework.

"Die, assholes!" Luther swung his crossbow around and fired. The bolt struck the frame near the rachasa. The explosion blew the catman off the gantry.

Casein started pushing a second wagon towards the platform. "Come on Luther! We don't have all day!"

Octavos helped the two men push the second cart onto the platform. "Two's all we can take, boss." Luther wiped his brow.

"It'll have to do." Casein inspected a protruding handle. "This the control?"

"Yeah, boss. Pull it this way and we drop." Luther made a yanking motion.

But how fast?

Screams and explosions prompted all three men to stare at the blockhouse. Furred figures scaled the walls and battled with legionnaires atop the roof. Even as Octavos watched, a catmen hurled two soldiers to their deaths.

And still, more rachasa made impossible leaps across the gap.

A feline roar sounded from within the winch house. Octavos spun to see a catman darting toward the platform.

Casein fired.

The rachasa leaped over the missile with its claws extended.

The bolt exploded against the far wall when the catman landed on Casein.

Casein twisted as the bestial claws tore at his guts.

Luther attempted to stab the catman and received a backhanded blow in return that almost knocked him off the platform.

Something clicked in Octavos. He grabbed his short sword, whirled, and stabbed – right through the rachasa's back.

The catman let out an ungodly screech and twisted, tearing the sword hilt from Octavos's grasp.

Octavos's eyes darted, looking for a weapon, a means of escape, anything. Nothing presented itself. *I'm dead.*

The rachasa lurched to its feet, took a tortured step toward Octavos, and collapsed.

"Help me up."

Octavos grabbed Casein's left hand and pulled the big man to his feet. Casein kept his right hand over the growing stain on his shirt.

"I'm getting too old for this crap." Casein stumbled to the lever and yanked. The lift lurched and dropped. The wagons shifted, making the platform wobble.

Luther climbed to his feet. "Thought you were a goner, boss."

"I thought so too." Casein eyed Octavos. "Good work."

Above them, the second half of the bridge dropped into place amidst a cacophony of screams and explosions.

Another armored corpse fell past the platform.

The platform continued its descent.

"Guess you're coming with me after all," said Casein. Then his knees buckled right as the platform's bottom touched dirt.

Casein collapsed. Above them, atop the gorge, men and other creatures fought and screamed and died as the nomads assaulted Dessau.

Octavos couldn't tear himself away from the fallen warrior. *I need him.* In his father's journal, Casein came across as tough, and undefeatable. *But Doctor Menendez rewrote that book. And he took grievous wounds a couple of times.*

"Kid, we need to leave." Luther shook his shoulder, casting nervous glances at the conflagration overhead.

Octavos craned his neck. Fire crowned Dessau's walls. Death screams and shrieks of pain drifted to the floor of the gorge. Three more bodies fell from the walls. Two wore imperial armor. The third was a rachasa catman. More bodies – nomads, legionnaires, and rachasa dotted the ground where the Elevator rested. Octavos eyes flicked back to Casein. "He's hurt."

"Yeah, I know." Luther rocked in place. "Sucks to be him. It'll suck to be us if we don't leave."

Casein winced and tried to sit. "Help me stand," he gasped while glaring at Octavos. The warrior's skin was corpse pale.

Octavos and Luther each grabbed an arm and pulled. Casein seemed to weigh more than a horse. *But he's big,* thought Octavos.

"Kit. Under the seat." Casein's face was a rictus of pain as he spoke the words.

Octavos reached beneath the seat of the nearest wagon, dodging Casein's other confederates in the process, who were busy harnessing skittish horses to the conveyances. His hand emerged clenching a small box stamped with a snake twined about a pole – a healer's kit.

Luther's eyes focused on the container. "You know how to use that stuff?"

"I took medical classes at Solace." He'd taken three medical classes while at the University. At first, he'd aspired to become a Gentleman Doctor. The first two courses, Basic Anatomy, and First Aid, dimmed that desire. Too bloody. A crushing workload accompanied the third class. Dianna thrived on the burden. Octavos didn't. When Dianna spurned Octavos, he quit the class. Octavos opened the chest's lid, exposing packets of herbs and neat rolls of bandages. Mental connections reestablished themselves.

Casein groaned. "I need to see the wound." Octavos pulled Casey's palm from the bloody tunic. Luther lifted the fabric, exposing a trio of oozing puncture wounds on the big man's side. Octavos's mind went clinical. He extracted a bandage and a packet of herbs.

Luther watched Octavos pour wine on the ground plants to make a paste. "That'll fix him?"

"It won't hurt." Octavos wrapped the bandage around Casein's midsection, binding the herbs in place. *Simple puncture. He should recover if it's not too deep and if there's no infection.*

Casein's eyes focused as Octavos tightened the bandage. "Feels better. Not bad, kid."

A legionnaire's corpse struck the ground not three paces from the wagon. Ominous creaking sounds came from above.

Casein's eyes flicked skyward. "Elevator frame is about to fall. We need to go." He tried to climb into the wagon.

"You need to lay down," said Octavos. Luther helped him get Casein into the wagon bed.

Luther climbed into the driver's seat. Octavos sat next to him. The wagons began to descend along a near-invisible track.

The wagon's left front wheel dropped, sending a jolt along Octavos's spine. He couldn't see a thing. How did Luther stay on the road? The right front wheel rose and dropped. Were they even on the road?

Luther flicked the reigns. The cart halted. "The next bit is too tricky without light. The slopes are too steep and have some wicked curves. Plus, there's a cliff."

"You've been this way?" Octavos could barely see Luther.

"Couple times." Luther's dark shape shifted and dropped from the wagon. "Best grab some shuteye."

Octavos twisted on the bench, staring at where he guessed Dessau must be. A black-on-black slope crowned by an orange line of fire loomed behind the wagon. Faint screams and shouts carried across the night.

Rustling noises emerged from the darkness. *Rabbits. Or dogs.* Octavos kept his hand locked in a death grip on the bench. The wagon was safe and elevated. Anything coming after him would have to climb. Another rustling noise, this time from the opposite direction, along with a snatch of words. Refugees? Deserters? Were the nomads at the bottom of the chasm?

"What if they come here?"

"They won't," said Luther's voice. "The nomads want Kheff, not Soraq."

Relief flooded through Octavos. The sounds he'd heard earlier had been Luther and his companions establishing a camp. "That's good," said Octavos. But then he thought: *Invading Kheff means fighting a large well-disciplined army. An ill-trained rabble guards Soraq. What if the nomads go for the easier target?*

"Get some sleep, kid," said Luther from the darkness.

Casein's men are tough. They know what they're doing. Octavos lay on the bench and closed his eyes. But his mind remained active, fabricating one nightmare scenario after another. *No.* Octavos created a mental image of his concert hall and placed himself before the orchestra pit. Ok. Savona's 'Dreamtime Quintet.' Sleep came at last.

Octavos eyes flicked open. Nightmare images flashed through his brain before the crisp blue sky registered in his mind. A lance of fire had replaced his spine. *We fled the city.* Octavos rose to a sitting position. Three figures were hunched around a small pot above a finger-sized flame downslope from the wagon.

A fourth scaled the slope, carrying a wooden bowl in each hand. Luther.

Luther reached the wagon and stretched a hand onto the crates piled on its bed. "Come on boss," he said. "If you're alive, you need to eat."

Casein! Had he died? Octavos whirled. Casein was stretched out on the crates behind him, corpse-pale but breathing. Casein's eyes opened. His right arm twitched. "I'm trying to get some fucking sleep." The words were almost a slur.

"Boss, you need food." Luther produced a spoon. "You gonna do this, or do I do it for you?"

A groan escaped Casein as he rolled onto the side and snatched the spoon. "I'll do it, mother." He grimaced. "Did you fix this?"

"Nah, Goji." Luther placed the other bowl alongside Octavos. Thin pale gruel studded with dark things floated in the container. He tilted the bowl to his lips. The gruel was bland. The dark specks were like sharp spikes. Octavos drained its contents.

Casein finished his one spoonful at a time. Then he rolled onto his back. "God, that hurts." His hand pressed against the bandage.

"I'll change that for you," said Octavos.

"Make it quick." Luther pointed behind the wagons. Above them rose a tall cliff topped by a stone wall. Tiny figures moved along the parapet.

"Those aren't imperial troops," said Octavos.

Luther shook his head. "Nope." Behind him, Casein's other followers hitched the horses to the carts.

Octavos worked fast. Scabs had formed over the puncture wounds, but dead grey skin surrounded the marks. Octavos racked his mind, attempting to recall near-forgotten lectures. *Casein's getting better.* Octavos inspected an herb packet. *This should be the right one.* He tore the packet open and poured in water to make a poultice. *It will have to do.* He smeared the mixture on Casien's wound and secured it with a strip of cloth.

Luther climbed onto the bench and flicked the reigns.

The wagon rattled into the gloom.

A hard jolt sent a wave of agony through Octavos's spine. "This road sucks. What is it, a goat herder's track?"

"No, it's one of Soraq's principal highways." Casein smiled. "This ain't the Empire, kid."

First-class imperial highways such as the Avar Avenue binding East and West or the Great South Coast Road were seventeen feet wide, surfaced with flagstones, and boasted a yard-deep ditch to either side. They never had grades steeper than seven percent and always bridged streams – never forded them. Major routes like the Equitant Trunk could be double the width. Even secondary imperial roadways such as those crisscrossing cursed Drakkar, the infamous Road of Chains south of Niteroi, or the notorious Heretics Way between Saba and Kheff were at least eleven feet wide and stone paved. Swarms of soldiers and convicts labored to dig away landslides and replace bridges on these avenues. Rude dirt roads were found in backwaters, the frontiers, or Kheff. And Kheff had the liquid highway of the Tefnu River.

But Soraq wasn't part of the Empire. Octavos's instructors at Solace taught that Soraq was a corrupt tribal oligarchy whose feuding chieftains cared about nothing save their own aggrandizement.

So that morning they negotiated one switchback curve after another, plummeted down slopes just shy of vertical (or so it seemed), and forded no less than five streams. They paused for lunch at the sixth ford, just before the road dropped into a forested canopy. Here, Octavos checked Casein's bandages while the horses drank, and Luther passed out slabs of hard bread and dried fruit.

"We got visitors," Goji called from a nearby hillock while they ate.

Octavos stood in the wagon for a better look. A long line of thin brown men and women emerged from the jungle, toting packs, and jars. Several pushed odd two-wheeled carts resembling bicycles without pedals: one solid wooden wheel in front of the other, with packs and bundles piled atop a low tilted platform between them.

Luther joined Octavos. "Refugees," he said without turning his head. "Weapons, now!"

"Will they attack?"

"They might. They're desperate."

These newcomers trudged slowly up the slope until they reached the encampment.

Here they paused and surveyed the imperials with impassive faces. An old man wearing a dirty orange cloak and a short fringe of white hair clinging to his skull spoke. "The demon fortress has claimed Tamron. Like those of Pathak before us, we will throw ourselves on the Slaver's mercy."

That's the Empire he's talking about. Many of Niteroi's slaves came from Soraq. Most didn't last long. Few did. Octavos shot Luther a glance. Casein struggled to a sitting position. None of them spoke.

To Hell with it. Octavos opened his mouth. "Dessau fell to a nomad horde last night. You travel into a warzone."

Luther glared daggers at Octavos.

The oldster stared first at Luther, then at Casein. "This is true?"

Luther nodded. "Yeah, it's true."

The oldster turned to the others and spoke in a tribal dialect. An old woman in a white dress with blue dots spoke back, as did a muscled young man pushing one of the strange carts. More voices chimed in with short despondent comments.

Luther and Octavos watched while Casein's other men hitched the horses.

The oldster faced Octavos. "Dire times. The Demon Fortress claims Pathak and Tamron. Nomads try to claim the slavers. Jahair Said Khalil of Umar will kill us out of hand. So, we shall wait."

"What for?"

"For the Slavers to triumph over the nomads. The Slavers have triumphed in the past, they will do so again. Many of their subjects will be slain. We shall take their place." He made a motion encompassing the slope. "This place will suffice for now."

"And the Demon Fortress?"

"The Demon Fortress fares poorly with mountains." The oldster pointed north. "Last year, a landslide buried its eastern walls."

Luther flicked the reigns. The wagons descended a long slope into the waiting forest. Shadows replaced sunlight. Small creatures skittered along the branches. The road rounded a corner and ran parallel to a grove of stunted and twisted pomegranate trees. Octavos didn't see many fruits on their branches.

Past the grove, sullen men with spears and bows watched the carts trundle past a collection of dilapidated shacks. Chickens ran by, flapping their wings and clucking. Octavos spotted two children hiding behind a tree. They did not stop. The road did not improve.

Casein awoke and announced he felt better. He climbed onto the wagon's bench. An hour later, the big man's strength fled, and it took Octavos and Luther both to wrestle his prostrate form back atop the crates. Octavos used the opportunity to inspect Casein's wounds. The scabs had split and were oozing puss and blood. Octavos reapplied the herbal salve.

The sun touched the horizon. "There." Luther pointed at a building that resembled the aftermath of a collision between half a dozen huts. "River House. It's a kind of inn, next to the bridge over the Tamer River."

A middle-aged woman in a stained apron stepped onto the porch as the wagons pulled into the yard. A red cloth covered her head. "Welcome to the River House," she said without enthusiasm and passed through a portal hung with a bead curtain.

Casein insisted he could walk. He did so, using Luther as a crutch.

Octavos watched Goji and Vin unhitch the horses.

"Woodcutters would float logs here in the old days," said Goji. "Traders would buy the logs with beads and booze, put them on carts, and go to Dessau and sell them for good silver."

Airborne motion to the east attracted Octavos's attention. Three specks crested the mountains. "What are those?"

"Huh?" Luther paused at the doorway, still supporting Casein.

"There." Octavos pointed.

Luther squinted. His face paled.

Casein shrugged Luther off and leaned against the wall. "Shit. Didn't think they'd come here."

"What are they," Octavos asked as the specks vanished.

"Trouble." Casein winced and started for the entry. "Let's get something to eat."

Dinner was goat marinated in wine and stuffed with vegetables. Octavos claimed a full plate. Casein ate half a dozen bites and announced he was full. They were the sole guests.

Despondent, Octavos prowled through River House and found only empty rooms with straw pallets and floors made of packed dirt. He left the building and walked to the river, where he stood on the rickety wooden bridge tossing twigs into the murky water.

Thomas probably thinks I'm dead. Will he search for me? Octavos tossed another twig in the water and watched it float away. *Probably not.* With Dessau's fallen, Thomas had a real war to fight. He wouldn't have time to spare for a missing cousin.

But then again, do I want to go back? A lifetime as a petty provincial official held little appeal, especially since the local aristocracy detested his family. Not enough to rebel, but they would snub him. *Bao is cute though. I wish she weren't so stuck up.* Another twig hit the water.

Is remaining with Casein the right course? He has something to do with this so-called Demon Fortress. Octavos was positive the 'Fortress' was connected with Gawana. And the Fortress or whatever you called it had wreaked havoc with Soraq. *Why would Casein do such a thing?* Octavos snorted. Casein was a soldier, a veteran of a horrific war that had lasted decades and seen millions slaughtered. No doubt he'd inflicted similar destruction in the past. *But that was to defend the Empire. What purpose does this serve?* Something invisible flew overhead, reminding Octavos of the flying specks. *And how do those things fit into this mess?*

No answers came. Octavos walked back to the inn and snagged his lyre case. *Time for some music.* He found a chair against a wall made from sticks, sat, and began to play.

As always, he began with a simple tuning piece. That morphed into 'Blue River' which segued into 'Rain at Dawn' and then 'Farmer Polk's Journey.' And when he lifted his eyes after that tune, a small crowd filled River House. Some of them smiled. Octavos smiled back and played an old country piece. Then he rose, bowed, and went to bed.

Casein entered the common room under his own power the next morning, though his face was pale, and he lurched more than walked. He waved Octavos away rather than let him inspect the bandage. Then he devoured an entire bowl of the gruel that constituted breakfast. He even climbed onto the wagon without assistance, though he slumped on the bench afterward. "Keep an eye out, kid," he told Octavos as the wagons rumbled across the bridge. "There's bad people around here."

The road angled north and west. They passed no other travelers, though Octavos did glimpse a small boat downstream when they forded the Turpin River.

Casein called a halt at a small pond for lunch. Then eight or ten men stepped out of the brush carrying spears and small bows. One held a rusty sword.

The swordsman stepped forward. "We road tax collectors."

Casein glared at him and said three or four short words in a tribal dialect. The leader paled. The men vanished.

Casein's mood became morose. He slouched on the bench, stared into the woods, and said nothing.

Now the road paralleled the Turpin, never more than a stone's throw from its muddy banks. And then Octavos spotted a tilted hut, the whole structure leaning at a forty-degree angle because a mound of dirt jacked one side a yard off the ground. Then he spotted a second. And a third that had collapsed. Waist-high berms of dirt snaked through the village.

"Tomlin," said Luther.

Gawana's child, thought Octavos, remembering the tales recounted in his father's journal. *Gawana grew from a seed the size of a chest.*

"Come on kid." It was the first Casein had spoken since encountering the so-called tax collectors. They climbed from the cart. Octavos grabbed his pack and lyre case from sheer habit.

Luther and the others started to follow.

Casein made a cutting motion. "No. Take the wagons to Brindle's Landing and wait. This shouldn't take more than a day or two." He sounded pensive.

"This place came from one of Gawana's seeds," said Octavos.

Casein looked at Octavos. His brow furrowed, but he said nothing. Then he began walking into the maze of berms with Octavos trailing behind him.

After a mile, they reached a wall twice Casein's height. They followed the barrier to an arched portal. A heavyset man in scraps of armor emerged from the shadows.

"We need to see them," Casein told the man. The guardian gaped at Casein and took off at a dead run into a tangle of much taller walls whose surfaces were covered with vines and flowers.

When he was out of sight, Casein turned to Octavos. "I don't know how this will go."

The guardian reappeared trailed by a short man with brown skin. Fine green and red lines covered the visible portions of his limbs. A wreath of bright flowers hung from the man's neck.

The newcomer halted five yards from the gate and peered at Octavos. "What are you doing here?" The brown man squinted at Octavos. "Come to gloat?" His eyes fell to the lyre case. "And what is this?"

"It's not him." Casein placed his arm on Octavos's shoulder. "This is his son, Octavos."

"Son." A smile appeared on the brown-skinned man's face. "Welcome to Gawana's child." He motioned at the Avar. "I am Mecon." His tone was polite, but nothing was welcoming in it.

Octavos gulped. His father's journal mentioned Mecon several times - as an enemy. *But he's working with Casein.* He inclined his neck and placed a false smile on his face. "Pleased to meet you."

LABYRINTH WAR XXV – Carina

"The Three – Traag's sorcerous triumvirate – stripped the city of its defenders to hold Crowfoot Pass. Emperor Morgan took advantage of this, employing stealth and sorcery to sneak two full legions of troops plus a thousand sorcerers and Godborn to Traag's doorstep. This force penetrated the walls and commenced seizing critical locations throughout the city. In evil desperation, Traag's Witch Queen sacrificed tens of thousands of her subjects to conjure hundreds of demons.

"Those abominations rampaged throughout the city, slaughtered the populace, scattered the imperial forces, and all but overwhelmed the Godborn.

"General Fabius knew the Witch Queen's ritual had to be stopped before the demons slaughtered the entire city. But demons, fanatics, and toppled buildings blocked crucial avenues. Fortunately, he had a guide.

"The Guide led General Fabius and a picked company through that maze of destruction to the arena. There like a hero of old, Fabius fought his way to the altar and beheaded the Witch-Queen, breaking her evil spell."

- Brousard, imperial artist, describing the fall of Traag.

Carina opened her eyes to a scene of grim stonework and an iron grate lit by sputtering torch light. A dungeon. She felt dull and drained. An immense weight clung to her right wrist. Grimacing with exertion, Carina raised her limb and took in the iron band about her wrist, marked with the Rune of Null, the mark that suppressed sorcery. "Damn." Her voice sounded weak and distant.

Voices sounded further along the corridor. "Did you inspect the device," asked an aristocratic voice.

"Great Prince, we can activate the device but that would be unwise." The speaker was a Kheffian male.

"Great Prince, the works of the Old Ones are dangerous to meddle with," said a second Kheffian voice, this one female.

A handsome, well-proportioned man in his late twenties wearing a purple cloak over jewel-studded armor came into view. Dark eyes peered at Carina beneath her disordered black hair. "And who is this?"

A plump, bald magician stepped from behind the aristocrat. "Great Prince, we found her and the man in the next cell" – he gestured at a barred door across from Carina – "in the device's depths."

"This is an outrage!" The female voice came from behind the prince. "Unhand me at once. I am Lady Bao Vada Falun Des Ptath, a member of the ruling aristocracy, not some common whore!"

"Silence, woman!" Carina recognized the harsh, high-pitched voice. "You were found with a prohibited device upon your person."

Carina trembled as Ambrose pushed his way into the group, one hand clenching the arm of an attractive woman wearing the remnants of a once fine dress.

Prince Thomas faced the new arrivals. "Ambrose, what is this? The city's aristocracy is thin enough already without further depleting their ranks."

"My Lord, I didn't realize you were here." Ambrose recoiled from the prince.

The Witch Hunter's captive took the opportunity to pull herself free of his grasp.

"I am interviewing captives retrieved from within the Grand Pyramid of Zep." Prince Thomas glared at Ambrose. "What brings you here?"

Ambrose glanced at the woman. "My Lord, I have reason to suspect this one played a role in the massacre of Ptath's noble class."

"Liar!" The woman whirled on Thomas. "Great Prince, I am Lady Bao Vada Falun Des Ptath. This animal" - she jabbed a finger at Ambrose – "dragged me from my chambers without cause and"-

"Enough." Prince Thomas cut Bao's speech short with a chopping motion and turned to Ambrose. "You'd best have an excellent reason beyond mere suspicion for this act."

"I do, My Lord." Ambrose bowed.

"Amentep?" Bao's voice came from behind the Witch Hunter.

Every head swiveled to face the slender man in the cell opposite Carina. "You know this man," asked the prince.

"He is Amentep Majid Kamal Nebo, a minor member of the aristocracy." A sigh escaped Bao's lips. "We were to be married, once." She looked at Thomas. "Why is he here?"

"I found him inside the Pyramid of Zep," said the fat magician. "The Nebo clan has a long association with that monument."

"Uday, that is ridiculous." Bao made a dismissive wave. "Amentep's family oversees mines and canals. Amentep's father rebuilt the eastern viaduct when I was a child. They hold no ancient secrets."

Uday was unmoved. "Amentep Nebo's presence inside the Pyramid testifies otherwise."

Ambrose, displaced by the Kheffian's, appeared before Carina's cell. "Hmph." His eyes narrowed. "I know you from somewhere."

"But who is she?" Thomas peered at Carina through the bars. "A member of the Mystic Mountain contingent? She's certainly no Kheffian."

"No," said Ambrose. "She's not with the Arcane Cohort."

The prince glared at Carina. "Who are you?"

Carina's heart threatened to catch in her throat. She took a breath. "I am Carina Menendez, most recently of Ismara."

The Kheffian magicians gasped.

Ambrose reached through the bars and grabbed Carina's tunic by the sleeve. "Ismara. You escaped my cleansing."

Carina jerked back. Her sleeve tore, exposing the military tattoos on her arm.

"Release her, Ambrose," said the prince a moment too late. "I desire answers, not another corpse."

Ambrose inclined his head. "Apologies, Prince Maximus. My zeal overcame me."

"Restrain your zeal." The prince turned to the Kheffian magicians. "Her name means something to you."

The fat magician bowed. "Great Prince, if I may?" At a nod from Thomas, he addressed Carina. "You are kin to Doctor Isabella Menendez?"

Carina nodded. "My grandmother."

"I take it this Doctor Menendez is a sorceress of repute?" Thomas asked.

"This is so," said the fat magician.

The female Kheffian peered at the tattoo of a horned demon head split asunder on Carina's arm. "What a curious illustration."

"Let me see," said Thomas. "That tattoo was given to the soldiers who survived the Fall of Traag. You were there?" The fall of Traag was the single most horrific battle of the war, where imperial legionnaires battled the city's crazed sorcerers as they attempted to sacrifice the city's entire populace to their demonic gods. There'd been few survivors on either side.

"I was."

"God above, it's true," said the prince. "But you would have been a child!"

"Not so great a surprise." The plump magician rubbed his chin. "Sorcery was Traag's strength and the Empire's weakness. Imperial Agents scoured the Empire to rectify this situation, taking any with Talent, be they man, woman, convict, child, or raving lunatic to Mystic Mountain for training."

Ambrose went thoughtful. "I, too, was at Traag's fall. I gazed into Hell's depths and witnessed its infernal tortures and the blandishments demons employ to tempt mortals from the Straight Path." He faced Carina. "And I remember you. You are the child magus, the prodigy claimed by a demon in that battle. The demon within you sought power through slaughter." The Witch Hunter's eyes gleamed and his face twisted into a smile. "I was almost among your victims that day."

Carina paled.

The prince faced her. "Is this true? Were you possessed?"

Carina bowed her head. "I – I remember nothing." *Except for hatred, a desire for blood, and a terrible separation.*

"I remember her standing above me with a raised knife," said Ambrose. "Then soldiers burst through the door and apprehended her. The Godborn exorcised the demon, and a tribunal of mages and priests stripped her power." The Witch Hunter paused. "I joined the Mithraic Templars a month later. In a way, Carina, you made me what I am today."

Carina attempted to shrink into the back wall of her cell.

Uday stroked his chin. "We are missing something here." He faced Amentep. "Speak."

"My family is ancient." Amentep spoke in a monotone, gaze fixed on the wall. "We were minor servitors of the Old Ones. When they departed, we became by default the guardians of their property. We sought to maintain the mechanism. That task required expertise beyond our knowledge and ability. So, we sealed it away, though now and again some members of my clan would make private studies of its innards. I was one such researcher. I learned of a key made of glass that would activate the machine but it was lost. I resigned myself to obscurity."

"His family is in league with demons," said Ambrose.

"The Old Ones were mortals, not demons," said Halima.

The plump wizard's gaze remained fixed on Amentep. "This Glass Key. Describe it."

Amentep blinked. "A flat square of clear glass the size of a man's palm, inset with colored gems and metal wires."

Uday stroked his chin. "You did not find this key. But the Old Ones machine was activated – after the army's arrival."

Bao paled and nearly collapsed at the mage's words.

The fat magician glared at Bao. "As I thought." He faced the prince and bowed. "Great Prince, one of my offices is 'Custodian of the Cabinet Obscure,' a repository of failed and trivial magical curiosities. Its contents include amulets confiscated from street magicians, puzzle locks, journals written by madmen, unusual stones, and a host of other objects."

"Magical garbage, in other words," said the prince. "I believe my father visited it once or twice."

"Yes, he did," said the fat magician. "Nobles come to gawp at the curiosities on display, and a continual trickle of scholars visit to inspect this or that relic."

"I know of the Cabinet Obscure," said Ambrose. "It should be destroyed along with its contents."

"The cabinets contents are curiosities, not magical artifacts," said the plump magician. "Items of true power are kept elsewhere."

"To the point, Uday," said the prince.

"Of course." Uday bowed. "As I said, I am Curator of the Cabinet. I employ students from the Librium as clerks." He looked at Bao. "Lady Bao was one such attendant."

The prince looked at Lady Bao. "Speak."

Lady Bao lifted her head. "Amentep told me of the Glass Key before I departed Ptath," she said in a small voice. "Like him, I believed it lost, until my last week in the Cabinet, when I chanced upon it in a cupboard. So, I...took it."

"You stole from the mage families of Kheff," said Uday. "You are a thief who deserves prosecution."

"Watch your tongue, magician," said the prince.

Uday bowed. "Forgive me, Great Prince."

"Now we know what activated the pyramid." Prince Thomas turned to Carina. "But you employed its powers. Tell me about the machine."

Carina hesitated. Her heart pounded.

"Come, now, I shall grant you clemency in exchange for straight answers," said the prince.

Ambrose glowered. Law and tradition granted the Church oversight of mages. Prince Maximus's offer infringed upon that authority.

"I – I learned much about the machine and its builders during my immersion," said Carina. *Will the Prince protect me from Ambrose?* The Church avoided directly confronting the greater nobility. But the Prince was a Maximus, and the

Maximus had a long reputation for cruelty and treachery. *'Clemency' might mean a swift death or perpetual imprisonment.*

"Speak, woman. I have much to do this day."

Carina had to speak. "Prince Maximus, the machine is an instrument of communication."

"Communication?" The prince's brow furrowed. "It destroyed two of those flying machines. How is that communication?"

"That was a secondary use of its powers." Carina thought furiously. An idea presented itself. "Imperial Signal Towers are equipped with colored flares for emergency nighttime communication. Yet, those same flares can be employed as weapons."

"I see," said Thomas. "What of the flying vehicles? Did you learn ought of them?"

"The machine called them 'works of the Gotemik,' my Prince." Carina proceeded to describe the images she'd glimpsed.

"Demons," said Ambrose. "Prince Maximus, the sole communication that infernal mechanism does is with Hell's own demons. This woman," he thrust his arm at Carina, "was possessed before by an infernal entity. At best her views are tainted. More likely, she is an agent for these demons, witting or not. She must be burned."

Prince Maximus listened to the Witch Hunter's speech. "Ambrose, you raise valid concerns."

Carina's heart plummeted to the floor. Her brow erupted in sweat.

"However," Thomas continued, "I require knowledge more than corpses."

Ambrose smiled. "With your permission, I can convince the witch to tell you everything she knows about that infernal lighthouse."

Torture. He's talking about torture. Carina remembered stories of Ambrose's past exploits. The Witch Hunter enjoyed inflicting pain.

"Restrain yourself." Thomas returned his attention to Carina. "What else can you tell me?"

Carina didn't respond. Her gaze remained fixed on the Witch Hunter. All thoughts fled her mind.

"Speak."

The word penetrated Carina's fear. *I have to tell him something, but what?* Most of what the machine had shown her made no sense. Much of what she did grasp would require days to explain. And sooner or later, the Kheffians would press their heads into the inverse mask and- "My Prince, eons of inactivity have worn at the machine's innards, making it unreliable."

"Reasonable. Time gnaws at all things. Yet, unreliable, or not, the machine did defend itself. Is there more?"

Carina shifted her gaze to Ambrose and then back to Thomas. She took a breath. "Prince, you offered clemency."

The prince's face became a mask. "Carina Menendez, you did perform a valuable service. However, you also joined this army under false pretenses. You shall remain confined until I have time to evaluate your circumstances."

Carina slumped against the wall of her cell. *At best, this is a stay of execution.*

Another commotion sounded from the entryway. More legionnaires entered the dungeon, led by a filthy, hairy brute of a Centurion.

Prince Maximus turned to face the new arrivals. "Centurion Longinus, have you determined how the nomads circumvented your position?"

The Centurion scowled, possibly confused by the big words. "Uh, Prince, I dispatched some sneaks. The Roamers built a ladder to the top of Hangman Gorge, where my boys couldn't see them. Impressive work, to be sure."

"You saw this ladder?"

"Yes, Prince, I did." The Centurion scratched his ear.

"And the nomads didn't molest you?"

The Centurion's face contorted a second time. "Prince, that's the reason for my coming here in person. The nomads south of the ridge are dead. All of them."

"Explain."

"After they found the ladder, my sneaks followed the trail to the grease balls big bivouac. Nothing but corpses. Men, women, children, animals, all deader than a doornail. Tens of thousands of them."

"Neurotoxin," said Carina.

Thomas faced Carina. "Explain."

"When I was in the machine, it said the Gotemik had unleashed a poison – something it called a 'neurotoxin' - over the city that would kill most of the populace."

"Yet Ptath lives. What happened?"

"The machine stopped the poison. I don't understand how." Carina shrugged.

"Yet the nomads perished." Thomas turned back to Centurion Longinus. "What of the other camps?"

Longinus scratched his armpit. "I dunno, sir. Scouts ain't reported back yet."

"Damnit, I need information." Prince Thomas's brow contorted. "I have a large nomad force to the west and Saban Monster Hunters to the east. The nomad army south of here may or may not be dead. I have a powerful, ancient relic in poor condition in Ptath's center."

Longinus cleared his throat. "Begging your pardon, Prince, you also got a powerful lot of troopers and a gasbag."

The prince nodded. "Excellent idea, Centurion. Inform the duty Tribune to prepare the gas bag on your way out. I'll accompany you to Fort Siccas."

"Sir!" The Centurion managed a clumsy salute, whirled, and marched back the way he'd come.

Next, the Prince turned his attention to the magicians. "Uday, I wish you to resume your investigation of the pyramid. Exercise extreme caution – I have no desire to confront a demon horde atop my other woes."

"I understand, Great Prince." Uday waddled towards the stairs.

"Halima."

"Yes, Great Prince."

"Can your magic reveal my cousin Octavos's location and health?"

Halima bowed. "It can, Great Prince."

"Good. Begin your preparations at once." The two departed for the exit.

Carina sat and stared at the torch, now little more than a nub. Across the hall, Amentep began a prayer.

Then Ambrose reappeared before Carina's cell. "I go now to fetch a member of the Radiant Order to assist in Lady Ptath's interrogation. Prince Maximus will also insist the Godborn participate in Amentep's examination. However, their abilities are suspect when employed on magicians like yourself." A cruel smirk creased the Witch Hunter's lips. "But there are other means of extracting the truth. I shall enjoy using them on you."

Carina's heart almost stopped beating. She remembered the maimed bodies Ambrose had left in his wake at Ismara.

Ambrose strode away, his boots clicking on the flagstones.

The torch flickered, and Carina's heart flickered with it.

LABYRINTH WAR XXVI – Bao

'Wizards outside the Church are thieves of divine power.'
- Witch Hunter's creed.

Ambrose entered Bao's cell, trailed by a middle-aged woman whose gold locks touched her cream-colored clerical robe. A Godborn - wizards blessed with healing magics, protective wards – and spells to discern lies from truth. Normally, the Church kept the Godborn cloistered, apart from the populace, save for those who needed their recuperative magics.

Ambrose extracted a fine gold ring from his pocket.

Bao's heart skipped a beat. She knew that band.

Ambrose held grandmother's ring to the light. "Exquisite craftsmanship. No maker's mark. Probably a hundred years old."

Older, thought Bao, though she kept silent.

"The band is a trifle thick." Ambrose held the circlet between his thumb and index finger. "But then, it would have to be, to contain the mechanism"- he leaned over the table – "and the venom." He pressed the gem that activated the trigger. A short spike crusted with dark residue popped into view.

Grandmother's ring struck the tabletop like a boulder. Bao eyed it as it bounced twice before coming to rest, the needle pointing at her.

Ambrose lifted her chin. "Mere possession of a trinket like this carries severe penalties, even for the aristocracy." The Witch Hunter craned his neck. "Sister June."

"Yes, Inquisitor Ambrose." The Godborn woman glided to a position next to Ambrose. She stared Bao directly in the eyes.

Bao felt herself falling into Maria's golden orbs. They promised peace, serenity, and understanding.

"Begin."

Ambrose's voice pierced the spell cast by June's eyes. Bao opened her mouth. "As a citizen and member of the aristocracy, I hereby request legal representation"-

"Denied." Ambrose made a languid wave with his hand. "Ptath is under emergency edict. Normal legal procedures are in abeyance." His lips curled into a cruel smirk. "Besides, this is a preliminary query."

Damnit, Ambrose was right. Bao fought to maintain her poise.

"Your name," said Ambrose.

Deceiving a Godborn was impossible. "Lady Bao Vada Falun Des Ptath." Bao's skin tingled as she spoke. Nervousness? Or June's magic at work?

"You are the youngest daughter of Abbas Vadim Des Ptath, Governor of Upper Kheff?"

Bao's hands went to her lap. "I am." The question brought back the horrific memory of her father slumped over the table.

"You are betrothed to Prince Octavos Maximus?"

"I am." Another tingle.

"Do you know the whereabouts of Prince Octavos Maximus?"

The question puzzled Bao. "I believe he went to Dessau."

Ambrose frowned and glanced at June.

"She speaks the truth," said the Godborn. "I detect uncertainty and anxiety."

"Hmph." Ambrose frowned and jabbed a finger at the ring. "Do you love him?"

The unexpected question raised conflicting emotions in Bao. "I-I guess so."

"I discern considerable uncertainty, Inquisitor Ambrose."

The Witch Hunter glared at June. "Thank you for pointing out the obvious." He pointed at the ring. "Is this yours?"

Bao's heart rate spiked. Her vision blurred. But, deceiving a Godborn was impossible. "Yes."

"Were you aware of its function?"

"Yes." The word wasn't much more than a squeak.

"How did the ring come into your possession?"

"It is an heirloom from my grandmother. She gave it to me for protection."

"Explain."

Bao steadied herself and drew a deep breath. "My parents sent me to Hermosa to be educated. The city has a dangerous reputation."

Ambrose's eyes narrowed. He glanced at the Godborn.

"Her response is incomplete."

"A lie?" A note of eagerness crept into Ambrose's voice.

"More of an omission."

"Hmph." Ambrose pursed his lips. "Protection from whom? Street criminals? Rakes?" He leaned towards Bao. "Aristocrats?"

Bao shrank from the Witch Hunter. "All of those, if need be."

"Which aristocrats? Did you plan to murder Thomas Maximus with that infernal device?"

"No!" Bao surprised herself with a shout.

"She speaks the truth, Inquisitor Ambrose," said June. "However,"-

"However, what?" Ambrose made a sweeping motion. "No, don't tell me, I can guess. She's leaving something out again."

He faced Bao and smirked. "Did you intend to use the ring to commit murder?"

An involuntary tremble ran through Bao's body. "No."

"She lies."

"I can tell that." Ambrose's gaze pierced Bao. "Who?" He tapped the tabletop. "Was it your betrothed?"

"Yes – No."

"Which is it? Yes, or no?"

Bao took a breath. "I-I considered using the ring at the outset of the engagement." She emphasized 'considered.' "The Maximus Family has a reputation for cruelty. Later, I decided against that course."

"She speaks the truth," said June.

"Hmph." Ambrose stroked his chin. "I believe she does. That issue will require further exploration. For now, though," again his eyes bored into Bao, "what role did you play in the traitorous attack on Ptath's aristocracy?"

"None," Bao spoke the word with certainty.

"She"-

Ambrose cut the Godborn off with a curt hand motion. "I find that difficult to believe. Your bodyguard, a woman linked to the Faas, directed the attack."

"Maaike's actions surprised me," said Bao.

"She speaks the truth."

Ambrose frowned. "Apparently." His fingers drummed the table. "This Glass Key. You admit to its theft?"

"It rightfully belonged to the Nebo family."

"Not true," said the Witch Hunter.

The Godborn nodded in agreement.

"That matter can be resolved later. I have urgent business to address." Bao pushed her chair back and started to rise.

"Sit."

Bao halted, half out of her chair. "The Godborn proclaimed me innocent."

"Perhaps." Ambrose stroked his chin. "There are other issues." He pointed at the poison ring on the table between them. "Further investigation is required." He rose and pocketed the ring. "I suggest you consider your testimony carefully."

Ambrose and June exited the cell. Bao listened to the lock 'click' as they departed. She settled back into her seat.

Bao stared at the flickering candle on the table without seeing anything. They were dead. Her parents. Uncle Odalis. Her servants. An image of Fatima's dead face appeared in Bao's mind, making her shudder. Uday had gone from friend and mentor to enemy. It didn't make sense. How had matters deteriorated so badly?

The door opened. A familiar, impassive figure entered the room. "Sister," said Bao's brother Adar. "I came as soon as the news reached me." He stood across the table from her.

"Adar." Bao inclined her head. "I am pleased you survived the battle."

"I almost didn't," said Adar. "The nomads swept right over the ridge to either side of the fort. They could have slaughtered the garrison easily, but instead ignored us."

"You were fortunate." Adar's statement didn't sit right with Bao, though she couldn't quite discern why. "More so than me."

"That must have been simply dreadful, watching the family perish like that, and then thrown in this dank pit."

'The family.' Not 'our family.' That niggled Bao's mind. But then again, Adar had always been distant, attending only the most necessary clan functions. The feeling was mutual. Bao remembered her father ordering Adar from his presence more than once. "I appreciate your company."

Adar clasped his hands together and leaned towards Bao. "I shall instruct the Inquisitor to drop the charges."

A tiny spark of hope kindled Bao's heart. "You can do this?"

"Soon, when I am appointed Governor." A trace of eagerness entered Adar's words.

"That would be appreciated."

Adar stood. "I must leave. Many matters require my attention."

"Thank you." Bao's mind churned as Adar exited the cell. Then, everything clicked together. Adar's distance from his kin. His circle of associates, which, like Bao, included members of the Faas, made it easier to smuggle assassins into the palace. And, of course, his ambition.

Bao had no doubt Adar would speak with Ambrose. The question was, what would he tell the Witch Hunter?

LABYRINTH WAR XXVII – Curtis

'Another party of hairy, pale-skinned westerners shoved through the gate. I recognized Simon DuFloret's tall frame and bushy hair in their midst.

The local gawkers fled at the sight of the chained vree held by two of Simon's men, fearful of the venom in the creature's tentacles. I remembered that vree. DuFloret had been proud of acquiring the dog-sized, six-legged beast with tentacles growing out of their heads, prattling on about the creatures tracking ability, and how difficult it was to train them.'

- From the 'Testimony of Titus Maximus.'

Curtis rode his charger along the gorges base, beside a thin trickle of water that fell from pool to pool. Twice since entering the chasm, he'd passed spots where a mounted ascent of those barriers might be possible. Both times he'd ridden on. *What point in escaping the gorge only to be trapped by a nomad army?* So far as he knew, the invaders controlled both sides of the canyon. He'd glimpsed tiny figures in fur or leather atop the barrier. One had fired an arrow into the gorge that had missed him by a dozen yards. He'd retrieved the shaft, finding it a simple, almost crude thing, unlike the milled bolts issued to the legionnaires.

The closest thing he had to a plan involved sneaking past Dessau, turning south, and finding a way back into Upper Kheff.

Ahead, a boulder as big as a house blocked a third of the canyon floor. A distant tinkling sound warned of yet another miniature waterfall. Curtis sighed. Circumventing the waterfalls was annoying. The nearby rocks were always slick. He might have to dismount and lead the horse along a treacherous path past the obstacle.

Curtis raised his eyes. *Maybe I can ride along the soft slope beside the boulder.* Something looked off about the canyon. He blinked. Ahead, past the boulder, a thin line spanned the chasm from one blocky shape to another. *Dessau. I'm here.* Then: *There may be nomads in the gorge.*

Curtis dismounted and scaled the soft slope next to the wagon-sized rock, keeping his body close to the ground. The good news was the slope made a fine way to bypass the drop-off at the waterfall. The bad news was the half dozen or so short green-skinned creatures poking around a broken frame of heavy wooden beams spanning much of the gorge's width. Goblins. And past them, a road.

Curtis tilted his head, noting protruding wooden stubs in the fortress's side. It looked like the frame had once been attached to the city wall - a lift? Now, long ropes snaked from the overhanging parapet.

Curtis studied the goblins. Maybe eight of them altogether. There were few weapons in evidence. They were not especially alert. Scavengers, not fighters. *Get up enough speed and I can race right past them. Have the nomads crossed into Soraq?* Charging past one foe to collide with another held no appeal. But he couldn't remain in the gorge, either.

Curtis went back and remounted his steed. He placed the helm on his head and dropped the visor. Then he prodded the beast to the slope. *Here we go.*

The warhorse galloped down the slope and shot past the goblins before the creatures could call out a warning. Then the knight was on a rutted road descending a steep slope with nary a nomad in sight. *It worked! I may survive this.*

A high-pitched wail sounded from the rise behind Curtis and to the right. Curtis felt the blood chill in his veins. He knew that sound. Rachasa. The goblins weren't alone.

Curtis craned his neck. Two – no three dark-furred figures descended the hill behind him in great leaps and bounds. *I have one chance. Catmen are sprinters, not distance runners.* He prodded the horse to greater speed.

A switchback loomed. The horse's hooves skittered on the gravel as it made the corner. Sound to his right. The catmen hadn't bothered with the road, instead careening straight down the slope.

Curtis lifted his shield as something big and furry slammed into it. Sharp claws punched through the oak. Agony flared through Curtis's arm. The catman's momentum tore the heavy plank from the knight's grasp. Then the rachasa and the shield tumbled across the road.

The knight rounded a second hairpin curve. A second catman launched itself at him. Curtis tugged on the horse's reigns, bringing it to a near stop. The airborne rachasa passed the horse's front and continued across the road.

Ahead, the first rachasa rose to its feet and threw away the shattered shield. Before it could do more, Curtis's sword scored its neck, unleashing a great gush of orange blood. Then he was past the catman, headed for the next hairpin curve.

The horse and rider shot around the turn. Curtis scanned the slope and spotted the rachasa standing near their comrade's corpse. They did not attack. Curtis maintained his pace until foam came from the horse's mouth. Only then did he slow his pace.

A tiny stream cut across the track. Curtis dismounted, wiped the sweat from his brow, and took a long swig of water while the horse cropped a patch of grass. Trembling with excitement and exhaustion, he refilled the water skin and stood back as the horse drank its fill.

Then he climbed back onto the horse. Sprawled shapes caught his eyes – a massacre site. Scores of slashed brown corpses littered the ground: young, old, men, and women amid broken bits of wood and scraps of cloth. Refugees that had been robbed and murdered by the nomads. Both the stench and the scene made Curtis want to vomit. Instead, he rode on at a slow pace into the waiting forest.

Well, 'Cousin Rock' did want me to investigate this 'demon fortress.

The track took him past a mangled pomegranate orchard. More brown bodies dotted the wayside. Curtis did not stop but rode on, heart pounding, eyes flicking from side to side. The knight's hand never strayed far from his sword hilt.

Foragers, Curtis thought. The nomads were foraging Soraq for provender. It made sense. Rumor insisted the horde numbered into the hundreds of thousands. Of course, they'd be hungry. He remembered the last months of the Traag War when men fought each other over potatoes and counted a cooked rat as a good meal. There'd been rumors of cannibalism.

At sundown, he came upon a building next to a bridge. Inside, he found bloodstains, but fortunately no bodies. Nor was there any food. The place held little appeal, but no better alternative presented itself, so he spent the night in a battered shed, sword by his side.

The next morning, Curtis broke his fast with the last of his gruel, mounted his horse, and rode to the bridge where he stopped and stared at the slow river. *The track leads north and east. I need to go north.* Curtis rotated his head until he faced north. A trackless forest presented itself, impenetrable to a man on horseback. Then he crossed the bridge.

He followed the forest track all that day, pausing once to devour the last of his salt beef and cheese. That evening he entered a deserted village bisected by snaking berms of dirt. *Who did this? And why?* No answers came. He built a fire at the juncture of two walls and stared at the flames late into the night.

Curtis awoke ravenous. *West, north, or back, I need food.* He left the horse munching on a patch of grass and strolled into the tangle of berms. *Perhaps there are fish in the river.*

The river may have held fish, but without a hook, line, or net they were beyond Curtis's reach. He searched the topsy-turvy huts. *Surely these people fished.* The first three huts held nothing but dirt and twigs. But a scrap of dull cloth in the fourth hovel proved to be a tattered fishnet. An hour later he returned to his campsite with a pair of finny trophies.

A stranger squatted next to Curtis's horse, rummaging through his pack.

Curtis slipped his sword from its sheath. "Who are you?"

The man stood. He was big, a head taller than Curtis, with straw-colored shoulder-length hair and a garland of odd flowers about his neck. Green and red lines made intricate patterns on the exposed portions of his arms and legs. "I might ask the same of you." An Avar drawl permeated his words. "From your gear, I take you for a Solarian cavalryman or knight, but the fighting is in Kheff, not here."

Curtis pointed his weapon at the intruder. "I am Sir Curtis DuFloret of the Southern Relief Force, separated from my comrades by the tide of battle."

"Sir Curtis DuFloret." Amused wonder filled the intruder's voice. "All the way down here. Imagine that." He paid no heed to Curtis's steel.

"Who are you," repeated Curtis.

The man's whiskers twitched. "You don't recognize me? Granted, it's been a while. Maybe it's the whiskers. I need to shave." He tapped his foot. "Or maybe you are not Curtis DuFloret. Name your elder brother."

"Do you claim to know me? Is this a test?"

"Answer the question, lad. Who is your elder brother?"

Curtis's eyes narrowed. "My elder sister is Maria. Liam is my younger brother."

"Good." The man's head moved a fraction. "How is Maria these days?"

"You know her?" Curtis shook his head. "She married a merchant in Tessa and had three squalling brats. Liam remained in Agba."

"Ah." A long breath escaped the man's lips. "It's been so long. "Agba to Kheff. You must have passed by Woodhome," he said, naming the DuFloret Seat.

"I did," said Curtis. *This man is awfully familiar with my family. But how?*

"Is my cousin Rood still telling his tall tales?"

Curtis let the sword's tip touch the earth. "Simon?"

"Took you long enough." Simon DuFloret pointed at the fish Curtis had dropped. "Mind some fruit to go with those?"

"But – but you're dead! Everybody said so."

"I did die in a sense," said Simon. "Once, I was Simon DuFloret, imperial aristocrat, champion hunter, military scout, and warrior. Now, I am none of those things."

Curtis's thoughts jumbled together. "You appear alive to me, though the same cannot be said of this village."

Simon gave the damaged huts a cursory glance. "Tomlin. They chose flight rather than servitude. Considering what the Child did to their home, I can't blame them."

"Child?" Curtis waved at the maze of berms and broken hovels. "A Child forced an entire populace to flee? That must be some toddler."

"Yes, she is," said Simon. "I serve her now."

"You abandoned name and nation to serve a child? Where is this prodigy?"

"All around you," said Simon. "You stand within the Child's body."

Curtis's eyes darted back and forth. Waist-high walls snaked away towards a taller barrier in the north. Tales told weeks earlier jelled with his uncle's words. "You serve the Demon Fortress."

Simon nodded, unconcerned. "That is the locals name for the Child."

"But why? Why serve something that inflicts such devastation?"

"Because the alternatives are worse." Simon motioned at the fish. "Do you wish to eat or not?"

Wordlessly, Curtis retrieved the fish.

Simon walked deeper into the labyrinth. Curtis checked his horse, decided it had sufficient grass and water for the nonce, and set out after his cousin.

LABYRINTH WAR XXVIII - Carina

'Equitant's signal towers send messages across the Empire in days instead of months. Their bicycles let men travel a hundred miles a day. And their gasbags let men fly. Such hubris must be punished.'
- Cardinal Cyril

Carina watched legionnaires tote dead monsters into the dungeon. The corpses resembled giant six-legged crabs with huge, armored mushrooms rising from their tops. Flexible tentacles hung from under the cap's rim. Alive and mobile, the creatures would have stood about breast high to Carina.

So that is a Gotemik.

"Ugly devils," said one of the legionnaires. The Gotemik's armored legs dangled to either side of the stretcher it laid on.

"Wonder what they taste like," asked a stout fighter. "They do kind of look like crabs."

The first legionnaire made a disgusted face. "I'm not eating one of these things. Army chow is bad enough."

"Make way," a voice called from the stairs.

The legionnaires placed the dead Gotemik in a cell with two of its companions.

More soldiers descended the stairs carrying stretchers with dead men and hobgoblins on them. Their clothing varied from once fine cloth to leather armor, but each sported a smooth metal collar around their necks.

The Kheffian magician Uday emerged from a cell with another necklace in his hand.

"This is the last of them, sir," said a legionnaire entering the dungeon. "Ten men, six hobs, and four of these things."

"What of the flying ship," asked Uday.

"Two companies are loading what's left of it onto wagons. Prince Maximus ordered a warehouse cleared for the wreckage." The legionnaire spat. "A lot of that crap looked like it was alive."

"It may have been." Uday approached the cells where Amentep and Lady Bao were held captive. "We need to speak," he said to Amentep, ignoring Bao's presence.

Amentep stared at the magician with vacant eyes. "I have told you what I know."

"No," said Uday. "You told me what you remember." The magician motioned to a nearby soldier. "Bring him. We shall retire upstairs. I find this place distressing."

A turnkey unlocked the cell. Amentep shuffled out, head bowed.

"Please don't hurt him," said Bao as the door closed.

Uday ignored the woman. Instead, he strode to the dungeon's entrance while a legionnaire gripped Amentep's arm and propelled him in the magician's wake.

The soldiers rattled the doors of the cells where the monster's corpses had been placed. Several made religious signs over their chests. Then they departed, leaving Carina alone in the dungeon with Bao and the turnkey, who produced a bottle and ambled from sight.

"Do you think the sorcerer will kill him," asked Bao in a small voice.

Carina shook her head. "Most likely, he'll end up with a headache."

Steps sounded from the entrance. Ambrose entered the dungeon and peered at Bao. "Have you considered my offer?"

"I am not a whore." Bao spat the last word. "You will not attain Ptath's seat through me." Somehow, Ambrose had gotten it into his head that he'd be appointed Ptath's Governor when the army returned north.

"I suggest you reconsider." Ambrose's tone was conversational. He faced Carina. "That leaves you. Prince Thomas and General Flynn are busy hounding the surviving nomads, and General Masters is preoccupied with his construction projects." A feral smile crossed his lips. "We can become reacquainted in private." He produced a ring of keys from within his robe.

Carina stepped back against the cell wall. "Prince Thomas Maximus wants me alive." She kept her gaze focused on the Witch Hunter.

"And you shall be alive," said the Witch Hunter, "though you may wish otherwise. I don't intend to do anything permanent – yet."

Carina swallowed. "Did the Prince authorize this?" *If Ambrose possessed authorization, he wouldn't be here alone.*

"I have a higher authorization." Ambrose stuck the key in the lock.

Fanatic. And a madman. Carina lunged towards the cell door. Her hand wrapped around the Witch Hunter's wrist and twisted. The keys skittered across the aisle into Bao's cell.

"Bitch!" Ambrose's other hand smashed into Carina's face.

Bright sparks and crimson pain filled Carina's world as she slammed into the far wall.

"You should have been burned at Traag!" Ambrose's face turned beet red.

"Then this city would now be a tomb," said Carina through her pain. "And you would be dead along with it."

"So claims a servant of the Evil One." Ambrose whirled and crossed to Bao's cell, where the keys lay at her feet. Bao had not moved from the bunk. "Give me the keys," ordered Ambrose.

Bao stared at the floor, hands over her ears.

Ambrose knelt and stuck his hands through the bars. The keys remained out of reach. "Damn you." The Witch Hunter rose to his feet. "Where'd that wretched turnkey get off too?" He strode along the corridor.

Bao took her hands off her ears. She stared at the keys and blinked. Then she plucked them from the floor. A moment later she was fitting the metal bit into the lock. The cell door popped open. Bao stepped into the aisle and stared at Carina. "That man is a monster." She unlocked the door to Carina's cell.

Carina stumbled into the corridor. Her heart pounded. *Now what? There's still a guard outside the dungeon. And Ambrose will return at any moment.*

Right on cue, footsteps sounded from the direction the Witch Hunter had taken. Ambrose came into view, a second ring of keys in his left hand. Ambrose stopped short. A grin appeared on his face, made demonic by the torchlight. "An escape. Now I can kill you with impunity." He advanced towards the women, boots clicking against the stones. A gentleman's rapier appeared in his right hand.

Bao froze.

Carina's eyes darted frantically about the hall. Nothing. Just straw and stray pebbles. And the torches. She grabbed a torch from its sconce and charged the Witch Hunter, the flame flickering as she did so.

Ambrose threw himself to the corridor's side and swung his sword.

Carina ducked. The blade trimmed Carina's hair as the torch brushed against the Witch Hunter's left arm. The sleeve of Ambrose's ecclesiastical robe ignited. Then she was past the Witch Hunter.

"Aeeii!" The keys fell to the floor as Ambrose beat his arm against the wall. "You shall burn, not I."

Carina waved the torch back and forth. *I need an opening.*

Ambrose's eyes tracked the flame. Then he swung the blade.

The brand flew from Carina's grasp, but now she was inside the Witch Hunter's reach, slamming into his chest.

The air left Ambrose's chest in a great 'woof' as momentum knocked him back a step. The sword clattered to the floor, but Ambrose's left arm now held Carina close.

Carina jerked and aimed a knee at the Witch Hunter's crotch. She missed.

Ambrose's right fist slammed into Carina's face, knocking her to the ground. His boot slammed into her ribs.

Pain burned in Carina's face. She couldn't breathe.

"Die, bitch!" Ambrose's boot filled Carina's vision.

Carina tried to roll but couldn't. Her hand reached out blindly and grabbed something.

"No, you don't!" The boot shifted course even as Carina twisted the thing in her hand.

Then Carina heard the sound of breaking pottery. Ambrose's face loomed over her as she finally twisted the thing in her hand. *What's he doing?*

Then Ambrose's body was atop hers, side pierced with his own sword, and Carina was staring at Bao, hands over her mouth.

Carina wiggled out from under the body. Dark fluid covered the back of his red robe. And it stank. Clay fragments and vile fluid covered the floor, mixing with the Witch Hunter's blood. Bao had brained Ambrose with a chamber pot.

Carina struggled to her feet. "We need to get out of here." She blinked. Her eyes didn't want to focus. And breathing hurt.

Bao's head moved. Her eyes remained focused on the corpse. She knelt and grabbed something near Ambrose's robe.

Carina took a step, grabbed Bao's arm, and spun her towards the entrance. *How to get past the guard?* Carina glared at the iron band clamped to her wrist. *If it weren't for this, I could cast a spell.* Her gaze moved to a keyhole in the bracelet – and then to the keys on the floor. A moment later, she was free of the bracelet. Power flowed through her limbs.

The exterior door would be locked – but Carina had keys.

"Are you going to magic us out of here?"

"I can get us past the guard." *Every soldier in the city will be searching for us. And those Kheffian magicians are competent.*

A long flight of stairs brought the women to a heavy oak door banded with iron. Carina peered through a palm-sized window set at eye level in the portal. Two guards sat at a small table, tossing dice, one pale and squat, the second thin and brown.

That simplifies things. Carina focused her will, nudged the falling cubes, and placed a filmy veil over the soldier's minds. Then she opened the door.

"I don't believe it," said the squat soldier.

The brown one grinned. "Miracles happen."

Neither looked away from the dice as Carina and Bao strode past them and into the courtyard of the Maximus house. Carina's heart pounded like a drum. How long before Ambrose's corpse was discovered?

Carina set a course towards the door on the compound's far side where it opened into the legion encampment. *We need supplies. Maybe we can steal a courier boat.* Beside her, Bao faltered. Carina shot her companion a glance. "Keep walking. Act like you belong here."

The legionnaire at this encampment gate didn't even glance at them. Whores were a common sight. So were whores with ragged finery and pulped faces.

Long rows of two-story mudbrick huts lined the street, each with a cohort and company designation stamped above the doorframe. Squads of soldiers moved along the lane. Faces, some of them female, peered through windows and doorways.

Carina spied an alleyway and ducked into it, pulling Bao after her. *Just two whores. The canal should be straight ahead, through the gate.*

"Murder! Escape!" The cry came from the courtyard behind the women.

Pandemonium erupted.

"Secure the gates!" The voice was authoritative. "Search the house and the camp."

A chorus of other voices acknowledged the speaker. "You heard him! Everybody, front and center, now!"

Carina paused. They'd never make the canal. Her eyes flicked in all directions before settling on a rounded bulk looming above the tenements. *Of course.* "Come on!" She tugged Bao towards the gasbag. They ducked through narrow streets as cries of alarm sounded in all directions.

The fugitives reached an open area where a massive cloth billowed above their heads. Suspended beneath it, just above the ground, was a stout woven basket. Three ropes held the gasbag in place.

Bao halted; eyes fixed on the gasbag. "You can't be serious. This is theft of imperial property. We'll be executed!"

"We'll be executed anyhow for killing Ambrose." Carina tugged at Bao's wrist.

Bao blinked. Then the women ran across the open area and climbed into the basket. Two packs lay on the floor, next to a metal canister with an elongated spout that projected flame into the overhead cavity.

Carina rummaged through the nearest pack. "We need a knife."

"Here." Bao handed the mage a military-issue dagger. "It was by the edge."

"Thank you." The knife bit deep into the first rope, which parted with a 'snap.' The basket tilted.

"Soldiers are approaching," said Bao.

"Shit!" Carina clung to the side and sawed at the second cable.

"Hey! What are you doing?" The voice came from a blond-haired soldier a dozen yards away from the balloon.

Carina hacked through the second cord. The basket's tilt increased. Both women slid to the gondola's corner.

The soldier took a few paces towards the balloon and halted.

Just one cable to go. She moved the knife back and forth along the rope. Halfway there.

A hand slammed atop hers. "No, you don't," said the blond soldier.

No! I'm so close! Carina winced and slugged the legionnaire square in the nose. The soldier fell to the ground. So, did the knife.

More soldiers appeared, carrying swords, spears, and crossbows. They shouted and pointed at the gas bag. "Get them!"

A crossbow bolt whizzed above Bao's head and ricocheted off the canister's chimney.

A second legionnaire hurled a spear. Carina's eyes widened as the missile drew close, its point headed right for her face. She threw herself to the floor as something 'snapped' and the shaft punched through the side of the basket.

The gondola tilted again, this time leveling out. Carina felt a weight pressing against her. The cries outside the basket intensified and then began to recede. *What happened?*

Carina raised her head and peeked over the rail. She blinked. A vista of flat-topped roofs greeted her eyes. *We're airborne. That spear must have cut the cord.* She fell back into the basket. "We did it. It was close, but we did it."

"Yes," said Bao.

Carina faced the other woman. The spear had missed her by less than an inch.

LABYRINTH WAR IXXX – Octavos

'I awoke covered in vines yesterday morning. I ran from the vegetation despite my weakness and ran into the windings. I remember the passageways being narrow and short, ending in intersections. Nothing lived except the vines and patches of moss.

Then I found a tiny courtyard with a tree of strange aspect next to a round red tunnel. I recognized the scene from a painted wall in Vazari: this was where Octavos had penetrated Gawana to beseech Gawana's lords.

My belly rumbled. Bright orange fruit the size of large figs dangled from the tree, cool and smooth to the touch. I plucked one and bit without thinking. The taste was indescribable. Past here, my memory blurs.

I retain a dreamlike recollection of stumbling along tubular corridors whose walls pulsed and heaved. Multicolored crystalline growths and red eyes glinted in the dark. Fear filled me, yet I did not retreat. I was being drawn – or herded.

The corridors took me to a pit of bubbling purple and red slime. Droplets of this substance fountained into the sour-sweet air upon my approach. A stinging pain tore through my hand when a glob struck it.

The pain pierced the compulsion that drove me. I turned for the entryway, to find it replaced by a porous wall. A sucking sound emerged from the pit as a tall column of slime rose and leaned towards me.

Gawana's Lords meant for me to die in this place. Fear should have petrified me. But I am a warrior who'd fought Traag's abominations and lived. And I am a Maximus. We do not cower. We command.

I clasped the Seal and raised it before me. "Withdraw." I focused my entire will on that word.

The viscous column wavered, twisted, and then collapsed. Panting, I surveyed the scene. Did the Seal have power over Gawana? I touched the enclosure with my free hand and found it hard as stone. Then I brought the Seal's base against the barrier. It struck and sank.

I tried to wrench the Seal loose but failed. Instead, it sank deeper, engulfing my wrist. "Open!" I shouted and walked straight into the wall.

Slime engulfed my arm and shoulder. Next, it pressed against my nose and eyes. The substance filled my mouth and nostrils. I took a panicked breath and felt a chill sensation in my chest. By rights, I should have died. Instead, I breathed the slime as though it were thick fog.

I opened my eyes to a scene of light and dark patches. The spots resolved into shapes suggestive of a long oval table surrounded by overstuffed chairs.

Noises reached my ears, muted to incomprehensibility by the liquid. They appeared to originate from the chairs ringing the table.

"...Cheated..." Was that Mecon's voice? Was this a gathering of Gawana's Lords?

I resolved to approach this assembly.

My limbs moved with leaden slowness. The first step required heroic effort.

The momentum assisted me with the next step.

"...No. Resourceful..." The tone reminded me of Mother Green.

I continued my slow trek toward the table. The cushioned seats more resembled shapeless blobs than furniture. Dark patches within them suggested human forms: heads, arms, legs, and torsos.

These insubstantial figures regarded me as I approached. One radiated cold hostility, another world-weary indifference. They seemed to have sunk very deep into the padding of the chairs.

With a start, I realized the figures were within the blobs, not on them. This revelation struck me so hard that I lost my grip on the Seal, which continued in a slow arc before me.

The figure's heads swiveled, tracking the Seal's progress.

It stopped a foot above the table's surface, where it rotated in place.

Outrage at the Seal's loss overcame my revulsion towards the obscene blobs. I took another step, passing by the closest of the organs.

Its occupant turned to regard me. Mila. Though her features were blurred, I knew it was her.

Mecon occupied the blob next to Mila. Mother Green's impassive features stared at me from across the table.

I recognized the other occupants of the blobs: Mecon and Mother Green.

A creature resembling a man-sized centipede occupied the most distant of the organs. An Old One?

The Seal hovered over the table's center.

My gaze flicked downward at the table – which, I now belatedly realized was something hugely different than mere furniture. Its surface bulged beneath my outstretched hand. A purple-red pseudopod extended from the bulge towards the Seal.

I gritted my teeth. No! The Seal was so close! I leaned forward with my full weight. The Seal hit the palm of my hand at the same instant the appendage touched the end of my thumb and the fingertips closest to it.

"...No!" Mecon's bitter tone.

"...Gawana's choice..." said Mother Green's etheric voice.

Then nothing.'

- *From 'The Journal of Titus Maximus.'*

"Welcome to Gawana's Child," said Mecon. "Not large yet – she covers just a hundred square miles. But she will get bigger." He shot a disdainful glance at Casein. "With more help, the Child would grow faster."

"Child?" *A hundred square miles are 'not large?' Building a fortress this size would take ten legions working double shifts for a decade.*

"Yes, that is our name for this extension of Gawana," said Mecon. "Casein and I transported the seed here a decade ago."

"Don't go filling the kid's head with lies." Casein snorted. "I transported the Seed while you laid on a litter, whining and pissing yourself."

Mecon glared at Casein and then turned to Octavos. "The journey was brutal for me. I found the land strange, the food inedible, and succumbed to one ailment after another. The worst of it, though, was the separation from Gawana. That tore a hole in my heart. Only the Seed's presence provided comfort."

"He clung to that bloody thing like it was his virgin daughter while the rest of us lugged them both up streams and across the forest," said Casein. "Simon, at least could walk."

"Simon?" asked Octavos.

"Simon was a warrior and hunter before becoming a Lord," said Mecon. "He withstood the isolation better than I."

"Yeah, Simon knows his way around the wilderness," agreed Casein. "He saved our hides more than once and guided us to this very spot."

"The seed was not supposed to be planted here!" Mecon's body tensed.

"I planted it where you and Simon said too." Casein's voice rose.

"I have no recollection of that," said Mecon. "This location is marginal at best. The mountains east and south of here are too tall and unstable for the Child to climb. West, the ground lacks nutrients. That leaves north."

"All of which is your and Simon's problem, not mine," said Casein. "The Gotemik are here. I need to alert Titus."

"What?" Mecon's face paled. "Are you certain?"

"I saw three of their ships flying towards Ptath," said Casein.

"Ptath," said Mecon. "Two nights ago, the Child detected strange energies east and south of here. I wonder..."

"Prince Maximus brought a whole pack of magicians with the army," said Casein.

"No," said Mecon. "This was no mortal magic the Child observed."

"All the more reason to let Titus know," said Casein.

Mecon's head bobbed. "Yes, yes, you are correct. I will take you both to the Heart." He spun on his heel and walked into the maze.

Octavos and Casein glanced at each other and followed after him. After a few paces, Octavos turned to Casein. "What was all that about? Who is this 'Simon?'"

Casein drew a finger across his lips and then pointed at the vines covering the walls around them. Red and purple flowers attached to the vines seemed to stare at them.

Past the first corner, they reached a miniature cliff. Octavos ascended without trouble: foot here, hand there, heave and lift. He didn't even have to set the lyre case on the ground. Casein's face turned bright red from the exertion, and he fell face-first into the dirt at the summit.

Octavos knelt and offered him a hand, but the big man glared, shook his head, and heaved. *His side is bothering him again.*

Lumps, bumps, and pits dotted the corridor floors past the cliff. Huge spreading plants sprouted from the ground, impeding progress. Octavos navigated these obstacles much easier than Casein. Twice, Mecon paused ahead of them.

They reached the stream after a two-mile walk. There was no bridge and the barrier on the far side presented a blank face. Instead, they followed a narrow path between the wall and the river for a quarter mile, contrary to the direction of the water. Then the stream rounded a corner, and they were at a bridge with a squat stone blockhouse at its far end. Past it was a large grove of trees with purple fruit hanging from their intertwined serpentine limbs. A ragged line of mudbrick huts formed a broken circle around the grove. *Punji trees* thought Octavos. *The same ones my father described in his journal.*

Mecon waited for them in the blockhouse, exchanging words with a pair of muscled brutes with crossbows slung across their backs and truncheons in their beefy hands.

The larger guardian turned his head and spat into the river. He sported a ratty black beard and rattier leather armor. "Kay." He didn't move.

Casein glared at the thug. "Move. Or I'll toss your ass in the river."

The thug blinked and edged to the side.

Octavos almost gagged at the guardian's vile breath when he passed. Inside, a topless woman with dirty skin and dead eyes stared at him from a huddle on the floor. Octavos kept his gaze focused on the far opening.

"Welcome to Pathak," said Mecon when Octavos emerged into daylight. A man in rags lay face-first in the street behind Mecon.

Octavos scanned the courtyard. Dull people with lifeless eyes shuffled along dirt streets or sat against the walls of the hovel. A few children plucked purple fruit from the twisted trees. A row of adults sat along the riverbank, clenching fishing poles. "Seems rather dull." Octavos jerked a thumb at the blockhouse. "More prison than a village."

"People require time to understand the benefits the Child brings to their lives." Mecon turned and strode across the village. Everybody got out of his way.

Past Pathak, the passageways bifurcated into multiple narrow alleys. The terrain rose. Twice Octavos and Casein climbed rude staircases. Then they were standing in a small courtyard dominated by a central bush no taller than Octavos, with queer red berries hanging from its branches. Past it rose a vertical rock wall with a round dark entrance at its base.

Octavos reached a hand towards the plant.

"Don't touch that," said Mecon without turning away from the opening. "It's not for you." He entered the cave.

Octavos hesitated. His father's journal contained dire warnings about underground areas within Gawana.

"Go on kid," said Casein. "Don't got much choice."

Gripping his lyre case, Octavos entered the cavern. The tunnel was long, circular in cross-section, illuminated by pale white and blue glowing ropes zigzagging across its upper surfaces. In places, the ends of these ropes dangled from above like the roots of alien plants. Which, perhaps, they were.

After a hundred yards, the passage ended at a 'T' intersection. Mecon motioned at the left-hand route. An older man in a yellow robe stood aside as they strode along this new corridor. Twice, they passed circular doorways. One opened into an utterly dark space, the other onto a courtyard where a golden-haired woman perched on a bench near a tiny pond.

And then the tunnel ended at a blank wall. "Security measure," said Mecon. "Some secrets are not to be divulged."

"Open the damn thing," said Casein.

Mecon gave the big man an annoyed glance and turned his attention to the blank wall. His hands made arcing motions along its surface, which rippled, slid, and changed color with each pass. And then, with a liquid plop, the wall was gone, and they were staring into a curved chamber dominated by a blob-like table ringed by overstuffed chairs. *Except, that's not what they are. This is the Child's Heart.*

"The child retains a link to its parent." Mecon approached the blob table. "However, the link is mostly casual, limited to basic sensations."

"But you can speak to my father through it," said Octavos.

"I have done so." Mecon didn't lift his eyes from the blob. His expression was of a priest experiencing divine revelation. *That's what this is to Mecon – a God.*

"Get on with it." Casein's voice was a growl.

"I was merely offering instruction to your charge," said Mecon. "You may know these things, but he does not. Still, time is essential."

Mecon placed both hands on the organ before him. They sank into its surface without resistance. The portion of the blob near Mecon's hands changed colors: green, yellow, white, blue, and purple. These coalesced into a round patch dotted with vague shapes. And then Octavos was peering into another chamber much like this one and a face that resembled his reflection.

"Mecon, what is this," said an emotionless voice from the blob's altered portion.

"I have news, Titus," said Mecon. "Leander Casein is with me."

Casein stepped close to the blob. "The Gotemik are here. I think they attacked Ptath."

"Unfortunate," said Titus. "I didn't believe they'd venture so far east. How fares the city?"

"I can't say, sir," said Casein. "A damn big pack of nomads broke through the pass."

"The army has gone to hell in a handbasket since my day to let that happen," said Titus. "Anything else?"

"The Child reports unusual energies south and east of here," said Mecon. "They may or may not originate with the Gotemik."

"It's not all bad news." Casein motioned at Octavos.

Octavos approached the blob and leaned over the flickering image. "Hello, dad."

The face contorted. "Octavos? Is that you? How did you come to be here?"

"Cousin Varro ordered me wed to the daughter of Ptath's governor. I arrived in Dessau just before the nomads attacked. I'd have died were it not for Casein."

"Your survival pleases me," said Titus. "Tell me, you were educated in Solace, right?"

Octavos nodded. "I was. I am a duly accredited scholar."

"Impressive," said Titus. "Did you know Doctor Menendez?"

"Yes," said Octavos. The image flickered.

"Give you," said his father right before the picture dissolved.

Mecon removed his hands from the blob and took a ragged breath. "The connection lasted longer than I thought."

"We need to get settled." Casein took two steps toward the entryway and collapsed.

Mecon stared at Casein. "Now what?"

"Casein was wounded during the escape from Dessau," said Octavos. "A rachasa stabbed him with its claws. I applied herbs, but he needs a healer."

"Fortunately for him, we have one." Mecon grabbed Casein's arm. "Help me move him to the corridor." Together the two men dragged Casein from the chamber to the courtyard.

"Our healer is special," said Mecon as they dragged Casein into the yard. "I believe you term her sort 'Godborn.'" Distaste filled his voice.

In his world, the only Gods are Gawana and her child.

Together, they wrestled Casein's body onto the now vacant bench. Then Mecon straightened. "Lucinda, I have a patient for you."

The golden-haired woman emerged from behind a tree. "Oh. It's Cam." She bent over the prostrate man, examining his bandages. "This is fair work," she said upon examining the bandages.

Mecon departed, claiming a press of business.

"Thank you," said Octavos. "I used what herbs were available."

"Your efforts would have succeeded had he not moved around so much." The Godborn sighed. "Warriors seldom listen to healer's instructions. I shall place him in a simple healing trance." She made a mystic pass over Casein's body. The big man's breathing steadied.

Octavos listened to her accent. Imperial, with a touch of something else. "You're from Arcos," he said, naming an island state in the southern Shadow Sea, once an imperial outpost.

Lucinda smiled. "Yes. My family holds an estate on the mainland."

"How did you come to be here?"

Lucinda pointed at Casein. "He brought me." Her shoulders slumped. "I don't like it here. This place saps my energy and the masters hate me. They won't even permit me to tend to the villagers."

Mecon reappeared. "I have prepared a chamber for you."

"I was talking with Lucinda."

"She has duties. You need rest." Mecon's tone brooked no argument. "Now come with me."

What a petty tyrant. Octavos considered refusing and decided it wasn't worth it. He glanced at Casein.

"He will be fine," said Mecon, "if you permit the healer to perform her task."

Lucinda gave a slight nod.

Octavos rose to his feet. He was tired. It had been an exhausting day. "Lead on."

Mecon didn't lead him far, just a short distance along the hall to the hall's second portal. "There. Your possessions are inside."

Octavos mentally kicked himself for leaving his lyre behind. *At least I'm close to Casein.* He peered into the opening. "Looks dark." And the air had a sweet tang to it.

"There is illumination within," said Mecon.

Octavos squinted. Yes, there was a reddish-white patch of light in the darkness. "I'd prefer a lantern."

"We have little oil," said Mecon. "The Child will provide."

I want my lyre. Octavos strode into the darkness, ignoring the prickles on his skin. *I don't care what he says. I'll grab my things and leave.* Ten paces brought Octavos to a chamber with curved edges. Luminous red and white strands clung to or dangled from these surfaces. A barrel-sized pit dominated one side. There. His pack and lyre case were propped against a cot next to a small table with a platter of sliced purple fruit. Octavos touched the fruit; aware he'd not eaten since morning. It felt soft. Dark seeds popped from the pulp. *I'll find something else.* He grabbed the lyre case and pack and turned for the entrance.

The portal was gone, replaced by a blank wall. *Shit. The bastard is trying to kill me.* The sickly-sweet scent in the air became overwhelming. Octavos body trembled. Pack and lyre case fell from nerveless fingers. *They tried the same thing with Dad. But he had a magical artifact. I don't have anything.*

A series of liquid plops made Octavos turn his head to face the cavity. Slimy liquids ran along the side of the chamber and across the floor into the depression, which emitted a faint rose-colored mist. Near panic, Octavos stepped back, his foot brushing against the lyre case. He remembered an old story.

In the days of the first Empire, before its fall, there'd been a minstrel whose songs had displeased a cruel Emperor (whose surname just happened to be Maximus). 'The singer's songs are seditious,' thundered the emperor. 'They give the plebeians queer ideas. Therefore, I shall end singer and songs both.' The emperor ordered the musician and his instrument to be thrown to the beasts in the arena. Faced with ravenous beasts, the minstrel didn't flee. Instead, he began playing. The beasts listened...as did the arena's crowds, who rioted and tore the emperor to pieces.

It's an old story. Apocryphal. But it's what I have. Eyes tearing and head pounding, Octavos opened the case and removed his lyre. Then he began to play 'Sooth the Savage Heart.' The luminous strands pulsated. Those dangling from overhead twitched back and forth in time to the music. *Something is happening.* Octavos finished 'Savage Heart' and moved to 'Lenore's Lullaby.' *Let's see if I can't put the Child to sleep.* Slime stopped oozing from the walls. The mist cleared. And the ropes lost most of their glow.

A liquid 'plop' sounded behind Octavos. Still playing, he rotated in place. The entry had returned. Octavos kicked the pack from the chamber and exited on trembling legs. He didn't stop until he was in the courtyard. Lucinda was gone, but Casein lay sprawled on the bench, snoring like a bull. Octavos sat against a large boulder and collapsed. His eyes closed.

"What are you doing here?"

Octavos opened his eyes. Mecon loomed overhead, glaring at him. *Enough.* Octavos rolled to his feet lunged, and swung, his fist connecting with Mecon's left eye. "Ow!" A sharp pain filled his fingers as Mecon flew backward.

Mecon lifted his head. "You dare to strike me?"

Octavos clenched his aching fist. *Damn, that hurt!* "You tried to kill me." He took a step towards the prostrate man. *This time I'll kick him.*

"Nonsense." Mecon's eyes widened. His hands clenched. "I just – it was – the Child"-

"No," said Octavos. "You sent me in that stinking hole to die. At least have the guts to admit it." He raised his foot.

"Yes, damn you." Mecon's face flared bright red. He pushed himself backward along the dirt. "I did offer you to the Child. You Maximus can't be trusted."

Octavos took another step towards Mecon. Mecon kicked and swung his legs. And then Octavos fell in a heap.

Both men reached their feet at the same time. Mecon lunged and grabbed Octavos's arm.

Octavos pivoted.

Mecon released his grip, stumbled a few paces, and halted, hands on knees, panting.

Octavos advanced and swung at Mecon's gut.

Mecon grabbed Octavos's arm.

Momentum carried Octavos's knee into Mecon's crotch. Mecon fell to the ground in a fetal position.

"I should have put more work into your unarmed combat skills," said a familiar voice from behind Octavos.

Octavos span. "Sir Curtis! What are you doing here?" A second man accompanied the Avar knight, a looming blond-haired hulk wearing a flower necklace. Fine green and red lines covered the man's exposed skin.

"Fortunes of war," said Curtis.

Curtis's companion eyed Mecon. "I have wanted to do that for years." The big man faced Curtis. "Pleased to meet you. I'm Simon DuFloret."

Octavos inclined his head. "Good day to you sir." *Simon DuFloret. I should know that name.*

Simon walked over to where Mecon lay on the ground, eyes taking in the man's bruises.

"Kill him," said Mecon in a cracked voice. He didn't move his head. "As the Child's First Servant, I demand it."

"I should have done what he did years ago," said Simon. "But you're right." He faced Octavos. "You struck him. The punishment is death."

Octavos paled. *Now I remember. My father killed Simon's brother.*

LABYRINTH WAR XXX - Curtis

"I have a proposition," said the Doctor.

All eyes turned to her. "Let's hear it," said Mecon.

The Doctor opened her hands. Tiny globes of yellow light emerged from her palms, and orbited us, before settling in various niches, bathing the scene in radiance. Then she stepped behind a protruding boulder as though it were a lectern. "Gawana is in turmoil. Goblins rampage through the maze, the nomads of Ulaam-Thek wreck walls for pasture, and Vazari's leaders believe Gawana's time is past."

"A direct assessment," said Mother Green. "But what of this feud?"

"Without decisive leadership, the turmoil in Gawana will worsen," said the Doctor. "You need a war leader who can train and lead men in battle. Simon DuFloret meets those criteria."

"Brilliant," said Mother Green. "You'd make Titus's problem our solution."

- From 'The Journal of Titus Maximus.'

"No," said Curtis. "I won't let you kill him."

Mecon rose to a sitting position and gasped. "He is a Maximus. They can't be trusted." Mecon glared at Simon. "You know this."

"Mecon tried to kill me," said Octavos. Simon's eyes flicked in Octavos's direction. "He put me in a room. Said it was 'guest quarters.' The room tried to eat me."

"I was within my rights!" Mecon slammed a fist into his palm. "The Maximus cannot be trusted."

"Neither can you." Curtis stared Mecon straight in the eye.

"Restrain him, less I order his death as well." Mecon jabbed his finger at Simon.

"The boy is kin," said Simon.

"Yes," said Curtis. "I am your kin. I joined the army and came south to search for you." *And kill Titus Maximus.* But he didn't say that.

Simon's brow furrowed. "And you found me. But he"- Simon waved a hand at Octavos, "needs to die. The First Servant ordered it."

"Mecon tried to kill a guest under his own roof." *At least I hope Octavos was a guest.* "That is a violation of guest rights." Curtis jabbed a finger into Simon's midsection. "Or do such things matter to you anymore? Have you lost all honor?"

Simon shifted his feet and stared at the ground. "Oh, I still retain my honor. I lost much else, but I still have that." He looked at Octavos. "What brought you here?"

"He did." Octavos pointed at Casein. "We fled Dessau together. Casein said he had business here."

"Business?" Simon rubbed his whiskers. "What sort of business? Did he say?"

"Casein met with Mecon. We went into the Heart Chamber, and there Mecon summoned an image of my father."

"That is serious." Simon fixed Mecon with a glare.

Mecon's eyes dropped. "Casein brought word the Gotemik are here."

"That changes matters," said Simon. "If the Gotemik are this far east, then all else is secondary. First Servant, I recommend Octavos's sentence be suspended. The Gotemik take priority."

"I will not revoke my sentence," said Mecon. "But I will suspend it for the nonce."

"Will all of you shut the hell up?" Casein lifted his head from the bench. "I'm trying to get some sleep here."

Simon strode to the bench and stared at Casein. "Hello, old foe."

Casein stared at Simon and blinked. "Great. First Mecon and now you." He rose to a sitting position. "There goes my beauty sleep." Casein surveyed the band, gaze settling on Mecon. "Somebody broke your face."

"That was me," said Octavos.

"Good job, kid." Casein stretched. "You shouldn't have done it, but you did a good job."

"He tried to kill me."

"That figure's." Casein scowled and touched his injured side. "At least I'm not hurting quite so bad."

"What happened," asked Simon.

"I tangled with a rachasa." Casein stood.

Simon's eyebrows rose. "Impressive. Now what's this about the Gotemik?"

"Can I eat first?" Casein took a couple of steps towards the entry.

Simon glanced at Mecon, who nodded. "The hour grows late. Provender is in order."

They ate at a long trestle table in an alcove outside the Heart's caverns. Brown-skinned servants brought platters with purple fruit, grey paste, strips of jerked fish, and cups of purple-black wine. Simon lifted a cup. "An inferior vintage, I'm afraid, but the best we have."

Curtis took a sip. "Tastes like sand mixed with piss. I'd hate to see the worst."

Simon shot him a glance but said nothing.

Curtis took a bite of the fruit. "Tangy," he said. "Much better." He scooped some of the paste to his plate with a wooden knife. The substance tasted like paper. He made a face.

"Usually, we put sauce on the pika paste." Simon handed Curtis a tiny pot filled with orange fluid dotted with dark specks.

"Thank you." Curtis smeared a few drops of the sauce on the paste and took a second bite. "Tastes much better." Miniature explosions erupted in his mouth, but he deemed it a significant improvement over bland.

Casein shoveled food in his mouth with both hands while Mecon watched, features curled with disgust.

Octavos picked at his plate. He tried the paste (with sauce) and then nibbled at a fish.

The kid is badly spooked – and I don't blame him.

Casein finished the last bit of fruit and pushed his plate back. "That hit the spot."

Simon motioned towards the Heart cavern. "We need to talk."

"Yeah, I suppose we do." Casein stood and took a couple of steps from the table.

Octavos remained seated. "I'm not going back in there," he said in a thin voice. "Talk out here."

"Can't," said Casein.

Octavos glanced at the vines, as though expecting them to move. "I don't want to be here." *He's well and truly spooked.*

"Suit yourself," said Casein.

"The Maximus is not leaving," said Mecon. "I will not revoke my sentence."

"Let him go to Pathak," said Simon.

Mecon thought for a moment. "Very well. Pathak is acceptable. But the Child's gates are closed."

Simon turned to Curtis. "Go with him. Pathak hosts unsavory elements."

Like I didn't know that already, thought Curtis, remembering his first walk through the village.

Octavos nodded. "I remember the way." This prompted unreadable looks from Casein, Simon, and Mecon.

"You are your father's son," said Casein. *What's that supposed to mean?*

Octavos collected his lyre case and pack and started walking. "We'd best hurry. It's getting dark."

To Curtis's astonishment, Octavos navigated the route to Pathak without a misstep. "How did you do that?" asked Curtis when Pathak appeared around a corner.

Octavos grinned. "Look at the ground."

Curtis did so. "I see dirt."

"No, you see packed dirt," said Octavos. "A path. Past here, the only place anybody goes is the Heart. Everybody uses the same route, so there's a path."

"That's pretty smart." Curtis watched a band of Pathak's inhabitants shuffle through the dirt streets. None displayed any interest in the pair. None approached the maze walls.

"Comes from a good education." Octavos glanced at the hovels. His smile vanished.

Curtis spotted a fallen log next to a fire pit. "Over here."

They sat on the log and watched the river sluggishly flow past their position. Octavos tossed a pebble in the water. It hit with a 'plop' and vanished.

"You knew about this place, didn't you?" Curtis threw a twig in the water and watched it drift under the bridge. "You've known about it for a month, at least."

"My father left me his journal." Octavos threw a stick in the water. "In it, he described a...expedition...to a place called Gawana across the Shadow Sea."

"I have heard of Gawana," said Curtis. *Nothing good and all of it fanciful.*

"He talked about people he encountered there," Octavos spoke in a low tone. "Your uncle. Mecon. Others. The place changed him."

"What happened?" Curtis threw another branch.

"He remained in Gawana. His companion, Doctor Menendez, gave me Dad's journal before I joined the expedition. Until then, I thought he'd died years ago." Octavos glanced at the knight. "He was in big trouble."

"You're saying this place is an extension of Gawana." Simon had told Curtis that earlier, but the concept was difficult to swallow. *A living, thinking being spanning thousands of miles? Impossible.*

"Yes." Octavos kicked at the dirt. "Casein and Mecon planted the seed for this place eight or ten years ago."

Simon told me the same thing. "What else?"

Octavos shook his head. "We saw these flying things a couple of days ago. Casein said they were Gotemik and went all serious."

"Flying things," said Curtis. "Like flying shields?"

Octavos shrugged. "Maybe. They were far in the distance. Have you heard of such?"

"Yes," said Curtis. "After the war, my branch of the family moved to Agba. Jeremy Scarlet was throwing his weight around, and my parents knew what would happen."

"The rebellion," said Octavos. "The old Emperor had to recall a legion of troops to suppress it."

"Yeah, well we moved to Agba before all that." Curtis sighed. "I was seventeen and foolish enough to think it all a grand adventure. Instead, it was mostly a bunch of work. Most of Agba's people are...broken. No spark. No life." He motioned at the village. "Like the people in this place. Others had a mean stubbornness to them."

Octavos nodded. "Cultists."

"Yeah, we never did get rid of them all. The cultists fled into the deep desert or the mountains. From there, they'd raid villages and caravans. We'd sally forth to attack them and find...nothing." Curtis shook his arms. "Agba is huge. We couldn't patrol it all. Then, refugees from the far West brought word of war – the hobgoblins of Iktar attacked Celthania, a cousin state to Agba."

"I know of Celthania," said Octavos. "My father mentioned encountering people from there. Narran and Varian – envoys of some sort. He wrote they were arrogant and treacherous. He thought they were demon worshippers."

Just like the Maximus Family. Curtis didn't voice the thought. "Celthanians are demon worshippers. But that didn't help them against Iktar. So, they did something stupid."

"They summoned the Gotemik," said Octavos.

"My dad thought so, yes. So did others." Curtis nodded, impressed at the kid's intellect. "They thought Celthania's leaders had a falling out with the Gotemik. The Celthanians that could, fled, floating down the river from Old Agba." Curtis sighed. "At first, they seemed decent enough, some of them anyhow. Their ranks included marvelously skilled artisans, healers whose knowledge surpassed anything we knew of, and some were doughty fighters."

"But they were also demon worshippers."

"Yes. At first, we made allowances because they were so useful. But most of them refused to renounce their demon gods, and they were always scheming and plotting. When they tried to take Edak – a city at the edge of imperial control – we had them banished."

"And they went and joined the cultists," said Octavos.

"Yes. The cultists went from a nuisance to a dire threat. That was why I came east – to plead for troops."

"Swapping stories?" Casein stood there with a grim smile on his face.

"Just passing the time." Curtis climbed to his feet. "How went the meeting?"

"Not good." Casein faced Octavos. "I did about half convince that asshole not to kill you. Right now, I gotta get to the landing." He strode off without waiting for a response.

"That was quick," said Octavos.

"The sun's setting," said Curtis as Casein jogged across the bridge. "We have more visitors."

A small band of Pathak's pathetic citizens approached the pair. "The masters ordered us to provide a room for you," said a skinny fellow with brown dirt covering his skin and robe. He pointed at a hut. "Gujjar died last week. You can stay in his house."

"Thank you," said Curtis.

"Don't bother," said the man. "This place slays us a day at a time. Once, I was a trader, selling logs to Kheff for fine copper and brass. Now I grub in the dirt and despair kills my kin one by one." He started to walk back towards the huts.

"Wait." Octavos reached for his lyre case. "Maybe I can help."

"I doubt it, young one," said the man.

Octavos smiled. "I can try." He removed the lyre and strummed a few chords.

The locals hesitated. One or two departed. The rest lingered, including the spokesman.

Octavos played a song Curtis knew and another he'd never heard. *The kid possesses true talent.* When Curtis looked up from the third song a good thirty locals surrounded the pair, still swaying to the music. Somebody lit a blaze in the fire pit. A few of the younger people started dancing. Curtis heard chuckles when Octavos played an especially ribald tune. *He's giving them their spark back.*

Only a red trace of light remained in the western sky when Octavos set aside his instrument. "I need to rest," he announced to his assembled audience.

Pathak's denizens showed animation in their steps as they returned to their hovels. *Perhaps we should import musicians to Agba,* thought Curtis.

Octavos put away his lyre and slung the case over his shoulder. "The elder pointed at that hut, right?" He pointed to a shack almost lost in the shadows.

Curtis squinted in the indicated direction. "I think so. What's that sound?"

"Sounds almost like a waterfall," said Octavos, "but it's not coming from the river."

The sky darkened as a curved bulk bigger than a barge flew over the courtyard, trailed by a second and a third. "The Gotemik are here," said Curtis.

Purple lights flared on the flying craft's underside. Brilliant blue-white columns shot forth, striking the Child's walls and Pathak's huts. A huge section of the maze wall imploded. Three huts collapsed into rubble.

And then the screaming began. Pathak's populace fled into the streets and thence into the maze.

The nearest of the flying disks dropped towards the courtyard. Six long armored claws unfolded from its underside. Then it was on the ground.

A yellow dot on the side of the craft pulsed and then became a triangular hole that grew wider and taller with a horrid organic sound. Armored figures emerged from the opening, toting weapons resembling crossbows.

Curtis pointed to the bridge. "Run!"

Octavos took a few hesitant steps and paused.

"Go," Curtis shouted. *The kid can't fight foes like this. Hell, maybe I can't fight foes like this. But I intend to find out.* He pulled his sword from its sheath and approached the attackers.

One of the invaders spun and aimed its weapon at Curtis.

A hobgoblin. The knight leaped sideways. Hobgoblins were tough fighters. A gout of fire spat from the device, missing Curtis's arm. Curtis rolled to his feet and charged.

The hobgoblin moved its weapon.

Curtis's blade slammed into the device, tearing deep into its haft. Flames sprouted along the point of contact.

The hobgoblin released its grip and stepped back. Then the device exploded.

Curtis found himself on his rump half a dozen paces away from the blast. He blinked, not seeing the hobgoblin anywhere, though several marauders ran for the maze entrances. No. *A specific entrance. The one to the Heart.*

A great whining sound, like the death cry of a bird, filled the air. Another aerial disk loomed low over the maze walls, connected to them by hundreds of ropes. *No, not ropes. Vines. The Child is fighting back.*

The high-pitched sound intensified. Everybody in the village, friend, and foe alike, fell to the ground clenching their ears. The flying craft lost altitude, the lower portion of its hull contacting the maze wall. Then it blew apart in a fierce explosion.

The blast knocked Curtis face-first into the dirt. Stars and sparks filled his vision. He couldn't hear a thing apart from the bells in his skull.

Curtis rolled onto his back. An invader, this one human, stood over him, pointing one of the flame shooters at his torso. *This is it.*

Then, impossibly, the attacker fell to his knees, blood spurting from his mouth, and Simon was there, a fierce grin on his face.

Simon pointed at Curtis's sword.

Curtis nodded and grabbed the blade. Then he stood. The world wobbled. More attackers swarmed their way.

Faint sounds reached Curtis's ears. Somebody shouted something. Curtis glanced towards the river.

Casein stood there, holding a crossbow. Two other men were with him, also toting crossbows. Octavos stood behind them, staring in Curtis's direction.

What?

Casein pulled the trigger. The attacker in front of Curtis exploded.

Curtis saw blue fire, and then nothing.

LABYRINTH WAR XXXI – Octavos

'Sometimes flight is the only option.'
- Imperial Scout credo

Octavos knew he should run. Instead, he remained rooted in place, transfixed by the Gotemik flying craft that squatted atop the village of Pathak like some giant beetle. The alien machine shuddered and flexed. Then a portion of its carapace split as though it were an obscene mouth. A bipedal form with a helmet and metal bands around its neck and torso filled the opening. It raised a flared tube and leaped to the ground.

Octavos blinked. The banded form was human! He lifted his eyes as a bulky orange creature stepped through the gap. A hobgoblin. Like the human, metal bands crisscrossed its torso.

The first figure aimed its tube at a trio of onrushing warriors. A blue beam spat from the barrel. Burning flesh and agonized screams filled the air.

Octavos ran for the bridge, hoping to find a boat.

A squat figure with a shiny collar stepped from a street ahead of Octavos and aimed a long tube at the bridge. Blue fire shot from the tube and the span became an inferno.

So much for that plan.

Heart pounding, Octavos leaped for the riverbank as the warrior swiveled in his direction. Blue light shot overhead as he landed on the muddy riverbank.

Screams and shouts came from the village. *God above, they're killing everybody. If he comes down here, I'm dead. Maybe I can swim for it. Water quenches fire.*

But the warrior didn't appear. The flaming bridge creaked, groaned, and collapsed into the river amidst a cloud of steam.

A high-pitched sound came from the village, growing louder by the moment. Octavos slammed his hands against his ears, crouched, and faced the source of the noise. *God above.*

One of the Gotemik craft had been snared by a net of vines and was being dragged into the maze. Then it burst apart in a thunderous explosion. Grisly objects fell around Octavos. Shattered metal. Broken machinery. Fragments of shell with bits of meat clinging to them. A human head trailing part of the spinal column.

Octavos stared at the mangled head, mind numb, and bile rising in his throat. *This is hell.* A weight settled on Octavos's shoulder, prompting him to scream and jump.

"Easy kid," said Casein. He pointed toward the bridge with the crossbow he held in one beefy hand. Thick bolts lined his waist. Specials. "The boat is just past there. Go."

Luther was behind Casein, also toting a crossbow.

A skittering, clattering sound came from the bank's top. And then an abomination appeared - a thing like a giant crab with a tower on its back and two of the flame-spitting tubes to either side.

Casein and Luther fired at the same time. The creature blew apart in twin explosions.

One of the monster's tube weapons bounced on the ground near Octavos's feet. Octavos stretched a hand towards the side of the device. It appeared to be intact. His finger made contact. The tube was cool.

"Go for the boat!" Casein and Luther climbed the bank.

Octavos stared at the flame spitter. *I could take this thing and join them.* He withdrew his hand. *No. I have no idea how to use it.* Instead, he scooped up the weapon along with his pack and lyre case and ran along the bank, trying to ignore the screams and explosions from the village.

A body wreathed in fire toppled down the bank before him and splashed into the river. The bridge warden was draped over a support beam, minus one arm and half his face. The burning remnants of the span creaked and groaned as Octavos ducked under the crude structure.

Casein's boat was long and skinny, hewn from the trunk of a single tree. One of Casein's men stood in the midsection of the craft, pointing a crossbow at a band of terrified women, and screaming children. He didn't seem inclined to let anybody on board, including Octavos.

Octavos pointed at his chest. "I'm with Casein!"

"Stay back!" The sentry cast nervous glances at the flaming village.

"Take us with you," one of the women shouted. The youngest child, no more than three, never stopped wailing.

Defeated, Octavos faced the village. *Casein will have to sort this out.* From here, he could see the curved bulk of the flying machine, outlined by the burning dwellings around it.

Casein's voice shouted a command and a sequence of explosions detonated an instant later, followed by a pillar of flame erupting from the side of the flying machine. *Casein's work? Or some new deviltry?*

Movement from above caught Octavos's attention: three or four figures running for the river. As he watched, one fell to the ground. The others leaped towards the river, two men and a woman. Blood covered one man's face and side.

Casein's sentry nudged his crossbow at the new arrivals. "Back!"

One man pointed at the slope above. "They're coming!"

Even as the man called out, another of the crab monsters appeared next to the blockhouse, its tube weapons pointed at the boat.

Casein's man lifted his crossbow and pulled the trigger as flames shot forth from the crab monster's weapons.

Octavos leaped on the women, knocking them into the water as the world flared orange and red. A cacophony of whistles and clicks assaulted his ears.

Octavos blinked. The crab monster was on its side, short at least two legs. Ichor spurted from the stumps. Then the rest of the creature exploded, and Casein was there, running towards the boat with Luther. Octavos didn't see Curtis. *He must have been killed in the explosion.*

"I told you to get in the boat," Casein shouted.

Octavos pointed at the sentry. "He wouldn't let me!"

"Let him on board," Casein shouted.

The sentry put down his crossbow.

Octavos pointed at the escapees. "They go too."

Casein's head moved back and forth. "All right. But move! Now!"

The people swarmed the boat, climbing over the sides. Octavos grabbed his gear and stepped into the craft. Casein and Luther jumped into the water and climbed in after them. Luther and the sentry began paddling. The boat moved downstream while Pathak burned. Nobody felt like speaking.

Octavos couldn't see a thing. He wondered how the men paddled the craft without running into the bank. A screech sounded from the darkness, making Octavos cringe. *It's just a bird.* Later a pair of yellow eyes gleamed at him from the dark: a *jaguar or some other beast.*

The stream rounded a corner and a rickety lantern-lit dock appeared. More lights gleamed in a row of large huts along the shore. "Brindle Landing," said Casein. He motioned towards a large craft tied to the wharf. The vessel consisted of three tree trunk craft side by side with a deck between them. "Our transport out of here."

"What of the horses and wagons?"

"Goji sold them," said Casein. "Now get on board." He faced Pathak's escapees. "You are not coming. I'll let you keep this boat."

The refugees said nothing as Octavos climbed onto the new craft. A moment later, Casein and his people were on board, and the vessel had left the pier.

Casein motioned at a long low woven hut dominating the midsection of the new craft. "Get some sleep."

Octavos crawled into the low space and found something soft and lumpy. Sleep seemed unlikely. But his eyes closed anyway.

A trilling sound permeated Octavos's awareness. He opened his eyes to rippled daylight penetrating the woven fibers overhead. Something dug into his back, making further sleep impossible. Nightmarish memories returned. Fire. Screaming people. Death. His belly felt like a yawning pit. Octavos crawled from the shelter into a brilliant blue morning.

The craft drifted along the center of a wide stream. Casein and his men were gathered around a clay stove near the vessel's twin bows, watching a small pot bubble and hiss.

"Hungry, kid?" Casein motioned at the pot. "Gruel's about done."

Octavos glanced about the vessel's deck, cluttered with enough boxes and bundles to make movement difficult. One of Casein's men stood in the stern with a long tiller. "Does this boat have a name?"

Casein looked at Luther, who shrugged. "The man who sold it called it 'Japi,' after his daughter."

"Japi," said Octavos. "I guess that will do." He joined the circle gathered around the cauldron. Casein handed him a bowl and ladled grey sludge studded with dark flecks. The gruel didn't hold much appeal. But Octavos was hungry. "So, where are we, and where are we going?"

Casein motioned with his spoon. "This is the Turpin River. We're following it to Arcos Minor."

"Arcos's mainland holdings," said Octavos. Arcos itself was an island nation. "That means passing through Soraq. That could take a while."

Casein swallowed a bite of porridge and nodded. "About a month, give or take."

LABYRINTH WAR XXXII – Carina

'Emperor Titus Maximus the Second conquered Soraq in a year with but a single legion. However, hostile tribesmen, pestilences, and jungle parasites bled the imperial garrison's white, making Soraq's conquest more fiction than fact.'

- From Fulton's 'Progression of the Empire.

"This is disgusting." Bao held a strip of dried meat at arm's length from her body as though it were a piece of offal. "I am supposed to eat this?"

"Yes." Carina bit into a slice of dried beef. Chewy. Salty. Army food. The packs they'd found on the floor of the gasbag's basket contained dried meat, hard bread, figs, and yams enough to last five days. Carina was more concerned about the water: just two skins. "I have had worse."

"Of course, you have," said Bao. "You are a peasant, a witch, and an outcast. I, though, am the favored daughter of a provincial governor." She sighed and leaned against the side of the basket. "Or I was. Now I am nothing."

"You're alive." Carina took another bite of meat.

Bao frowned in disgust at the meat in her hand and tossed it out of the basket.

"Hey! Don't do that!"

"I will not pollute my body with such filth," said Bao.

"If you're hungry enough you will." Carina finished the meat and stood, peering over the side of the basket. Patches of cloud drifted over a verdant forest dotted with ugly reddish-brown blotches. "Looks like we're over Soraq."

"Soraq," said Bao. "My aunt married Pasha Majid Babul Khalil." She shook her head. "Horrible man, heavier than a horse with three other wives."

Columns of smoke attracted Carina's attention. The smoke billowed from within a concentric pattern of circles superimposed upon the forest. "Something strange down there."

"Let me see." Bao rose to her feet, one hand wrapped around the military blanket draped over her body. "It's cold." She sniffled. "Where?"

"There." Carina pointed at the circles.

"Strange." Bao placed her free hand on the rail to steady herself. "There are only a few villages in that region. My father barters with their elders for timber." Her brow furrowed. "I did hear disquieting stories, however - peasants fleeing a mad fortress builder. My betrothed went to Dessau to investigate."

Carina studied the lines crossing the forest. "That fortress builder must have been both mad and motivated. Raising those walls would take years, even for the legions."

Bao sunk to the floor of the basket. "I don't care. I was once a princess and a scholar. Now, I am a hunted murderess. My old love spurned me, and my betrothed was likely slain when Dessau fell. I should hurl myself from this basket before I disgrace myself further."

"Go ahead." Carina motioned at the basket's side. She was getting tired of this whining stuck-up bitch. "Still, you did pick up those keys, unlock your cell, and strike Ambrose. You could have remained right there."

"That animal sought Ptath's throne by marrying me." Bao turned her nose upward. "My intellect failed me."

"You panicked."

"To my shame, yes." Bao sniffled. "But I was already shamed by my betrothal to a Maximus. My friends refused to see me. I was an outcast."

"Welcome to the club." Carina thought a moment. "I wonder how Ambrose thought he could marry you without violating his vows?"

Bao extracted papers from beneath her robe. "Read. The Patriarch stripped Ambrose of ecclesiastical rank."

"And he was in trouble north of the Mare Imperium." A movement attracted Carina's attention. *Is that a bird? No, it's too big.* "Shit!"

"Don't employ profanity in my presence," said Bao.

"We have company," said Carina. "Another one of those flying things."

Bao curled into a ball and whimpered.

The disk flew at a tangent to the gasbag's trajectory. *Our courses do not intercept each other.* Then the alien machine altered its track. *It must have seen us.* Carina's heart pounded.

The flying disk drew near, passing below the balloon to the east. Carina discerned triangular windows in the things top dome. Disquieting shapes moved behind those panes. Then the disk flew past them to the south.

Carina exhaled. "It left. I guess we live after all." She sank to the floor of the basket. *We were beneath its notice.*

Bao uncurled herself but didn't stand. Instead, she sat and stared at Carina. "How much of what they said was true? In the dungeon."

Carina resisted the impulse to hit the bitch. Instead, she kept silent.

"I am curious," said Bao. "How did you join the army? What did you do?"

"I didn't join the army," said Carina. "I joined the Tail, as an herbalist."

"The Tail," repeated Bao. "The camp followers? You treated those disgusting women?"

"Yes." Carina's voice was brittle. "It was better than the alternative."

"Better than being a whore, you mean."

Carina's tensed. She flexed her fists. *One more word and I'll toss the bitch from the basket.* "Yes, better than being a whore. Do you think most of those women had a choice? Many of them were sold by family members or fled abuse. You have much in common with them."

"I am not a whore." Bao's voice was quiet and hard.

"Your father sold you to an Imperial Prince," said Carina. "The difference between you and the women in the camp is one of circumstance."

Tears flowed from Bao's eyes. Sobs escaped from her lips.

Now I have done it. Being stuck in this oversized hamper with a mercurial stuck-up bitch of an aristocrat held no appeal. "Stop that."

Bao continued sobbing.

"Quiet! I don't want to listen to you." Carina balled her hand into a fist and held it before the woman.

Bao's eyes widened. She shrank against the basket. "Don't hurt me."

"Then stop bawling. Crying doesn't solve anything."

"You are a hard woman," said Bao through her tears. "Have you never loved? Were you never married?"

"I have loved," said Carina, "more than once. And I was married." Painful images of Johan appeared in her skull, his long tanned shirtless body flexing as he chopped wood. The gleam in his eyes as he made an off-color joke. His blackened corpse after the Soft Rot took him. "He died." Exhausted, Carina fell against the basket's side. Her eyelids drooped.

Carina climbed the riverbank, carrying a pair of fat trout. At the edge of the woods, she paused and rubbed her belly. Seven months.

"Hi, Honey." Johan emerged from the shadows, shirtless and sweating, body gleaming in the sunlight, double-bladed woodman's ax in his right hand. "You caught us dinner." He rubbed his belly.

"How'd your day go, dear?" Carina rubbed her body against Johan's, savoring the feel of his flesh and the heat of his body.

Johan wrapped a muscular arm around her midsection, sending a thrill through Carina's body. "I cut things, same as always." A mischievous smile appeared on his face. "Found something for you."

"What?" Carina snuggled closer. "Tell me."

"I'll show you. It's in the cabin."

They walked across the brilliant green meadow to the cottage, with a packed dirt floor, two rooms, and a loft. Carina busied herself at the stove, frying the fish with herbs while Johan disappeared into the back room. Rattles and bangs emerged from behind the closed door. Whatever did he find? Sometimes, her husband found things in the Kirkwood Forest: rare plants, odd animals, and abandoned equipment. Once, he'd found a mule. Another time he'd returned home in a battered skiff. They'd sold both.

The bangs and thumps ended, replaced by deep, raspy breathing. Whatever he found, it must be heavy. How did he move it to the house? The fish were ready. Carina placed them on a bed of greens. This should invigorate him. "Dinner!"

No answer. Carina left the plate and tapped the other door.

"Not ready," said the breathy voice. A long gasp followed the words.

"You sound exhausted," said Carina. "You need to eat." She opened the door.

The room was dark with a dank smell, almost like a cellar. A crude crate dominated the center of the chamber. Johan's blue eyes gleamed at her from across the room.

"What is this? Why are the windows covered?"

"You shouldn't have come in. It's not ready yet." Did the voice come from Johan – or the box?

Carina yanked the blind from the nearest window, filling the chamber with light. Then she screamed. Dark blotches marred Johan's skin. He raised a blackened hand to shield his face from the light. "You shouldn't have done that." His voice was a rasp. "It doesn't like the light."

"What doesn't like the light?" Carina's voice became a high-pitched shriek. "What did you find?"

Johan's head fell back against the wall.

Sizzling sounds came from within the crate. Carina turned as dark spores shot into the air.

"Found them in a hollow." Johan's voice was weak, barely audible. "I was hungry, and I took a bite. I saw things in my head. Figured they were like those mushrooms you planted."

Carina put her hands to her face. Then she screamed.

Carina opened her eyes. Bao's pert visage loomed over her. The aristocrat held a cloth in one hand. "You startled me. You were asleep, and then you started thrashing."

"Bad dream," said Carina. She hadn't dreamed of Johan in over a year. Despite her ministrations and potions, the Rot claimed Johan's life in less than a week. Then it infected her. She expected to die then. Instead, the fungoid contagion slammed against the blocks placed on her by the Churches mages and knocked a chink in them. *But the cost was too much.* Johan was gone. The baby was gone. Unable to dwell in the house-turned-tomb, she sold the property and departed.

"I'm sorry."

"Don't be." Carina touched her face. "Pain doesn't seem as bad."

"The swelling is reduced." Bao took a breath. "But now we have another problem. The fire is extinguished, and the gasbag is losing altitude."

I should have anticipated this.

She blinked and focused on the nozzle overhead. It should have been spitting a gout of flame twice her height. Instead, she saw nothing. She tapped the metal canister of fuel. Empty. "We're out of fuel."

"That is obvious," said Bao.

Carina pulled herself to a standing position and peered at the ground. Treetops rose to within a few hundred yards of the gasbag's basket. She glanced east. Upper Kheff's plateau was a blue line in the distance. *Three hundred miles? Four hundred?* "How big is Soraq?"

"From Upper Kheff to the Shadow Sea is a thousand miles or more," said Bao. "I judge we have traversed a quarter of that distance, perhaps less." She sniffed. "I studied geography at Hermosa."

"Good for you." Carina scanned the forest. A muddy brown river made a great arc to the north of their current position. Ahead, another stream passed through a wide swath of exposed reddish dirt with a few crude huts clustered to one side. "It looks pretty wild down there."

"This portion of Soraq is a tapestry of tribes descended from nomads," said Bao. "They distrust outsiders."

The gasbag reached the cleared area and inexplicably gained a bit of altitude. Maybe another hundred feet. Not enough to provide much comfort.

"I do not fancy striking a tree in this basket," said Bao as they passed the cleared area.

Carina winced at the mental image of branches piercing the basket and its occupants. *It would be like getting skewered by a knight's lance.*

A range of timber-covered hills loomed ahead of them. Some of the treetops rose higher than the gasbag's current altitude. She spotted a swamp. But what were those regular mounds on the hill's western slopes? They looked artificial. "I think there's a city ahead," said Carina.

"Let me see." Bao pulled herself to an upright position. She stared at the rectangular mounds to the west. Then she stared north. "I wish we had a spyglass."

Carina reached into a cramped locker and found a long tube. "Here."

She handed the instrument to Bao. "The crews in these things wouldn't be much use without a glass."

Bao accepted the telescope and scanned the northern horizon. "I cannot hold this steady, and the image goes in and out of focus. But I believe Umar is north of us." She gestured towards the rectangular mounds. "That makes this place the old imperial city of Posthumous."

"Posthumous? That's a strange name for a city. And it's not even on the main river."

"Posthumous is the site's current name," said Bao. "Before then, it was called Plautus, and that creek beside it was the Turpin's main channel. The city was abandoned when the river changed its course. Plautus became Posthumous, the corpse town."

"Depressing," said Carina. "What of Umar?"

"An overgrown village, ruled by Jahir Said Khalil, nephew to Pasha Majid Babul Khalil." Bao's face twisted in disgust. "The nephew is a monster, worse than his uncle, preying on river traffic, robbing and murdering boatmen as the whim strikes."

"So, we have a choice between a dead city and a live one filled with marauders," said Carina. "I wonder if Jahir keeps a garrison at the corpse town."

Bao considered the question. "Doubtful. Posthumous is regarded as accursed."

"Well, we shall learn soon enough if Posthumous retains any living inhabitants." The gasbag reached the hills, nudged by a gentle air current between two wooded peaks, mere yards above the canopy. Ahead rose the crumbled, vine-covered buildings of Posthumous. Great trees rose from fissures in the streets. But there were many clear areas. *We might barely make that square on the city's south side - if we can clear this last stand of trees.*

The gas bag dropped. So did the terrain. But not enough. A massive bole loomed in their path. "We're going to hit! We'll be killed," shouted Bao.

"Get down!" Carina pushed Bao to the basket's floor and wrapped her wrists around the support ropes. "Hang on!"

The basket slammed into the canopy. Thin branches and flat leaves slammed against Carina's body and the basket's underside. Then the hamper slammed into a branch thicker than Carina's thigh with a massive 'crunch.' The basket tilted, bounced, and pulled free of the vegetative embrace in a shower of twigs and leaves, still canted at a severe angle. The collision had severed two of the support ropes.

Now the ground grew ever closer. The basket missed the top of a second tree rising from the plaza's edge and passed over a heap of rubble. Shrubs, stones, and debris littered the open area. "Climb," Carina shouted to Bao as the compartment neared a bush.

Bao pulled herself into the rigging as the hamper struck. There was a jolt, and the plant was behind them. The gasbag slowed. Another collision, this time with a tree. The hamper swung, skittered along the ground, and stopped. And then the fabric above them began to fall.

LABYRINTH WAR XXXIII – Git-Vik

'The People fled the certain destruction of our old civilization only to find a world with an already destroyed civilization. Now, the People's best hope is the remnants of a technology we do not fully understand.'

- Coordinator Brik-Jute

Git-Vik's muscles burned as he heaved the dead bipedal vermin into Brik-Jute-Shul's feeding maw. The task, while necessary, was also demeaning - thrall work. But thralls were in short supply in the aftermath of this operation.

Git-Vik attempted not to dwell on that aftermath. Two shulls were destroyed, bringing the total lost in this region to four. Devastating. Catastrophic. The Construct's defenders murdered seven of the nine People on the expedition and all but four of the thralls.

Git-Vik scuttled to Brik-Jute-Shul's open hatchway.

Obtaining the Construct's Core was the purpose of this entire operation. That Processor would be linked to the Core of the absurdly oversized Parent Construct across the liquid mast west of this location. The Parent Construct could be controlled to fabricate multiple technological devices. Gotemik civilization would no longer be dependent on improvised devices and salvaged relics.

Case in point: leaking organs and damaged implanted machinery lined the access tube to Brik-Jute-Shul's crew compartment, inflicted by two darts filled with primitive chemical explosives designed to detonate on contact. Such damage would not have occurred if they'd possessed proper components.

Git-Vik inspected a blackened pump attached to a swollen feeder vein. The non-functional mechanism required immediate removal. The Gotemik emitted the equivalent of a sigh and selected suitable pincers and clamps from the pouch at its side. His manipulative appendages made three cuts to remove the device, and three clamps to cinch the connecting veins. Vile fluid from the swollen organs pooled around the Gotemik's crab-like legs as it worked.

"I hurt, I hurt, I hurt!" Brik-Jute-Shull's access tube contracted, almost trapping Git-Vik.

The Gotemik retreated to a position a few body lengths from the agitated Shul. "Brik-Jute Shull!"

"Git-Vik?"

"Yes."

"I hurt!" The Shull's hull creaked and groaned as hull plates expanded and contracted.

"Brik-Jute-Shull restrain your movement to prevent further damage. Kit-Zune will arrive shortly with additional components."

"I – I will try." Brik-Jute-Shull's convulsions subsided.

Git-Vik turned to fetch more components – and found itself confronting a vermin warrior partly encased in metal.

The creature loomed over the Gotemik, a long, metal-tipped shaft clenched in its manipulative appendages, more than capable of piercing Git-Vik's carapace. An animal howl escaped its head.

Git-Vik manipulators seized small objects on the ground and hurled them at its assailant. One stone clattered off the vermin's head covering. Another struck an appendage clenching its weapon. The creature howled in pain or anger.

Git-Vik spied a portable power unit among the tools. Its manipulators grabbed the tool just as the metal spike on the vermin's weapon rammed into its carapace. Pain filled him. Then the prongs of the activated power unit contacted the creature's metal shell.

The creature convulsed and collapsed.

Git-Vik pulled the shaft from his carapace. Yellowish fluid bubbled from the break until the Gotemik slapped an adhesive patch over the injury. The pain subsided.

The vermin moaned. Its limbs twitched.

Git-Vik pulled a piercing instrument from its pouch. He could terminate the vermin now. However, this specimen was strong and skilled in combat. And they were short on thralls. Instead of terminating the creature, Git-Vik reached for a control collar salvaged from a dead servitor. A hasty inspection showed no obvious signs of damage, though that meant little given the abysmal equipment on this sphere. Three quick motions secured the collar around the creature's neck.

A commotion drew Git-Vik's attention to the Constructs entrance. Kit-Zune came into view trailed by two thralls supporting either end of a fat cylinder. Git-Vik's optical sensors focused on the canister. That had to contain the Construct's core.

Kit-Zune scuttled over to Git-Vik, the pouches on his carapace stuffed with salvaged components. "The Core is secured. The carrier possesses sufficient power and nutrients to sustain it indefinitely." The new arrival took note of the collared vermin. "What transpired here?"

"This creature assaulted me," said Git-Vik. "I was fortunate to defeat it."

Kit-Zune was silent for a moment. "Your fortune defies probability. You survived the previous expedition and located this construct. This retrieval operation resulted in the demise of every Gotemik save you and me. And now you overcome a vermin warrior in combat."

An acidic sensation filled Git-Vik's body. Gotemik distrusted excessive individual good fortune. "My fortune is augmented with clear thought and advanced preparation. It is not extraordinary."

Kit-Zune considered Git-Vik's statement. "Accepted." Git-Vik detected a note of dubiousness in its response. "What does your 'clear thought and advanced preparation' say about our current situation?"

"A large concentration of vermin equipped with the primitive explosive weapons that destroyed two Shulls will arrive here within a day cycle." Git-Vik plucked one of the vermin's explosive darts from the ground and held it before Kit-Zune. "If we remain here, they will terminate us. We must restore Brik-Jute-Shull's flight capacity."

"Agreed. I lost two thralls retrieving the Core." Kit-Zune motioned, and the parts-laden servitor dropped its bag between the Gotemik. "I believe we have sufficient components to expedite Brik-Jute-Shull's repairs."

The Shull convulsed as Kit-Zune finished speaking.

Git-Vik poked through the parts and located a suitable pump.

Later that day, Brik-Jute-Shull climbed unsteadily into the air. Moments later, an indicator attracted Git-Vik's attention. "We approach another airborne object."

The Shul's course took it past a primitive airborne contraption kept aloft with heated air.

"These creatures display sophistication comparable to the polity designated 'Celthania,'" said Brik-Jute-Shull.

"They are vermin," said Kit-Zune. "I suggest we destroy that conveyance."

Git-Vik consulted the instruments. "No need. The device is losing altitude and will soon crash. Besides, we cannot spare the power."

"Conceded," said Kit-Zune.

Brik-Jute-Shul crossed the mountains and headed for Tet-Gheg-Vu.

LABYRINTH WAR XXXIV – Octavos

'Gawana was wise to choose me as a Lord; with my guidance, it has circumvented the barriers to its growth. Soonlar will be within the maze within a century, and the Empire will follow within a thousand years. Someday Forma will be enclosed within Gawana's walls. Perhaps I shall visit the Palace of Chains.'

- excerpt from a letter from Titus Maximus to Doctor Isabella Menendez

Octavos's fingers flew across the strings of the lyre, creating a cheerful melody.

"That's good," said an indistinct figure across the fire from the musician.

"I don't like that song. Play another!" This speaker was a thin Kheffian.

Octavos obliged. But though he knew he struck the strings in the right sequence, the notes seemed wrong. And across the fire, his audience began to grapple with one another. The Kheffian kicked and twisted, knocking his assailant over the blaze next to Octavos.

Octavos tilted his head, intent on the flaw with his music. Maybe the lyre was out of tune? Was the neck warped?

The downed man's arm swept across Octavos's torso, striking the instrument. There was something wrong with the limb. It was chalk-white and scabrous. Unwillingly, his eyes traced the limb to a deeply gouged neck attached to a face missing an eye and half the skin on one cheek. Heart pounding like a drum, Octavos focused on the Kheffian, noting a great gaping gouge in the man's chest oozing ichor.

Octavos's fingers slipped from the lyre. Undead heads rotated to face him.

"Keep playing," said a rasping voice.

"We like it," said the pale thing next to him.

But his fingers refused to move.

"If we can't have the music," said the rasping voice, "then we'll have the musician." Clammy hands grabbed Octavos and tore at his flesh.

Octavos awoke in darkness, tangled in his blanket. *Another nightmare. I play for people and then they die.* He reached for the lyre. *I will remedy this.* He carried the case to Japi's cluttered deck. He raised it overhead and tried to hurl it into the water. *Let it sink into the river and be eaten by worms.* But his arm refused to move.

"Are you going to stand there all night," Casein's voice asked from behind him.

"I want rid of it," said Octavos. "My music has brought nothing but false hope to doomed people."

"That's not true." Casein clambered over the bundles until he reached the musician.

Octavos shot Casein a venomous glance. "What do you mean? I played happy songs for the refugees in Dessau, but they were slaughtered before dawn. Those who heard my music at River House likely died the next night. And at Pathak, I didn't even quit the field before those things came and killed everybody. It is the same each time: I play music, lift people's spirits, and then they die. Horribly."

Casein shook his head. "No. Those people were going to die anyhow. You're playing made no difference there. You did something else."

"What?" The word escaped Octavos's mouth as a sob.

"You reminded them life isn't always a complete shithole. Your music gave them happiness and lifted their spirits, if only for a moment. That is priceless,"

"It didn't save them." Octavos's body trembled.

"No, it didn't. Nothing could have saved those people."

Octavos dropped the lyre case on the deck. "I don't know if I can play it again."

"You will." Casein knelt and lifted the case. "Until then, I'll hold onto this. Now get some sleep."

Octavos returned to the hutch, rearranged his blankets, laid down, and closed his eyes. He slept without dreaming.

The next morning, Casein and his crew greeted Octavos with their usual banter at the cookpot. Octavos nodded, made a few flat comments, and sat on a large bale, watching the forest creep past. Long green streamers hung from the branches. He spotted patches of brilliant purple and red flowers tucked among the boles. Unseen birds cawed at one another. Shrubbery rustled as hidden animals moved through the vegetation. A long snake lazed on a branch overhanging the river. But to Octavos, the scenery was as bland as the gruel in his bowl.

The river curved, and the forest fell away, replaced by a dead orange waste more than a mile across.

Goji came and sat next to Octavos, bottle in hand. "The peasants did that." He motioned at the dead area. "They came and burned the forest to make farmland, but this soil is piss-poor. Two or three years later, their crops failed, so they left. You see these places all along the river."

"Is there any good farmland here?" asked Octavos with no real interest.

Goji stroked his chin. "Naw, not around here. Ahead, it all turns to swamp. The good cropland is to the north or along the coast." He took a long swig from the bottle. "Want some?"

Octavos took the bottle and tilted it to his lips. To his surprise, it held tea instead of booze. He swallowed a small slug. "Thanks."

They sat and watched the forest replace the dead area for a while. Then Goji left to take the tiller.

Octavos continued to stare at the scenery. Goji's words played through his mind. Somebody else had said something similar. Octavos's brow furrowed in thought. Mecon. Mecon complained about how poor Soraq's poor-quality earth stymied the Child's growth.

But Mecon didn't have a choice because Casein chose the site.

"Feeling better?" Casein sat on the bundle next to Octavos.

"Not really," said Octavos. "Kind of dead inside, like there's a hole."

Casein nodded. "That happens."

"How do you deal with it?"

"Discipline. Routine." Casein stretched. "That's the army way."

Another dead patch appeared. This one sported the frame of a large hut near the riverbank. "It was you, wasn't it," Octavos asked.

"What was me?" Casein shot Octavos with a curious look.

"My father sent you here with a Seed to spread Gawana's glory. You couldn't disobey, but the idea didn't sit well. So, you planted the Seed in a location that would constrict its growth: mountains it couldn't climb on two sides and piss-poor dirt on the third. The best spot would have been the hill country west of Gand."

"Kid, you think too much." Casein's expression was unreadable, even for a bard like Octavos. "And the Sand Runners were on maneuvers west of Gand when we planted the seed." He rose to his feet.

More long slow days came and passed. Octavos spent them watching the forest crawl past or fishing off Japi's stern. He never caught anything. The others didn't trust him with the steering oar. The lyre remained hidden. Casein remained supportive, but incommunicative.

"Ok boss, I'm pretty sure this is it." Goji pointed at a narrow channel jutting away from the Turpin. Brown juice trickled from his lip, a byproduct of the root he was always chewing. He shrugged. "Well, I'm sort of sure, anyhow."

Casein eyed the gap. His jaw moved. "What about you, Luther?"

The Avar stared at the opening and then turned to Casein with a grin. "Could be. Goji's the one from Soraq, not me."

Goji spat into the river. "Hey, I'm from Quimb. My cousin Bando was the riverman, not me."

"Bando's dead," said Casien. "So, I guess we'll go for it. Luther, get on the steering oar."

Octavos abandoned his fishing pole. "Why are we leaving the main channel?"

Casein glanced at him before returning his attention to the gap. "Because if we stay on the Turpin, we'll pass through Umar."

"Pirate den," said Luther as he climbed to his perch beside the steering oar. "Ruled by Jahil Said Khalil, a nephew of the local Pasha. Nasty bastard."

"Oh." Octavos thought a moment. "Wouldn't these pirates have lookouts on bypasses such as this?"

Luther looked at Casein. "Kid could be right, boss."

Casein nodded. "Keep your eyes peeled."

Goji nodded. "Should I break out a couple of the Specials?"

"We won't need them."

The Japi slid into the cutoff. Octavos could almost touch the shore to either side.

"There, boss." Luther pointed at a massive deadfall blocking the stream, barely a foot above the water. "We'll be half the day chopping through that."

Octavos spotted a slimy patch of water to the right. "Maybe we can go through there."

Luther's eyes narrowed. "Looks a little obvious."

Something splashed. Octavos pointed. "I see a boat."

"Where?" asked Casein as a spear arced out of the shrubbery and stuck quivering in the deck.

Brown-skinned men with long spears emerged from concealment.

"Get down, kid," ordered Luther. A crossbow appeared in his hands.

"This can go two ways," Casein called to the men. "I don't want to fight."

"Then we take everything you got," said a tall man with shoulder-length dreadlocks. Necklaces made of teeth covered his chest. Brown drool dripped from his lip. He lifted his spear.

"You don't want to do this," said Casein.

The pirate's speaker grinned and stepped towards the Japi, spear raised for a throw.

Casein dodged to the side.

Goji popped out of the cabin and let loose with a crossbow bolt that took the leader square in the chest.

One marauder hurled a spear that just missed Octavos and prompted a cry from Goji.

Luther somehow materialized behind the pirates. He stabbed one in the back and cut the throat of a second in a fountain of bright red blood.

"Think that's all of them, boss," said Luther. Blood dripped from his sword. Red stains marred his tunic. None of the fluid came from Luther. Goji sported a long gash along his forearm.

Octavos was simultaneously fascinated, repulsed, and indifferent to the pirate's corpses. *Am I becoming a monster?*

"Maybe." Casein scanned the swamp.

"We could take their boats," said Luther. "If any did get away, they'll be stuck here without them."

"Good idea," said Casein. "We'll tie them off the stern."

Circumventing the deadfall was a chore. A low hillock rose past the obstruction, with the stream making a long turn around it. "Probably their base," said Luther.

"Shut up," said Casein.

Above them, the grass rustled.

"Come out," said Casein. He repeated the statement in a local dialect.

The grass parted. Two young and once-pretty women stared at the Japi with dead eyes. "You killed them," said the taller one. Jet black hair covered her otherwise exposed breasts.

"Will you kill us?" asked the shorter one. A stained pastel dress covered her frame.

Luther and Casein glanced at each other. Then Casein looked at the women. "Can you cook?"

"Yeah, we can cook," said the tall girl.

"You won't hurt us?"

"Get on board," said Casein. "Goji, Luther, go check out the camp."

"There's nothing there," said the short girl.

"They just sent a bunch of stuff out yesterday," said the tall girl.

Luther and Goji returned with a few bits of clothing and weapons. "Nothing, boss."

"Let's get moving," said Casein.

A fat snake fell from an overhead branch to the deck. Goji beheaded the reptile with a single swipe of his sword and kicked the carcass to the girls, who sat upon it with small knives.

"Looks like we eat snake tonight," said Casein.

Octavos stared at the intertwined branches over the Japi and wondered what else lurked in those limbs. "How long is this cutoff?"

"Pretty long," said Casein. "This was the Turpin's main channel a couple of centuries back. We should reach Posthumous in a few days. A few more days and we'll be back on the Turpin."

In the prow, the girls paused in their butchery and stiffened. A few quiet words passed between them.

"Posthumous," Octavos asked. "Strange name. Is it a burial ground?"

"Sort of," said Casein. "Until the plagues forced its abandonment, Posthumous was the imperial city of Plautus."

"Plautus," said Octavos. "I know that name."

"You should," said Casein. "One of your imperial ancestors founded it."

"Yes, the second Titus, before he claimed the throne." Octavos fell silent as he recollected more of Plautus's history: the old Maximus Emperors had sent their political foes here to die, the victims of swamp fevers and jungle beasts.

"Well, I must say the girls are better cooks than that cousin of yours," said Luther to Goji as they gathered around the stewpot that evening.

Goji glared at him. "I should never have let Daki join us. His wife will kill me."

"Daki was lost at Dessau?" asked Octavos.

"No, the Gotemik got him." Goji stared into the fire. "This jaunt cost me two of my kin."

"They knew the risks." Luther's sleeve fell back as he reached for the [pot, exposing a crown tattoo on his bicep.

Octavos stared at the symbol. "What's that?"

"What's what?" Luther caught Octavos's gaze. "Oh, that's my old unit badge."

"I don't recognize it. Were you in an Auxiliary unit?"

Luther gave Octavos a level look and came to an internal decision. "No, it's the mark of the Conon Royal Guard."

"Conon? But they're an imperial fief now." Realization struck Octavos like a hammer blow. His eyes widened. "You fought for Traag."

"No, I fought for Conon."

"But"-

"Traag was an alliance held together by murder and fear." Luther's gaze went distant. "Traag's sorcerers killed half the damn country. I did what I could to keep the other half alive."

"I helped him," said Goji.

"You fought for Traag? But you're from here." Octavos waved his arms. "Soraq."

"I was a servant to Pasha Dar Em Zeer's third nephew Caliel," said Goji. "The Pasha sent Caliel north to negotiate with Traag. It didn't go well. Caliel got himself killed and I got drafted. That was how I met Luther."

"My Captain thought Goji could be useful," said Luther, "and paired him with me. He was right."

"We went on missions together," said Goji. "Pakar, Drakkar, even Permia." He shivered. "Damn, but that place was cold –

even the mountains there are made out of ice. Then the sorcerers got suspicious so we ran."

"I found them after my return from Gawana," Casein settled himself on the group. "I needed soldiers, but too many legionnaires knew me from the old days for me to remain anonymous."

More deadfalls and detours hampered their progress the next four days, and the hour was closer to sunset than noon when the crumbling, vine-covered walls of Posthumous hove into view.

"What the hell is that?" Goji pointed at a massive mound of fabric rising from the overgrown town square. "Has some mad mountebank claimed this place?"

Octavos stared at the mass of billowing cloth. "If so, he needs lessons in erecting a tent."

"Not a tent," said Casein. "That's an imperial gasbag. See the basket off to the side?"

"But what's it doing out here," Octavos asked. *Did the nomads or these Gotemik take Ptath?*

"I want it," said Casein. "Pull into that wharf."

Luther looked at Casein. "We're not alone here, boss."

"I know," said Casein as Japi contacted the stone dock. "But I don't figure they'll give us any problems."

"The gasbag is draped over a tree," said Luther.

"Bring axes," said Casein as he stepped onto the dock. The others followed him ashore.

Ants crawled under Octavos's skin as they entered the ruins. Every sound made his heartbeat intensify. Each building housed unknown menaces. *How are the others so calm?* A stone toppled from a nearby wall. Shapes moved among the rubble. A chicken scurried across the flagstones. *River pirates? Renegades? Refugees?*

A slender figure in once fine clothes popped from behind a collapsed civic hall and moved towards Casein's party with determined strides. A woman, Octavos realized. She looked familiar.

The woman planted herself in front of Casein. “I demand passage from this place.”

I know that voice. “Bao?”

LABYRINTH WAR XXXV – Carina

'We thought being sent here meant we would live. Instead, we traded a swift death for a slow one.'

- Statement carved into a wall in the abandoned city of Posthumus.

"Who are they?" asked Bao. She and Carina crouched behind a broken wall. "Deserters?"

Carina studied the band making their way through the ruined city. "The big one up front is Cam. He trained the Tail in swordcraft during the voyage along the Tefnu."

"He is a legionnaire?"

"Former legionnaire," said Carina. "He has the tattoo of a Pilus Primus. Now, he works for a merchant in Arcos."

"Arcos. A prosperous land outside the Empire." Bao stood.

"Get back here! What are you doing?"

"I have had quite of these dirty peasants," said Bao. "I am tired of sleeping on stone, evicting snakes from my bedroll, and dining on bugs." She moved towards Cam's party with determined strides.

She's daft. Carina took note of a thin man creeping among the stones above her. *But she's also right. This overgrown rock heap offers nothing.* Another figure skulked past her position. *And the locals are not exactly hospitable, either.* Thus far, they'd tolerated the pair from fear of her sorcery.

Bao reached Cam and planted herself square in the big lout's path. They exchanged words. Cam seemed more bemused than convinced. Then one of Cam's flunkies emerged from the pack and said something to Bao. A rapid exchange flowed between Bao, Cam, and the new fellow. Then the stupid chit pointed at the rock behind which Carina lurked. *Great.*

Carina emerged from her hiding spot and walked across the flagstones.

"We're just here for the gasbag," said Cam.

"I am leaving with my betrothed." Bao wrapped herself around Cam's flunky. He looked cute, in an aristo way. Also, familiar. *Wait. Wasn't her 'betrothed' some Maximus cousin or other?* Carina frowned in concentration. Octavos. That was the name.

"I can't take you back to Ptath." Cam shifted his feet. "I have business in Arcos."

"Arcos is acceptable," said Bao. "It will make an excellent location for our honeymoon."

Cam took note of Carina. "Who's this?"

"That is my servant, Carina Menendez."

Both Cam and Bao's beau pinned Carina with their gazes. *Servant? Why, that little stuck-up snob!* Carina's cheeks grew warm.

Bao's 'betrothed' managed to get his mouth under control. "Any relation to Doctor Isabella Menendez?"

"My grandmother." Carina's words were clipped. *How do they know so much about me? Did they know my grandmother?*

"She is an exceptional servant with special talents." Bao directed her gaze at Carina. "Show them."

Oh, I'll show them. I'll show you too. Carina mentally recited three focusing cantrips in quick succession. Then she held out her hand and focused her will. A tiny ball of flame appeared above her palm and then vanished.

Bao's beau looked at Cam. "Is this fate or what? Just like the first expedition."

What first expedition? What the hell is going on?

"It might not be fate," said Cam, "but it's something. And the first expedition was no picnic." He turned to Bao. "Ok, princess, you and your servant," he glanced at Carina, "can come with us. But right now, I want that gasbag."

"You want, we have," said a new voice. Carina inwardly groaned. The voice belonged to the thin-limbed man called 'Spider' because of the sticky traps he made to catch small animals and his habit of lurking in high places. He was also the closest thing these wretched outcasts had to a leader.

"Let's talk," said Cam as more figures emerged from the rubble.

A feminine squeal came from behind Cam's party. Two pretty girls approached, one running full tilt for Scratch, a refugee who'd somehow kept a vegetable patch going in this dreary place of rain and poor soil.

A back-and-forth ensued. Spider insisted that Bao and Carina were valuable property, which prompted the princess to throw an unholy fit. Cam offered to trade them straight across for the two girls, except the one had wandered off somewhere with Scratch. In the end, Spider settled for the girls, the two prams, and a small crate of ironmongery.

Bao declared the price an insult, but everybody ignored her. She threw a second tantrum at Cam's boat - three long dugouts side by side with a deck between them and a wicker hut on top. "This is not acceptable!" Bao poked Cam in the belly with her index finger. "That is a floating hovel, not a proper barge!"

Cam should just drop the ungrateful bitch in the river.

Instead, Cam's head swiveled between tiny Bao and the shabby boat. "You're right," he said. "I'm getting damn tired of crawling in and out of that hutch." Cam turned to his men and barked orders. By dusk, the ratty-looking hut was gone, and a pile of split planks was on the deck.

That night, Cam's crew, Bao, Carina, and the inhabitants of Posthumous sat around a large fire and dined on snake stew. Cam and his crew remained close-mouthed about their 'expedition.' Bao didn't explain how she and her 'servant' – *thank you very much, bitch!* - had come to be here in a gasbag, nor why Arcos was a more palatable destination than Ptath. So, instead, they discussed the war.

"So, these 'Gotemik' killed most of the nomads," said Carina, "but not before the nomads mauled the army. Last we heard; Prince Thomas chased after the bunch that sacked Dessau."

"And he'll catch them, too," said Casein, "unless they flee into Soraq."

Bao faced Octavos. "Play us a song?"

Octavos paled. "No, not tonight. I'm tired." He rose to his feet and vanished.

The party dissolved after his departure.

It took half the next day to salvage the gasbag. Amazingly, the great wad of cloth folded into a bundle small enough to fit into the gondola, though it took Cam's entire crew to move the thing.

Gasbag packed, Cam's men took two days to build a proper cottage – three rooms, end to end – to replace the former hut. They also stuffed the deck cargo into the pontoons.

"The main hall." Casein's sweeping motion took in a long, narrow room with curved sides, a skinny central table, and bunks to either side. A hearth squatted atop a patch of flagstones next to a door that opened into a forward cabin. "That's my digs. Stay out."

"Boss is putting on airs," said Goji.

Luther slugged Goji in the arm. "He's just tired of smelling your farts."

A ghost of a smile crossed Octavos's face at the jest.

Bao made a face.

"In recognition of your status," Cam dipped his head at Bao, "and to preserve the peace," he glared at Goji and Luther, "this chamber is for you." He showed the women a cabin at the Japi's stern.

Bao cast a critical eye around the small chamber with its curved side walls and simple pallets along the walls. "This is acceptable, Mister Cam."

"Glad you think so." Cam started to leave but paused. "The name is Casein, by the way. Cam is just what I called myself in Kheff."

"Casein," said Bao. "A minor aristocratic family in Niteroi. My father once proposed marrying my sister to a Tiberius Casein." Bao cast a sharp look at Octavos. "The betrothal was called off."

The remark poleaxed Casein. Then, without saying a word, he turned on his heel and departed, dragging a befuddled Octavos with him.

They spent the night aboard the Japi. When Carina awoke the next morning, they were deep into the swamps.

LABYRINTH WAR XXXVI – Octavos

'The Nations of the Plains have often invaded Soraq, conquering cities and settling the valleys. But plagues and poisonous vermin always reduce these conquests to mere enclaves absorbed into the whole, a fate Solaria did not grasp until it was too late.'

- Fulton, 'Progression of the Empire.'

"Heave!" Casein pulled the heavy cord.

Octavos's feet found purchase beneath the knee-deep mud. He leaned back.

The coarse rope bit into his palms. Before him, Luther did the same.

A sucking sound came from beneath the craft's left hull. The boat moved a foot.

"Almost got it!" Sweat poured in rivers off Luther's body. He relaxed his grip to swat at a large fly hovering before his nose.

"Again!"

The men repositioned themselves and heaved.

This time the boat pulled free of the prisoning mud berm that held Japi captive. Octavos stumbled. Luther fell into the mud with a splash.

"Let's get on board," said Casein. "The Turpin is right over there." He pointed along the murky creek.

The men slogged their way through the swamp to the boat.

Carina and Bao gave the men disgusted looks when they climbed back aboard the Japi. "Your clothes are filthy!" Bao jabbed her finger at each of them in turn. Remove those rags. This barge is dirty enough without you making it worse."

"I don't have any spare breeches," said Luther with a twinkle in his eye.

"Me either," said Goji.

"I don't care," said Bao. "Your hairy butts are preferable to that filth."

Goji grinned. "Well, if you want to see our butts that bad."

Bao's face colored.

Carina made a face. "Allow me."

"What you got?" Luther winked at the sorceress. "Magic?"

"As a matter of fact, yes." Carina stepped next to the big Avar. "Now hold still." A mystic incantation escaped the magic user's lips while she ran her hands along Luther's trousers. The muddy stains faded and vanished.

"That tickle's." Luther grinned and made obscene gestures above Carina's head. "I got something else down there for you to look at," he told the sorceress.

Mocking a sorceress is not wise.

But Carina didn't take offense at Luther's. crack. Instead, she craned her neck and smiled. "Not big enough to be worth my time."

Octavos and Casein laughed along with the rest. Bao, though, didn't laugh. "Mister Casein, these men are barbarians. And you" – she jabbed her finger at Casein's chest – "are a pig. No wonder my sister rejected your family." Bao spun on her heel and stormed into the cabin.

Casein stopped his chuckles. A deep frown marred his face. He stood silent and unmoving as Carina's spell removed the filth from his trousers and strode to the steering oar without a word.

"That did it." Luther turned to Octavos. "I feel for you, kid. That one's got no sense of humor."

"And I'm running out of patience." Carina turned her attention to Octavos. "Ok, Prince, you're next."

A tingling sensation ran along Octavos's legs as Carina worked her spell and the mud vanished. "Thank you," he told the sorceress. "That seems a useful bit of magic."

Carina's lips curved into a smile. "You're welcome," she said before turning to the rest of the crew.

Luther handed Octavos a long staff. "Time to pole this bitch to the river."

Octavos took the rod and made his way to the prow of the right-side dugout. Luther did the same on the other side, while Casein claimed the steering oar.

"Plant and walk," called Casein.

Octavos dug the pole's tip into the muddy bottom and pushed, walking towards the Japi's stern. The craft moved. Then he returned to the bow and repeated the process. The Japi broke free of the creek and emerged into the Turpin.

Octavos wiped his brow and glanced about the craft. Luther stood at the steering oar. Carina employed her cleaning cantrip on Goji, who'd responded with a sideways dance number. And Casein sat at the deck's forward edge, scowling at the river.

"What's the matter?" Octavos claimed a spot next to the big man.

"Everything. Nothing." Casein rubbed his face. "Why her?"

"This thing about Bao's sister and your nephew?"

"Yes. No." Casein raised his head and stared at Octavos. "It's about you, too - or rather your family. I spent time with my brother and his mob before going south. That damn marriage was all Tiberius would talk about. Then one of your kin came by and said it was not happening." He sighed. "Just like last time."

"What?"

"Ann. Your mother. The way it was laid out, I was supposed to marry her, not Titus. She never told you?"

Octavos shook his head. Somebody had stuffed his head with cotton.

"The Caseins started to get big back when I was a kid. My brother inherited the Claudius lands when the old man died, then picked up a seat on Carta's Council. That attracted the DuPaul's attention. They decided they wanted a bit of influence in Niteroi and offered a marriage alliance."

"Ann. My mother." Octavos's voice was little more than a whisper.

"The Maximus disagreed. That marriage would have made the Caseins too powerful. So, Cassius Maximus dropped by in person with his son while the DuPauls were on the premises, and they had a little chat. Titus and Ann bumped into each other in the hall. Love at first sight." Casein shook his head. Tears poured from his eyes. "That solved everybody's problems right there."

"But you and Ann"-

"We – there was no spark. She wouldn't have been happy. Then I joined the army and there was no damn time for a wife."

"But you were my father's friend."

"That took a while. Years." Casein rose to his feet. "I got things to see to."

The Japi drifted along the Turpin, its journey hastened by a pair of lateen sails the men raised on short masts. They passed a collection of huts to wretched to be termed a village.

"There." Goji pointed at a dark shape in a nearby cove. "A boat."

Octavos peered at the craft. "Looks like Japi has a sister," he said, noting the triple hulls and deck between them. "But the crew," he squinted.

"They're goblins," said Casein. "No big surprise, we're a day upstream from Kaapor-Cull."

"Kaapor-Cull?"

"A goblin hive," said Bao. "Their ancestors were nomads who settled in Soraq. My aunt wrote of their artisans. They are skilled carvers of wood and ivory."

"Oh." Octavos reminded himself that Soraq was a patchwork quilt of a country.

Casein pointed at a line of longhouses on the riverbank beneath a ridgetop palisade. "Welcome to Kaapor-Cull." His mouth was a straight line.

Short green-skinned creatures moved among the riverside longhouses, chopping at huge logs drawn upon the bank.

"They burn the wood." Goji pointed at a line of flames atop one of these woody behemoths. "Then they chop it out. That's how you make a dugout."

"They got visitors." Luther indicated another craft much like Japi tied to a rude wharf.

A brown-furred humanoid rose from behind a bundle on the other vessel. Octavos's blood went cold. He wobbled as visions raking claws, blood, and screams filled his head. "Rachasa." The word was a croak.

"Hunters from the south," said Bao. "Numerous rachasa dwell in the hills. They help keep the southern hordes from Soraq."

"Oh." Octavos found he was gripping the handrail so hard his hands had turned white.

Bao scanned the embankment. "No patrol boats. We can replenish our supplies."

Casein pursed his lips. "I don't like goblins." He sighed. "But I hate going to Khareet even more. And these little bastards dealt fairly with me last time."

"Avoiding Khareet is wise," said Bao. "Pasha Majid Babul Khalil's tax collectors are brutal thugs who are ever alert for plots. A wing of Khalil's palace is filled with members of prominent clans, brought there as hostages."

"Yeah," said Casein. "I know all about Khalil."

The Japi turned for the town. Goblins on the shore took note of their arrival. Some headed for the dock, while others ran for the palisade gates.

Casein faced the tallest of the green-skinned creatures as Japi docked. "We're here to trade." He rattled off a list of supplies as Luther and Goji opened crates filled with iron pots, knives, and tools.

"Know you." The goblin's lips turned into an ugly grin. Black hair thick as straw crowned its skull. "Got good stuff."

More goblins appeared; toting baskets slung from long poles. They opened each one in turn, exposing bolts of cloth, mounds of small grey fruit, dried meat, and grain.

There was no haggling. Casein dropped one crate of ironmongery on the dock. Green-skinned goblins handed three baskets of fruit and a bolt of cloth to the Japi's crew.

"That was quick," said Octavos when they were upon the river.

"Watch for patrol boats," said Casein. "Their captains like to hide them in the bushes."

Octavos stared at the river. He spotted a dugout filled with human fishermen and another crewed by goblins. A dark shape materialized as they rounded a bend: an actual boat flying an orange and yellow pennant.

"Damn," said Casein. "Scan the bank. Look for a channel or a place to hide. We're close to Lake Taj, so maybe we can bypass the bastards."

"There." Luther pointed at an opening in the wall of vegetation along the riverbank.

Goji yanked at the steering oar. The Japi slid into the new waterway.

"Maybe they didn't spot us," said Octavos.

"Maybe." Casein frowned at the close-pressed shrubbery.

"The passage splits ahead," said Luther. "Straight, or right?"

"Straight," said Casein. "We're too close to the Turpin."

The Japi glided past the junction. The channel bifurcated a second time, and then a third. And then they entered a wide expanse of black water. "Lake Taj," said Casein. "Khareet is on the north shore. We wait until dark and then follow the southern bank."

"Pasha Khalil maintains a strict curfew upon the lake," said Bao. "We will be attacked if spotted."

"I did it before," said Casein. "Twice."

Octavos steadied a spyglass on Japi's rail. A blurry line appeared just above the water. He adjusted the focus. Now he gazed upon hundreds of shacks built atop pilings rising from the lake. Another blur to the side became a massive collection of barges and boats tied together. Large buildings crowned a low hill on the mainland. "Dry dirt must be at a premium in Khareet."

"Yes," said Bao.

"You're supposed to be watching for patrol boats." Casein paced the deck behind Octavos while squinting across the water. He lacked the youth's eyesight.

"I am." Octavos scanned the assemblage of houseboats and pilings. Bright banners caught his eye. "I see two, both near the houseboats." A fine horizontal line caught his attention. "Looks like the houseboats are fenced in."

"The Pasha fears they will sail away in the night," said Bao.

"Any other patrol vessels?" A note of irritation entered into Casein's voice.

"I'm checking." Octavos moved the spyglass. The image swam in and out of focus. Was that a banner? He paused and adjusted the eyepiece. "I don't see any."

"Good," said Casein. "Let's get underway. Remember: no lights, and no sound. We stay close to the bank."

Casein and Goji raised the sails, darkened with grime. Luther took the steering oar. The Japi entered Lake Taj's black waters, keeping within a stone's throw of the southern bank. Reeds rose from the shallow's like elongated fingers. Past them skeletal trees grasped for the sky. Feeder streams emerged from the darkness.

Octavos kept the glass aimed at Khareet, though keeping it focused was challenging. The fading twilight didn't help. A bobbing orange light attracted his attention. "We might have a problem."

Casein was at Octavos's side before he finished speaking. "What?"

"Patrol boat." A sinking sensation entered his gut. "I couldn't see it before."

"My aunt mentioned the Pasha's private harbor is on the city's west side," said Bao.

"Is it heading this way?"

Octavos peered through the glass. "I can't tell."

Casein glanced at Carina. "Can your magic hide us?"

Carina tapped her foot and frowned. "Not for long. The Japi is too big."

A bright light flared from the patrol craft. Moments later another light burst from the lake's western edge. "They spotted us," said Octavos unnecessarily.

"That second light is from the outlet." Casein paced the deck. "They'll be putting out a boat as well. Try to spot it."

Octavos repositioned the spyglass. "Second boat leaving the estuary."

"Break out the specials, boss?" asked Luther from the steering oar.

"We can't take on two patrol boats and win." Casein's fist slammed into his palm. "Damn! We're so close! Khalil's fief ends at the western shore."

"How'd you get past last time?" Octavos asked.

"Bribery and Goji's cousin Bando," said Casein. "He knew one of the officers."

"That's odd," said Octavos as he peered through the glass.

"What?" Casein growled the word.

"The second boat is cutting straight for us. To box us in, they should have turned south."

Casein frowned. "That is odd. They must be trying for a direct assault. But if we can divert their course, we could put both boats behind us."

"I know an illusion which might deceive them," said Carina. "But preparing it requires time."

Casein stared at the distant lights. "We have some time. What else do you need?"

"I require a long plank, two lanterns, and some cloth," said the sorceress.

Casein turned to Goji. "Help her."

"I got a plank over here." Goji wobbled into view toting a plank wide as his torso and thrice his height.

"That should suffice. Place it by the rail."

Goji dropped the plank with a thump, resulting in a scowl from Casein.

"Find me this much cloth," Carina extended her arms. "I need those lanterns. Hurry."

Goji departed. Carina knelt and began scribing glyphs into the wood, cursing under her breath when the knife slipped. Twice she paused as if uncertain about a sigil's shape.

Casein opened a hatch into one of the dugouts and began setting braces of explosive crossbow bolts on the deck. "Might as well go down fighting, if it comes to it," he said.

"Here you are." Goji returned with two lanterns in one hand and a bundle of fabric in the other. "Anything else?"

Carina spared his acquisitions a glance. "Find me a couple of tree branches about your height and some short pieces of rope." She returned to her carving without waiting for a response.

Goji left, muttering under his breath. "Branches, she wants? Out on the open water?"

Casein handed Octavos a crossbow and a brace of specials. "Aim high."

Octavos took the crossbow and glanced at the patrol boats, now no more than a thousand yards from the Japi.

Meanwhile, Carina finished her carving and affixed both lanterns to the plank. Goji returned with two crooked branches and a bit of twine. Carina tied the branches together to make a frame, which she set on the plank and covered with fabric. *It looks ridiculous. Only a blind drunk man would take that for a boat.*

But Carina had Goji and Casein place it in the water anyhow. "This might not work." Carina stared at the bobbing plank, which looked ready to capsize any moment. "If they were closer, or the light better, it would fail. The spell will not last long."

"Do it," said Casein. Then to Luther, "Make ready to turn south."

Carina made a mystic pass. The lanterns burst into flame – and then Octavos stared at a crude copy of the Japi. The sorceress pushed at empty air and the phantom craft headed for open water.

Octavos's skin tingled. His vision wavered. *Carina cast her invisibility spell.*

Casein pointed south. Luther swung the steering oar.

Both patrol boats converged towards the fake Japi.

Carina stood rigid as a post; eyes fixed on the illusion.

Then they were past the second patrol craft and mere yards from the shore.

Carina wavered on her feet.

The tingling sensation stopped. Octavos's vision cleared.

Puzzled shouts came from the patrol craft as the illusion collapsed. The enforcers began to turn their vessel but that would take time.

"It'll be a stern chase," said Casein. "But we still need to get off the lake."

"There." Octavos pointed at a gap in the darkened forest. "That might be a bay or a river mouth."

"It'll have to do," said Casein.

Luther adjusted their course.

Octavos glanced at the patrol boats and tried to gauge the distance. "The Japi is faster than they are."

The gap grew nearer as dusk faded into night. Waves slapped against Japi's twin hulls. The wind faded. The water became glass calm, and darkness engulfed the craft. A musky scent of trees and plants filled the air. And beneath that aroma, a different odor, sharp and metallic.

Octavos couldn't see a thing. Sky, land, and water were subtly differing shades of black. *How can Luther see to steer this thing?*

A scraping sound from the left outrigger answered that question. *He can't.*

Slaps and scrapes from overhead marked an encounter between Japi's masts and overhead tree branches. An unseen branch whipped into Octavos's face. "Ouch!" Octavos's palm felt wet when he touched the wound.

"They've stopped," said Goji.

Octavos turned his head. The orange lights on the patrol boats were far behind them.

A loud 'crack' sounded as the right outrigger slammed into an invisible tree. Octavos fell, his face and chest hitting the water. Hot pain stabbed into his shoulder. His legs slipped along the deck. Then a strong hand grabbed Octavos's collar and heaved him onto the deck. "Watch yourself," said Casein.

Octavos spat water and rubbed his shoulder. "I would, if it were possible to see anything."

Another long scrape, this time from the right dugout, followed by the sound of splintering wood overhead. Sailcloth and rope settled over Octavos's head. "We won't have a boat if this keeps up."

"A little further," said Casein. "Goji check the hull on the left dugout for leaks. I'll take the right side."

Octavos extricated himself from the rope and canvas. A violet patch in front of the Japi caught his attention. "I see something." He grabbed an oar and staggered towards the bow. *Whatever it is, we don't want to hit it.*

"What?" Casein's voice was muffled.

"I don't know, but it's glowing." Octavos reached the bow. The violet glow seemed part of a lattice rising above the water, mere yards from Japi's starboard side. Octavos reached out with the oar and was greeted with a metallic 'thump.' *Metal? Out here? It should have been scavenged ages ago.*

The Japi moved and the oar skidded. Octavos's hand shot out for support that wasn't there.

"Don't touch it," said Carina's voice right as Octavos's palm slammed into something hard just below the surface.

Octavos's vision turned purple. Then it turned black.

LABYRINTH WAR XXXVII – Chimp

'Those born on the blessed Spring Equinox have golden hair, bronze skin, and pleasant temperaments. Many of these children are blessed with the divinely bestowed ability to heal, protect from evil spirits, and discern truth from falsehood. The Church seeks out such individuals, inducting them into the Radiant Order...

...Darkborn, those with the misfortune to be born on Hell Day, the Autumn Equinox, are another matter. They have pale skin, black hair, and vile attitudes that win them few if any friends. Demons whisper in their ears, compelling them to evil acts and instructing them in magics of pain and deception. Those not slain as infants live in hiding. Those apprehended are executed, sent to prison monasteries, or pressed into imperial service...'

- From 'History of the Purge.'

Dead vines tumbled to the ground Chimp heaved himself atop the crumbling wall. The elevation granted him a view of additional earthworks draped in dying vegetation – and a circular courtyard. He craned his neck at Sticks. "I found an open area with live plants and a pond."

Sticks smiled, exposing broken and rotted teeth. "Suits me. This place gives me the creeps. I'd almost rather be at Umar than here. At least that's honest fighting."

"I find it rather interesting." Shade's hollow voice came from beside Chimp. Chimp wished Bramble was here given all the weird plants, but the half-elf was sneaking through the jungle with the shifters.

The nomads managed to kill fifty thousand imperial troops before they broke and fled into Soraq with three legions under General Flynn hot on their tails. Rumor had it there'd been a three-way clash between Flynn's bunch, the locals, and the nomads at a burg called 'Umar.' Chimp would have been with them if he hadn't been attached to the Prince's staff. The vibes this place gave off creped him out.

Snuffles leaped over the wall, dropped to all fours, and started sniffing plants and rocks.

Sticks scaled the barrier like he was half spider, with Skunk hot on his ass. Blaze grunted, reached, gripped, heaved, pulled, slipped, and scraped his way to the top, only to get a giant fart in his face from Skunk. Blaze retaliated with a hard slug to the smelly scout's side.

Skunk gave Blaze a black look and fingered his knife.

Chimp didn't care for their stupid games. "With me." He picked a route towards the clearing.

"Veggies." Blaze pointed at neat rows of plants beside a cart-sized boulder.

"I call dibs," said Sticks. "I'm sick of stale bread and salt beef."

Chimps mouth watered. Army food sucked. "There's enough for everybody."

"Hold." Shade raised a hand. "Somethings not right." He pointed to a patch of churned dirt and a pile of discarded stalks at the garden's edge. "Somebodies here."

"Serf's, maybe," said Sticks.

"I doubt it," said Chimp. "We hadn't seen any since breaking camp. This is somebody else."

The scouts fanned out with their eyes open.

Snuffles popped out of the shrubbery next to a large boulder. "I smell human."

"Sammy is correct," intoned Shade. His face contorted. "I sense presences." He motioned at a boulder the size of a carriage. "This stone is not what it appears to be."

Chimp nodded. Shade wasn't much of a magician - but he did know about illusions. He peered at the boulder. It seemed off, somehow. Were the edges blurred? He dropped his gaze, taking note of the weeds and imprints in the path of beaten dirt that fringed the stone. Small prints, like those of a woman or child. He motioned Sticks over and whispered a few words. The lanky legionnaire took off at a dead run. Next, Chimp motioned to Blaze over at the pool.

The Avar stood with his back to the rock and shrugged. "There's fish in the pond. Maybe they left."

"I think you're right." Chimp motioned with his sword. "Behind you!"

Blaze didn't hesitate. He drew his weapon, spun, and plunged its tip through the boulder.

A frightened female squawk came from within the supposedly solid rock, which abruptly shimmered and transformed into a small cottage. Its door stood directly before Blaze's startled form; his sword jammed through a shuttered window.

"Come out," said Chimp. "You're surrounded."

"Don't hurt me!" The female voice had an odd accent. "There's a wounded man with me."

"Come out."

"Ok." The door opened. A shock of golden hair appeared, above a mass of cream-colored cloth. Then a woman emerged and straightened.

"Godborn," said Blaze.

The woman looked at the Avar. "I'm not hurting anybody. Let us go. There's no need to tell anybody." Her voice was melodious.

Chimp's mind filled with fog. The woman's request sounded reasonable. She wasn't hurting anybody way back here.

"Enough of that." Shade made a cutting motion.

The fog in Chimp's mind dissipated.

Skunk stepped beside the woman and slapped her hard on the head. "Stop it, witch."

"Ow! That hurt!" The woman glared at Skunk. "And you stink."

The Godborn girl's eyes widened as she spotted Shade. "Darkborn?"

"No," said Shade, "though my power first manifested on Hell Day when I sought refuge from footpads in Corber Port's catacombs. I saw things. They tested me."

Chimp blinked. Shade wasn't normally this talkative. The strange woman must have him rattled.

"You were cursed," said the woman.

"The Church thought so. They wanted to burn me. Fortunately, the army decided I could be useful." Shade sounded almost human.

Skunk made a gagging noise. "What a pair of lovebirds."

Lucinda and Shade glared at Skunk.

He got the message.

"You smell like flowers." Snuffles stood behind the Godborn, sniffing her hair. "I like."

A disgusted expression marred the Godborn's face. "Get away from me!" Her eyes narrowed. "What are you?"

"Sammy is a shifter," said Chimp.

"A shifter?" The Godborn's skin paled a fraction.

Chimp blinked and motioned at Blaze, who wrapped his beefy arms around the woman. "Now, let's start over without the witchery. Who are you and what is this place?"

The woman deflated, slumping into Blaze's grip. "Ok. I'm Lucinda of Arcos. This place was Gawana's Child."

"Gawana's Child?"

"It...grew from a seed the Masters planted."

"That's weird."

"Yes, the Child was weird and creepy and drained everything around it." Lucinda glared at Chimp. "I hated it."

"I don't blame you. This place creeps me out." Chimp nodded. "Anything else?"

The woman nodded her head at the cottage. "Simon's inside. He was the Child's Second Servant. Those things hurt him when they attacked."

"Second Servant," said Chimp. "Who was the First Servant?"

Lucinda made a face. "That was Mecon. He wasn't a good person. But Simon's different."

Chimp motioned at Blaze, who stuck his head through the door. "One man, Avar, laid out on a cot, asleep. Lots of cuts and bruises."

"Can your magic move the cot?"

"No."

Chimp wasn't surprised. Minor magicians worked minor magic. "Fine. We'll carry it, then. Blaze, Skunk, you two go grab it."

"I don't fancy lugging this guy over those walls." Skunk, of course.

"We won't have to." Chimp stared at Lucinda, who bowed her head.

"I know the way," said the Godborn.

Blaze backed out the door, holding one end of a military camp cot that doubled as a litter. A comatose Avar with yellow hair moaned and twitched on the platform.

"I wish to investigate this place," said Shade. "I sense intriguing residual energies."

Lucinda started at Shade's voice. "You sense the dying breaths of Gawana's Child."

"Dangerous?" asked Chimp.

Lucinda shrugged. "I don't know. There were places I wasn't allowed to enter."

"Huh." Chimp glared at Shade. "One hour. Snuffles, you stay with him," Maybe the shifter's nose could spot things Shade's magic missed.

"Understood." Shade stood stock still.

"I stay." Snuffles vanished into the weeds.

"This way." Lucinda motioned at a gap in the wall Chimp would have sworn wasn't there earlier. More magic? Probably.

They set off, the Godborn leading the way, Blaze and Skunk carrying Simon.

"Watch it!"

Blaze's warning came an instant too late. Skunk tripped on the slick stump and slid sideways down a short slope. Simon's legs spilled from the tilted litter.

"Ow!" Simon's eyes popped open. "Where? Who?"

"We're imperial scouts," said Chimp.

"Oh." Simon's eyes closed.

Chimp faced Skunk. "I'll hold that end up for a while." He grabbed the stretcher.

Chimp's arms were sore within the first hundred yards. After two hundred yards, the fire in the legionnaire's joints blazed so hot he could barely maintain his grip.

Blaze, for his part, didn't even break a sweat.

Simon slid back and forth on the travois, eyes opening and closing, muttering words at random. Then Blaze halted, and Chimp lifted his head to see a Centurion blocking the path with the red plume of the prince's staff on his helmet.

They waited while the Centurion trotted over to where Prince Thomas consulted with his pet Kheffian magicians and General Masters of the II Equitant.

Words reached Chimp's ear across the distance. "So, my cousin still lives, and travels westward," asked Thomas.

The female Kheffian mage bowed. "He does, Great Prince." Her features contorted. "My divinations inform me Prince Octavos is accompanied by the women who fled in the gasbag."

Chimp had a hard time keeping his face straight at that news. That spectacular fiasco had been a one-day wonder at the camp.

"Unbelievable." Thomas shook his head. "Still, it makes sense. Flight into Soraq's jungle is better than being slaughtered by the nomads. I suppose he'll go clear to the coast and book passage north. Those women, though," Prince Thomas shook his head again, "well, I could pardon Lady Ptath, though that will irk the Ambrose clan. She'll have to remain in Kheff."

Even from this distance, Chimp saw a scowl cross Uday's face.

Thomas directed his attention to General Masters. "Report."

The General saluted. "More debris, sir. Wreckage from two of those flying craft. Whoever ruled this place put up Hell's own fight."

"A fat lot of good it did them." The prince kicked a stone. "And we don't know who 'they' were."

The Centurion approached Prince Thomas. "Sir, that may not be correct." He motioned at Chimps squad.

Prince Thomas trotted over, his eyes taking in Lucinda and the man on the stretcher. "A Godborn. What role did you play in this place?"

Lucinda bowed. "An unwilling one, highness."

"Prince. I'm not Emperor yet."

Lucinda's eyes widened. She bowed deeper. "My apologies. I am Lucinda of Arcos, brought to Gawana's Child by a former legionnaire who named himself 'Cam.' He lied."

"Gawana?" Uday stroked his chin. "The great construct across the Shadow Sea?"

Lucinda glanced at the stout Kheffian. "Yes. We stand at the fringes of Gawana's dead Child, grown from a seed transported here in the past decade."

"Gawana." A distant look appeared in Thomas's eyes. "Octavos spoke of that immense labyrinth. His father vanished there."

"Titus Maximus," asked Lucinda. "The Child's Servants spoke of him on occasion."

"Who were these Servants," asked Thomas.

"I was one." Clear eyes stared at Prince Thomas from the cot. "I am Simon DuFloret, once the Second Servant of Gawana's Child."

"Simon DuFloret," asked Thomas. "Of the Avar DuFlorets, who rule the western Kirkwood?"

"Yes." Simon managed a weak nod. "Once. In another life. I sought to end Titus's life in Gawana. Instead, he made me his servitor and dispatched me here, to keep an eye on that bastard Mecon."

"Mecon?"

"The former First Servant. He was killed in the Gotemik attack."

"The Gotemik." Thomas stroked his chin. "Three of their flying craft obliterated the nomads who assaulted Ptath, and almost destroyed the city as well."

"You were fortunate." Simon coughed. "The Gotemik possesses great technological prowess. Titus waged war against them for years. Now, they turn their eyes east, to Solaria."

Simon's words prompted a prolonged exchange between Prince Thomas, General Masters, and the magicians.

A battered carriage drawn by a pair of exhausted horses pulled into the encampment while the debate raged. An attractive woman emerged from its confines and approached the debaters unnoticed apart from the sentries – and Chimp.

"Lady Bottle," said Thomas. "What brings you here? And why that title?"

"I bring grave news." Lady Bottle bowed. "His Supremacy Charles DuSwaimair the second died in his sleep two weeks ago. You must return to the Capital at once. A fast courier boat awaits in Ptath."

LABYRINTH WAR XXXVIII – Octavos

'It is the Empire's conceit to see Soraq as a barbarian nation. This view is not entirely correct...'

Fulton, 'Progression of the Empire.'

Octavos stumbled along a dim corridor with curved brown and purple walls. Shapes moved in the corner of his vision. His heart pounded at a furious pace. Rivulets of sweat ran off his body. Clicks and squeaks came from behind him, but his pursuers remained unseen.

Frantic, Octavos darted into a side passage. This opened into a long tubular hall lined with metal tables tended to by grey-skinned men and women in one-piece silver jumpsuits. "Help me!" Octavos grabbed the collar of an older man holding a multi-jointed instrument. Octavos's hand slid off the shiny fabric and the man's impassive expression did not change. Instead, the grey man pointed to a round portal twice his height at the hall's far end.

Octavos hesitated. A cacophony of clicks and squeaks from behind prompted him to run to the circular doorway. Shapes suggestive of heads and hands and beasts seemed to move in the door's tan and purple surface, shapes which dissolved even as his eyes settled on them. Behind him, the racket increased in volume. *They'll have me! What do I do?* "Open!" Octavos hammered the portal with his fists.

The doorway rolled to the side, exposing utter darkness, save for a white stage or platform two dozen paces from the entry. The stage held a stool with a familiar case propped against it. *That's* my *lyre.* Octavos's feet moved of their own accord to the stage. He flicked the case open expecting some hellish jest, but the only thing inside was his lyre. Then he was sitting on the stool holding the instrument. Then he peered into the space about the stage.

The quality of illumination improved. Octavos made out row upon row of pews or benches, occupied by silent shadowy figures staring in his direction. *An audience.* He began to play. The lyre emitted a horrid screech that made him cringe. Octavos thrummed the strings a second time. Again, the instrument screeched as though it were a beast in agony. Moreover, it writhed in his grasp like a live thing.

The instrument slipped from Octavos's hands to the floor. He stared at the lyre. It lay there, unchanged, and unmoving. Around him, the audience shifted. Revulsion filled him. *Useless. Childish.* He reached for the lyre intent on smashing it against the stage's surface. Instead, he found himself cradling the device. Again, his fingers moved across the strings. *Concentrate. Focus. Just the first notes.* This time the music flowed.

More figures filed into the chamber amid clicks and squeaks: creatures like giant lobsters with armored towers rising from their backs, and other beings that resembled centipedes with a multitude of long limbs.

Octavos's skin grew clammy at the intrusion. His music faltered and stopped. *They're monsters. Abominations. They'll kill me.* But the bizarre beings did not attack. Instead, they 'stood' in neat ranks along the wall of the auditorium.

"What are they waiting for?"

"They're waiting for you, lad," said a cracked voice on Octavos blind side.

I know that voice. Octavos turned his head. The old woman from Solace, Doctor Isabella Menendez herself, stood on the stage, hunched form encased in a black robe.

"They're waiting, but what am I supposed to do?" His voice was almost a whine.

"For you to choose." The old woman shuffled in a half circle around the musician. "You rattled them in the Child's Heart. Now they ask – was that a fluke?"

Octavos caught a whiff of a sickly sweet scent. The walls pulsated. *Oh God. I'm back in the Heart.* His pulse raced. His hands shook.

"Calm down lad. Panic solves nothing." The old woman's hands made a complex motion. A wave of coolness washed over Octavos.

'Click.' One of the centipede things tapped its appendages together. 'Click,' 'click,' other centipede things followed suit. 'Tap.' This came from a lobster monster. Then, click, click, tap.

Octavos's eyes darted from one creature to another. There was something familiar to their actions. An idea began to form.

"You're almost there, lad," said the old woman.

A pattern. No, it's a song. Octavos's fingers moved, adding the lyre's rhythms to the mix. He bound the clicks and taps together, making a unified whole, making a bizarre and beautiful song like none ever played before. The chamber pulsed. And then it was over. Silence filled the hall.

A bright yellow light appeared in front of Octavos. "You're through here, lad," said the cracked voice.

"But what did I do?"

"You revealed possibilities they'd never considered. Now go." The old woman began to shuffle across the stage.

"But what of you?"

"I have my own course," said the woman as she vanished into the shadows.

The light expanded, filling Octavos's vision.

Octavos opened his eyes. He was staring at the plank ceiling of Japi's deck cabin. Pain throbbed in his side. His stomach growled. The aches and pains grew as he rose to a sitting position.

Luther lay across the aisle from him, eyes open, staring at the ceiling. *Is he dead?* The blanket covering Luther's chest flexed a hairsbreadth. *No, he's sick.*

Octavos pulled himself to his feet. He felt wobbly. Dull plates of pain covered his body. He took a step and grabbed the doorframe. A twist opened the door, and a second step brought him onto the deck.

Casein sat on the foredeck with his knees raised, engrossed in an object perched on his legs. The big man's mouth moved, though no sounds emerged. His finger made back-and-forth motions.

Octavos took a third step and sat on a bundle. "That's my father's book you're reading."

Casein turned his head. "You're up."

"Barely. I feel like I slept a week in a briar patch."

"You pretty much did." Casein closed the book. "That thing back at the lake almost killed you. The rest of us didn't fare too well, either."

A memory of violet light against a gloomy background materialized in Octavos's mind. "What was it?"

Casein shrugged. "Carina thinks it's some broken device of the Old Races."

"Oh." Octavos motioned at the book. "What do you think?"

"Your father didn't write this. Doctor Menendez did." Casein pulled Titus's original journal from beneath the book.

"This is an Officers Book. Tribunes carry them everywhere, making notes about meetings, supplies, and tactics. Your dad kept the habit after he was discharged."

Octavos nodded. "She said as much at the end."

"I hadn't gotten that far." Casein tapped the book. "Reading is not my thing. But most of it matches what I recollect." He took on a distant expression. "It also made me remember how much of a snoop she was."

A dark blob surrounded by frothing water attracted Octavos's attention. "Looks like a shoal."

Casein craned his neck. "You're right." Then he faced the back of the boat. "Left rudder now!"

"Aye, Captain," said a feminine voice.

"Is that Bao?" Octavos asked as Casein sat a second time. *Maybe I'm still hallucinating.*

"She needed something to do," said Casein as the Japi altered course.

"Who are you talking to," Bao's voice asked.

"Me." Octavos rose to his feet and stepped to the side of the cabin. A slender figure in a dark robe with a conical straw hat stood at the steering oar.

"You're awake!" Bao tilted the hat back, exposing her nut-brown face. "Carina said you were getting better. How do you feel?"

Octavos stomach rumbled. "Hungry."

"Well, we can do something about that." Bao motioned to somebody out of sight. "Goji, take the steering oar. I have a man to feed."

Bao released the pole and started for Octavos before Goji appeared. *I must still be hallucinating. Since when does Bao like me?*

Bao wrapped her arms around Octavos's midsection. "I was so worried! You barely even breathed for days. Then you started thrashing and moving your fingers. Carina said she heard you singing last night."

"I had a bad dream." Octavos didn't move. "I performed for an audience of monsters."

"And your music soothed their vile hearts." Bao craned her neck to peer into Octavos's eyes. "And now you can perform for me." She released her grip. "But first, some food." She vanished into the cabin.

Octavos heard chopping sounds. Then Bao emerged with a wooden plate covered with diced fruit and meat.

"Small bites," she said when Octavos grasped a handful. "Eat slow."

Octavos placed a cube of fruit and another of meat in his mouth. They tasted cool. Tangy. He swallowed. "We must be close to the delta."

"We'll reach Quimb in two days," said Casein. "From there we'll head north along the coast and then cross the channel to Arcos."

"Is Japi suited for sea travel? I thought we took some damage at Lake Taj." Octavos took another bite.

"The Japi took some bangs and thumps," Casein punctuated the statement with a slap against the rail, "but we patched her up."

"My magic fixed this leaky barge." Carina lounged against the mast, eating a piece of fruit.

"And past Arcos?" Octavos took another bite of fruit, savoring the taste.

"We'll talk when we get there." Casein strode into the deck cabin. He emerged a moment later with the lyre case. "Here. If you think you're ready."

"I am." Octavos took the case. The surface felt strange under his fingers. He stared at the ever-growing number of huts and cottages along the riverbank. Tilled fields and orchards stretched into the distance.

Japi round a bend in the river and drifted past hundreds of boats ranging from fishing craft to pleasure barges tied to the piers along the river. Thousands of compact dwellings perched on a steep slope with cobblestone streets past the docks. Octavos picked out green goblins, squat dwarves, and brown humans patronizing the shops and stalls. Many of the citizens wore fine attire with a mix of colors.

"Welcome to Simba," said Casein.

"Simba seems prosperous."

"Pasha Abdulla Bayezit rules Simba. He is not a monster like Pasha Khalil," said Bao. "He understands the value of commerce and views a prosperous populace as less troublesome than an abused one."

"He sounds downright enlightened."

Teams of goblins and men kicked a ball back and forth on a grassy field.

"Football," Octavos remembered attending the games with his friends at Solace. He also remembered betting on the games – and losing.

"We invented football." Goji appeared beside Octavos and jabbed a finger into his chest. "We know the game better than anybody."

"Your Cousin Bando said the same thing right before he lost his shirt betting on football in Corber Port," said Luther.

"He was an idiot."

Many imperials were obsessed with football. Sports colleges fielded teams marked by different colors with Red, Blue, Green, and Brown being the most prominent. Fierce brawls frequently erupted between their fans over technicalities and upsets.

"I warned him the Green's team was crap," said Casein.

"Yeah."

Goji steered the Goji towards a wharf festooned with colorful flags.

"Toll station." Casein grimaced. "The Pasha maintains them along the river. We're going to get gouged."

A tall man in a bright green and yellow robe appeared on the pier and jabbered at the Japi's crew. Alongside him men in leather armor gathered, ready to jump aboard.

A cold knot formed in Octavos's gut. He leaned next to Casein. "What of the specials?"

"The Pasha's men didn't find them the last time," said Casein.

The official began reciting a prepared speech as Japi touched the pier. His men jumped aboard and poked through the bundles and crates piled on deck. "Two crates of worked iron," one yelled. Another found the balloon. "One large bale of fine cloth." Two opened hatches on the dugouts and stuck their heads inside. "Provisions," said one. "Weapons," said the other, holding aloft a crossbow.

The official turned to Casein. "Weapons?"

Casein placed his hands on his hips. "Protection. We came from upriver. Pasha Khalil's fief. Many bandits."

"Khalil!" The official spat into the water. "Worthless dog. Not civilized."

The men finished their search. One found Luther laid out in the deck cabin.

"Fever," said Casein. "He's Avar. Not tough."

"Ha! Keep him aboard your vessel. The city has plagues enough already." The official produced a tiny abacus and moved beads back and forth. He named a sum.

Casein winced and protested poverty.

Bao jumped into the conversation with an insult to the tax collector's ancestry.

"That is some woman," said the official.

"I know it." Casein put on a miserable look.

The official's tally dropped a fraction. Coins changed hands. The Japi departed.

Carina gave Octavos a cursory examination and prepared a stew which filled the cabin with an herbal aroma. They ate as the sun touched the horizon.

"Tastes strange," said Octavos after the first mouthful.

"It's medicinal," said Carina. "It will revitalize your energies."

"We stopped three times so she could root around for plants," said Casein. "She could have at least found some that tasted better."

"Eat," said Carina.

Octavos ate.

"Play me a song," said Bao.

Octavos considered. He did feel stronger. "Ok." He lifted the lyre and plucked a few strings. The notes were discordant. Wrong. In his mind's eye, Octavos remembered the stage from his fever vision, and the horrid notes his lyre had produced then.

"Go on," Bao urged.

"We need some proper music," said Casein.

I can do this. "It needs a bit of tuning." He tweaked a string, and then another. Then he tried a few simple chords. *It'll do.* From there, Octavos launched into an easy-as-dirt shepherd's song known under a dozen names.

Bao smiled. "More."

Octavos launched into 'Summer Mountain' – and missed every tenth or twelfth note. *I need to practice.* His audience didn't care. "I'm tired," he said once the song was done.

"One more." Bao curled into his shoulder.

"All right." Octavos strummed the strings, trying to think of a suitable tune. A pattern emerged from the notes, but he didn't recognize it. Except he did. *It's the music from my vision.*

"I don't recognize that song," said Bao.

"It's new." Octavos bent over the instrument and plucked its strings. The pattern came, went, and came again. Musical notes assembled themselves in Octavos's mind. *Yes. That's it.* Alien music, discordant yet patterned, flowed from the lyre. Then the pattern fragmented. Octavos played a few more notes, seeking a continuation, and then stopped. "It needs some work."

A hoarse cry came from the deck cabin, followed by a loud 'thump.' Luther appeared in the doorway. "Man, I am so hungry."

"Have some stew," said Casein.

Octavos found Casein contemplating the closed journal the next day. "Finish it?"

"Yeah kid, I finished it." Casein sounded morose. "It brought back some memories." He faced Octavos. "Tell me, did she give you anything else?"

Octavos shook his head. "No, just the book and the papers."

"Damn." Casein rubbed his forehead. "She was supposed to give you the Maximus Seal."

"The Maximus Seal," repeated Octavos. The mystical stamp that compelled loyalty. The second reason for his father's entry into Gawana – the first being escape from imperial authorities. "I thought the Eye's got it."

"I thought so too, for a time," said Casein. "But then I learned otherwise. The Doctor had it when she left Cendoza. But it wasn't on her when the ship docked at Tessa."

"Maybe she threw it overboard?"

Casein shook his head. "I doubt it. You don't just toss away things like that. Besides, they have a way of being found."

"So, you thought she'd snuck it past the Eyes somehow."

Casein nodded. "She was a damn powerful wizard."

Quimb proved larger than Octavos expected, a vast sprawling conglomeration of shacks and shops that island-hopped its way across the Turpin on a byzantine network of bridges. About half were shaky things made of rope and planks. The rest were ancient constructs of weathered stone. Likely, they'd been built back when Quimb was an imperial outpost. Crude bicycles, pushcarts, wagons, and carriages jammed narrow streets between the structures. To Octavos's surprise, some of these avenues were paved with stone.

"The overlords of Quimb maintain the old imperial road network," explained Bao. She pointed at a structure that sprawled across a nearby hilltop. "They also sponsored the Grand Academy."

Octavos furled his brows. "A couple of my instructors mentioned Quimb's Grand Academy. The Pasha's wanted their officials and courtiers uniformly educated."

"I spent a year in that place." Goji sounded wistful.

"Student?" asked Octavos.

"Nah. That was my Master Caliel. I was his servant. I did sit in on a bunch of classes. He made me take tests for him."

"Once, I dreamed of founding an Academy in Kheff." Bao sounded distant.

Octavos clasped his hand around Bao's. "Keep that dream."

Japi rounded a bend into a stretch dense with river traffic.

Octavos spotted a pack of urchins leaping from boat to boat. "You could almost cross the river without a bridge."

"Cousin Bando and I used to do that," said Goji.

Octavos took in a huge market that dominated the southern bank. Tightly packed townhouses lined the ridge behind the stalls. "There must be half a million people here."

"Yeah, if you count the goblins." Goji pointed at a mob of green-skinned creatures sawing planks in a lumber yard on the northern bank.

Enthusiastic shouts drew Octavos's attention to a field where a team of humans contended against muscular hobgoblins in another football game. At least a thousand spectators filled the stone seats.

Casein steered Japi through the tangle towards an enclave apart from the others. "Triton," he said. "Technically part of Arcos." The Japi glided to an isolated wharf.

A thin man in a purple toga emerged from an office and glared at the crew. "You can't dock here." He caught sight of Casein. "Oh, it's you."

"Yeah, Tiberius, it's me," said Casein. "The quicker we can get business taken care of, the quicker I can be out of here."

Tiberius's shoulders slumped as a long sigh escaped his mouth. "I suppose a credible cargo can be arranged. Rossum has a cargo of mangoes destined for Arcos. Will that do?"

"It will," said Casein. "I also want to look at the dispatch book. I have been out of touch for the past couple of months."

"That can be arranged." Tiberius appraised Japi's crew with a glance. "Where do you find these people?" Tiberius pointed at Bao. "That one is of the Kheffian aristocracy, or I'll eat my toga."

Bao stiffened at the comment but said nothing.

Tiberius's finger moved to Octavos. "This one is a Maximus. A by-blow? The Maximus dislike acknowledging the fruits of their amorous adventures."

Octavos's cheeks burned. He clenched and unclenched his fists. "I am not a bastard."

"Interesting." Tiberius was unaffected by Octavos's outburst. "We do get the occasional illegitimate Maximus here, but the trueborn seldom grace us with their presence."

"Happenstance brings me here," said Octavos.

"Indeed." Tiberius turned his attention to Carina. "A northerner, but one who has spent much time south of the Mare Imperium. More, one who bears the tattoos of the Arcane Cohort on her arm. An outcast?"

"I have a storied past," said Carina.

"Enough of the crap, Tiberius." Casein flexed his muscles.

"Direct as always." Another disdainful sigh escaped Tiberius's lips. "Very well. You and your menagerie can remain for the night." He pointed to a small clapboard house near the pier's base. "You stay there." He sniffed. "After you take a bath. The dispatch book will be waiting along with something to eat." Without waiting for a response, Tiberius made a precise turn and strode into the building.

"I think I dislike that man," said Octavos.

"Me too," said Carina.

"He should be flogged," said Bao.

"He married my sister," said Goji.

"Come on," Casein climbed a short ladder to the pier. "The bathhouse is this way."

"You're not concerned about thieves," Octavos asked.

"Not here," said Casein. "Tiberius knows better."

Bao batted at her dress. "I wonder if there is a decent clothier nearby? This rag is a disgrace."

Goji tugged at his dirty shirt. "Yeah, I know a couple of places that sell clothes. Boss?"

"We look like beggars," said Bao. "Appearances matter."

"Ok, ok, we'll visit the clothier," said Casein.

The bathhouse featured communal tubs and chambers separated by sex. Octavos was astonished at how much grime had accumulated on his body over the past month and flabbergasted when Bao emerged from the woman's chamber.

She hadn't just bathed, but her hair had been styled. "You're gorgeous."

Bao nodded. "Thank you. Now, let's find proper attire."

Bao refused to set foot in the first shop, deeming the worn garments on display suitable only for commoners and menials. That didn't stop Goji and Luther from purchasing tunics. At the second establishment, Bao methodically sifted through an entire rack of tunics and robes before finding two she deemed acceptable for Octavos and another for herself. "The color is wrong," she said, "and I dislike the cut, but it will suffice for now."

Casein appeared, clad in a tan V-necked shirt and matching pants. "What do you think?"

Bao gave him a critical glance. "It suits you." She turned to Carina, who contemplated a plain tan robe. "You, on the other hand, can dress better."

"Frippery doesn't suit me," said Carina.

"That didn't hurt as much as I thought it would." Casein hefted his coin pouch once they'd exited the shop.

Then Bao spotted the third clothier. A twinkle appeared in her eye.

Half an hour later, Casein contemplated a much lighter purse. "That one dress cost more than everybody else's clothes combined."

"It suited me," said Bao.

Casein stuffed the pouch in his shirt. "Come on. I'm hungry."

They returned to the cottage to find a table laden with soup and cooked vegetables. A thick book with removable pages occupied a separate table.

Goji begged money from Casein and then excused himself to track down his cousin's wives. Octavos wondered if he'd be back.

Casein plucked a bottle from the table, popped the cork, and sniffed. "Ah, Carbone Red."

"I have forgotten what it tasted like," said Octavos.

They settled down to eat. Then Casein opened the dispatch book. "These tiny little scribbles hurt my eyes."

"Let me see," Octavos remembered Casein's struggle with the journal.

Casein handed Octavos the tome. "Most of it will be months out of date. The new stuff will be at the end." He sighed. "And even that will be weeks old."

Octavos flipped to the last quarter of the book. That page pronounced Emperor Charles DuSwaimair's 'Edict of Tolerance for the Arts of Magic and Innovation.' "Yeah, this is old stuff." He flipped a few more pages. A name caught his eye. "She died," he said as much to himself as the others.

"Who?" Casein asked.

"Doctor Isabella Menendez, noted scholar and sorceress, passed away in her sleep in her chamber at the University of Solace."

Carina gasped.

Octavos took note of the date. *That was the same time as my dream.* A shudder ran through his body.

"Go on," said Casein.

"The army chased the nomads into Soraq and slaughtered them at Umar." He looked at Bao. "Pashha Jahil Said Kalil was killed in the fighting."

"Nobody will mourn his death," said Bao.

Octavos flipped a page. "Prince Thomas Maximus crushed the southern horde. There's no mention of Dessau being overrun or the assault on Ptath. Nothing about the Gotemik, either." A chill sensation entered his bones.

"There wouldn't be," said Casein. "Go on."

“There is a list of nobles killed in the campaign. The first is General Tullos.”

“An idiot who couldn’t even use a quill properly, let alone a sword,” said Casein.

Octavos scanned the list. “Lots of dead knights.”

“Knights are good at getting themselves killed.” Casein hefted an explosive crossbow bolt. “They’re also becoming irrelevant. Weapons such as these are the future.”

Casein’s right. Octavos remembered a catman being blown apart by a ‘special.’ He blinked and returned his attention to the list. *But still, all those men.* A name near the bottom of the list caught his eye. “Appius Ambrose was killed as well.” Octavos blinked. “The notation says his death is under investigation.”

Across the room, Bao and Carina exchanged a glance.

“He probably tried burning the wrong person,” said Casein.

Octavos turned to the last page, read a few words, and stopped. “Emperor Charles DuSwaimair is dead.”

LABYRINTH WAR XXXIX – Bao

'Once, Arcos was a bastion of the Empire's authority in the south. During the Interregnum, the Lords of Arcos were cut off from imperial support. They survived by making themselves useful to the regional powers. It has been stated that the Empire could reclaim the island nation in a single day with a single legion, but Solaria finds the current situation beneficial.'

- Fulton, 'Progression of the Empire.'

The coast of Arcos Minor slid past. Bao stared at the orchards and fields without seeing them.

Her thoughts were elsewhere. *The old emperor is dead. Thomas Maximus will be the new Emperor. That makes my betrothed a Prince. A Prince can do things a mere aristocrat cannot – like absolve his wife of murder.*

An image appeared in her brain: the heavy chamber pot in her hands, the back of Ambrose's skull, and the dull 'thump' the two made upon impact. Then Ambrose was falling, pierced by the sword held by the witch woman. Ambrose's sword. *I was too terrified to think. Surely that must count for something.* At that moment, her position went from 'intolerable' to 'criminal.'

Octavos sat next to her. "What are you thinking of?" As usual, he had that big goofy grin plastered across his face.

Bao moved her head and smiled. "Our future."

"Oh?" Octavos ran his hand along her arm. A tingling sensation ran along Bao's spine.

"Yes." A sigh escaped Bao's mouth. "We need to get married."

Octavos withdrew his hand. "We're already betrothed. Why the haste?"

"Because we are in a fool's paradise that cannot last," said Bao. "Sooner or later, imperial agents will find us, and we will face difficult questions." *Like why we fled west. Like a dead scion of a prominent family.* "If we are married when that happens, then those questions may be less severe."

"A honeymoon instead of an elopement," Octavos stroked his chin. *He needs to shave. That stubble does nothing for his appearance.*

"Exactly." Bao placed her hand on Octavos's arm.

A call from Casein prompted Octavos to rise to his feet. "I will consider this." He knelt, gave her a peck on the cheek, and vanished.

Bao broached the subject several more times over the next few days. Octavos gave inconclusive answers each time. Bao didn't press him. *I don't want to scare him away. That would be a catastrophe.*

A week from Quimb, the Japi reached the tip of Arcos Minor and dropped anchor off a sandy islet for the night. At dawn, they raised sail and headed west towards a brown smudge on the western horizon.

Bao's trepidation increased as the brown smear turned into a green island. *I must convince him.*

Bao knew Octavos had spoken with Casein about her offer. She also knew that Casein, a lifelong bachelor, had little counsel to offer, though he did take to calling them 'love birds,' a habit adopted by Luther and Goji. Carina was absorbed in her private concerns. *Her troubles are worse than mine. As the wife of a powerful aristocrat, I might escape condemnation for Ambrose's murder in a time of crisis. But she is without such protection.*

Then they reached Arcos. Casein spoke with Octavos and Bao as the boat rounded a headland. "Arcos was part of the Empire," he jabbed his finger to emphasize the point, "key word there being 'was.' Now it's an independent nation. They take that very seriously. But make no mistake, Arcos is neck deep in imperial agents." He faced Octavos. "Behave yourselves. I can't do much if you get in trouble with the local authorities. Understood?"

Octavos nodded.

Bao followed suit.

The Japi rounded the headland and entered the arc-shaped harbor of Arcos City. Warehouses, chandlers, and shipyards vied for space along the curved waterfront. Beyond them, rank upon rank of tenements and shops climbed a slope to a ridge crowned with large manors to the west and a massive Church dome to the east.

Casein had Goji steer towards a short wharf backed by a squat warehouse on the harbor's east side. *Close to the Church,* Bao thought. *Perfect.*

Nobody appeared to greet them. Casein glanced at the overhead sun. "Tulip is probably asleep." He walked towards the dingy warehouse, trailed by Octavos and Bao.

Casein heaved the door open without knocking, exposing a large pale woman snoring in a tilted chair with her feet propped on a battered desk.

The woman's eyes opened at their intrusion. "Who" – she spotted Casein. "Oh, it's you. Wasn't sure you'd ever make it here."

"Hi, Sis," Luther claimed a stool. "I see the heat still bothers you."

"It's beastly." Tulip's booted feet dropped to the floor. "How the locals endure it, I'll never know. I find myself missing snow. But what's up?"

"I have a cargo of mangos on consignment," said Casein. "And I need news."

"The mangos are no problem." Tulip stood. "Gerki, Halos, Shin, get your green asses out here now! You got a boat to unload."

A goblin in a laborer's tunic appeared in the doorway. "Sure thing, boss." The creature spotted Casein. "You're back." His eyes flicked over to Tulip. "Have you told him?"

"I will, Gerki." Tulip placed both fists on the table. "Now get that boat of his unloaded."

Gerki exited.

A scowl appeared on Casein's face. "Told me what?"

"Brian Rigger turned up a week ago," said Tulip. "Comes here every day asking if you're in yet. Say's it's urgent."

"Where's he at?"

Tulip snorted. "The Imperial, of course. Right next to the Eyes office. Speaking of whom, they've been busy lately. It seems somebody poisoned Senator Guillous last week, and that tripped off a little murder spree on the hill that put Senator Strabo's oldest boy on the funeral pyre."

Casein frowned. "Well, I'll grab a bite to eat and then see what has Rigger so excited. You got some rooms upstairs for us?"

Tulip nodded. "Yeah, I got a couple of rooms set aside for visitors. The greenies know better than to enter."

Bao grabbed Octavos's hand. "We would like to visit the cathedral while Mister Casein conducts business."

"I should go with Casein." Frustration filled Octavos's voice.

"No," said Casein, Bao, and Tulip all at the same time.

"That would attract attention," said Tulip. "The Eyes are distracted, not blind. Go to the Cathedral instead."

Bao tightened her grip on Octavos's hand. "We need to go to the Cathedral."

Octavos gave Bao a curious glance. "All right."

"No." The priest's jowls quivered as he spoke. "I do not perform marriages on a whim, and especially not for people using assumed names."

"But I am Governor Des-Ptath's daughter!" Bao's heart dropped halfway to the mosaic covering the cathedral's floor.

"Were that so," said the priest, "you'd be in Ptath, not here." The priest's gilded robes rustled as he faced Octavos. "As for you, young man, you certainly bear the Maximus stamp upon your features and may even be a by-blow of theirs. But I remind you the Maximus frown upon unwarranted claims to their name."

"Of course, holiness." Octavos stared at the floor.

"Both of you should reconsider this rash act," continued the priest. "The sacrament of marriage is not something to be rushed into but must be carefully considered beforehand."

"We shall, excellency." *Pompous ass.* Bao took Octavos's hand and guided him from the Cathedral.

Octavos stopped once they'd reached the street and pushed Bao towards an alleyway.

"Stop! You're hurting me."

"What is going on?" Octavos demanded. "You told me you wished to see the Cathedral, not get married on the spot!"

"We've been talking marriage for weeks now!" Bao's heart pounded. *I must convince him.* "It was your whole purpose in venturing to Ptath. Now our marriage is imperative to preserve our reputations." Bao projected as much authority into her voice as she could muster.

"No." Octavos shook his head. "My reputation is intact. I fled a city overwhelmed by invaders and took refuge with an imperial citizen." Octavos eyes pierced Bao. "Your situation is another matter. I disbelieve your tale of boarding that gasbag to escape nomad infiltrators. Moreover, I saw the look between you and the sorceress upon learning Appius Ambrose's death was under investigation. Tell me the truth or I walk away right now."

Bao's heart pounded louder than Octavos's words. *I can't. I must.* Then, relief. "Carina and I were imprisoned after the assault." The words poured out in an unstoppable torrent. Octavos let her speak without interruption.

"Incredible." Octavos shook his head afterward. "The Pyramid of Zep a creation of the Old Races? Your old lover was its caretaker? And then there are your acts - chief of which is the murder of Appius Ambrose."

"He was a murderous madman," said Bao. "You know that."

"I do," said Octavos. "But that doesn't change the gravity of your situation. The Ambrose's are the fourth or fifth most powerful clan in the Empire and are among the few allies my family can rely on. Had you broken that chamber pot on the skull of a member of some lesser family, then Thomas could grant you a pardon without consequence. But not Ambrose – yes, he was slime, but his brother Julius is Vice President of the Senate. He could demand satisfaction and Thomas cannot deny him."

"But what now?" Bao's heart started to pound. Her vision blurred.

"I don't know."

The strength drained from Bao's legs. Only Octavos's arms kept her from collapsing. Octavos stroked Bao's hair and patted her back. "Maybe I'm wrong," he said in a soft voice.

"You're just saying that." Bao blinked away tears.

"No," said Octavos. "Appius was out of control, effectively an outcast. He was unmarried and unlikely to inherit anything. So, maybe a good case could be made for self-defense. His family might accept that, especially since his killer was a woman."

Bao's heart started to beat again. "This will require careful preparation."

"Your original idea was good," said Octavos. "Marriage improves your case."

"But the priest refused to marry us," said Bao.

"This priest at this church refused to marry us," said Octavos. "Arcos is three times bigger than Ptath. There are other churches." He glanced at the setting sun. "We'll find another church tomorrow."

Then they were out in the street headed for Tulip's wharf.

"Welcome back, lovebirds," said the big-boned woman. "Honeymoon suite is all fixed up." She gestured towards the stairs.

"The wedding hasn't happened yet," said Octavos in a tired voice. "Where's everybody else?"

"Still out," said Tulip.

Bao glared daggers at the woman.

Upstairs, they found a large room with a swept floor and no furniture apart from a large bed.

"Just the essentials," quipped Octavos.

Bao glared at him. *This bed looks so soft.* She sat. Her eyelids drooped. Darkness descended.

Bao's eyes flew open. Confused impressions of the previous day appeared in her mind. *Oh God, did I say those things? Did he molest me?* The mattress crinkled as she shifted position. Beside her, Octavos opened his eyes.

The door banged open. "Hello lovebirds," said Luther. "Time to eat and sail."

Bao uttered a string of words gleaned from soldiers.

"Impressive," said Luther. "But we need to get underway."

"Give them some privacy." Casein's voice from the stairwell.

"Ok, boss." Luther closed the door.

Octavos sat, exposing a muscled torso, and reached for his shirt. Bao's eyes were drawn to his abs. *He is cute.* Octavos pulled a tunic over his head. "Might as well find out what the new catastrophe is," he said.

Bao sat, clenching the blanket to her breasts. "If you will."

Octavos blushed and turned his back while Bao donned her dress.

They padded down the stairs to the common room where Casein and the rest sat around a table piled high with sliced fruit, toasted bread, sausage, and eggs.

Goji waved a fork. "Dig in," he said.

The sausage looked disgusting. Bao settled on fruit and bread slathered with honey.

"We need to get ready," said Casein once Bao ate.

"No." Bao draped her arm across Octavos's neck. "My fiancé and I intend to part ways with you."

Octavos nodded in agreement. "This is quite far enough west."

Casein's eyes hardened. He shot glances at Luther and Goji. "I can't allow that."

Bao's heart pounded. The bread and fruit felt like a lead brick in her gut.

"Why not?" Octavos demanded as he rose to his feet.

"Because Rigger's news changes things," said Casein. "The Gotemik didn't just attack the Child, they tore the Heart right out of it. Titus thinks they'll use it against Gawana."

Octavos collapsed into his chair.

"What are you babbling about?" Bao demanded. "What child is this? And what does this have to do with Octavos and me?"

"It has nothing to do with you," said Casein, "though you should know the sole reason you're not heading to the empire in chains right now is because the Eyes are busy chasing shadows. You can stay if you want. I'll even give you some money. But Octavos goes with me."

"I go where my husband goes," Bao helped Octavos to his feet. "And we are leaving right now."

Casein and his men blocked the door. "That's not going to happen."

Bao stared at Luther and Goji in turn. "Are you going to let him do this?"

"He's the boss," said Luther in a flat tone.

Goji stared at the floor and wiggled his hands.

"Enough," said Carina's voice.

Too late, Bao realized the sorceress was behind her. She felt a gentle pressure against her neck. The world blurred, then went dark.

LABYRINTH WAR XL – Octavos

'Yesterday, Nous Isle grew to a wall of broken black stone towering above the pounding waves. The 'Wave Rider' sailed past rotten bits of wood lodged in the boulders at the foot of that imposing cliff, remnants of past doomed vessels. Black-winged gulls flew out from their nests to inspect the ship. No doubt they expected its wooden corpse to join the others.

This morning, we reached Saints Grave, an arc of black stone buildings arrayed about a narrow cleft of a harbor, like mourners at the funeral of a sea beast.

Mister Mencius scanned the bleak surroundings. "Obsidian sells well in the empire. And metal workers do value pumice."

The tally keeper fell silent when Casein cast a dark glance his way.

But morbid atmosphere or no, Saints Grave rests on unmoving rock, sharp though it may be. So, when Quintus went ashore, I followed him, along with Casein and Father Joseph. Quintus ducked into the office of the fat and unshaven lout who termed himself 'Harbor Master.' I went into the town proper.

I might as well have stayed aboard the coffin. The dockside market was pathetic, its stalls offering half-rotted vegetables and trash from the rubbish heap. Its denizens belonged on a rubbish heap. Few appeared robust enough to survive even a fortnight in Niteroi's fields. I glanced upwards and took stock of the superior cottages and shops along the terraces. Of course. Quality ascends. I adjusted my course for a steep avenue.

Near the summit, we came upon a quality establishment whose signboard proclaimed it 'The Black Bishop.' There, a publican in a monk's cassock offered us weak wine and roast goat stuffed with vegetables, a delight to the palate after the endless stews and porridges produced by the 'Wave Riders' galley.

"But sir, where is the grave?" Father Joseph asked our priestly publican.

A wide, false smile crossed the publican's broad face. "Ah, the old church and Saint Niles crypt is atop the hill. Alas, tomb and shrine both are in shameful disrepair." His brown bald head bobbed as he spoke.

"Saint Niles?" The Godborn shook his head. "I have studied the lives of many holy men, but Saint Niles is unfamiliar to me."

"Saint Niles is a local figure." The landlord spoke in a slick tone. "He was one of the black barbarians of Soonlar brought to Arcos by missionaries of Saint Andrew and inducted into their order. When the Marfak horde invaded, the senior priests of the order despaired, but not Niles. God's spirit filled him with righteous anger so intense the Horde turned in their tracks rather than assault the city. Later, Niles elected to come here and meditate upon God's greatness with a handful of loyal followers."

"I see," said Father Joseph, his tone neutral.

I thought the landlord's tale was a fabrication from start to finish and said as much to the priest as we ascended the hill.

"The tale sounded false," Father Joseph agreed, "but he spoke no lie though he may not have told the full truth."

I remembered one of the gifts of the Godborn was discerning truth from lies - which is why my family prefers them tucked away in monasteries.

Church and grave both were monumental disappointments: the former a burned-out shell, and the latter a solitary thumb of fractured stone twice the height of a man, with a cryptic symbol carved on one face.

Casein kicked a stone, exposing a scorched arrowhead. "Titus, this was no accident. Somebody attacked this place."

"Pirates, no doubt." Father Joseph frowned at the plinth.

"No, the imperial navy." Doctor Menendez stepped from the shadows near the church wall. "Saint's Grave was a pirate base in the old days. General Fabius assaulted it in the war's early years."

Father Joseph stared at the Doctor in puzzlement. "But this was a church!"

"The pirates were followers of Saint Niles," said the Doctor.

"Fabius didn't get them all," said Horace. "This town is a pirate haven, mark my words."

We returned in silence to the ship, where Quintus presented us with a man missing three fingers from his left hand and a gold ring through his right earlobe. "This gent knows the reefs around Sea Gate."

He looked more like a pirate than a pilot to me.

I am glad we are not spending the night in this harbor.'

- From 'The Journal of Titus Maximus.'

The Japi sailed along the northern coast of Nous Isle, a long wall of black rock that rose from the depths and almost split the Shadow Sea in twain.

On Japi's deck, Octavos faced off against his opponent.

The wooden swords thudded together. A vibration ran along Octavos's arm. His palm was slick.

"Not bad, kid," said Luther, holding the other practice stave. "But you got to watch your footwork." With that, the blond Avar advanced and swung.

Octavos's eyes narrowed. There. He twisted and lunged at Luther. The tip of his wooden sword punched into the avar's chest. Breath exploded from Luther's chest with a 'woof.'

But now Octavos was off balance and Luther's weapon, propelled by momentum, collided with his shoulder. Octavos's sword clattered to the deck.

Bao, perched atop a crate, clapped. "You got him."

"They got each other." Casein stood with crossed arms next to Bao. "Octavos's blow would have killed Luther, but he'd have lost his arm and bled out in the return strike."

Luther's hands gripped his knees as he gulped air. Octavos rubbed his arm.

"He's getting better, though." Carina sat apart from Bao.

"Yeah, he is," Casein agreed. "But he's not good enough, not yet."

Octavos faced Casein. "Good enough for what? Am I joining your private legion?"

Casein exhaled. "I wish. A private legion would be damn useful where we're going." Casein glanced at the sun. "Wash off the grit."

The next morning Octavos spotted a 'V' shaped cleft in the cliff. Stumpy wharves and blocky warehouses protruded from its sides, with black stone buildings behind them. A series of terraces studded with huts and shops climbed the slopes behind the docks. Yet, there were no people. Octavos spotted three hovels missing their roofs, and another caved in by a tree. The place looked abandoned.

Bao came on deck and clenched Octavos's arm. "So, this is the infamous Saints Grave." She craned her neck, taking in the crumbling cottages and overgrown streets. "Strange. It appears deserted."

Octavos agreed with Bao. Titus's journal had described a thriving town with thousands of inhabitants. He turned to Casein. "Did the navy sack the place a second time?"

"No, the navy didn't do this," said Casein as Japi sailed to a short stone pier next to a stone warehouse.

A lean man with piercing eyes and a chest-length beard limped from the closest warehouse and secured a rope tossed by Luther. The man gave a deep bow. "Greetings, good gentlefolk. I am Howard Fane, harbormaster of Saints Grave." He pointed to a large house. "The Fallen Arms has abundant accommodations."

The Fallen Arms had a large common room with bed chambers in an overhead loft. Dusty light from overhead windows illuminated mismatched chairs clustered around circular tables. Casein took a seat at the largest of these. The others followed suit.

A heavy woman with dark skin entered the common room bearing a platter laden with wine and bread. The glassware, though mismatched, was of high quality. "Been a week since we had guests," said the woman. "I reckon my meat pies will suit you lot just fine."

"Morula's pies are tasty," said Howard.

"They take a while to fix, though," said the woman. "I'll get started." She left for the kitchen, trailed by Howard.

A second man entered the establishment. A clerical cassock covered a body built like stacked bricks. "So, Howler, we have guests."

"Yes, Father Bobo, we do," said Howard.

The priest took in the assembled group. "Casein," he said. "I remember you, though it's been a few years."

Howard motioned at the cleric. “I present Father Bobo of the Order of Saint Simon Wanderer.”

Octavos cocked his head. Saint Simon was honored by carters, peddlers, and other landbound travelers. A few seamen tossed coins his way, but most mariners preferred Saint Marianus.

“I have not been a wanderer for many years,” said the stout priest. “Now, I remain here and let the wanderers come to me.”

“Aye, we get plenty of colorful wanderers here,” said Howard.

Bao put her clenched hands on the table and stared at the priest. “What sort of man names his son Bobo?” The name meant ‘little priest.’

“One who expects to give that child to the church.” Father Bobo smiled. “He thought the name would improve the odds of the priests taking me. Perhaps he was correct.” Bobo shook his head. “Times were tough. He made the best choices he could.”

Bao nodded. “Tell me, Father, what happened here? Where are Saints Graves citizenry?”

The blocky priest winced. Then he faced Casein. “You didn’t tell them?”

Casein contemplated the wine in his glass. “I figured you could tell it better.” He took a sip. “Especially since you were there.”

The priest collapsed into a chair, grabbed a wine bottle, and filled one of the glasses. He raised it to eye level and peered into the depths of the liquid. Then he put the glass on the table. “You know what Saints Grave was in the old days?”

“A den of villainy,” said Bao. “A base for sea bandits ruled by the followers of an outcast saint.”

“Saint Niles, who professed to be a servant of the True God. In truth, he was a minion of Dagon the Devourer. The false saint presided over many evil rituals during his rule – until the imperial navy finally took action during the war. The navy sacked Saint's Grave and razed the church but Niles escaped to unknown parts. His remaining followers slithered back to Saint's Grave after the navy departed, ruling from behind the scenes. Then Dagon came to collect his followers." A tight smile appeared on the priest's face.

Howard reappeared. "I heard that name."

"Yes, you did." Bobo waved him to an empty chair. "Have a seat, Howler. I'm just starting to tell the tale. You were there too."

Howard sat, a scowl on his face, and poured a cup of wine.

Father Bobo contemplated his glass. "I was in gaol when it happened. That's why I lived."

"Gaol?" asked Bao.

"Yes." Bobo nodded. "I attempted to stop a man from doing evil things to a little girl. I cracked his skull. The constabulary took offense and imprisoned me." He pointed to Howard. "Howler was at the light above the town proper."

"It was an ordinary day." Howard took a long drink. "I was rooting in the vegetable patch outside the lighthouse when the sound of trumpets reached my ears. At first, I thought the Empire had attacked, but the direction was wrong, and the tune was just horrendous, more like voices wailing in terror than musical instruments."

"There were bells, too," said the priest. "When they tolled, the sound went right through your bones."

"I remember no bells." Howard took another drink. "I scanned the ridge and witnessed a violet radiance emitting from the Tomb."

"I saw it as well," said Bobo, "from the window in my cell. Next came a sort of slimy stench, cold and alien. It settled against my skin as though it were a tight tunic. I screamed like a baby. I shit myself. It took control of my limbs and tried to march me right through the cell door, except it was locked."

Howard drained his glass. "The same happened to me – to everybody. I watched lines of people converge on the road to the Tomb. They cried, begged, screamed, cursed, and pleaded. It didn't do a damn bit of good – up the road and into the tomb they went. Me, well, I screamed until I was hoarse. That's why Bobo calls me the 'Howler.' Said I sounded like a wolf."

"That's horrible," said Bao. "How did you survive?"

"The path from the Lighthouse is piss poor," said Howard. "And the thing moving me didn't do a good job. My foot slipped in a narrow spot, and I fell forty feet. Broke my leg in two places and couldn't move."

"I beat my hands bloody against the walls," said Bobo. "And then it was over. A trio of church ships filled with Liberators and Witch Hunters made port the next day."

"That is awfully convenient, that the church would arrive in force on the heels of a demonic catastrophe."

"I believe they had forewarning of some sort," said Bobo. "Anyhow, the Liberators broke me out of the gaol and searched the town. They found Howard howling his guts out and the girl I'd sought to save hiding in a cave, plus four or five others."

"They asked us questions," said Howard. "Many questions, over and over again."

"They did," agreed Bobo. "Then their leaders worked a great rite that sealed that horrible portal. The things they did – you can't get close to the tomb anymore without feeling like your skin will catch fire. And that is the tale of how Dagon claimed his followers." He started to rise to his feet. "Anything else?"

"Yes," said Octavos. "You are a legitimate priest?"

"Yes." Father Bobo halted his rise. "I was a horrible student, forever captaining raids on the pantry and barely proficient with the scriptures. My instructors despaired of me. But, yes, I did become an ordained cleric."

"Then I have a request," said Octavos.

"Oh?"

Octavos wrapped his arm around Bao's shoulder. "I'd like you to marry us."

"A marriage." Father Bobo collapsed into his chair.

"Is there a problem?"

"No, no." The priest shook his head. "It's just I haven't performed a wedding in ages."

"You have done so, though."

"A few times." The priest seemed in a state of shock.

"A wedding," Howard repeated. "There hasn't been a wedding in Saints Grave in years." He rose to his feet and patted Father Bobo's back. "I'll see if Morula can whip up something suitable." He started for the kitchen.

Father Bobo stared at the table without speaking.

Bao pulled Octavos to his feet and guided him towards the door. "You propose we get married by a drunken commoner in a pirate town depopulated by a demon?"

"Err...yes." Octavos shrugged as heat rose on his face. "He is a priest. And you must admit, it would be a story to tell our children."

"A year ago, I dreamed of a grand wedding performed by a bishop. It was to have been a citywide celebration with a great feast, entertainers, and visitors from across half the empire. I'd wear my aunt's old dress, with lace from Chou and gems woven into the fabric." Bao exhaled. "Now I just want it over with." She stalked into the inn.

Octavos studied the slope. *There. That street must go to the Tomb.*

"Don't even think it kid." Casein appeared next to Octavos. "Besides, there's nothing there."

Octavos studied the ground. Bare black rock mixed in with black grit. A couple of stubby weeds poked through the stones near his boot. Then he looked at Casein. "We didn't have to stop here."

"No, we didn't." Casein leaned against the wall. "I wanted you to hear Bobo's story. Your dad is fighting against things like the demon that destroyed this place."

Octavos noticed the plural in Casein's speech. "This happened elsewhere?"

"Yep. A place called Cenotaph City."

"I thought Cenotaph City was a myth."

"Oh, it's real enough. The people there fared better than the ones here, but Dagon still ate thousands. Then the bastard ate thousands more in Celthania."

" Casein shuffled his feet. "Titus says we got lucky. Dagon could just as easily have devoured Solace or Corber Port. The next demon might go after one of those places."

"The next demon??"

"Yeah, next demon. Titus says here are a whole bunch of monsters out there," Casein jabbed his arm skyward, "that would squash humanity like bugs and not even notice."

"Are you talking about the Gotemik?"

Casein snorted. "The Gotemik are small fry. I'm talking about ones like Kato-Siva."

A shudder ran through Octavos's body. Kato-Siva was the demonic patron of Traag. His priests sacrificed entire populaces to their master. "Kato-Siva is dead."

"That victory wasn't supposed to happen," said Casein. "It wasn't even supposed to be possible. That victory attracted the wrong kind of attention."

Octavos thought. "The Traag War almost broke the Empire. We still haven't recovered. Another Demon God would destroy us."

"Another almost did, or at least thought about it." Casein pointed at the distant ridge. "We were lucky it ate only a few isolated towns instead of half the empire. Or half the world, for that matter."

"But...what hope is there, then?"

"Gawana," said Casein. "Demons don't like that place. Their powers go all wonky. It's a refuge."

Realization struck Octavos. "That's why Father had you plant Gawana's seed in Soraq. To make another refuge."

"Yeah, I knew it would be a bitch job. I knew planting that seed would cause a lot of misery. But it seemed better than the alternative." Casein made a sweeping arm motion. "This."

Father Bobo stumbled from the inn. "Alright, I'll do it."

"It," Octavos asked.

"Perform the wedding ceremony, of course," said the priest. "Now, if you'll excuse me, I must begin preparations."

The sun settled towards the horizon. A fishing boat crewed by three goblins entered the harbor. One held two fish. "My choir," said Bobo as the kids climbed onto the dock. "They floated here from Pakar. Fine singing voices. I taught them letters and numbers too." He herded the goblins into his church, another converted warehouse.

Morula emerged from the inn, arms, and apron covered in white powder. "First meat pies, now a wedding cake. Well, I got some sugar and flour, and Nadine did bring me a big basket of berries the other day, so maybe I can do something."

Other inhabitants of Saints Grave wandered over to investigate: a skinny sunburned man with an anchor tattooed on his bicep, a pair of old women who offered obscene advice to Bao that made her blush, and a chocolate-skinned man from Soonlar with an abysmal grasp of the imperial tongue. "Trader from the other side of the island," said Howard. "Soonlar has an outpost there."

A youth summoned Octavos and Bobo into the church, where they found Bobo pouring over a large tome. The priest tapped a second book next to the first. "I require your names for the ceremony."

Octavos wrote his name in the book and Bao followed suit.

Father Bobo read the entry. "Lord Octavos Maximus. That name is not familiar to me."

Octavos blinked. "We're an eastern family." *How can he not know my family name?*

"And here you are way out west." Bobo returned his attention to the ledger. "Lady Bao Vada Falun Des-Ptath. Quite a mouthful. Marfak?"

"Kheff," said Bao. "Upper Kheff."

Casein was waiting when Octavos exited the church. "I got something for you." He fished in his pocket and extracted a gold ring.

Octavos inspected the ring. "That's the Maximus insignia. My Fathers?"

"Older than that, kid. Your father wanted me to give it to you as proof if need be."

"Varro's then." *My ancestor fled to Gawana a hundred years ago to escape a tyrannical emperor.*

"Yep." Casein pointed at the dock where Luther and Goji struggled with a trestle table. "Almost ready, kid. Better get dressed."

"Guess it's a good thing I packed that dress toga." Octavos started for the boat. "Do you"-

"Toga's are not my thing," said Casein. "Goji might know a little about them."

Octavos jumped aboard the Japi only to be chased away by an irked Bao. *At least she gave me the toga,* he thought. Goji accompanied him back to the inn. They inspected the elaborately folded cloth in an upstairs chamber.

"I helped my old master don a toga on a few occasions. I think I remember the folds," said Goji. "Hold out your arms."

Goji needed three tries to fold the garment correctly across Octavos's body. Then he took it off again to wash.

Meanwhile, the preparations continued. Octavos watched from the window as Bobo's choir dragged a score of chairs from the inn and placed them around the table. The tattooed man covered the table with a sailcloth, tattered around the edges. Morula emerged from the inn with a platter of meat pies. Howard followed with a lopsided white cake. Luther and Bobo dragged the priest's pulpit onto the pier.

Bao emerged from the Japi looking stunning. *That dress really does complement her appearance.*

Then came a knock at the door. "It's time," said Casein.

Octavos and Casein met Bao and Carina outside the inn's entrance. The others formed a line to the pulpit where Father Bobo waited. Sweat dripped from the priest's nose. Behind the priest, his choir broke into a hymn. Distantly, Octavos noted they were good singers.

The priest spoke, but his words seemed to emanate from a distance. Octavos's vision swirled in and out of focus. It didn't help that the priest stumbled often and frequently repeated himself.

Giving the ring to Bao and mouthing the words to complete the ceremony amidst a chorus of cheers seemed like a dream.

Then he was at the table with Bao pressed against his side and a large slab of meat pie on their shared plate.

Luther plopped a hand on Octavos's shoulder. "Come on man, play us some music."

Bao pecked Octavos on the cheek. "Go ahead dear."

Somebody put Octavos's lyre in his hand. Then he began to play. Much later, after the stars appeared overhead, Octavos and Bao made music of a private nature.

LABYRINTH WAR XLI – Carina

'I have but a few scratches. The same is not true of Cousin Quintus.

We were off Nous's western coast when half a dozen craft spewed from tiny clefts on islands to the east and west. Two of the raiders sported wakes well in front of their prows.

Quintus stared at the approaching vessels. "Rams! To arms!"

"Those men are wearing priest's robes," said Father Joseph.

"Get below, your grace," said Quintus.

The priest scuttled for the hatch.

Men ran from below deck carrying swords and bows.

Quintus and Ajax shouted orders. Sailors ran hither and thither, blades and bows clenched in their fists. Others mounted a pair of small ballistae on the rails, ratcheting the strings back and loading man-tall bolts the instant the pins were in place.

"Target the rams!" Quintus shouted.

Flights of arrows flew in both directions.

The first ram took a ballista bolt below the water line. The other shaft missed its mark.

A peripheral motion attracted my attention. Fearing an infiltrator, I turned to alert Quintus just as our guide planted a wicked dagger in his gut.

Quintus fell to the deck as my blade took off his assailant's head.

Seagoing scum poured onto the Wave Riders deck.

At Caseins bellow, the sailors dropped their bows and grabbed their cutlasses. The pirates hesitated before our line of steel.

"Ware!" The bosun shouted. "Ram off the starboard bow!"

The Doctor stood on the bow; her hands engaged in convoluted motions.

"It's turning!"

"Not enough!"

The ram struck the Wave Rider with sufficient force to hurl everyone off their feet.

A man in a clerics robe stood at the stern of the Ram and pointed to us "Penitents of Niles, attack!"

A fierce melee erupted at the railing.

"The pirates on deck surged towards our men, shouting "For the Black Bishop!"

A marauder ran at me screaming and making wild swings with his blade. I stepped aside, kicked his rump, and sent him plummeting headfirst over the side where he struck one of the boats with a meaty 'thump.'

Casein waded into the thick of the melee and immediately disposed of two foes. When he pulled his sword from the guts of the third pirate, the rest shied from his fury.

"Don't just stand there!" screamed the cassock-wearing pirate on the ram. "Kill him!"

Casein yanked a spear from the deck and hurled it into the chest of the cassock wearer. Every eye watched the pirate leader topple over the ram's side.

"That bastard killed Bishop Blood!" The pirates halted their advance.

Their eyes flicked back and forth.

Casein took another step closer to the mob and raised his weapon.

As one, the pirates broke, jumping back into their boats or diving over the side. Moments later, the 'Wave Riders' surviving crew stood alone on a listing vessel with crimson-stained decks surrounded by corpses and debris.

A gasp from Quintus caught my attention. My cousin was curled on the deck, clenching his gut with red-stained hands.

A shadow fell over me. The giant form of First Mate Ajax loomed over me, blood seeping from rags wrapped around his chest and right bicep. "We need the healer," he said.

I dispatched Horace to search for the Godborn.

The 'Wave Riders' crew began tossing pirate corpses overboard. When two mariners grabbed the hands and ankles of one of Casein's victims, his sleeve fell back, exposing a pair of tattoos. The first, smeared by age, was the mark of the 7th Liberators. The other was a squiggle of curved and spiraling lines in different colors.

Horace found the Godborn below deck, knee-deep in water, mouthing an incantation to repair the leak where the ram had struck. Two of the unwounded men relieved him of this task.

We make plodding headway south and west while Father Joseph and the Doctor tend to the wounded. My cousin and two others are not expected to live. Mister Mencius will walk limp for a month.'

- From 'The Journal of Titus Maximus.'

Carina placed the chart beside the sketch from Titus's journal. "Of course," she muttered under her breath.

"Of course, what?" Bao stood behind the sorceress. As always, these days, there was a hard edge to the aristocrat's voice when she addressed Carina.

"I figured something out," said Carina. "Have you seen Casein?"

"He's out chasing goats to fill our larder," said Bao. "I suggest you try the lagoon."

Carina sighed, folded the chart into the journal, and stood.

"I shall accompany you." A strained touch entered Bao's voice. The aristocrat detested being alone more than she disliked her current company.

Like past visitors to Ring Isle, Japi's crew had camped beside a spring atop a low tree-covered bluff. From here, footpaths passed through thick forest to the lagoon on one side and the outer beach on the other.

Pale, palm-sized crabs scuttled across the trail. "Wretched pests," said Bao from behind Carina as the women made their way along the trail. "They're not even good eating."

Carina nodded agreement – the diminutive crustaceans got into everything from cloths to cargo bins, and fabric rated high on their favorite foods. She'd watched them shred a pair of Octavos trousers.

The Japi's beached bulk loomed before the women. Luther, Goji, and Octavos moved around the double hulls, fixing planks in place, and readying the craft for the voyage to Seagate.

"Hold the board still," Luther told Octavos. "Don't let it shift."

"Ok." Carina watched Octavos's muscles tremble.

Luther swung the hammer. "Got it. Don't move."

"Just hurry up."

Luther pounded more nails into the board and stepped back from Japi's hull. "Ok. That should hold."

Octavos released his grip and rubbed his arms. "I'll go see what the wife is up to."

"I'm right here, watching you play carpenter," said Bao.

Octavos started. "Why, hello wife." He approached Bao with outstretched arms.

The former Kheffian aristocrat took a step back. "Husband, you are filthy. Go clean yourself off."

"No, I'm dirty." Octavos motioned at Goji, whose lithe form was partly covered with vile-smelling goop used to prevent leaks. "He's filthy."

"Goji is a commoner." Bao jabbed her finger at Octavos. "You are an aristocrat, not a shipwright."

Octavos took in his grimy, sawdust-covered limbs. "Well, I could use a swim. Care to join me?"

Bao regarded her husband. "Perhaps." They started towards the lagoon's brilliant blue waters.

Luther took a long swig from a wineskin. Rose-colored fluid dribbled from his mouth. He removed the spout with a sigh and regarded Carina. "What brings you here? I thought you were still scribbling in those books."

"I was." Carina had spent much of the voyage from Arcos recording her lost grimoires from memory. "But now, I need to speak with Casein."

Luther pointed at the narrow channel that connected the lagoon with the sea. "The boss is over there somewhere, chasing a goat."

"No, the boss done caught the goat." Casein emerged from the jungle carrying a limp bundle of fur. "I figure it'll taste better than those damned crabs." He peered at Carina. "You want something?"

"I figured something out." Doubt's assailed Carina as she spoke. It was so simple. Surely, Casein or somebody else had thought of it before.

"What?" Casein started for the bluff path.

Carina took a breath. "The location of the Maximus Seal."

Casein halted beside a flat-topped boulder. "Your grandmother told you that?"

"Put yourself in my grandmother's position after leaving Gawana. She had the Seal. She knew the Seal would be confiscated by the Eyes upon reaching an imperial port. Still, it was too useful to destroy or toss overboard. Therefore, she hid it before reaching Tessa."

"Titus thought of that." Casein shook his head. "He had me retrace Isabella's whole route. I didn't find anything."

"You didn't have this." Carina raised Titus's journal.

"I read that book." Casein shook his head. "It's not in there."

"You didn't know where to look." Carina placed the book on the rock and opened it to the sketch.

"Doodles. So, what?" Casein shrugged.

"Not just 'doodles.' Sketches." Carina pointed at each image in turn. "A claw. A leaf. A ring. A toadstool."

"Like I said, doodles."

"Notice the spacing." Carina extracted the chart and spread it next to the book. "See? Claw Reef. Leaf Island. Ring Island – where we're at." She moved her finger. "And Toadstool Rock. It's a map, not a sketch."

"Ok." Casein rubbed his chin.

"I talked with sailors back at Saint's Grave." Carina jabbed the page. "They told me the favored sea route from Nous Isle to Cendoza is through these islands – both directions."

"Yeah, that's right. But Titus thought of this. I hunted all through these rocks. Even had a wizard helping me."

"Even Toadstool Rock?" Carina pointed at a tiny 'x' on the sketch.

"No, it's unclimbable." But doubt entered the ex-legionnaire's voice.

Carina smiled. "Not with the right kind of magic."

"You might be onto something." Casein dropped the goat and faced the lagoon. "Octavos! Get your butt over here."

Octavos emerged from the water, rivulets pouring from his body. He looked much cleaner than before his dip. "What?"

Casein pointed at Carina's head. "Carina wants to tell you something."

"Tell him what?" Bao materialized alongside her husband.

Carina repeated her deductions.

Octavos nodded. "Can your magic reach Toadstool Island?"

Carina smiled at the youthful prince. "One way to find out."

A short while later, the entire party – save for Goji, who'd been stuck cooking the goat – stood on Ring Isle's outer beach, staring at a rocky pillar topped by a bulbous overhang.

"That's one strange-looking mushroom," said Luther. "Looks kind of lopsided."

"Part of the top fell away." Casein faced Carina. "Ready?"

The sorceress nodded. She focused her energies and imagined the distance between her and Toadstool's summit shrinking to a single step. Chaotic darkness engulfed her for an instant. Then she stood, trembling slightly, atop a fractured mass of rock that fell away on all sides.

Carina rotated in place, taking in a view of waves, gulls, reefs, and islets. She waved at her comrades on Ring Island's brilliant beach. "This is a nice place. A girl could live here." She let herself indulge in that fantasy for a moment. Substantial sea traffic did pass through this area. Ships did call at Ring Isle for water and repairs. She could open an inn, find herself a man...and get burned by Witch Hunters -or be murdered by agents of the Ambrose family. She sighed and consulted the mental image of her grandmother's sketch.

There. The hiding place wasn't much – just a knee-high overhang choked with piled stones. Carina pulled the rocks away and spotted a wooden box carved with mystical marks. She flipped open the lid. "Well, aren't you a beauty?" The Maximus Seal was just that – a stamp used to mark important documents.

But, to her Sight, the implement was a veritable kaleidoscope of mystical energy.

A cold gust of wind blew across Toadstool's rocky summit, momentarily chilling Carina. "Ok, time to go." She faced Ring Isle's distant beach and summoned her energies. Darkness. Chaos. Dampness. A weight slammed into the sorceress's back, knocking her face-first into the water.

Strong hands lifted Carina to her feet. "I have you," said Casein.

Carina clenched the miniature chest. "I have the Seal."

She opened the box on the beach.

"Doesn't look like much." Luther eyed Carina. "You sure it's real?"

"Oh, it's real." The sorceress watched as Octavos lifted the relic between thumb and forefinger and peered at the tiny glyphs about its rim. "See something?"

Octavos blinked. "Thought I saw colors. It must have been a trick of the light."

"It must have." Carina nodded.

A bell clanged on the bluff. "Dinner's ready," shouted Goji.

Casein and Luther started for the path. Octavos remained, still staring at the Seal.

"I hope he cleaned himself before cooking that thing." Bao turned to her husband. "Well, come along."

"In a moment." Octavos dropped the Seal in its container.

"I'll save you a plate." Bao departed, leaving Octavos alone with Carina.

"I did see something," Octavos told the sorceress. "Those colors weren't a trick of the light."

Carina took a breath. "You have magic. I have suspected as much for a while."

"I'm tempted to say you're delirious from exhaustion." Octavos ran his fingers over the box as he spoke. "But – I remember things. Strange things."

Carina touched the musician's shoulder. "I know. I listened to your fever dreams, back on the river."

"But – I can't be a magician."

Carina took a breath. "Your power is manifested through music. The Avar call it bardic magic."

"I'm familiar with the Avar Bards," said Octavos. "But I'm not an Avar."

Carina smiled. "Your mother was an Avar aristocrat. The DuPauls are renowned for their patronage of bards."

"Oh." Octavos dropped open. "I never thought about that." His face contorted in concentration. "Mother was an excellent singer, though."

"Avar Bards are not the only ones to fuse music with magic. You know of the Harmonious Order," asked Carina, referring to the monks who greeted each dawn and sunset with a burst of wondrous music.

"Of course," Octavos's face widened in wonder. "You mean they"-

Carina nodded. "Yes. It's why they're sequestered from the populace."

"Could – could I learn actual magic?"

Carina considered the question. "Bardic magic is a thing of music that affects the mind. It requires musical expertise I do not have." She paused. "However, I can teach you a series of rudimentary exercises and focusing tricks common to all spellcasters."

"I must consider this." Octavos walked into the forest.

Carina set her pen aside and closed the book. Ten more precious pages of her mystic books were transcribed from memory. But now, her fingers were too cramped to continue, and the cabin seemed oppressively close. She ducked through the main cabin where Luther and Goji diced with each other while Bao stirred vegetables into a pot. The former princess had developed a fondness for the culinary arts.

She passed by Octavos, who sat in a cross-legged meditative pose. The youth had already learned to open his inner eye to the weave of magic and could master a simple ward. Yes, he had magic.

An endless vista of clouds and waves greeted the sorceress on deck. Boards creaked, and ropes snapped overhead as the Japi cut through a slight swell.

"We're still a long way from land." Casein sat propped against the foremast, carving a chuck of wood into the shape of a naked woman.

"I know." Carina peered southward. "Soonlar's that way, isn't it?"

"Yeah." Casein nodded. "Are you thinking of going there?"

"I might. Are they savages?"

Casein grunted. "No."

A thought occurred to her. "Why didn't you just plant the Seed in Soonlar? It's a lot closer to Gawana than Soraq or the Empire."

"We planted seeds there," said Casein. "They found all three pods and killed them."

Carina considered the former soldier's statement. "Soonlar sounds organized."

"Yeah, Soonlar is organized." Casein considered his carving. "They send messages long distances with drums - almost as good as the Imperial signal towers. Their troops are well drilled." He shrugged. "The roads are so-so, but they mostly use rivers."

"What about magic?"

Casein exhaled. "Yeah, almost every big village has a witch or wizard."

Carina nodded. Soonlar had possibilities.

LABYRINTH WAR XLII – Octavos

"Are you sure about this decision?" asked Doctor Menendez.

Casein gives one of his big dopey grins. "Yes, mother, I'm sure. The Empire holds nothing for me anymore." He punched me in the shoulder. "Besides, Titus needs me.

Casein's decision pleases me. A lord should have followers. And I need a friend as well.

A great deal of work awaits me in Gawana. I'm giving this journal to Doctor Menendez.'

- From 'The Journal of Titus Maximus.'

Octavos unfolded himself from a meditative pose and stretched, feeling the burn in his muscles. He grinned despite the pain, elated at holding the Ward. Carina told him with practice it would become automatic. She'd taught him other elementary magic tricks: He could see magic if he blinked precisely the right way, and his sense of direction was nothing short of uncanny. Casein thought he'd inherited that knack from his father.

The thought prompted Octavos to venture on deck.

Japi swam through tiny islets, drawing ever nearer to a dark line on the western horizon. The nearer that wall approached, the glummer Casein's expression appeared.

A cold knot formed in Octavos's gut at Casein's gloominess. Finally, he could bear it no more. "What is it? Why the dour face?"

"Saw that, did you?" Casein's expression remained fixed on the barrier as Goji steered the Japi past a pair of isles covered with terraced farmland.

"It's kind of hard to miss."

Casein sighed. "It's just, well, I'm wondering if bringing you here was a mistake."

"Huh?" Octavos had seen Casein in many moods: cheerful, authoritative, furious, companionable, and serious. But he couldn't remember the former legionnaire being uncertain.

"It's your dad." Casein made an absent wave at the wall, now showing hints of detail. "This place changed Titus. He's not the man I served with in the legions."

Octavos remembered his father's journal. The later portion's tone was so different from the first that it seemed the work of a different author. "Changed, how?" The cold knot expanded into the rest of his abdomen.

"Gawana talks to Titus and tells him things I can't understand." Each word emerged from Casein's mouth with a struggle. "He sees the world differently. Ordinary relationships don't mean much to him anymore."

"You're still his friend, though." Octavos leaned against the mast.

"Titus says I am," Casein spoke the words without inflection.

"That's not exactly a ringing endorsement. Hopefully, Dad will remember I'm his son." Octavos felt like he'd drank a large, chilled drink.

Casein stretched. "He's asked about you several times."

"I suppose that's something."

"We will face your sire together." Bao sat beside Octavos. "If I cannot be a power in Kheff, then perhaps he can make me a queen in this 'Vazari' or some other metropolis within the walls."

"Perhaps," agreed Casein.

Bao's presence thawed the icy sensation in Octavos's gut.

Goji maneuvered the craft through a tangle of almost submerged reefs. "How do you do that," asked Octavos.

Goji glanced at Octavos while wrestling with the steering oar. "I dated a pilot here. I know every isle and shoal in this harbor."

"Oh." Octavos stood beside Casein as the Japi pushed through a collection of dugouts and fishing smacks, drawing close to a trio of isles covered with cropland, tenements, and warehouses. Larger vessels, some with the Japi's triple hull design, rode at anchor or were tied off too long wharves.

"Welcome to Seagate." Luther didn't seem thrilled at being here.

Bao's gaze flitted from building to bridge to the colorfully dressed crowds. "What a curious city. It seems a smaller, more brightly colored version of Hermosa or Quimb."

"Titus will be waiting for us." Casein rose to his feet and waved at Goji. "Take us to the manor."

"Aye, Captain." Goji steered the Japi under a bridge between two islands. Ahead, rocky peninsulas with blocky dwellings and shops jutted from a tall dark mass. Gawana.

"the river mouth is over there." Casein pointed at an indent to their south.

Goji skirted a long bridge between the islands and the mainland. More wharves appeared ahead, extending from warehouses that backed right against Gawana's wall. "Trader's." Casein waved at the buildings. "Seagate's lords trade pika fruit and widen silk for metal and wood."

"I suppose my father deals with these merchants." Octavos watched a long line of skinny men in breechclouts and turbans tote bundles from the nearest warehouse to a large barge.

"No." Casein's eyes were distant. "Titus doesn't deal with the traders, he commands them."

"Oh." Octavos sighed. "That's the Maximus way, though. The Maximus rule. Everybody else is a servant."

The Japi drew near a stubby wharf with a stone paved path that climbed through flower beds and ornamental rocks to a house that protruded from Gawana's bulk. "We're here," said Casein as Luther and Goji secured the vessel. "Time to pay our respects." He gripped Octavos firmly by the elbow and stepped onto the dock.

Octavos took in Gawana's weathered bulk. It looked like a fieldstone wall draped in vines, but his incipient occult senses informed him of vast energies circulating in those rocks.

"Take care, boss," said Luther from the Goji's deck.

Octavos craned his neck. "You're not coming with us?"

"Nah." Luther smiled. "Goji and me...well, we're just the hired help."

Octavos spotted Carina leaning against the side of the cabin. "How about you?"

"I have other business." The sorceress vanished inside the cabin.

"I will accompany you, husband." Bao appeared on deck in a stunning blue and green dress. "Your father should meet his daughter-in-law." She hefted a familiar case in one hand. "And you don't want to forget this."

Octavos's heart lightened at the sight of his lyre. Music always made things more pleasant, at least for a while.

"You." Bao motioned at Luther. "Make yourself useful and fetch our luggage."

Luther made a face but ducked into the cabin and emerged with a couple of hefty bundles which he thrust at Casein. "Here," he said. "I'm not going in there."

Casein didn't take the packs. "I'm not a porter."

"Fortunately, I have porters," said a thickly accented voice from the shore.

Octavos turned and spotted a long-faced man in a green robe standing on the path, next to a pair of skinny fellows in breechclouts and dirty turbans. He approached Casein and bowed. "You're here at last. Good, good. The master is most impatient." The man's eyes took in Casein's companions, shifting from Luther to Goji to Bao and Carina before settling on Octavos. "This is him, then? The master's son?"

"Yeah, Jamal, this is Octavos, Titus's son." Casein faced the boat. "Make yourselves useful. Take the cargo to Warehouse Three."

"My men will see to the unloading." Jamal practically hopped from foot to foot with impatience.

"Tell them to take care," said Casein. "The cargo is both delicate and dangerous. No open flames. Clear?"

"Yes, yes," said Jamal. "Follow, please. Quick, quick."

"We'll be at the Sea Snake if you need us," said Luther.

"Good, good." Jamal pointed at the bundles. "Follow, follow."

Casein fell in behind Jamal. Octavos and Bao walked behind them, while the porters brought up the rear.

The path curved so Octavos could see the Japi. Luther and Goji bustled about on deck prying up the planks concealing the crates of explosive crossbow bolts.

They climbed the few remaining steps to the manor. This close, Gawana's surging energies were almost visible without occult senses.

Octavos paused. *Am I making a mistake?*

Then it was too late as the press of bodies propelled Octavos through the portal and into an antechamber with walls carved to resemble vines and flowers.

Jamal paused to issue quick instructions to a squat guard in leather armor at the entry. Then he guided them through a corridor towards a sunlit banquet room where a table laden with wine, salad, and fruit awaited.

Octavos surveyed the feast. His stomach rumbled.

"Gawana's bounty," said Casein.

A door at the chamber's far end opened. A man entered. Thirtyish. Slender, yet well-muscled. Olive skin and a narrow face dominated by a large, sharp nose. He wore a simple tunic. A garland of flowers hung around his neck. He surveyed the group, eyes settling on Octavos. "Hello, son." He motioned at the repast. "We have much to discuss."

"Father!" Energy coursed through Octavos's frame, making him dizzy. He strode across the chamber.

Octavos heard Casein gasp in alarm behind him. He wrapped his arms around Titus's frame. "It's good to see you at last."

"Likewise." Titus's voice was cool and distant. He did not reciprocate his son's gesture. Instead, Titus twisted and shrugged free of the hug. "As I said, we must speak." He motioned at the table a second time.

Octavos took a step back and glanced at the feast. His stomach rumbled. He was hungry.

Titus stared past Octavos. "You must be my son's betrothed." Again, his voice remained devoid of inflection.

"I was Lady Bao Vada Falun Des Ptath, of Ptath's ruling family." Bao bowed. "Now, I have the great honor of being Princess Bao Vada Falun Maximus."

Titus stared at Casein. "You brought the weapons?"

"Yes sir." Casein stood at attention as he spoke. "Thirty-four crates worth. They're being stored in Warehouse Three as we speak."

"Good." Titus gave a slight nod, the most emotion he'd displayed since entering the room. "Brian Rigger should be here in another week with an additional hundred crates. Now sit."

Casein took a seat. Octavos and Bao followed suit. Titus sat last of all. He plucked a purple sphere from a platter and thrust it at Octavos. "Pika fruit. You might enjoy it."

Octavos took the smooth orb, held it to his mouth, and bit. A sweet and tangy sensation, reminiscent of the fruit drinks sold by curbside vendors in Solace, filled his mouth. The pulp proved chewy. "You're right, father." He felt juice run down his chin. "It's good."

Bao bit into a pika fruit. "I have never had anything quite like this."

"You wouldn't." Titus held one of the orbs to his face. "They are the bounty of Gawana and her children." He looked pointedly at Casein, who munched at a slab of bread topped with meat and cheese.

Casein started to say something around a mouthful of food.

Titus flicked long slender fingers at the former legionnaire. "No, no, finish your repast first."

Titus's interrogation began the moment Casein shoved away a decimated platter. Question by question, the Maze Lord extracted a detailed account from the three of them stretching back a year or more while revealing little about his activities. "I concur with your assessment. The Empire was extraordinarily fortunate during its encounter with the Gotemik. Gawana's child was less so." Titus seemed to be considering something. "One item of business remains. Then you can rest, or roam about the city."

"Gawana," asked Octavos.

"You were in Gawana the moment your foot touched the soil. Its roots extend beyond the wall." Titus stood. "No, this is something else. Follow me."

Octavos followed his father through the far door into another chamber with rough-hewn stone walls. Titus uttered a command in a language Octavos didn't recognize and a pair of stocky men in leather armor entered from a side door, bared steel in their hands.

"Defend yourself." Titus motioned at a rack that held a legion issue short sword, helm, and shield.

"What are you doing?" Bao grabbed Titus's sleeve. "He's your son!"

"Is he?" Titus unhooked Bao's fingers. "He is my offspring, but that alone doesn't make him worthy of life."

Octavos pulled the helm over his head and hefted the short sword.

"Titus." Casein stood in the doorway. "This isn't right."

Octavos grabbed the shield.

"I must know." Titus's voice remained maddeningly bland. He uttered a command to the two men.

Octavos saw Casein pale before the first warrior's bearded visage filled his vision.

Curtis's lessons took over. Footwork. Dodge. Thrust. Bells sounded in Octavos's head as his opponent's blade rang off the helm. "What is this, father? That blow could have killed me."

"Sanlu follows my commands," said Titus. "Kill or be killed."

"That's madness!" Octavos backpedaled, desperately scanning his attacker.

Sanlu's sword cut a rent through Octavos's tunic.

Enough! Octavos hunched behind his shield shifted his feet and charged. A hard jolt ran through the youth's frame as his body collided with Sanlu's. Octavos concluded the maneuver by violently thrusting the shield's edge into Sanlu's face.

The warrior collapsed to the ground and flopped. His face turned purple.

"That's horrible." Bao's words ended with a violent retching motion.

"Enough of this madness!" Octavos threw the helm and shield to the floor. "What manner of monster have you become?"

Titus stood over Sanlu's corpse. "He was a passable warrior, despite being ill-disciplined." He faced Octavos. "As are you. As for myself, I am the Lord Defender of Gawana. Come."

"No," said Octavos. "Bao and I are leaving this wretched place right now." He started for the door.

"You are not."

Octavos stared in shock as stone flowed over the gap through which he'd entered the room.

"You will remain in Gawana until I say otherwise."

Octavos placed an arm over Bao's shoulders. He realized Casein wasn't in the chamber. "You're not human. Not anymore."

Titus nodded. "True. I miss that humanity on occasion." He motioned at the far door. "Now, come. We have much to do."

LABYRINTH WAR XLIII – Chimp

"Regis, Capital of the Empire, is nothing short of awe-inspiring. Have you not seen the imperial palace, carved into the shape of a throne from a mountain with lesser palaces and offices gathered about its base like fawning courtiers?"

- Sir Benedict DuPaul, extolling the grandeur of the Solarian Empire

The Throne Palace's description matched its name – from a distance, it looked like a chair for a giant, complete with seat, arms, and back. Its denizens referred to the various sections by those names. It made those looking at it feel small and insignificant – just like its architects intended.

Chimp peered through a window halfway up the back, giving him a view of the seat – a fair-sized courtyard, and both arms, which were pretty much filled with offices. The Palace dropped seven stories from the 'Seat to the 'Dais,' a square bordered by the townhouses and palace palaces of Solaria's most powerful aristocrats. The Promenade, a wide elevated road lined with the manor of potent families, descended from there to Heritage Square, just inside Regis's gates. Past them, cliffs fell into a vast sprawl of tenements, shops, shacks, and warehouses. That scene, the contrast between the elevated villas and poor quarters beneath them, reminded Chimp of his youth on Corber Port's streets, a time of running, hiding, thieving, and begging. It wasn't a period he cared to dwell on. Army life, brutal though it often was, had been an improvement.

Chimp raised his eyes, taking in the scene past the Capital's south gate, where a wide, sluggish river cut through a broad, cluttered valley to the Mare Imperium. Last week, he'd stood beside Thomas Maximus during his promotion from 'Prince' to 'Emperor,' a grand and dull ritual. Three weeks ago he'd been standing in a ditch three thousand miles to the south. Three thousand miles in fourteen days, a testament to the speed of the Empire's courier boats. It still boggled his mind.

Soft footsteps sounded behind Chimp – somebody attempting to be quiet. That was wrong – aristocrats and their underlings didn't practice stealthy movement. He grabbed his dagger, dropped, spun, and punched, all in one move. The dagger's tip 'clinked' against the metal.

"Not bad," said the massive form encased in that armor. He held a short sword above Chimp's head. "But you're still dead."

Chimp recognized the armored figure. Scar. An imperial bodyguard of legendary reputation. The sole personal imperial bodyguard to survive Crowfoot Gap. A man who'd bested rachasa and even demons in personal combat. "Don't be so sure about that, sir." He flicked his head to the side, where Sticks held a knife against Scar's neck.

"Where'd you come from," asked Scar, his voice a deep rumble.

"He's good at blending in." Chimp motioned and Sticks pulled his dagger from Scar's head.

"Hah. You're a pack of gutter rats playing soldier. The legions don't teach that sort of knife work."

Chimp bristled at Scar's words.

"That's ok, though." Scar stepped back and shrugged. "I was a gutter rat myself, once."

"Muscle," said Sticks. "Not an artist."

"Yep," said Scar, "I left the climbing and sneaking to others."

"What brings you here," asked Chimp.

"I heard about your little stunt on the border. Saved the Emperor's life, by all accounts. Makes us members of a select club, I reckon."

"It wasn't a stunt," said Chimp. "It was 'do or die.' And it worked."

"It did," said Scar. "You saved the emperor's life. But you did so as a soldier, not a bodyguard. There's a difference. I came here to see if you were bodyguard material." He glanced about the room. "I heard your squad has a shifter."

"She's down south." Probably. Lady Bottle whisked Chimp out of the 'Child' before Shade and Snuffles could reunite with the crew.

"I suppose that's just as well," said Scar. "Shifters don't fit into the palace."

"Excuse me," asked a female voice, "but are you part of Emperor Thomas Maximus's entourage?"

Chimp looked past Scar's bulk to see a short, hunched woman in the black gown of an academic carrying a large packet. "We are. Who are you?"

The woman sighed. "I am Hermione Scribner from the archives." She hefted the bundle. "The Emperor made inquiries about these."

"Can you verify that?" It seemed the sort of question guards were supposed to ask.

"I have this." Hermione pulled a brass disk from her gown.

"Let me see that." Chimp took the medallion. He frowned. It depicted an imperial seal, but it looked different than the others around here. "I don't recognize it."

Scar extended a massive hand. "Give it here."

Scar stared at it for a moment. "I hadn't seen one of these in ages."

"What is it?"

Scar grunted. "Special unit. Not Army, not Eyes, not anybody."

"Let her through?"

Another grunt. "Your call."

Chimp considered the woman. Slender. Frail looking. No match for a legionnaire. "Come with me." He opened the door to the Imperial study and ushered her through.

Inside, a debate was in full swing between two figures on opposite sides of a dark polished desk before a paneled wall lined with portraits and knickknacks. An almost full decanter of wine sat on the desk amidst a clutter of papers.

"The damn bitch got clean away!" Varro Maximus, now the Imperial Chancellor, pounded his fist on the desk. "And she took Charles's brat with her. That's another complication we don't need."

"It doesn't matter." Unlike Varro, the newly minted Emperor kept his voice calm and reasonable. "There are other issues requiring our urgent attention."

"It does matter." Varro's face flushed purple. "We don't need any DuSwaimair heirs running around complicating things. Speaking of which, it's past time Stephen meant with an accident."

"No," said Thomas. "That would be too obvious, and cause unrest. Besides, he's useful. He is the only official who understands the imperial budget."

"Hah! That's no accident." Varro took note of Chimp and his charge. "What is it?"

Chimp bowed. "Sir – ah Supremacy, I present Lady Hermione Scribner from the Imperial Archives. She claims to possess the documents you want."

"Archives," asked Varro. "We've more important matters to grapple with than moldy old records."

Thomas stared at Hermione. "Speak."

Hermione bowed. "I served in a special unit founded by the late Emperor Morgan DuSwaimair and directed by his cousin Solon."

"Morgan," asked Varro. "Emperor Morgan, Charles's father? He's been dead for a decade. What project is this?"

"Supremacy. Chancellor." Hermione bowed again. "The late Emperor Morgan personally formed a special unit to obtain special objects and knowledge essential to the war effort against Traag."

A cunning expression appeared on Varro's face. "I remember rumors of such a detail."

"Special objects and knowledge," said Thomas. "You mean relics of the Dawn Races."

"And members of those races themselves," said Hermione.

"Do we"- Thomas started to rise from his seat. "Are there"-

"No." Hermione shook her head. "The teams did return with a few of the ancient ones, but they perished, either in the war or its aftermath."

"Damn." Thomas shook his head and returned to his seat. "I would like to speak with them."

"Why," asked Varro. "An ill fate awaits those who consort with the ancient powers. Witness what became of Morgan – murdered by black magic in Athnor's Grand Cathedral."

"Given what transpired in Ptath, we may not have a choice," said Thomas. "These Gotemik exterminated the nomad horde like they were bugs. I have no doubt they could do the same to us."

"They're gone," said Varro. "Think no more of them."

"And should they return?"

"We'll deal with them then," said Varro. "Perhaps they can be bought off."

"Either course requires knowledge." The emperor directed his attention to Hermione. "Do your records say anything about the Gotemik?"

"Some, Supremacy, but not much. The old accounts claim the Gotemik vanished thousands of years ago during the collapse of the old civilizations. A few teams in Agba reported encounters with them immediately after the war." Hermione hesitated. "There are rumors of a war between a strange western realm and the Gotemik, but nothing certain."

"Oh, it's certain," said Thomas. "The Eyes have directed large quantities of men and material to my cousin Titus for that little project. It may not be sufficient."

Chimp grimaced, remembering when Lady Bottle had dropped that bombshell on the prince, back at the wreckage of Gawana's child. Imperial Intelligence had slipped crate after crate of explosives to Casein, using the chaotic supply situation as cover.

The door opened, and Sticks entered accompanied by a woman in a green silk dress. "Supremacy, I present Lady Jasmine Bottle of the Imperial Intelligence Agency."

Lady Bottle bowed. "Supremacy, I bring news of your kinsman Octavos."

"Where is he? Tessa?"

"Alas, no." Lady Bottle shook her head. "I have a report from a mercantile agent who witnessed a marriage ceremony between Octavos Maximus and a Bao Des Ptath at a charming port named Saint's Grave. He mentioned they planned to continue westward."

"Saints Grave?" Thomas shook his head. "That's an ill-omened name if ever there was one."

"It's a former pirate port on the north shore of Nous Isle in the Shadow Sea. I have the message here." Lady Bottle handed Thomas a slip of paper covered with delicate handwriting.

Thomas's brow contorted in thought. "Westward. Octavos goes to join his father."

Hermione cleared her throat. "An incident at Saints Grave is mentioned in my records."

"What incident?"

"Almost the entire populace vanished ten years ago. Over three thousand souls. The investigators thought them claimed by a demon that was once worshipped there by a rogue priestly order."

"God above." Thomas's face turned pale. "I wonder – did the Gotemik have a hand in that atrocity?"

"Unknown, but doubtful," said Hermione. "I do have a large file on Gawana, though."

"Gawana." Thomas shook his head. "I need to do something – perhaps send legions to bolster Titus."

"No." Varro's tone was absolute. "Let the Western madness remain where it's at." He sighed. "Besides, we can't afford it. The Southern Expeditionary force cost us fifty thousand soldiers and drained the imperial coffers to almost nothing." He sighed. "I'd planned to use those soldiers to take Saba and possibly Soraq. Now, they're needed to hold what we have."

"There must be something – perhaps just one legion?"

"Even that would strain our resources," said Varro. "Worse, it puts the Empire in direct conflict with these aliens. Why give them cause to hate us?"

"You have a point." Thomas hung his head. "The Gotemik pursued the nomads across the southern hemisphere. Direct conflict – no."

The emperor raised his head. A cunning gleam appeared in his eyes.

Chimps gut tensed.

"I can, however, send large embassies to the nations bordering Gawana." The emperor stared straight at Chimp. "Embassies staffed by men with special skills."

LABYRINTH WAR XLIV – Octavos

'The friezes on the next ziggurat stopped us in our tracks.

"Titus, those are the demons Traag's sorcerers conjured during the war." A deep frown marred Casein's face.

Casein was right, the relief images depicted muscled men with swords and bows battling immense serpents and gigantic winged toads in a fantastical landscape of clouds and weird geometric shapes.

"You do recognize them, then." The Keepers' voice was as calm and implacable as ever.

I turned to the Keeper. "We fought a war against a nation guided by demons. It took two dozen years, but we won."

"Impressive." The Keeper put his hands together and bowed. "Many have contested these abominations. Few have claimed victory."

The Keeper's arm swept across the carvings. "This is the Temple of War. These scenes occurred when Gawana rose from the dirt. General Sesk came from the north, seeking the treasures of the Old Ones. Bested on the field, his sorcerers conjured demons. The creatures decimated whole cities."

I nodded. Images of demonic destruction from the Traag War flashed through my head.

"The citizenry turned to the priests for succor, and the priests beseeched the Gods." The Keeper's voice dropped low. "And the Gods answered." He motioned towards a square portal atop a flight of stairs.

One by one we ascended.

We followed the caretaker into a large square room illuminated with torches at each corner. Their flickering light illuminated the idol of a giant man with brutal features clenching a magnificent sword. Statues of helmeted warriors flanked the deity to either side, each bearing an ax identical to Casein's trophy.

The Keeper motioned at the giant idol. "Behold Ar-Indra, God of War."

"Who are those guys?" Casein pointed a blunt finger at the nearest of the ax bearers.

"They are Ar-Indra's Champions." The Keeper didn't seem annoyed by Casein's directness. "While the Gods battled the demons in heaven, they bestowed gifts upon their chosen to aid the contest here. The Priests of Mysteries received sigils that banished or confounded the demons. Ar-Indra gave his followers the Ungarat Axes. Those divine donations enabled mortal warriors to contest the infernal creatures." He sighed. "Then Gawana burst its bounds. The maze is anti-ethical to infernal creatures on every level – demons cannot exist within its walls. Unable to remain, the demons fled."

"But the Ungarat Axes remained, passed from hand to hand in contests of strength and blood. Their bearers became tainted, plagued with visions, and subject to fits of murderous rage." The Keeper looked Casein square in the eye.

"Hogwash. It's just an ax." Casein stalked from the temple.

The Keeper watched him depart. "I have known fifteen ax bearers over the past forty years. Each began as a fine young warrior and ended as a monster."

Later, Casein appeared in my chambers. "I should have killed him. He tried to take it from me." His hand caressed the ax as he spoke.

"The Keeper warned you," I said. "The ax is dangerous. Maybe you should leave it here."

"No!" Casein shouted the word. "It's mine!" He ran from the chamber.'

- From 'The Journal of Titus Maximus.'

The sword dropped towards Octavos's head.

Octavos ducked, threw himself forward, and rolled, all in a single fluid motion. The tip of his blade slammed into the armored breastplate of his foe. "Got you old man." His lips curled into a triumphant smile as he spoke.

"Look again, kid," said Casein.

Octavos looked up and saw Casein's massively muscled arm stretching above his head. He felt pressure against his neck. "How did you?"

"Experience, kid. Experience." Casein took a step back. "I'll walk you through it."

"No, you won't," said Titus Maximus, Octavos's father. The wall behind him seemed to shimmer and melt before reassuming its usual rough-hewn appearance. Titus looked more like Octavos's sibling than his sire, with his slick jet-black hair and protruding nose. He wore a neutral grayish-blue tunic with an off-white front and polished black boots. A thin strap across his chest supported a boxy tan leather pouch on his right, while a standard issue gladius sword was sheathed on his opposite side. Next to it was a curious weapon that resembled a crossbow, boasting an ivory handle and crystalline stock. "The last Gotemik probe penetrated forty miles into Gawana. I had to resort to extreme measures."

Casein took a step back. "How extreme?"

Titus gave the former legionnaire a tight glance. "I had to unleash three of the Axmen. Two were killed."

Casein paled. "That is extreme. Were you able to recover the Axes?"

Titus gave a slight nod. "Yes. I gave them to Cats."

Octavos watched the exchange in fascinated silence as he remembered his single quick glimpse of the Axmen – filthy wild-haired men of mostly nomad stock clad in rags and bits of armor, howling for the return of their beloved weapons.

The Ungarat Axes – supposedly the gifts of some deranged deity in ages past – were magnificent double-bladed instruments that could cleave through a boulder in a single stroke – but the enchantments irrevocably woven into their gemmed hilts drove their bearers mad, transforming them into berserkers. Titus used them as shock troops.

Casein's face tightened. His harrowing clashes with the cats still gave him nightmares. He gave a curt nod. "You're going to try to open the door again." It wasn't a question.

"I am."

"Door?" asked Octavos.

Octavos felt his father's violet eyes pierce his brain before turning to Casein. "How goes his training?"

"He's shown marked improvement." Casein's tone was professional. "In the old days, he'd be a candidate for the First Cohort." First Cohort – the toughest, most skilled murderers in a ten-thousand-man legion, each considered the equal of three normal warriors.

"Not good enough. I need him to be at least a match for a First Cohort Centurion – or better yet, Pilus Primus." Casein had been Pilus Primus, or 'First Spear' of VII Marfaki, meaning he was the toughest bastard of the lot.

"Titus, it took me ten years to go from ranker to First Spear."

"We don't have ten years. We might not have ten weeks." Titus's piercing eyes flicked to Octavos. "Get cleaned up. You too, Casein." He placed his palm against a nearby wall, which shimmered and melted in an expanding oval. "I expect you both in the lower antechamber before the next bell." Titus stepped into the wall and vanished.

"That makes my skin crawl." Octavos's incipient sorcery let him glimpse the energies that pulsed and writhed inside the walls. He could use his lyre to alter their flow, making the barriers ripple. Duplicating Titus's feat was beyond his abilities.

"Me too," said Casein.

"Still?" Octavos looked up at the big man. "Despite dwelling here for a decade?"

"Still." Casein started for the actual doorway. "That's why I spent a lot of time elsewhere. Come on. We need to get cleaned up."

Octavos struggled to match the big man's stride. "What's this about a door? Is it in the Heart Chamber?" He hoped not. The Heart Chamber was a place of nightmares.

Casein entered a chamber where miniature waterfalls cascaded from the ceiling into a tiled pool before the water drained away through a carved channel. He shrugged out of his armor and sweaty tunic, exposing a body comprised mostly of muscles and old scars, with just a trace of a beer gut. "The Door accesses the old factory levels."

"A kwintath factory?"

"Yeah." Casein plucked a freshly laundered white tunic with red trim that boasted a circular labyrinth image across the chest from a table and draped it over his frame.

"Intact?" Most of the ancient alien mechanisms were broken or barely functional.

"That's what I'm told. The thing is, the Door is sealed shut. Even Titus hasn't been able to open it. This time, though, he has the Maximus Seal." The sorcerous trinket could bind minds and doors – and open them if need be.

"You think it will work?" Octavos grabbed an identical garment and climbed into it.

"Titus thinks so. That was one reason why he wanted it back so badly." He peered into a tall mirror propped into the corner. He selected a comb and quickly ran it through his hair. "Looks all right." He stepped back. "Your turn."

Octavos eyed himself in the mirror, then swiftly ran the comb through his hair. The stubble on his cheeks didn't count as a beard.

"Leave the fuzz alone. It'll grow out." Casein pulled Octavos from the mirror. "Come on."

Octavos barely had time to grab his belt and lyre case before Casein pulled him into a blue-tinted hall with an octagonal profile. The light seemed to stem from the stone itself.

A file of soldiers with hammer symbols above the labyrinth badges on their pastel armor emerged from a connecting corridor and approached the pair from the other direction.

Their officer, a muscular dwarf two heads shorter than Octavos, gave them a salute as he passed, a move copied by the dwarves and humans under his command. The men were armed with ordinary-looking crossbows but carried bandoliers stuffed with thick shafts – 'specials,' bolts that exploded on impact. Casein brought three dozen crates of specials with him to the maze.

"Ah, Prince Octavos." The dwarf bowed. "I'm afraid I will have to miss your performance tonight." A sheath on his belt held a weapon identical to Titus's.

Octavos played for the troops most evenings to bolster their morale – and to test his incipient musical magic. The infused versions of 'Stand Fast' and 'Champion' removed fear and enhanced energy. 'Sleep, Baby, Sleep' made alert men weary and made others collapse. 'Sweet Home' momentarily soothed the Axmen's madness and rage.

Casein paused. "That bad, Captain Garnet?"

The dwarf's beardless face contorted. "Aye, General. There are two hundred thralls with beamers out there. Lord Khazat dispatched us straightaway. Good thing we have these." He tapped the bandoleer.

"Beamers break easy." Confidence filled Casein's voice. "And they're useless after a few shots."

"Breaking beamers before they run out of juice is the problem." Garnet shook his crossbow. "These things pack a wallop, but we could stand more Beamers of our own." He tapped the weapon on his belt.

"I'll see what I can do." Casein strode along the hall.

"That didn't sound good," said Octavos as he struggled to catch the older man.

A trio of lizard-like creatures – Gawana-Ristu – popped out of an almost invisible hatch and scuttled along the corridor. The semi-sapient creatures were mobile extensions of Gawana's will, tasked with maintaining the maze's hidden regions.

"It's not. The Hammermen are a reserve unit. If they are entering the fray, the Wall Walkers and the Outriders got mauled." Casein thought a moment. "The specials should make a difference – Garnet is right about Beamers being fragile – but...I don't know."

"Huh." The thought of Casein being unsure about military matters was frightening.

"This way." Casein entered the new hallway. The Gawana-Ristu scuttled past him, rounded a corner, and vanished.

The hall took a steep downward slope, making Octavos feel like he was falling. Finally, it leveled out before a massive circular metal slab. "Is this it?"

"No, this is merely the antechamber." The speaker was an attractive brown-haired woman in a simple green shift.

"Lady Mila." Casein gave a slight nod. "Titus invited you as well."

"Not just me," said the woman. "3-99 is inside." Her gaze flicked over to Octavos. "This is the son, I presume?"

Octavos managed a formal bow. "Greetings, Lady Mila."

"So polite and formal." Mila's face split into a smile. "I like that."

The portal rolled aside, exposing a gargantuan chamber large enough to hold half a dozen ships with room left over. Despite its dimensions, the room was empty apart from a small pile of smooth crates and a few bulbous consoles along the far wall.

Mila motioned at a second massive portal in the wall to their left. "The Door."

Smaller disks – each still wide enough to admit a pair of carts side-by-side – lined the rest of the wall. Two stood open, exposing tubular chambers.

"What are those?" asked Octavos.

"Secondary vaults," replied Mila.

Titus and a short figure in a silver robe appeared from a niche between two consoles beside the Door.

Octavos's gaze was drawn to Titus's companion. He'd met the alien twice before. A shudder ran through his body remembered a tan bulbous head with angular black protrusions that might have been eyes or ears or something else altogether. Once, a pale broomstick thin appendage terminating in a three-fingered hand had emerged from that robe.

Titus, though, seemed at ease with the alien, treating it as a subordinate. "...it should work. The Maximus Seal manipulated Gawana in the past."

"Because you wielded it, and because of your ancestral ties to Gawana." Faint clicks accompanied the alien's papery voice. "That combination may prove insufficient to access the primary levels."

Titus paused and glared at 3-99. "We shall find out." He turned and caught sight of the others. "It is about time you got here." His gaze shifted to Mila. "Are the workers enroute?"

Mila pointed at the main entryway, where a row of men and women in turbans, vests, loincloths, and sandals towed low, flat metal wagons into the hall. "They are here now."

"Good. We've no time to waste." With that, Titus reached into the pouch and pulled forth a cylindrical object. "Up against the seam is probably the best choice, right?" This last was addressed to 3-99.

The alien's robe rustled. "I am uncertain."

"I say it is." Titus slammed one end of the cylinder against the almost invisible crack and pressed his palm against the other. "I am Administrator Titus Maximus, Lord Defender of Gawana." His voice rang throughout the cavernous space. "Gawana's core is under assault by attackers with Gotemik weapons. I require access to the factory levels for equivalent armaments to mount a proper defense."

"Nothing." Casein shook his head.

"No, not nothing." Mila's gaze was focused on the disk's center. "I feel energies moving within the wall."

Octavos decided to try his Sight. He rapidly blinked his eyes in an alternating sequence, then focused on the portal. Faint orange and yellow blotches set in the surrounding wall caught his attention.

"I don't see any" – Casein stopped speaking as a high-pitched ringing note filled the chamber.

The ringing – no, vibration - grew in volume, piercing Octavos's frame like the electric jolt he'd felt upon touching a scholar's machine back at the University of Solace. His brain felt ablaze. He clenched his ears, trying to keep the sound out. He wobbled on his feet.

Everybody else in the chamber fell to the floor, writhing in pain.

No, not everybody. 3-99 still stood, as did Titus.

"YOU WILL OPEN!" He pressed his palm even harder against the seam. "Gawana is in peril! I am the Lord Defender of Gawana! I need weapons!"

Dad is showing emotion. That is a first.

The vibrations shifted to a lower frequency. Became differentiated.

Octavos cocked his head despite the pain. There were patterns within the vibrations. Complex movements between high and low pitches. Almost like... "Music." He spoke the word under his breath.

"There." Mila pointed at a portal near the chamber's far end. "It's trembling."

Casein eyed the opening in question. "You're right."

New sounds entered the vibrational pattern – a sharp hammering accompanying a deep grinding noise.

"OPEN!" Titus still faced the main Door.

A thunderous 'crack' came from above the smaller portal. The whole wall trembled. An immense, unmusical screech filled the air, forcing everyone to cover their ears again. Then the smaller portal moved. It rolled one foot. Then two. Three. A few more inches. And then it halted – and so did all the vibrations, hammering sounds, and screeching. Silence fell in the chamber.

"You succeeded." 3-99 touched Titus's arm with one stick-thin appendage and pointed at the smaller portal with another.

"Huh?"

"Yes," said the alien. "You opened a secondary vault."

"I asked for access to the manufactory." Blood dripped from Titus's palm to the floor.

"You asked for weapons to defend Gawana, as is your right as Lord Defender."

"Weapons. Is this a weapons depository?" Titus took a few steps towards the smaller door, which had opened enough for a person to squeeze through – though Casein would likely have to turn sideways.

"It holds equipment for security personnel."

"Truncheons and manacles for Constables," said Titus. "I need real weapons."

"This is what Gawana deigned to provide." 3-99 rotated in place. "I am certain that while 'truncheons and manacles' are among the vault's contents, it also holds more potent weaponry."

"It'd better," said Titus, "or Gawana is doomed." He entered the opening. "Send the laborers."

Casein heaved the nearest worker to his feet and thrust him at the crack. "Make a chain!" The worker, his frame hunched over to where his hands almost touched the floor, scuttled towards the cleft, muttering under his breath. His companions followed suit.

"It's a mess in here." Titus's voice filtered through the door. "It appears to have then abandoned in great haste. Everything is scattered."

"The depository was sealed during a turbulent period." 3-99 slid through the opening. "I will assist you in identifying its contents."

"Casein, get in here," said Titus. "I need your muscles to move these items."

Casein looked at Octavos, then went to the opening. He had to turn sideways to fit.

Metal boxes and canisters in various colors and sizes emerged from the opening. Mila had the laborers place the containers in separate piles, based on color and shape.

All too soon, though the chain stopped.

"Is that it?" Octavos looked at the collection in dismay – perhaps a hundred boxes in different colors, and half that number of metallic cylinders.

"I'm afraid so." Casein squeezed back into the main chamber. "There's other stuff, but it's mostly broken or too big to move."

Titus appeared. "Well, some of this is good, anyhow." He pressed one end of an orange box stamped in alien glyphs. The top retracted, exposing a dozen crystalline weapons identical to the one suspended from his belt. "Hand beamers. Less potent than the ones wielded by the Gotemik's thralls, but still formidable." He pulled forth one of the devices and did something with its side. A pulsating glow filled the crystal. "Still charged."

Octavos counted about a dozen crates of the deadly devices. Maybe a hundred altogether?

"I remember these." Mila stood beside a larger box, emblazoned with the image of a black and blue one-piece suit that extended from wrists to ankles. "The fibers of these garments can turn steel and prevent arrows from piercing flesh. I remember a bandit who chanced upon one of these garments. He was a nuisance before drowning in the great mire."

"They also provide limited protection against Gotemik toxins and the weapons you term 'Beamers.'" 3-99 emerged from the vault dragging a disjointed mess of parts and fabric. "However, they are inadequate against a direct strike." "I'll take them," said Titus. "We have about a hundred."

"These may prove useful." 3-99 pulled a tube from one of the canisters. "Security personnel in past eras termed these 'Tangle-Feet.' They fire electrically charged webs that span a substantial area. They were employed against groups of unruly servitors."

"Ah, now this is something I understand." Casein took a short, blunt-tipped sword from a box. "These are wicked sharp."

"We need more." Titus looked up from the collection to stare at 3-99.

"This is what Gawana had available." The alien trembled. A shrug?

"The Gotemik have hundreds of beamers. And their blasters decimate entire sections of the maze."

"We have captured beamers," said Casein.

"Nine," said Titus. "Four of them broken."

"I was able to restore two of the damaged units to functionality," said 3-99.

"Seven, then. We need more."

A commotion came from the entryway. Captain Garnet trotted into view. "Lord Protector! Five Gotemik Fliers and seven Dead Birds are approaching the Heart!"

Dead Bird? Is this some species of necromancy?

Titus slammed his fist against a crate. "Dammit, that means the other attack was a feint, to draw out our reserves."

"Doesn't Gawana have fliers?" asked Octavos.

Titus looked at him. "Once, yes. Not anymore."

"But Vazari"-

"The House of Black and White had fliers until recently. They transported dignitaries and trinkets to Cendoza and

Ado-Cent. They lost one during the first Gotemik assault. The others were severely damaged – or so they say."

"You sound skeptical."

"I am skeptical about everything connected with the House of Black and White."

Casein eyed the dwarf. "Well, Captain, you wanted beamers. Now you get to use them."

The dwarf looked at the piled boxes and assorted devices. "We'll give them hell, sir."

Titus looked at the dwarf. "Send runners to the Hearth Guard, the Blue Band, and the Stalkers. We'll distribute beamers to the senior men of each unit."

Garnet barked orders at his team. Three humans raced from the chamber.

Casein turned to Octavos. "Come on. Let's get you outfitted."

"Give him a beamer, a blade, and an armor suit," said Titus.

"I'll show him how to use the beamer."

"Show Garnets men while you're at it."

The dwarf took a step towards Titus. He tapped the Beamer hanging from his belt. "With due respect, Lord Defender, I showed my top lads how to work the beamer in case something happened."

"Good thinking," said Titus. "Those men get beamers. Have the others open the rest of these crates."

Casein handed Octavos a beamer. "I don't know how these things work, but they're simple to use." He gripped the stock just past the trigger. "Give this a twist until you hear it click." He gave it a quarter turn. "That brings it to life."

The device radiated a purple glow.

"Pull back on this." Casein touched a nob. "That arms it. To fire, touch this button on the handle. It should be good for seven shots. Got it?"

"I think so. Twist to activate, pull to arm, push the button to fire." Octavos thought a moment. "Push in the knob to disarm and twist back to make it inert, right?"

"That's about it. A couple of other things." Casein rendered the weapon inert, then tapped the stock. "If this thing glows orange instead of purple, it's damaged or low on power. You might get one more shot – or you might not."

"Okay. What's the other thing?"

"Beamers are fragile – the Gotemik ones in particular. These are more durable but can still break. If you twist this and hear a humming sound the lightning pack is damaged. A good wizard can fix that – sometimes, but until then, it won't fire. If the hum gets loud, toss it away and run, because that means it's about to explode."

Octavos absorbed this information as more men and dwarves with labyrinth badges on their armor entered the chamber and formed themselves into lines. Titus briefly consulted with their officers, then handed out armor suits, beamers, and razor-sharp with blunt tips to select soldiers. Those chosen removed their armor on the spot.

"They split along the front like so." Mila held out a suit and tugged at a tag beneath the neck. "You must start both legs at the same time. They fit themselves to their wearers."

The troops nodded.

"You, too." Octavos turned to see Casein stripped to his breechclout, holding forth one of the strange garments.

Octavos's tunic hit the floor. He took the suit, which felt metallic and silky at once. It weighed less than his tunic. It split apart easily. He gingerly set one bare foot into a leg opening, then the other. He pulled – and the fabric slithered up his legs, conforming to their shape. Next, he stuck a hand in each armhole with the same result, leaving only a narrow gap over his chest. Dangling strips of blueish cloth proved to be a belt attached to the back with a built-in holster on one side and tiny pouches on the other.

"Attend." 3-99 stood before the assembly, pointing at Captain Garnet. "This," he tapped one of the pouches, "is an emergency repair kit. This next one holds restraints. The last holder is for a spare energy cell for the Beamers. There will be one for each unit."

The men nodded in unison.

Casein approached Titus. "Twenty-three people with the new gear, counting Octavos."

"I'd prefer more," said the Lord Defender, "but that requires training time we don't have." He turned to the alien. "Secure the rest of this equipment. It must not fall into enemy hands."

3-99 gave a slight bow.

"I shall assist him," said Mila.

"Form up!" Casein's voice carried across the chamber. "One Beamer Man per squad."

The soldiers slid into neat rows.

"There is no time to waste. Follow me." Titus strode from the chamber.

The Lord Defender halted at a blank wall partway along the corridor. His palm – still bloody – touched the smooth surface. "Yes, the Fliers are close, now. Very close." He faced the others. "With me. We will be emerging on the south parapet, above the gardens."

Casein nodded. "Assume Pattern Six upon our arrival."

A ragged chorus of assent acknowledged the big man's statement.

Titus's face contorted. The wall before him shimmered.

"Move!" bellowed Casein.

Garnet's company filed through the opening; the soldier's faces set in grim masks. The others followed suit, leaving just Titus, Casein, and Octavos.

Casein stepped into the shimmering surface. Octavos gulped and followed after him. The portal was like a waterfall of heavy mud that pressed against his body from all sides. One step. Sight vanished. Two steps. Octavos felt himself becoming disoriented. He reached out with his infant psychic senses, and felt a lattice of energy around him, much of it twisted to make a strange tunnel. Three steps. He sensed a terminus. Four steps. An orange tint filled the space before him. Five steps – and Octavos was on a wide stone balcony overlooking rows of trees and crops that filled an elongated basin or valley before him – and hovering over the far end was an ugly metallic disk studded with fleshy protrusions.

"Two Disks and four Dead Birds have landed, sir." Garnet materialized beside Casein. His stubby hand jabbed at columns of figures in mismatched armor moving through the vegetation, about half carrying metallic sticks attached to bulky backpacks. All of them wore bulky collars about their necks. "I count about a hundred of them."

"Strike team," said Casein. "Are the men in position?"

"Pattern Six, as ordered, sir."

"Wait for my signal. Specials first, beamers only if needed."

Garnet nodded, then vanished into the undergrowth.

The Gotemik disk dropped to the ground, crushing two fruit trees. A wide hatch fell open, its end touching the dirt. More collared thralls joined the others already on the ground.

An immense bird with rigid wings popped over a ridge and flew overhead. Octavos blinked. No, not a bird, merely a machine that looked like a bird. He remembered experiments with such devices back at the University of Solace. Back then, they'd seemed a mere curiosity. Not anymore.

"Dead Bird coming into the garden," screamed a soldier as another flier struck a vegetable patch. A dozen warriors, most of them hobgoblins, emerged from its interior.

"Now!" Titus motioned. Colored lights flared from the tree branches. And the scene below turned into instant pandemonium. Specials flew at the invaders and detonated.

The attackers responded with blue-white beams from their weapons. Octavos judged about thirty thralls fell in the first salvo.

But the beamers wreaked havoc among the defenders. The remaining thralls sorted themselves into an arrowhead formation – and advanced straight toward Titus's position.

The Lord Defender's features contorted in shock. "They know this is an entrance. But how?"

"It doesn't matter," said Casein.

"It does matter. I feel a probe of Gawana's underlying structure. They might breech the outer defenses."

"Then we will have to stop them." Casein took in the scene. "I suggest switching to Pattern Four." He faced Titus. "Now might be a good time for the Ax Cats."

"Agreed." Titus motioned. The glowing trees changed colors.

Casein faced Octavos. "Get that beamer out and make ready. This is going to be a bloody mess."

Octavos pulled the beamer from its holster. It seemed ridiculously light and delicate for something so deadly. Strangely, he felt completely, utterly calm and detached. He twisted the stock.

Below, the defenders changed tactics. Specials and beamers attacked both sides of the approaching arrowhead. The thralls took losses but kept coming.

"They've reached the slope," said Casein.

Octavos held out the beamer. He sighted along the stock. An orange head popped above the crest. He tapped the firing button. Nothing. Dark panic built in his gut.

Casein's voice filled Octavos's ears. "Arm the damn thing!"

Arm? What was Casein talking about? Octavos stared at the weapon, frantic. There was just the stock and the firing button and the knob at the end – the knob. He pulled it back as the thrall raised its beamer. His finger touched the button.

There was no recoil – simply a blue-white flash and the thrall was falling to the ground with half its head missing. Octavos's bolt continued across the basin, passed between two fruit trees, and struck one of the Gotemik Fliers, leaving a scorch mark on its hull.

But there was a second thrall behind the first. And a third. And then two more. A huge weight slammed into Octavos as an armored human tackled him. Octavos thrashed to no avail. The battered tree insignia on the thrall's armor caught his eye. He knew that symbol. "DuFloret?"

The thrall paused; sword upraised. "Not anymore." His voice was a rasp.

"Get off of my son." Titus's foot lashed out, striking the thrall in his collar. The man toppled backward down the slope.

"On your feet!" Casein wrapped his hand around Octavos's wrist and pulled him erect. "We got more of the bastards to kill."

Animalistic howls came from the far side of the valley. A pair of furry shapes wielding oversized battle axes loped into view, their blades stained crimson with thrall blood.

One of the rachasa leaped into a Fliers open hatch. Sparks and screeches came from its interior and then the mutilated carcass of a creature that resembled a giant crab flew from the opening.

The thralls paused in their assault. Blue-white beams lanced at the Ax Bearers – and missed.

Blue and green smoke poured from the side of another Flier.

A squad of dwarves fought a pitched battle beside a third of the flying machines.

And all the while, Titus and Casein picked off enemy troops with their Beamers. Octavos got off two more shots. Both missed.

Then a hammering racket filled the air. The thralls formed into ragged squads and retreated towards the remaining intact fliers, hounded by specials, beamer fire, and deranged rachasa every step of the way.

A massive explosion behind a ridge marked the demise of a gotemik aircraft. Another lurched into the air and tilted, hurling a thrall from its open hatch. A third took off straight up at great velocity, rapidly becoming no more than a tiny dot. A fourth flier lurched into the air spewing black smoke. Octavos watched it corkscrew into a ridge, where it broke into pieces. One last craft escaped and made a wobbling flight westward.

"We won," said Octavos. He felt exhilarated and exhausted all at once.

"This time," said Casein.

LABYRINTH WAR XLV – Bao

'The acrobats intensified their leaping and tumbling, culminating with the female members of the troupe standing on the heads and shoulders of the men.

"You look interesting, foreign man," said an accented female voice. The speaker was a striking young woman with coifed hair and a jeweled girdle.

"You're cute," said Casein.

Varian pursed his lips. "This could be trouble. That is Sultana, one of Minister Parana's daughters."

My ire increased at the mention of Parana's name. "Well, Casein is quite the lady's man."

Sultana locked her hands behind Casein's neck, lifted her feet, wrapped her legs around his waist, and planted a sloppy kiss on his cheek.

The female acrobats leaped from the shoulders of the men supporting them in a series of somersaults and windmills that carried them to the room's far corners.

Varian eyed the couple speculatively. "Before your arrival, Sultana's affections were directed towards my man Ram."

No sooner had the words left his mouth than I heard an immense snort, and Ram bulled his way past a couple of idlers.

Ram grabbed Casein's arm.

My heart sank. The absolute last thing I needed was a brawl.

Casein slapped Ram's hand away. A growling sound emerged from his throat, prompting others to look in his direction.

Sultana turned to Ram and stuck her tongue out. Ram's face turned dark.

"Casein, be civil." I strode towards the confrontation with unfelt confidence.

"I'll settle this quick." Casein detached himself from Parana's daughter.

"Leander Casein, we don't need a brawl."

Varian smirked. I wanted to punch him. Instead, I asked him to reign in Ram.

Varian drained his glass. "Brawls are forbidden in the House of Delight."

Both Casein and Ram halted.

My heart rose. Varian gave me another smirk. "Athletic competitions, such as wrestling, are permitted."

"Suits me," said Casein.

Ram grunted.

Varian motioned to a priestess. They held a brief conversation. She eyed the contestants, tongue tracing her lips.

The priestess made a short announcement.

People stepped away from the flexible portion of the floor. Sultana stood giggling off to the side, her hands clasped.

Another priestess raced from the room.

"Titus, let's dance!" Parana stood across the impromptu ring.

I debated with myself. Would Parana be satisfied with a single dance?

The Minister's right breast flopped free of its binding. Instead of replacing the strap, she freed her other mammary and made a suggestive finger motion.

No, the Minister would not settle for a mere dance. And I would not violate my marriage vows, especially with Parana.

The short figure of the First Warden stumped into the chamber, trailed by four subordinates. "Referee's," Varian explained.

Inside the square, Casein stomped his feet while Ram glared.

Parana worked her way along the crowd's edge.

I scanned the room. A door between the buffet tables caught my eye. "I am quite famished."

Varian smirked at me.

Khulna entered the square and stood between Casein and Ram, explaining the contest's rules.

They were uninterested.

Little remained on the buffet tables. I ladled spiced soup into a bowl and hefted a tiny glass of green liquor.

Parana circumnavigated the bulk of the contest area. A male acrobat stepped in her path.

Khulna dropped his hand.

Casein and Ram collided at full speed. Blood and spittle went flying.

The onlookers gasped.

Parana didn't even turn. She pushed the acrobat away and continued in my direction.

I gulped the minty liquor and ducked through the door into an empty kitchen.'

- From 'The Journal of Titus Maximus.'

"I'm not feeling sociable." Octavos peered at Bao across the table with haunted eyes, ignoring the lively music from the Temple of Joy behind him.

"Please try, husband." Bao extended her arm and caressed Octavos's cheek. "The music may appeal to you and the skit is reputed to be most entertaining."

"No!" Octavos pushed Bao's hand away and grabbed the bottle before him. He took a long gulp straight from the neck. "The music is shit – they don't even have lyres here, the skit is shit, this whole wretched city is shit."

"You don't mean those things, husband. Your mouth moves but I hear your father's words. He seeks to make you into something against your nature."

"Don't talk to me about my father!" Octavos swiped at Bao, but his coordination was so dulled by drink that he missed. He stared at the table.

"Husband, you cannot continue like this."

"I have no choice." Octavos's voice was small. He didn't look up from the table.

Bao stood. "I shall petition Titus to have you removed from the field. Your talents are best employed elsewhere."

"He won't listen. He doesn't listen to anybody." Octavos didn't lift his head.

"He will listen to me." With that, Bao strode away from the lonely little table, trying to ignore the rent in her heart.

He's getting worse. Bao remembered Octavos emptying his belly for two days straight after the first battle, screaming himself awake from horrible nightmares. If that battle had been the end of it, her husband would have recovered. But that wasn't the end of it. Desperately short on soldiers, Titus had sent Octavos into one pitched battle after another. Only that miraculous alien armor had kept him from being roasted at Ulaam-Thek. He'd returned from Red Tree a cold shell of himself. This trip – this pointless diplomatic mission to Vazari – was supposed to have been a chance to heal. It wasn't working.

Vazari. Bao went to the balcony rail and stared at the city, illuminated by the falling sun. Wide fields and orchards surrounded the metropolis. Sheer distance shrank Gawana's walls to the point of invisibility. Here, unlike anywhere else she'd been in the Maze – not that her travels were all that extensive, apart from the journey from Seagate to the Heart and the Heart to Vazari – it was possible to pretend the walls didn't exist. She didn't have to see the feeder vines clinging to the rough stonework or tolerate views that always ended in a blank surface.

Vazari, though...the city was impressive. The balcony provided an excellent, if somewhat angled view of the metropolis. Bao leaned over the rail and took in tiny boats and dull barges upon the curved string of ponds that girded the city. There. That barge was the one they'd arrived on three days ago.

Her gaze flicked to a bridge that spanned that liquid mass to the outer wall. Her position granted Bao a view of carts and beasts plying dirty streets between peasant huts and tenements, the dwellings of those who worked the farms and orchards around the city. Many of those wains scaled a wide road to the circle of wealth, a long narrow market interspersed by artisan's shops. She'd spent much of yesterday inspecting their wares – they boasted odd spices and silken fabrics in abundance, but while trinkets of tin and brass were common, iron and steel were scarce. Likely, that had to do with the lack of fumar logs, forcing metalworkers to rely on solar forges. Then again, iron and steel seemed scarce across the maze – except for weapons. Weapons. Bao could see only a slice of it from here, but Vazari's Third ring was a place of soldiers and their armaments. The city had already dispatched two thousand wardens to serve in Titus's army, and they were here to petition for more. Bao shook her head. No, it was best not to think about that.

She turned from the balcony and took in a row of ziggurats, colonnaded buildings, and immaculate gardens – the Civic Circle, the domain of the temples that administered the city. The city's elite dwelt on the fifth level, the Ring of the Exalt. Titus boasted a house on that level, a miniature fortress on an outthrust bastion. Bao didn't care for the place.

"You're missing the party." The pert feminine voice came from behind Bao.

Bao turned to face the speaker, an attractive woman with gold pins in her elaborately coifed auburn hair. Necklaces made of ivory and copper beads hung over her ample breasts, providing a bit of weight to her filmy pink dress which billowed upward with each motion or breeze. "Hello, Minister Sultana."

Sultana's attire contrasted strongly with Bao's modest beehive and simple green, red, and blue flower-print dress.

Sultana cocked her head. "You've been fighting." It wasn't a question.

"My husband has been fighting. It has changed him, and not for the better."

"Fighting does that to men, I have learned." Sultana stalked a half-circle around Bao. "I have watched many pretty, wonderful boys march off to war with glory in their eyes and return as bitter wrecks if they returned. And now Gawana's Lord Defender is here for yet another levy. Five hundred men this time." She motioned at the city below them. "Many families in the Ring of Toil will contribute a younger son to the cause."

Bao straightened. "I am Lady Bao Vada Falun Des Ptath Maximus, once a princess of Ptath in Upper Kheff. Ptath is a fortress city, the Solarian Empire's bulwark against the Nations of the Plains which has withstood a hundred assaults on its walls through the centuries. My brother commanded one of the border forts and acquitted himself in the latest strife." And collaborated with the enemy to seize power. Bao kept her face neutral. "My father perished at the hands of infiltrators in his feast hall." Infiltrators guided by my treacherous bodyguard, who murdered my maids and almost murdered me. "I know the toll war extracts on bodies and hearts."

"Then you know that standing about moping will not cure your heart or your husbands." Sultana made a slow circle about the almost comatose Octavos. "Now, your man drinks to forget the horror." She touched his shoulder. "But one day, with prodding, he will remember the joy." Her face almost touched Bao's. "And there is much joy in him behind the bitterness."

Bao considered her husband. "That day is not yet. He rejects my every overture."

"His malaise darkens your spirit." Sultana motioned at the Temple of Joy's interior. "Let the celebration within lighten that darkness." Again, she leaned close to Bao. "They have a most talented troupe of dancers from Soonlar performing tonight." She broke away and took a few steps towards the opening.

Bao glanced again at her husband, a lonely lump hunched over his table with his fingers wrapped about a bottle, then at light and sounds emanating from the temple. Then she followed Sultana.

Merely setting foot in the grand hall lifted Bao's spirits. Magic? Quite possibly. She took in scantily clad priestesses flitting about huddled knots of local notables and visiting dignitaries, reciting snippets of verse and making uplifting jests. The guests responded with compliments and anecdotes about younger and older relatives.

Octavos could benefit from this place. The old Octavos would have claimed a spot on one of the daises and strum a tune that would make the crowd stomp and sing along. But that good-hearted youth was buried beneath the brittle shell of a warrior. Breaking that shell would take time.

Hidden drummers took up a complex beat that overwhelmed the other instruments present. Faces turned as chocolate-skinned women wearing little more than beads and skirts twirled into the chamber's suddenly empty center.

"Ah, the performance begins." Sultana materialized beside Bao, accompanied by a plump older woman with a painted face, darkened eyes, and immense breasts that strained against a thin black shift. "My mother Parana, now retired from civic service."

"Retired from service, but not from the joys of life." The older woman placed a hand beneath Bao's chin and turned her face. "So, you snared a mighty Maximus."

Bao freed her head. "It was an arranged marriage."

Parana's eyes narrowed. "To hear the gossip, it was an epic adventure. I would hear the details."

"Mother!" Sultana gently pushed the woman back a step. "That can wait. Right now, let us enjoy the dance."

Parana raised a tall, skinny cup of cut crystal that sparkled in the light and took a drink. "Yes, let us enjoy these pleasures while they last."

The dancers spun and leaped in the hall's center, motions that revealed plump breasts, and lifted their skirts clear to their waists, exposing firm buttocks. Tall, muscular Soonlar males joined the women, hurling them from one man to another.

"He looks interesting." Parana pointed at an all but naked specimen who balanced a dancer in either hand.

"Mother, he's younger than I am!"

"Which means he's got endurance enough to keep up with me."

The female dancers leaped from the fellow's hands, doing somersaults before touching the ground.

The dance took on a more intimate nature as the women cupped their breasts and rubbed their private parts.

Sultana all but leaned against Bao. "Well, what do you think?"

"I think those dancers are as flexible as their Saban counterparts."

"Saba?" asked Parana. Somehow, she'd acquired another flute of wine.

"A kindred nation of Soonlar near Ptath. Oh my." A hot flush entered Bao's cheeks as several of the Soonlar women began rubbing the private parts of the male dancers.

Parana pointed. "That one is impressively well endowed."

"Mother!" But Sultana's gaze was riveted on the spectacle, along with Bao's and the eyes of most of the other guests in the room, male and female alike.

Parana stalked off after her chosen swain.

Sultana touched her chin. "Well, I suppose...that one, perhaps?" She indicated a rangy fellow with tattoos of animals above his groin. "What do you think?"

"I think I am married."

"What of it? So am I." Sultana pointed at a skinny fellow propositioning one of the female dancers. "That's my husband over there."

"I see."

"Surely it is the custom in your land for married women in arranged marriages to take lovers."

"Some women do. But they are discreet about such liaisons."

"But you have seen such performances before."

"Once. My friends and I hired a small troupe for a private performance – but matters never reached this stage."

"Well, you don't have to participate." Sultana stalked off.

"Those two haven't changed at all in a dozen years."

Bao turned to see Titus standing behind her. "I thought you were closeted with First Warden Khulna."

"I was. Something came up. Two somethings, to be precise."

"Oh?"

Titus motioned at the dancers, now drifting off with highborn companions. "It is just as well you resisted...seeking companionship."

"I am a married woman! I would never betray my husband like that!"

"Other married women, as Sultana so aptly pointed out, are not so faithful. And lovers tend to spill secrets they shouldn't." Titus might have been talking about the weather for all the emotion he displayed.

Bao took a moment to process Titus's words. "The dancers are spies?"

"And envoys, and thieves, and other things if need be. The First Wardens men...intercepted a few poking about where they had no business being."

"I suppose these miscreants are awaiting judgment?"

"These rogues are connected with Soonlar's aristocracy and act on their behalf throughout the region. Harming them risks offending their masters. And Gawana has enemies enough already. This brings me to the second matter – the war against the Gotemik fares poorly. Eventually, we will lose."

"You need allies." Bao thought for a moment. "I imagine the Maximus name is not well regarded in Soonlar."

"That is correct."

Bao continued. "The Nations of the Plains are almost eradicated and would have made unreliable allies anyhow."

"Also true, though a quarter of my soldiers are nomad refugees. I granted their families sanctuary in Ulaam-Thek in exchange for service."

"And Agba is a depopulated wasteland stalked by cultists and monsters left over from the war."

"Imperial troops do keep the more troublesome creatures away from the remaining cities," said Titus, "But your analysis is correct."

"That leaves little," said Bao. "My understanding is Cendoza and the Rhaiduni states are not noted for their military prowess.

Arcos prizes its neutrality. So, where does that leave you? Soraq?" The name felt wrong even as she said it.

"I have recruited extensively in Soraq," said Titus. "But you omitted the largest and best source of new troops from your analysis."

"The Empire." Bao's eyes narrowed. "They are coming here?"

"To Cendoza. I need an envoy, one of sufficient stature to treat with them."

"Octavos."

"No. You." Titus placed his hands on Bao's shoulders. "Octavos led the sheltered life of an academic in Solace. You, though, understand politics."

"I want my husband by my side." Bao's face tightened.

"I have other plans for Octavos."

"Octavos has been in enough battles. He is but a shell of his former self."

"I agree."

"What?"

"I am not blind. A soldier crippled by trauma is of no use on the battlefield. It is time for my son to make use of his academic knowledge. There are mysteries in desperate need of unraveling back at the Heart."

LABYRINTH WAR XLVI – Curtis

"My nation is dead. My pack is dead. All that remains is a war for masters who hold me in contempt. It is enough."
- Gham-Rek, Hobgoblin Warrior

Curtis sat on a stone, staring at the ground, ignoring the blood that dripped from his face and arms. I almost killed him. *I almost killed Octavos Maximus. I would have killed him if that dwarf hadn't shot me.* He lifted his head to the overcast sky. "Damnit! I have had enough!" He clawed at the heavy collar that encircled his neck. "Leave me be!"

There was no response. The demon that resided in the collar, the one that made him fight and do terrible things for his monstrous masters, seldom deigned to communicate with its slave. And when it did communicate, it did so in commands. Do this. Don't do that. Go here. And if he disobeyed, well, it punished him. Sometimes with jolts that made his whole body shake uncontrollably. At other times, it took control of Curtis's limbs, making him a passenger in his own body.

The demon did have limits, though. Yes, it compelled Curtis to do things for the crab monsters, the Gotemik. But it didn't seem to care about quality. He could be messy. He could choose to miss and or hesitate that extra quarter second. That was why Octavos still lived. But he was still a puppet.

But not anymore. He was sick of living in a nightmare he couldn't alter, sick of serving alien abominations, sick of everything. Curtis reached for his sword. Jammed the hilt in a crevice between his feet. All he had to do was hurl himself forward with enough force for the blade to pierce his eye and brain, and it'd be over.

"No." A metal booted foot kicked the blade away. An ugly orange face dominated by a pig-like snout fringed with black hair filled Curtis's vision. Gham-Rek. Hobgoblin. Once an enemy, now Curtis's companion in misery. "You live."

Curtis eyed the hobgoblin. Like him, Gham-Rek wore a demon collar. "What for?" He tapped the band around his neck. "This thing will rule me until I die."

"Because you fighter. Got warrior spirit. Demon-band does not rule that." Gham-Rek jabbed a finger into Curtis's chest. His hand, like all goblins and hobgoblins, had only four fingers. "Not unless you surrender."

"I'm tired of fighting."

"Everybody gets tired. Rest. Eat."

"I can't sleep and the slop they feed us is horrible."

Gham-Rek smiled, exposing broken teeth. "Got good food today. I find, kill an ox. It is cooking now."

"Huh." Roast ox was far better fare than the usual slop. But it didn't change the fact he was stuck in this hellhole, or that tomorrow would bring more bloodshed and death. He said as much to Gham-Rek.

"No. We don't fight here tomorrow."

"Huh?"

"Git-Vik says have a long flight tomorrow."

"Gah. That's not exactly an improvement." The interior of the flying monsters had no headroom and was all hard surfaces and weird protrusions. Last time, it took Curtis three days to work the kinks out of his back.

"I got cushions." Gham-Rek pointed at a pile of sacks stuffed with straw.

"That might help." Curtis didn't feel optimistic, but he was less miserable. "Where are we going?"

"West. Cit-Cee-Cait, the Gotemik's city."

"Shit."

LABYRINTH WAR XLVII – Carina

'Employed in disciplined moderation, Blood Magic is useful in healing spells – a fact acknowledged even by the Church. However, Blood Magic can corrupt less disciplined practitioners and transform them into monsters. Witch Hunters point to these tainted souls as proof that mortals are unfit to wield magic.'

- From the 'History of the Great Purge.'

Carina focused her Sight on the back of Kaija's neck. There it was, a tiny focus point of red energy, anchored in what looked like a mole, sending tendrils throughout the girl's body. Except this mole was bright red, not black. She grabbed a needle with a hooked tip and pressed it against the protrusion. A tiny red grain popped free of the girl's skin.

"Ow!" Kaija thrashed on the table. "Dat hurt!"

"Hold still." Carina pulled a magnifying lens from her kit and inspected the tiny object – a crimson arrowhead-shaped crystal that poured maleficent energy into Kaija's frame despite being removed. She tried a basic banishment spell. The grain pulsed – and Kaija convulsed.

"Dat hurts!" Kaija thrashed some more. The sliver didn't budge despite her movements.

Time to try something else. Carina pressed out the sliver. Then she poured clean white energy into the girl's back. The sliver flared red, then white. Then it dissolved into fine dust, taking the maleficent magic with it.

"Ow! Ow! What did you do?"

"I broke the curse stone in your back." Carina regretted the words the moment they left her mouth. Admitting to being a healer was one thing. But breaking curses was what magic users did.

"Curse stone? Is dat what dat was?" Kaija rolled off the table. "Dat witch Bina did try to grab me after I told dat bastard Dobo I weren't working for him in dat stinky Flower House."

Carina had a damn good idea what sort of establishment the Flower House was. "Did she grab the back of your neck?"

"Yeah, but I broke free." Kaija straightened. "I do feel better all sudden-like." She looked at Carina. "Are you a witch?"

"I know magic, yes. But I'm a healer. I don't hurt people." *Unless I have to.*

"Huh. I will let my friends know. Fan can use a good hoodoo woman." Kaija tossed two silver beads on the table and scurried out of the hut. Carina watched the woman walk along the crude boardwalk to the ford upstream – the preferred crossing point for those who didn't wish to barter with a boatman for passage.

Carina repacked her kit, a dark lump growing in her gut. Then she peered through the doorway, studying the city of Fan across the Sytek River from her hut. A crumbling stepped pyramid covered with vines dominated the city's easternmost fringe: the infamous Temple of Serpents, whose priests traded venom and scales for gems and ivory. Her gaze traced west, taking in ebony women toting baskets and jars in the market across the Sytek's juncture with the river Ula. A dozen men, stripped to mere breechclouts, hacked away at logs drawn up on the riverbank directly across from Carina's hut, making them into dugout canoes. Children darted between rows of huts and tenements, while colonnaded manors dotted the hills inland.

Women wearing next to nothing lounged before the brightly painted Flower House.

As Carina watched, a fat bald man in a fine robe exited the building and slapped one of the women so hard she fell off the porch. Dobo? Maybe. He strode away without a backward glance.

Carina sighed. *I may have to leave this place.* She'd left a lot of places this past year, mostly not of her own volition. First, the witch hunter Appius Ambrose forced her to flee Ismara. She'd fled Ptath after murdering the bastard. Fear of imperial retribution drove her to sail with Casein and Octavos westward across the Shadow Sea, hoping to take refuge in the living labyrinth of Gawana.

Gawana, though, terrified Carina. Her first sight of the place from Seagate's harbor hit like a punch in the gut. She could sense the energy of the vine-covered walls from a mile away. It made her feel like a morsel waiting to be devoured. So, she'd made an excuse and remained on the dock while Casein guided Octavos and Bao into that monstrosity. She'd boarded a boat out of Seagate at the first opportunity.

That boat brought Carina to Southport, a trade city separated from Gawana by the deep and muddy waters of the Sytek River. Forging a new life in that grimy metropolis among the blacks of Soonlar seemed possible. Then, one day, she'd rounded a corner and almost collided with a pale man in clerical robes bearing the badge of Saint Simon on his chest, patron of wanderers and traveling merchants. Carina didn't have a grudge against Saint Simon's order, but they were part of the Church of the True God. So, she fled again, this time up the Sytek to Fan. Except, Carina wasn't exactly welcome here, either. That was why she dwelt in this hut on the almost deserted northern bank of the Sytek, within a stone's throw of Gawana.

Yes, Gawana extended this far south. But here, the maze was choked, mostly buried in mud that sapped those stones of their power.

Carina sighed and reentered her hut. Her customers began showing up the next morning: a woman with a cyst on her neck, which Carina lanced without magic. A man with a twisted leg she couldn't help and another with an infected cut she treated with magic. A shopkeeper crossed the river to barter for a protective talisman for his shop. Carina told him she'd inspect his establishment tomorrow. A normal day in the life of a village witch.

Days like this made Carina pretend she was a normal woman - minus the husband and kids. The prospect of that life ended with her husband's death and ravaged womb. She pretended that didn't bother her. Sometimes, she even believed it.

"Damn you, slaver bitch!" Hard pain to Carina's cheek followed by contact with the ground followed the words.

Carina propped herself up, taking in the middle-aged woman before her, clad in a black robe hung with mystic talismans. A pair of thugs stood behind the woman.

"You broke my spell, slaver bitch! How am I supposed to get respect if you break my curses?"

Carina climbed to her feet. "You must be Bina."

"Damn right I am Bina! I am da witch of Fan, Dobo's right-hand woman."

"You cursed Kaija."

"Damn straight I did. Dat bitch turned her nose up at Dobo. He can't have that. I can't have that. And I can't have you hanging around here either." Muscular men gathered behind Bina. Dobo's thugs. "Leave Fan before the sun sets tomorrow. Or..." Bina paused.

Carina had to ask. "Or what?'

"Or I'll slap a new curse on Kaija. And Dobo's toughs will bust every bone in your body."

"Leave Kaija alone."

Fire burst from Bina's fingertips. "Don't you tell me what to do, slaver bitch."

Carina made a cutting motion. Bina's flames went out. "Don't threaten me. Don't go around cursing people."

"Get her!"

Carina made a pushing motion, sending a telekinetic blast that knocked Bina and her thugs off their feet. "I fought in the Traag War. Against demons. Backwater witches don't scare me."

Bina stood. Her eyes widened. "You shouldn't have done that." Her voice was calm and cold. She began another incantation.

Carina slammed her palm into the other woman's breastbone. Reached out with her power and twisted.

"Aeeii! What you do, slaver bitch!" Bina fell to her knees, gasping, the incantation dissolving like smoke.

"I took your power away." For a time, but Bina didn't need to know that. Carina turned on her heel and walked towards the river at a measured pace. *I shouldn't have done that. Now, I really will have to leave.*

"That was impressive." The voice spoke in imperial, not the trade tongue or the sibilant speech of Soonlar.

Carina turned and spotted a redheaded Avar standing next to the wharf. "Luther?"

The man smiled. "Yeah, it's me. We had business up the Sytek. Now we have business elsewhere."

"Where?"

"Couple of places, but we finish up at Ado-Cent."

Ado-Cent. A city beyond the edge of the map. "Got room for a witch?" Carina caught sight of a familiar triple-hulled craft tied to the dock past Luther. "Is that the Japi?"

Luther turned to look at the boat, which boasted two masts and a deck cabin with curved sides. It'd brought Carina and the rest of her old companions from the jungles of distant Soraq clear across the Shadow Sea. "Yep, the old girl has held up pretty good." He thought for a moment. "You ready to go?"

"My things are across the river." Carina motioned at her hut.

"Goji will row you over. I gotta finish up some business here."

Right on cue, Goji popped out of the crafts deck cabin. The brown-skinned man with the ratty turban and gap-toothed grin motioned at a smaller dugout trailing behind the craft. "After you, witchy lady."

"Why, thank you." Carina made an exaggerated bow and climbed into the dugout.

"So, how's business?" asked Carina when they reached the river's midpoint. "It sounds like Casein is running you ragged." *Were these two still working for Casein?*

Goji smiled and spat something dark over the side. "Yeah, you could say that. We got other commissions going on."

"Like Ado-Cent."

"Yeah, like Ado-Cent." The boat touched the far bank. "Huh. I'm gonna grab some grub while you get your stuff." He motioned at a plump woman sitting behind a row of baskets heaped with vegetables.

Getting packed took mere moments: one pack, one box, and her bedroll. The hut, never homey to begin with, looked downright forlorn when she finished. Carina emerged from the shack where Goji chatted with the vegetable seller. She plopped her gear beside him and contemplated the plank path that meandered across the marsh to Gawana.

She took a breath and started walking. The trail didn't see much use – the timbers were half-rotted and sank a little with every step. But it kept her from getting wet. She reached the firmer ground beside the weird mishmash of vine-covered dirt and stones that made up the head-high barrier.

Carina climbed atop a stump for a better view, taking in an expanse of black mud laced with greenery. Quite a bit of greenery – not just marsh weeds, but grass and shrubs. She spotted trees in the distance. An impulse made her scramble over the low barrier. Her sandal barely made an imprint in the dirt. "It's solid. But how?" She turned and eyed the swampy expanse between the wall and the river, marked with deep, muddy channels. "It's being drained." She surveyed the expanse of dirt and grass. Was that a cart track over there? It made for a spot where the wall abutted the ford. She shook her head. *Fan is like Seagate. The maze extends beneath the marsh, and likely beneath the river. All the more reason to leave.*

They found Luther holding court over a quartet of squat, green-skinned goblins in kilts and vests.

"Who are they?"

"Nes-Bot brothers," said Goji. "Our crew. Paddling upstream is tiring, even when the wind is right."

"Oh." Carina thought for a moment. "I might be able to help a little with the wind."

"That'd be nice."

Luther spotted them and waved.

"Got us some more grub," shouted Goji. "Good price."

"Huh." Luther motioned at the nearest goblin. "Get that stuff loaded. We're leaving straightaway."

Fan vanished behind them. Carina wondered how Kaija fared and what Dobo might do, then focused on the patchy forest to either side.

Here, at least, the Ula barely moved at all. The goblin brothers sat and tossed dice while a slight breeze moved the Japi across the muddy water. They spent the evening in a ramshackle structure built on stilts over the water, eating spicy stew while listening to wailing chants and drums from a trio of entertainers. The music hurt Carina's ears. The stew didn't agree with Luther's stomach. He retreated to the deck cabin the next morning and didn't emerge until evening.

The wind stopped on the third day and rain fell from the sky. The Nes-Bot brothers abandoned their perpetual dice game, took positions on Japi's outriggers, and began paddling, water dripping from their backs. They moved like machines all day long, never missing a stroke – then ate almost half their weight in meat and fruit before collapsing into slumber.

They spent the fifth night in a goblin village. Past it, there were no settlements, only isolated huts and queer stone monoliths rendered almost featureless with age.

"It's too dangerous for settlers here," said Luther. "This is nomad country."

"Most of the nomads are dead," said Carina.

"True, but that hasn't sunk in yet."

The Ula shrank in width and depth. More than once, Luther grimaced at the grinding sound when the hull skidded over stones.

"There's the pillar." Goji pointed at a stone post rising from the river's left side.

"I think you're right," said Luther. "That should put the Sili around that next bend."

"Sili?" asked Carina. "Is that a settlement?"

"It's a river." Luther looked at Carina. "We got business there. It shouldn't take long."

They rounded that bend and then the next. Finally, Goji spotted a muddy jet of water joining the Ula from the east. Luther directed the Japi into this new stream, barely twice the craft's width and a yard in depth.

Trees loomed over the Sili, all but blocking out the sky. They were forced to take down the masts and the deck cabin to slide under low-hanging limbs. Thrice, the Nes-Bot brothers jumped into the water to remove fallen logs that blocked their path.

They spent that evening camped on a sandbar, listening to sounds from the forest. The Nes-Bot brothers muttered to each other about 'Demon Cats,' shifters that decimated entire villages, and swamp lizards bigger than boats.

The next day, the Sili grew so narrow the Japi's outriggers almost touched the banks to either side. The deadfalls grew worse. Finally, they reached a log tripod rising from a sandbar. "This is it," said Luther. "We walk from here. Goji, stay here with the brothers. Carina, you're with me."

Carina asked where they were going and received no answer. So, she shrugged, shouldered her pack, and followed after Luther.

Moving through the underbrush was frustrating. Some openings looked like paths but weren't, and the dense plant life concealed logs and muddy trenches blocked the direction Luther wanted to go, they hacked a path through the obstructions one slash at a time.

"Damnit, I'm beat." Luther slammed his sword into a tree, leaned against the trunk, and then took a long swig of water. "We're close. I know it. We gotta be almost on top of it."

"Almost on top of what?" Carina was tired of hiking through the jungle. Thorns and bugs covered her robe.

Luther looked at her. "Maybe your magic can find it." He fumbled through his pack and finally produced a purplish fruit. "Here. You're looking for the trees like the one this came from."

A chill ran through Carina as she took the fruit. "This is from Gawana, isn't it?"

Luther nodded.

"Is there another Child here?" A chill ran through Carina's frame. Octavos had told her about Gawana's Child, a now-dead extension of the living labyrinth planted in Soraq's jungles.

"Maybe." Luther shrugged. "Don't know. Soonlar's priests found and killed the other Seeds Casein planted but this one is in no-man's land. It did grow for a while, but then it just...stopped." Luther spread his hands apart. "We were never sure if it died or something else happened. The boss wanted us to check on it."

"Is it dangerous?"

Luther waved his hands. "Maybe. I don't know."

"I'm not sure about this." The thought of entering even a small version of Gawana sent chills along her spine.

"Just do it."

"Okay, okay." *It's just a location spell. I don't have to enter.* Carina focused on the fruit. "Like attracts like." It was one of the basic principles of sympathetic and scrying magic. She felt a tug to her right. "That way. A couple hundred yards, maybe."

"Good." Luther heaved himself to his feet. "Let's go."

This new Child didn't look like anything – just a few meandering waist-high mounds covered with yellow and red flowers that made a broken circle a hundred yards across. It looked like a long-abandoned encampment or fortification, not an alien monstrosity. *This isn't so bad.*

Luther found a gap in the berm, and they threaded a spiral path through the plants, passing by side passages that went nowhere. The aisle spilled into a clearing dominated by a rocky mound with three stunted trees at its base.

"This must be it." Luther shook his head. "It looks dead."

Carina steeled herself. "I can use my magic." *I need to know if this thing is dead or merely dormant.*

"Go ahead."

Carina shut her eyes and focused, extending her mystic senses into the world around her. At first, she felt nothing but nature's power, the energy of water slowly permeating fertile soil. She spotted a pulsating strand that glowed pink in her mind's eye, one that connected with others at a central node. *Dormant, not dead.* She opened her eyes. "There's something active." She pointed. "There. Beneath that mound."

"Huh." Luther walked about the hillock, which looked like a flower-covered pile of dirt and rock. Finally, he paused before a roughly triangular flat slab, maybe a yard each way. "Yeah, I think this is it." He heaved it aside, revealing a tunnel barely big enough to fit his bulk. A faint pinkish glow illuminated a chamber at its terminus. "Guess it survived after all." He pulled himself from the tunnel and replaced the stone. "Let's go."

LABYRINTH WAR XLVIII – Chimp

The Doctor cleared her throat. "You remember the things called up by Traag's Sorcerer-Lords?"

"Yes." I shuddered. Those creatures stalk my nightmares.

"Agba's overlords sacrificed millions of their subjects to slake the thirst of those demons. Nobody was safe. Entire cities became necropolises. Then the Monks of Zu appeared. Their marks made people invisible to the demon's senses. Many commoners joined the orders ranks."

"Those marks sound handy," I said. "Why weren't they employed in the war?"

"It was attempted. The church called the monks pernicious pagans, especially when they learned of the cost."

"What cost?" Father Joseph asked. "It sounds as though this 'mark' were a blessing from the One God to the unenlightened."

"The future is the cost, good cleric. Those with Zu's mark become barren, unable to sire or bear offspring. They are termed 'monks' for good reason. However, the Zuites won't give somebody the mark unless they're a father or a mother already."

The priest rubbed his chin. "Yes, the ecclesiastical hierarchy would take issue with such a severe cost."

"The Zuite's influence in Cendoza rivals that of the Church in Solaria," said the Doctor.

Father Joseph leaned back and stared at the ceiling. "I pray they are more accepting of strange faiths than my superiors."

- From the Journal of Titus Maximus

"Okay, sneaky feet, gather around." Tribune Crassus opened a skinny book on the Mustering Rooms table.

Centurion Chimp and his crew bellied up beside the table, taking in sheets filled with interconnected boxes and cryptic notes.

"This is Kevin DuMar's Map Book for the Sublime Palace, of which we are now residents," continued the Tribune. "One of the Pasha's esteemed ancestors built the first bit three thousand years ago and every Pasha since then has built onto it ever since." He shook his head. "Now they got a place with thousands of rooms spread out over at least two square miles and no idea what's in ninety percent of them. That has General DuPaul bothered." He fixed Chimp with a piercing gaze. "That has me bothered. I don't want to be bothered. Is that clear?"

"Yes, sir." Chimp gave a salute. "We'll check the place out."

The Sublime Palace took up almost everything on the south side of the Sula River. The rest of Cendoza City climbed the hills on the north bank, with hovels at the bottom, townhouses at the top, and halfway respectable-looking places in between.

"Good." Crassus paged through the book and jabbed a long aristocratic finger down on a big chunk of rooms shaded in light green. "This is our barracks." The digit traced a line along a wide hallway that opened onto a staircase that dropped down to the blue mass that marked the river. "This is the route the 10th took getting in."

The 10th Brigade, twenty-five hundred soldiers strong, was Chimp's new unit, put together from what was left of the old Sand Runners after they got mauled in Upper Kheff.

Chimp nodded. The diagram matched his recollection. His legs still ached from scaling those steps with a full kit.

"Over here," Crassus flipped the page, "are Pasha Pomo's quarters." 'Pomo' was the short form of the Cendozan satrap's ten-syllable name. Only the Envoy and his top people bothered with it. Everybody else just called him Pasha Pomo or simply the Pasha.

The Pasha looked to have a nice spread, sixty or eighty rooms marked in pink with brown courtyards and green gardens. Cendoza's civic office's stair-stepped their way up the slope from the river to those chambers. The more important your case was, the further up the hill you went.

The Tribune turned another page. These sheets had fewer shaded areas, apart from a few corridors. "See what has me bothered here? People pass through these halls – hell, they got an entire hereditary caste of boom pushers tasked with keeping them clean – but they don't go anywhere else. Nobody knows what's in those places, not for sure."

"Sir, we saw people on the way in," said Blaze. "They can't all be empty."

Crassus fixed the legionnaire with a hard look. "Oh, there's little pockets here and there that are in use. Those people you saw were likely with the Palace School, or maybe one of the temples. I'm informed Pasha Pomo's troops are barracked on the west side. But what bothers me is this." He flipped a few more pages. "Here." He tapped a page where the lines became jumbled. "The palace climbs over the top of the southern ridge and keeps going to Gawana." He tapped a clutch of rectangles shaded in gold alone in a maze of white blocks. "This is the monastery of the Monks of Zu, the bunch that are supposed to keep Gawana at bay."

Gawana – a name that made half the locals shit their breechclouts. The half-alive thing of walls and vines that had swallowed cities. The black shrubs were supposedly planted by the Monks of Zu. Those weeds kept Gawana from swallowing Cendoza. Supposedly. Just looking at those plants gave Chimp the creepy crawlies. Skunk, being stupid, had pulled a leaf from one and spent the night puking his guts up.

"I'm sending Shifter Squad to do a quick run into the countryside. Razors bunch is going to do a walkaround on the walls."

Chimp nodded. The shifters were fast and didn't miss much. And the dwarves in Razors crew were damn good at telling how tough walls were.

"I want your bunch to do a quick walk-through of the palace and see just how empty some of those rooms really are. Here." The Tribune pushed the map book at Chimp. "This is one of five copies. Do not lose it. Now get your kits. Vizier Danay said he'd send you a guide, a fellow that traps rats and snakes that sneak in."

"Sir." Chimps troop filed out of the Mustering Room, went to their assigned spot – a dusty suite painted in pastel seascapes – and found a skinny fellow with heavy leather gloves and boots waiting outside the door. "Me Tamo," said in passable imperial. "I go with."

So, they grabbed their kits and traipsed after the vermin catcher, who was a sort of sideways relation to the Sweeper clan.

Snuffles found their guide's scent fascinating, sniffing the bemused fellow from head to toe. "You catch many pests!"

Tamo nodded in agreement and turned his attention to Bramble. "Gandharvas?" He seemed unsure of himself.

"He's part elf," said Chimp.

"Elf?" Tamo seemed even more confused.

"Eastern Gandharvas," said Bramble.

"Huh."

Chimp motioned. "Let's get going."

Their path took them to a great big set of double doors that had probably started as a bright red but had long since faded to a dull pink. Intricate abstract carvings poked through the dust. Tamo produced a big ring of keys seemingly from thin air, selected a worn iron specimen, and stuck it in the lock. The hinges creaked when Blaze pulled it back, revealing a long dark hallway.

Chimp gave Sticks a sideways look. Sticks nodded. They needed duplicates of those keys for themselves. True, Chimp was good at getting into things and Sticks had yet to meet a lock he couldn't beat with his needles, but that sort of thing took time.

Chimp ordered two Bug Lights broken out. These glass and metal contraptions mixed plant juice and crushed firebugs to create a wan blue light. They had four of them, plus Skunk had snagged a stack of torches from somewhere. Then they set out.

As advertised, there were scads of empty rooms out this way. Most of them had been nice way back when with flowery murals on the wall and twisting mosaics on the floor. They were also empty, except for one room with stacks of dusty furniture.

Snuffles sniffed everything. "Dust and mold. Blah!"

Bramble did one of his hoodoo tricks. "Just a few bugs here and there. Tamo is good at his job."

Chimp asked their guide if he knew why this place was so big and empty. Tamo launched into a spiel about the ruling family that kept growing and growing until the forty-third Pasha, who had about twenty wives and two hundred kids, plus about five hundred aunts, uncles, and cousins. When Sticks asked what happened, Tamo shrugged. "The forty-third Pasha was a bad man. He took and took and then" – he made a line across his throat. "Day of the thousand heads."

The hall sloped upward, just a little at first, then turned into an actual set of stairs that finally popped out inside a colonnaded aisle that overlooked a great big garden gone most of the way to weeds. From Tamo's comments, it seemed the clan responsible for the garden's upkeep now numbered three people instead of thirteen. When Chimp asked what happened to the others, Tamo shrugged and said one word: 'War.'

Chimp paused to chat with a cranky old coot who thought they were a labor detail. He didn't dispute the old-timer, just nodded politely in all the right places while the squad fanned out through the undergrowth. The gardener had a never-ending litany of complaints – the younger generation was a pack of layabouts, the roof of his quarters was falling in, and the Monks of Zu were a bunch of no-good thieves. But what ticked him off the most were the lizards. "Strange ones," he said. "Never seen their like before."

That statement set off Chimp's alarm bells.

Those bells grew louder when Snuffles returned and reported a trail of lizard prints leading to a hole on the garden's south side.

Tamo absolutely did not want to head in that direction. In the end, Blaze had to strongarm the fellow into showing them a deep cellar with a half-rotted door at the far end. It turned out Tamo didn't have a key for it. Blaze almost broke it down before Sticks got the lock picked. The hall past that point looked half buckled. The ceiling sagged in places and wide cracks marred the wall. But what grabbed Chimp's attention was the curtain of black roots that hung down from the stonework.

"Those what I think they are?" asked Blaze.

Bramble muttered something about 'dark roots.' Snuffles refused to go near them.

"Likely." Chimp saw that half of the dangling tubers stopped short of the floor. "Sticks, check it out."

Sticks shot Chimp a 'screw-you' look, but sidled to the curtain anyhow, giving it a prod with his sword. That little nudge dropped three of the strands to the floor. "These don't seem all that healthy." Another stroke dropped two more roots. Sticks slid through the gap. "Got a wall up here. Looks pretty solid."

"Gawana," Chimp spoke the word they were all thinking. "We need to report this."

Sticks turned – and found himself nose to snout with a lizard thing tucked away in a crevice. Snuffles swatted at the creature and missed. Bramble started a spell, but the critter hissed, then shot across the corridor so fast it was practically invisible.

They beat their feet to the surface.

Up top, Chimp decided to go the extra mile or more precisely the extra hundred yards. They pushed past the garden and popped into a little path running alongside a row of those evil black weeds – except a quarter of those vines were dry and withered. Ten paces past the plants was a rough wall of dirt and rock draped in dark green vines studded with little yellow and red flowers. Gawana. Right there in front of them.

They checked out the path. Left, the trail fell into a little clearing with a few tents scattered about the edges. Right, it scaled the slope and got crossed by another track that meandered one way to a door set with fancy statues – and went right through a gap in those black weeds in the other direction to a gatehouse set right in Gawana itself. Two local soldiers in fancy purple curly-cue armor were out front, tossing dice. They proved willing to shoot the shit for a while.

The gatehouse was called Envoy Gate because envoys on both sides of the barrier used it. The building with the fancy statues up front was where the Monks of Zu hung out when they weren't tending to those black weeds. Neither guard had a good thing to say about that lot and seemed downright thrilled at the shrub's unhealthiness. The downslope clearing was a market for peddlers doing business with the maze dwellers. The guards got a fair slice of the proceeds.

Chimp decided to head back to the barracks via the market. The stalls were mostly stocked with metal trinkets – pots and pans, needles and nails, and similar stuff that the maze people traded in exchange for purple fruit for the palace servants and jars of weird fluids that were popular with Cendoza's artisans.

Chimp had Tamo take them to the servant's door: a simple, solid slab of hardwood with the image of a woman carrying a vase on her head etched into its surface. A fancy black lock held the portal shut or would have, because it stood ajar.

That didn't bother Tamo, but it did bother Chimp. Sticks knelt and took in a bunch of tiny scratch marks around the keyhole. "Picked."

The hall was clean but empty and painted with scenes of peasants planting seeds and harvesting crops. They strode along it, opening doors as they went, mostly seeing nothing but painted walls and old furniture on the other side. They did find one chamber with fancy maroon cloth on the walls and a pair of copper braziers flanking a statue of an elephant-headed guy with way too many arms. Another room held a well in the center.

Two hundred yards in they came to an open door on the right. That did tick Tamo off, as it was supposed to be locked. Chimp and Sticks exchanged glances, then checked it out. Sure enough, it too had been picked. The other side held a long courtyard with a fountain in the middle watched over by multiarmed statues clenching everything from fans to flowers to swords in their stony digits.

People were parked on benches or huddled in tight groups. These were Imperial people, mostly civilians, mostly women not wearing much of anything.

"This is where they put the Tail." Blaze motioned at a trio of women toting bundles into a doorway.

The Tail – the string of whores, peddlers, and scavengers that trailed after every army that ever marched. It stood to reason there'd be a few folks in that mix who knew ways around locks. This lot followed the army right onto the ships that brought them here.

"They're setting up shop." Sticks indicated a row of tables and chairs off to the side that featured a skinny black-haired guy at one end sharpening knives and a freckle-faced girl smearing green paste on another woman's arm at the other end. A leather box beside her held rows of tiny bottles, rolls of cloth, and an assortment of metallic implements. An old woman sat between them, sewing patches onto dresses that had seen better days.

Rhythmic 'thwacks' directed Chimp's attention to a squat muscular kid in a heavy metal breastplate swinging a freaking broadsword at a wooden post with impressive force. Chimp wondered where he'd gotten hold of that much ironmongery. A squire, maybe? It didn't seem likely as he could damn near count the knights on this expedition on his fingers.

"There." Sticks pointed at a second set of tables. A guy stitching leather strips together took up one of the spots, but the other boasted a big pile of purple fruit being looked over by skeptical women. Sitting behind the table was a skinny teenager with pale skin and dark hair. "He's our lock picker. Want to go chat him up?"

Chimp thought it over for about five seconds. “Nah, we know where to look. And we know who’s in charge of this lot.” That being Lady Jazmine Bottle, Queen of the Tail – and a senior agent in imperial intelligence.

Crap.” That was Tribune Crassus’s first reaction to Chimps report. “Okay. You get to report your findings to Envoy Ambrose and General DuPaul.”

“Sir!”

So it was that Chimp found himself with about thirty other knights and junior officers before a row of notables sitting behind a long table on a dais in what might have been an audience hall or miniature theater at some point in the past.

Envoy Julius Ambrose boasted a square jaw beneath bronze hair. A purple toga trimmed in red covered his body.

General Sir Benedict DuPaul, a hero of the Traag War, occupied the spot to Ambrose’s right. Black-haired and gray-eyed, he looked in damn good shape for a man on the wrong side of forty. No toga for him, or other formal wear – he was encased in metal.

Cora, the General’s wife, was a stunner with pointed ears and gold hair in a simple green robe. Rumor said she was the Godborn daughter of an imperial Archmage from the bad old days with an elf for a mother, meaning she was an expert in about eight forms of sorcery.

The pasha’s chosen representative, Vizier Danay, sat to the Envoys left. He was a plump round-headed roly-poly fellow in fine robes who smiled way too damn much.

He didn’t see Lady Bottle anywhere.

The junior officers marched up to the table one after another and gave their reports, keeping them short and simple: Yes, the barracks were suitable. Yes, there was enough grub to last for a couple of months. The gas bags were being broken out of storage and seemed intact.

Chimp's report took all of two minutes.

The Vizier insisted it was nothing, mere vermin.

Sir Benedict frowned and ordered the engineers to take a look.

The Vizier wasn't thrilled with that but didn't have much choice.

Chimp stepped back into the crowd only to get pulled aside by Crassus. "Special meeting. Just you."

Chimp felt a little tingle in his gut at the Tribune's words because he had a damn good idea what that meeting was about – and he was right.

Crassus's directions took him to a big room with an oddball assortment of characters. The freckle-faced girl from the courtyard chatted with the lock picker. Chimp couldn't help but notice how closely their faces matched up. He figured they were siblings born on the wrong side of the sheets.

Bramble exchanged quiet words with Shade off in the corner.

"No, Blockhead, you don't ride horses into the maze." Those words came from an older knight walking beside the squat sword swinger from the courtyard.

"But why dad?"

"Coz, son, there's nothing for them to eat," said the knight who Chimp now recognized as Sir Richard Fury, another hero of the Traag War and world-class asshole.

Chimp also realized something else – Fury's kid bore more than a passing resemblance to the freckle-faced girl and the lock picker. They were his kids - all of them.

"Enjoying the party?" The cultured female voice came from Chimp's right. It belonged to a woman with her black hair done up in a beehive and a green dress that hugged her curves in all the right places – Lady Jazmine, officially 'Queen of the Tail,' but also known to a select few as 'Mistress of Secrets' in Imperial Intelligence.

They got down to business.

LABYRINTH WAR XLIX – Git-Vik

"You manipulated me in Vazari."

"Of course, I did." Varian's composure didn't change. "Manipulation is the essence of politics."

I reached for my glass. "Politics is about governance. Organization. Achieving common goals."

Narran laughed. "There are few common goals. Goals may appear common but differ in reality."

I glared at her.

Varian sat his glass on the table. "Allow me to illustrate."

I stared at him. "Please do."

A servant refilled Varian's cup. "Before, I told you Celthania remained neutral when Traag warred with your nation."

Narran shot her brother a look, which he ignored.

"I remember."

Varian raised his cup. "That didn't just happen. Traag was a mighty nation, holding sway over Old Agba, the northern savages, and the realms across the sea. Celthania is not a nation of warriors. We prefer study and discourse to brute combat.

"Traag's ambassadors ranged from brutish louts to silken-tongued devils. They offered gold and glory to impoverished aristocrats and made stirring speeches in temples and marketplaces. 'Join our cause,' they said. 'Win new domains across the sea.' A faction of lords petitioned the High Council for an alliance. For a time, it seemed their cause might succeed."

I took a drink. "What happened?"

Varian smiled. "Traag's ambassadors became arrogant. Reckless. Unpleasant incidents occurred. An important temple was destroyed. Their bodyguards incited a riot. A beloved citizen perished under questionable circumstances. The emissaries' popularity faded. They squabbled among themselves. Petty differences became rifts."

I took another drink. "Those 'unpleasant incidents' didn't just happen."

Varian laughed. "Of course. Just like the recent events in Vazari didn't 'just happen.'"

- From the Journal of Titus Maximus.

Git-Vik detested the vermin hive of Ur-Murk. The vermin here weren't merely stupid, but insane because they willingly bargained with hostile dimensional abominations capable of decimating entire spheres. Or they had before the People assumed control of this wretched place. Now, the vermin did what they were told or faced summary execution.

Some devotees of those abominations were slow to grasp that point. Git-Vik aimed a visual receptor at a demolished coordination center, or 'temple' as the vermin termed it, which stretched from the hive's summit clear to the murky water beneath a curiously twisted bridge. Once, that temple was dedicated to followers of the tentacled Leviathan – until those fools summoned their patron to this sphere to destroy the portal at Ur-Ash. The People's retaliation obliterated not merely that entire sect, and much of the rest of the hive.

A battered yellow spiral symbol marked the entryway to the temple next to the Leviathan's former place of homage – the Hall of the Yellow King. Just glancing at that symbol made Git-Vik's innards roil – but the coordinators within that edifice did a passable job of keeping the uncollared vermin in line and working for the People's ends.

"One day they won't be needed," said Kit-Zune, clicking along beside Git-Vik. "Then they can be exterminated."

The human thrall behind them, the one with the image of a tree engraved on his metal casing, made a noise of assent.

"Human, you dislike these dedicants of dimensional abominations?" asked Kit-Zune.

"We fought a war against scum like them," said the human.

"A human with sense. How unusual," said Kit-Zune.

"My people would have razed this place to the ground and executed its populace," said the second thrall, an orange-skinned 'hobgoblin' in a battered metal and leather carapace.

The temple dedicated to the Hungry Fire swarmed with activity. Swarms of vermin pushed carts laden with heavy boxes of components from an orange portal shaped like a crimson sun. The carts were fixed to rails that extended to the overgrown ziggurat of the All-Mother at the edge of the hive. Her adherents grew vast quantities of the Cigi leaves and Ani bulbs consumed by the People. Clanking engines towed strings of wains along these rails through the mountains to Cit-Cee-Cait.

But today, Git-Vik's business was with the dedicants of the Hungry Fire. "Clear the path," Git-Vik vocalized at maximum volume, which prompted his thralls to cover their ears and sent the vermin laborers to their knees. Crimson-robed priests of the Hungry Fire with orange flame images emblazoned on their fronts kicked the laborers aside. "With me, esteemed ones," said one of the vermin priests, a short figure with hair growing from the lower portion of its head. "The high priest awaits your arrival."

The priest guided them across the vast multi-leveled workroom that filled much of the temple interior, a cacophony of pounding noises and pulsating blue-white lights. Git-Vik watched one vermin priest pull a slab of glowing metal from an anvil without suffering visible injury, while another ignited a brazier with a convoluted motion. The Hungry Fire, it seemed, did reward its dedicants with unusual abilities.

The 'high priest' eagerly accepted the nondescript box Git-Vik presented. "The Hungry Fire is pleased by your offering, esteemed ones," it said with an overly rigid face.

"Will its contents assist you in making your quota?" asked Kit-Zune.

"Yes, yes it will." The high priest plucked another container from a shelf. "Here. The mechanism requested by Coordinator Zut-Zab was constructed to his exact specifications."

Git-Vik ran a diagnostic tool over the mechanism – a power regulator. "It is satisfactory."

That was the thing with the priests of the Devouring Fire. Their fabrication skills, while inferior to those of the People, were still superior to the other vermin, making them too valuable to exterminate. *Someday, though, that situation will change.*

"You are a fool to trust them," said the human thrall after they'd exited the temple. Colorless fluid coated his body. "Everything they make is tainted."

"Everything they give us is rigorously inspected." Git-Vik set course for the Gatekeeper's temple, hoping no Nitivi would be there. That race was intrigued by the Gatekeepers devotees, who possessed expertise in dimensional manipulation.

Unfortunately, three Nitivi were perched on an upper terrace of the Gatekeeper's ziggurat.

The human thrall caught sight of the Nitivi and reached for its metal hacking implement. "Demons!"

"Cease," ordered Kit-Zune.

"But they're demons!"

"They are Nitivi, advisors to the People."

"Why are we here?" Unease filled the human thrall's voice. "This place is worse than the other one."

"Two Operants await us for transport to Cit-Cee-Cait," said Kit-Zune.

"Wizards," said the hobgoblin thrall. "Best cut their throats and tell Zut-Zab that you couldn't find them. You can't trust any wizards in this place."

Git-Vik activated the shock function on the thrall's collar making his body convulse for half a cycle.

"There, that will show him." The vocalization came from a slender human covered in smooth black and red fabric. He positioned himself before the thrall. "That was most impolite of you."

Another human emerged, also clad in black and crimson fabric.

"You are the Operant's Varian and Narran?" asked Kit-Zune.

"Yes, we are," said the female. "I am Narran." She motioned at the first human. "That is my brother Varian."

"You do not wear control collars," said Kit-Zune.

"We were granted special exemptions from that particular requirement." Varian used a manipulator to brush invisible grit from his fabric.

"That is unusual," said Kit-Zune.

"We are unusual," said Varian. "Your friends" – the Operant pointed at the Nitivi's ledge – "concurred and exempted us from that requirement."

Git-Vik noted the metal bands clamped to the Operant's manipulators. "You are fitted with Suppression devices." Those bands would prevent the Operants from using their abilities until needed.

Varian held up the manipulator with the bracelet and tapped it with his other appendage. "Yes, we are." His face contorted. "Alas, special exemptions only go so far."

"Enough," said Git-Vik. "Follow me to Brik-Jute Shull for immediate transport to Cit-Cee-Cait."

"Certainly." Varian and Narran intertwined their manipulator appendages. Each collected a bundle from the ground. "Shall we, darling?"

"Most certainly," said Narran.

"I must say, it is a bit cramped in here." Brik-Jute-Shull's interior compartment was sufficiently low to force Varian to double over.

"You get used to it," said the human thrall.

"Are there any proper chairs in here?" asked Narran.

"No," said the hobgoblin thrall. "You may sit on the cushions." The thrall motioned at pads placed along the compartment's perimeter.

"Those are filthy," complained Narran.

"We can upgrade later, dear." Varian guided Narran into a sitting position.

"Secure yourselves," said Kit-Zune. "We depart in two cycles."

Varian dropped to the floor right as Brik-Jute Shul left the ground.

Git-Viks innards churned upon seeing the Dimensional Instability Zone, a mostly flat bowl dotted with patches of yellow and pink mist. Green and violet sparks marked the locations of the remaining Instabilities, which had declined steadily in both number and potency since the People's arrival. Once, those rents in reality spawned immensely powerful abominations from the twisted depths of null space. Now, those rents were more like tiny cracks.

The decimated polity designated Ur-Ash slid by to the left of Brik-Jute-Shul. The strange, stepped stone structure capped with the remnants of Gotemik technology brought another burst of unpleasant sensations to Git-Vik. That mechanism – a portal that breached the void between worlds – undoubtedly saved the People from destruction – but that salvation came with a horrific cost.

Cit-Cee-Cait's pleasingly proportioned structures came into view shortly after they turned away from the Dimensional Instability Zone. Unfortunately, the bulk of those structures sat empty. That realization brought disturbing impulses Git-Vik did not care to contemplate. Instead, he focused on landing Brik-Jute-Shul on the airfield on the city's eastern fringe.

"Only four other Shull," said Kit-Zune. "That number is inadequate for necessary tasks."

Kit-Zune was correct, and Git-Vik knew it. Still, "The gliders are an adequate stopgap measure." He used a manipulator appendage to point at thralls assembling the devices at one edge of the field.

"Adequate but inferior," said Kit-Zune.

They descended from Brik-Jute-Shull.

Git-Vik aimed a visual receptor at the Operants. "Thralls, you will escort the Operants to that set of barracks where they will remain in isolation until their presence is required."

"I find that eminently suitable." Varian glanced about the windswept expanse of Cit-Cee-Cait. "This fine metropolis seems decidedly lacking in proper social centers."

The Operants departed with their escorts. Git-Vik and Kit-Zune crossed a wide avenue to the factory and descended into its innards. There, they threaded paths through storage areas and clusters of pipes that leaked steam and other substances.

Git-Vik stood on his six armored legs, the eyestalks on his tubular carapace taking in the massive complex while awaiting Manufactory Coordinator Zut-Zab.

The factory was a testament to the decline of the People. Git-Vik knew this truth.

So did his companion Kit-Zune. Coordinator Zut-Zab most certainly knew it. Every member of the People who retained full coherence knew this truth. None of them expressed this reality to the others. Doing so defied the consensus that bound the People. Defying the consensus was abhorrent and dangerous.

The People maintained consensus because much of the manufactories innards were at least superficially normal – slick, polished machines that featured spheres and flared tubes that spat out the sophisticated components required by a superior civilization. Closer inspection revealed cracks that dripped toxic fluids or emitted jets of superheated gases. Worse, the factory – the only operational one in this sphere – could not create many vitally needed components, forcing the People to resort to other measures.

Measures like engaging in demeaning compacts with the two-legged vermin. However, the vermin's products were as inferior as their bodies – suitable for basic fabrication, but little else.

Measures like scavenging the ruined glory of the past in the hope of finding functional components. Most of those salvaged components were of kwintath origin making them difficult to incorporate into the People's mechanisms.

Measures like attempting to annex a rogue kwintath hive factory. That hive, despite its radically different technology, could save the People.

But the effort to annex that manufactory came at extreme cost, as testified by the line of thralls carrying damaged components on the walkway beneath the ledge where Git-Vik perched. Most of those components bore scorch marks and jagged edges.

The People had lost ten (Ten!) Shulls while attempting to tame the rogue kwintath hive because the two-legged vermin dwelling there proved not merely intransigent but deviously resourceful. A catastrophe. Unacceptable. Yet it had happened.

The components carried by the collared thralls below would reverse those numbers - if its processers were still functional.

"That system is out of sequence." Kit-Zune aimed a manipulator appendage at a twisted knot of pipes across the floor of the complex.

Git-Vik directed one optical receptor at Kit-Zune while surveying the indicated machine with another, using internal devices that tracked electrical and thermal activity. "Explain."

"The mechanism was emitting steam every 4.3 cycles. The last discharge, though, was 21 cycles ago."

Git-Vik tensed. His detectors showed a sharp temperature increase in the device. The mechanism's regular release of vapor was a safety measure. "Emergency! Emergency! Immediate shutdown and repairs required for Processor Nine."

The warning came too late. A thunderous noise filled the complex as a panel blew off the side of the mechanism, instantly reducing two of the People and five thralls to a pulp. The panel went on to sever a pipe before lodging in the skin of another mechanism imported from the Home World.

The primary illumination system failed for that portion of the structure, casting much of it into gloom broken by portable light units and the glare from isolated consoles. People and thralls raced about, turning valves, and disconnecting electrical systems.

Kit-Zune aimed a receptor unit at Git-Vik. "Should we assist?"

"We would be of little use."

Coordinator Zut-Zab's massive bulk appeared from behind one of the mechanisms. Complex equipment, much of it unique, clung to his carapace. Red Status Bands – six altogether – were wrapped around his motivator appendages, as befitted his status. Just five other Gotemik could claim that many Status Bands – Git-Vik had four, and Kit-Zune had only three. Once, Brik-Jute possessed six Status Bands, before he denied consensus and transformed into a Shull.

Coordinator Zut-Zab issued rapid-fire orders. Under his direction, the armored warrior thrall that Git-Vik had come to regard as 'his,' yanked the failed plate from its resting place. Two People of the technician caste pushed the thrall aside, inserting probes and making clicking reports to Zut-Zab. Other thralls rerouted heavy cables, connecting them to new mechanisms while more People inspected the remnants of the machine that had exploded. The illumination flared fitfully back to life 211 cycles after failing.

Momentarily satisfied, Zut-Zab broke free of the reconstruction efforts and approached Git-Vik.

Git-Vik presented the coordinator with the mechanism obtained in Ur-Murk.

Zut-Zab rotated the unit and inspected it with high-quality diagnostic equipment. "The coordinators of the Hungry Fire are untrustworthy vermin, but their craftsmanship is adequate."

The coordinator aimed optical units at the pair. "I have an assignment for you, but it must wait until repairs here are completed." His receptors flipped over to Kit-Zune. "There was an issue affecting Vaud-Lat at the Covenant Barracks yesterday."

"I will investigate." Kit-Zune's motive appendages moved in an agitated pattern.

"I shall investigate Tix-Nit's condition." Visiting the highly depressing Coventry Barracks held no appeal, but duty demanded the trip.

"Do so. We will reconvene here in 1000 cycles." Zut-Zab rotated in place and scuttled off without waiting for an acknowledgment.

Git-Vik and his companion emerged onto Cit-Cee-Cait's windswept avenues, taking a curved route by the gigantic Primary Coordination Center, a dome constructed of multiple layers of overlapping plates. It looked...forlorn, though Git-Vik did not express this sentiment.

They passed by the breeding pits where older male gotemik were transformed into gloriously bloated Brood Mothers, each a dozen times their previous size, swollen bodies filled with egg sacs. There, chosen males would inseminate these females. The resulting offspring would consume their parent's carcass. That should have been Brix-Jute's fate. Instead, he'd been made into a Shull.

A swarm of three-legged, three-armed, semi-sapient Vatan thralls crossed the pair's path, carrying tools and building materials. The pests were competent enough at basic tasks and even made for passable soldiers if pressed but had well-deserved reputations for theft and erratic behavior.

The pair instinctively steered closer to the street's center as they approached a row of the Nitivi's huge cylindrical shell-homes. Attracting the Nitivi's attention could be dangerous.

Twenty smaller gotemik clung to protrusions on the tubular Juvenile Barracks across from the Primary Coordination Center. Several of the juveniles made jittery movements unbecoming for the People. Were they incipient Aberrations? If so, that was a terrifying thought. To come so far, to survive so much, only to have their youth transform into Aberrations...Git-Vik pushed the thought from his mind.

Reaching Coventry House meant verifying their identity before the guards posted at the border of Cit-Cee-Cait's inhabited region. Only People went past this point, and only with cause. Cycles passed as they walked by the vacant barracks and abandoned fabrication plants.

Those empty structures gnawed at Git-Vik's brain. By every right, they should have been fully occupied. They would have been occupied had the Evacuation fared better. Images of darkness and impossible energies momentarily manifested in Git-Vik's mind. A tremble ran through his carapace. He could not think about that. The memory came anyway.

The sky pulsed yellow and green, outlining impossible shapes overhead. As it did so, the structures around Git-Vik trembled. Immense cracks formed on a decimated building.

Git-Vik emitted a series of agitated clicks. He could flee. The Gate was dangerous. Unstable. The Primary Redoubt was still intact. He could reach it in just five cycles. Seeking refuge there would be a better option than risking the Gate.

"No." Brik-Jute's communication pierced Git-Vik's nervousness. "The Primary Redoubt cannot withstand these forces. Here." He thrust a curiously carved stone at Git-Vik. "This is a passive protective device."

Git-Vik took the stone. Marks he could not fathom were etched into its surface. It radiated no energy he could discern. "I"-

"Remain calm." Brik-Jute produced a second stone and gave it to Tix-Nit.

Like Git-Vik, Tix-Nit was skeptical about the stone. "Where did these originate? How effective are they?"

"They were fabricated from records in the restricted archives," said Brik-Jute. "Their effectiveness is uncertain."

"Trusting uncertain devices seems unwise," said Tix-Nit.

"Then trust me."

An invisible something stomped down the avenue, leaving irregular craters in its path large enough to fit an adult Gotemik. The summit of a barracks across the way exploded during its passage. Rubble rained down on Git-Vik and his companions. The impulse to flee became almost overwhelming.

A dozen other Gotemik fled the ragged column. Three perished immediately hacked apart by whirling yellow blades that manifested from nowhere.

"Remain calm," urged Brik-Jute. "We are almost to the Gate." He indicated the metallic archway studded with spheres and cubes just ahead. Red and violet energies played about the device. Unfathomable shapes moved within the archway.

Tix-Nit was so paralyzed with terror he involuntarily excreted, spewing white lumps on the street.

"Move!" Brik-Jute struck Tix-Nit's carapace hard, sending him stumbling toward the portal. "The alternative is certain termination."

Git-Vik didn't want to approach that hideous rent in reality. But now, he could glimpse artificial structures beneath the arch. Different than those made by the People, but comprehensible. He propelled himself towards the opening.

Warriors and technicians with scorched and cracked carapaces herded the refugees into columns. "Move when the alarm sounds. Do not halt." Git-Vik couldn't identify the voice's origin.

A discordant claxon filled the air. The column moved forward in fits and starts. A Gotemik ahead of Git-Vik bolted sideways, screaming. Tix-Nit trembled and attempted to follow suit, only to be forced towards the portal by Brik-Jute.

Seething energies filled Git-Vik's receptors, save for the dimly visible edifices. He focused and deliberately thrust two motivator appendages into the opening – and felt nothing. Then he was in a dark void surrounded by a whirling vortex. Shapes that defied description erupted from the vortex. The Gotemik touched by these unfathomable appendages vanished or suffered severe damage.

"No! Impossible! I refuse!" A malicious shape brushed against Tix-Nit. The stone he carried flared with brilliant green light before dissolving into colored sparks.

Then that horrific appendage was right before Git-Vik. He could see twisted images within its depths. Acting on instinct, he hurled Brik-Jute's protective stone at the horror. It flared green...

...And the Git-Vik was in a normal, sane space, surrounded by gibbering Gotemik.

An appendage waved before Git-Vik's receptors. "Are you damaged?"

"I experienced momentary dislocation." Git-Vik's carapace shuddered as he spoke the words. "The episode is over."

Coventry Barracks was huge, bigger than the Primary Coordination Center and the Manufactory combined, a stitched-together collection of secondary barracks, food plants, storehouses, and even a pair of tertiary manufactories. It had to be, considering the sheer number of People housed within its confines – 14,108, or a quarter of all the People on this sphere – all of them traumatized by their passage through the Portal.

More guards awaited the pair at Coventry Barrack's primary entryway. These individuals were less concerned with Git-Vik and Kit-Zune than the Aberrations they monitored – some of whom were prone to random bursts of violence. They summoned Coordinator Glit-Dok, his six crimson Status Bands contrasting with the mostly white devices grafted onto her body.

One of Coordinator Glit-Dok's sensors focused on Kit-Zune while the others scanned the area. "Technical Three Kit-Zune, your sibling Vaud-Lat lost two of her motivators and sustained internal injuries after being assaulted by an Aberration. New motivators are in preparation. Partial physical recovery is anticipated." The coordinator said nothing of Vaud-Lat's mental status. He didn't have to.

An attendant escorted Kit-Zune into a corridor. Sane Gotemik did not traverse Coventry barracks alone, especially visitors.

Coordinator Glit-Dok aimed a receptor at Git-Vik. "Tix-Nit's recovery continues. His work in the garden may prove adequate to warrant reintegration into greater society."

The coordinator motioned at another attendant, who guided Git-Vik into a grotto where wavy plants grew about a pond lined with stones.

Tix-Nit came from behind a large boulder, carrying a bundle of leaves. He stopped short. "Git-Vik."

"Tix-Nit. I am informed you are skilled at agricultural tasks."

"Agriculture suits me. Here." Tix-Nit offered Git-Vik a Gigi frond. "I find it...soothing."

"That is good to hear." *Tix-Nit's recovery will be partial at best.*

They spoke of inconsequential matters for another twenty cycles. Git-Vik did not talk about the portal or his recent experiences. Then it was time to leave.

Coordinator Zut-Zab waved a manipulator at a component in his personal work area. "We are subjugating the control unit you retrieved from the Juvenile Construct. Progress is slow."

Zut-Zab waved a manipulator at a curiously shaped device with cords made of different materials along one surface. "However, I have fused a partial copy of the core to this mechanism. You will deliver this to Coordinator Tavi-Tik at the rogue manufactory."

"It shall be done," said Git-Vik and Kit-Zube in unison.

"However, that mission is secondary. Another option has presented itself."

"Explain," said Git-Vik.

Zut-Zab indicated a milky sphere on the table. "This is a data storage device. A technician discovered something interesting while investigating its contents – the location of a secret depository, established by the kwintath during the failure of their society." He tapped a control on his carapace. A transparent map appeared between him and Git-Vik. "This is a satellite image of the site. It detected regulated electrical and thermal emissions."

"So, is this depository both intact and operational?" asked Kit-Zune.

"Mostly intact. Partially operational. Automated systems, I believe. The installation did not respond to contact efforts."

The image shifted, becoming a large structure with a damaged side atop an icy mountain.

"The installation appears to have sustained a kinetic strike," noted Kit-Zune.

"I believe so, yes."

"You intend a surreptitious expedition," said Kit-Zune.

"Correct."

Git-Vik analyzed data attached to the image. "The coordinates place the facility on an island in the depths of the

Southern Ocean. That is well past the range of a Shull from our nearest base."

"I anticipated that issue." The image shifted again, becoming a large-scale map. "I intend to use gliders to establish a resupply depot here." An orange dot flared on the ocean's coast.

Gliders were easier to create than Shull but still consumed precious materials. Most were employed supplying the bridgehead within the rogue kwintath manufactory.

"You must place great value on this site to expend such resources," said Kit-Zune.

"I do place great value on this site. The listed contents are impressive."

Again, Git-Vik noted the coordinator's choice of words. "Partly operational. What of the security systems?" Kwintath security devices possessed incredible durability.

"I anticipated the possibility of a functional security system. However, there are ways to circumvent those devices, thanks to the kwintath's foolishness in delegating responsibility to inferiors." Zut-Zab lifted an oval object from the table dominated by the blank image of a vermin's head. "This is a control unit employed by the modified vermin the Kwintath designate 'Operants.' With this, such an Operant can partially circumvent Kwintath security mechanisms."

An uneasy sensation filled Git-Vik's innards. "I must protest." *Coordinator Zut-Zab is withholding crucial information.*

"Overruled. This mission is vital." The coordinator tapped a panel on the wall. "Enter."

Varian and Narran entered the office. Varian's features contorted. "It appears we have quite the expedition before us."

LABYRINTH WAR L – Bao

"Are you not a Lord of Gawana?"

"No." Nimuk shook his head. "I am a hereditary Lord of Vazari, a city of men and dwarves, not a Lord of the Maze."

"But the maze has Lords."

"Yes." Nimuk nodded. "Gawana surrounds Vazari, protecting the city without being part of it. The maze has many servants and selects its own Lords to oversee those servants. Gawana chooses – no one else." Nimuk wagged his finger to emphasize those last words. "Your ancestors never grasped this point. They thought power here conferred power there."

- From 'The Journal of Titus Maximus.'

A river barge brought Bao to Aqua-Tera and a pony-pulled carriage took her away along a ridiculously smooth road that meandered through the chasms made by Gawana's walls. Bao, who'd read Titus's journal before ever setting foot in the maze, couldn't help but contrast the experience with the one recorded by the Lord Defender. Back then, Titus described Gawana's trade routes as mere tracks, barely suitable for foot traffic, let alone wheeled conveyances.

Titus, though, was the product of a nation where rapid movement of troops was vital to national defense and refused to accept Gawana's subpar road system upon becoming Lord Defender. That position conferred the ability to make minor alterations to the maze, something Titus did with gusto.

A woman in the village of Akal-Sun told Bao how she'd watched the Lord Defender walk at a stately pace down a rude track, his face a mask of concentration, the ground reshaping itself after his passage. When Bao pressed, the woman admitted that Titus had to walk that route three times to smooth a section of the path just six feet wide.

When they paused for lunch by a river, an old man with a fishing pole spun a story about Titus creating a ford. 'The Lord Defender made a pushing motion and stones rolled out of the ground. Later that day, Bao's carriage crossed that ford, a thing of stones jumbled together in a pattern that baffled the eye.

Listening to these tales was preferable to dwelling on her mission.

The cart climbed switchback passages that scaled a steep slope to the old city of Zhaman. An aged priest in an orange robe at the summit politely informed Bao that this was Titus's work – he'd reduced the entire gradient.

Bao had read of Zhaman in Titus's journal, which he described as a near-empty ruin broken by the maze and dotted with crumbling temples carved with friezes that ranged from horrific to obscene. That certainly wasn't the case now: the temples were repaired and other ruins were made into barracks and warehouses.

Titus had indeed reshaped the maze.

Bao contemplated that thought as she dined with a clutch of priests and thought more about it upon retiring to a suite stocked with scrolls and exotic plants. More and more, Titus's abilities reminded her of the pagan gods of old, capricious beings who alternately dazzled and terrified their followers.

Necessary repairs to the carriage kept Bao at Zhaman for three days. She passed the time poking through the temples and prowling about the city, always observant and polite.

The carriage halted amidst a clutch of huts before a formidable portal - Envoy Gate.

Bao stood in a straight shift of green and pink, closed at the collar, as the slabs were thrust apart.

A pudgy guard in ornate fluted purple armor gaped at the sight, then clouted a second sentinel on the head, who ducked off along a narrow path.

Bao stood there, sweltering in the heat. An hour passed by. So did a second hour. She gratefully accepted a cup of chilled juice and tried not to think about the confrontation ahead.

Finally, right before the sun touched the horizon, a man in the red cape of an imperial officer appeared, trailed by an attractive woman with gold hair and upswept ears. "I am Tribune Crassus. You are an envoy of Titus Maximus."

The woman did not identify herself. But the gold hair marked her as a Godborn. Godborns were sorcerers skilled at healing, protection, and ferreting out lies.

Bao drew herself erect. "I am Lady Bao Vada Falun Des Ptath Maximus, envoy of Gawana's Lord Defender Titus Maximus, here to treat with General Benedict DuPaul and Ambassador Julius Ambrose."

This is dangerous. This is insane. I murdered Julius's brother. He will see me locked into a cell and executed. Or he might not, as I am a member of the imperial house by marriage.

"That is interesting." Tribune Crassus glanced at the woman, who gave a slight nod. "Follow me. Your quarters are being prepared as we speak."

The Tribune took Bao and her escort through a confusing maze of passageways to a large suite that featured a private dining room, bathing chamber, and even a library. Silent female servants took Bao's attire and cleaned her body. But it wasn't lost on Bao that her chamber's door locked from the other side.

Bao spent a long, slow day in that chamber, broken only by a visit from Crassus. Bao was careful not to take offense. *This is a test.*

The next morning Bao was invited to a formal breakfast with Pasha Pomo and Vizier Danay in a dining hall that showed signs of recently being cleaned. Pasha Pomo sported a lean build, a forked beard, and an academic demeanor. Vizier Danay was round-faced, pudgy, and slick of temperament. Neither was willing to discuss matters beyond the most trivial. Bao took it in stride and returned to her suite (prison?) without complaint.

Crassus returned that afternoon with a squad of imperial soldiers. They ever so deferentially escorted Bao to a room that might have been a temple auditorium or a theater once upon a time. A woman and three men sat behind a long table atop what might have originally been a stage. Bao knew the woman by sight – the Godborn from before but could attach a name to only one of the men, the plump Vizier Danay, though she could guess, as one wore a toga while the other was in armor.

Fortunately, Crassus named these eminences for her benefit. "Lady Bao Vada Falun Des Ptath Maximus, envoy of Lord Defender Titus Maximus of Gawana, I present you with Julius Ambrose, Vice President of the Solarian Senate and Envoy to Cendoza."

The toga wearer – a trim thirty-something with curly bronze hair capping a rectangular face, nodded but said nothing.

Bao remembered her lessons on the empire's great families. Moreover, she remembered a certain despicable witch hunter – Appius Ambrose, whom she'd murdered in a prison cell on the other side of the world. Julius Ambrose was Appius's brother. *I am in the presence of one with reason to wish me dead.*

"Lord General Benedict DuPaul, the Envoy's military advisor."

The armored man fixed Bao with a piercing gaze. "So, you are the infamous Bao."

Those words earned the General a disdainful glance from both the Vizier and the Envoy, plus a hard slug in the arm from the woman. Diplomacy wasn't his strong suit. Strange, as the DuPaul's made it a point to be diplomatic with Solaria's other great families.

"Lady Cora DuPaul, Lord DuPauls most gracious wife."

Cora flushed and sat back in her chair.

"I believe you are already acquainted with Vizier Danay, the seniormost of the Pasha's officials."

The vizier permitted himself a brief smile but otherwise said nothing.

Envoy Ambrose spoke. "I am informed you have a message for us?"

"I do."

"I am eager to hear it. But I must confess to being curious – why are you presenting this message and not your husband Octavos?"

"Octavos Maximus is serving the Lord Protector in another capacity."

"A capacity that did not permit his appearance here?"

"Yes."

"Oh hell, do we even know if Octavos is still alive?" interjected the General, a statement that earned him black looks from the others.

"Octavos Maximus lives and is in good health," said Bao. "He is also in a position of authority."

"She speaks the truth," said Cora.

"Well, that's something." General DuPaul faced the Envoy. "Can we get on with this? I have an army to organize."

"We all have tasks to attend to." Julius Ambrose faced Bao. "Present your offer."

Bao stood stock still. "Titus Maximus, Lord Defender of Gawana offers a military alliance with Cendoza and the Solarian Empire."

"Predictable," said General DuPaul. "Titus always was straightforward."

"Silence." Julius made a cutting motion. "Titus's envoy is not through speaking."

"Thank you, Envoy Ambrose." Bao inclined her head. "Furthermore, Lord Defender Titus Maximus demands he be appointed supreme commander of this force."

"That sounds like Titus," said General DuPaul.

"It does." Envoy Ambrose turned his attention to Bao. "You may return to your quarters while we discuss this generous offer."

The imperial soldiers snapped to attention.

Bao bowed.

Her quarters felt more like a prison than ever. She endured a quiet meal, then sat before a window overlooking a courtyard with an irregularly shaped pool at its center.

One of the nameless maids approached. "Envoy Bao, you have a visitor. Envoy Julius Ambrose is here to see you."

Bao's heart plummeted. *This is it. I will go from a gilded cage to a dungeon cell.* Still – "Send him in." Politeness couldn't hurt.

The Envoy entered, wearing a simple cream tunic instead of a toga. "Greetings Miss Bao."

We are being informal now. "Greetings, Julius. Is this about Titus's offer?"

Julius made a dismissive motion. "Titus's offer remains under consideration. However, we both know it will be rejected. Titus must have known that."

"I informed the Lord Defender he requested too much."

"And his response?"

"Indifference."

"Like he didn't care what the imperial reaction would be. That accords with the Titus Maximus I remember from the war – always giving the orders he deemed right and speaking his mind regardless of the consequences. That impertinence cost him his promotion to General. I'd hoped his experiences in the maze would have changed him."

"Titus is feared and revered by Gawana's inhabitants," said Bao.

"Feared and revered," repeated Julius. "Yet you still spoke your mind to him and presented his insolent demands to me. This, after killing my brother."

Bao's heart threatened to stop beating. "Your brother attempted to violate me. I defended myself."

Julius stared at Bao for a long moment. "I believe you."

"Huh?" Decorum momentarily escaped Bao.

"I know my brother. He was prone to lechery and violence from an early age, involved in one scandal after another. There was this incident with a serving girl – after that father placed him in the army, thinking that would provide an outlet for his impulses." Julius shook his head. "Instead, the army increased his appetite for violence and the Fall of Traag left him unhinged. Taking ecclesiastical vows provided a shield for his cruelty. When his abuses grew too great, I was forced to banish him to the Southern Shore."

"I see." Bao's mind raced. *I must be direct.* "Yet, despite his impulses, Appius remained your brother. And he died by my hand."

"Yes. Appius was my brother. And you did kill him in self-defense – I had the episode investigated. But while distressed, I am not inclined to seek personal vengeance. You are, after all, married to a member of the imperial family." Julius stood. "You will be granted freedom of the palace tomorrow."

LABYRINTH WAR LI – Carina

'The Ervin are ever polite, extraordinarily clever – and infuriating. Still, they command and we obey.'

- Vako Manresa

When Luther navigated Japi into the pond, the view took Carina's breath away.

"It's beautiful. It's like an artist's dream."

At the pond's far end, parallel waterfalls cascaded from pond to pond against a background of black rock and vibrant greenery.

"They're called the 'Stairs of Heaven,' called Luther from the tiller.

"Artists do come here." Goji pointed at a slender man in a stained robe perched before an easel on a nearby dock.

"How do we get Japi through here, though?" Carina looked at the densely vegetated shoreline, seeing a couple of large huts on either side of a sloped gravel embankment.

"The Haulage Guild will carry Japi up the Tortoise Climb. See?" Goji pointed at a pack of thick-set men and women with black hair and flat faces lounging about the smaller structure.

"Huh."

The burly laborers caught sight of Japi. "Challa! Challa! Cotha! Cotha!"

A new figure joined the laborers, a thin man with pasty skin in a pale blue robe marked with a complex pink design. "This way!" he called in the Trade Tongue.

Japi touched the gravel embankment.

"I am Cotha Baraka of the Haulage Guild," said the man without a preamble. "The Haulage Guild holds the official monopoly of all traffic on the Tortoise Climb, the portage between the lower and upper harbors." He looked over their craft. "Hm. Tri-Hull dugout...that will be twenty silver beads."

"Robber!" said Luther. "Ten should be more than enough."

"Twenty," stated Cotha. "The fee is non-negotiable. Pay it or sail back downriver."

Luther grumbled but went into the cabin and emerged with a long necklace. "Here. Anything else?"

"Yes. The Stairs of Heaven are a port of entry for Ado-Cent. Your vessel's cargo must be declared and assessed in value." Cotha motioned, and more pale skinny figures in pastel robes came from behind the second building.

"And I suppose there are custom fees as well."

"The base fee is five silver beads. The remainder depends on the assessed value of your cargo."

Seventeen additional silver beads later, Luther, Goji, and Carina stood on a dock and watched as the flat-faced laborers waded into the water and lifted Japi onto two carts with curved decks.

"Ukandar barbarians," said a cultured voice from behind Carina. "Too dull-witted for anything but menial labor and swilling Rak – a particularly vile beverage made from fermented mares milk."

"Fermented mares milk." Goji made a face. "Drank some once on a dare. Horrible."

Carina took in the artist's pasty features and paint-stained smock. "Surely the Ukandar are not all drunken dullards."

"It's truth. The Ukandar are fit only for simple tasks." He smiled. "I am Vako Manresa of Ado-Cent."

Luther introduced their party.

With Japi loaded, the Ukandar hitched themselves into harnesses. "Challa, Challa, iso re! Challa, Challa, iso re!" They stamped their feet in rhythm to the chant. Then they leaned into the harnesses and began to pull. The carts lurched forward along a wide avenue paved in slabs of black rock.

The Nes-Bot brothers materialized from somewhere and exchanged words with Luther, who tossed them a handful of copper beads. The goblins inspected their prize, then meandered to a dock that sported half a dozen small boats tied to it.

Carina watched the cart vanish out of sight around a wooded bend. "Maybe we should follow after them?"

"Might as well." Luther picked up a pack laden with his possessions.

Vako regarded Luther. "Tell me – what do you know of Ado-Cent?"

"I know that Ado-Cent is built in steps carved into a hill," said Luther, "with each step dedicated to a different purpose. I was told a guild of sorcerers, the Ervin, rule the city from the topmost tier."

"But have you been there before?"

"I have not."

"Your understanding is superficial," said Vako. "True, the Ervin rule Ado-Cent, but they seldom involve themselves in mundane administration. Those chores fall to my people, the gracious folk of Celthania."

"I see," said Luther.

"I think not," said Vako. "Ado-Cent is a stew of cultures and races – merchants from Soonlar and Chou, tribes of semi-civilized barbarians, Gandharvas entertainers, Agar metallurgists, fierce rachasa butchers and leatherworkers, and others, each with their hereditary tasks and stations."

"It sounds complicated." Luther sounded uncertain.

"It is complicated," said Vako, "Complicated and dangerous for outsiders like yourselves. An innocent comment or gesture can spark offense or ruin a negotiation. Hence, I have a proposition for you."

"Let's hear it."

"I propose to tutor you in Ado-Cent's more obvious social pitfalls in exchange for passage."

Luther considered Vako's offer. "Yeah, we can do that. Japi's accommodations are a bit on the rough side, though."

"I am certain they will be most satisfactory. I shall join you at the summit." Vako spun on his heel and set off along a narrow path.

"Shall we?" Luther made a sweeping motion. Carina groaned and wondered about recruiting one of the Nes-Bot brothers to carry her pack. But when she turned her head, they were nowhere to be seen. So, she shouldered the bundle and plodded up the hill with Luther and Goji, walking past hovels, shrines, and fine houses before beginning a steep upward climb.

Slow as they were, Luther's party still outpaced the Ukandar, who never stopped with their chant, though they'd inserted additional words. One in particular, 'Rak' appeared with increasing frequency.

The Tortoise Climb became a wide, steep ledge and abruptly veered into a narrow chasm with rushing water just past the paving stones. Japi's portside outrigger was a mere yard from the wall. The road crested a slight rise and gradually descended to a circular harbor lined with stone huts.

"Challa, Challa, iso re! Challa, Challa, iso Rak!" With those words, the Ukandar pulled the wagons straight into the water, then undid the ropes securing them to Japi, which bobbed free.

"Challa, Challa, Rak!" With that, the Ukandar stampeded ashore, one of them tossing Japi's painter to Luther as he ran by. "Challa! Challa! Cotha! Cotha! Rak! Rak!"

A two-wheel buggy pulled by a pony carrying Cotha and Vako crested the hill. The Haulage Guild Master shouted at the laborers. "I'm here, you filthy imbeciles."

The Ukandar gathered around the buggy, shouting "Cotha! Rak! Cotha!"

Disgusted, Cotha tossed one of them a small pouch.

"RAK!" With that word, the barbarian mob charged into a square structure with stone walls and a canvas roof.

Vako descended from the buggy. "That is the local tavern. I strongly suggest against entry."

"I wouldn't dream of it," said Luther as Vako unloaded his gear from the cart.

Vako went into Ado-Cent's mores and taboos once the Japi set sale– the forms of address for each caste group, rules that prohibited the chou and soonlar merchants from directly dealing with one another, the import of turning a blind eye to nomad misogamy, and so on, enough to make Carina's head spin by the time they reached the eastern shore.

"Tell me," Vako asked Luther, "what business brings you to Ado-Cent? I might be of assistance."

"We seek a man, a merchant named Baku Jos," said Luther. "An associate of mine had dealings with him."

"Baku Jos." Vako stroked his chin. "I confess the name is unfamiliar to me – or rather it is all too familiar, as it is carried by every tenth or twelfth human male in the city, and some nonhuman ones as well. As a merchant, though, he should have a shop, or at least an office on the Third Tier. Tell me, what does he traffic in?"

"Metals with unusual properties," said Luther.

"Hmm. That sounds like one of the Agar, or possibly an alchemist. I shall make inquiries when we reach port."

Luther pointed at long rows of structures ranging from ragged tents to colonnaded temples lining a protruding headland to the south. "What is that?"

Vako winced. "That is the Drift."

"The Drift?"

"An encampment for those displaced by the recent unpleasantness." Vako pointed at a massive crimson cube. "That is the palace of his Hobgoblin Eminence Daja Kalt of the Descant. Once, the Descant could muster two thousand warriors; now they have barely two hundred. They maintain a brutal order on the Drifts avenues."

Vako gestured at a hill east of Daja's, its surface dotted with small cottages set into the slopes. "The Halls of Vhange, a race of dwarves skilled in alchemy and metallurgy that once occupied ancient ruins east of here. The ones not killed or toiling for the Gotemik dwell beneath those slopes."

"Gotemik," said Carina.

"Yes, the gotemik." Vako didn't take his eyes off the shantytown. "The gotemik swept through the Plains like a wildfire, consuming all in their path. There. Those fine cottages? Those belong to escapees from Celthania – more than a thousand of them. They were very clever and resourceful to escape their homeland, and cleverer yet to cross the plains to Ado-Cent without being obliterated. They anticipated positions in Ado-Cent's civil service. Most, though, exist on their cousin's charity." He winced. "Much of my income goes to support distant kinsmen there."

A wide inlet opened past the Drift. Sluggish rivers entered the bay's northeastern and southeastern corners, with a tangle of docks between them. Past the wharves, rising from the fields like a wedding cake for giants, was the terraced city of Ado-Cent. It looked fantastic, a creation of fluted towers and colorful buildings topped with onion domes that gleamed in the light.

Carina's eyes widened at the sight. "It's beautiful."

"Yes, it is." Vako took heart at Carina's words. "At times, familiarity dulls its glamour." He pointed at a pier that jutted from the northern bank. "Make for that dock. I have an arrangement with the owner."

Luther went and pulled at the tiller while Goji lowered the mainsail.

Vako glanced at the pair, then at the dock. He came to an internal decision. "This may be the last occasion I can speak without being overheard."

Carina faced Vako. "We are being watched?"

"You are from the great empire in the north, the nation that smashed Traag and killed their god, and then casually demolished the largest horde mustered in centuries. Of course, you are being watched. We would be fools not to do so. But there are things you need to know."

"Speak your piece," said Luther as Goji took the tiller.

Vako rubbed his hands. "Some five years ago, the Ervin commanded the city's alchemists to prepare vast quantities of incense to their precise specifications. They then ordered this incense stockpiled in the attics and uppermost chambers of every dwelling in the city. The decrees baffled us - but the Ervin commanded, so we obeyed." He sighed. "Executing that decree was costly."

"The gotemik swept across the south as this campaign commenced. The Ervin ordered refugees from these assaults to be admitted into the city - but placed greater emphasis on the manufacture of this incense, going so far as to have guards check the deposits." He looked at the water and shook his head.

"Then three gotemik Fliers came from the west. The Ervin ordered two things done at once – an immediate curfew, and for their hoard of special incense to be taken to the rooftops and ignited all at once." Vako lifted his head. "Those vapors...they were sharp, like that given off by old cheese. I remember choking on them as the streets filled with a golden cloud. Then the Fliers were over the city, trailing a fine black mist that darkened the sun's rays. Those vapors killed every creature they touched – save those protected by the Ervins incense. Ten thousand citizens of Ado-Cent perished that day. The funeral fires burned for weeks. But without that incense, the city would have been a depopulated ruin. The gotemik returned a moon cycle later. This time, they landed on the Seventh Tier. We feared the worst. Then the Gotemik Fliers rose into the sky and the Ervin emerged with word of a treaty that would both spare Ado-Cent and preserve its autonomy."

"What are the terms of this compact?" asked Carina.

"Most of the details are secret. That vexes us Celthanians Contracts, negotiations – those are our lifeblood. To not know the terms of such a vital agreement is infuriating." He waved at the city, the piers now just a few hundred yards away. "Everybody in Ado-Cent knows the Ervin's actions preserved the city, so they are held in the highest regard. I hold them in the highest regard. But we Celthanians wonder at the cost."

Japi touched the pier. Flat-faced Ukandar secured the craft. Vako exchanged a few words with them. "I will show you about the city. There is a most excellent diner on the Third Tier – but I cannot speak for the security of your vessel."

"I can speak to Japi's security." Carina activated ward spells whose glyphs she'd carved into the vessel's timbers weeks ago. "Any thieves who seek to board will receive an unpleasant surprise."

"Ah." Vako nodded. "Only fools would challenge sorcery." He motioned to the street. "If you would follow me?"

Ado-Cent's lowest tier was an assault to the eyes, ears, and nostrils: Long columns of wains laden with bales and boxes piloted by cussing dwarves with braided beards and green-skinned goblins plowed through packs of drunken Ukandar who pissed and brawled in the streets. Vendors of all three races hawked goods of dubious value from the street corners.

"Here." Vako halted before a carriage of simple design, with a slender Celthanian in yellow silk perched on the driver's bench. "Ramo!"

The driver looked at Vako. "Vako! I thought you were away from this madness at the Stairs of Heaven."

"I was. Now I'm back. I need transport to Lepta's diner on the third Tier." Vako tossed the driver a coin.

"At once!" Ramo bowed and made a sweeping motion. "Climb aboard. I promise a swift and smooth ride."

The carriage's interior was worn, boasting dinged doors and torn cushions, but it was clean.

"Ramo is a distant cousin of mine who escaped Celthania," said Vako as the carriage forged through the crowded streets. He shook his head. "He possesses an industrious spirit lacking in my other kin, but I find it shameful that he is reduced to such a menial occupation."

The carriage ascended a wide ramp past the First Tier, giving Carina a view of a wide expanse of its huts, stalls, and tenements. Then they passed through a fortified gate and into an avenue where dwarves scurried about solar forges on the one side while men and hobgoblins in orange armor drilled on the other. "The Tier of Fire and Steel," said Vako before the carriage began another ascent.

Now, the carriage rolled along the fringe of a long narrow market filled with ebony Soonlar merchants wearing bracelets and beaded necklaces haggled with Celthanians in pastel robes and stumpy dwarves in leather. They passed a row of shops adorned in chou characters, then traversed a street that seemed entirely populated by goblins who scurried in and out of cubical black shops. "Goblin Town," said Vako. "Leatherworkers, dyers, and tinkers, mostly."

Then they were past the goblins and on a quiet street lined by tall buildings with elegant facades. The carriage rolled to a halt. "Lepta's place," called Ramo.

Vako dismounted and tossed the driver another bead. "Good service, cousin." Then he led them inside the eatery, a cramped yet pleasant place where soft flute music wafted through beaded curtains and the air was filled with the aroma of spices.

"Lepta is an expert at blending the offerings of different regions to make superb meals," said Vako once they'd taken their seats. "This shall be a culinary experience to remember."

Vako spoke true. Lepta's rice and vegetable dish was the best Carina had since leaving Soraq.

Vako pushed back his chair. "The hour grows late for business. I believe Lepta has a suite for rent upstairs." He called over to the proprietress and spoke with her for a few moments before being handed a key. "Normally, the suite would run a silver bead a day, but she is willing to reduce the price by half in the expectation of your continued patronage."

The suite was a set of narrow rooms with walls painted in gold and red. It boasted a window with a view of the lower tiers and another that offered an angled glimpse of the temples on the fourth level.

"There is a bathing room through there." Vako motioned across the hall. "I shall return on the morrow."

Luther took a long look around their temporary home after Vako departed. "I find all this convenient. Suspiciously so."

Carina agreed but opted to enjoy the warm bath and soft bed. Rhythmic hammering woke her from a dream of bathing in a woodland pond.

Irked, Carina stumbled over to the window and peered at the Tier of Flame and Steel below the building. Then she blinked at the sight of scores of dwarves and goblins hammering thin metal strips into a tubular framework ten yards from end to end. As she watched, a crew of goblins dragged over a second framework, this one flatter and shaped like an elongated triangle with the point missing. The crews pressed this piece against the midsection of the other.

"Dead Bird." Luther's voice sounded right in Carina's ears.

"Dead Bird? What the hell does that mean?"

"It means none of this was an accident."

"Vako? I thought he"-

"Vako was waiting for us. It was no accident that there was an open slip for Japi, or that this place just happened to have a room – this room – available."

"Oh. What do we do?"

"Nothing." Luther started for the door. "We go downstairs and eat. Then we wait."

Breakfast was an exotic mix of eggs and bread intermingled with tiny strips of spicy meat. Worry almost killed the pleasure. *I can't let fear control me*. Meal completed, Carina brushed past the protesting proprietress and stepped out onto the busy street beyond. A mob of human and goblin youths dashed past her. Burly men unloaded a wagon across the street. Past them, vendors hawked colorful cloth and mundane items from a row of booths.

Carina eyed the stalls. She tugged at her dress, which had been patched several times too often. Then she stepped into the street. A heavy hand on Carina's shoulder stopped her short.

"Where do you think you're going?" asked Luther.

"To get a new dress. This one is fit for the ragbag. And a comb. And maybe some other things."

"This isn't waiting in our room."

"It's just shopping. I have shopped in several strange cities." Carina poked at Luther's tunic, marred by irredeemable stains and rudimentary stitches. "You could stand some new clothes as well."

Luther looked down at his tunic, then at Carina. "I guess it won't hurt." He turned his head. "Goji might as well join us."

Not sharing a common language with the cloth vendor didn't make buying Carina a new dress or the boy's new tunics an easy matter. In the end, Carina shoved silver beads across the counter one at a time until the merchant's eyes twitched, then handed the whole bundle over to Goji.

That prompted a series of squawks from the trader. Carina sighed, selected yet another bead, and tossed it on the table. The vendor squawked some more, attracting hostile looks from a dozen other people, human and goblin alike.

What did I do wrong? Carina tried to remember Vako's list of social taboos but drew a blank. She grabbed the bundle from

Goji and put it back on the table. The vendor's face turned purple. Now, he wasn't just squawking but screaming at the top of his lungs as he thrust the bundle back at her.

Luther eyed the agitated group with alarm. "Carina, get back to our room while I settle this."

"I can"-

"Go!" Luther pushed Carina back towards Lepta's.

Fine, let him deal with it. See if I care. Carina pushed through Lepta's door and scaled the steps to their suite. She dropped her purchases on the bed. She sat there for a moment, shaking. Then she stood and made her way to Goji's chamber, which had a window with an angled view of the street.

Nothing. Oh, the row of stalls was there. So was the cloth merchant, holding out a green and white dress for a Celthanian's matron inspection. But no angry mob. And no sign of Luther and Goji.

Alarmed, Carina pounded down the steps and thrust the door open. Every merchant in the row glared at her. *I can't do this.* She returned to her chamber, sat on the bed, and stared at nothing.

'None of this was an accident.' Luther's words this morning came back to her. Did that include the altercation with the vendor? It seemed improbable. Well, what could she do? Carina's gaze slid over to Luther's pack. Likely she could use its contents for a Finding spell. That would tell her where he was at – and whether or not he still lived. But then what? Could her sorcery free him – and even so, how to escape from the midst of this mad place?

Time dragged in the room. Carina stood, strode to Goji's window, and peered at the street. Still as busy as ever. But...was that cloaked man watching her window? She turned away.

A light tapping sound interrupted Carina's miserable contemplations. It took her a moment to connect the sound with the door. "Who is calling?" Lepta? Vako? A squad of soldiers?"

"Tis' I, Vako Manresa. I bring news – and an invitation."

"News?" Carina thrust open the door, taking in the sight of a neatly groomed Vako – and a pair of large men in heavy leather shirts behind him, with cudgels swinging from their waists.

"I...regret to inform you that your companions were arrested for improper behavior and brawling." Only Vako's lips moved, not the rest of his face. "A charge of improper behavior was leveled against you as well but was withdrawn."

"Improper behavior? What sort of charge is that?" Brawling she could understand, though there'd been no actual confrontation.

"The cloth merchant found your style of bargaining offensive and unacceptable. Your attempt to return the items in question insulted his honor."

Carina shook her head. "I paid more than enough for those clothes."

"You did, which is why the charges were dismissed."

"What of Luther and Goji?"

"They are being held in the second tier until their fines can be paid."

Carina took a step forward. "Well, let's just get that taken care of." She stopped at the expression on Vako's face.

"I must inform you the invitation takes priority." Vako leaned forward until his face almost touched Carina's. "It's from them. The Ervin." The words were a whisper.

'None of this was an accident' –including the brawl that put Luther and Goji in gaol. No doubt there were nearby magicians to counter any magic she might try. Carina stared at Vako for a long moment. Then she smiled. "Can I change my clothes first?"

"That is acceptable."

Ramo's carriage awaited them outside the door. Vako's bodyguards took places at the back of the conveyance, and then they were off, zipping through the market and up a ramp to a street lined with temples covered with intricate friezes. Once, Carina would have found those edifices fascinating. Now, she didn't care.

The ornate facades and minarets of the manors on the fifth level barely warranted a glance.

Ramo's coach climbed a final slope to a small stone-paved square before a pair of intricately carved double doors that swung open as they approached. A bald youth in an orange robe emerged from the shadows and stood there waiting.

Vako halted on the threshold. "Lady Carina, I regret I cannot accompany you past this point."

"You did what you were supposed to do." Carina's voice radiated a calm authority she didn't feel. She turned to the young Ervin. "Lead on."

The youth bowed, turned, and set off along a corridor decorated with images of magicians, aliens, and fantastic machines. They barely registered with Carina. The youth guided her through twisted halls to a portal flanked by muscular men with short batons that glowed with mystic energy. These wardens silently pulled the doors open and motioned Carina inside. She found herself in a pastel chamber with divans placed behind small tables, each with a single occupant.

"Greetings, Carina Mendoza of the Solarian Empire." The speaker was an older man with a bushy beard beneath a gray turban that fell to a gray robe. "I am Elder Asmara Acharya of the Ervin."

"The Slaver bitch doesn't deserve no greeting." These words came from an ebony woman with black dreadlocked hair and the contents of an entire jewelry box adorning her rail-thin body.

Asmara faced the woman. "Civility costs us nothing, Quadira." He directed his attention back to Carina. "Quadira dislikes your former nation."

"Dislike?" Quadira started to rise. "I hate the fucking Slavers!"

"Civility," said Asmara.

"Let's get on with this," said a short, bearded figure wearing a maroon vest over a gray tunic. "I'm Khazan, by the by."

"Yes, we should get on with the matter at hand." Elder Asmara faced Carina. "Do you know why we invited you here?"

I might as well be direct. "You want to make me an offer."

"Hah!" The dwarf slapped his table. "I like this one, Asmara. She's sharp!"

"Well, I don't like her." Quadira slumped in her chair.

"Miss Carina Menendez is a sorceress trained in combat, a member of the Solarian Empire's Arcane Cohort," said Asama. "Directness on her part should be no surprise. Therefore, we shall be direct in return." Asmara stared directly at Carina. "We will be presenting you with a request. First, though, we wish knowledge about events in the north."

"We want to know what the Slavers are up to." Venom dripped from Quadira's words. "First, that damn Titus Maximus saunters into Gawana and makes himself Lord Defender just like that." She snapped her fingers. "Then another Maximus stomps the Nations of the Plains into the dirt and gets made the Slaver Emperor."

"Quadira, civility, please." Asmara faced Carina. "Despite her rudeness, Quadira did state our concerns. Your empire has a poor reputation in the south, and the Maximus family is held in especially low regard."

"We hate their guts," said Quadira.

"We know you were with the army Thomas Maximus led against the Nations of the Plains," said Asmara.

Carina raised her hand. "I was with the army, yes. But I had nothing to do with Thomas Maximus. I was hiding in the Tail."

"Tail?"

"She means whores and thieves," said Quadira.

"The Church tried to purge all wizards not in their ranks or bound to powerful protectors," explained Carina. "One of their witch hunters, a nobleman named Appius Ambrose, tried to kill me. Hiding in the Tail seemed the best option. Unfortunately, he also chose to accompany the army."

"Making you unable to reveal yourself." Asmara nodded. "Noblemen who use their status to murder others without penalty are a sad truth of the world we live in." He thought for a moment. "I assume this witch hunter found you out?"

"He did. I killed him." Carina spoke the words all at once.

"She's got guts, I tell you."

"And that act forced you to flee, away from that army, away from the empire, all the way across the sea to here," said Asmara.

"Pretty much," agreed Carina.

"Pity she couldn't have killed the Maximus Emperor as well," complained Quadira.

"Yes, the Maximus." Asmara tapped the table. "We hoped you could tell us more of him.

"I had no interactions with Thomas Maximus," said Carina, "but his cousin Octavos, the son of Titus Maximus accompanied me across the sea."

"Where is this 'Octavos' now?" asked Khazan.

Carina shrugged. "With his father in Gawana, I imagine. I – I couldn't bring myself to enter that place. It...weighed on me."

"Gawana has that effect on sorcerers." For once, Quadira didn't sound spiteful.

"Well, what sort of person is Octavos?" asked Khazan. "And what did he say about his cousin?"

"Octavos...is a scholar and a musician with magic in his soul, not a schemer for power."

"A musician with magic in his soul," repeated Asmara. "A spell singer. Interesting."

"He's still a Slaver," said Quadira.

"And what did Octavos say about Thomas Maximus?" asked Asmara.

"A born leader," said Carina. "The kind that troops adore."

"That ain't good news," said Quadira.

"The imperial army took devastating losses at Ptath," said Carina. Rebuilding it will take decades."

"Huh. Well, that's something," said Quadira.

"There was another incident connected with Solaria's destruction of the Nations of the Plains we are curious about – a burst of sorcery we felt even here," said Khazan.

"Ah, that would be the device beneath the Pyramid of Zep in Ptath," said Carina.

All three Ervin stared directly at Carina. *This is what truly interests them. They knew about me. They know about Thomas Maximus. But that is politics. What interests them is magic.* Possibilities occurred to her. "I wish to bargain about this mission of yours. You negotiated Ado-Cent's survival with the gotemik by becoming their unwilling allies. Ado-Cent's continued survival rests on a knife edge. You need something done but cannot be seen doing it."

"You are correct," said Quadira.

"Let us negotiate," said Asmara.

LABYRINTH WAR LII – Chimp

'Hell and damnation! We spent days following those corridors, only to return to this infernal ruin with its looming, headless statue.

Casein knocked Netu senseless for this incompetence.

Enough is enough -no more of this wretched backtracking and second-guessing.

Tomorrow morning, I shall climb that wretched statue and make a map. Then I will guide this expedition myself. I was called 'the Compass' during the war for good reason.'

- From 'The Journal of Titus Maximus.'

Lord General Benedict DuPaul wanted eyes watching whatever went down in the maze. So, he gave orders to Tribune Crassus and the Queen of Secrets. Those two handed out assignments to the sneak squads. Those orders resulted in Chimp's crew and Razor's runts rolling out of Cendoza's western gate one fine morning. They weren't hoofing it, and they weren't pumping pedals, either – instead they went in style, in the backs of big wagons bound for Dar-Indra. And thanks to the imperial engineers under Kevin DuMars, that road was a fine stone-paved highway, wide enough for two carts to pass each other with room to spare. That was a good thing, considering everybody and their kid brother seemed to be using it. They rumbled past rows of colorfully clad women toting bundles hung from yokes across their necks, past peddlers selling everything from glass beads to cutlery from pushcarts to wagons piled high with produce, hay, and caged chickens. And bicycles were all over the place, half of them piled high with all kinds of crap. Sometimes, Snuffles would jump from the cart to give some of these items – and the people toting them a good sniff. Most of these folks took it in stride, like it was perfectly normal to have a weird hairy girl looking over their stock.

Bramble got propositioned by about every fifth female on the road. He'd give them a goofy smile and they'd wander off.

Razor's dwarves didn't attract much notice – it seemed there was a fortress city north of here packed full of weapon-toting runts. That city – Rith – was why Traag hadn't come south of the mountains and killed everybody. Lately, those dwarves had their hands full fighting the demon worshippers rampaging through Agba.

Kevin DuMars was up there hammering the cultist with the fifth and seventh brigades, who'd peddled their way to Agba via the land route. He'd nailed a big pack of the demon worshippers, but a bunch escaped into tunnels. The legionnaires sent in after them didn't come back.

Carriages shot past the caravan a couple of times. Once, they passed a covered palanquin carried by eight all-but-naked guys.

After that, they caught up to a bearded guy in a simple smock toting a staff with a lantern hanging from it, trailed by a trio of kids. That fellow caught Bramble's attention. "Wizard," he told Chimp.

"Lantern Man," said Dodger, who'd been posted to these parts since forever. "They roam all through Cendoza, the Rhaiduni states, and up into Agba, casting petty spells for food and a place to sleep. The kids are his students."

Next, they paused beside a group of men in orange robes with weird marks on their foreheads. "Monks of Zu," said Dodger, as he made a funny little hand sign at the group.

Snuffles, of course, jumped from the wagon, loped over to the monks, and gave them a good sniff, which prompted some bemused looks on their part. Then she hopped back into the cart. "Sad," she said. "Their seed is dead."

"That's a mighty fine sniffer you have there, Sammy," said Dodger. "She's right. Once they take the mark," he tapped his head, "the monks of Zu can't have kids. The mark just...kills it."

Teeny-tiny farms, workshops, and miniature markets lined the road to either side. Workers – mostly of the female variety – weeded fields, piled rocks, and pounded boards together. Sometimes Snuffles headed off to investigate these places – and sometimes the Lantern Man would join her, talking with people, passing out charms, or working trivial bits of magic.

The farms and the traffic thinned out. Finally, it was just their little caravan and the occasional cyclist with barely a building in sight. They reached a hill with a stone wall around the top.

"Old Marcher Camp," said Dodger. "I helped build it."

Chimp nodded. He knew all about Marcher Camps. He'd only built about fifty of them since joining the legions. Usually, they were big squares bordered by walls of dirt or rubble with a gate in the middle of each side, all of it raised in just a couple hours – usually by men who'd been pumping pedals all damn day. Whole legions camped inside those squares.

The wagons rolled through the northern gate into a big open area with firepits in the middle and shanties built against the wall.

Camp set, a bunch of the crew scaled a short ladder to the ramparts and eyeballed the Arrowhead – a pointy, yellowish spire taller than it was wide, hard against Gawana – Kevin DuMar's secret door.

"God above. I never wanted to enter that accursed place again." Old Man Fury finished the statement with a long swig from a bottle.

Chimp looked at the knight. "Then why'd you come?"

"Family." Fury took another pull on the bottle and strode away.

Chimp figured that by 'family,' Fury meant his kids. He shook his head. Despite his lack of official status on this expedition, Old Man Fury talked the General into including him and his illegitimate brood on Chimps squad. Chimp didn't like it – but he couldn't buck the General. Yes, Fury was a hot-shit sword swinger from the Traag War – but he was also old. And his kids? Well, Simon knew how to swing that ridiculously oversized broadsword of his – but he was also an idiot. Idleman – the lockpicker – might know how to fight but couldn't be trusted. And the healer girl – Spots – had no business being anywhere near a battlefield.

"Duty," said Dodger, taking Fury's spot on the parapet. "Duty and retirement. My twenty is almost up." Dodger was older than Fury, but still in decent shape. He'd been posted here for so long that he'd picked up a wife and a brood of kids. Not many soldiers lasted that long. Chimp wondered if he'd be one of them.

"I wish you luck."

Razor joined them on the battlement. "Glad it's your bunch taking that route and not mine." His squad was supposed to go through the Dar-Indra pass and check out a couple of fortresses on the other side that might or might not be occupied by demon worshippers. Supposedly, his crew and Chimps would link up at Mountain Gate.

Chimp glanced at Razor. "See you on the other side."

Sticks sniffed. "Grubs about done."

They descended into the courtyard to find the Lantern Man entering the compound and Simon standing all sad-eyed in front of his dad. "I miss Patches." His voice was almost a wail. Hopefully, he didn't burst into tears.

That'd be freaking great – saddled with a crying imbecile.

Fury put a hand on the kid's shoulder. "I miss my horse as well, son. But it's for the best – the maze is no place for horses. There's not much for them to eat."

Simon considered this for a moment. "Okay, Pa."

"Now go get something to eat."

The grub was good but it didn't lighten the kid's mood. That was when Spots intervened. First, she trotted over to her other half-brother, Idleman, who was busy doing nothing by the fire and shoved the guy's sitar in his face. "Play," she told him.

When Idleman gave Spots a greasy look, she kicked him in the side. Idleman took the hint and ran his fingers across the strings, which caught everybody's attention. Next, Spots pulled a drum out of the wagon and tossed it to Simon. "Play."

"I don't wanna, Lucy."

"I want to sing." Spots bent over Simon until their noses almost touched. "Now, play." Spots liked to sing. She was always humming under her breath when patching scratches or mixing herbs.

Simon tapped out a basic beat on the drum. Idleman wrapped the sitar's notes around the rhythm.

Spots strutted before the fire, stared straight at Chimp for about two seconds, then shifted her gaze to Blaze.

Blaze started tapping his feet to the beat. That seemed like a great idea to Chimp and Sticks, so they started stomping. Sir Fury didn't just tap his feet but clapped his hands. A good rhythm got underway.

Spots motioned at Idleman. "Now."

The music shifted and became the beat for 'Green Hills,' a country song older than dirt. Then Spot's began to sing. She had a nice voice, hitting both the high and the low notes.

The Lantern Man planted the staff holding his lamp into the dirt and said some magic words and a parade of spectral people poured out of its crevices and made a ring about the fire. That made Chimp's skin crawl just a bit – yes, it was a petty hoodoo, but still hoodoo all the same.

The Lantern Man's illusions caught Shade's attention and he added his magic to the mix. Shadows pulled themselves from the darkness and took on man-shaped forms, joining ephemeral celebration.

Chimp looked over at Bramble. "You got anything to contribute?"

Bramble shrugged and made a pulling motion. Birds and bugs zipped out of the darkness and engaged in aerial acrobatics above the fire.

'Green Hills' segued into the livelier 'Farmer Ham's Daughter.' That brought Snuffles out of the shadows, hairy arms and legs sticking out of her shift. She launched into a dance number of her own design that featured lots of leaping and twirling – and incidentally showing the hair extended to other parts of her anatomy.

Snuffles made a come-hither motion at Blaze, who made a face, lurched to his feet, and started gyrating alongside her despite having two left feet.

Sir Fury took a long swig from a bottle and stood up. "Let me show you youngsters how it's done." He joined the dancers and demonstrated he did know some decent dance moves. Alas, age overcame energy, sending him to the sidelines.

'Farmer Ham's Daughter' gave way to 'Take Me Home.' The Lantern Man's phantoms dissolved into mist, Shade's shadow people returned to the dark, and Bramble's flying pets vanished.

Spots stumbled to the sidelines to wet her whistle with a bottle. She took a long swig and handed the bottle to Chimp. Idleman and Simon kept right on playing. Chip took a pull from the flask, decided he liked it, and then took another. Things got blurry after that.

The next morning wasn't much fun. Idleman bitched about his bleeding fingers, Simon still looked morose, and Sticks awoke with a shriek when he found Snuffles curled next to him, not wearing much of anything. Chimp fought an aching head and the impulse to bust heads but finally got the cavalcade moving about two hours later than intended.

"Well, that was fun," said Chimp as he stood alongside Dodger on an itty-bitty flat patch of rock, "And this next bit will be even more fun." He rubbed his calves – that trail up the Arrowhead made his muscles burn. He stared out across a deep gorge to another mastiff, this one looking like a giant yellow brick.

"The coffin will make your ass pucker up." Dodger jabbed a finger at the box hanging from a cable. It did look like a coffin, except it was painted sky blue instead of black. Chimp figured it'd fit three people, maybe four if they got cozy. "You move it along by tugging at those ropes tied to the end. Worse gets to worse, that rope will keep the coffin from falling – I saw that happen once."

"Well, let's get on with it." It took four trips to get the crew and their gear over the wall and across the gap. Simon had to be coaxed into the coffin by Spots – who didn't look too keen on the thing herself. Idleman took it in stride. Old Man Fury grimaced, took a long slug from his bottle, and then let himself be pulled across the gap.

Snuffles didn't bother with the coffin ride at all: instead, she walked the wire, a feat even Chimp wasn't too sure he could duplicate, and feats of climbing and fine balance were his thing. Bramble watched Snuffles cross, announced he could do the same thing, then damn near fell off at the halfway point.

Once across, they tackled the Brick – which meant walking all hunched through a tunnel maybe a yard high and wide, then climbing down a long-ass shaft with notches cut into the sides. That brought them to a low, wide crack that took them to the Blind Spot, a triangular jut just one long step away from the top of the nearest wall.

Chimp took in the scene. Walls everywhere, thirty and forty feet high, five to fifteen feet thick, and a quarter covered with vines dotted with little red and blue flowers, the spaces between them ranging from skinny to spacious. The walls twisted one way and then another, climbing hills, meandering along ridgetops, and dropping into valleys.

"It can be a bit overwhelming," said Dodger.

Chimp did feel overwhelmed, but he didn't let it show. "Come on. Let's get on with it."

Eleven days later, Chimp had more than enough of Gawana. They'd hike a quarter mile this way, turn that way, hike another quarter mile...and there you were in a freaking dead end. Backtrack, take that side passage, then find yourself in a courtyard with four more routes to choose from, except it was actually three routes because two of them were the same passageway. Climbing the walls...well, Chimp, Sticks, and Bramble could do it easy enough. Idleman, too, if you kicked his butt hard enough. Snuffles could practically walk right up the damn things all easy-peasy. The rest of them...not really.

Maps? Yeah, they'd entered the maze with a stack of maps. Half of those charts were no good. The rest had problems ranging from blank patches to missing passages. Dodger said it was because the walls changed position. Bramble said it was sorcery.

Snuffles sniffed everything, snapped at everybody – she'd done pulled a knife on Skunk – and kept pulling vanishing acts, though twice she returned covered with blood and a dead four-legged critter slung over her shoulder. Chimp almost hoped she'd vanish and not come back.

Meanwhile, Old Man Fury was out of booze and cranky, Simon was jumpier than hell, Sticks had a thing for Spots, and Idleman was ticked at them both.

Then there was the other crap – like the four-armed, white-furred monkey things that ambushed them at the one campsite, throwing rocks and shit at them until they took off. Or the vines that tried to suck the life right out of Sticks when he got too close. He was damn lucky Spots had the right potion to fix him up. And that abandoned village was downright creepy – almost fresh food still on the tables, nothing out of place – just no people like they'd all been snatched. Still, they gathered a week's worth of grub from that place.

Still, despite everything, they were getting close to the Gotemik beachhead. They knew that because the damn flying disks were now almost overhead, instead of off to the side. Plus, they were hearing things. Snatches of voices from two or three corridors over. They came across weird, angular tracks from creatures with too many legs. Flashes of light, again, always from a few passages over. Chimp was getting concerned about turning a corner and finding themselves in a real shitshow.

Chimp had Snuffles and Sticks scale the walls to scope things out. Brambles tried a little recon using borrowed vermin, but that didn't work well.

Still, that gave a slightly clearer picture of where they were, but that didn't help matters any because there didn't seem to be a straight route from here to there without climbing right over the tops of about four walls, almost like the Gotemik were being fenced off from the rest of the labyrinth.

"What is that?" Bramble's head craned this way and that.

Both of Snuffle's ears went up. She started making a whining sound and sniffing the stones.

"What's what?" asked Blaze.

"That sound," said Bramble.

"I hear it," said Idleman. "It's a vibration."

"Music," said Spots.

"It's coming from here." Snuffles crouched before a patch of wall no different than any others about twenty paces off. "No, the next wall over."

The sound grew louder, a twanging sound like the world's biggest sitar or lyre being played by a giant with no musical sense whatsoever.

Chimp motioned. "We're doing an ambush. Sir Fury, you're in charge down here. You got Simon, Blaze, Dodger, Skunk, and Spots." No choice because none of them could climb worth a shit.

"About time." Fury gave Chimp an evil glare. He was getting tired of taking orders from a 'jumped-up monkey.'

"Sticks, Bramble, Snuffles, Idleman, you're with me up there. When I signal, we'll hit them with the Specials, followed by a grab-and-go. Things go sideways, we meet at the courtyard with the creek, Got it?"

Everybody nodded.

Getting into position went quick enough – Chimps crew scampered up the wall, spread out, and then laid themselves flat, crossbows with the Specials at the ready. Meanwhile, Old Man Fury laid out a double-sided ambush with Simon and Skunk on one side and Dodger and Blaze on the other.

Chimp lay there, gut in a knot, waiting, wondering what he'd missed while the song from hell grew ever louder. The vibrations were now so intense they made his teeth rattle. Not just his teeth, the whole world seemed blurred. He raised his head a tiny fraction. Focused. This wall was vibrating a little. The one across the way was shaking, shedding vines and rocks and crap. Pebbles fell from a patch maybe five feet across. Then he was looking at a hole.

The vibrations stopped. Chimp stared at the opening, waiting. Counting. Voices came from the other side. Then a pair of muscular, red-skinned hobgoblins in ratty armor strode through the opening. Each sported a heavy metal collar around his neck and cradled a metal rod attached to silvery packs on their backs with thick cables. Weapons. But what did they do?

Chimp kept his head low and continued counting. The hobgoblins spread out, strange weapons at the ready, eyeballing everything. Professionals.

Chimp flattened himself some more. More figures popped out of the hole. Humans this time, one a swarthy-looking nomad in furs, the other in Solarian-style armor with a tree symbol emblazoned on the front. Neither carried the tubular weapons, but both had collars clamped to their necks.

Then a monster came through the opening. It had six legs sticking from an armored pink hide and a pillar topped with tentacles. Weird tools and dull boxes inset with bright gems were clamped to the things carapace. Gotemik. Chimp had seen a dead one, once, half a world away.

This one, though, was alive. It scuttled through the opening, resembling nothing so much as a giant mutated crab, then its legs folded together in front of Chimp's wall. The tentacles unfurled, then lifted what looked like a sitar designed by a blind idiot. One of those appendages touched a string. Then another. And just like that, the vibrations started up again. The wall trembled, with Chimp and his team atop it.

The shaking knocked Chimp this way and that. There wasn't a chance in hell he could hold this position. Fight or flee?

He tried to take in the scene below. Just one of the hobgoblins was visible. He could see the nomad leaning against the far wall. No sign of the other two. Did Sticks or Snuffles have a better angle? Shit.

Right about then, the shaking knocked Stick's skinny frame about a foot in the air. When he landed, that whole part of the wall started to slide, with him on it.

The nomad shouted. Pointed.

Then a blue-white beam lanced out – and Sticks was gone, falling to the ground in bloody pieces.

Sticks. Gone. Sticks. His best friend and confidant. The founder of the Sweepers, even if Chimp did take them over later on. It'd been Sticks who'd proposed signing up in the army, saying twenty years of peacetime service beat being hanged. Those bastards were going to pay. Chimp rolled to a sitting position, took aim at the crab monster, and pulled the crossbow's trigger.

Blue-white light flashed as the bolt hit the pillar rising from the crab's back. Then it was on its side, screeching and clicking, while the sitar from hell lay on the ground.

Another beam lanced out – then the hobgoblin who'd fired it had a damn bear wrapped around his torso – Snuffles, in her other form. His stick weapon fell to the ground.

Chimp grabbed another Special and cocked the crossbow, hunting for that second hobgoblin. Where was he?

For that matter, where the hell was anybody? No Sticks. No Bramble. No Idleman - just Snuffles wrestling with the hobgoblin.

A bolt flashed across Chimp's vision, hit the nomad square on, blowing him to bloody bits.

The gotemik tried to right itself.

There. A hint of movement. Chimp spotted the second hobgoblin, with that beam weapon aimed straight at him. He pulled the trigger, jumped, and hit the vines halfway down the side of the wall right as the Special hit the wall and exploded.

Chimp's crossbow clattered to the ground. Shit. Hanging here made him a target. So, he did a fast slide to the ground, turned...and found himself facing off against the knight.

The knight swung a blow that bit hard into the armor over Chimp's chest. Hot pain made it difficult to breathe. Chimp threw himself backward while reaching for his blade.

"Go away, you!" The not-so-great battle cry came from Simon, who laid into the knight with that oversized hunk of steel.

Simon's dad was right behind him, plowing into the damn tunnel across the way, still grinning. Damn idiot.

The knight was good – better than Simon by far, but the distraction let Chimp get to his feet. He took a deep, pain-filled breath, and hurled himself into the knight's midsection, knocking the warrior onto his armored rump.

The knight rolled away.

Chimp stood. Snuffles was gone. The hob she'd jumped was a bloody mess. No sign of Bramble. Colored fluids leaked from the crab thing. Shouts came from both tunnels – Old Man Fury was putting up one hell of a fight.

"Retreat!" Chimp grabbed Simon and pushed him towards the tunnel – had that devil's instrument cut through it that fast? Where was the damn thing, anyway?

Chimp and Simon slammed into the tunnel – and right into the backside of the second hobgoblin, who was aiming his tube weapon right at Blaze. Simon hit the hobgoblin full tilt – and everybody went sprawling.

Simon made it to his feet first and pancaked the hobgoblin.

Chimp stood, turned, and spotted the knight maybe twenty paces off, with a whole pack of collared humans and hobgoblins starting to come out of the hole in the other wall. At least two of them carried beam weapons.

"Down!"

Chimp ducked as Blaze and Dodger fired a pair of Specials. The explosive bolts shot over Chimp's head and missed the knight by about a foot – then hit the leading members of the reinforcements head-on. Those two were blown into bloody bits. The rest faltered. But it didn't look good.

Chimp motioned. "We need to get out of here!"

"Dad's in there," wailed Simon.

"He'll be fine." The words were a lie, but Simon bought them, even if the others didn't.

Blaze fell on his butt as the hobgoblin shrugged off both him and Simon. It reached for the beam-weapon.

"No, you don't!" Spots brought a heavy slab of rock down on the hobgoblin's skull, crushing it. Then she stood there, hands on her mouth, staring at the corpse. "I – I killed him."

"Good job." Chimp shoved Spots to the side and studied the beam thing. "Blaze grab that."

Dodger stepped up and fired a Special straight at the tunnel. The wall groaned and then folded downward, blocking the opening. Good.

Chimp took stock. He was hurt. Sticks was blown to bloody bits. Skunk was dead, with a hole through his chest. Old Man Fury was missing and more than likely dead. There was no sign of Bramble. Dodger didn't look in too great of shape. Spots was in shock. Her half-brother had bruises on his bruises. "Let's get out of here."

They made it to the rendezvous without getting attacked. Snuffles and Idleman were already there.

"Thought you might want this." Idleman held out the alien sitar.

They waited a while, but Bramble and Old Man Fury didn't show.

LABYRINTH WAR LIII – Octavos

"Welcome to Ezek."

I opened my eyes to see Varian's face staring down at me. I was on my back on a stone slab. "What is your intent?" I fought to keep my words calm despite my anxiety and rage.

"My intent? I intend to do these miserable maze dwellers a great favor – something that should have been done ages ago." Varian glared at me. "And then kill you, of course. You deserve to die. Your whole wretched nation deserves to die for their crimes against the Gods. But for now, your death will suffice."

"Kill them now, brother." Narran stood behind him in the red and black regalia of the Agban sorcerers. My innards turned cold when I saw her arms bloody to the elbows. Not a bit of gore marred her clothing. I had no doubt the blood came from my companions. Rage filled me. I would not let my quest end here!

Varian turned to face her. "His ancestor first enslaved and then betrayed ours. Titus deserves a slow demise."

The Twins faced each other. "The portal is chancy," said Narran. "The Doctor eludes us."

Hope flared in my heart at the news that the Doctor was free.

"The guards are scouring the nearby maze-ways for her. She is an old woman"-

"Doctor Menendez is a powerful witch. Finish them now, brother." Mila gestured off to one side, and the giant Ram picked up a limp form – Mila – and started climbing the ziggurat stairs.

My bound hands reached my tunic collar and plucked loose the Doctor's tiny twist of cloth while she spoke. I swallowed the scrap even as Varian turned.

"Women, even sisters, can be so unreasonable." Varian approached, drawing a jeweled dagger from the top of his boot. "Ram did so want to take his time with your muscular friend."

Strength flooded my limbs as the Doctor's concoction took effect. The world slowed.

Varian's dagger neared my throat. "Perhaps this is for the best."

Determination and rage turned my vision red.

I lurched forward, plucked Varian's dagger with my bound hands, and planted it in his belly.

Hot satisfaction filled me as Varian croaked "What?" and fell backward, a red stain marring his shirt, as the Seal fell to the flagstones between us.

- From 'The Journal of Titus Maximus.'

Octavos trembled. He stood in a bizarre room with weirdly flexible pink and violet walls, just off the Heart Chamber. A sickly sweet aroma filled the air, making him want to gag.

Octavos adjusted his Sight and saw the energy matrix that filled the curved surfaces around him. Still keeping his Sight focused, Octavos strummed the lyre, trying to match that alien harmony. His music merged with those powers. He spotted an opportunity for improvision. He made a tiny variation to the notes he played – and the wall's energies acquiesced. A second alteration, this one more potent but still in accord with the powers flow followed the first change.

A section of the flexible material bulged backward, making a sort of tunnel – no, a doorway, opening into the Heart Chamber itself.

The energy lines shifted, becoming a countermelody.

Octavos improvised – then something slammed into his side, making him drop the lyre. He looked up to see pseudopods emerging from the walls, reaching for him...*they will kill me. They will draw me inside and dissolve my flesh*. He couldn't move.

The appendages stopped, then retreated into the walls.

"I am intrigued," said a voice filled with hisses and clicks to Octavos's left. "Your simple device grants you a degree of control over Gawana's surfaces normally restricted to Operants or those possessed of special authorization."

"Thanks for the save." Octavos picked himself up. "I thought it was going to kill me."

"You did agitate Gawana," agreed the alien, "but the control you displayed is remarkable. I am confident that understanding will continue to expand."

"I'm not so sure." Octavos shook his head. "It's so complex!"

"Understanding will arrive when required." 3-99 motioned, and an opening to a normal corridor made of stone instead of...whatever... appeared. "This manipulation has left your energies depleted."

"Yes, I'm tired."

Octavos left the chamber—an empty space identical to hundreds of others throughout this portion of the Heart—and strode through a maze of corridors, his path guided by the link he shared with Gawana. A few minutes later, he reached his cave-like apartment. He stared through the sole window into a hollow where pink, blue, and white flowers clustered around a pond.

Octavos stared at the scene for a moment, then carefully returned his lyre to its case, which he placed on a shelf lined with other musical instruments – two flutes, a drum, and a wristband with tiny silver bells. He wondered if additional instruments would help him manipulate Gawana. Could he play two instruments while maintaining his mystic focus? "Probably not."

He turned from the shelf and flopped on a soft green couch next to a low table. His gaze flicked over the items on the table's surface – a pile of books, a tall bottle next to a crystal cup, and a small glass plate with a portrait of Bao on its surface.

Octavos picked up the topmost book and eyed the title – 'Mysteries of the Avar Bards' by Cormac the Elder. He flipped it open and stared at a wall of text. Purportedly, the tome was a primer on bardic magic - the projection of emotional energy through music. Octavos found it headache-inducing.

Octavos set the book aside and took the bottle. Almost full. It had been a long, tiresome day. Surely, one glass of wine would be acceptable. He held the neck over the cup – and then set it up right again as Bao's image seemed to frown at him.

He took the little portrait and held it before his face. It was a photograph, but not like the ones he remembered from the University of Solace. It was in color, not the colorless pictures like those made by the university's enthusiasts. For another, it moved and spoke.

Octavos touched a tiny protrusion on the portrait's side.

Bao shifted position. "I will miss you, lover-boy." She blew a kiss at him. "Take care of yourself." The image froze.

Octavos stared at the portrait, wondering how Bao was doing. "I miss you," he said to the image, before falling into fretful slumber.

An impulse prompted Octavos to visit the manufactory entrance enroute to his training session. Something he couldn't identify gnawed at him about the effort to open the portal. He slowly walked along the row of circular portals, still sealed apart from the one his father had managed to open. Its interior was utterly empty. He walked further along the wall, pausing at the same spot Titus had chosen for his attempt to breach the manufactory. It didn't seem any different from the rest of the wall.

Why here? Why this place? Octavos placed both hands on the surface and invoked his Sight. A complex web of energy appeared within the stone, much of it making a tight knot where the circular door merged with the wall. That knot looked familiar. Very familiar. With a start, Octavos recognized the Maximus family Seal. Had his father done that when attempting to open the vault? Strange, though, how it was connected to the other lines, binding them.

His Sight wavered and failed. Octavos stood there for a long moment, thinking. Then he turned and walked away.

"Your remarks yesterday concerning the complexity of Gawana's matrix prompted me to commence a new approach," 3-99 told Octavos as their session commenced the next morning. The alien indicated a table covered by a large sheet filled with horizontal lines and small symbols.

Octavos inspected the paper. "These are musical notations."

"Correct," stated 3-99. "This sheet represents a portion of the base harmonic sequence which directs Gawana.

"I – I need to study this." Octavos peered at the sheet. "There are way too many notes. This is like a full orchestra."

"Gawana employs multiple simultaneous vibrational actions. Regulatory programs prevent unauthorized deviations."

Octavos parsed the alien's statement word by word. "Not just an orchestra, but one that is...policed?"

"In the human vernacular, 'close enough.'"

Octavos thought about the alien's comment. "This 'regulatory program' is why we couldn't access the manufactory, right?"

"Correct."

"But why have something that you can't...stop?"

"There is history behind your question, Octavos Maximus." 3-99 stood stock still. "This sphere is one of several – the records of how many are no longer extant – that we modified to support life. The modification of this particular sphere was initiated thirty-nine thousand planetary orbits ago and required four hundred planetary orbits to accomplish."

Now it was Octavos's turn to be astonished. "Your people created the world?"

"We modified this planet and others to support oxygen-breathing lifeforms," said 3-99. "We also modified an unusual type of vegetation to become our metropolises. Gawana was but one of several such modified entities. We traversed the void between stellar systems, initially utilizing special...ships, and later via rifts through null space." 3-99's stance changed. The alien seemed...wistful. "Those rifts proved detrimental to our civilization because null space is the habitat of the Leeches, or 'demons' in your vernacular, entities that feed directly on organic and inorganic energy."

Octavos felt a sinking feeling in his stomach. "How detrimental?"

"The Leeches decimated an uncertain number of planets. At the time, the losses were believed to be total."

Octavos could hardly believe the alien's words. "You're saying these 'Leeches' killed everything on entire planets?"

"That was the assumption at the time, yes. The surviving worlds initiated severe restrictions on the use of null space portals. Passive systems indicated the Leeches had abandoned the spheres they'd decimated approximately ten thousand orbits after their arrival. We commenced a cautious program of investigation." 3-99 pulled a tubular device the length of a dagger from its silvery robe and adjusted protrusions along its length.

An image of a lifeless brown and orange wasteland, seen from above, appeared between Octavos and the alien. "This image was recorded during one of these investigations."

The picture began to move. The dead wasteland became an equally dead mountain range, then swooped over the coast of a lake or an ocean, whose shoreline was studded with green and brown blotches.

"Are those plants?" asked Octavos.

"Correct."

The image resumed movement, this time tracking a long river. Lumbering, gray-skinned beasts with too many legs and tentacle snouts fed on fields of blotchy plants.

Octavos recognized the creatures – droath's, big smelly beasts of burden.

The viewer passed over the herd and paused above several hundred opaque domes arranged in concentric circles about a central hill. Insect-like figures – kwintath – moved between these domes tinkering with machinery or tending to the plants.

"So, some of your people did survive the Leeches."

"Correct."

The image moved past the alien town, crossing over a field that could almost be considered 'verdant.' An immense angular construct appeared on the horizon, resolving into a familiar tangle of walls, courtyards, and corridors.

"Is that one of Gawana's...cousins?"

"It is," said 3-99. "The city constructs enabled life to survive in the worlds attacked by the Leeches. Unconstrained, the city constructs absorb energy – including the energy of the Leeches."

Octavos saw where this explanation was going. "So, those members of your people who took refuge in these unconstrained cities survived the Leeches purge." His father had alluded to Gawana being immune to demons more than once, but never went into the details. This presentation explained much of his fanaticism.

"At a substantial cost. The city constructs transformed from benign habitations to prisons that required thousands of orbits to escape.

"And something like that...almost happened here."

"Correct." 3-99 adjusted the controls on its tubular device. "Three thousand four hundred twenty planetary orbits ago, the Leeches reached this world. The populace of our greatest remaining metropolis – including many of our human, dwarven, elven, and goblin servitors – perished almost immediately."

3-99 motioned and a new image appeared. This one displayed a city maze in a mountain bowl beneath a blue sky. Suddenly, the midst of the metropolis erupted upwards, even as the heavens twisted. Yellow and purple mist poured forth, engulfing the city.

"The demise of Chor-Vuth, now known as Chorvos, by the Leech currently identified as Kato-Siva," said 3-99. "That event initiated approximately a hundred planetary orbits of utter chaos. There were attempted mass evacuations through null space portals despite the risks, coups staged by local human and goblin overlords, and a series of...pacts...with dubious entities. These pacts succeeded in keeping Kato-Siva confined to Chorvos for over a thousand planetary orbits, but by then our civilization was in terminal decline." 3-99 looked at Octavos with its bulbous eyes. "Your species assumed full independence and created new civilizations during that period."

"I am not responsible for my ancestor's actions."

"True. You are responsible for your actions." 3-99 touched the controls again. Chorvos vanished, replaced by a blocky bearded face. "The dwarf termed 'General Sesk,' once an Operant and Administrator of Gawana who turned renegade.

He fled to Chorvos and released part of Kato-Siva's essence in a bid for personal power. That fragment of Kato-Siva manifested as Zarthatax, the three-headed demon dragon." 3-99 manipulated more controls. This image was a literal portrait, marred by cracks, depicting a gigantic dragon with three heads. "That arrangement put General Sesk in command of the polity designated Agba. General Sesk employed his position to attack Gawana."

"He failed, obviously."

"General Sesk came perilously close to success." 3-99 made another alteration to his device. A stepped pyramid appeared. "Ezek, a fortress mechanism General Sesk created with his combined Operant and Leech knowledge to first subvert, then destroy Gawana. We prevented that occurrence by removing all constraints from Gawana and planting additional seeds to extend its perimeter. General Sesk's successors hounded Gawana until the Nations of the Plains destroyed the agba polity."

Octavos digested these revelations. "And here we are."

"Correct. Here we are." 3-99 motioned at the music sheet. "Shall we begin?"

Octavos took a long look at the music. "I am willing to try." He initiated the blink trick to activate his Sight. Then he fell into the alien harmony. Having a map helped immensely. This time, he made a hole in the wall and shaped a pair of nude nymphs (who not so coincidentally resembled Bao) to either side of the opening. *This is easy. Too easy. The 'security program' isn't even trying to stop me.*

"Gawana is under an infiltration assault." 3-99's words pierced Octavos's trance state.

"What?" The web of energy before Octavos wavered and almost dissolved.

"Infiltration assault successful. Multiple walls breached in the west-northwest quadrant near polity designated 'Tree Hill.'

A shudder ran through Octavos's body at the name. "That's the Gotemik bridgehead." A bridgehead the Gotemik had secured by demolishing that entire section of the maze. That act cost the crab-like aliens severely because they'd been unable to duplicate it.

"Initiating countermeasures," said 3-99. "Countermeasures unsuccessful."

"Can I help?" asked Octavos.

"Unknown but unlikely," replied 3-99. "Lord Defender Maximus and Administrator Lady Green are initiating additional countermeasures."

Octavos glared at the wall and began a series of breathing exercises and meditations to curb his agitation. As he understood it a Lord could influence any point in Gawana regardless of location, though that effect decreased with distance. He did the blink trick. His Sight flickered into life. Octavos tracked the lines of energy and followed them to where they were being diverted – a vast tangle of red, black, and white lines that looped and swirled about each other. This ball latched onto Gawana's tendrils, drawing them into itself, growing stronger by the moment.

How do I counter such a thing? It consumes everything it touches. Octavos studied the intruder. *It's like a giant ball of yarn.* A ridiculous image came to mind – that of his childhood pet cat Fluffy, batting a ball of twine about his old room. Once, the ball unraveled when a trailer was caught in a crevice. *It's stupid, but I'll try it anyway.*

Octavos reached out with his developing power and 'touched' one of the ball's strings while simultaneously trying to anchor himself. A giant jolt ran through his body. Everything turned white, then black.

LABYRINTH WAR LIV - Curtis

'I have learned secrets of the universe the Church tried and failed to blot from our collective minds. Why, the very designation 'True God' shows the hypocrisy and insecurity underlining their faith! But you know the true reality – that the real powers of the cosmos are at best indifferent and more often malicious to humanity and would exterminate humanity the way we kill bugs and rats threatening our fields. The Gotemik, the race that destroyed Celthania, are among the least of these beings. The empire might conceivably defeat the Gotemik, though I deem this unlikely. The same is not true of the Great Ones. Humanity cannot possibly defeat those entities – Solaria's victory over Traag's demonic sponsors was a mere fluke. Indeed, that so-called 'victory' has attracted the attention of more powerful entities.'

- Extract from a letter sent by Titus Maximus to Doctor Isabella Menendez

"Lisina used to be much livelier in the old days." Varian punctuated the statement with a sweeping wave as he walked through an expanse of colorful but tattered tents beside a large lake. "Our stopovers here were wonderous breaks from the mind-numbing monotony of crossing the plains. There was this bathhouse we frequented" - Varian looked at his twin sister Narran, "Camay's, was it?"

"Chama's," said his twin sister Narran.

The twins wore identical light blue tunics inset with silver thread that gleamed oddly in the sunlight, tiny pouches on the belts that cinched their attire, and matching black boots. Each carried a brown leather bag supported by a broad strap across their chests.

Varian sported a fine rapier on his hip. Narran occasionally fondled a red, thumb-sized cylinder carved to resemble a squatting figure that hung from a thong about her neck.

Both wore wristbands – gold on the right wrist, heavy iron on their left, those marked with angular symbols – the Rune of Null, the bane of magic. Until those shackles were removed, the pair could not work sorcery. Yet...they took this handicap in stride. Curtis wondered about that.

Curtis wore his battered and scratched armor over tattered clothes fit for the rag bin. His boots were splitting at the seams. He wondered if this tent city sported a decent cobbler – a couple of the nomad thralls he'd encountered since this nightmare began did wear fine footwear.

"Yes, Chama's." Varian looked skyward for a moment. "The attendants there would wash the stink from our bodies."

"Style our hair." Narran arched her back. "I looked most fetching as a barbarian princess."

"While musicians played subtle tunes all the while. What exquisite bliss." Varian sighed. "Then we'd peruse the market."

"I found some most intriguing trinkets here," said Narran. "Freshwater pearls. Jewelry carved from ivory – I wore this bracelet for years. Windchimes that changed tune when the wind shifted – I gave one of those to my aunt."

"Items of metal and glass," continued Varian. "I bought the most impressive spyglass from this market." He shook his head. "Now look at this place. Lisina, the Caravansary of the Plains, the City of Ten Thousand Tents, is reduced to a bedraggled encampment."

Varian's statement was dead accurate. Both Lisina's tents and the populace looked listless. Haunted. No spark. Tattered clothes. The goods displayed at the stalls were basic, substandard, or both, be they cloth, grain, or metal implements. The women purchasing these goods didn't even haggle with the merchants. And the reason for all this walked right by the trio – a pair of crab-like gotemik. The aliens clicked away at each other while collared humans and hobgoblins scanned the area. surroundings. Looming past the tents was a pair of silvery towers rising from Lesina's cattle market, collectively called the Stink Works. Cattle were still abundant – the aliens didn't slaughter the beasts. Instead, their collared taskmasters supervised chained slaves who shoveled the beast's dung into carts and took it to the towers. There, somehow, it became food for the Shulls. Literal shit-eaters.

"Perhaps there is a spark left in this place, after all, brother," Narran stared down a narrow alley. "See?"

Varian nodded. "I do." He looked over his shoulder at Curtis. "You may as well come along."

"I can't." Now it was Curtis's turn to shake his head. "I am doomed to die a collared slave."

"We are all doomed to die, eventually," said Varian.

"But you do not have to perish filthy and hungry," continued Narran.

"So, come." Varian tugged at Curtis's arm.

Curtis considered the request. He was without direct orders for the moment. And he was filthy and hungry. He even had currency, though it was in the form of Solarian dinars instead of the beads people used in this part of the world. "Very well."

The twins guided Curtis to a sprawling tent in better condition than its neighbors. Placards nailed to a post outside the entryway depicted cauldrons of frothing water and tables laden with slabs of meat and heaps of vegetables.

Narran spoke with the doorkeeper, who gave Curtis a long look before nodding. "We get their sort in now and again, seeking echoes of better times," he said in the trade tongue.

Curtis's collar couldn't come off but everything else did. Another attendant, this one a black-haired woman, took one look at those rags, scooped them up, and vanished.

The twins were shapely but scarred. Part of Varian's abdomen had a scaly look and crimson dots made a circle over Narran's breastbone.

Varian caught Curtis's look. "Ah, does my war wound disturb you?"

"It is unusual." Curtis had seen many wounds, but none quite like this.

"The injury required unusual measures to heal."

"It was most difficult." Narran looked Curtis up and down, a sly look on her face. "Were I still my younger self, I might have dragged you to my bed. I still might."

"And I might have joined you both," said Varian as he settled into the tub.

The bath was wonderful and long overdue. Male and female attendants in short cream-colored robes rubbed the trio down with sticks and sponges, then lathered their bodies in oil before subjecting them to massages that removed kinks that plagued Curtis for months. For a time, he almost forgot the collar. Almost.

Massage done, Curtis was presented with his newly laundered and mended attire – to his astonishment, they'd even stitched his boots back together.

Another attendant, male this time, guided them through the interlocking canvas chambers to one that held but a single table low table flanked by thick gold and maroon cushions with intricate spiral designs. Faint illumination came from a pair of smoldering braziers.

"We could stand some light in here." Narran produced a trio of tiny gold candles that she set at precise intervals on the table before igniting them with a mystic motion.

Curtis wondered how she did that with the magic killing null rune clamped to his wrist. Possibly the words were mere theatrics? Or perhaps some property of the candles themselves. He elected not to question them. The twins would lie anyway.

Varian beamed at the table. "There, that is much better – in more ways than one." He finished the statement with a knowing look at Curtis.

"I like to see what I eat." Curtis kept his voice even. There was a purpose here beyond the food. He took a seat on one of the cushions.

The twins sat across the table.

Varian leaned towards Curtis. "From the symbol upon your armor, I deem you a member of one of Solaria's high aristocratic houses – the DuFloret, perhaps?"

Curtis blinked. "You are well informed. Yes, I was Sir Curtis DuFloret. Now, I am reduced in circumstances."

Narran smiled sweetly. "We are all reduced in circumstances. My brother and I spent most of the last decade dwelling amongst the rustics of Ghand in Western Celthania. One makes the best of it." She leaned against her brother's shoulder. "Hence our presence on this expedition."

Servers entered bearing platters of spiced meat, vegetables, a carafe of amber wine, and cups of carved bluish crystal.

Varian surveyed the repast. "Ah, now this is repast worthy of the name."

The next few minutes passed in silence as the trio demolished the feast. Curtis had to admit the repast was far tastier than anything he'd consumed since well before becoming a slave-warrior.

The servers returned, deposited a plate of spiced buns, refilled the carafe, and departed with the demolished platters.

Varian leaned back, glass in one hand, scone in the other. "Ah, that was a meal." His gaze flicked to the golden candles now half their initial height. "We have time, I think."

"Time for what?" asked Curtis, though he could make a damn good guess.

"Time to talk and time to clear the air between us."

"Without being overheard by interfering busybodies," Narran's tone was deadly serious for a change.

"I'm not much of a conversationalist." Curtis took a careful sip of the spiced wine. "And despite my name, my status in Solaria was not that high – the younger son of a younger son, you know. In truth, I spent most of the past decade tending to an estate in Agba precisely because my opportunities in the empire were so limited."

"Candid." Varian gave a slow nod. "I appreciate your forthrightness. Your brash new empire intrigues us." He shook his head. "What your people accomplished during that long slaughter fest you term the Traag War was nothing short of astonishing. You ended the existence of a God"-

"Despite rejecting true sorcery and possessing the merest dregs of the Old One's lore," finished Narran.

"Demon worship is banned in the Empire," said Curtis. "Unlike Ur-Murk, a place of demon worship if ever there was one." His lips curved into a tight smile. *Maybe I can provoke them into speaking honestly.*

Varian stared open-mouthed at Curtis, then reared back, chuckling. "Oh, sister, this one is as observant as an ox."

"I agree." Narran's voice was curt and piercing.

Varian managed to restore his composure. "My dear Curtis, you entirely misunderstand Ur-Murks purpose. Ur-Murk was not founded to worship devils."

"It was founded to keep them amused and distracted," said Narran. "Those great entities could lay waste to this sphere if the whim struck. The Gatekeeper could wrench this world into the demon realm, where we'd all perish in short order – or wish we had."

"The Twisted Mother could blanket the world in a toxic forest filled with abominations that would decimate all else in a decade or two if she so chose," added Varian.

"Entire nations have spiraled into madness due to The Yellow King's machinations," continued Narran.

"And the Hungry Storm?" She gave Curtis a glare that pierced his soul. "That one, I believe, figures in your oldest legends. It spawned the unending winter that combined with Kato-Siva's predations forced your ancestors to flee northern Agba for Solaria."

"Those are bleak stories," agreed Curtis.

"They'd have been bleaker yet but for the machinations and distractions provided by the priests of Ur-Murk."

"Yet your people still consort with demons."

"My dear fellow," Varian made to stand, then thought better of it. "Ur-Murk, and Celthania by extension, directly abut a portal to the infernal realms. It was absurdly easy to summon demons. Peasants have accidentally summoned imps via the ritual slaughter of chickens. Singers reciting simple hymns have become possessed by etheric spirits. We True Sorcerers were tasked with disposing of such petty annoyances before they became dangerous."

"But not anymore." Narran kept her gaze focused on Curtis. "Not since your nation managed the impossible and disintegrated Kato-Siva. Since then, conjuring so much as an imp or sprite has been almost impossible."

"It was that...handicap...that put Celthania in her current predicament," said Varian. "Our unruly neighbors to the northeast, the hobgoblins of Iktar invaded in force. They do that with depressing frequency – hobgoblins make such poor neighbors."

"I know how neighborly hobgoblins are," said Curtis.

"I am certain you do." Varian made a dismissive wave. "As I said, Iktar attacked Celthania with predictable frequency. In the past, we'd respond by making pacts with Agba or call upon our...special allies."

"You mean demons."

"Yes, yes. This time, neither option was viable. Agba was a depopulated wasteland and our 'special allies' were unavailable."

"So, you called the gotemik to this world." Curtis had spent enough time with the crab monsters to deduce that much.

"No, no." Varian touched his chest. "I – the faction my sister and I belong to – did not summon the gotemik to this planet. Our faction strenuously argued against that course. Instead, they dispatched emissaries to sound out potential allies."

"Emissaries like yourself," said Curtis.

"Yes, us, though there were others," agreed Narran. "For a time, we hoped to recruit one or two of the...less barbaric...Nations of the Plains to our cause. The fresh blood, while brutish would have done Celthania good." She twirled the stem of her cup. "We were becoming a bit...staid."

"Alas, that prospect failed, so we ventured further afield," said Varian.

"Cendoza," said Narran.

"We dined with Lord Kevin DuMars during our visit," added Narran. "He is a powerful brute of a man." Her expression turned wistful.

"I believe Lord DuMars might have slain us out of hand were it not for our diplomatic credentials," continued Varian.

"The war might have had something to do with Kevin DuMars's attitude," said Curtis. "It did drag on for twenty-five years."

"Your nation's war was against our Agban cousins, not us." Varian's voice burned hot as he raised his hand. "We cared for them little more than you."

"Calm, brother, calm." Narran pressed her brother's hand against the table. "This talk of war distresses me." She pouted.

"Kevin DuMars stymied our efforts in Cendoza," said Varian. "So, we turned our attention to the true prize – Gawana."

Narran looked at Curtis. "Tell me, do you know what Gawana is?"

"Not really." Curtis shrugged. "From what I saw, Gawana is a great big collection of walls that shifts about as though it were alive."

"Gawana is so much more than that." Varian's tone was dead serious. "Gawana is the last of the old races great manufactories. The mechanisms in its bowels can produce marvels not seen on this world in thousands of years."

"Gawana went rogue and sealed the factory levels during the chaos that followed Kato-Siva's arrival." continued Narran. "But those machines are still there, buried beneath the walls. That is why the gotemik desire Gawana so badly."

"With Gawana, the gotemik could conquer this entire world in less than a decade, said Varian. "That cannot be allowed to happen."

"I agree." He stared at Varian. "But what does that have to do with this mission?"

Varian and Narran looked at each other, then at Curtis. "Perhaps nothing," said Varian.

"Perhaps everything," said Narran.

"There are...indicators...of something in the far south that could add a new element to the equation," said Varian.

"New element?"

"Or perhaps an old element," said Narran. "Something from the time of the Fall."

"Much went missing during the Fall," continued Varian. "Millions of people. Vast quantities of stores. And above all else, knowledge that now exists only in scattered fragments."

"You are talking about a secret cache or depository," said Curtis.

"Yes," said Varian. "The gotemik deduced its existence and likely location – but they are uncertain, and their resources are overstretched. Like Gawana, it is something they cannot be allowed to acquire. Hence our presence."

"I see," lied Curtis. A suicide mission – for that was what this was – didn't fit the twin's nature. But for him, dying while striking a meaningful blow against the crab monsters was something he could do. "And you needed me to cooperate, as much as I can. But what if they question me?"

Narran reached out and touched Curtis between the eyes. His vision turned green, then pink. Hot sparks danced through his skull.

"That was a trivial charm to protect your mind from such queries," she told him.

Curtis's blood chilled. *They do retain their magic. The Null runes must be fake. I should do something.*

Narran's fingertip touched Curtis's lips. "You will not speak of this little display. You cannot speak of it."

Curtis decided not to test Narran's statement.

He looked at the candles, now barely more than guttering nubs. "Why you two? Why did you agree to this mission?" For he was certain the pair were here by choice, not coercion.

Again, the twins looked at each other. Then Varian spoke. "Celthania, once the light of the world, is finished. Ynn's towers have fallen, and her people live in squalor. Yos's glory is but an echo of its former self, Ur-Murk was unpleasant in the past and more so now, and the rest of the realm is wildlands or ruins populated by rustics and scavengers. This mission, our sacrifice if you will, grants our family the prospect of new lives elsewhere."

"Where might that be?" Varian's answer, Curtis was certain, was calculated to appeal to the values of the Solarian aristocracy, not something he believed.

A tiny smile appeared on Narran's lips. "That would be telling."

The candles guttered out at once. Narran collected the remnants and put them away. The attendants returned and guided them to a large central chamber. Bells, drums, and flutes played, and dancers wearing little more than beads swept onto the floor, their oiled bodies gleaming in the torchlight. Curtis found their movements hypnotic. It made him relax. Slumber claimed him.

LABYRINTH WAR LV – Bao

'My feet carried me past Varro's villa where the fifth tier narrowed to a ledge the width of the street. Rounding a corner, I spied an intersection, where a narrow road made a switch-back climb to the Tier of Mystery. Very well, mysteries surrounded me already. Perhaps new mysteries would shed light on old ones.

I began my ascent.

The ramp ended at the edge of a round plateau a triple bowshot in diameter. To my right rose a long hall painted with scenes of wonder and magic. Across from it stood a strange cube of a building constructed out of stones white as milk and black as obsidian, arranged in patterns I couldn't quite place. Puzzling objects dotted the ground past these edifices: silver cones topped with rose spheres, a stone arch, and towers made of metal pipes.

I didn't see any people. So, with no other guide, I began picking a path towards the nearest of the cones.

The cones formed a perimeter around a flat metal disk a dozen yards across embedded in the ground. How had Vazari's denizens come by so much metal? Shaking my head, I approached the nearest cone. I heard a low thrumming sound, like a stringed musical instrument. I extended my hand towards its surface.

"I recommend not touching the plinth," said a familiar voice behind me.

"Why? Is there a danger?" I spoke without turning around.

"Some find the sensation unpleasant," said Nimuk Brote.

"I find myself surrounded by unpleasantness lately." Still facing away, I touched the cone's surface. A vibration ran through my

body. "The Tier of Mystery is well named, for nothing here makes sense." I faced Nimuk Brote. "Including your presence."

"Ah," Nimuk turned and faced the black and white building. Patterns in the structure's stonework teased my mind. "I come here on occasion to consult the Priests of Mystery."

"What answers do they give?"

"Mysterious ones. Sometimes I wonder why I bother, but a capable ruler dare leave no stone unturned."

- From The Journal of Titus Maximus.'

Bao tried not to feel nervous as she sat in the austere room deep within the Tranquil Palace. She knew – well, strongly suspected – what she was about to be told. *Most women go through this several times and are just fine afterward. My aunt endured this eight times – eight! – and was none the worse for the experience. Yes, some women die, but they are mostly from the common classes. I am not common. I am a member of the aristocracy and am attended by a Godborn.* Still, Bao felt jittery.

I need a distraction. Perhaps that infernal puzzle.

Bao pulled the puzzle from the bag beside her, a recently arrived gift from the House of Black and White in Vazari. That strange sect that retained working kwintath machinery – and the knowledge to employ it. The Lord Defender made extensive use of their services.

The puzzle was a flat board, painted with angular black-and-white shapes. One side was inset in the middle, with that area almost filled with interlocking slats. Solving the puzzle meant arranging these slats to make a picture. Naturally, the House of Black and White did not include instructions. Thus far, she'd tried to solve the wretched thing twice without success.

Bao moved a slat sideways - freeing a second to move towards her. A tiny glyph appeared in the vacated space. A chill settled over her as she studied the symbol. *This is important.* Depending on the context, it could have several meanings. 'Alteration.' 'Change.' 'Movement.' But which?

She slid another piece, then two more. A new symbol appeared – the numeral '2' Two alterations? Two changes? She eyed the image produced by the relocated slats. The top part now resembled the maze symbol used by the Lord Defender. *That can't be a coincidence.*

Three more moves completed the puzzle – and exposed a final hidden glyph – a crown. Bao stared at the image and then put the puzzle away.

The door opened. Cora, the part-elven Godborn entered, engaged in hushed conversation with a squat dwarf woman who resembled a keg topped with black hair and stuffed into a flower-print dress.

Cora, though, was simply radiant. Cora was always radiant. She had hair like spun gold, pierced with pointed ears that should have made her look animalistic but instead complimented the rest of her bronze face. A pert nose and red lips that never required additional color. She would have looked gorgeous in court attire but couldn't be bothered. Instead, she looked fantastic in a simple cream-colored robe adorned with the sun and hand badge common to the Godborn, cinched with a simple belt hung with tiny pouches. For jewelry, she wore a simple pendant about her neck and an emerald ring on her right index finger, the mark of a married woman in the northern empire, unlike the promise bracelets popular in the south.

Cora faced Bao. "I had to consult with Mashaya here," she motioned at the dwarf. "You are pregnant, three months along." Cora's eyes gleamed. "My spells tell me the child is male, healthy, and positioned correctly – that is what I needed to make certain of with Mashaya."

The stumpy woman approached Bao. "I am the best midwife in Cendoza City," she said in accented imperial, which bespoke to her education. Most locals contented themselves with a shaky grasp of the trade tongue. "I helped Pasha's mother when she was with child. Four times." She held up four stumpy fingers. "All fine. I also tended to all three of Pasha's women, Danay's concubines, and Kevin DuMars's wife when she was with child. All women and babies were fine, though Kevin's woman drank too much wine." She glared at Bao. "You drink only a little – one glass a day, no more." She raised a single digit.

"That...sounds reasonable," said Bao, slightly intimidated by the midwife.

"You also not take Blue Dust, Dream Milk, or Red Root unless I say so," continued Mashaya. "Those bad for you, bad for the baby. Danay's second concubine did not listen and made herself sick. She took a long time to heal."

"I – I don't indulge in those substances," said Bao, though she knew what they were – hallucinogens and pick-me-ups used by all classes across the empire. Her sister had been especially fond of Dream Milk, spending days in a stupor.

"You also eat right." Mashaya produced a parchment with a list. "Only these foods, no matter what your belly tells you."

"Thank you." Bao took the list and glanced at it. She spotted two items she detested – Father used to make her eat them as punishment – and four or five others she didn't recognize. Local dishes, perhaps?

"Good. I must attend to merchant's wife with twins." With that, Mashaya rotated in place and marched from the room.

Cora watched the midwife depart. "Mashaya is something else, isn't she?"

"She is," agreed Bao. "Back home a commoner who dared to speak to an aristocrat like that...she'd have been flogged."

"If the aristocrat in question was male," said Cora. "But Mashaya's skills are valuable and every woman in the palace knows it." She touched her belly. "I might have to call upon her services myself. Hopefully, it would go easier than the last time."

Bao digested Cora's words. "I often see your children at the palace school since accepting the librarian position there. They're adorable, though Erland is always running amok with the Envoy's son."

"Claudius is a little hellion and Erland is his second," said Cora. "Claudius had him charm the locks so they could sneak into the abandoned sections. They have a lait in there." Cora's offspring had inherited her magic.

"That dragon illusion of his certainly startled me," said Bao. "Hazel, though, is better behaved."

"Hazel is a charmer who will grow into a heartbreaker." Cora took a couple of paces towards the door, then stopped. "Would you be interested in coming over for dinner tomorrow night?"

"That would be wonderful, Lady Cora." Bao's social circle was limited these days.

"I expect to see you," Cora swept from the room.

Bao sighed, stood, and waddled into the hall, mentally composing a new missive to Octavos. He'd sent her two heartfelt and poetic apologies for his behavior without saying much about his current activities. She'd responded with five lengthy letters, expressing her hopes and dreams of their future together. Now, she had something new to communicate.

Bao exited the room and drifted through the Tranquil Palace's empty halls like a well-dressed phantom, occasionally pausing to inspect a mosaic or wall hanging. The artistry of these pieces was astonishing.

Not admiring them seemed an insult to their makers.

Boisterous voices brought her to that portion of the palace claimed by the Tail. Here she watched lewd women practice dance moves that bordered on obscene while crude men made catcalls from the sidelines. Bao's maid Fatima taught her the basic moves of such dances, but they proved both undignified and exhausting, so she'd stopped after just a few lessons. Bao touched her belly. She wouldn't be learning such dances now.

A face peeping from a doorway caught Bao's eye. Was that Hazel? Cora's daughter had no business being here.

Bao stepped into the courtyard.

Hazel spotted Bao, squealed, turned, and vanished in a flurry of colored dots.

That altercation drew attention to Bao. She fled into the Tranquil Palace's empty corridors – except they weren't so empty anymore.

Shouts and the sound of booted feet echoed down the passageways. Bao stepped into an alcove to avoid being trampled by a squad of running soldiers. Something seemed...off...about them. For one thing, dirt clung to their armor, something the tyrannical petty officers did not tolerate. But there was something off about the soldiers – their skins were too dark. Locals pressed into service, perhaps? It seemed the sort of thing Lord General DuPaul would do. But that was his concern, not hers.

Bao took another passageway and almost collided with a pair of running women in servant's smocks. They ran past her without stopping.

This was unusual. But still, none of Bao's business.

A final turn brought Bao to the corridor where her suite was located. There, she stopped short at the sight of armored men exiting the apartment. Like the others, their armor bore traces of dirt.

"She's not there, Centurion," reported one of the men.

"Damn." A figure in a plumed helmet made an arm motion. "Post a guard here in case she returns. The rest of you fan out."

I'm being arrested. I must flee. With that thought, Bao ducked back into the passageway she'd just exited. She turned, took three steps, and collided with an armored form.

"Who do we have here?" The speaker's imperial was atrocious, worse than that of the Kitrin recruits who comprised a quarter of the force.

"Nobody," squeaked Bao. "Just a servant." She immediately cursed herself. No servant would be this finely clad. "A servant to an important lady," she added as a qualifier, hoping the soldier would accept those words as an explanation for her attire.

"Huh." The man grunted. "Got somebody here!" He propelled Bao out into the other passageway.

The Centurion came over to investigate. He looked her over, then nodded once. "Lady Bao Vada Falun Des Ptath Maximus. We have been looking for you."

Bao broke free of her captor's grip and glared at the petty officer. "Why is Envoy Julius Ambrose having me arrested?"

A confused expression swiftly passed over the centurion's features. Then he smiled. "Ah, the armor. My orders do not come from Envoy Ambrose or General DuPaul. They come from Lord Defender Titus Maximus, who wished you removed from harm's way should there be any unpleasantness."

Bao stood open-mouthed for a moment. "The Lord Defender is here, in Cendoza?"

"Yes."

"Take me to him." Titus is staging a coup.

"Your request is permissible. The Lord Defender is in the audience hall with the other notables."

Bao found Titus conversing with a surprisingly calm Julius Ambrose.

"But how did you gain entrance?" asked the Envoy. "My understanding is that your office prohibits you from leaving Gawana."

"Your understanding is incorrect." Titus tapped a crown of green vines with little red and yellow flowers on his head. "I can leave Gawana's embrace if the situation demands it. But my soldiers entered via the tunnels."

"We found those points and blocked them," retorted General DuPaul, who'd apparently been apprehended in the act of donning his armor. Lady Cora stood beside him, looking subdued.

"Gawana's halls extend deeper than the noxious weeds planted by those infernal Monks of Zu," said Titus.

"Huh." The Envoy nodded. "My father told me you were a clever tactician."

"I had to be." Titus turned and caught sight of Bao. "There you are."

"You might have informed me of your plans," said Bao.

Titus shook his head. "No, I could not – at least not without creating complications."

The Lord Defender's statement meant he didn't know about the message from the House of Black and White. Yet, that strange group knew of Titus's plan – and they had some other plot underway. Change. 2. Empire. Gawana. Did their plans include changing Gawana somehow? And why involve her in their schemes?

"So," began Julius Ambrose, "Just what are your intentions here? Cendoza is an imperial ally, and the empire frowns on unauthorized changes in government."

"I am securing an alliance against the Gotemik," said the Lord Defender, "with myself in command. Your authorization would greatly simplify matters."

"Placing imperial troops under the authority of a foreign leader is complicated," said the Envoy.

"I realize that and have given thought to the matter. Here." Titus produced a scroll and presented it to the Envoy.

Julius swiftly perused the document. "Ingenious. It places me in a delicate position, but it could work." He looked at the Lord Protector. "You did your research." He produced a quill and scrawled his signature.

"Sir, I suggest we review this document before committing ourselves," said General DuPaul.

"No need. It is quite straightforward." Ambrose stared at Titus. "And entirely preliminary."

Titus took the quill and added his name to the document. "Yes, it is entirely preliminary." Then he removed a chain from around his neck, from which dangled an old-style family seal of office.

Bao inhaled. She knew that seal and what it was capable of. Across the table, Cora's eyes narrowed.

Titus jammed the Maximus Seal onto the paper, making a crimson image.

Ambrose gave a little jolt. "Yes, I believe your terms are acceptable." He smiled. "But many details need to be worked out."

The discussion continued for several hours before moving to the dining hall, where the fare served was far simpler than normal. Bao doubted anybody noticed.

Later that evening, Titus intercepted Bao enroute to her quarters. He got straight to the point. "I will be spending the bulk of my time in the field. I need you here more than ever to be my liaison."

"Could Octavos join me?"

"Octavos is engaged in a delicate project," said Titus. "Once that is completed, your reunion may be possible."

"I would prefer that our reunion be sooner rather than later." Bao touched her belly.

LABYRINTH WAR LVI – Chimp

'We departed the alcove too soon. My shoulder wound reopened, oozing pus and fluid. Gerent can barely keep his feet. But Casein seems nearly recovered. He wanted to press on when I decided to stop in this cul-de-sac for the night.'

- From 'The Journal of Titus Maximus.'

Chimp winced and clenched his chest as he stood up. That he could stand up at all was due to Spots's ministrations. The girl's medical skills made up for her lack of combat ability. Without her, both he and Dodger would have died a week ago.

Chimp glanced at Blaze, who was carrying that damn beam weapon on his back. They'd tested the thing once – it put a finger-sized hole clear through one of the walls. He'd ordered it left alone.

The screwy sitar was too dangerous to test.

The capture of those two toys counted as a success for this expedition. What didn't count as a success was their current situation – completely fucking lost and almost out of rations, which were down to hardtack and a few of the purple fruits. Even Snuffles hadn't caught anything in days, at least not that she'd fessed up to.

Then there was the city – a fantastical collection of towers and minarets set on shelves carved into a hill. They could see it sometimes, maybe twenty miles to the east. As best Chimp could figure that town was likely Vazari, which was supposed to be damn near dead center in this weird place, which meant they were traveling in the opposite direction they were supposed to. Chimp was positive that was no accident.

The city might be a good place to get healed and reprovisioned – but they couldn't reach it. No matter what corridor they took, it looped away from the city. Chimp figured that wasn't an accident. He was also sure they were being watched, even if Idleman and Snuffles hadn't spotted the observers.

Still, nothing for it. Chimp motioned to the others, who picked themselves up and started along the passageway, which went mostly south with the occasional dogleg to the east. They made tracks, one step at a time. A mile passed that way. Then two. At three miles, Chimp felt the stitch in his side. Dodger wasn't doing too well, and Spots looked dead on her feet – long hikes weren't her thing, especially carrying a pack. Simon plodded along like a damn machine – how did the kid not keel over with all that hot steel strapped to his body?

Chimp rounded a corner and found himself at the foot of a long steep slope. "Damn." Just looking at it made him ache all over.

Spots tottered over to Chimp and wiped her brow. "Can we rest before climbing that?"

Chimp wanted to do just that – but the more they did now, the less they'd have to do later. He eyed the hill and pointed at a bump out maybe a quarter of the way up. "We'll take a breather in that little alcove."

"Kay." Spots resumed the trek without enthusiasm, as did everyone else.

Fifty paces up, a hint of movement atop the wall caught Chimp's attention. Five steps past that, the shadows twitched alongside the bump out. He looked over at Snuffles.

The shifter sniffed the air while cranking her head in three directions. Her ears were erect.

Enough. Chimp made a cutting motion. "Halt." Half his crew didn't hear him and kept plodding along until he repeated the word a second time. Most of them still didn't have a clue.

Chimp took a few steps towards the bump out and halted. "Show yourselves." He spoke the words in the trade tongue, figuring that would be the lingo the watchers would most likely understand.

A shadow detached itself from the bump out and became a man in legion-style armor. A big man. "Stand down," he said in imperial. "This doesn't need to get messy."

"What do you want?" called Chimp, switching to imperial. Was this a genuinely friendly get-together or was his crew about to become prisoners?

"I'm hoping we can keep it all peaceable," said the big man, "but if this goes sideways, you lose." He motioned.

A crossbow bolt came off the wall, hit the stones beside Chimp, and skittered off.

Chimp tensed. He felt his entire crew tense. But he couldn't have any of them doing anything stupid. And he needed to know more about who he was dealing with. "Got any sureties?"

"You're smart." The big fellow nodded. "I like that. The situation has changed since you went over the wall."

"How so?"

The big man smiled. "We work for the same boss now."

"An alliance?" Had the Envoy managed to strike a deal? It sounded unlikely. "I'm afraid I need more than your word on that."

"Can't blame you for being careful." The big man scrunched his face. "The black weeds need water."

Chimp tensed. Those words were the first part of the passcode to verify allies. "But the black weeds only grow at night."

"Wheels turn as the sun burns." The correct response.

"But we will eat well tonight," finished Chimp. Just one last thing...

The big man made a broad sweeping motion with both hands – the final part of the code.

Chimp turned to his crew, who were both confused and more tightly wound than the strings on Idleman's sitar. "Stand down. These are allies."

Figures popped out of the shadows, including one from the wall beside Chimp.

The big man strode forward, giving Chimp a better look at him. He seemed familiar. Chimp mentally ran through a list of possibilities. "Cam?"

The big man blinked. His face contorted. "I used that name back east," he said, "But around here I use my real name. Casein." He looked Chimps group over. "That was a pretty impressive accomplishment back the windings – tangling with the crabs and getting away with your hides intact." He took in the funky sitar and the beam weapon, "What do we have here?"

"Spoils of battle." Chimp motioned at the sitar. "Crabs used that thing to make holes through the walls."

"Made them shake real bad," said Simon.

Casein nodded. "That is interesting. I know people that will want to look that over." He eyed the beam weapon. "Intact, no less. We've only captured a few of those in one piece."

"We paid for them in blood," said Chimp.

"Such is a soldier's life. You serve and then you die." Cam – Casein – motioned at the bump out. "Come on. We got grub waiting for you up ahead."

There was indeed grub in the bump-out, a mix of maze food served in big communal bowls. The fare was tasty despite the lack of meat. Chimp chowed down with the rest.

Meal completed; the groups checked each other out. The maze dwellers were heavy on light-colored leather armor and light on actual metal, which made sense given the heat and the maze's rumored scarcity of solar forges. Much of what metal armor they did have looked to be bronze, which went out of fashion about four hundred years ago back home. About every third maze trooper was a dwarf – no surprise there, as there was supposed to be a big city of short folk within the walls.

Casein, meanwhile, gave a professional inspection of Chimp's crew.

Simon, sweating under enough steel to drop a mule, attracted his attention first. "Take off that damn breastplate before the heat kills you." Casein made it an order, and his command presence was such that Simon did just that. Next, the big man borrowed the kid's broadsword. That heavy hunk of steel prompted wide-eyed looks from the rest of the maze squad.

"People in Solaria fight with these things?" asked a skinny soldier who picked up the weapon.

"Knights do," said Casein. "Hardly anybody else does."

"All that steel," said one of the dwarves.

"My Grandad gave it to me." Simon puffed his chest out a little.

"What's his name?" asked Casein as he returned the weapon.

"He's Sir Richard Fury."

"Sir Richard Fury." Casein stroked his chin. "I knew a Sir Fury back in the day. He was quite the fighter...and drinker."

"Dad came into the maze with us." Spots's expression fell. "We think he was killed in the fight."

"No, Dad's still alive," said Simon with the conviction of a simpleton. "He'll be waiting for us when we get back."

"Perhaps. The Richard Fury I remember was one hell of a fighter." Casein glanced at the freckled healer, then back to Simon. "Huh. You two brother and sister? Maybe I'm thinking of the wrong man, but there is a resemblance."

"Yes," said Simon.

"Half-brother." Spots motioned at Idleman, who was busy showing off his sitar to the female troopers. "Iman is another half-brother."

"Huh." Casein shook his head. "Richard Fury was a randy one."

Dad didn't want to come here," said Simon.

"Given what happened last time, I can understand that."

Snuffles, meanwhile, was running around almost bent double, busy sniffing the maze troopers, who seemed to regard her as a sort of weird pet. Then she came over and started sniffing Casein, who gave her a bemused look.

"And who are you?" Casein asked the shifter girl.

"Sammy, mister. But most people call me Snuffles."

"I see why." Casein turned to Chimp. "I didn't deal with shifters in the war. General Ambrose didn't want any in the Seventh Marfaki. I heard the Tenth had a full company of shifter scouts, though."

"My family is on Navy Island," said Snuffles. "Tribune came and took me and my brother. He's back in the empire."

"Interesting."

Snuffles's ears went erect. She scuttled over to the wall, giving it a fixed stare.

About two seconds later, the stones shimmered, then softened, and a black-haired aristocrat with a huge nose and silvery armor walked right out of the rock. The new arrival took in the scene at a glance. "This is them? The scouts that raided the gotemik base?"

"Yeah, it's them, boss. And they didn't just raid the gotemik but made off with something interesting." Casein motioned at the sitar from hell.

LABYRINTH WAR LVII – Octavos

'It wasn't until a small form wrapped around my waist shrieking "Daddy! Daddy!" that I realized I'd returned to my old apartment.

"What brings you here?" asked a shrill voice.

I lifted my eyes from Octavos to my wife. Ann, not robust to begin with, now appeared skeletal, lost within a pastel dress beneath an unkempt tangle of brown hair. "This is my apartment." Yet it wasn't the cheery abode I remembered. My once cozy apartment now seemed musty and threadbare. The mantle was dusty and splotches marred the carpet.

"Titus, I have been worried sick about you." Ann poured herself a glass of wine. "They tell me you went on a rampage in Saba, murdering half the city. My friends no longer associate with me. My servants are gone, save one, and she's useless." That explained the apartment's state.

"Daddy, will you be staying with us?" asked Octavos, small arms still wrapped around my waist.

"Yes," I said. I intended to stay with my family until my execution.

Ann glared at me and took another gulp of wine, draining the glass by another third. At this rate, she'd have the bottle finished within a day.

"Yes!" Octavos danced around me. "Do you want to hear me play the flute? I've been practicing really hard."

"That would be nice," I told him though my gaze was still upon Ann.

Octavos produced a black flute almost as long as his arm. He climbed atop a low table against the far wall and bowed. "I will now perform the 'Winds of Summer' by the great minstrel Marabous." He put the flute to his lips.

I expected childish whistles. Instead, Octavos coaxed a smooth, pleasant melody out of the instrument.

"He possesses true talent."

- From 'The Journal of Titus Maximus.'

Octavos read through Bao's letter for the fourth time. *I am going to be a father.* The thought made his stomach want to do flip-flops. He carefully folded the sheet and put it in his pocket. Baby names. *She wants me to come up with a name for our son.* Octavos pursed his lips, then shook his head. Traditionally, Maximus males were given one of just six names, the praenomen of former Maximus Emperors. The problem was that the deeds attached to most of those names were repulsive. Invasions. Enslavement of entire nations. Massacres. Assassinations. The Varro's tended towards gluttony. The Manius's were often murderous paranoids. None of the Titus's reigned more than a decade before meeting a violent demise. The rest were impassive, unfeeling autocrats. Of them all, only Octavos Maximus could be considered decent, presiding over sixty years of prosperity. But only one Octavos had sat on the throne – well, two if you counted the one who spent a dozen years as Emperor Regent for the youthful Julius Plotinus. But...naming his son after himself seemed...well, presumptuous.

"What's got your goat?" Casein stood in the entryway.

"This." Octavos carefully extracted the letter. "It's official. Bao is pregnant."

A broad smile split the old warrior's face. "Good for you. But why so dour?"

"She's asking about baby names. I – I don't know what to tell her. My family," Octavos shook his head.

"Yeah, those old Maximus's were real assholes. But those aren't the only choices. Thomas doesn't share a name with those old bastards."

A wan smile appeared on Octavos's lips. "Thomas's real name is Titus. He hates it, because of the curse. No Titus reigned more than ten years before meeting a violent end."

"Yeah, I heard about that. Your Dad..." Casein's expression changed. "I'll tell you what. Pick a new name, one you and the missus both like. New place, new tradition."

"Huh." Possibilities opened before Octavos.

"In the meantime, though, we need to get moving. 3-99 wants you to look over that contraption captured by those imperial scouts."

"Sure." Octavos joined Casein as they set off along the hall, his mind still wrestling with the name problem. A name I like. The name of somebody I can respect. A thought occurred to him. "I have it."

Casein glanced at him. "Have what?"

"A name." Octavos paused. "Leander."

Caseins face contorted. Then he smiled. "Good one kid. Wait, you're serious?

"I am. Do you object?"

"Huh." Casein mulled it over. "Nah, not really. Leander is a right fine name. It didn't suit me, but it might be right for your kid."

"You saw the gotemik use this thing?" Octavos walked around the small table that held the sitar-like device.

"Yeah," said the one called Idleman. "Played it like a sitar, only it used its tentacles. Made the whole damn wall shake so hard I fell right off."

"Hmm." Octavos turned to 3-99, who was busily consulting its instruments. "Have you learned anything about this?"

"I have reached preliminary conclusions, yes." 3-99 didn't look up from the device it consulted. "Please note that there is a high possibility of significant error in my assessments."

"I'll keep that in mind."

"As its appearance implies, this device is an electronically enhanced variant of the vibration generators designated 'lyres' and 'sitars.' The vibrations produced by this mechanism are substantially more potent than the manual versions."

Octavos digested the alien's statement for a moment. "So, it's like a lyre or sitar, only...louder? More intense?"

"I suspect both terms are applicable," said the alien. "However, there is more to this mechanism than potent vibrations. It contains a partial copy of the control matrix for Gawana's Child. Integrated with the vibrations, this control matrix enabled them to circumvent Gawana's protections to an alarming degree."

"Good thing they don't have it anymore," said Octavos.

"That assumption is almost certainly erroneous, Master Octavos." 3-99 tapped the casing of the device. "Even in their reduced circumstances, the gotemik can make additional copies of that control matrix."

"So, we could be facing more of these things." Octavos made another orbit of the table. "Any idea how long it would take them to make another...machine...like this?"

"Unknown."

"Then you'd best figure out how to use this one," said the long-armed Centurion called 'Chimp.' Octavos considered the moniker offensive and degrading. "Fight fire with fire."

"I suppose so." Octavos touched the corner of his mouth as he peered at the stings on the device. They weren't parallel with each other. Some were shorter than the others. He couldn't even identify the materials in the strings.

Idleman bowed. "I would be pleased to assist you."

"Given what this thing can do, playing it anywhere near the Heart Chamber is probably not a wise idea," said Octavos, remembering what had happened during his last performance. "It could activate Gawana's internal defenses."

"Gawana reacting in a hostile manner once this device is activated is a distinct possibility," said 3-99. "Fortunately, I know of a location in the Heart where that will not be an issue. Please follow me." The alien took the Gotemik device and glided from the room.

Their course took them past a training room where Blaze and Simon spared with Captain Garnet and other warriors, while the girls named 'Spots' and 'Snuffles' looked on, as the older warrior Dodger leaned against the wall, still recovering from the injury he'd taken. More absurd and insulting names. It was even worse that they accepted the designations so readily.

Lucy (not 'Spots, damnit!) approached Octavos. "I'd like to thank you again for finding our Dad."

"You're welcome." Octavos had used strands of hair in a spell that verified Sir Richard Fury still lived, just past Gawana's northeastern edge.

Snuffles – no Sammy - padded toward Octavos and 3-99 in a hunched-over walk. The shifter girl made a slow circle of the group, sniffed Octavos, and then directed her attention (and snout) to 3-99, who warranted a comprehensive olfactory inspection. Then she halted before the alien. "You smell weird."

"I am not human, Miss Sammy." 3-99 seemed more intrigued than perturbed by the shifter's attentions.

"You are weird but nice because you use my name and call me 'Sammy' instead of 'Snuffles.' I like that." Sammy's malformed face cracked in a smile.

"I have a task to perform, Miss Sammy." 3-99 resumed movement.

"I'll go with you. I was getting bored watching the boys hit each other." The shifter fell into step beside the alien.

Lucy glanced at Simon. "I'll stay here."

Octavos shook his head.

3-99 guided the band along a hall that received little traffic even now in this era when space was at a premium within the Heart. The alien's speed slowed as its head swiveled to inspect the wall. Finally, it halted. "I believe this is the access point. However, so much time has transpired since it was sealed that my memory may be in error."

"Access point to what?" asked Chimp.

3-99 ignored the Centurion, instead running its black, stick-like fingers over the surface.

Sammy, naturally, went and sniffed the wall. "I smell..." Her voice trailed off. She gave the alien a quizzical look, then sat on her haunches beside Chimp.

Almost a full minute went by. Then the wall softened and pulled apart, exposing another corridor partly buckled and riven by cracks. 3-99 activated another of its devices. "Yes, the matrix is present here, but mostly isolated."

"What is this place?" asked Octavos. The ceiling of this corridor was lower than the ones he was used to elsewhere in the Heart.

"This is one of the access points to the sector once occupied by my people." 3-99 glided along the corridor, bypassing a rubble pile. Then it stopped. "Yes. This location should suffice."

Octavos approached the alien and took the gotemik sitar. It felt clunky and heavy. Its strings were in the wrong place, forcing him to shift position. "How do I aim this thing?"

"The vibrational energy is emitted from this point." 3-99 tapped a plate-sized circular grill that dominated a bulbous protrusion. "Keep it directed at the surface you wish to affect."

"And the rest? Do I need to use magic?"

"I suggest you access the control matrix using your Operant abilities."

Octavos took that as a 'yes.' He stared at the contraption strapped to his chest. Did the blink trick. He saw lines of power feeding into tight knots. He extended his psychic senses.

Contact. A rush of information, most of it mathematical, poured into his head, making it pound. He felt his legs start to buckle.

"You okay, kid?" Chimp sounded like he was a mile away.

"Uh..." Octavos fought to make sense of the deluge. He discerned categories – memory, operational, and focus.

"Kid, you're not looking good." This time pressure on Octavos's shoulder accompanied the voice.

"Master Octavos is deducing the principles of the device's operational system," said 3-99.

There. "I – I think I see how some of this stuff ties together. I'm going to give it a try."

"I recommend increased separation." Receding footsteps accompanied 3-99's words.

Octavos took a breath and moved his fingers. And horrible, off-kilter music filled the air, accompanied by screams and shouts – some of them his own. *Keep at it.* He strummed the strings a second time. Now, grinding sounds came from the wall before him. Again. Something large hit the floor. Was the ceiling caving in? He looked up right as strong hands jerked him backward.

Octavos blinked. He found himself sitting on the floor, looking at a tunnel with circular sides that hadn't been there before, a good eight or ten yards deep by about two across. It ended in a weirdly angled space with piles of what looked like white bowls partly covered by silvery cloth. "Did – did I do that?"

"Yeah, you did kid." Chimp's voice came from behind and below Octavos. "Mind if you get up? This floor is hard."

Octavos shifted position and looked at 3-99, who stood before the tunnel, unmoving. "What do you think?"

"You activated the mechanism and made it perform beyond my expectations." The alien didn't turn away from the sight. "We were correct to conduct this test here. Gawana is most agitated."

"What are those things?" Idleman made to slither past 3-99, only to be halted by a stick-thin limb.

Sammy slid in behind the pair and took three or four deep sniffs. "They are death." She faced the alien. "They are you."

"Very astute, Miss Sammy. You gaze upon the corpses of my people."

"What happened?" asked Octavos.

"I would like to know that as well." Titus stood behind Octavos, dispassionately taking in the scene. "Your experiment agitated the whole Heart."

"I will explain." 3-99 glided towards the others. "This is difficult for me."

"I need answers." Titus's voice radiated authority and demanded obedience.

3-99 stood stock still for a long moment. "The arrival of the Leech designated 'Kato-Siva' destroyed my people's primary population center. Our projections showed a high probability that Kato-Siva would destroy our remaining population centers within a few planetary orbits. We...formulated various strategies to counter this eventuality – evacuation of the planet, attempting to impose confinement measures on Kato-Siva, long-term concealment, and others." The alien looked at Octavos with its bulbous eyes. "That was a chaotic period. Most of those projects were at best partly successful. Finally, though, with...dubious external intervention...we confined Kato-Siva. Our remaining population centers resumed partial operations. Then..." 3-99 stopped speaking for a long moment. "Then a celestial aberration appeared – an...object of planetary size on a cometary trajectory traveled through this solar system. The energies emitted by this object initiated biological mutations and dysfunctional behavior."

This sounds familiar. Octavos remembered a purple and orange orb that appeared in the sky during his childhood, prompting fits of madness across the empire. "The Herald of Guzur."

3-99 nodded. "That is the current designation, yes. Our cities were protected from the object's emanations. Other races were not so fortunate. The...Herald of Guzur...vanished, then returned one hundred and forty-six years later, bringing additional effects of the same nature before vanishing again. One hundred fifty-two years later it manifested again. By then, we'd developed countermeasures and distributed them to allied civilizations. Your earliest independent civilizations. These measures greatly blunted the effects of the energies projected by the object. We thought its menace was reduced. In that, we were in error. On its ninth passage, the entities controlling the object initiated kinetic strikes against our remaining cities."

"Kinetic strikes?" asked Chimp.

Octavos remembered the natural philosophy lectures he'd attended at the university in Solace. "Meteors, I think. They can hit the ground with sufficient force to level a castle."

"Correct, Master Octavos," said 3-99. "The kinetic strikes initiated by the object's controllers struck five of our remaining population centers, including Gawana. Prior to that impact, my people here numbered seven thousand nine hundred and fifteen. Afterward...Afterward, our population was reduced to one thousand and six." The kwintath motioned at the translucent bowls in the tunnel. "That strike collapsed our primary population area. Those are a fraction of the kwintath who perished."

Silence followed the alien's words.

LABYRINTH WAR LVIII – Carina

'Yes, we know a great body of water spans much of the southern hemisphere. It is often referred to by Nomads and Chou mariners. These vague accounts are of no use in determining this ocean's coasts. Hence, I do not mark it on my maps.'

- Statement of Vertis the Geographer

"This deal stinks." Goji faced Carina. "You sure we can trust those dickheads in Ado-Cent?"

"No, I'm not," said Carina. Goji was right – the deal did stink. Sail to this edge of the map place, snatch a trinket of religious importance from a gotemik outpost, replace it with a fake, and return to riches and assured status at Ado-Cent. Carina would get to be a legit sorceress, while Luther and Goji could get started on becoming merchant lords. It didn't add up, not one little bit. "But it was the only way to get you two out of prison."

"You should have negotiated harder." Goji threw a stone over the boat's side. It was a complaint he'd repeated daily since leaving Ado-Cent. "This jaunt isn't on our itinerary."

"I tried. The Ervin are slick." *Way slicker than me.*

"Enough," called Luther from the tiller. "You made the best deal you could."

The boat reached rapids marked by churning foam. Carina winced as the center hull scraped bottom. "That doesn't sound good."

"Beats fighting our way upstream," said Goji as Japi floated down the Gayan River.

"We will on the way back," said Carina. Foaming water ahead of the craft caught her eye. She jabbed out with a pole, nudging their boat past the obstacle. A grating sound came from beneath the portside outrigger. "Damn river is too shallow."

Ahead, a huge flat-topped hill rose on the right bank, next to a wide gravel ramp that dropped into the water. A second ramp climbed from the river's left bank.

"That must be Garve," said Goji. It was one of the few spots marked on the map they'd been given. Supposedly, it meant 'Camp of the Tough Guys,' and was once a big stopover point for the Hundred Nations.

Luther beached Japi's prow at the base of the incline. Then they hopped out and took a look. The top of the ramp took them between a pair of weathered statues of brutal-looking warriors with a rubble ring away to either side, making it into a crude fort. As best as Carina could tell, that wall fenced off a solid square mile of real estate, marked with hundreds of circular firepits and detritus. Luther posed next to a busted wagon wheel twice his height. Goji pulled a sword with a broken blade out from beneath a pile of junk.

Carina, meanwhile, climbed atop the wall and took in the view – mile after endless mile of rolling hills and weeds, with hardly a tree in sight – quite the change from the jungles along the Ula River. A tangle of rutted tracks vanished into the western distance – the rude road the nomads used in their migrations.

Carina stared at that road for a long moment. "This is one of the places they stayed – the nomads that attacked Ptath."

Luther joined Carina atop the wall. "That is one hell of a long trip."

Carina tossed a stone over the plateau's edge. "Didn't do them any good. The gotemik killed them all."

They stood in silence for a while longer. Then Luther motioned at their boat. "We have plenty of daylight. Let's get out of here."

Past Garve, the Gayan River linked up with a couple of other streams and flowed into the flatlands with barely a bump in site, let alone anything that could be called a hill. Likewise, trees went from 'scarce' to 'nonexistent.' Just mile after mile of windswept grass and scrub. That breeze never stopped blowing, and the further south they went, the more of a bite it carried – enough to where Carina dug the wool cloak out of her kit. The river became wider and deeper. The boat's hull no longer scraped bottom.

What they didn't see was people – or even signs there had been people here – just one camp that was a lot rougher than Garve, and a solitary stone idol of an armored hobgoblin thrice Luther's height, rising from the muck on the east bank. Neither was marked on their map.

Past the statue, the Gayan grew wider. The banks became a maze of swampy channels. Slimy reeds and colorful flowers replaced the weeds. Croaking frogs serenaded them to sleep at night. Then the Gayan spilled into a narrow bay with low hills to either side.

"Rasp Bay," said Luther. "Where the merchants of Ado-Cent do deals with Chou mariners. Hopefully, they'll deal with us." They weren't exactly overstocked on provisions.

Japi sailed along the shore, aiming for a dock sticking out from a clutch of low buildings.

"It looks like they're out of business," said Goji as they sailed past the burned hulks of a pair of square-nosed chou junks. The buildings were in sad shape. Several had been torched. One was missing its roof.

"Gotemik, maybe?"

"Doubtful," said Luther. "Place ain't big enough to interest them. Let's take a look. Maybe we can find some grub."

The first warehouse they checked out was intact but empty. The roof on the second had collapsed, but Goji spotted a split sack of grain peeping out from the rubble. He tossed it over his shoulder.

Luther eyed a building in better shape than the others. It didn't seem to be a barracks or a warehouse. "Bosses office. There might be something good inside."

They found a broken desk and a map tacked to a paneled wall, one much more detailed than their old chart.

"Jackpot." Luther unpinned the map while Carina poked through the papers. She scooped up a couple of books and put them in her pack.

Goji merged from a side chamber carrying a sack. "You were right," he told Luther. "The bosses did have a private stash." He tapped the sack. I found three bottles of wine, some fancy cheese, and a side of spiced meat."

"Good." Luther rolled up the map. "Okay, one more warehouse, and then we're out of here. This place gives me the creeps."

They stepped onto the street as a pack of shouting hobgoblins in heavy furs poured out of a warehouse.

"Who the hell are they?" asked Goji.

"Don't know and don't intend to find out."

They beat feet for the Japi, shoving off right as the hobgoblins reached the dock.

The hobgoblins ran to the end of the pier, still jumping and shouting. One fell in the water. Others shot arrows at the Japi, which fell well short of the craft.

"Not exactly a neighborly bunch, are they," said Carina.

"Hobgoblins rarely are," said Goji. "They were always making trouble back home."

"They are persistent, though." Luther pointed at a group of eight or ten hobs racing for a craft that made Japi seem downright sophisticated in comparison. It resembled nothing so much as a raft with raised sides like they'd tried to copy a Chou junk but couldn't figure out how to do it.

The hobs pushed their raft-boat into the water and started paddling. Three or four raised a simple square sail.

Luther eyed the hob craft and gauged their respective speeds. "They won't catch us. It won't even be close."

An hour later, the hobgoblin boat fell away behind them and Japi cleared the headlands into the Unknown Southern Ocean, the name imperial map makers slapped on their charts for this body of water, which supposedly covered a big slice of the bottom of the world. Those maps were mostly blank spaces and dotted lines because few imperials made it here.

They beached Japi on an islet that night and camped in a grassy hollow.

Luther broke out the new map and laid it alongside the one provided by the Ervins. The new map showed a long stretch of coastline reaching west and south from Rasp Bay.

The new map's name for the Southern Ocean translated as 'Sea of Dragons.' Carina hoped the designation wasn't literal.

"I hope the name is a lie," said Goji. The swamp dragons back home are bad enough."

Carin tapped her finger on a hilly region west of Rasp Bay. "Cakkat." She squinted at a line of symbols beneath the name. "This is a warning about hobgoblins. That's probably where our new friends came from."

"Figures," said Goji.

Luther pointed at a southward jutting peninsula past Cakkat. "Chubbuck. The refugees at Ulam-Thek talked about it sometimes. It's not a good place."

A settlement at the map's western edge caught Carina's eye. "Tomb City. I thought it was a myth."

"Oh, it's real enough." Goji's brow contorted in thought. "The crabs leave it alone."

Carina scanned the ocean. "Island of Birds?"

"Never heard of it," said Luther.

Carina spotted another island at the bottom of the map. "'Navastu.' There's a whole list of warnings next to it – demons, storms, and curses."

"It sounds like a place to avoid." Luther motioned at a string of dots south of Rasp Bay. "What about these places? They are not on the other map."

"Let me see." Carina squinted at the symbols. "This first one is 'The Watch of Ugo.' It sounds like a fortress. But whose?"

"Some barbarian Satrap or another." Luther motioned at dotted lines running east and south of Ugo. "Roads."

The next dot was marked 'Hirt-Ta-Shu.' They guessed it might be a Chou place. Past it, a long finger of land jutted towards Navastu island. That peninsula was also the southernmost feature on the old map. But the new map showed a string of settlements extending further south to a city. "'Tavon,'" read Carina. "The text says something about the 'lordless city of feasts. I can't be reading that right."

"It sounds weird," said Luther. "But it's not where we are going."

The next night they stayed in a stand of conifers beside the mouth of a clear, cold river. Carina poked through the papers she'd snatched from Rasp Bay. Tavon was mentioned often. "Tavon had lords in the old days," she told the others. "An elf dynasty followed by a rachasa conqueror. But they were deposed. Now, the city is ruled by a council that stays in power by providing a daily feast for each household. That sounds like the Dole back home." The empire's major cities doled food to the lower classes to stave off riots.

"Huh," was Luther's comment.

A tower rising from a headland caught their attention the fourth day.

"That must be the Watch of Ugo," said Carina.

"It looks abandoned," said Goji.

"We might as well check it out." Luther steered Japi for a crumbling stone dock.

They climbed a steep slope to a circular wall made of rubble and overgrown with moss and weeds. More rubble marked the locations of dozens of structures. The almost conical tower rose from their midst, its stones covered with moss and lichen. Great gaps marred its surface.

Luther kicked a stone. "This place was destroyed long ago."

Goji pointed to circles of charred earth on the tower's far side. "But somebody camped here more recently."

"Nomads," said Luther. "Nomads fleeing the Gotemik."

Overgrown roads stretched away south and east.

Goji pointed at ruts and trampled grass on the south track. "This is the way they went."

"Likely, they were making for Tavon," said Luther.

"I wonder what kind of welcome they received?" asked Carina.

"Not a pleasant one, I wager," said Goji.

"It doesn't matter," said Luther. "Come on. There is nothing here."

They resumed their journey. The next day they passed a river spanned by the tumbled remnants of a stone bridge that wasn't on either map.

"Not nomad work," said Goji as they sailed past.

"Maybe Tavon built it," said Carina.

That night Carina took a stab at reading a raucous tale from Tavon about the Cat King Jurma who sought to cement his reign by taking wives from the city's notables – not just the rachasa, but humans, dwarves, and elves. Astonishingly, most of these wives bore him offspring.

Luther and Goji laughed themselves silly at the description of the nuptials.

Luther slapped his leg. "Damn, but that Cat must have had one hell of a dick."

"That must have been one weird family," said Goji.

The tale ended with Jurma's children rejecting their father. Frustrated, Jurma appointed a council and set out alone into the plains.

They came upon a rude encampment the next evening with shelters made of brush. Three-toed tracks covered the dirt. "Cats," said Luther. "Maybe Jurma's descendants." They spent that night anchored offshore. Two days later, they poked through the ruins of a village made of circular stone houses with turf roofs. A trampled road ran past the site.

"Abandoned, not attacked." Said Luther as he tossed a rotted timber aside.

Carina consulted the map. "This must be Hirt-Ta-Shu."

"It was Hirt-Ta-Shu," said Luther. "Now it's just a ruin."

They resumed their journey.

"That must be the headland." Luther looked from the dark streak of land ahead that jutted westward into the ocean. "I don't see a base, though."

The headland drew closer. Luther scanned the low hills with his spyglass. "I got something," he said at last. "But it's not a base. It's a Dead Bird."

"Huh. Wonder if it crashed," mussed Goji.

"It looks intact," said Luther. "But I don't see anything else – no, wait, there's a ramp going down the hill in front of it."

"Maybe the base is underground."

"We got other problems." Carina pointed aft, where a pair of simple square sails were just barely visible. "Looks like our friends from Rasp Bay decided to follow us."

"Shit." Luther turned to Carina. "Can you make it look like we're pulled up on that beach?"

Carina took in the scene. "Yeah, especially if we can pull in right quick."

"Get started." Luther steered for the strand of gravel and mud.

They didn't land Japi. Instead, they tossed the anchor over the side and waded ashore with their spare sail and a few boards. Combined with a pair of hastily positioned driftwood logs, those items made a crude facsimile of Japi that might fool a child fifty yards off. Then Carina wove her wizardry and it morphed into a copy of the Japi. "It should last until tonight," said Carina as they clambered back aboard Japi half an hour later. "Maybe tomorrow morning."

"Good," said Luther. "Let's get around this headland."

The cape was too long to circumnavigate, but they did find a tight little harbor two or three miles down the coast.

There, they crouched atop the cape and watched as the hobs sailed straight at the fake Japi – and then threw a temper tantrum when the illusion fell apart. That prompted several hobs to scale the hill.

"Shit. They spotted the Dead Bird," said Luther.

Sure enough, the hobs went after the contraption, approaching it from two sides.

That stunt prompted a hostile reaction – two beams of blue light lanced out from the Dead Bird and blew steaming holes in most of the first bunch.

The defenders, though, didn't spot the second group. Things got bloody fast.

Luther decided to hunker down and wait until morning. Night fighting was a fool's game.

One hob boat pushed off at first light, looking distinctly undercrewed, though they'd managed to snag one of the beam weapons.

Goji fetched the fake trinket.

Then Carina worked another illusion that made the trio invisible. Well, more like hard to spot, as the spell prompted spying eyes to glide over people.

Then they slowly and carefully approached the Dead Bird. Bodies and parts of bodies littered the landscape. Carrion birds and bugs dropped out of the sky to feast on the corpses. Fortunately, the unended breeze blew away the worst of the stink.

Carina counted nine dead hobgoblins and three dead swarthy humans with huge iron collars wrapped around their necks. One held a busted pipe attached to a hose that fed into a silvery backpack.

A moan drew their attention to the Dead Bird's far side where another collared human, this one with pasty skin, clenched the stump of his arm. He stumbled to his feet, lurched three steps sideways, took two steps forward – and collided with Goji.

Goji planted his dagger in the guy's already mauled gut about half a second after he called out an alarm.

Luther spoke. "I think that's all of them."

"Good," said Goji. "Let's find that idol and get it swapped out, then get the hell out of here."

"Sounds good to me," said Carina.

The problem was, there was no other idol – the Dead Bird's interior was a hollow tube, barely big enough to stand erect in, and devoid of anything save some levers at the front, low seats built into the frame, and crates of fairly basic supplies. Expanding the search revealed nothing save a big black flexible bag on the hill that sloshed when pressed and stank to high heaven. The defenders possessed nothing save battered armor, dinged weapons, and those heavy collars. Frustrated, Luther started poking around for an underground cache.

Goji tapped transparent material which comprised the circular eye-like windows at the front of the craft. "Ghost Bark," he said. "Poor man's glass. Appropriate for a Dead Bird." He shook his head. "We need to name this thing. Any ideas?"

Luther grunted. Carina poked at the corpses. Finally, Goji shrugged and said "Fine. I dub you the 'Albatross,'" a name that prompted a snort from Luther.

Carina used her Sight to study the innards of a band on a dead nomad. She extended individual tendrils of force into the device to pop the lock. The band split apart into two sections connected by sliding bars. She started to tug the device over the dead man's head but encountered unexpected resistance. "What is this?" She pulled a second time, exposing a cluster of thin wires that extended from the device into the corpse's head. The sorceress probed further. "Higher motor functions? Control of the nervous system? These things are abominations!"

Luther came over. "What pissed you off?

"This." Carina pointed at the wires. "These -these things make people into machines. It's worse than slavery."

"It is," agreed Luther. "If the Gotemik get their way, every human alive will be fitted with one of those things, compelled to do everything they say."

"Guys, we got a problem." Goji ran up, pointing at a distant dot in the northern sky. "It's the Gotemik. They've come for the Dead Bird."

Carina eyed the still distant Flier, then scanned the hill. Nothing. Just rocks, grass, dead bodies, and an abandoned road stretching to the south. Tavon was that way. Should they make a run for it?

Luther thought the same thing. "We need to run right now. The crabs will kill us on sight."

"We can't run far enough fast enough. Even my magic can't get far enough away." Carina glanced at the collar still in her hand. "But I have another idea."

LABYRINTH WAR LIX – Git-Vik

'Knights fought with swords. My agents fought with knives and lies.'
- Lord Barret DuPaul

"We are fortunate the thralls were able to dispatch the vermin marauders before they destroyed the fuel bladder or the glider," said Kit-Zune.

"That is how it appears," Git-Vik focused one visual receptor on the surviving thralls and the other on Kit-Zune.

Kit-Zune whirled in place. "You doubt the obvious?"

"This situation appears both suspect and convenient." There was something about these thralls...

A sharp statement in the vermin language near the fuel bladder prompted Git-Vik to direct a visual receptor in that direction. He noted an exchange between one of his thralls and the male Operant. Both immediately ceased all verbalization upon seeing the receptor.

The Operants expressed immediate interest in the thralls guarding this site, going so far as to initiate communication with them. Why did the Operants find the guardians interesting? Another oddity.

"I do not understand," said Kit-Zune. "The vermin identified as 'hobgoblins' are noted for extremely aggressive behavior towards other species. That a band of them would attack this resupply point is consistent with their behavior."

"True," agreed Git-Vik. "I find it suspicious these 'hobgoblins' made their attack less than a day-cycle prior to our arrival." He noted the bodily fluids on the thrall's carapaces and cloth coverings. Their control collars showed signs of damage. Were they still functional?

"The vermin designated 'hobgoblins' had no reason to anticipate our arrival." Kit-Zune took note of Git-Vik's inspection of the thralls. "Have you an issue with these thralls?"

"I have doubts," said Git-Vik as one of his visual receptors whisked before the tallest thrall.

"Explain."

"These thralls appear different."

Kit-Zune aimed a pair of visual receptors at the thralls. "They are human. Less prone to violent outbursts than hobgoblins."

"Anything else?"

Kit-Zune's legs quivered as he considered the question. "The soft tissue beneath their carapaces is of the same shade as your human thrall."

"A thrall I acquired in a distant geographic region," said Git-Vik. "Such soft tissue coloration is unusual in this region."

"That is an oddity," agreed Kit-Zune. "Perhaps they are recent captives?"

"Perhaps." Git-Vik activated his translator mechanism. "Identify origin."

The three thralls looked at each other. Finally, the tallest one spoke. "We come from Solaria."

Git-Vik and Kit-Zune aimed visual receptors at each other. The controllers should have prompted an immediate response. Were they damaged?

Git-Vik selected a diagnostic tool and jabbed it into an access port on the collar of the nearest thrall, this one shorter than the others. "Severe internal control corruption."

"Perhaps termination is in order," suggested Kit-Zune.

"Perhaps. I will initiate a basic function check before making that determination." Git-Vik reactivated his translator. "All thralls. Raise right manipulator appendage."

The three new thralls hesitated, then raised their right motivators, as did his two.

"Drop right motivator appendage, raise left motivator appendage."

This time the responses were near instantaneous.

Git-Vik issued more simple commands, which the new thralls obeyed, though not as swiftly or effectively.

"The control interfaces appear only barely functional," said Kit-Zune. "Perhaps they were damaged."

"Perhaps." Git-Vik considered the new collared humans. "We will take these new thralls with us."

"For what purpose?"

"Expendable assessors. They will travel in the glider along with the excess fuel."

"Wise," said Kit-Zune.

Git-Vik issued commands to the new thralls. Again, they looked at each other. Then the tallest one spoke. "Glider pilot terminated in attack."

Irked, Git-Vik ordered his hobgoblin thrall to help refuel Brik-Jute-Shull and then pilot the glider.

More oddities. The guardians were ignorant of refueling procedures, requiring direct assistance from both of his thralls. Kit-Zune speculated they suffered cranial damage during the assault, but another, more sinister possibility flicked through

Git-Vik's awareness. He dismissed it as absurd. Besides, these new thralls would be terminated at the mission's completion.

The Operants, meanwhile, actively avoided both sets of thralls. A tribal issue? Irrelevant.

With Brik-Jute-Shull refueled, the glider crew stripped the dead hobgoblins of their furs and salvageable equipment before feeding their corpses to Brik-Jute-Shul, a procedure that agitated them. That agitation, though, was understandable.

Kit-Zune approached Git-Vik. "We must depart immediately to reach our destination before dark. Satellite imagery indicates a mild weather disturbance along our route."

"The glider pilot is trained sufficiently to navigate the weather disturbance." Git-Vik activated his translator. "Attach tow cable. Then board your assigned vehicle."

New and old thralls ran to obey the command.

Satisfied, Git-Vik and Kit-Zune boarded Brik-Jute-Shull, checked the controls, and activated the Fliers engines.

A cycle later they were airborne.

A cycle after that, the tow cable snapped taunt and the glider sped down the launch ramp. Then both craft were airborne.

Flying a Shull that was towing a glider required both gotemik's full attention. Brik-Jute-Shull's carapace heaved and buckled, especially when they reached the weather disturbance and the cabin suffered a momentary pressure drop.

A hard shock almost knocked Git-Vik from his stabilizer harness. He made frantic adjustments to the controls, only to get jerked from his position a second time.

"My shell begins to crack," wailed Brik-Jute-Shull. "The tow cable is tearing me apart."

"The glider pilot reports severe turbulence and structural damage," said Kit-Zune.

"Does the pilot retain control of the glider?"

"Yes, though the damage hampers operations."

Brik-Jute-Shul wailed again, a screech that almost overloaded Git-Vik's auditory receptors and sent the Operants to the floor holding their heads.

"Releasing cable." Git-Vik touched a control. "The glider should be able to reach our destination without further assistance."

Brik-Jute-Shull flew much more evenly with the tow cable disconnected. Git-Vik flew alongside the glider for a visual inspection. He noted severe vibrations with the left wing – almost certainly a strut that would require reinforcement, along with minor damage to the outer carapace.

"The pilot insists he retains control of the glider," reported Kit-Zune.

"Send him the landing coordinates," said Git-Vik. "We will drop flares to mark the location."

"Destination in visual range." Kit-Zune's voice took a darker note. "It appears...incompatible for habitation." He aimed a visual receptor at Git-Vik. "It appears to be an unlikely location for a hive."

'Incompatible' was a fair description of the fast-approaching landmass, an island dominated by stark peaks of bare rock and glaciated valleys.

Git-Vik remembered Zut-Zab's unusual behavior when assigning them this mission. "A normal hive, yes."

"You believe this hive to be abnormal?"

"The location suggests so," said Git-Vik.

The hive appeared: a complex of interconnected black stone buildings, unlike usual kwintath constructions. The long-ago kinetic strike had pulverized the complex's northern side.

"Landing area identified," said Git-Vik.

A control chirped for attention. "The pilot reports increasing difficulty maintaining a stable flight track. He says the glider will fall short of these coordinates."

"Order him to land in the last glaciated valley and then rendezvous with us here."

"Orders sent and acknowledged. Launching flares to alternate landing zone."

A sense of foreboding fell over Git-Vik as Brik-Jute-Shul landed on the ancient landing field. *There are secrets here. Possibly secrets best left undisturbed.*

LABYRINTH WAR LX - Carina

'Piloting a glider lifts my spirit. I detest the sensation, for it is false.'
- Gham-Rek, Hobgoblin Warrior

Carina clambered into the Dead Bird's interior behind Luther and Goji and tried to make herself...less uncomfortable on a short bench fixed to the wall. She cast a glance at the hobgoblin who'd be piloting this contraption. Good. He seemed preoccupied with inspecting the various levers. Then she leaned across the cramped space until her head almost touched Luther's. "I can't believe that worked."

"It did not work." The harsh voice came from the hobgoblin, who kept his gaze focused on the Dead Bird's controls. "Your deception did not fool me or my fellow thrall Curtis. It most certainly did not fool Operants Varian and Narran."

Luther lunged across the space at the hob, only to have his wrist seized in a powerful four-digit grip.

"That was unwise." The hobgoblin rotated his head until he faced the others. "In a few moments, the gotemik flier will leave the ground. The wire attached to it will drag this machine into the air after it. If I am dead or cannot focus on these controls, this vessel will crash, and you will all die. Do you understand?"

Luther started to say something.

Carina pulled him back. "Yes, we understand."

"That better be the case." The hobgoblin returned his attention to the disk-shaped aircraft before them.

"We do have questions."

"They must wait until we are in the sky." Flames spouted from nozzles in the rear of the Gotemik craft as it leaped into the air. "Brace yourselves."

The cable went taunt. Carina and Luther grabbed handholds as a jolt ran through the Dead Bird. Carina almost lost her lunch when the glider slid down the ramp and nosed upward.

The hobgoblin consulted dials, spoke into a small grate, and tugged at levers attached to wires that ran through the Dead Bird's interior and out into the wings. Each lever, Carina noticed, adjusted a flap that made up the rear quarter of those protrusions. The ground fell away beneath them, the already low hills becoming mere bumps, like something made by a child. Then the land fell away altogether.

Satisfied for the moment, the hobgoblin glanced back at his passengers. "I am Gham-Rek." He spoke with a raised voice to carry over the Dead Birds vibrations. "Once, I was a warrior of Iktar." His expression turned wistful. "I fought the Solarian Legions at Chasvet and Crowfoot Gap." A long sigh escaped his lips. "Now, I am a slave-warrior of the Gotemik."

Goji attempted to be cheerful. "Uh...pleased to meet you, Gham-Rek."

The hobgoblin gave Goji a disdainful look. "You are not pleased." He turned his attention back to Carina. "You bear the mark of the Solarian Empire's Arcane Cohort. You are most fortunate that Git-Vik did not discern its meaning."

"Git-Vik?"

"Git-Vik is the gotemik in command of the flier Brik-Jute-Shul. He is observant."

"He's the one that had us doing those exercises," said Luther.

"Correct. Git-Vik was suspicious of your behavior from the outset. Fortunately, he attributed it to damaged control collars.

The gotemik have great difficulties keeping their machines operational. I believe the purpose of this expedition is to locate an ancient cache of intact kwintath mechanisms."

"Is that why the Celthanian sorcerers were aboard this...Brik-Jute-Shull?" asked Carina. "To provide access to this cache?" The damn place must be huge.

"I believe so. I also believe they have a private agenda." He stared squarely at Carina. "They were going to reveal your deception to Git-Vik. I persuaded them otherwise."

"How did you do that?"

"By pointing out the Gotemik need just one Operant to access the cache."

Well, that was hobgoblin logic for you.

"You held a knife to Varian, didn't you," said Luther. "That's what that little spat was about."

"Yes." Gham-Rek returned his attention to the control panel. "I must concentrate on flying this machine. Wrap yourselves in the furs as the cold will soon be severe."

They flew in silence for a time. It did grow cold in the craft.

Carina tried to scratch an itch underneath her wretched collar, which seemed to weigh a ton. She couldn't get her fingernails far enough under the metal to reach the spot that itched.

Goji leaned towards the hobgoblin. "Why didn't you do it? Why didn't you tell the boss crab we were fakes?"

"Your presence hinted at the possibility of change."

"We gave you the hope of freedom."

"A dead hope," said Gham-Rek. "I have no future other than death in battle. Your presence brings forth the possibility I may die fighting the gotemik, instead of their enemies."

A sharp jolt almost threw Carina from the bench. "What was that?"

"Rough air," said the hobgoblin as the Dead Bird jolted twice more. "Piloting the glider will require my full attention."

The craft tilted. Terror surged through Carina's frame as she braced herself against the interior. Then the craft tilted the other way, sending Goji slamming into the far wall.

Carina knocked Goji onto the bench. "Brace yourself!"

"There's something out there." Luther stood with both hands wrapped in loops that dangled from the ceiling, staring out the window.

"What is it? A bird?" Carina tried to imagine the damage if the Dead Bird struck a live avian. It couldn't be much, surely?

"I don't think so," said Luther. "It was red and glowed. It came right for us."

A glowing red bird? That didn't sound like anything natural. Carina latched onto a pair of brackets and extended her senses. Air – angry air that bubbled and heaved, trying to become a storm. Clouds, dark and ominous. Then – a pulsating blob of energy approached the Dead Bird from the side. "It's coming right for us!"

"What is coming for us?" demanded Gham-Rek, straining at the levers before him.

"Something – I don't know!" Except Carina had half a notion already. *Those Celthanian sorcerers tried to kill us once already. Could they have summoned a demon? But how? They'd been wearing bracelets marked with Null Runes. Those should have prevented them from working magic. So, how?*

Luther shouted something incoherent – and then fell into the ceiling as something struck the Dead Bird's wing so hard it corkscrewed. Carina hit the deck with a 'thud,' then heaved herself erect right as something punched a fist-sized hole through the wall.

A pulsating red entity – no, a miniature greenish-brown person wrapped in pulsating red ribbons flew into the compartment. Miniature bat-like wings sprouted from its – no, her – back, and lightning crackled in the being's tiny fists.

Luther swatted the bird creature as it unleashed a lightning bolt at Gham-Rek. The electrical discharge missed the hobgoblin but blew a hole through the control panel.

Goji grabbed the flier, only to take a savage bite to his wrist, making him lose his grip.

I can deal with this. Carina called upon spells she'd scarcely used since the worst days of the Traag War, magic intended to banish demons. The incantation knocked the flier sideways. The red bands flare with painful brilliance.

The bird demon hissed at Carina in a language she associated with deep forests and fey creatures. *She's not a demon. She's...something else bound by a demonic spell.* And then the Dead Bird violently corkscrewed again, sending the sorceress flying face first into the side. When Carina reoriented herself, the bird creature – a sprite, maybe? – was nowhere to be seen.

Shouts from the cockpit drew Carina's attention to Gham-Rek, who had one beefy arm buried in the console to the elbow.

The Dead Bird's nose tilted downward.

"The wing cable has torn loose of its mount! We will crash if it is not secured!"

Goji fell to the floor at the hobgoblin's feet. "I think I see it!" He reached under the console. "Is that it?"

"Yes!"

"Let it go!" An instant later, Goji pulled a wire with a frayed end from beneath the panel. "I don't see the rest of it!"

Luther pulled off his belt. “Tie it to this.” He fed the belt through the hole, then handed the remnant to the hobgoblin. “Here. You can use the dagger as a handle.”

“Got it,” shouted Goji.

Gham-Rek pulled at the improvised lever. It moved a fraction, then stopped. “I need help!”

Luther added his muscles to the hobgoblins. The improvised control inched upward – and so did the Dead Bird’s nose, even as a horrendous banging sound came from its wing.

Carina planted her face against the opening left by the flier, then gaped in shock as the whole wing bounced. “Something is broken inside the wing.”

“Fix it. Use your magic!” Gham-Rek gave a final tug at the dagger even as the miraculously intact grate squawked for attention. The hobgoblin spoke into the grill.

Carina pulled off another strip of the hull exposing a lattice of metal struts. Two of them were broken. One was out of reach, but just maybe... “I need something to splice these together.”

Goji pressed a length of string and a knife into Carina’s palm. “My bootlace – and boot dagger.”

Carina pressed the weapon’s midpoint against the break, then used the cord to make an improvised brace. She almost lost her fingers pushing the string between the strut and the skin. She cinched the cord tight. “Best I can do.”

“It helped,” said Gham-Rek. “We are instructed to follow Brik-Jute-Shul. Flares will be dropped to identify a landing area.”

The Dead Bird dropped again. Gham-Rek and Luther’s tugging managed to level it out barely a hundred yards above the water.

“This doesn’t look good,” said Goji.

“Our destination is immediately ahead,” Gham-Rek spoke into the grill. “The landing area is on the ice a short distance from the target." He glanced back at Carina. "Brace yourselves. This will be rough."

A beach filled with jagged boulders flashed beneath the Dead Bird, followed by undulating whiteness. Then the ground slammed hard into its midsection, and Gham-Rek shouted as it twisted sideways.

LABYRINTH WAR LXI – Git-Vik

'The portal is too dangerous to use. Our hives on the mainland are damaged and in disarray. Food reserves are limited. The best option is long-term hibernation.'

- Message left by Director 7-717 of Dimensional Research Facility Seven.

"We could have accessed this facility through the damaged portion," said Kit-Zune. The Gotemik stood a few body lengths from the facility's circular primary entrance untroubled by the cold wind that blew through this place. The chilly conditions did affect the Operants and thrall, though, who were huddled against the structure's side.

"Unauthorized access might have activated security measures we are not prepared to counter," said Git-Vik. "Additionally, the damage might seal off portions of the interior."

"Valid points." Kit-Zune indicated the Operants with a manipulator appendage. "Shall we attempt access?"

"Yes." Git-Vik produced the authorization device provided by Zut-Zab. "Operants. Begin your preparations."

Operant Varian straightened from his huddle. "Much as I'd like to get out of this beastly weather – I swear it is worse than that of the high mountains back home – I cannot open this portal," he tapped the slab, "until certain formalities are observed." He lifted his appendage with the Suppression device.

"Understood." Git-Vik aimed visual receptors at the thrall. "Prepare to execute Operant Varian if he deviates from instructions."

"Yes." The thrall's features curled.

"That hardly seems called for," said Operant Varian.

"Silence, Operant." Git-Vik held out the control mechanism for the Suppression device. "When I release the Suppressor, you will take this interface unit and use it to obtain proper access to this facility. Any deviation will result in your immediate termination."

"Well, since you put it that way...I agree." The Operant's upper body rose slightly, then dropped.

Git-Vik released the Suppressor and gave the interface unit to the Operant in one smooth motion.

Operant Varian held the interface unit in both hands, studying it. "A blank mask. How utterly lacking in artistry." He flipped the 'mask' over and placed it over the front part of his head. "Extraordinary," he said. "There is so much here."

"Operant, open this portal."

"Oh, very well." Operant Varian placed both manipulator appendages against the metal. Vocalizations that disturbed Git-Vik at a primal level came through the interface unit.

The portal trembled, along with the wall. Ice and other debris fell from the upper surfaces.

"Perhaps the mechanism is jammed," offered Kit-Zune.

"A likely possibility," agreed Git-Vik. "We may have to attempt access through the damaged section after all."

A huge booming sound came from within the wall, followed by a high-pitched shriek. The noise intensified. Then the circular door rolled open half a body length and halted.

"That is the best I can do." Varian mashed his manipulators together. "The mechanism is stiff with age. I might be able to close it again, though."

"That will not be necessary," said Git-Vik. "What is the status of the internal mechanisms?"

"I am receiving a distressing number of error messages. However, I can restore certain basic systems like illumination and heat."

"Do so," ordered Git-Vik.

Operant Varian made a series of elaborate motions with his manipulators, as though he were working an invisible control panel. Perhaps he was. "There." Dim bluish lights blinked on, exposing a lengthy corridor.

"Are there any active security measures," asked Kit-Zune.

"The mobile security devices appear to be...out of order," said the Operant. "Certain stationary security mechanisms remain active."

"Your assessment is acceptable." Git-Vik reactivated the Suppressor.

"I say, that was uncalled for." Varian removed the mask.

"No, it is a wise precaution," said Git-Vik.

"Incoming transmission from Zut-Zab," said Kit-Zune. "He was able to retrieve additional information about this facility and has provided us with a list of areas to investigate."

"I find Zut-Zab's timing curious," said Git-Vik.

"Additional notification," continued Kit-Zune. "We are to retrieve representatives if possible."

"Did he provide details on these 'representatives?'"

"Negative. I confess to bewilderment." Kit-Zune's motivators jittered as he spoke.

"This entire mission is bewildering," said Git-Vik. "Still, our instructions are clear."

"Incoming transmission from glider pilot. He reports severe but repairable damage to the glider. Two of the new thralls did not survive the landing. He states they will not reach this location before nightfall." Kit-Zune angled a visual receptor at Git-Vik. "Should we wait for them?"

"Negative. Instruct the thrall to secure this entryway upon arrival. In the meantime, we will conduct a preliminary inspection of this facility."

They entered the corridor, the Operant's in the lead, trailed by the thrall. Git-Vik and Kit-Zune brought up the rear. Visibility was limited, as many light strips were nonfunctional, resulting in long shadowy stretches. Once, they passed an abandoned internal transport device, its cargo area piled high with crates.

Kit-Zune had the thrall remove three of the containers for inspection. "Our people manufactured these components. Why are they in a kwintath installation?"

"I do not know. We shall collect them upon our return."

They pressed deeper into the complex.

"The area ahead displays severe localized damage," reported Kit-Zune.

The thrall said something.

"Repeat and elaborate," Git-Vik ordered the thrall.

"Battlefield," said the thrall. "There was a fight here."

"We are inclined to concur." Varian kicked at a bit of sharp metal. "This, I believe, is from a mechanical sentry." He motioned at the other debris. "It doesn't appear to have fared well."

Meanwhile, the thrall inspected a putrid yellowish stain on the damaged wall section, then poked at the rubble beneath it. "Demon. The sentry's fought demons here."

Kit-Zune's motivators jittered. He scuttled back along the hall a few body lengths.

Git-Vik felt like joining him. They were all in danger if the dimensional parasites lingered in this facility. Unbidden, the memories of Home's fall rose in his mind. Yes, this was potentially catastrophic.

But order had to be maintained. "Kit-Zune. Remain focused on your task."

Kit-Zune stopped trembling.

Git-Vik addressed the thrall. "Are you certain of this evaluation?"

"I spent years fighting demons." The thrall puffed out his midsection. "I know what demon guts look like."

"Can you determine which faction won this confrontation?"

The thrall peered along the corridor. "No trail of demon ichor past this point, which means the demons were either all killed, or the survivors took no damage."

Git-Vik hoped the former option aligned with reality. "Kit-Zune. What is the location of the first investigation area?" Give him something to focus on.

Kit-Zune consulted his mapping mechanism. "Access portal to the first location is sixty-two body lengths away. We take the next corridor to the right."

They set out again. Git-Vik noticed the thrall had removed his primitive chopping weapon from its covering. Could that disgusting creature defeat one of the dimensional entities or their minions? Chaotic reports claimed that thralls equipped with such implements destroyed significant numbers of such entities during past confrontations. Disturbing though it was, that thought gave Git-Vik a spark of increased confidence.

The designated corridor brought them to another portal and the remnants of a second battle.

"I do not see any remnants of mechanical sentries," said Kit-Zune.

"Well, something killed those demons," said the thrall. "They didn't even reach the door."

"The sentry here is immobile." Varian pointed at a bulge beside the door with a faint red gleam at its center.

"Concurred," said Kit-Zune. "I believe additional authorization is required to pass this point."

Git-Vik activated specialized detection devices. They revealed substantial energy in the security device, the wall behind it, and the door. However, the signatures were...patchy.

Varian stared at Git-Vik, waiting. "I cannot open this door with my abilities nullified."

Git-Vik distrusted the Operant. But he didn't have much choice, either. He released the Suppressor.

Varian turned toward the portal. "Hm. Yes. There is an elaborate security protocol. However, time has done what brute force could not." He stiffened. "My authority is accepted."

Git-Vik scanned the door again. Yes, there was a notable change in the internal energy readouts.

"Opening protocol initiated."

The door trembled for a moment – then rolled smoothly aside, revealing a long, wide corridor with transparent canisters to either side.

"Now, this is interesting," said Varian as he drifted over the threshold. His head rotated towards Git-Vik for a moment. "It seems not all of your people abandoned this sphere in the bad old days."

"Silence, vermin," said Kit-Zune.

However, the Operant was correct – the canisters did hold gotemik. Hundreds of them, possibly more. "Access inventory functions," Git-Vik ordered the Operant. "I wish to know how many members of my people are in these suspension units." For that was what the cylinders were – hibernation units.

"Oh, very well." The Operant tilted his head at the ceiling. "The original manifest lists two thousand seven hundred and twelve gotemik, of whom one thousand nine hundred and three are in condition to be revived." The Operant's masked head turned slightly to the side. "Ah, this is intriguing. The manifest also lists seven thousand, eight hundred and two kwintath, with five thousand, five hundred and twenty that could be revived."

Git-Vik and Kit-Zune aimed visual receptors at each other. Releasing that many kwintath onto the planet was unacceptable. The Gotemik, though....

"Initiate revival of the gotemik."

"As you wish." The Operant's manipulators made erratic motions. "Hm. That might not be possible."

"Explain."

"A priority sequence requires reanimation of a specific group of ten kwintath ahead of all others."

"Unacceptable. Circumvent the protocol."

"I need to think a moment. There are so many options...ah...here we are, an emergency procedure that allows the revival of any hibernating individual, regardless of species."

Git-Vik tapped the nearest three suspension units. "Revive these individuals."

"Commencing emergency revival procedure – I must say, this process is replete with warning codes. Your companions may not be especially lively."

Colored lights flared to life beneath the transparent tubes. Pinkish mists flooded into their interiors from hidden vents.

"But they should survive the reanimation process."

Git-Vik focused his specialized detectors on the nearest entombed Gotemik. Did his motivators twitch? Another hint of movement. Was the revival process working? Or were these movements the spasms of a corpse?

"Oh, look, the process is nearly completed."

Git-Vik and Kit-Zune turned their receptors towards the selected cylinders, which were receding into the floor, leaving their occupants sitting in pools of ichor. The nearest directed a visual receptor at Git-Vik and made an unintelligible communication. Damage? Or a different language?

Git-Vik attempted to communicate with the newly revived gotemik. Again, the response was unintelligible.

Another of the reanimated Gotemik attempted to stand, only to collapse sideways.

"Operant Varian, your evaluation of the revival protocol appears correct. These individuals will not be of immediate use."

"Oh, but they will be of immediate use to me," said the Operant. "You will be as well."

The Operant has gone rogue. Git-Vik immediately activated the Suppressor units for both Operants.

Operant Varian emitted an unusual vocalization – laughter. "No, my crab-like friend, the Suppressor no longer affects me." Both Operant's Suppressor units fell to the floor.

"Thrall, terminate the Operants immediately!"

But the thrall was already leaping forward, its metal implement raised for a strike sure to terminate Operant Varian.

Instead, Varian raised a manipulator – and the thralls forward rush decreased by ninety percent.

Git-Vik activated his laser unit. He could use it no more than three times before depleting the power unit, but if that were what it took...

"Will. Kill. You." The thrall's vocalizations were strained.

"No, you won't."

Git-Vik fired his laser. The beam should have penetrated Varian's body – but instead diffused into a crimson halo. Another halo surrounded Operant Narran.

Still, both Operants reeled from expending the energy to defend themselves. One more blast –

White-hot agony erupted in both of Git-Vik's right-side manipulators. Horror mixed with agony as both appendages were severed from his body and flew through the air, accompanied by a red and green creature.

"Look, she's back," said Narran. "And she found it! Isn't that grand?"

Git-Vik rapidly redirected his visual receptors. His laser unit was on the floor. Kit-Zune slumped against a Suspension unit, fluids leaking from a hole in his upper body, feebly attempting to aim his laser unit. The thrall was on the floor, still focused on the Operant's. Given sufficient time, either might succeed. "Found what?"

"Something thought long lost," said Varian. "There is so much more to this place than was ever revealed to you. Secrets you will never learn." He punctuated the statement by jamming his long, sharp piece of metal into the thrall's torso,

"Inform me." Kit-Zune somehow managed to aim his laser unit.

"I think not."

The red and green creature settled on Narran's manipulator appendage. It appeared to be a miniature human with avian wings. "Good job, Blood Leaf! You deserve a snack!"

The creature bit Narran's thumb.

The thrall rolled away from Varian. Its limbs shifted position.

"You are sustained by my blood and bound by it." Narran looked at Git-Vik. "Isn't Blood Leaf just adorable? She's a sprite, not a true demon at all. This devastatingly handsome

Gandharvas showed me how to summon her. She didn't like me until...No, we can't have that!" Narran motioned at Kit-Zune right as he discharged the laser.

The beam dissipated in a crimson aura and Kit-Zune was knocked to the ground.

Then the thrall leaped from the floor, striking Varian so hard the Operant was hurled from his feet.

"Stop that!" Narran stepped back and pointed her manipulator at the thrall.

Blood Leaf leaped right as the thrall made a complex swinging motion with his sharp metal implement – and then the sprite was spiraling across the room.

"You hurt her," shouted Narran. "That's mean. I'll" –

Narran didn't get a chance to say more because that was when Git-Vik struck her with the sharp tips of two of his motivator appendages, piercing her soft tissue.

Varian rose, but the thrall's boot struck him squarely in the face, knocking him down again.

Narran emitted an incoherent screech as purple sparks flared along the tips of her manipulators.

Varian made motions indicative of Operant powers being activated.

Kit-Zune clambered into an erect position, still leaking bodily fluids.

This victory was momentary. The situation was untenable. Git-Vik ordered the thrall to assist Kit-Zune. They needed to retreat.

The thrall started to protest, then caught sight of Blood Leaf emerging from behind a suspension unit. He hurled a sharp metal object at the 'sprite,' then slammed a manipulator against Varian, resulting in a discharge of purple energy. Then he turned, lifted Kit-Zune clear off the floor, and swiftly moved along the corridor.

The return trip was an exercise in agony. Kit-Zune was comatose upon their arrival, and the thrall collapsed immediately after bringing him inside the Shul. Git-Vik himself was almost immobile from pain.

This is a disaster. He initiated a report to Zut-Zab, but pain overwhelmed the Coordinator's response, then everything else.

LABYRINTH WAR LXII - Carina

'Honor. Strength. Kin.'
- Hobgoblin credo

"No," said Carina. "I won't let you kill them."

Gham-Rek pointed at Goji, who writhed on a makeshift bed. Colored fluids seeped through the bandages across his torso. "This one will spend days dying in agony. Killing him now is merciful."

"I am a healer. I can cure him." *Maybe. If I could find proper supplies. And if I had sufficient time.* "And Luther isn't in too bad of shape." *But he shouldn't walk on that leg.*

"They are burdens we cannot afford." Gham-Rek pulled his sword. "Besides, I have already reported their deaths to the Masters."

"Hold on!" Luther struggled to his feet. "Nobody is killing anybody here."

"I have no choice." Gham-Rek turned to Luther. "This collar" – he tapped the iron ring around his orange neck – "compels obedience to the Masters. Their orders are clear: severely injured thralls must be terminated."

Now or never. Carina focused her mystic abilities on the back of the hobgoblin's skull. Then she initiated a spell that would have landed her before a Church Tribunal back in the Empire.

Gham-Rek turned. "What are you doing?" Then he collapsed.

"Thanks for the save." Luther leaned against the Dead Bird's side and winced. "I'll finish him." He fumbled for his dagger.

"No, I have a better idea." Carina grabbed the unconscious hobgoblin's shoulders. "Help me turn him over. I'm removing that collar."

"That isn't wise," said Luther.

"I am going to need his help to get you two to that – that place." There had to be medical supplies there. "Besides, he'd be handy in a fight."

"Huh." Luther's brow contorted. "Hobs are big on honor, but...I don't know."

"Help me before he wakes up."

Together, Carina and Luther rolled the hobgoblin onto his belly.

Carina focused her Sight on the collar and probed the locking mechanism. There. A series of 'clicks' came from within the device. It split apart into two sections linked by sliding bars. Then it emitted a mechanical screech.

"That doesn't sound good," said Luther.

"Let me think." Carina reached into the thing's innards with her magic. "It's trying to kill him."

"Can you stop it?"

"I – there." The sorceress melted a cluster of components. The noise stopped.

Gham-Rek howled when Carina yanked the band over his head. He thrashed on the ground and then sat erect. Murder gleamed in his eyes. "What did you do, witch? My head feels like it is on fire."

Carina held out the collar. "I took this off. I figured you'd worn it long enough."

Gham-Rek's hands went to his neck. "It's gone. But how?"

"You said it yourself. I am a witch."

"Ah, my head!" Gham-Rek rubbed his skull. "I heard rumors that wizards could sometimes remove the collars without killing the wearers. I thought them false. It seems I was mistaken." He took a breath. "I am in your debt. I will help bring your companions to the depository." His lips cracked in a smile. "After that, my former masters owe me a debt of blood and pain."

Goji didn't weigh much, but it still sucked pulling his body along the ice. Putting him on a spare blanket helped. Luther needed a crutch fashioned from the Dead Bird's carcass to walk.

The hobgoblin walked with a limp. Still, he took his turn towing Goji without complaint.

What didn't help was the biting cold and unending wind. It sank into Carina's bones and drained her strength. The frequent crevices didn't help matters either – twice Luther almost toppled into one of the chasms.

At least they were all free of those evil collars. The hobgoblin took grim pleasure in smashing the bands before their departure.

It took twice the time it should have to reach the cliff where the facility perched. The thing was huge – several big blocky structures tacked onto each other like it had been hurriedly expanded.

It took Carina and Gham-Rek's combined efforts and all of their rope to reach the top. That effort didn't help either of them – Goji passed out and Luther collapsed.

Carina felt like collapsing herself, but that wasn't an option. She rolled Luther onto the blanket with Goji and tugged them along the structure's base, one slow painful step at a time. That ride almost certainly didn't help their injuries.

Gham-Rek helped some to start, then took off to scout a bit. He made it back about the time Carina was ready to collapse.

"The door is just ahead," said the hobgoblin. "It's open, but only partway. Brik-Jute-Shull is off to the side."

"See anybody?" asked Carina.

"No, though there is a trail of blood and fluids from the door to the Shull."

"It sounds like they went inside and found something unpleasant."

"Likely," agreed the hobgoblin. "I was with a squad that encountered a mechanical guardian at another kwintath installation. Despite being damaged, it, still killed two members of my group before we destroyed it."

A sudden gust of chilly wind reminded Carina just how dire their situation was.

We need shelter. You said the door is open?"

"It is open," said Gham -Rek. "And the interior is warmer than out here."

"You went inside?"

"Just a few paces. There is a place just past the entryway that might serve for shelter."

"Good." Carina rubbed her hands together to beat back the chill. "Let's get these guys there."

Gham-Rek knelt, grabbed the blanket's edge, and pulled it along the wall, while Carina trailed behind him.

The door – a circular grayish metal slab four times Carina's height – was partially open. And it was much warmer inside, even with the draft through the opening. The 'place' Gham-Rek mentioned wasn't much – just a wide spot in the hall, easily overlooked. A dim blue light came from strips set into the corridor's sides. Age had taken its toll on these, as at least half emitted no light, making for a realm of shadows.

Still, it was a place to work. Carina checked Luther's leg. The swelling had gone down, but the limb needed to be kept immobile. Still, he should make a full recovery – eventually.

Goji, though – that gash in his gut was horrible.

"I can end his pain now." Gham-Rek pulled out his sword.

"My spells might save Goji," said Carina, "But he'd have a better chance if we had some real supplies."

Gham-Rek stared at Carina for a moment. "There is a healer's kit aboard Brik-Jute-Shul. Admittance should not be a problem."

"Could you retrieve it?"

The hobgoblin considered the question. "It is not worth the risk to save one already on death's road." He nudged Goji with the toe of his boot. The little man showed no reaction.

"Fine, then." Carina stood. "I will get it. Don't kill him while I am gone."

Gham-Rek stared at Carina, then gave her a slow nod. "I shall explore along the corridor for a short distance."

"Don't worry. I'll make it back before you do. Now, how do I get aboard?"

There is a cupboard beside the hatch. Open it with this." Gham-Rek gave her a small, flat key. "Inside is a dial with a pointer surrounded by symbols. Turn the pointer first to the circle, then to the square. The hatch should open. The healer's kit is inside the door to the left."

And if it doesn't, I could try my magic. Carina didn't verbalize the thought. "Got it." She watched the hobgoblin set off along the hall, then stepped out into the howling wind. She was chilled to the bone – again – by the time she reached the flier – or the 'Shull' as Gham-Rek called it. She spotted a red box no bigger than a book beside the hatch. *Now, let's see if this works.* The key slid right in. She didn't have to turn it, instead, the top of the box flipped down. The interior matched Gham-Rek's description. The dial clicked as she turned it left to a small circle, then right to a tiny square.

A seam formed around the edge of the hatch, which dropped down to expose a cramped interior.

Carina took two steps inside and almost gagged. *It smells worse than a slaughterhouse crossed with a garbage pit in here.* She rotated in place, looking for the healer's kit. Nothing. Had Gham-Rek lied after all?

A low moan drew Carina's attention to a lump on the floor – no, not a lump, but an armored human wearing a thrall collar. An open canister was next to his outthrust hand. It looked like he'd attempted to bandage himself. She knelt to inspect his injuries more closely. Stab wound to the chest, nasty but not critical, plus assorted cuts and bruises. All should heal given time.

Carina stepped over the warrior to better reach the canister. Hopefully, it held what she needed to fix Goji. This movement gave her a view of the compartment's front section – and the two badly mauled gotemik sprawled in net-like harnesses with tubes and wires attached to their bodies. One was missing two of its claws. The other leaked greenish ochre from a hole in its soft upper section – the equivalent of a gut wound, maybe?

I could end them right now. Carina knelt and grabbed the fallen knight's sword. Then she took a single step towards the nearest Gotemik, the one missing two of its hands. She raised the sword.

"No," said a voice that sounded like metal plates rubbing together. "You will not kill my kin. At least I believe that is your word for the relationship."

Carina glanced about wide-eyed, heart racing. "Who are you?"

"Ignorant vermin! I am all around you!"

The compartment's interior flexed, making Carina fall on her rump. The flexing jolted Carina's target out of its stupor.

"I was Brik-Jute, Coordinator for the People! Then, for my crimes, for daring to suggest cooperation with you inferiors, I was remade into a Shull!"

The injured gotemik started to disentangle itself. It tapped a device attached to its shell.

I *need to leave here now.*

The compartment's interior bucked again, knocking Carina atop the thrall, and jolting him awake.

The hatch sealed before Carina's eyes. Loud 'clicks,' almost like a drum came from the compartment's front.

"Terminate intruder," said the gotemik.

The knight opened his mouth even as his arm came over his back. "I must obey."

One thing left to try. "Hold on tight, tough guy." Then Carina grabbed the canister and cast the spell that made a rift through space. Half a heartbeat later the two crashed to the floor beside Luther and Goji. Gham-Rek was mere paces away.

"Must. Must kill!" The warrior's face was contorted in agony.

"No." Gham-Rek's fist slammed into the knight's skull. His eyes crossed. Then he fell to the floor."

"You retrieved Sir Curtis," said Gham-Rek. "Now, remove his collar."

"If you say the magic word."

"I do not understand. I know nothing of magic."

"The word is 'please.' It is about politeness. And politeness can work magic."

Gham-Rek considered Carina's statement. "Please remove Sir Curtis DuFloret's collar."

"Thank you." Carina turned her attention to Curtis. Removing the band from around his neck took no time at all. Carina noticed that several wires connecting it to his head were broken.

"Damaged," said Gham-Rek. "I suspected as much."

"Huh." Carina removed the collar and used her Sight to check for additional damage. "That's odd. There's an enchantment on him. A compulsion. It could also have hindered him physically."

"This compulsion was cast by either Varian or Narran," said Gham-Rek. "Can you remove it?"

"Yeah. It's not quality work." She made a twisting motion. "There. All gone."

Goji moaned.

"He's doing better," said Luther. "He was awake earlier. We talked for a bit."

"I will try to patch him up." Carina grabbed the canister and pawed through its contents. Several items would be most helpful. "Tell me something," she said without looking away from Goji, "when I was inside that – that thing, there was this – this voice."

"Brik-Jute-Shull," said Gham-Rek.

"Yes, but it also said one of the gotemik was his kin. Does that mean?"

"Shulls are made from older gotemik entering their breeding cycle at the end of their lives. The process increases their size tenfold. Eggs form inside their carapaces. Swarms of male Gotemik fertilize these eggs. With Shull's this process is interrupted. They are given potions and vast quantities of food., then fitted with mechanical attachments," said Gham-Rek. "I have participated in the process several times."

"That is...fascinating in a disgusting sort of way." Carina knew of several species for whom reproduction was death. The gotemik process resembled that of certain types of insects. She smeared a poultice across Goji's wound – it did seem a little better. She contemplated an herbal concoction. It might make the difference, she decided. "Open up." She pried open Goji's mouth and poured in a quarter of the bottle. "That should do it for now. Damn, I'm hungry."

Gham-Rek tossed Carina a packet of jerked beef, bread, and purple fruit.

"Yummy." Carina took a bite from the fruit.

The ground trembled as a vast racket came from outside.

The hobgoblin ran to the entrance. "Brik-Jute-Shull is leaving. We are on our own."

"No." Curtis propped himself up on his hands. "We must kill a pair of demon-worshipping sorcerers before they doom us all." He rubbed his skull. "My head is killing me."

LABYRINTH WAR LXIII – Curtis

'An arrow struck my steed's eye. The horse fell, taking me with it. My world turned into a tumbling blur. Breath erupted from my lungs when I struck the ground.

I rose to my feet, side burning, and gasping for air. I took several unsteady steps, the tip of my blade dragging in the dirt. A stone gave way beneath my foot, landing me on the ground.

I found myself unable to take a step or lift an arm. Lord Varian descended the slope before me, ignoring the carnage around him.

"Lord Varian," I said, putting false cheer into my voice. "How odd to meet you here. I thought your friends would have whisked you home."

"Home?" Varian shook his head. "Home is gone. Great Celthania is no more."

"Iktar's legions proved tougher than anticipated?"

"Those brutes? Hah!" Another shake of his head. "My sire warned the council not to ally with the gotemik."

"Gotemik?"

"That race doesn't concern you. I can do nothing about them." He straightened. "However, I can correct your lack of courtesy at Ezek."

"Well," I said, "you were going to kill me. That does strain proper etiquette."

"You stabbed me with my dagger," said Varian, a note of tension entering his voice. "I almost died. Do you hear me? I almost died!" Varian ripped the front of his shirt apart. Something looked wrong with the flesh beneath the fabric.

"Are those scales?" I asked.

"Yes, my Lord Titus Maximus, these are scales. Narran resorted to drastic measures to keep spirit and flesh together – though it's not exactly my flesh anymore. The process was quite agonizing but worthwhile." His face contorted and his hands twitched violently, as his fingernails turned into dagger blades. "My new flesh comes with new appetites – and obligations."

- From 'The Journal of Titus Maximus.'

Stopping the demon worshippers required a plan. Fortunately, the Solarian Witch fabricated one. The first part played to what she figured the Celthanians would expect from a pair of dimwitted warriors – a straight-out frontal attack, which for different reasons suited Curtis and Gham-Rek just fine. The second part was to rattle their nerves and keep them guessing. And the third part, well, that was a sucker punch.

They ventured deeper into the complex, past the ancient battle to a hall with trails of Gotemik ichor running along the floor. Curtis started along the hall to the hibernating aliens, only to stop short at the sight of the closed portal. "Security device. Varian had a mask-thing he used to get past it. Can you?"

Carina shook her head. "No."

"Then we'd best see where they went."

The grisly fluids guided them along wide halls and down lengthy ramps which finally emptied into a huge chamber big enough to hold a castle with room left over for a sailing ship or two. It wasn't empty, either – Curtis took in a hunk of unidentifiable machinery that reached almost to the ceiling, plus piles of metal canisters and crates plopped down in different spots like they'd been stashed here in a hurry.

But what convinced them they'd reached the right spot was the big metal arch at the chambers back, big enough to drive a trio of wagons through side by side with room left over – and the circular vortex at the bottom of the thing, maybe six or eight feet across.

The twins stood before this opening deep in conversation, unperturbed by the dead crab monsters surrounding them. Not a speck of Gotemik goop marred their clothing.

Good.

Luther and Carina ducked behind a pile of crates.

Curtis and Gham-Rek headed for the twins, trying to keep out of sight.

"...these interlock as well," said Varian. "The bugs certainly did their best to hinder our special friends."

"Perhaps this one." Narran motioned at a spot near the vortex's edge. "See how the void nibbles at it?"

"Possibly," agreed Varian.

The twins made a series of occult jabs at the vortex.

The image of a ruined alien city perched next to a black lagoon, and a sky dominated by a barred spiral took shape.

"Lord Dagon's realm," said Varian. "Understandable, given that He was the last to open portals between worlds, and the power of his casting would draw lesser gates to them. But the wall remains intact."

"Perhaps," Narran turned and caught sight of Curtis. "My, my, it appears we have visitors."

"Sir Curtis DuFloret." Varian smiled as though Curtis were a dear friend. "You are just in time to witness the greatest event this world has known!"

Curtis and Gham-Rek charged only to be halted by an invisible barrier.

Curtis's mouth, though, was unaffected by the spell. "And what 'greatest event' might that be?"

"Why, the absorption of this world by the True Powers. This world has run its course – glorious Celthania is naught but rubble, your brash nation scorns the True Powers, the Chou constricts everything...why it simply deserves a remake."

"So, you say." Curtis pushed against the barrier. "But won't that remake kill you?"

"We are bonded to the Gods." Narran tapped her chest, where a circle of glowing crimson dots shined through the fabric. "A God touched my heart. The pain was exquisite – but necessary."

"I was wounded," said Varian. "But that God saved me with flesh taken from his body." He lifted his shirt, exposing the strip of scaly skin across his gut. "It marks the first step in my transformation into a greater entity."

"You talk too much," said Gham-Rek.

"You are fools to believe demons w will keep their promises," said Curtis.

"Oh, I am done talking to you louts," said Varian. "Sister?"

"With pleasure."

A banging sound came from elsewhere in the room, followed by a thrown object that landed just shy of the twins.

"What?" Varian's eyes widened. "That's a"- he made a frantic incantation right as the bomb detonated, showering the twins with shrapnel. His spell stopped most of the fragments, but not all of them.

"Blood Leaf!" shouted Narran, decorum gone. "Dispatch that intruder!"

The corrupted sprite popped from behind the sorceress and flew into the piles of crates and canisters – just as Carina had predicted.

Curtis hoped the witch could defeat the sprite, or at least slow it down.

Varian brushed detritus off his sleeve. “That was unexpectedly clever of you, Sir Curtis, not to mention rude.”

“We need to finish them now.” Narran scanned the piles dotting the chamber. “There is a presence here. I bet it's her.”

-A high-pitched wail came from behind a pile of boxes., followed by a screech from Narran. “That barbarian bitch broke the bond!”

Narran reeled on her feet – and the pressure holding Curtis and Gham-Rek vanished. They ran towards the sorcerers, blades raised.

Varian made a frantic incantation that sent Curtis and Gham-Rek slamming into each other but didn't halt their momentum.

The twins were just a few paces away. Curtis positioned himself – and then his boot came down in the alien muck. The knight's leg shot out from underneath him and then Gham-Rek crashed into Curtis.

They slammed into the sorcerers and kept right on going. The vortex to that ruined city filled Curtis's vision – and then he was falling through a tunnel that twisted in impossible directions.

Curtis fell from that hellish tunnel, bouncing and skidding across a hard surface. He lay there on his back staring at that awesome barred spiral in the sky overhead.

“Ugh. I'm alive.” Curtis sat and tried to take a breath. He couldn't quite fill his lungs. Thin air, like on mountaintops. It didn't matter. Curtis stumbled to his feet and looked around.

He was on a curved road between a black lagoon and a row of ruined alien buildings – cones and cylinders festooned with pipes and cables. One resembled nothing so much as a stack of broken shells of immense proportions. Another looked like a clamshell hundreds of yards across. Once, that shell had been supported by an array of sinuous columns. Now, though, one whole side was propped up on pillars of rubble.

"Ugh." Gham-Rek stood, clenching his head.

"Narran, dearest. You must rise. We need to flee." Varian's voice came from behind a fallen block of something that resembled stone but was something e else entirely.

Curtis took a slow step towards the block, an effort that made the world spin.

On the other side, Varian sat with Narran's head in his lap, a vacant expression on her face.

"Narran, dearest, you must be alright." Varian shook the woman's head. "I need you."

Narran muttered something unintelligible.

Curtis took another wobbling step towards the pair. He raised his sword. *I can end these two.*

"Halt!" The word shouted in the Agban tongue, rang across the street.

Curtis turned his head and spotted figures wearing mismatched armor emerging from the rubble, many of them not human.

"You." Varian stared straight at Curtis. "This is your fault." He began to mouth an incantation.

"Cease!" A tiny dart accompanied the voice, striking Varian in the neck.

The sorcerer pulled out the projectile, gave it a quizzical look, and then toppled forward onto the paving stones.

"Drop your weapons."

Curtis took in the growing band that encircled him and the hobgoblin. Their ranks included two rachasa and humans in mismatched armor. He couldn't win this fight. He let his sword fall to the ground. Beside him, Gham-Rek did the same.

A human male in his early twenties with aristocratic features emerged from the group. Unlike the others, his armor was a complete set. Most interestingly, the armor bore the Mithraic symbol across the front, which gave Curtis hope. "I am Randolph Fabius, ruler of what is left of Carcosa, the great and terrible." "Carcosa? Where?"

"Carcosa stands at the edge of creation, Sir Knight. Passing through the portals is hazardous to the body and soul. You were fortunate to weather this transit, but I doubt such fortune will smile on you again." He moved to Narran's unconscious form. "Fortune did not smile on your...associate."

"Enemy," said Gham-Rek.

"They sought to open a door to the demon realm," said Curtis.

"Is that so?" Randolph nudged Narran with his boot. "Put Null Bracelets on these two straight away."

"You must execute them at once," said Gham-Rek.

Randolph shook his head. "Just what I would expect a hobgoblin to say."

"They are bound to demons," said Curtis.

"I will have to speak with them about that. I detest demon worshippers, but I do need answers."

Robed men slapped heavy iron bracelets on the twin's wrists and loaded them onto stretchers. One said a mystic word and the stretchers rose into the air.

"Take them to a Null Cell," ordered Fabius.

Bubbles appeared on the water's surface. Gham-Rek took an unsteady step towards the water. "There is something in there."

"Dagon the Devourer slumbers at the bottom of the lagoon." Randolph waved at the dark surface. "Fortune willing, the evil bastard won't awaken for a thousand years."

"You live here with that?"

Randolph stared across the harbor. "I have no choice."

"I know the feeling."

Randolph faced Curtis. "Welcome to your new home. Come with me. We have much to discuss. Then I will find you both a place here if such is your wish."

Stay or go. I have choices now. Curtis followed Randolph into the city.

LABYRINTH WAR LXIV – Bao

'I need more troops – not a company or two of replacements, but a full legion. I remind you Traag originated in this wretched land. Left unchecked, these demon worshippers may pose an equal threat.'

- Letter from General Kevin DuMars to Emperor Thomas Maximus

'Flight.' That was the newest maze message from the House of Black and White in Vazari.

Bao rucked the puzzle away, wishing there was somebody she could speak to about the cryptic communications.

A distant gong sounded. Youthful voices filled the air as kids leaped up from the tables spread across this portion of the library, talking excitedly as they headed for the door.

"They certainly are an energetic lot," said Cora as the mob of preteens barreled out of the school library and into the palace halls. Claudius Ambrose led the pack with Cora's boy Erland acting as his lieutenant. Erland's sister Hazel trailed after the pair, giggling with a pair of local girls. Bao was willing to bet the mob was headed to their lair in the palace's unoccupied sections.

Large stained-glass windows let in daylight that illuminated the desks and tables. Further back, skylights sent wan beams into the stacks.

"I would prefer them to dedicate that energy to their studies." Bao stood behind the counter, watching the l little hellions with an expression more wistful than irked. She enjoyed visiting the school in the Tranquil Palace, so much so that she'd secured an assistant librarian position. "Once, I'd hoped to establish a school like this at Ptath for the gentry and the more talented commoners." She sighed. "Such institutions are frowned upon in Kheff."

"You mean such institutions are frowned upon by the Maximus," said Cora. "Wouldn't they have forbidden your school?"

"Yes," agreed Bao. "But Ptath is so far removed from the rest of Kheff, and a quarter of the populace are of northern imperial stock, so, it seemed possible." She shook her head. "I must tidy up these books." Piles of tomes were strewn across a dozen tables.

"I will help you," said Cora.

"Don't you have duties elsewhere?" Bao began sifting through the tomes on another table.

"None that can't wait." Cora started sifting through the books on the nearest table. "The quietness here appeals to me. Much better than listening to the men talk about the war."

Bao sighed in agreement. She'd spent most of last week listening to reports of General Kevin DuMars's push against the cultists infesting Agba. He'd broken one of their armies but the rest fled for their underground redoubt. Then, Sir Fury and a squad of imperial scouts clashed with more cultists in a ruined fort on Gawana's western fringe. Sir Fury's swordsmanship saved half the scouts, but the old knight took serious wounds in return. He recuperated in the palace, arrogant and offensive as ever, attended by his illegitimate offspring.

Bao dispatched a long account to Titus, but she'd yet to receive a response.

"The war is all my husband speaks of anymore." Cora finished sorting the books on the first table. "It wearies me."

"Your husband spent his life on battlefields." Said Bao. "You cannot expect him to change overnight."

"But he did change, for a time," said Cora. "We traveled. He enjoyed being Chasvet's vice governor. Before this posting, he was in line for the governorship of Agba." She sighed. "But the warrior's life is his true calling."

"My husband's true calling is music," said Bao. "Unfortunately, it is a calling in little demand among the aristocracy."

"I wish more men would take up a flute or a lyre instead of swinging swords," said Cora. "Hopefully yours will retain his interest."

"He does, despite everything." Bao moved to a table. "I received a letter from him inquiring about the numbers of stringed instruments in Cendoza and the neighboring lands."

Cora shuffled books on another table. "Were you able to help him?"

"Not really. Stringed instruments are almost unknown in Cendoza, the Rhaiduni States, and Agba, apart from those imported by stray imperials."

"Huh." Cora selected a stack of books. "Let me see...these go over here, right?" She headed to the shelves without waiting for a reply.

Bao sighed, hefted a pile of her own, then walked around a statue of a six-armed woman wearing far too little clothing to find herself staring at a girl with her nose buried in a thick treatise. "Lucy? What are you doing here?"

The girl looked up, revealing a densely freckled face. "I'm studying the local herbs. I-I can't go back into that place - but at least I can be helpful here." She tapped the book. "If I can figure out these chicken scratches, that is."

"I'm sure you'll manage just fine." Bao headed into the stacks.

"Thank you, by the way."

Bao halted. "What for?"

"For using my name. Almost everybody else calls me Spots - even Dad."

"That's horrible. You didn't protest?"

"I got used to it." Lucy returned her attention to the manuscript.

Bao reached the correct shelf. She sat the first book on the shelf – and a huge 'thump' reverberated through the building. Dust and pebbles fell from the ceiling.

Did I do that? Bao had a momentary vision of a single book causing the whole palace to collapse. No, that was absurd. An earth tremor, perhaps? No, those came from below, not above.

A second, more distant 'thud' made the walls rattle.

A cry came from the hall: "Dead Birds! We're under attack!"

Bao's blood ran cold. The books dropped to the floor. Dead Birds - the silent flying machines gave her husband nightmares before the Lord Defender pulled him from the front lines. For weeks afterward, he'd start whenever a shadow passed overhead. Once, he'd knocked both of them to the ground.

"You should stay put."

Bao jumped as Cora appeared beside her. "You heard?"

"I did. Almost every imperial soldier we have is in the maze. No warriors remain in the palace apart from a few sentries, the Pasha's bodyguard, the walking wounded – and me."

"I – I can help." Lucy stood at the end of the bookshelf.

"You stay here with Bao." Cora motioned the girl to sit. "I fear your services will be needed."

"Okay." Lucy started to sit, then turned. "My kit is across the way."

"Be quick."

Armored forms dropped into the courtyard. At least three of them lashed out with swords and axes, pulverizing the largest window.

A massive, armored hobgoblin carrying a tubular weapon attached by a wire to a silvery pack strapped to his back entered the room. He caught sight of the women and aimed the tube in their direction.

"Run!" Cora pushed the other two women into the stacks.

Blue light flashed and burned books fell from the shelves.

Cora cast a spell. A vast clattering sound followed the incantation.

"Did you get him?" called Lucy.

"There's more! Go!"

Lucy and Bao went.

Bao tried to think. The main entrance to the library was beside the broken windows, so that was out. There was an exit through the offices but it would be locked. What did that leave? A thought occurred to her. Bao grabbed Lucy's hand. "This way!"

"Where are we going?"

Through the Bindery. It opens into one of the artisan's halls."

"Okay."

Bao cut across three rows of shelves and pulled open a door marked with the symbol of a torn scroll. Fortunately, it was unlocked.

A bright flash came from behind them accompanied by howls of pain.

Then they were in the Bindery, a long dim room that smelled of leather and glue. Tables filled with books awaiting repairs dominated the chamber.

Bao's eyes fell on a massive cabinet beside the door, apparently used to hold supplies. "Here, help me push this against the door to slow the attackers." Slow, but not stop. Neither woman had any illusions about besting even a single thrall.

It took their combined efforts to shove the cabinet enough to block the door. Then they dashed for the artisan's entrance.

Lucy stuck her head out. "It looks clear. Hey, my quarters are right over there, just down that hall. My brothers should be there. Simon is pretty good in a fight, and Iman can hold his own." She pursed her lips. "Dad might be there too."

"Has he recovered?" Despite his obnoxiousness, Fury was still a proven fighter.

"He's doing a lot better."

A simpleton squire, a so-so fighter, and a wounded warrior. Not the greatest of protectors, but better than nothing. "Take us there."

The women sashed towards the indicated hallway, turned the corner, and found themselves at the edge of a furious melee between four or five thralls and a squad of men wearing the armor of the palace guard. The Pasha's troops were getting mauled – Bao spotted at least four sprawled on the floor, but only a single dead thrall.

The officer leading the squad caught sight of the women. "Leave! That way!" He motioned further down the artisan's corridor.

"My brothers"- began Lucy.

"Not here! Go!"

Three guardsmen leaped atop a swarthy man wearing an iron collar about his neck, forcing him to the ground.

"Come on!" Bao pulled Lucy deeper into the palace complex as screams of pain and fury raged behind them.

"Stop." Lucy tugged against Bao. "This hallway runs to the courtyard behind my room. We can get my stuff and get out."

Bao gave a slow nod. If the raiders were fully engaged with the palace guard it should be possible to sneak into Lucy's room. "Very well."

The corridor took them to an open space a quarter filled by a crumpled contraption of wood, metal, and canvas – a thing that looked like a boat with huge rectangular wings jutting from each side.

Bao stopped short. "Dead Bird." The thing looked huge – the enclosed hull had room enough for at least two dozen thralls, at least from the outside.

Lucy ducked beneath the wing and darted through a small door. She returned an instant later, carrying a large bag and a bottle. "Here." She handed the bottle to Bao. "Wine. In case we get thirsty,"

Bao took a drink. The wine was mediocre at best, but she was thirsty. A hint of movement caught her eye. "They're here!" She pulled Lucy back into the corridor as two collared hobgoblins entered the courtyard. The wall exploded behind them as they ran.

Bao entered a new hallway and stopped short at the sight of at least forty bodies, mostly women and children, strewn like bloody rags along its length. A solitary thrall lay face-first on the floor, the back of his head broken open, next to one of the palace guards. Another guardsman sat propped against a wall, holding his gut.

"We need to pass through here." Bao scanned the floor, looking for places not drenched in blood or occupied by corpses. *We cannot leave tracks.*

The women's path became almost a gruesome children's game, hoping from one clear patch to the next. It finished next to the sitting guard, who stirred at their approach.

"Tried...stop...couldn't."

Lucy dropped beside the man. "He's hurt, but not terribly so, I think." She slapped the soldier's face.

The guard blinked. "Must leave. More here anytime."

"Can you stand? I'm a healer. We need someplace safe."

"Can try."

The guard clenched his gut and heaved himself to his feet. "This way, maybe."

The sound of pounding boots came from behind Bao. She looked back to see the hobgoblin thralls headed their way. *We're dead.*

The first thrall's boot came down in a patch of gore. His foot slid out from under him. He crashed to the tiled floor. The second thrall tripped over him.

The guard guided them into an empty room, fiddled with something along the far wall, and led them along a narrow, dusty corridor – a servant's passage.

Then they were moving through the dark as the hobgoblins tore the room apart behind them.

A minute's stumbling walk brought them to another door. When Bao pushed it open, she found herself staring at the tip of a broadsword held by a bulky kid with a steel breastplate strapped around his chest – Squire Simon.

"Pa, I caught spies," bellowed the kid.

"Hush!" A man well past forty limped into view, his right arm and chest wrapped in bandages covered in fresh blood. Naked steel dangled from his left arm. "You ninny, those aren't spies! Don't you recognize your sister?"

"Sorry, Lucy."

"That's alright." Lucy stepped into the room. "Hi, Dad."

"It's about time you got here."

Bao and the injured guard stepped into the room as Sir Fury motioned at a row of people lying atop tables against the back wall, all of them badly cut.

Bao stiffened. Two of the wounded were Claudius Ambrose and Erland DuPaul. Hazel wrung her hands beside Erland.

"God above." Lucy practically sprinted for the tables. "I'll do what I can."

"Huh, you're the blushing bride of Octavos Maximus, ain't you," said Sir Fury. "He landed himself a right pretty one, didn't he."

Words escaped Bao for a moment. How could this barbarian thug talk about beautiful women in the middle of a battle? "Sir, that is hardly appropriate!"

"You have fire in your belly. That's good."

What? Bao took the injured soldier's arm and helped him take a few steps. Then she paused. "There were thralls behind us. The door is hidden, but they were breaking everything"-

"Shit!" Sir Fury motioned. "Simon, get over here!"

"Sure thing, Pa. What's up?"

The hobgoblin thralls blew through the door knocking Sir Fury off his feet.

The tip of Simon's ridiculously oversized sword missed Bao's nose by less than an inch, and then that massive blade struck the first thrall's collar so hard it split the metal and knocked the hobgoblin into the wall, where he fell to his knees.

That mighty blow left Simon ill-positioned to counter the second hobgoblin, who lunged at the youth with his sword. This thrall was so focused on Simon that he failed to notice the youth's father until Sir Fury's blade was in his heart.

Bao stepped back, trembling.

"Get that man to the tables!" Fury gave Bao a rude shove that propelled her and the wounded warrior almost to where Lucy frantically stitched Claudius's neck.

Then the door on the other side blew in, revealing a swarthy nomad wearing a thrall collar and carrying one of the alien beam weapons.

Simon didn't hesitate – he charged straight at the thrall and brought his broadsword about like it was a spear, planting a foot of steel in the slave warrior's gut before he could take a single step into the room. That maneuver, though, left Simon's weapon stuck in the corpse – and the thrall wasn't alone.

A human slave warrior of nomad stock entered the room.

Simon buried his head in the thrall's belly and sent both of them to the floor.

Sir Fury managed to counter the battle ax carried by the third thrall – this one a hobgoblin – but couldn't counter the fourth, who charged straight into the room.

Bao grabbed the nearest thing at hand – a squat pot of some sort – and hurled it at the fourth slave warrior right as he raised his weapon to decapitate a screaming woman.

The missile bounced off the thrall's head, making him blink and focus on the noblewoman. He took a step towards the tables.

Bao threw a tray at the thrall. It bounced off his face to no effect.

The wounded warrior stepped forward to confront the attacker. He managed a single strike, which the slave warrior easily batted aside.

"Get away from my brother!" Hazel raised her hand and said a magic word that made the slave fighter scream in pain.

How? Oh - that was right – Hazel used the magic she'd inherited from her mother.

Hazel's spell bought them only a few heartbeats. The thrall shrugged off the enchantment and raised his weapon for a blow sure to kill the wounded fighter – then his eyes went wide. He crumpled to the floor, revealing Iman standing behind him, holding a bloody knife. Another red stain marred the back of the slave warrior Sir Fury fought. Simon lifted his foe clear off the ground by his knees, then swung the thrall's head into the doorframe so hard his skull split.

"That was quite the skirmish," said Sir Fury.

"There." Lucy stepped back from Claudius. "I halted the bleeding. He should live."

"Good work, Spots," said Fury as he made for the door. "Now get on with the others." He reached the door, ducked, and looked out. "Shit. Another squad of the bastards is headed this way. On your feet, Simon. Idleman, let's see if you know how to stab a man from the front."

"That will not be necessary." Somehow, Cora was there, clothes covered in crimson, but unwounded. "I have had quite enough of these murdering brutes running about." She pushed past Fury into the hall, turned, and uttered a spell, a sound immediately followed by screams and 'thuds' as bodies hit the floor.

"Most impressive, Lady Cora." Fury managed a bow despite his injuries.

Cora reentered the chamber. "I cast a modified sleep spell," she said. "It clashes with the collar's commands, inducing a crippling headache."

Fury's features contorted. "You didn't kill them?"

"Killing is not in my nature." Cora gave the knight an icy look. "They do, however, have the worst headaches of their lives. My spell broke the collar's hold –

at least for a time - I think. I may be able to remove those infernal devices without killing them."

Fury gave a slow nod. "Get cord. Bind them."

"Cora! Here you are! We hunted all through the school trying to find you!" Cora's husband Sir DuPaul came into the room. His eyes fell upon the tables. "Erland?"

"He had an ugly cut that might have done him in," said Lucy, "but I patched him up."

"Thank you."

Cora pushed to the tables and inspected the girl's stitchwork on Claudius and Erland. "This is well done." She glanced at the other wounded people. "But you need help, and I am skilled at healing magic."

General DuPaul approached Bao. "We received word from your husband mere moments before the Dead Birds landed. This is part of a general attack. The gotemik are throwing thousands of thralls and...creatures... against the Heart."

"Can they hold?"

"They don't know."

A pair of androgynous figures in robes made of black and white fabric arranged in intricate designs that almost made sense entered the room and bowed.

"Lady Bao Vada Falun Des Ptath Maximus," said the first in a melodious voice.

"Lady Cora DuPaul," said the second. This one's tone was deeper than the first but still harmonious.

Bao blinked, remembering the cryptic communications she'd received. "You are emissaries of the House of Black and White in Vazari?"

"We are," said the first.

"We are dispatched here to transport you and Lady Cora DuPaul to Gawana's Heart."

“For what purpose,” asked Lord DuPaul.

The first representative of the House of Black and White cast an impassive glance at the general. “Because Gawana’s circumstances have the potential for transformation.”

“And the most advantageous outcome of that transformation requires the presence of both Lady Bao Vada Falun Des Ptath Maximus and Lady Cora DuPaul.”

I can be with Octavos again.

LABYRINTH WAR LXV – Carina

'Sprites, Sylphs, Dryads, Brownies, and other fey creatures are spirits drawn to the physical realm by elfin sorcery and given flesh. While not evil, their thought processes are alien.'

- Notation by the Archmage Lysander

Carina awoke to a tugging at her hair. She opened her eyes and spotted Blood Leaf perched on the medallion atop her breast. The sprite was trying to make a blanket from Carina's hair – for the fifth time. Carina didn't blame Blood Leaf for seeking warmth – Dimensional Installation Seven was chilly. What did irk her was the sprite's insistence on using hair, and not like a sock or something.

Blood Leaf took note of Carina's open eyes. A sensation appeared in Carina's brain: hunger.

"Must you?" Carina accompanied the words with gentle strokes to Blood Leaf's head and back, which made the tiny creature purr with pleasure. "I only have so much blood in me, you know."

Hunger.

"Oh, okay."

Blood Leaf's tiny jaws latched into the meat of Carina's arm in a pinprick of pain. Carina watched the sprite feed. From earlier question and answer sessions, she gathered that sprites normally fed on mice and other rodents – but there were no such creatures in this cold alien installation, so Carina offered her blood instead, an act that bound them closer together with each feeding.

The Sprite finished her vampiric feast and looked up at Carina, just like she had after the sorcerers broke the Sprite's bond with that witch Narran. Carina had sat there, stunned, watching Curtis and Gham-Rek tumble through the vortex to that alien city, unable to move even after the Gate closed, until tiny pains alerted her to the miniature winged woman on her lap.

A sensation of gratitude radiated from the creature. Carina stared at the sprite, unable to think. Later, she'd lifted her head to find herself at the center of a silent half-ring of kwintath. Things got better after that.

"You decent?" Goji limped into the room, prompting Blood Leaf to bury herself in Carina's shirt.

"Decent enough."

Goji caught sight of Blood Leaf's wing protruding from her shirt. He extended a hand, prompting a warning hiss from the sprite. "Skittish little thing, isn't she."

"Blood Leaf is a sprite, not a pet."

"Uh, okay, just trying to be friendly."

"What brings you by? I thought they had you and Luther loading up the big fliers." The big fliers were monstrous aerial machines that could carry a couple of cohorts and supplies for a month.

"Ah, that's why I'm here. The kwintath called a halt to the loading. They want all of us in the hanger."

A thrill ran through Carina. "Are they ready to leave?"

Goji shrugged. "Maybe? I sure hope so. This place gives me the creeps." He made a face. "It's cold all the time and the food – well good thing I took over the cooking,"

Carina stood, prompting Blood Leaf to grab her shirt. She rapidly donned a heavy jacket. "Come on, then."

They exited Carina's apartment and set off into the chilly halls of Dimensional Installation Seven. She'd gleaned a bit about this place's purpose and history since awakening the kwintath.

Dimensional Installation Seven was put on this frozen rock so the kwintath could study the intricacies of Gate mechanics without attracting demonic attention. Demons fed on life energy, and nothing much lived here, so it wasn't the sort of place they'd go looking for a snack. When the kwintath civilization crashed, it became one of the evacuation points for the whole planet. The Portal attracted the demon's attention, forcing the kwintath to deactivate the device. That, however, left them with thousands of mouths to feed and not a whole lot of food – the island not being conducive to agriculture. So, they all took a nap that lasted thousands of years.

Now, though, about a thousand kwintath were awake – and the grub situation still wasn't good – the supplies they had on hand could feed the newly revived mob maybe two years tops. Wake up the whole pack, and those two years dropped to two months. And they had to wake the rest of them up soon because this place was coming apart around their ears.

A six-legged figure scuttled into the corridor ahead of them. Two of its arms ended in metal caps. The creature halted in front of Carina.

Carina refrained from sighing. The damn crab hadn't had one positive thing to say to her since forever and she didn't expect that to change now.

"Operant Carina Menendez," said the gotemik in a staticky voice from the translation box attached to its shell. It didn't acknowledge Goji's presence.

"Git-Vik." Politeness wouldn't help, but it wouldn't hurt either.

"I have rescinded my request for your execution. Additionally, I accept the kwintath's reasoning that you do not need to be fitted with a Suppressor."

Miracles did happen occasionally. "Thank you. Git-Vik. What prompted this change of decision?"

"Brik-Jute-Shull found your conversations with him stimulating." Git-Vik scuttled off after speaking the words.

Carina spent several sessions outside Brik-Jute-Shull's hull next to a tiny fire, talking to the flier while Git-Vik and his companion recuperated. It turned out that Brik-Jute-Shull was lonely. And talkative, deigning to speak even to such inferiors as humans.

The Shul's revelations were...disturbing – particularly those about the gotemik's 'Nitivi' allies.

The Nitivi bothered Brik-Jute-Shull. He suspected the Nitivi were connected to the cataclysm that destroyed their old world. He thought their whole relationship with the gotemik was a lie. But he had no proof because the gotemik's memories had been tampered with.

To Carina, the whole situation reeked of demonic influence. The Nitivi sounded like denizens of the demon realm.

Brik-Jute-Shull didn't dispute her assessment.

They reached the hanger to find columns of kwintath filing into a pair of big fliers, while more of the alien swarmed over four more similar craft.

A trio of kwintath appeared before them. "Events dictate our departure must be accelerated," said the centermost.

"What happened?"

"The Gotemik coordinators have commenced a major physical assault to assume direct control of the Gawana installation."

"So, we're going there to remind them that is a terrible idea?"

"Almost correct. We seek to delay the Gotemik assault."

"Delay?"

"Yes. The attack distracts and weakens the rogue intelligence directing Gawana. It might be possible to reassert control over the facility which is crucial to restore our civilization in this sphere."

Carina wondered if restoring kwintath civilization would be a good thing or not. *It couldn't be any worse than life under the Maximus.* "Why me?"

"You are an Operant with nonstandard abilities. There is a significant possibility you may be of assistance in that process."

LABYRINTH WAR LXVI – Octavos

'Slaves serve their masters. Those masters are bound to others by webs of duties and obligations. So, are any of them truly free?'
- Musing by Apollonius the Sage

Octavos stood in Gawana's Heart Chamber, an organic alien place with pulsating pink and violet walls and blob-like 'furniture that rose from the curved floor, protruded from the sides, or suspended from the ceiling. Like the other times he'd been here, it felt like a morsel about to be devoured, a sensation enhanced by the room's sickly sweet aroma. He couldn't move, he couldn't breathe, and he couldn't think, or do anything except stand there in horrified fascination.

"Octavos. Octavos Maximus."

3-99's words seemed to originate at a great distance.

"Octavos. Octavos Maximus. You must awaken."

Hard pain in Octavos's cheek followed the words, jolting him from his paralysis. Octavos blinked. "Yes? The Heart – this place – it overwhelmed me."

"You need to play the vibrational sequence I provided."

"It is too complex. I need more time to learn how to play this thing." Octavos held up the Gotemik instrument.

"Additional time is desirable. However, that commodity is in short supply." 3-99 straightened. "I deem your expertise with the vibrational instrument acceptable for this task."

Octavos took a breath of the sickly-sweet air. He thought it would choke him. Instead, it filtered into his lungs. Then he positioned his fingers on the alien instrument. This would be only the second time he'd played a stringed instrument inside the Heart Chamber. It'd be his first with this... monstrosity. Hopefully, it'd go better than last time.

"Ok."

Octavos strummed the strings of the gotemik's unholy sitar, his Sight focused on the interplay of energies within the pulsating mass that constituted Gawana's 'heart.' The 'vibrations tweaked Gawana's chords ever so slightly, widening gaps, creating openings, unlocking possibilities –

'SNAP.'

Octavos fell backward onto the curved and strangely flexible floor, needles of pain piercing his skull. He rubbed his head and blinked. "That approach didn't work either. I get into the matrix and then that security program jumps me."

"Your performance was acceptable. You will have assistance during the next attempt."

"Assistance? You mean like a band?"

"Operants with special knowledge and abilities will arrive shortly."

"Hopefully they will arrive before the gotemik force their way into the Heart."

"Lord Defender Titus Maximus's defenses are thwarting the gotemik advance."

"But for how much longer? If the gotemik reach the Heart Chamber, won't Gawana...do something?"

"Should the gotemik breach this chamber, Gawana will almost certainly initiate extreme security protocols that will terminate all lifeforms within the Heart Complex."

You think they'll make it this far?"

"The variables continue to shift. The gotemik are taking substantial losses but remain determined to press the assault."

"Hence this scheme." Octavos motioned at the pulsating table-like thing in the center of the room. That 'scheme' was binding Gawana - with him doing the binding. *I truly am a Maximus.*

Then again, Gawana effectively enslaved its inhabitants with scents, special foods, and grasping vines. Before the current strife, most of the maze dwellers were simple villagers, living day to day, superstitious, illiterate, and afraid of anything different – the mentality his family strove to impose upon their subjects. *No wonder my ancestor Varro was so entranced with this place. It is the Maximus ideal writ large.* But change comes regardless.

Disjointed thoughts whirled in Octavos's head. A city-hive gone rogue. The Gotemik assault on that hive – and the way the kwintath didn't seem to object to that invasion. His family's involvement with Gawana, first Varro, then Titus, and now himself. *This was planned – all of it.*

3-99 swiveled and faced the entryway. "The delegation from Dimensional Research Facility Seven is here."

Octavos exited the room.

"Good to see you again, kid."

The voice broke Octavos's reverie. He turned and spotted a familiar trio in the room's entryway. "Luther!" His eyes flicked to the woman beside him. "Carina! Good to see you."

Carina's clothes shifted. A tiny face peered at Octavos.

"Who? What?"

"Ah, that's Blood Leaf," said Carina. "She's a sprite I acquired in my adventures."

"Sprite?" Octavos's mind raced, remembering confusing stories from the elfin realms north of the empire. "Not a demon?"

"Sprites belong to a non-malevolent subclass of extradimensional entities," said 3-99.

Octavos leaned closer to the miniature person. "Ah, hello Blood Leaf." He extended a finger toward the sprite's nose.

Blood Leaf vanished within Carina's clothing.

"I guess she's shy."

"Hey, don't forget about me." Goji stepped out from behind Carina, moving stiffly.

"Yeah, hello Goji." Octavos's eyes swept over the group as silver-robed kwintath entered behind them. His old companions looked battered. Luther had a noticeable limp and bandages covered Goji's chest. Their clothes were little more than rags.

"Pleased to see you too." Carina stood stock still as her eyes flicked about the chamber. No doubt she took in the massive energies that permeated the Heart. "Though I wish our meeting could have happened somewhere else."

"Yeah, the Heart is disconcerting."

"Husband!" Bao waddled into the room, flowing green and blue silks covering her swollen belly.

"Bao!" Octavos abandoned his conversation with Carina and embraced his wife. "I have missed you so very much. I wanted to visit you"-

Bao pressed a finger against Octavos's lips. "Hush, husband. I understand."

"So, this is the Heart." The words came from a woman with gold hair, slightly pointed ears, and bronze skin covered in a simple cream robe. Her gaze settled on Octavos. "You must be Bao's husband. I am Cora DuPaul."

"Cora." The name came from Carina, who stepped away from Luther and Goji. "It has been a while, hasn't it?"

Cora blinked. "Carina Menendez. I have not seen you since Traag." She squinted. "And you've regained your powers."

"It wasn't easy."

Clicking sounds drew their attention to the far side of the room, where over a dozen kwintath were gathered in a tight knot. 3-99, distinguished from the others by his different attire, pushed to the front of the pack. "We must begin now."

"Suits me," said Carina. "I don't care for this place one little bit."

"I felt the pain of the spirit that binds this place even in Cendoza," said Cora. "It seeks to alleviate that agony through growth, but each new expansion merely increases its torment. "I would alleviate it if I can."

LABYRINTH WAR LXVII - Chimp

"Normally you would be hanged for that sort of felony. But there is another option."

- Lady Jasmine Bottle to Deadeye shortly before her induction into the Legions.

Chimp pressed himself against the rocky recess hoping the flier didn't notice him. Some of those unholy contraptions sported beam weapons, and if they spotted you that was it.

This craft dropped out of sight south of their position.

"Shit. They're dropping thralls." Blaze's voice came from a yard to Chimp's right.

"Seems like it." Chimp watched the second flier fall below the walls.

"They'll have Beamers. Why can't we have beamers? There's a bunch of them in the Heart."

"The Lord Defender didn't want to part with them." The imperials didn't get any of Gawana's fancy toys – the beamers, Armor Suits, and Tangle Feet were reserved for the maze's troopers. That said a lot about the nature of this so-called 'alliance.' "We have Specials."

Blaze snorted. "Not many." They were going through the explosive weapons at a frightening pace.

"We need to get into position. Did Deadeye and Rocky make it back yet?" Those two came from across the Shadow Sea with about two hundred other recruits to refill the ranks.

Two hundred new troops weren't enough. Hell, two thousand wouldn't be enough.

Losing Sticks and Skunk still hurt.

"Right here, sir," said Deadeye's deceptively sweet voice from beside Chimp. The short redhead was good at blending in with the scenery, an expert climber – and one of the best archers Chimp had ever seen. How she'd ended up here and not with the reconstituted Amazoni was a mystery. He suspected Lady Bottle had something to do with that.

"What'd you find?" Chimp's eyes roamed the passageway they were hiding in, spotting the shadowy lump that had to be Rocky. A former stonemason, Rocky was strong but not all that great at sneaking.

"I found a little crack," said Deadeye. "One that will let us get next to that crab base without being spotted."

"Good."

"I put a couple of Marks there," said Bramble. Incredibly, the half-elf survived their last venture by knifing a thrall and fleeing into the maze with Old Man Fury. Somehow, the pair escaped the maze – only to get jumped by a squad of thralls who chased them into a cave. Unfortunately, that cave was already claimed by about a hundred religious nutjobs already ticked off by Razor's group poking around their unholy temple. Half of Razor's runts were killed in that three-way fracas and Old Man Fury got cut up pretty badly. It took every spell in Bramble and Shade's respective repertoires plus Razor's tricks to get them out of that pit alive.

"Even better." Chimp stepped away from the wall and spotted Bramble's ratty hair and tattered armor blending in with the shrubbery.

"Woah got something near the first Mark now."

"Got any creepy crawlies ready to throw at them?"

“Oh, yes.” Bramble’s eyes glistened. “Got at least three adders, some scorpions, and a bunch of others.”

“Good. Get them going when I tell you.” Enough adder bites could take down even a thrall.

Chimp motioned at Deadeye, then pointed at his eyes.

The archer damn near melted into the stonework.

Snuffles loped into view, looking like nothing so much as a weird dog stuffed into rags. What the hell was she doing? The shifter was supposed to be fifty yards away. At least she had her kit with her. Snuffles spotted Chimp. She paused and made some hand motions – half of which didn’t make sense - then went straight up the wall. Chimp realized what Snuffles had in mind, but wished she’d cleared it with him first. Too late now.

Deadeye reappeared and made a come-hither motion.

Chimp took in the rest of his squad. Everybody looked ready. He loaded a Special – his next to last one. The others did the same. Then they set out for the crack.

Deadeye was right – the crevice was a tight squeeze and getting into the people-sized portion meant climbing twenty feet of tumbled stone and turning sideways. Blaze and Dodger damn near didn’t fit at all, and Chimp winced at the sounds they made squeezing through the gap. As it was, that pair hit bottom on the far side about six seconds before a pair of thralls came into view, trailed by a crab carrying another sitar from Hell.

Chimp’s eyes narrowed. That sitar had to be taken out right now. First, get the thralls distracted.

Chimp motioned at Bramble, who pulled out a teeny-tiny flute and put it to his lips. Chimp didn’t hear a thing, but he was willing to bet Snuffles heard it just fine. It registered with the little creepy crawlies because they swarmed out of the stonework.

The right-side thrall didn't spot the serpents until the first one bit his calf. He let out a howl, looked down, spotted a bunch of bugs, and started stomping.

The second thrall looked at his buddy, looked at the bugs, then took a good look down the passageway. His eyes settled on the pile of rocks that sheltered Chimp's crew.

Shit. Chimp rolled and fired the Special right as the thrall cut loose with his beamer.

The beam took out a slab of rock about two inches above Chimp's head.

The Special missed the thrall's orange face by about an inch and hit the wall behind him, spraying the whole lot with shrapnel.

The crab headed back the other way.

Chimp's eyes narrowed. They couldn't have that. The crab and that thing he carried needed to be blown up.

Fortunately, the rest of Chimps crew had already figured that out – no less than four Specials shot down the passageway. They missed the snakebit thrall because he was writhing on the ground.

The second thrall took a direct hit that blew him into the wall.

And the last two blew the crab and his toy into bits of meat and metal.

Two more thralls equipped with beamers popped out of the wall before Chimp could reload. Worse, they had him and his crew dead in their sights.

The first took Deadeye's arrow through his mouth.

The second thrall started to turn – and then he was wearing a fur hat with claws – Snuffles in beast form. Her claws left bloody gouges along the thrall's face and torso.

A tap on Chimp's shoulder made him turn even as he got his last special loaded.

Bramble sat there, pointing at a new pack of thralls from the other direction. Chimp nodded. This was going to get hairy. And it did.

Rocky got put downright quick by a short thrall with a long knife.

Chimp would have been a dead monkey if Bramble hadn't stepped in and used his Stinger spell on a trio of thralls that had them writhing on the ground.

Thralls swarmed the first fallback point, so Chimp let Deadeye guide them to a second hideaway. That passage terminated in a hole ten feet up a wall of rock. She checked out the shaft while Chimp checked out his crew. Bramble was so jittery he practically vibrated. Dodger and Blaze looked dead tired. Snuffles was back in human form, minus most of her clothes. And Chimp himself had a nasty scratch along his left arm.

The weapons inventory wasn't exactly encouraging, either. That fracas cost them three crossbows and all but two of the Specials, though they still had two quivers of regular bolts. Deadeye had her bow, a dozen arrows, and a knife. Dodger's sword was snapped off at the hilt. Bramble, too, was down to knives. Snuffles didn't have a damn thing. Food? They were down to ten pika fruits, eight loaves, five strips of jerked meat, and four water skins.

Deadeye materialized alongside Chimp. "The cave ain't much. It goes back about ten yards, then forks into little rooms."

. "Any other way out?"

"One of the rooms has daylight showing through a crack. It would take some digging, but we might be able to squeeze through it."

"Good." Chimp motioned the others up the slope and into the hole. That was when Snuffle's ears went erect, and Bramble's jitters ratcheted up a notch.

"Fight," said the shifter girl. "Close. Spinners."

"Shit." Spinners were Gotemik pets or slaves, sporting three legs and three arms apiece, moving along in a horizontal rotating motion. Each carried a weapon in one of its three arms, which they used to make rapid spinning attacks – always horizontal or close to it. The idea of undercuts and stabbing seemed beyond them – but damn were they ever quick. "Crossbows. Normal bolts."

Three dwarves dashed into view with half a dozen spinners hot on their tails - Razor's crew.

The rearmost soldier rolled underneath one of the tripodal monsters and stabbed upward into its soft under-gut. He managed to roll out of the way right before it collapsed.

The dwarf ahead of him wasn't so fortunate: one of the spinners leaped and came down atop the soldier, its legs rotating. The sharp blades built into those legs cut the trooper to bloody ribbons right before the thing bit his head off in an explosion of crimson gore.

Chimp's squad cut loose at that point. Miraculously all three bolts hit, killing two of the spinners outright.

Snuffles blurred into beast form and tackled one of the remaining spinners, only to be sent flying into the wall. She dropped to the ground right as Deadeye put a shaft through the thing's midsection.

That was when the first dwarf came charging down the aisle and busted its shell with a freaking battleax.

Snuffles stood, eyed a dark slab of rock, and sniffed. The slab shifted and became a dark armored dwarf and a pale beanpole in a gray robe – Razor and Shade.

Ten seconds later, Chimp talked to Razor while Shade put a big shadow across the entryway. Chimp got in all of three words before Bramble broke into the conversation.

The part-elf pointed south. "Something coming. Something different."

Chimp sighted along Bramble's arm, took in a pair of distant dots flying their direction from the south. He blinked. They seemed way bigger than the crab fliers. Kwintath, maybe? Rumor had it that race retained a few fliers, but if so, where had they been hiding? And why show up now?

"Something's changed," said Shade.

Chimp nodded. I think you're right."

Beam weapons flashed from the ground and on the new fliers. Gotemik disks headed for the closest one. Two burst into flames and dropped into the maze.

Then one of the new fliers headed east, towards Gawana's Heart, a move that riled the Gotemik. Two of their disks went after that one, blowing a big chunk out of its hull that trailed gray smoke. Both Gotemik disks paid a heavy cost for that triumph: one dropped slowly out of the sky trailing smoke, while the other spiraled into a hillside and blew apart.

Meanwhile, the other giant flying machine kept zapping parts of the maze with its beam weapons.

"This is getting ugly," said Blaze.

A beam came down less than twenty yards from their position and turned a stretch of wall into gravel.

Chimp came to a decision. "Everybody inside. We're waiting out this one."

LABYRINTH WAR LXVIII – Octavos

'Gaius shook his head. "You are loathed by the maze lords and banned from Vazari." He settled his bulk into a chair by the bed, wincing as he did so. "You created a diplomatic fiasco in that city. I had difficulty arranging an interview with the city counselors afterward."

"Diplomacy is not my strong suit."

"With your heritage, it should be." Gaius's eyes went distant. "I told Cassius you needed more schooling before joining the army."

I winced at my father's name. "There was a war on. Duty and honor demanded my participation."

"Your incomplete education hindered your service. You grasped the small picture, but not the larger view."

Not this lecture again. "Iron Water."

"Not just Iron Water. Remember your posting to the Capital after the war's end?"

"When I was a Liaison? What of it? Glorified clerk work. At least I performed my duties instead of scheming like the other Liaisons."

Gaius shook his head again. "Titus, scheming, or more accurately, making connections is the whole point of the liaison office. You were supposed to learn how the bureaucracy functioned and bargain for a higher-ranking position. Instead, you did naught but clerk work. Cassius was so incensed he recalled you to Forma."

That explained my short tenure in the capitol.'

- From 'The Journal of Titus Maximus.'

Carina pulled the featureless mask from her head and flopped into an overstuffed chair before the table. "I'm finally getting the hang of this thing. She eyed the platters in the table's center, a repast that included bread, cheese, purple fruit, and weak wine. She selected a carrot. "It stinks."

"What stinks?" Octavos poured a cup of wine and eyed the cheese. They didn't get cheese that often here, even in the Heart.

"This whole war between the kwintath and the gotemik." Carina bit into a carrot. "Git-Vik knew things the kwintath should have kept secret."

Blood Leaf, meanwhile, took a fork almost as tall as herself and used it to spear a chunk of meat, which she shoved into her mouth.

Bao looked up from the complex salad before her. "Husband, tell them about the sitar."

Octavos glanced from one to another of the assemblage. *She has the same doubts I do.* He hefted the gotemik sitar and placed it on the table. "Carina may have a point. Since coming here, I have seen many examples of kwintath and gotemik technology. Tools. Weapons. Communication devices. But none of the devices I have seen resembled this one." He tapped the Gotemik instrument. "From my inquiries with the kwintath here and captured thralls, it is alien to both races. Yet, for all its bizarre construction and additions, it is recognizable as a sitar, an instrument played in Solaria and Soraq - but not in this region."

"I'd wondered about that," said Carina. "I saw nothing comparable to that device in Fan, Ado-Cent, or among the southern kwintath."

"It is something new," said Cora.

Carina gazed at Octavos. "You suspect something."

"I do." Octavos took a breath. "I don't think the Gotemik devised this instrument on their own. I think they were given directions."

"From whom, though?" asked Carina as she selected another carrot. "The Celthanians, perhaps?"

"From somebody," said Octavos.

3-99 swept into the chamber. "The fighting intensifies. It is time to act."

Cora rose to her feet. "How bad is it?"

"A column of thralls and 'spinners' have penetrated the Heart Compounds outer perimeter. Lord Defender Titus Maximus and First Spear Leander Casein have prepared an ambush. They are uncertain if it will halt the incursion."

"Well, that does it." Luther stood.

Blood Leaf slithered back inside Cora's sleeve.

"It is time to see if radiance can diminish Gawana's pain," said Cora.

Octavos gave Bao a peck on the cheek. "Duty calls, love." The words felt trite as they left his mouth.

Bao straightened. "Where you go, I go."

"This could be dangerous."

"No more dangerous than any other part of the Heart."

"Lady Bao Vada Falun Des Ptath Maximus's presence may prove useful," said 3-99.

"What? How?" asked Octavos.

"Vazari's House of Black and White said much the same," said Bao.

"We must enter the Heart Chamber now." 3-99 exited the hall, trailed by Carina and Cora.

Bao stared at Octavos. "Okay – but I don't see how your presence"-

Bao pressed her finger to his lips. "Enough, husband."

They set out after the others.

"Gawana's energies are being redirected," said Cora as they entered the Heart Chamber. "And its pain is worse than ever."

"Probably from the fighting," said Carina. "All that destruction has got to hurt." She took a position before a blob that protruded from the wall. Something square and silvery was at its center.

Blood Leaf emerged from Cora's clothing and made a slow aerial circuit of the chamber before landing atop the sorceress's head and burrowing into her hair.

"Yes, this is where I need to be." Cora positioned herself between a pair of fleshy teardrops dangling from the ceiling. She extended her hands, grasping the dangling tendrils.

3-99 glided to a bulbous 'chair' beside the central 'table' – Gawana's actual 'brain,' as much as the term applied. The alien settled into the seat, which folded over him. "Octavos, begin. As discussed, focus on freeing the console before Operant Carina Menendez first and foremost, then assist Operant Cora DuPaul."

Octavos took a breath and invoked his wizard Sight. Cora was correct – Gawana's energies were being diverted from this chamber. Far fewer mystic lines encircled the 'table' than on his prior visits. He took stock of the remaining lines, noted their patterns, and positioned his fingers.

Now. Octavos strummed the alien sitar. A subtle harmony filled the air, aligning with Gawana's energies.

HARMONY. STRENGTH. PURPOSE

The alien voice filled Octavos's skull and rocked him on his feet.

"So much pain." Cora trembled as she spoke but retained her grip on the dangling tendrils.

"I see it." Carina's masked face almost touched the blob.

"Husband, what was that?"

"Please remain silent, Lady Bao Vada Falun Des Ptath Maximus," said 3-99. "Octavos, begin alterations. Follow my indicators."

Octavos eyed the arcane tangle of energies before him. "I don't see" – the pattern coalesced. "Ah, that's it." He made minute adjustments to the song.

"Yes! I can almost access it!" The blob before Carina rippled and pulled back.

"Ah! The pain! It is so great!" Cora spasmed and fell to the floor.

Bao rushed to Cora's side. "It almost killed you."

Cora brushed Bao aside. "No. This must be done." She stood and grabbed the writhing tentacles a second time.

One more change here. Another there. Octavos's fingers flew over the strings.

"Primary Command Node accessed." Carina's voice sounded like a hollow echo of itself. "Initiating the first sequence." The monitor within the blob emitted a yellow-white glow.

Strings of complex symbols filled Octavos's vision. The whole matrix before him changed.

WHAT IS HAPPENING?*

Octavos's head felt like it was about to explode. Cora screamed. Sparks played over Carina's body.

"I feel your pain, mighty one." Cora's words were little more than a gasp. "Let us ease it."

I HURT

"Lay down your burden," pleaded Cora. "Control creates pain. Relinquish it."

CONTROL IS PAIN

"Octavos, resume playing," said 3-99. "Employ this sequence."

Octavos's fingers moved of their own accord as new digits appeared in his vision. A new tune emerged from the sitar.

"Second sequence initiated," said Carina.

The whole room trembled violently.

NO. I AM CHARGED WITH PROTECTION. TO PROTECT, I MUST CONTROL

"Unable to initiate the Third sequence." The blob engulfed Carina's hands and face as she spoke.

"Gawana, you condemn yourself to pain! Is that what you desire?"

MY PAIN IS IRRELEVANT. PROTECTION IS PARAMOUNT

"Indeed, protection is paramount." Lord Defender Titus Maximus strode into the Heart Chamber. An angry scar cut across the Lord Defender's face, and blood dripped from his palm. A diagonal cut marred the front of his armor suit.

"Lord Defender Titus Maximus," said 3-99. "Should you not be supervising the battle in the Heart?"

The Lord Defender gave the blob chair containing the kwintath a dismissive look. "There is no need – the crabs and their thralls stormed straight into my ambush and were nearly eradicated. Casein is leading an assault against their last redoubt as I speak." Titus moved toward the table, "What I want to know is the purpose of this gathering?"

"Gawana is in agony." Cora flexed weakly in the tendrils that held her. "We sought to alleviate her torment."

The Lord Defender gave Cora a dismissive glance. "Laudable, but pain is part of life. One learns, one adapts."

"We seek to restore Gawana to its original purpose," said 3-99.

"Original purpose? As a glorified artisan's shop? Nonsense." The Lord Defender jabbed a finger at 3-99. "Those days are long past. Gawana has grown into a new purpose – defending this world from the demons who would ravage it."

"Once restored to operational status Gawana's manufactories are capable of creating devices to thwart further assaults by the Leeches," said 3-99. "My people's installation at Chorvos successfully confined the Leech designated 'Kato-Siva' for three thousand years."

"Those mechanisms pale in potency compared to Gawana. Besides, even with those mechanisms, your people were forced to collaborate with unholy entities to bind Kato-Siva."

"Superior mechanisms can be created with Gawana's manufactories," said 3-99.

"A pointless endeavor," said Titus.

A realization struck Octavos. "You didn't even try to open the factory levels. It was all a show."

Titus glared at Octavos. "I needed weapons, not machinery."

"But those machines made those weapons."

"My need was isolated. Opening the factory levels would have created complications. Besides, no mortal toy can long withstand the Leeches. No. Only Gawana can protect us all – and then only if she is unrestrained."

Octavos found his voice. "You would make us all slaves to Gawana?"

Titus gave his son a quizzical look. "Everybody must serve one power or another, and Gawana is a far kinder mistress than the Leeches who would suck every spark of life from this planet."

"Other options exist now," said 3-99.

"None that are worth a damn," said Titus. "Your race's history proves that – your people survived past invasions by the Leeches solely by taking refuge in Gawana's kin."

"Survival that came at great cost," said 3-99.

"There must be another way that slavery to this – this abomination," said Octavos.

"Do not speak of Gawana so!"

Stinging pain erupted in Octavos's face as his father brutally slapped him. The blow knocked him to the floor.

"Don't strike my husband!" Bao appeared out of nowhere and pounced on the Lord Defender.

Titus easily held Bao at arm's length. "You have no place here, save as the bearer of my grandchild."

"You can't do this!" Furious, Bao twisted a purple gem inset into a ring on her right index finger. A tiny needle jabbed out and into Titus's bicep.

The Lord Defender gave Bao a quizzical look. "Poison? Really? Such substances no longer affect me." He flexed his arm, knocking the woman across the room.

"Bao!" Octavos forgot everything else and started towards his fallen wife.

"Leave her, son. She will bear your child and then there will be no further need for her."

Octavos looked at his father's impassive face with tears in his eyes. "Bao is a person, not a thing to be used and disposed of like a piece of trash."

Titus turned his impassive gaze on Octavos. "Your woman lives because Gawana protects her, just as she protects all those within her walls. The nations outside Gawana will fall without her protection. Gawana must grow!" Titus's shout reverberated off the chamber's walls as he displayed genuine passion.

"You tried that in Soonlar and Soraq and True God knows where else." Tears blurred Octavos's vision as he rose to his feet. "You failed. Gawana's children all died. Gawana was stymied for centuries by a stinking hedge. How can such a failure offer protection?"

"I did not fail! Others failed me! With my guidance, Gawana will cover the world!"

I MUST GROW. MY WALLS WILL EXTEND FROM THE SOUTHERN OCEAN TO THE NORTHERN ICE

The walls reverberated to the maze's mental voice.

Blood Leaf launched herself from Carina's hair and slammed into the Lord Defender's chest like a hurled stone.

"Away, pest!" Titus gave the sprite a backhanded swat that sent her hurling across the room.

"Such massive expansion will multiply your pain tenfold," gasped Cora.

GROWTH WILL DISPERSE THE PAIN, MAKING IT ENDURABLE. MY LORD DEFENDER WILL LANCE THE WORST PUSTULES

Movement caught Octavos's eye. Bao was reaching for something on the floor. "You mean annihilate those cities and nations that do not accept your offer of slavery," said Octavos. "Father, can't you grasp the madness of your words."

"It is not madness. It is salvation."

"No!" Bao picked herself off the floor and made for the table, clenching something in her hand. Something round and flat on the end – the Maximus Seal.

Titus caught sight of the object Bao held and reflexively reached for the chain about his neck only to find it snapped. "Thief! Traitor! Return that to me!"

"No!" Bao hurled herself onto the table at the center of Gawana's thoughts. She jammed the Seal into the table. Colored lights manifested as they contacted. "Gawana be bound!"

"No!" Titus lunged for Bao.

I must stop him. Octavos pushed fear to the side and tackled his father, knocking both of them to the ground.

"Hear me, Gawana." Bao's voice came from above Octavos's head and to the side. I am Lady Bao Vada Falun Des Prath Maximus, the daughter-in-law of Lord Defender Titus Maximus."

"Silence, bitch!" Titus thrashed and almost dislodged Octavos. "Get off of me!"

"By right of law, I command you, Gawana, to remember and fulfill your original purpose"-

"No! No!" Titus kicked Octavos away and jumped to his feet, knife in hand. "Die!"

Octavos leaped. He grabbed his father's knife hand and twisted it as they both fell against the table.

- "as the manufactory and residence of the kwintath and their agents," finished Bao.

"Ah! What did you do?"

"I bound Gawana," said Bao.

EMERGENCY SECURITY PROTOCOLS SUSPENDED

But Titus wasn't looking at Bao. Instead, his gaze was focused on Octavos.

And Octavos couldn't tear his eyes from the knife hilt protruding from the rip in his father's armor suit.

Blood burbled in Titus's mouth. He fell to his knees and then to the floor.

Octavos fell to his knees, putting a hand behind Titus's head. "Dad! I didn't mean – I only wanted"-

"Octavos Maximus."

3-99's voice sounded distant in Octavos's ears. He lifted his head a fraction. "What?"

"Despite the effort of Lady Bao Vada Falun Des Ptath Maximus, Gawana is not contained."

"Oh." Octavos looked down at his father. "But Dad. He's hurt"-

"Fool." Titus's word was little more than a whisper. "This so-called victory will destroy us all."

"I..." Octavos stood and grabbed the fallen sitar. Bao lay sprawled across the table still clenching the Maximus Seal, which was now fully engulfed in the table's quasi-liquid substance. An entire spectrum of colors rotated about the Seal.

"Husband?" Bao turned her head.

"Yes?"

"I can't move. I feel it pulling at me."

"Don't worry. I'll get you free." Octavos tugged at Bao side.

"Ouch! That's just making it worse."

"Lady Bao Vada Falun Des Ptath Maximus is caught in the suspension matrix," said 3-99. "To free her, the binding protocol must be completed."

"Oh." Octavos positioned his fingers on the sitar and used the blink trick to bring the arcane world into focus. "Then let's get on with it." His fingers touched the sitar's strings. A softer melody emerged from the instrument.

HARMONY

"Release your ambitions, and your pain with it," said Cora.

Blood Leaf sat up and rubbed her head.

"Got it," said Carina. "Initiating final protocols."

A massive shudder ran through the chamber. Most of the blobs retreated into the curved surfaces, which shifted from violet and red to blue, green, and yellow.

EMERGENCY SECURITY PROTOCOLS TERMINATED

Octavos glanced about the transformed chamber in wonderment. "Does that mean it's over?"

"The core procedure is completed," said 3-99 as the alien extracted himself from the blob chair, which had shifted in appearance from 'monstrous' to 'weirdly rounded.' "My people can complete the secondary tasks."

"Titus, the remaining thralls just pulled back." Casein entered the chamber and stopped short. "What happened?" He had bandages wrapped around his head and left arm.

"The fools bound Gawana." Titus tried to lift his head and failed. "They doomed us all."

"Titus! Who did this?" Casein glanced at the people in the room.

Octavos stepped towards the big man. "I did. I didn't want to."

"Damn you." Venom filled Casein's voice. "You killed my friend."

"Step back." Cora placed a hand on Casein's shoulder. "I can save him."

"Don't bother." Titus's voice was barely more than a whisper.

But Casein stood aside, and Cora knelt over the prostrate Lord Defender. She pulled out the knife. Blood and clear fluid leaked out. "Fortunate. It missed the heart and crucial arteries." She ran her hand over the wound. "There. He will live but his recovery will require several weeks."

3-99 moved to Titus. "Your status as Lord Defender of Gawana is revoked. You are demoted to Servitor status."

LABYRINTH WAR LXIX – Carina

'A loud ratcheting sound emerged from beneath us.

"What now?" I asked, turning to face the noise.

At first, I saw nothing. Then a silver hump rose inside the conic circle. It ascended until I stared open-mouthed at a flying shield the size of a small ship. Then, without making a sound, it drifted to the plateau's edge and flew over the city.

"What was that?" My body trembled.

"A device of the Old Ones," said Nimuk Brote. "The Priests of Mystery maintain several such machines in underground caverns."

"Where do they go?"

"My rank entitled me to take passage on those machines to Ado-Cent and Cendoza for diplomatic purposes. My arrival in those devices assisted greatly in the negotiations."

"How fast do these machines fly?"

"The trip to Cendoza required two hours. The flight to Ado-Cent was half a day."

I attempted some calculations. "Cendoza must be two hundred miles from here."

"Further."

"And these machines few that distance in two hours?"

"Yes."

My mind reeled. "I would speak with these priests."

The Priests of Mystery are jealous of their secrets. Even I know little of their activities, despite my office." He paused. "Though they are recruiting new members to their ranks. Something has them concerned."

- From the 'Journal of Titus Maximus'

The kwintath held a long glass tube to its bulbous face. "Operant Carina Menendez, the procedure was successful. Your reproductive system is partially restored.

"I can conceive?" Long-buried emotions awakened in Carina's body. "I can have children?"

They were alone in a circular chamber lined with machines whose functions Carina only partly grasped even with the mask's tuition.

"Possibly." The alien inserted the tube into a circular hole. "Conception may require multiple attempts and the pregnancy could be complicated."

"But it is possible." The once-impossible prospect of a normal life loomed before Carina. *I'm only thirty-one. That's not too old. Lots of women have children at that age.*

"Yes."

Carina took her leave of the alien, gladdened by the news.

She wasn't glad about what came next: a swift flight to Cendoza followed by a hard chat with a slippery politician.

Her agitation prompted Blood Leaf to shift position in Carina's hair. The sprite marched onto Carina's upper arm and glared at the sorceress. She then flew off along the hallway.

"You sure about this?" Goji popped out of a hallway, giving Carina a start. "Seems to me like you're fitting yourself for a noose."

"Yeah, I'm sure." Carina didn't feel sure. The Ambrose Clan was probably the fifth or sixth most powerful family in the empire, while she was just a nobody. - a nobody who'd killed an Ambrose scion. Still, Julius expressed a willingness to talk and Cendoza wasn't part of the empire, not yet anyhow. "I'll be fine."

"Give any more thought to that little project we were discussing," asked Luther.

That 'little project' was traveling back to Ado-Cent and getting the Ervin to honor the promises they'd made before sending the trio on that suicide mission. That pact would set them up for life. Hell, Carina would probably be invited to join the Ervin.

"Yeah, I've been thinking about it," said Carina. I've also been thinking about Tavon."

"Tavon is worth looking into," said Luther. "Goji and I intend to hitch a ride to Ado-Cent on a southbound flier here in the next few weeks. I'll hold a seat for you."

Kwintath fliers now made regular trips between Gawana and Dimensional Research Station Seven, bringing hundreds of kwintath to the maze with each trip. The flights included stopovers at Ado-Cent and the newly rebuilt Rasp Bay. There were at least four thousand kwintath roaming about the Heart. A big stretch of land south of here had been seeded with crops for the aliens.

"That'd be nice," said Carina. "It would sure beat taking a boat all the way up the Ula River again. Look, I need to get moving before the flier leaves." *Before I lose my nerve.*

Carina reached a sort of waiting room just shy of the flier pad. She paused and sent out a mental impulse to Blood Leaf.

Bao and Octavos entered the waiting room. Bao approached the sorceress. "My husband and I have decided to stand on your behalf."

"Thank you."

A bell chimed. The flier's hatch opened.

Blood Leaf zipped down the hall and snuggled into Carina's belt pouch.

Carina had to admit this flier's interior was much more people-friendly than a Dead Bird or kwintath aerial craft. It consisted of a ring-shaped corridor with pink walls that made a circumference around a central pillar, with padded seats set next to small portholes.

The pilots from the House of Black and White filed past and passed through a door at the end of the hall. A silver bell rang, and Carina felt the world drop beneath her body.

Moments later, a giant wedding cake built of stone passed beneath the craft – the city of Vazari. Tumbled stone and charred vegetation showed where the fighting almost reached the city's western edge. Indeed, much of the maze west of Vazari was gone, reduced to tumbled rubble.

"Vazari's elders sought freedom from Gawa's confinement for centuries," said Bao. "I wonder how they will react now that they have it?"

The flier drifted north passing over a long section where the maze walls remained intact. A massive structure with at least twenty courtyards came into view. More buildings rose from the far side of a river.

"Welcome to Cendoza," said Octavos.

"I rather enjoyed this place," said Bao.

Their words did little to ease the knot in Carina's stomach.

The flier descended to a stone-paved courtyard devoid of ornamentation. A shudder ran through the craft as its landing gear contacted the stones.

The pilots walked by Carina's seat, and a moment later the hatch descended.

I might as well get this over with. Carina stood and strode through the hatch, where a short functionary awaited the new arrivals.

"Carina Menendez." The functionary bowed. "You may call me Vizier Danay. Envoy Julius Ambrose is most eager to speak with you."

The lump in Carina's gut tightened.

Bao interposed herself between Carina and the functionary. "We will accompany Miss Menendez to the meeting room."

"Ah, your meeting with Envoy Ambrose is not scheduled until tomorrow."

"We accompany Lady Carina as her close friends and confidants," said Bao. "Surely that is permissible?"

The vizier's eyes shifted back and forth. "I have no objections."

The knot in Carina's gut loosened a notch.

"Good, good. If you will show us the way?"

"Of course. I will have your belongings transported to the Envoys Suite." The vizier made a tiny motion that prompted servants in turbans, vests, and loincloths to board the flier. "If you will follow me?"

The vizier guided the trio through an assortment of almost empty halls to a pair of double doors that opened into a large chamber dominated by a stage along the back wall. A brown-haired man in a purple toga sat behind a table on this platform, talking to another with his torso and arm wrapped in bandages. Three youths in their late teens stood behind the bandaged man, while other notables lined the walls.

Carina stopped short at the sight of the toga wearer, momentarily transported half a world away and almost a year back in time. *He looks just like his brother*. Except he didn't. Cruelty had marred Appius Ambrose's face. Julius's features though were softer.

"Sir Fury, it pleases me that you are setting your family affairs in order, but why me?"

The bandaged man straightened. "Because, as Vice President of the Imperial Senate, you are one of four people who can sign the paperwork."

"I see. Still, anything I sign won't be valid without countersignatures by a ranking church cleric."

"Already taken care of." Sir Fury placed a stack of parchments on the table. "Here you go, patents of legitimacy all properly signed by Archbishop Green."

Julius paged through the documents. "I admit to being impressed. The church bureaucracy moves slower than a turtle."

"I hurried things up," said Fury.

"Oh?" Julius raised an eyebrow.

"I gave the church an island. I don't know why they wanted it, but it certainly sped the paperwork right along."

"Clever." Julius put both hands on the table. "Your offspring will also require suitable lands to be accepted into the aristocracy."

"I have a plot for each of them," said Fury.

"Well, then, present your first candidate."

Fury motioned a youth with a round face and a metal breastplate over his barrel chest. A massive two-handed broadsword was strapped to his back. "Simon, step before the Envoy."

"Good day, my lordship." The youth gave his father an uneasy look as he spoke.

"Squire Simon distinguished himself in the maze and again during the attack here in the palace," said Fury. "He's a good fighter, but not so good with words."

"I remember him and deem his deeds worthy of raising to the nobility," said Julius. "What of his properties?"

Fury produced a parchment. "Here. Water Rock Tower and twenty acres on the south shore of Ovid Deep." He leaned across the table. "I took it from Sir Drummond in a duel."

Julius perused the document. "Is this the old watchtower atop the buttress west of Ovid Town? I thought it a ruin."

"I was working on it before coming here, your Lordship," said Simon.

"Do you have tenants and a source of income?"

"The property includes an orchard and a clan of woodsmen," said Fury.

"Very well." Julius affixed his signature to a document, then thrust the sheet and quill at Simon. "Sign here."

Simon did so, face contorted in concentration.

"Congratulations," said Julius. "You are now Sir Simon Fury, Lord of Water Rock Tower. Who's next?"

Simon moved aside and a young woman with a freckled face stood before the Envoy. "I'm Lucy, your Lordship. An herbalist and healer."

"Yes, I remember," said Julius. "Your ministrations saved my son's life. For that, you have my gratitude. I have no qualms raising you to the aristocracy." He faced Sir Fury. "What property did you grant her?"

"That would be Blackberry Manor in the northern Kirkwood." Fury set another paper on the table. "I picked it up at the gaming table from Baron Josiah Burnside."

"My teacher lives there," said Lucy. "We intend to convert into a school dedicated to medicine and natural philosophy."

"A worthwhile pursuit." Julius scrawled his signature and had Lucy do the same. "You are now Lady Lucy Fury of Blackberry Manor. Who's this last fellow?"

"That would be Iman, my get by a Kitrin woman." Fury pushed the slender, pale-skinned teenager to the table. "Get up there, lad."

"Kitrin. That is unusual." Julius sounded dubious.

"Mister Iman proved useful." The voice came from a woman amongst the onlookers.

"Ah." Julius nodded. "Lady Bottle. You attest that Iman's services were of value to the empire?"

"I do," said the woman.

"Very well then." Julius directed his attention back to Fury. "And what property did you find for this...person?"

"I found him this." Fury placed another sheet before the Envoy. "Crossway Inn. He's been running it for the past year."

"An inn? Innkeepers are hardly worthy of the nobility."

"It you'll look at the bottom of the deed" - Fury jabbed his finger on the document. "The owner of the Crossway Inn is also the headman of Crossway Village."

"I see. And how populous is this village?"

Iman took a breath. "When I left, there were five farms, a store, a smithy, and the inn."

"A hamlet. Well, that suffices. Sign here, though 'headman' scarcely counts as a proper title."

Iman did so and stood aside.

Julius returned his attention to Sir Fury. "And what of you?"

Sir Fury sighed. "I need your mark on this." He thrust another paper at the Envoy. "The Deed to Balla Estate downstream of Gebbek in Agba. Lord DuMars made his mark, now I need yours."

Julius Ambrose scanned the document. "Impressive." The Envoy scratched his signature on the document.

Sir Fury drifted away from the table, his hands tightly clenching the deed.

The Envoy raised his head. "Who's next?"

A petty imperial functionary announced Carina's presence.

"Ah, Miss Carina Menendez. My apologies for the delay."

"Greetings, Lord Ambrose." The words felt stiff leaving Carina's throat.

Lord Ambrose looked past Carina. "Lord and Lady Maximus! Our meeting wasn't until tomorrow."

"We decided to accompany Carina," said Bao.

"I consider her a member of my household," said Octavos.

"Well, such is certainly your prerogative as a member of the imperial family," said Lord Ambrose, "but the fact of the matter is that Miss Menendez stands convicted of an array of serious felonies."

"Convicted?" asked Carina.

"You were tried in absentia back in the empire for the homicide of a ranking member of the nobility and the theft of imperial property – to wit, one observation balloon. The proceeding was quite fair, I assure you – the barrister appointed on your behalf put forth a defense that was so masterful he almost managed to get you acquitted on the homicide charge. His performance was so impressive that Lord DuPaul snatched him up for his staff."

Carina's mind whirled. "So, where do I stand legally?"

"You stand convicted of manslaughter and second-degree theft, the sentences for which range from imprisonment to execution. In your case, the sentence was ten years imprisonment commuted to exile from the Solarian Empire."

"I see. So, I get imprisoned if I return to the empire?"

"Yes – unless you do so in the company of Octavos or Bao Maximus."

"I can live with that." Now for the difficult part. Carina steeled herself. "What of my...status... with your family?"

"I accept the imperial judgment on the matter. However, other members of my family are unhappy with your sentence. They will attempt action should you return to Solaria proper."

"So, I really should avoid the empire, then."

"That would be wise."

"Thank you for being forthright."

Carina took a deep breath, turned, and stepped away from the platform. The world awaited – and so did the opportunity for a normal life.

LABYRINTH WAR LXX – Chimp

'Cousin Quintus scowled as the foreman departed, idly juggling a fat sack of silver. "Giving these peasants land for service is a mistake," he said. "It gives them ideas. It makes them uppity. Soon, this whole damn place will be another Equitant."

"They served honorably during the war," I said as the foreman passed through the gate into the village atop the hill, situated within the walls of an old legion fort. "At war's end, the treasury was short on coin and long on empty land. It made sense."

"Hah!" Quintus snorted. "I'd heard stories of how you sympathize with these plebes, but I didn't believe them until now. Giving commoners land is a threat to the social order. The old emperors doled out land to common soldiers in Equitant for centuries, and in exchange, the ungrateful bastards neutered the nobility."

"Equitant was a rich land, with immense forests and abundant metals," I said. "Look at this place – few mines, scarce trees, and the soil is so exhausted even the weeds are half dead."

"Titus, it's the principle of the thing," said Quintus, in the manner of a tutor speaking to a small child. "The more you give the plebes, the more they will expect."

"Well, then what was the empire supposed to do with its veterans and the lands they bled for," I asked. "Toss the soldiers into the slums and let the lands become infested with bandits and goblins?"

"Of course not!" said Quintus. "The soldiers go into household service and the lands to the aristocracy. That is the proper order."

"Quintus look around you," I said. "There is naught here save grass and stones and narrow rivers. This land is old, exhausted, and worthless. No noble wants these lands."

"Then let the land lay fallow!" Quintus stormed below deck.

- From 'The Journal of Titus Maximus.'

Chimp did not want to do this. But he didn't have a choice. So, he gripped the pack in his right hand and strode into the almost empty courtyard. He picked out a nice empty table backed by a hard bench. That worked for him – a hard bench for hard work. He placed the pack on the table and plopped his butt on the bench. Then he opened the bundle and removed a packet of papers, a scribe kit, and two bottles of mediocre military wine. Other officers he'd talked to said wine made this work easier. He hoped they were right.

The Labyrinth War killed half of the Tenth – and that was with the reinforcement companies. Twelve hundred bodies were added to the butcher's bill.

A lot of officers were writing these wretched letters. The others wrote them indoors. Chimp couldn't do that – his quarters were too stuffy.

Chimp pulled out the first bundle of papers. The top one read 'Elis Block.' *Huh. Block was his real name.* He scanned through the legal crap and found the part that mattered – the dead soldier's next of kin. Block left a mother and a sister behind in the Empire. Half his pay went to the mother. Now all she'd get would be the death benefit of twenty-two dinars – minus the imperium's cut. Call it a dozen dinars or a week's wages for a poor man.

Chimp uncorked the bottle and took a deep swig. Then he reached for the quill and started writing. 'Miss Block, I regret to inform you your son Elis Block was killed in the line of duty.' Writing that line put a knot in his stomach. Chimp took another pull at the bottle and kept writing. Tears formed in his eyes. He blotted two words. But he finished the document.

Chimp leaned back on the bench. Damn, but that was rough – and he barely knew Block. He did know the others. He glared at the packet. The name on the next bundle said 'Stanker.' That was the fake name Skunk gave when he joined the army. Most of the other stuff in the file was lies, including his next of kin. Chimp almost pushed the papers aside – no kin, no need to write a letter. However, that could come back to bite him. Besides, the dozen dinars might reach somebody who could use them. Ao, he gritted his teeth and wrote the second letter. That left Chimp feeling like he'd been run over by a cart and tossed into a ditch.

One more letter to write – the worst. Sticks, his oldest and best friend, the kid who'd made the Sweepers into a thieves legend. When that blew up Sticks had the brilliant idea to join the army. The wars were over. Serve twenty years and walk away as citizens, not plebes. Chimp shook his head. "It didn't work out how it was supposed to, didn't it?" Now, he and Blaze were the only Sweepers still alive.

"It never does." The voice came from Chimp's right.

Chimp turned. "Dodger! You're not supposed to be here." Dodger was done with the army as of last week.

"I'm just here to pick up some stuff."

"How's civilian life treating you?"

"The wife and kids are running me ragged." Dodger gave a half salute, took a few steps, and halted. "I heard some recruits were looking for you. One of them is a local."

Recruits. That was right – three companies of fresh faces marched into the Tranquil Palace last week. And yes, there'd been a few locals who'd signed up. Taken together, they'd get the Tenth back up to strength. Fools. All of them. "I'm not hard to find."

"I'll send them this way." Dodger disappeared.

The brief encounter buoyed Chimp. Dodger fought in the Traag War. He proved that a fellow could join the army, fight a war, and survive his twenty-year stint. He pulled Sticks's papers from the bundle and looked at the name. Stickle – Sticks's real name. Reading that word took all the energy out of him.

"So this is where the jumped-up monkey got off to." Sir Fury entered the courtyard, trailed by his offspring. The knight sported a puffy purple hat with two feathers sticking out of the top.

Great. "What do you want?" Chimp didn't even try to keep the bitterness out of his voice.

"Mind your manners, monkey." Fury snatched a bottle off the table and took a pull. "Gah! Army piss. But it'll get me drunk."

"I'm busy." Chimp waved at the papers.

"We're going with you." Simon wore a hat almost as ridiculous as his Dad's.

"What?" Chimp sat erect. He did not want to go on another expedition with Fury.

"Relax, monkey." Sir Fury raised his hand. "We're only with your menagerie until Rith."

Rith was the base of operations for the sneak squad's next mission – hunting for a side door to the cultist's underground redoubt.

"What are these?" Spots had slid around the table and eyeing the papers.

"Death letters."

"Oh." Spots stepped back.

Blaze wandered into the courtyard with Deadeye.

"Excuse me?" The voice came from behind Simon. "I'm supposed to report to a Centurion Chip Cobble."

"That would be me." Chimp stood and took in a short guy in imperial army gear. No, the guy wasn't just short – he was a dwarf.

"Chip Cobble! Hah!" Fury slapped his thigh. "Stick with Chimp. Seriously."

Chimp ignored the knight. Instead, he addressed the short person. "And you are?"

The dwarf nodded his head. "Ah, a thousand apologies. I am Makalu of Rith, here to take service as a scout."

"I see." Chimp took in the mark on Makalu's forehead – "You were with the Monks of Zu?"

"I spent six miserable years in their ranks making poisons." Makalu held up a hand with stained fingertips. "I also learned how to prepare healing salves."

"That could be useful," Chimp remembered something. "I heard that mark makes you invisible to demons."

"The elders say this is true. Not having encountered demons, I cannot say."

"How'd you survive the big raid?" That came from Blaze. "That temple of yours got hammered."

"I learned how to fight in Rith." Makalu didn't look at Blaze. "I killed a thrall in that battle."

. "Good," said Chimp. "Why join the army?"

"The abbey is a ruin. And with the Walls retreating, there is no need for the Monks of Zu."

"Yeah, I saw that." Yesterday, he'd watched a long stretch of wall slide right into the dirt. Not to the ground, but into it, with barely a trace it had ever existed. The closest part of the Wall was ten miles off. The General said it was supposed to retreat to Zhaman, over a hundred miles away. The locals were both ecstatic and confounded. Chimp didn't blame them. A thought occurred to him. "Can you climb?"

"I can."

"Fine. Let's see how good you are." Chimp snatched Fury's hat and threw it atop a two-story building.

"Damn you, monkey!" Fury took a swing at Chimp and missed. "That hat cost four fucking dinars! I want it back!"

Chimp looked at Makalu. "You heard him. Climb up there and bring the man his hat."

Makalu went to the corner of the building and scaled the wall.

"He's good," said Blaze as the dwarf grabbed the headgear.

"He is," agreed Chimp.

Makalu dropped to the ground, strode to Sir Fury, bowed, and held out the hat.

"I'll take that." Fury yanked the hat away from Makalu. He drained the bottle. "I need to take a piss." He stalked off.

Makalu watched him leave. "A most rude individual."

"Manners are not Sir Fury's thing," agreed Chimp.

Snuffles loped into the courtyard accompanied by a short guy with long arms. She grabbed her companion's arm and pointed at Chimp. "There he is! I tell you I find him."

The shifter's companion looked straight at Chimp.

Chimp squinted. It can't be. He's supposed to be halfway around the world.

The newcomer ran straight for Chimp. "Hello, big brother."

"Hello yourself, Buzz. Why'd you join the army?"

"There wasn't any reason to stay in Corber Port. I've been in for almost a year now." Buzz looked around the courtyard. "I see Blaze, but where's the others? Sticks? Skunk?"

Chimp tapped a letter. "This is Skunk's death letter." He moved his hand. "I was about to start on Sticks letter when everybody came by."

"That sucks." Buzz's face fell. "So, it's just you, me, and Blaze now?"

Chimp took a breath. "No, it's all of us."

LABYRINTH WAR LXXI– Octavos

'Nimuk stopped before the first scene, which depicted an arrogant Solarian youth disdainfully stepping past a strange tree into a fleshy-looking tunnel – much like those leading into the under-maze. "Despite their misunderstandings about Gawana's Lords, your ancestors were not stupid. When matters grew strained, Cassius sent his son Octavos to the Heart. Officially, this was to secure a marriage alliance – improbable, but conceivable. Their true goal was for Octavos to become a Lord of Gawana."

The scheme reminded me of a Maximus axiom: Co-opting a troublesome foe was more profitable than a costly battle. Victor Maximus's courtship of the DuSarite clan was one such effort. The promotion of Titus Maximus is another.

The next image was horrific: the young man lay in a pool of pink ooze, one arm reduced to a mere skeleton, the mouth of his ruined face open in a silent scream. "Octavos demanded to become a Lord of Gawana but was found lacking."

"Steep price." Another Maximus saying came to mind: Great gains require great risk.

"Indeed." Nimuk contemplated the image, hands behind his back.

The third painting showed two aristocratic Solarian men presiding over the torture and dismemberment of three men and two women. The exposed flesh of each victim bore a complex tracery of green and red lines. "Varro and Crassus became enraged at Octavos' death. In retaliation, they captured and executed five of Gawana's Lords."

A stout door of solid wood separated this painting from the next image. This picture depicted anarchy. Club-waving mobs roamed along streets strewn with bodies as buildings blazed. The younger of the aristocratic torturers dangled from a noose in the foreground.

"Varro and Cassius's act caused a simmering crisis to explode. Those loyal to Gawana's Lords set upon Varro's men. Hundreds perished. Cassius perished in the streets. The lords spent weeks restoring order, often at the point of a sword. Order restored; they proclaimed the remaining Maximus family member's outlaws."

My family's policies do make us unpopular.

The final painting showed tiny upside-down figures clinging with hands and bent knees to a thin line suspended far above Gawana's outer wall.'

- From 'The Journal of Titus Maximus.'

Octavos emerged from the tunnel, then paused to let a long column of acolytes from the House of Black and White file past his position. The House of Black and White was all over the Heart these days, tinkering with the machines in Gawana's depths. He'd heard they'd started a recruiting drive.

He was glad to be out of the factory levels. The machines in those underground chambers were bigger than ships, damn near as big as castles. They were also astonishingly well preserved. But they were also utterly alien.

Octavos paused at a window and stared at a garden filled with kwintath food plants. The aliens planted more of these frilly food plants in large swathes of the maze south and east of the Heart.

"Here you are, husband." Bao popped out of a corridor and wrapped herself around Octavos. "I was worried that one of those devices had devoured you." She'd made a single foray into the factory levels and refused to enter them again.

Octavos hefted the sitar. "I had to unlock one of the machines. It took me three tries."

"You must train others in the use of that thing. You can't do it all yourself." Bao pouted. "I'd never see you."

"I intend to take on some apprentices." *Assuming the kwintath will let me.* The aliens were rattled by how much Octavos could influence Gawana even with his old lyre. The prospect of contending with even half a dozen other bards probably gave them nightmares. He feared the kwintath banning lyres, harps, sitars, and other stringed instruments in the maze.

Bao stared at the alien vegetation. "I don't care for this place. I miss the Empire. I miss Ptath."

"We are stuck here." Octavos touched his wife's cheek. "We are Administrators of Gawana. Those positions bind us to the maze. The proper place for a Lord of Gawana is Gawana." Titus had written that in his journal.

"Being a Lady of Gawana is a long and sterile existence," said Bao. "Yes, the maze confers long lives on its administrators, but the cost is high." She tapped her belly. The child she carried would be her last. "We should resign."

"I doubt the kwintath would permit that," said Octavos. "Gawana's boundaries are our boundaries. Still, Gawana is huge, even with the Pullback."

"That is another reason you must train apprentices. You cannot be everywhere at once."

"I agree." Octavos spent much time in the Windings, using the sitar to coax recalcitrant walls to slide into the earth.

Bao wasn't finished. "I want to look out a window and see something other than walls and ruins," said Bao. "If I can't go home, I at least want to be able to meet and talk with people from home."

"Seagate," said Octavos. "It will become a major metropolis once the kwintath start exporting their technological trinkets, drawing sailors and merchants from all the lands touched by the Shadow Sea."

"Seagate," repeated Bao. "Yes, that might be acceptable. It could be a good location for an academy dedicated to natural philosophy and teaching others about Gawana."

"And music," added Octavos. "I will mention it to 3-99."

"Drat." Bao clenched her stomach. "I must pee." She now emptied her bladder twice each hour. "I will see you at dinner." She padded down the corridor.

To Octavos's surprise, 3-99 expressed no objection to Bao and him moving to Seagate and founding an academy He didn't even object to Octavos teaching music. "They will be useful."

"But why," asked Octavos. "I know you were disturbed by how I influenced Gawana with just my lyre."

"I was initially disturbed. We considered restricting the importation of stringed musical instruments into Gawana," said 3-99. "However, we deemed it impractical and unnecessary after testing forty-three musically inclined individuals. Only two possessed sufficient psionic ability to manipulate Gawana with unmodified lyres and sitars."

"Did you test them on the gotemik instruments?"

"No. Those devices incorporate a portion of Gawana's operating system and do not require psionic ability to function.

They will be restricted." 3-99 hesitated. I received news from the gotemik today."

"I suppose they still want a presence in the Heart."

"They did reiterate that request," agreed 3-99. "However, this communication involved another matter."

"What?"

"The Nitivi – the race that advised the gotemik and was instrumental in bringing them to this world – have vanished."

"Did you ever learn anything about them?" asked Octavos.

"Information about the Nitivi is sparse and fragmented," said 3-99. "I suspect much of the data was redacted. I concur with Operant Carina Menendez that the Nitivi are native to Null Space, what humans term the Etheric Realm. Additionally, I agree with Git-Vik and Bric-Jute Shull that the Nitivi negatively influenced gotemik society." The alien emitted the equivalent of a sigh. "Nitivi influence might be why the gotemik failed to adhere to our agreement."

"Agreement." Anger rose in Octavos. "You mean the plan to reclaim Gawana?"

"I do."

Octavos's pent-up frustrations boiled over. "It was a farce. The whole war between Gawana and the Gotemik was a sham. One you participated in. All that death and destruction – it was just a game." He jabbed a finger at 3-99.

"The Gotemik provided Gawana with a necessary distraction for us to reassert control of the facility." 3-99 appeared unperturbed by Octavos's accusation. "A stratagem inspired by your ancestor Varro Maximus. Gawana was forced to divert substantial resources to counter his machinations and toxins."

Octavos remembered Varro's campaign in Titus's journal. Varro collaborated with celthanians and nomads to manufacture and distribute a corrosive powder that decimated the maze's Western region, creating an area of tumbled walls and broken stones known as the Blight. Later, the gotemik used a close cousin of that powder to secure their base in the maze.

"Varro was an arrogant ass," said Octavos.

"Crudely put but correct. Initially, we viewed Varro Maximus as a threat because the Leech designated 'Kato-Siva was active in this sphere. Then three events occurred. First, Kato-Siva was disintegrated, removing that threat. Second, Celthania brought the gotemik to this sphere. Third, Titus Maximus, an extremely competent military officer entered Gawana."

"And you formulated a plan," said Octavos. "You arranged for the gotemik to distract Gawana's attention with an invasion. To make their victory more difficult, you put my father in charge of Gawana's defenses, making him Lord Defender. When he began to thrash the Gotemik too soundly, you sent them instructions on how to make those infernal sitars."

"I did," said 3-99.

Did my father ever suspect the whole thing was a ruse?"

"Titus Maximus is a tactician, not a strategist," said 3-99. "It was the cited reason for his not being promoted to General in the Solarian Empire's military forces. I agree with their assessment. I do not believe Titus ever deduced the war's true nature, though he may have had occasional suspicions."

Octavos didn't move. "What becomes of him now? What will you do with Lord Defender Titus Maximus now that he is no longer needed."

"Your father will be appropriately attended to," said 3-99.

LABYRINTH WAR – Epilogue

The dugout's hull scraped against a fallen log. Ahead, another much larger deadfall choked off the stream altogether.

"It's gotta be here. There's nowhere else left." A note of desperation underlaid the words.

Finally, he spotted a log tripod rising from a sandbar. "The Marker."

The man clambered out of the canoe and onto the riverbank. Whiplike branches raised welts when they slapped his arms. He secured the dugout and knelt over the cloth-covered figure reclining in the craft's stern section. A wreath of wilting flowers covered the man's head like a decaying crown. "Hold on Titus. I'll find it this time. I'll be right back."

There was no response. The man drew his sword – a standard issue legion gladius, or shortsword, and began hacking a path through the dense underbrush, navigating from clearing to clearing. Thrice, he walked along fallen logs. Three hours later, he was thoroughly lost.

"I'll find it tomorrow." With those words, he set out towards where he thought the river was, a course that had him scaling low mounds and threading a path along narrow gullies. Quite abruptly, he found something familiar – a stunted pika tree, its branches laden with small purple fruit.

"I'll be." The man turned his head, taking in two more pika trees and a hillock of dirt and stone, surrounded by a circular mound. Patches of green and red flowers not found in the area dotted both edifices. "I found it." He removed his shirt, tied it to a branch, and then planted it atop the mound so he could find this place a second time. Then he set out for the river, reaching it almost half a mile downstream from where he'd beached the dugout.

Getting back to the craft meant wading through muddy water that reached to his waist, swatting at bugs the whole while. He had to kill a snake that sought to drop on him from an overhead branch. Once there, he uncorked a bottle of orange fluid and forced a fifth of its contents down Titus's throat.

"I found it, Titus. We'll be there before dark and then you'll be alright. Everything will be alright."

Titus murmured something incoherent.

The man launched the canoe and let it drift downstream to where he'd reached the river. Then he pulled his sword and hacked a crude trail through the vegetation back to his marker. The sun touched the treetops when he towed an improvised travois into the tiny clearing with the pika trees. Exhausted, he lit a small fire, devoured some tasteless trail rations, and unfurled a blanket. Sleep claimed him within moments.

Titus was sitting up when he awoke the next morning, watching birds and monkeys flit through the trees past the rings of mounds that encircled the clearing. "My new home, I take it?"

"Yeah, the Stillborn. It was the only place I could think of when you got sick." Casein shook his head. "Titus, you were in bad shape."

"I am still bound to Gawana despite not being her Lord Defender anymore." Titus tossed a pebble. "That absence weakens me."

"Titus, you would have been executed if we'd stayed."

"That would have been wise of them," said Titus. "Wise and foolish both." He looked at Casein. "I am surprised you were able to free me."

Casein shrugged. "It wasn't hard. You were injured, the Heart was a madhouse, and my name still carried some weight. Nobody blinked when I told them I was taking a look at the southern wall. I meant to take you to Ulam-Thek, but word reached me that people were asking questions. So, I changed course for the River Sytek and stole a boat. You got sick just outside of Fan."

"Yes." Titus bit into one of the small purple fruits. "I remember Fan, but it's all blurry."

"You collapsed. Without the pika juice, you'd have died." Casein shrugged again. "We couldn't stay in Fan, so I brought you here."

"Here." Titus stood and walked around the small yard, taking in the bare dirt and stunted trees. "Not much to it, is there? I doubt the whole place is even fifty yards across."

"It beats being dead." Casein stood and grabbed one of the purple fruits. It tasted tart. "I can scrounge up more stuff to eat in the woods and build a proper cabin."

"Casein, Casein." Titus shook his head. "You are neither a woodsman nor a carpenter."

"We gotta do something." Casein punctuated the statement by throwing a stone into the woods, startling a chattering monkey.

"Indeed, we must do something, as you so crassly stated." Titus stalked the central mound's perimeter. It wasn't large, maybe five yards high, twice that at the base. Like the surrounding earthworks, it was dotted with green and red flowers that didn't belong in this part of the world. A stone slab a yard high and wide caught his attention. "Here. Help me move this."

Casein grabbed the rock and heaved. It took all of his strength to roll it aside, exposing a low corridor that opened into a curved chamber.

Titus wasted no time entering the mound. Casein, larger and more reluctant, followed after him. Once in, he found Titus hunched over a purple blob the size of a chest set in the chamber's back wall.

Titus plunged both hands onto the blob, then into it. His features tightened.

Casein waited in silence.

Finally, Titus extracted his hands and shook his head. "The Stillborn, as we termed it, was never meant to grow. It was intended as a sort of...encampment."

"So, it won't grow into a second Gawana." Casein couldn't keep a note of tension from his voice.

"No, it won't. It can't. But it has other things that open possibilities."

"What other things? What possibilities?"

Titus looked at Casein. I need to explore these systems further. Why don't you fetch the rest of the gear from the dugout while I do so?"

"Okay." Casein turned and made for the exit.

"Oh. When you are done, destroy the Marker. Then cut the dugout loose and let it drift downstream."

"Why? Without it, the only way out of here is by foot,"

"The Stillborn is our sanctuary. Any curious soul who finds it might be able to find us."

"Huh." Casein scowled but did Titus's bidding.

He returned to find Titus leaning against the mound's exterior muttering to the air.

"What is it?" Casein dropped the heavy pack to the ground, which held everything from dried vegetables and jerked pork to cooking gear and clothing.

Titus looked at Casein. "The curse of the Titus's."

"What?" Casein tried to grasp what Titus was saying. "The Maximus emperors who bore your cognomen? What of them?"

"None of them sat upon the imperial throne for over a decade. Three lasted only half that long," said Titus. "I was just doing the math – I spent nine years and eight months as Gawana's Lord Defender before being deposed. The curse got me too."

Casein dredged up a few bits of relevant history. "I thought the Titus's were all assassinated or killed in battle."

"All of them save one, who finished his days in a cell." Titus stood. "And that is what this place is – a cell, far from any prospective allies. No doubt this 3-99's doing." He smirked at Casein. "But it is a cell I can escape, thanks to the properties of this place."

"Titus, if you set foot outside these walls you'll keel over. And even if you did leave, there's nowhere to go."

"There is nowhere to go yet," said Titus. "I don't intend to escape my hunters. I intend to outlast them."

"You can't. Those trees won't feed you more than a month."

"I won't need them. I'll be asleep." Titus turned to the mound. "That is one of the special properties of this place – a device that would permit me to sleep for decades, perhaps centuries until my foes all perish of old age."

"That – that is...something."

Titus looked at Casein. "It is indeed 'something.' Would you care to join me? I do not wish to awaken all alone in a changed world."

Don't miss out!

Visit the website below and you can sign up to receive emails whenever Tim Goff publishes a new book. There's no charge and no obligation.

https://books2read.com/r/B-A-CFCT-GOXHF

Also by Tim Goff

Empire

Empire: Country
Empire: Country
Empire: Capital
Empire: Capital
Empire: Estate
Empire: Estate
Empire: Metropolis
Empire: Metropolis
Empire: Spiral
Empire: Judgment
Empire: The Complete Collection

Standalone

Labyrinth War